Ethereal Legacy:
Part One-
The Expedition

Written by William F. James
Edited by Avonlea Gardner
Artwork done by Akash Sk

ISBN-13: 978-0692144411
www.EtherealLegacy.net

This Book is dedicated to:
My Grandmother Lorainne "Bear" Webb
and to my faithful and trusted Steed Egghead.

I lost you both way too soon and each day that passes I miss you more.
I Love you.

William F. James

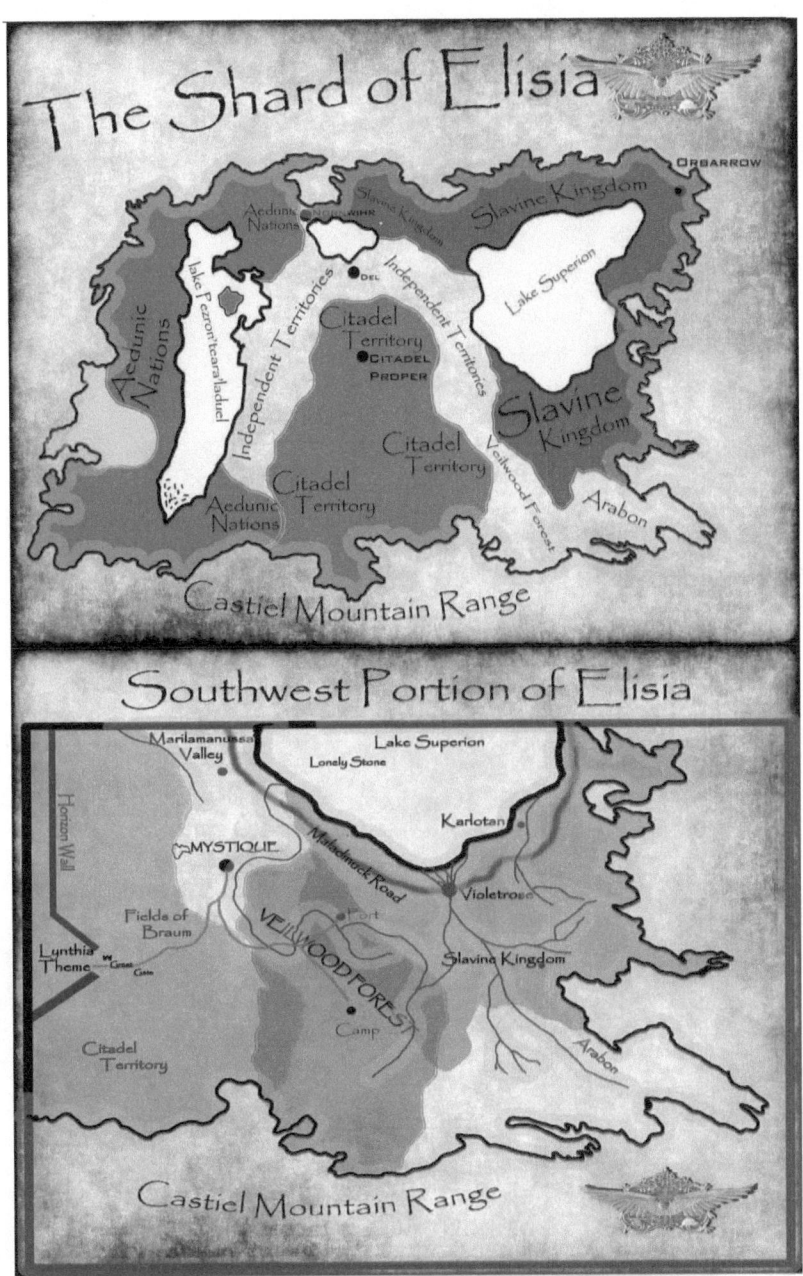

Professor Belladon's Expedition Path -----------

Ethereal Legacy Timeline

PREEXISTENCE

- **The Maker**
  (Before Creation)

- **First Creation**

  (The Celestials)

- **Second Creation**
  (The universe and all other forms of life)

EXISTENCE

- **The Question**

- **The Celestial War**

  Progenitor Era

- **The Barren Age**
  (Echo from the Past)

- **The Great Cataclysm**

- **The Dark Era**

  The Age of Shards

- **Citadel: King's Era**

- **Citadel: Steward's Era**

Table of Contents

Author's Note

"Writing is not merely placing words on a page. Its creating- Creating life in a world we may only dream to live in."
W.F.J.

Congratulations humble reader,

You are about to read something very special. Something that has taken me the better part of four years to write and edit. Ethereal Legacy has become more than just a single book, but a trilogy within a trilogy. What started as a simple idea has blossomed into something far grander than I could have originally imagined.

I told myself that the last thing I would do before publishing would be to write the Author's note. I wanted it to be the last thoughts as I finally submit my work to the world. In a few days' time this book will be read by more than just myself and my advance readers. This thought is both terrifying and exhilarating. During the writing process there were long periods of time I never thought I would ever complete this novel. There were days I feared that all this time spent in front of this computer was just a hobby that annoyed my family with all the time it took up. Perseverance, dedication, and sheer strength of will though has made this dream into a reality.

It is hard for me to sum up Ethereal Legacy, its basic premise breeds complexity and diversity. This series is more than just a single high fantasy steampunk adventure. It is a grand universe that goes beyond what you will read in Part One. I pray that you will enjoy reading this book as much as I have had creating the setting, the characters, and the lore. This novel is the first in many more to come. The Potential of Ethereal Legacy goes beyond this story line. I look forward to bringing you as much depth and creation as I can. In the coming months and years, I hope the books and stories you read will allow you to escape into a reality that is fun and adventurous.

When you begin any adventure, you may know the end game. But it's the path, though that makes the story. The path is where all the chaos and fun usually happen. Writing this book, I knew right away I wanted pictures of my characters. Drawing is a hobby of mine, but never draw what you write about, it's never exactly as you see in your head and its never good enough.

William F. James

    I was told about a website (fiverr- Thank you my wonderful wife, Lisa) where I could find an artist who could draw my characters off the descriptions I gave. That one piece of advice changed my life. That's when I met Akash Sk.. I live in Florida, Akash lives in Sri Lanka. We literally live on the opposite sides of the world. Despite all the harm and chaos, the internet provides, the best thing it really does is to bring people together. Friends for four years now, Akash and I have colluded and written (Akash directed) four short films together and have entered many different film festivals including San Diego Comic Con. (The first film ever to be selected from Sri Lanka!) It's been a roller coaster of fun and something I never thought I would be a part of! That is the beauty of going on an adventure. I cannot thank Akash enough for all the artwork and helping me bring these characters to life!

    Before I go any further I must thank several people without their help and support I don't know if I could have finished this book. First off to my mother, you have always been my rock and greatest fan. My life is what it is because of all the things you have done for me. Thank you for all the times you listened to me rant about my book and the advice you have given me. To my Lisa, I did it. I finished something I started, thank you for all your patience. To my aunt, thank you, I don't think you thought that small young boy who thought comedy and jokes were all about hurling tomatoes (I blame the Muppets for that) would one day write a fantasy novel. It has been a great comfort in life to know you are always there for me. To my dad, we work together every day and yet somehow you are still willing to read any rough draft I handed to you, no matter how bad it really was, Thank you!

Now to the people who deserve not just a thank you but probably a noble prize or a free therapy session. Writing is a skill, and when I first began writing Ethereal Legacy it was probably a skill I couldn't really claim for myself. Four years is a long time to work on that skill, but to my editors I apologize! My first editor Nicole, thank you for getting me started. I am sorry we didn't work out, but I really did love the work we did together. To my cousin Amanda Bruch, you were one of the first people to read through the original draft and to endure all my run-on sentences. I am sorry, so, so sorry! Your sacrifice though, did help me greatly. Without seeing how often I did write a run-on sentence, I probably would have never learned to stop. My next, thank you goes to my other cousin Allie Russell- Allie you are my "Gozer of Grammaria", you beat my grammar with a hammer! So, if anyone sees a grammar issue please email her at Allieyoumissedthisgrammarmistake@ethereallegacy.com (it's not a real email). And maybe one day soon, you will be the best lawyer ever. Good luck in law school! Now to Avonlea Gardner, thank you, thank you, thank you! Your editing was the fine detail work that was needed to make a good novel into an amazing one! I enjoyed going to that small coffee shop and talking to you about the story, the characters, and about life itself. I am very thankful that you offered to help me and thank you to your family who probably had to put up with hearing all the mistakes I made. No words that I can write could adequately describe how much I appreciate your help. I cannot wait to continue our work together.

One of the unique things about this book is that all the horses are real. Every horse was or is a real living horse in my life. My father is a farrier, I have become one as well. Each horse (Except for Poncho- for reasons) is a horse that was important to me. Some of them, I or my family owned. Like Halki the grey son of the two Lord horses was a perfect purebred Arabian that belong to my mother. The bond those two shared was simply amazing, and his ability to knock me off his back with every tree branch as a kid was eerily perfect. Other horses like Moose the large and goofy bay were horses that belonged to my clientele and they were simply great horses that I enjoyed being around. Horses are an important part of my life and I hope you can feel that as well.

Of all the horses though, there is one that stands above the rest. That horse is Egghead. He was my horse for many years. Like many horses he was more than just a pet, he became part of the family. He was one of those special horses that you just connect with spiritually. The bond that we shared was amazing and something I will always cherish. A year before I began to write this book I lost my Eggers to an illness. He was my best friend and noble Steed (to steal from Shrek). I was not prepared to let him go and when you have been together for as long as we had its never the right time. Geoffrey Chaucer wrote one of the saddest and truest of verses ever written- "All good things must come to an end". The void you feel losing a member of your family is a hole you can never fully fill. You learn to walk around the hole, but it's always there. After I lost my horse I thought our journey together was over. I didn't see how we could continue, but through these pages, I have found a way to bring the joy, happiness, and companionship I felt with my Eggers back. Without Egghead this novel, this series, would not have come to fruition.

One point about the book I would like to clarify, you will see the word **shard** a lot. In this book the entirety of the story takes place on the Shard of Elisia. A shard is a very large floating landmass in space. Think of an island orbiting a sun instead of an entire planet. (Spoiler alert- move to the next paragraph if you don't want to know) While reading Part One, you will learn about the Planet Aurelia- Aurelia was a massive planet (Think Jupiter size) that was eventually ripped apart by celestial forces. Crumbling and breaking the planet into millions of shards. Not every shard contains life, but the ones that do no longer remember a time when they were once a planet. After thousands of years of drifting apart they have developed their own cultures and histories. After the first book, we will see adventures beyond the shard of Elisia.

Part one, is a three-part series that will form Book one of a three book trilogy. I know that sounds confusing but trust me it will all make sense in the end. I broke up this book because of the overwhelming size it was becoming. It was entering Game of Thrones size novel and I wanted Ethereal Legacy to be a bit more digestible to the reader. While writing the main plot line, smaller books based on other parts of the universe will be published as well. For example, stay tuned for a novel that will take place on an entirely different shard with all new characters, cultures, and histories (spoiler alert it will have steampunk Egyptian like culture and Vikingesque pirates). While another book will be a prequel to the main plot line about the Steward and how he became the ruler of the Citadel.

Thank you so much for purchasing this book, I hope you believe the money you spent was well worth it. Please leave a kind review on Amazon if you enjoyed this book. Please like and share on Facebook @ Facebook.com/ethereallegacy Or check out the official Ethereal Legacy Website EtherealLegacy.net, there you can read short stories not found in the novels.

Thank you so much for reading Ethereal Legacy

William F. James

P.S. Every book sold will benefit a child in need. I want to give back to the community and one of the greatest things we can do is bring joy and laughter to children who are suffering. By buying this book and other Ethereal Legacy related material you will help kids with life threatening illnesses travel to the happiest place on earth, DISNEY WORLD Via the Make a Wish Foundation.

William F. James

Andrastii "Andi" Kimbol

Chapter One

From the first scroll of Zakarael, chapter 29 verse 11:
"Trust in me, for I know the plan I have set for you," declared the Maker. "Even in your greatest calamity, have faith in me. For my plan for you is not to harm, but to give you hope."

Andrastii's day began like every other-begrudgingly waking to the sounds of bronze metal gears grinding against one another. These precursory morning alerts acted as an alarm to prepare her for the muffled whine of pistons, whistles, steam release valves, and an assortment of other chaotic mechanical devices. These common but disruptive noises were part of the price everyone paid to live within the nation now simply known as the Citadel.

Like clockwork, these abrupt mechanical noises seamlessly found their way into Andi's 12th story bedroom window. Yawning mildly, she stretched out her arms, brushed away the golden blonde hair matted to her face, and tried to blink away the hazy sleep which muddled the vision of her pale green eyes. Sitting up, she pulled the closest lever on the wall and set into motion a number of bronze gears which were fused perfectly within the dark green marble facade along the corner of her room. Out from one of the walls came a long mechanical arm holding a tray of convenient breakfast items. She relished in the aroma of the hot peppermint tea and a cream cheese pastry, her favorite. On the opposite wall, an audible click indicated the automatic doors to Andi's closet were opening. She eyed the assortment of hanging clothes, many of which were standard Citadel issue garb, 'respectable for any occasion' just like the many billboards outside stated.

Andi hastily brushed past the standard clothing. Personally, she hated the long dresses and the rigidity of girdles women were expected to wear, but it was the preferred look of Citadel society women. The clothing rod extended left, displaying some of Andi's favored outfits. As she browsed through her options, she took a sip of her Peppermint tea and appreciated the feeling of its warmth as it ran down her throat. Unlike many of her female peers, Andi had the privilege to attend the Citadel's prestigious university; this allowed her a more diverse range of apparel. She donned a long-sleeved baby blue shirt, her favorite pair of rugged, loose fitting tan leather pants and threw on her favorite jacket with too many pockets. Why many women's outfit lacked pockets was beyond Andi's reasoning, designed by men was her guess.

Hurriedly dressing, Andi paused at the bay window to survey the familiar pile of parchments and scrolls covering a bench, remnants of a civilization long since dead. She reflected on her father's life mission, discovering the secrets of their progenitor race. Soon her gaze was drawn to the tarnished bronze pendant hanging from a faded painting of her parents beside the recently polished glass. Its hand engraving of a honey comb and a hammer, her father's own workmanship, which reminded her as she grabbed the patina chain to recite what, had become her morning mantra, "I'll find you someday, Dad. I promise!"

Andi glanced again over her father's scrolls. Over the last 8 years, she had tried hopelessly to decipher them, but none of it was clear. Andi believed that one day she would see the connection that her father so easily understood. Andi clung to a faded memory. The night before he left, she recalled how he wished her goodnight, lovingly kissed her forehead, and whispered a riddle; at the time it had been a silly notion, an enigmatic secret. "The key to unlock the truth is held within the planet." Andi mumbled it slowly. Hearing the word planet always made her smirk. Andi had been brought up like everyone else in the Citadel, to think of planets as superstition, as fairy tale, a world where you could travel all the way around its surface and end up where you first began. It seemed childish to her and everyone else, but she suspected her father had taken it seriously and maybe even quite literally.

Andi reached down and moved several parchments aside, revealing her father's old map depicting the Shard of Elisia, the landmass on which all life in the universe resided. At least, that is what the professors at the university taught everyone. Andi remembered her father believing very differently. Staring at the map past her father's hastily scribbled notes in a yet un-deciphered code, she saw in the middle of the page was the Citadel. The Citadel was once the Five Kingdoms of Civilized Man. Centuries before Andi was born, a great threat loomed over the Five Kingdoms. For the very survival of mankind, the Kingdoms merged together forming the Citadel. Andi followed the large dotted lines that once marked each of the five kingdom's borders. The kingdoms were now known as Themes. To the north and east of the Citadel lay the lands of the Slavine, historically one of mankind's mortal enemies. To the west were the Lands of the Lake where the Aedunic nations had settled.

Deep in thought, she was startled by the sound of her bedroom door flying open. It was her younger brother, "Good morning Andi!"

"Good morning, Glut," Andi responded smiling.

Andi's brother was flustered, "You know how much I hate that name!"

"That's your name, deal with it!" Andi laughed. "Telling everyone that your name is Garrett is not going to end well, especially when I'm usually the one that has to tell them the truth!"

Glut threw his leather backpack onto Andi's bed. "Whatever you say, sister. You're *so* much wiser than me."

Glut rolled his eyes once he caught sight of the painting of his parents. He hated watching his sister waste her life trying to untangle the writings of a mad man. Glut had few memories of his parents. He was only three when they disappeared. There were times when Glut wondered what his life would have been like with two loving, caring parents there for him. Though he would like to know what happened to them, he had long given up hope of ever actually meeting them again.

Glut knew he had to break Andi's concentration or she would spend hours staring at those wretched papers. "Anyway, I packed all of the supplies we'll need for Professor Belladon's expedition. I expect—"

Andi broke her gaze from the parchments and interrupted her brother, "Did you pack the rest of this week's C.P.s? I sent the market our temporary suspension letter to hold our Citadel Provisions. As the billboards say- *Don't Waste Food.*"

Glut looked at his sister with contempt, "I am not a child! I know not to waste food! Yes! I packed the rest of our C.P.s in our bags. Like I was saying, I expect the professor is eager to get going before we raise any suspicion about our true destination."

"*Us* raise suspicion?" Andi mused in disbelief. The first letter she received from the professor was quite clear about the urgency and importance of keeping everything a secret. When the second letter arrived with the time of departure, it struck both Andi and Glut as odd. They had expected to depart in the late evening or early morning, but the letter clearly stated that the departure time would be in the middle of the day. Still, the most peculiar thing in the letter was where they were to meet.

> *...Secrecy is key; we must not let the Steward or anyone in the Citadel know about our expedition. Please meet me fully packed and ready to leave at the central forum in the Southern Theme of Diamin in three days' time early afternoon. The proper paper work for travel will be delivered to you within twenty-four hours of departure. Look forward to seeing you both soon. Do not be late, Time is of the Essence!*

> *Most sincerely,*
> *Professor Nikola Belladon*

"He wants to leave in broad daylight, and in the middle of the central forum of Diamin Theme. If it's anything like the central forum here in Parnia, there will be thousands of people there! How is that secret?"

Glut nodded, "Maybe there aren't a lot of people in Diamin? I've never been to that Theme before now that I think about it."

Andi paused for a moment, realizing she had never been to Diamin either, "It's one of the central forums of the Five Themes. There must be people and government officials there. How can we expect to start there and not be caught? The Citadel bureaucracy might be extremely slow and dim witted but come on. They're not that blind. What is the professor thinking?"

"The professor has his reasons," answered Glut assuredly. "Who are we to judge?"

Glut produced two leather bound scrolls tightly rolled and sealed with a wax infinity symbol, representative of the Citadel University.

"The professor's letter says our usual papers won't work, we'll need these." Andi grabbed them and looked at them oddly.

"When did these arrive?"

Glut shrugged, "Sometime last night. They were waiting right outside the apartment door with instructions to use these at the Cross-Road Station."

Andi nodded. She eyed the scrolls, annoyed. *Papers to prove where we live, where we go to school, papers for food, clothing, and other essentials, how many papers do we damn need?* She placed the leather-bound scrolls in her backpack near the top for easy access. *Maker knows how many times we will have to show them to the Citadel Bureaucracy.*

Leaving her backpack on her bed and taking a moment for herself, Andi grabbed her pastry and walked out to the small balcony overlooking the main road in Dupree. This part of the city was teeming with life. Her residence in one of the tallest buildings in the immediate area gave Andi a panoramic view of the neighborhood's multi-level streets, buildings, shops, and best of all, people.

Andi looked north towards a single topless mountain, once called the King's Plateau. Now it was simply referred to as the Citadel Proper where the rich, affluent, and powerful of society lived. For many, the mountain stood as a reminder of everything they would never have. The mountain's peak had been mined and quarried for its pristine white stone, one of the key materials in Citadel architecture. Thousands of years ago, Servius Tullius Theodus the First, first king of the Citadel, ordered his palace, the castles, and mansions of his royal court be built on top of the mountain's plateau. In today's Citadel, with the bloodline of the King broken, the Steward and his cronies lived on its heights.

The most remarkable part of the Citadel Proper was the Grand Wall. Acting as a barrier between civilized man and the rest of the barbaric world, the wall was massive in height and width, stretching from the high mountain plateau and wrapping around the entirety of the twelve hundred square miles of the Citadel. There was no denying its marvel; even the reptilian apes of the Slavine could not deny the sheer ingenuity and skill necessary for its construction. At three thousand feet tall, it loomed as the tallest structure in the Citadel. Only the buildings on top of the mountain enjoyed a higher view.

Due to one's ability to see part of the Grand Wall from anywhere inside the Citadel, the structure was more commonly referred to by the people as the Horizon.

Andi followed part of the eastern wall with her eyes and pondered how thousands of years ago anyone could build such a wonder without the help of the steam powered luxuries and equipment they had the benefit of today. *What threat could scare a people so badly that a wall of such amazing size and proportions was ever conceived?*

Andi chewed silently on her pastry, reveling in its subtle taste. "It never ceases to amaze me..."

"What?" asked Glut, standing in the balcony's doorway?

"Five million people living inside the Horizon..." Andi paused and thought for a moment trying to comprehend the numbers. "It's remarkable really if you think about it. That's nearly three thousand people per square mile if we were evenly distributed."

Glut met her next to the balcony's edge, "Evenly distributed? That's not nearly the case. I heard several residential buildings are being expanded ten more stories next year to meet the population shifts. Families are losing their farms to the agro corps and are leaving the countryside of the southeast to come north to the urban areas looking for jobs. Look at those buildings over there," Glut pointed northwest towards a set of white stone buildings near the edge of the Horizon. "A year ago, they were barely visible, now they are plain as day, we are definitely growing higher."

Andi was looking north, but she wasn't paying attention to the stone white buildings on the ground level. Her eyes were still set on the single topless mountain. She wondered what it looked like whole. She imagined its green peaks touching the skies, reaching towards the heavens.

Andi could make out trees and several smaller buildings upon the former Royal Plateau, but the most stunning was the large white marbled towers of the Palace. Rumor had it that even while at the southernmost part of the city, you could see parts of the Palace towers looming over its domain.

"Do you remember Father taking Mother and us to Citadel Proper for the Giving festival?" asked Andi breaking her gaze.

Glut shook his head, "I'm sorry, I don't."

Andi smiled fondly, "I forget how young you were. Father had somehow gotten tickets for the whole family. It's amazing, everything is so clean and bright on top of the mountain, the flowers are the purest blue and the truest of reds, and there are these ornate marble fountains that cascade down an unending promenade, and—"

"Did we walk past the King's Fountain? Was it filled with water?"

Andi shook her head. Glut was referring to a grand fountain adorning the front courtyard outside the doors of Mithridaties, commissioned and built by the Citadel's first King, Servius Tullius Theodus. Supposedly, the Maker's priests blessed the fountain. From its spouts flowed water holy and divine. For as long as the King reigned justly, the fountain would run. The King's fountain continued to pour its brilliantly clear blue water for thousands of years but ran dry when Good King Magnus the last king of the Citadel, died. Nearly forty years had passed since *the Night of Blood*, when the king and most of his court were massacred by Slavine assassins.

"What else do you remember?"

"Well, the view was amazing, and I remember the dresses the women wore, they were so extravagant and elegant; mother was totally underdressed. So was I, for that matter."

"So, nothing has changed then," teased Glut.

Andi slapped his arm and leaned down on the balcony railing, "It was such a treat to be there!" Andi recalled, remembering better times.

"I wish I could remember. One good memory of our parents would be better than none," pined Glut, equally angry at his missing parents and embarrassed at his feelings in front of his sister.

Andi's eyes burned, "It was one of the last times we were all together. If I had known, I would have-- I would have been more focused on Mother and Father, not those pretty fountains."

"If you had known then, you wouldn't have let them leave," Glut placed an arm around his big sister, "Just remember you have me, little sister, I'm not going anywhere!"

Andi giggled slightly, "Thanks, Glut. You may not be the best brother in the whole shard," Glut gave his sister an odd look, "but you are mine, and I will always love you. All we have is each other until we find our parents."

Glut stayed silent and allowed his gazed to drift. He wanted to tell Andi his true feelings; the parents he was too young to even remember were gone and never coming back. But Glut held back, he knew how much his sister needed to hold on to her last bit of hope. "One day we will," he said kindly, lying to his sister.

The siblings ate the last of their C.P. rationed breakfast and finished packing their bags. They left their cat with their crotchety old landlord and explained they were heading to the opposite end of the Citadel to visit relatives. They would be back in two days' time. At least, that's what they told their landlord. They approached the apartment's bronze-caged lift. It wasn't the most reliable contraption, but they were eager to begin their journey and were running slightly too late to take the stairs down twelve floors. Glut smirked at his sister and without hesitation pulled the lever with all his might. The lift shook violently until they hit the ground floor.

"This thing is a Death Trap!" yelled Andi snidely exiting.

They made their way down the building's steep stone steps. The immense government billboard above them reminded them to stay within their neighborhood. *Everything an upstanding citizen needs is within their reach. Ration your food responsibly!*

Many parts of the Citadel, especially in the ever-growing urban areas like Dupree, had become so densely populated that the Steward had issued laws to help alleviate street congestion. The Steward's answer was to build taller buildings and connect them through sky-tiers, an enclosed maze connecting the buildings. The ground floor was dedicated to citizens with last names beginning with A-M. Those with last names beginning with N-Z did their shopping above. Andrastii and Glut Kimbal had access to the ground floor only. Between the sky platforms and the ground ran tracks for steam powered bikes and horseless carriages for those who could afford to travel in private. Scads of signs bordered the streets, reminders from the Steward to remain orderly and report suspicious activity to the Citadel Officer Guard ship or C.O.G.s.

Recently, many of the ground level shops and stores had begun to expand upwards, buying and renovating the floors above them, trying to reach the N-Z customers, just as the upper stores were descending to reach A-M. The government quickly put a stop to that, fearing it too easy for consumers to move between the different levels. Many of the renovations were left unfinished.

Andi and Glut passed Leo de Ponce's *General Goods and Exotic Rare Commodities*. Scaffolding remained around the outside of the building, despite the fact the C.O.G.s had ordered Ponce to cease and desist his renovations towards the sky-tier platform.

"Do you think Leo will take all this down?" asked Glut, marveling the height of the platforms.

Andi shrugged, "Probably not. I heard Fred Sorell say that Silvia de Ponce was told by Leo that unless the Steward reimbursed him for the money already invested into the project, the scaffolding would stay up forever."

"Or until the C.O.G.s come and tear it down," replied Glut.

Andi shrugged again, "You're probably right. Damn C.O.G.s, they're more bullies than police."

"Shut up, Andi!" whispered Glut harshly, pointing down the street. An officer in black stood near the street corner, holding a club, "Don't let them hear you or we'll spend a day in the stockades!"

Andi's face turned red, and she ducked her face away as she walked past the Citadel Officer quickly. The corner of Andi's eye though caught something new along the wall of the building behind the Officer. She couldn't help by look up; it was an I.M.W. Independent Marshal Wanted poster. The Marshals were an independent group of Lawmen that worked in the neutral and independent areas of the shard that share no influence with the Citadel, Slavine, or Aedunic nations. The poster was unique which was why it caught Andi's attention. The words *WANTED- BAND OF DANGEROUS HORSEMEN- DEAD OR ALIVE* was written across the top. Below the title was a penned drawing of an evil looking man dressed in black carrying a deadly harpoon like spear. He was astride a large, intimidating black horse with fierce, unnatural eyes and a scar down its long neck. At the very bottom of the poster it said, *Extremely Dangerous wanted for, Robbery, Mayham, Kidnapping, Horse Killing, Murder, Massacre, and Treason against the States of the Citadel and the Slavine Kingdom.*

Andi stared at the poster far too long, the Citadel officer glared at her, "Move along now!"

Frightened, Andi grabber her brother and scurried a crossed the street and headed south. This particular block was slightly more prosperous. A councilman named Thames owned the entire area, and many of the stores were fully upgraded with the latest inventions to come out of the Inventorii, the Steward's personal squad of engineers, inventors, and thinkers.

"Turn down Magnus Street," insisted Glut.

Andi looked at her brother confused, "Why? It's faster to go down Appian Way."

"I know, I just love going this way," answered Glut, turning the corner. Andi simply smiled and followed her brother's lead, passing under one of several large glass spheres that hung from *The White Hard Inn*. Glut paused and looked straight up at the glass sphere. The globe was glowing with a charged blue brilliance, in contrast to the establishment's name scrawled in stunning calligraphy. "How do they do that? No matter where you are standing, you can see the name perfectly," exclaimed Glut in astonishment.

"Why don't you ask the professor, I think he invented it," replied Andi. Her brother wasn't listening though; he was too busy staring at the other signs on the street. *Lionel's Apothecary* was written in red, *Longburrow's Herbs, Vegetables, and Spices* in green, and *Clearwater Pub Distillery* in white. The distillery sign was several hundred feet away, yet still clearly visible.

As they were leaving Magnus street, Glut turned his gaze skyward. This particular section of road lacked a sky-tier platform above, but the steam and smoke coming from the buildings was so thick that in some areas the sky was hardly visible. The people in the Citadel who lived on the lower levels probably had not seen the sky in some time, especially if their last name began with an A-M.

"I miss the sky," said Glut to himself, wondering if anyone else even noticed the missing sky, and if this, the price for allowing the people to have their comfortable way of life was worth it?

A large group of women were standing tightly around themselves wearing formal standard issued dresses. There was only a slight variation in color and hair style that kept these women apart and not looking like one large, cohesive glob. They were all surrounding particularly large woman wearing a jewel collar, a clear sign of her station as a person who lived in the Citadel Proper. One of them near the edge of the group noticed Andi's non-standard outfit and glared at her insidiously. Andi rolled her eyes and ignored the stare, but she couldn't help but overhear some of the words the women were saying.

A tall woman with a very high-pitched voice was speaking, "There was another massacre near the fields of Braum! Seventeen people, men, women, and children slaughtered, including their HORSES! Only a small boy survived."

"Gracious! That's the third massacre I have heard of!" remarked the large woman, annoyed. "Are the Marshals or the Citadel guards going to do anything to stop these atrocities?"

"The boy said they were attacked by a group of black dressed riders" insisted another woman, "and their leader's horse' eyes glowed red and its jugular had been sliced open. "

"Goodness" announced the larger woman, dismayed. "The jugular? The creature had to have been dying."

"No, the boy said that the leader's horse slaughtered several of the people with its own teeth." answered the tall woman; she then leaned in as if to whisper. "The wound was cleary cut down the neck and around the jugular, the boy said it pulsed like a beating heart and he heard the screams of hundreds of dead horses."

"Oh please, Ellie- I think you are having a little too much to drink at night now." The larger woman began to laugh, the other women followed suit. "My dear HAHA- a wound that pulsed? Lunacy I tell you!"

"It's not lunacy," insisted the woman who had stared Andi down, "my husband says it has to be a Hell Horse and he said- "

"Pipe down Addison" demanded the larger woman, "Your good-for-nothing husband is no stranger to the bottle as well!"

Andi secretly smiled at hearing the larger woman snap at Addison; though she began to wonder what truth there was to the massacres and the wanted poster she saw. *I hope the professor's expedition doesn't have to go near Braum*, said Andi inside her head.

Andi brushed off the thought, she had faith the professor knew what he was doing. As brother and sister arrived at the end of the street, they noticed a group of people gathered around a small stage. From the blue curtain emerged a man wearing a garish brown suit. He spoke to the crowd in a charismatic voice. The man was an Orator for the Inventorii. He presented a steam powered machine that could produce fresh oxygen for the bedridden. The Inventorii introduced new contraptions weekly, some revolutionized the entire Citadel, but most simply made life a little more convenient. Last week's exhibit had displayed glass tubing that when placed all through your house would light up as you passed by it. No need to turn lights on or off again.

Andi was sure by the end of the year the tubes would be installed in every home. She noticed the time and grabbed her brother by the arm. "We don't want to miss our shuttle!" So many people had gathered around the Orator. That it was hard for them to push through the throngs of people enchanted by the new inventions.

"ANDI! Oh my, Andi! Is that you?" A young voice pierced through the dense crowd of people.

Andi recognized the voice coming from a tall, young woman who had only recently started mixing with Professor Belladon's group in the history department. Deep red waves of hair reached down to the thin bends of her arms. Her physique was one of perfection, and her face was pure without flaw, long and elegant with a bewitching smile. Andi knew her eyes, such beautiful blue eyes. Oh, how Andi disliked this person. Not so much for anything she had said or done, but for the audacity of being born with such natural amazing beauty. She reminded Andi of her own insecurities, she felt her own appearance mousy and without grace.

Andi tried to grab her brother and lead him away, as if she hadn't heard the voice screaming her name, but Glut had already made eye contact with the woman, and neither he nor any other man would dare miss a chance to talk to Leora.

"Andi! It's so good to see you!"

Andi produced a strained smile, "Leora, how are you?"

Leora approached, wearing a newly tanned, bulky leather coat. She held a sizable bound book in her hand.

"Oh, I am fantastic! The apothecary off of Magnus Street has this new elixir that is just amazing! It's filled with bubbles and tickles your nose as you drink it. It's supposed to give you energy. I think the apothecary called it a 'carbonator drink' or something like that!" said Leora never missing a breath. Her brilliant smile seemed to shine brighter. Andi had to blink several times in disbelief at her beauty, "Oh and my father just bought me this amazing journal, he wants me to write down everything new that I learn!

"That's...uh...that's...um...uh...you're amazing," stammered Glut, awestruck.

Andi rolled her eyes, "What my brother is trying to say, is that we have to get going, we have some business to attend to for the professor," said Andi puffing up her chest with pride.

"Me too!" Leora quietly added, "Are you guys going on the expedition?"

"Yes! Yes, we are!" exclaimed Glut. Catching himself and realizing his outburst, he leaned in closer to Leora, this time talking quietly, "You're coming too?!"

"Yes, I am. I cannot wait! My first expedition!" answered Leora, hardly able to contain her excitement. Glut heard Andi let out a huge sigh of exasperation. "I am going to learn so many things, I love learning, and I am going to write my adventures in this journal. Maybe someday I will publish it! Well, parts of it at least! I am sure there will be some parts I won't want anyone to know about!"

Leora either didn't notice or didn't care about Andi's reaction, her excitement was palpable.

"You two have to see this!" smiled Leora jovially.

Leora stood straight, excited to show her friends what she had made. Undoing the buttons of her coat she revealed a leather outfit that formed to every curve of her body. Glut and Andi's eyes widened for two very different reasons. Andi was astonished; Leora had every tool you could possibly think of in the many pockets sewn to the inside of her coat. She also had gadgets attached to her leather vest and hanging on her belt were tools which seemed to float on her hips. Glut stared too, but at the fabric hugging Leora's bust.

"The instructions the professor gave me stated to only bring what you can carry on your person. What do you guys think? I made it all myself. It's a little heavy, but it has everything I could possibly need! Where do you guys keep your tools?" Leora looked up and down their outfits, "Hidden pockets?"

Andi rolled her eyes in disbelief. She turned and indicated her backpack.

"Oh, is that considered on your person?" She gave the backpack a dirty look, "And that has everything you need right there?"

Andi nodded.

"Man, should have thought of that," replied Leora smiling slightly, "Sometimes I take things too literally! Oh, I'll have to write that in my journal."

Leora scribbled in her notebook, looked up and smiled brightly, "No matter, at least I'm stylish, even if this pick keeps poking me" she half-groaned, half-laughed rubbing her side.

There followed an awkward silence which made all three of them grow tense. Glut finally spoke up.

"We…We 're, heading to the station to jump on a shuttle to meet the professor! Care to…to join…uh, come along with us?"

Leora smiled brightly. Andi felt faint. The words *Please do not let this woman join us* rang in her head.

"I'd love to Garrett, but the professor has me on an errand before I meet up with the rest of the team. I'll see you both there! I can't wait for the adventure!" sang Leora enthusiastically, as she bluntly waved good bye and set off.

Andi was momentarily relieved but quickly spun around and shot Glut a reproachful glare.

"What?"

Andi kept starring.

"WHAT!?" asked Glut again.

"Garrett!" mocked Andi, "You told her your name is Garrett?!"

"It's darn better than Glut!"

Andi had to agree with him, but pensively. It was still the name their parents gave him. "I've warned you, people aren't going to like it when they realize you've been lying to them. Come on let's just *go* already!"

Glut shrugged it off, but in the back of his mind he did worry slightly about people discovering the truth.

Within minutes, Andi forgot all about Leora and was focused on the steamed wonders they had just seen. "What do you think the Inventorii's will showcase next week?"

Glut looked down at his sister and shrugged, still miffed at her. After several minutes of walking, they arrived to the closest Cross-Road Station. Over the past thirty years the Citadel had built hundreds of C.R.S.s in every Theme, city, and neighborhood. C.R.S.s had become the central hubs of transportation for goods and people. Millions used the Citadel Shuttles to get to every part of the Citadel, if you had the proper papers of course.

The station in Dupree had become one of the more highly trafficked stations and had recently gained a sky-tier level to accommodate the high volume. Once nothing more than a few small tracks leading to other stations for people to disembark and re-embark on shuttle lines, it had become a labyrinth of elevated bridges and sky-tier platforms all leading to alleys where the shuttles would arrive. To Andi's and Glut's dismay, the place was busier than Dupree's streets. Thousands of people crisscrossed and bumped into each other trying to get to their particular shuttle line, hurrying to inevitably stand in other lines to wait for their transport to arrive.

High pitched whistles blew, and so many release valves bellowed out white smoke that steam became a constant companion. When Andi was young, her Father would take her to the C.R.S. to eat lunch and people watch. Andi avoided the Cross-Roads when she could now.

Each Citadel neighborhood had its own Cross-Road station. Some were smaller, and others were twice as large as this one, but they were all decorated by countless large banners of the Citadel, the red flag with a yellow depiction of the King's fountain wrapped in a laurel crown had been replaced with a single yellow fist. The other commonality between every crossroad was the numerous signs reminding everyone of their duties as a citizen, including, *The Steward provides you with Utopia! Don't just work, Sacrifice! Food is precious, Don't Waste it! Greed kills. A Citadel Citizens Fights for his Steward.* Andi watched several COGs place two new signs on the wall. The first one was a new declaration, a new law or standing order from the Steward. Effective immediately all armed and independent cavalry units are now illegal and must turn themselves in to the nearest Citadel Officer Guard. *They must really fear those black riders* thought Andi.

Andi began to read the second sign "Look!" she declared patting Glut's shoulder pointing at the second sign. *Know your rights! No one shall go hungry! No one shall be cold! See your nearest Citadel Officer of the Community today!"*

Glut snorted, "Wow, how stupid must they be to put up a sign like that? Do they honestly think the drifters can read?"

Andi looked at him angrily.

"Oh, come on sis, we have COGs, now we have CO—"

"That's enough, I get it, I don't want to hear my brother say that!" replied Andi finding it horrifying and hilarious at the same time. "Some of my friends at the university told me that their neighborhoods have these offices now. There are a lot of desperate people and families flocking to them, and they say that those who go in never return."

"I am sure they are just being relocated to other neighborhoods that have work," assured Glut despite his own thoughts on the subject.

As they made their way through the crowd, Andi looked for the giant electric sign hanging above the entrance of the southernmost shuttle which read To: *Diamin.*

Andi pointed at the sign, "This is the one we want!"

Glut furrowed his brow, "Are you sure about that?"

Andi stared down the alley. Unlike the other lines, this one had armed guards from the Citadel. These were not normal COGs, these were Citadel soldiers. They held their standard issue Tesla rifles over their shoulders, large bulky power packs were strapped to their backs. They wore dark brown rubber jackets to protect them from any random discharge from the power pack or gun, and the steward's closed fist symbol was stitched over their forearms.

As they walked closer, Andi and Glut noticed a crowd of about 15 people grouped around a man standing on a box. The old man probably hadn't shaved or combed his hair in over a decade. Andi felt uncomfortable under his gaze.

"Repent! Repent now! The end times have come, and the Great Evil will soon be released! His minions of darkness have already begun plundering the outer lands of our very own Elisia. Soon the city will be surrounded!" The man held out one of his hands and pointed at individuals in the crowd before turning his sights and pointing straight to Andi. "HAVE FAITH CHILD! FIND STRENGTH! DO NOT LET THE DARKNESS CONSUME YOUR EVERLASTING SOUL!"

Andi turned away, unable to look at the old man. *Why is he singling me out?* Looking over at her brother she expected him to have noticed the old man's outburst towards her. Glut showed no signs that he had, still listening to the man.

"Evil is all around us, we are surrounded! Will you all stand by and let our Shard succumb to darkness?"

The mob buzzed at the allegation.

"Look upon the very people who lead us to our doom! The Citadel does nothing to prevent the coming apocalypse! Look! I SAID LOOK at them!" cried the old man on the box as he pointed at the two guards. "They stand there blindly following the orders of fools and crooks! Their blind allegiance to the false Steward and their mighty Citadel will lead us all to ruin!"

The crowd's buzzing escalated into shouts of anger. One man reacted to the energy and anxiety of the crowd; he picked up a rock and threw it at the nearest guard, striking him in the face. Blood flew from his cheek. "You will not lead us to our ruin!" screeched the man with conviction.

The other guard calmly lowered his Tesla Rifle and took aim. A brilliant bluish white beam shot towards the man and in less than a second, he was lying on the ground, dead, a hole through the center of his chest smoking profusely. The smell of burning flesh made everyone cover their faces.

"Bless the Maker!" gasped Andi as she surged forward.

Glut seized her shoulder, she strained against him, rage in her eyes.

"We can't just stand by and let this happen!" she panted, "He could have stunned him, he didn't have to kill him."

"Are you kidding me?" hissed Glut, with genuine fear in his voice, "What are we going to do?! They have Teslas and the man had it coming. He threw a rock at the guards! What did he expect would happen? There is nothing we can do now."

The growing hysteria of the crowd attracted an entire platoon of guards who began forcefully dispersing those standing in the street. Huddled against the wall, the siblings were forced to wait for the commotion to die down. In all their lives, they had never once seen so many guards in a C.R.S. or such acts of aggression towards guards occur.

Once the crowd had dissipated and the platoon had left, Andi and Glut handed the Diamin shuttle guard a leather bound scroll the professor had given them. The guard broke the seal and read through it.

"You may pass!" replied a guard, the smell of burnt flesh still in the air.

The only other person in line was their good acquaintance Dean. A man of short stature, he and Andi stood at the same height. Andi admired how well-kept Dean was. She especially liked how his hair was so neatly cut and combed to the right.

"Hey guys, I'm glad you're here, I thought maybe I was late and missed the shuttle!" Dean held out his hand to shake both Andi and Glut's.

"All ready for you know what?" whispered Andi.

Glut and Dean's eyes widened.

"Damn it Andi, hush up or someone might hear you!" whispered Dean harshly. "The guards just shot a man! Don't do anything that may…" Dean looked around to make sure no one was listening, "jeopardize the professor's expedition."

The three waited in silence. Several minutes passed before the steel streamlined shape of a Citadel shuttle arrived, bellowing smoke and screeching to a halt. The trio climbed aboard, thankful to be leaving the platform and its recent events behind them. Andi glanced back at the spot where the man had been shot. Only a stain of blood and some ash remained. *I hope this isn't an omen of what is to come.* She pushed the thought away. The cabin inside the shuttle was barren. They were the only three passengers on board. Andi, Glut, and Dean took their seats and waited. The shuttle's horn signaled, and the large metal wheels began to propel down the steel track. Andi smiled as her body was forced backwards into her seat, excited for this adventure to begin.

***

The shuttle ride was either moving very slowly or very quickly. No one was really ever sure since none of the shuttles had windows; neither did they have clocks. Time seemed frozen in a Citadel shuttle. Andi read while Glut dozed, and Dean sat fidgeting, consumed with anxiety.

It didn't take long for Dean to break the silence. "Does anyone else think this is all odd?"

Andi closed her leather-bound book and slipped it into her bag. "What do you mean odd?" A slight snore filled the cabin. Glut was fast asleep.

"You know, all this secrecy, guards patrolling a random shuttle line, this sudden and mysterious expedition, the three of us being asked to accompany the professor--it's been almost six years since I graduated from the university and never has the professor himself requested I come on an expedition!"

"The professor asked you personally?" asked Andi. "He sent us a letter of request."

"I happened to be helping some Mech students with a new design. The professor walked by and noticed me. He was in a hurry, a bit frantic, and he asked me to stop by his office later. That's when he asked me to join this expedition. I will say this though, when I walked into his office, he seemed whiter than white, like something had really spooked him."

"Did he say anything about where we're going?"

"Only that it was of the utmost importance we attend, and imperative we meet him in Diamin at a very specific time!"

"I hate all this mysteriousness, but I'm hardly surprised we were asked. The professor has been like a father to my brother and me..." Andi trailed off.

"After your parents went missing?" offered Dean.

Andi gave Dean a very abrupt look of anger.

"Oh, I'm sorry, that wasn't meant to sound rude."

Andi nodded, "Oh, you've heard the gossip. My parents went missing after leaving on their own expedition, and the professor took us in. He made sure we were properly taken care of and schooled. I probably wasn't as grateful as I should have been. I was so young when my world went upside down, and for a long time I was angry."

"Wow, so the professor raised you?" Dean was impressed.

Andi's face went a little red, "He did not raise us, per say, you know how busy he is. He invented practically every contraption we use in society today. If he wasn't inventing or writing a book on some new theory of his, he was off excavating a progenitor sight on the other side of the shard. He was around as often as he was able to be, but we were mostly raised by many different nannies and governesses that he paid for."

"Why many?" asked Dean.

Andi's face turned a shade brighter. "Let's just say my little brother and I were not the most proper of children! Glut barely remembers our parents and followed my example of being a complete brat. All I wanted to do was escape from home. I didn't care about schooling or etiquette. All I wanted to do was go searching for my parents. I knew if I was given the chance, I could find them..."Andi trailed off, embarrassed at her sudden openness.

"That's really tough, Andi." Dean tried to sound supportive, "Maybe one day you will find them, or at least find out what happened to them."

"I will," said Andi.

"Have you found anything so far?" asked Dean.

Andi straightened against her seat and contemplated how much she should really tell Dean. Although they had known each other for a long time, she had never talked to him about her past, nor had he asked. "Well to be honest, and you are going to think this a little foolish, but my father was a big proponent of the Planet Theory. He had made a huge discovery. He arrived home with this strange stone that I think he had gotten from a merchant one day, adamant that it would prove his hypothesis correct."

"What did it look like?"

Andi shrugged. "It wasn't remarkable. It was small. It nestled perfectly in my palm. I do recall thinking it was kind of pretty for a rough old stone. I kept placing it on my chest and I tried to break it with my teeth." Andi's face burned bright red. She had no clue why she told him that last part. "It was about half the size of this." Andi reached into her shirt and pulled out her bronze pendant and handed it to Dean.

Dean admired the craftsmanship and looked for a manufacturing mark, "the design is amazing, the beehive is a symbol for industry, order, and the results of people's toil over the soil"

Andi cocked her head slightly.

Dean's face turned red slightly, "Sorry, I went to a church school, many of the older cathedrals that date back during the Five Kingdoms have beehive symbols and anvils chiseled on every door."

"Anvils?" asked Andi surprised, "my father made this pendant and a matching one as well; except his had an Anvil on his."

Dean nodded, "We must have gone to the same church school."

Andi sniffed the air slightly, her mind falling back to the past. "Just days after finding the stone, my mother and father left to discover where it had originated, and they never came back. We are not even sure if they reached their destination, which was supposed to be Anclor, a small village near the Aedunic nation in the valley south of the city of Nornwihr. What I have gathered is that they turned eastward. My assumption is they turned towards the lonely stone in Lake Superion, but that's a guess from some scribbled notes I found in one of my father's journals. The day he left he knelt down and handed me this pendant and made me promise to always keep it close to me. He then kissed me on the forehead and mumbled 'The key to unlock the truth is in the planet.' I have been trying to determine what that means for years. Personally, I think it means—"

"It means NOTHING!" said Glut half asleep, "They are gone, they left us because some kind of special rock said to go. What kind of parents do that? They are not coming back and that's that!" Glut turned in his seat and went back to sleep.

Gluts sudden outburst left Andi utterly embarrassed, she fell silent.

Dean felt obligated to ease the tension; he suggested they discuss something a little less intense, to which Andi politely nodded. Glut slept as they made small talk.

"Did you hear about the massacres near Braum?" asked Andi, Dean shook his head. "I overheard people talking about a group of horsemen slaughtering and killing innocents and that the leader, believe it or not rode a Hell Horse! An actual Hell Horse, can you believe it? How do people really believe such nonsense?"

Dean shrugged, "I don't really like horses, I don't know anything about them. What is a Hell Horse?"

"Does it matter?" remarked Andi sarcastically, "It's a mythological story- it's not real. Like a planet it doesn't exist."

The small talk continued until eventually, the shuttle slowed. They were somewhat disoriented while exiting. Since the shuttle had no windows, it was difficult to determine which direction they were facing. The Cross-Road Station was barely a station at all. It was a small shed with an overhang and single path leading between two buildings. Andi immediately noticed the arrival sign was painted rather than electric, it was made from a large piece of rotting wood. These signs were typically made from stone or metal. It all felt unnatural to her. The sign read: *Welcome to Diamin.*

Andi looked around at the shabby station, "I don't think I have ever been this far south in the city before." Both boys nodded.

What made the area so foreign was not the architecture. The white grey stone common in all citadel construction surrounded them. Missing were the bright red banners of the Citadel. Not a single giant billboard message from the Steward could be found. More unfamiliar was the silence. No gears or contraptions could be heard. Andi looked up, expecting to see signs of the mechanical life they had become so use to, but there was no sign that any of these buildings had been updated. The walls were bare, not a single steam release valve to speak of, and nothing was sticking up out of the surrounding buildings bellowing smoke.

"Everything looks so... so desolate!" stated Andi. Windows and doors stood open and many hung on a single hinge. Green moss, dust, and dirt saturated the signs and windowsills. It had been a very long time since anyone had occupied these buildings. Muck and covered the streets, one could hardly distinguish the stone road from the sidewalk. A wild dog ran across the road into an alleyway where three more waited.

All of this paled when Andi noticed the clarity of the sky. It was absolutely breathtaking. Scattered across the azure eternity were lofty white clouds that floated like cotton candy in the breeze. She realized the air was also not as heavy. Even with the pungent odor of decay in the street, the air smelled sweet.

As Andi reveled in the area's natural beauty, a flock of birds soared majestically above. It reminded her of the time her father took her camping along the farm fields in the Lynthia Theme, just so they could watch the birds and see the stars. Unconsciously, Andi grabbed her necklace, and started to rub her thumb over the honey comb emblem.

"Andi, look at this!" Glut called from the corner of the street, snapping Andi out of her trance.

"What is it?" she asked

"Look at this temple, it's the Temple to the Lady Arcadia, I thought it had been completely torn down!"

Arcadia was the Maker's first creation, the original Ethereal. Arcadia is believed to be the smartest and most beautiful and the powerfulest of all the Maker's creation. It was because of her beauty and brilliance the Maker created more life in the universe. Of the several temples built in her honor only one stood in the Citadel. The temple was old, and it did not look safe to enter. Its large bronze doors were lying on the ground, their hinges rusted.

Glut started up the steps.

Andi was about to protest when,

"Over here!" Dean stood near a large mounted plaque on the structure's wall. It bore a map of Diamin and its relation to the entire Citadel.

"Whoa," said Glut, pointing at a symbol on the map's north east corner. "This map still has the Grand Horse track in the Parnian Theme. It was demolished and moved to the Lynthia Theme almost fifty years ago. This map is an antique!"

Andi perused the criss-crossing streets and consecutive buildings. The massive Citadel was constantly changing, old structures replaced by newer and taller ones, theme borders slightly reimagined, and people shuffled. On this map, the Parnian Theme wasn't quite as large as it was today. According to these borders, Andi, Glut and Dean would be considered Azarian and not Parnian. Andi chuckled at the thought of being a no good Azarian. Much of the map, though, was current. The Grand Bazaar still stood in the center, the heart of the Citadel. It was the greatest economic hub on the shard, a giant market place that seemed to never sleep. The Bazaar was the size of many small villages, all five Themes of the Citadel touched it. Andi ran her finger along the map to the north of the Grand Bazaar, to the Mighty Gates of Astronomicus, through those gates and up the Great Corridor to the Royal Plateau. That's when Andi let out a small gasp.

"Look at this..." Andi pointed to the symbol on the Citadel fortress. "It's a crown. This map is from the time of the monarchy-before the Steward took over."

The trio stood quiet, invested in their own thoughts. Lurid silence pulled at Andi, and she looked quickly to her left and right. Everything was off. Her soul felt odd. She stared at a broken glass jar on the ground. She realized suddenly what was wrong: it was the vast emptiness. In Dupree, thousands of people walked the streets daily, but here in Diamin, she hadn't seen a single person.

"Something isn't right." Dean's voice was cold. He too had noticed the emptiness and it was beginning to get on his nerves. "How can an entire area like this be abandoned," he stared at the crown on the map, "for over *fifty years*? Why haven't we heard about it, and where are all the people? Furthermore, where is the professor? He's supposed to meet us here."

"I know the Citadel is huge, but I thought all the districts had been upgraded. That's what the banners told us." Glut turned to Andi.

"Why upgrade part of the city nobody lives in?" sniffed Andi.

"The professor has to be here somewhere," insisted Dean. "We just have to find the Forum."

The three pushed down the street, lost in the silence.

Dean stopped abruptly, "Obviously, the Citadel propaganda doesn't want people to know about this."

"Not know about what, though?" asked Andi. "Where is everybody? What happened here?"

"Guys- shut up. Can you hear that?" Glut motioned to the street. The whistle and hum of machines was noticeably absent.

"Look at the sky!" Dean's usually strong voice cracked. Andi followed his gaze to the southern mountain range towering over the Horizon wall.

The sky had changed. It was both blue and black coalescing like an oil painting. The sun reflected on the steel grey Castiel mountain range, the well-known barrier of existence. Its mountainous peaks ran a circle around the entire shard of Elisia, but these ridges seemed to take on a life all of their own. Andi realized the wind had shifted. It was blowing hot and arid. *This is too sudden,* Andi thought to herself.

The smell, previously enchanting, was now stale. The emptiness now seemed worrisome. The change, whatever this change was, was enough to make the trio unconsciously gather together. All three of them felt like they were being stalked by an unknown predator, but unlike a wild animal surviving for food, this predator, this new life, had a darkness to it. A presence so evil, that it was almost tangible. Fear crept towards them and with it a sudden burst of light and a cacophony of sound. The echo from the stone buildings multiplied the screech and they heard the dogs began to howl and whine, louder and closer than before. Birds flying overhead began thudding to the ground, and the dog pack appeared, ripping their small flightless bodies into shreds. The small hoard noticed the three, and stared, with a hunger in their eyes so desperate it seemed maddening. Several of them slowly approached, growling low and snarling sharply. Dean pushed the siblings behind him, summoned his full height, and tried to look intimidating.

The wind grew in strength, ripping around, blasting sand and dust. The clouds danced like a sea of violent waves crashing on a cliff. The three looked towards the mountains, and somehow their perception was warped. The mountains filled the sky and grew larger still. The peeks pulsated, red bursting from every precipice and out of the red light came an emerald flame. The fire was miles away, but it seemed to fly closer. The all-consuming blaze arose from the mountains. Inside it were eyes, evil, demonic, life sucking eyes of creatures and abominations. They were hideous and grotesque and appeared as a legion, multitudinous slits staring fiercely. Andi, Glut, and Dean's hearts fell to their feet, and their stomachs churned. A sinking feeling of pure dread overwhelmed them.

"The man was right, there is evil!" whispered Andi, her face twisted in dismay. "What are we going to do?"

The three stood locked in place, unable, perhaps unwilling to comprehend the danger and fear that wracked their bodies. Tears poured from Andi's face, but the wind ripped them from her cheeks. Dean shielded a paralyzed Glut. Never had any of them felt such emptiness. A gentle voice broke them from their daze.

"Be calm, breathe deeply." At once, the mountains died down, and soft blue replaced the painted dark sky. The air was clear and less than a remnant of red remained at the peaks of the mountains. The dogs were mollified and slunk back to their cracks and holes.

"My dear Andi, I may not have the full answer to your question, but I promise you, we won't die saying we didn't try!"

The three were relieved to see Professor Nikola Belladon standing behind them in his oversized cow hide duster. A large monocle adorned his obscenely tall top hat, held in place by a brass rod jutting from its brim, and his beard was short, full, and grey.

"Professor, what was that?" Dean's voice was beyond strained.

Andi wiped the remaining tears from her face. "What did we just see?"

"What you have just experienced is the very reason no one lives in Diamin. Decades ago, people started having problems, vivid hallucinations, obscene fear. Stress was cited, and bed rest prescribed. But the meltdowns spread. Entire streets would witness the mountains rising. Soon, everyone could see it and as years passed, it became more common. The people were moved away by the Steward. Now, if you are anywhere near the southern mountain range, you will witness this once a day."

Andi didn't understand. "I don't understand. Why would the Citadel keep this secret from us? How could the Steward think someone would not figure out an entire Theme was deserted?"

"I have only recently discovered this phenomenon myself." The professor leaned on a wooden cane with a polished red crook. "Tell me something, children. How much of our country have you explored? Is this the farthest you've been from Dupree?"

"Everything a good citizen needs is within his reach," Glut cited automatically.

The professor returned Glut's statement with a half-smile, "So would you consider it a personal choice to stay close to home? Or do you think it's something that's been pushed upon you?"

Glut looked at his feet, unsure how to answer the professor. Dean was more confused, realizing the truth in the professor's words.

Andi shook her head and tapped her foot impatiently, "What does all this mean professor? What did we just witness?"

"I am afraid, Andi, what you all have witnessed is the beginning of the end!" answered the professor, monotone and matter of fact, leaning on his cane. "I knew you wouldn't believe me unless you witnessed this for yourself."

The three stood in front of the professor dumbfounded.

"Don't you realize, now that you have seen this anomaly, that this is the whole purpose of our expedition? Why I have asked you all to join me? You are some of my closest alumni! I can't trust just anybody with this truth, and I need your help!"

Dean's eyes opened wide, "Whoa, help with what, professor? You can't expect us to be able to stop that! How could we stop those … those… THINGS?!"

"Well Dean, we are either going to save this spherical planet, re-imprison this evil, or take a front row seat straight to Hell. Either way, it will be an exciting adventure!" the professor proclaimed with almost childlike delight.

Dean stumbled forward, dropping his bag to the ground. "Exciting? How can that be exciting?!"

Glut looked confused. "Did you say planet?"

The professor cautiously took a step forward, using his cane for support. "Ah, yes, Glut…"

"The name is Garrett," reminded Glut, annoyed.

"A planet, *Glut,* is what we used to be. This shard is one of many shards that have broken apart from one another, and evil has crept its way out of the depths and found its way here!"

"But why here?"

"I'm not sure. I'm not really sure what has been preventing them from venturing past the mountain range. That still is very much a mystery to me, but it is a mystery I am definitely thankful for!"

Dean felt like his whole body was so tense it was going to break from the stress. "Why are you thankful?"

Belladon grabbed Dean's shoulders and spoke softly, "Because it means there is still time to fix it!"

"professor, you aren't making any sense!" fussed Andi, feeling like a child losing her parents again. The professor used the one word Andi could not hear and remain unmoved emotionally. "Planets are myths spouted by generations of superstitious illiterates. You can't expect us to believe any of that nonsense now!"

The professor's gaze was stern and unyielding. His blue eyes sparked against the sun's rays.

"My girl, I thought you, of all people, would appreciate the implication all of this has on the inhabitants of the Shard. Look! Look at the horizon and explain the evil that we see emanating from the rocks. I brought you all here to see what I have seen. Do you not feel the fear, the rage, and the utter emptiness?! That, my dear, is the look of pure evil, and it's trying to break through. I fear other shards have already been taken!"

Dean threw up his hands and pointed in the direction of the mountain range. "How can we manage to deal with whatever that was? I doubt the entire Army of the Citadel can fight against an evil like that!"

The professor's calmness was beginning to weigh heavily on the group.

"Follow me, everyone. We have a lot to do," instructed the professor, turning about and marching off, assuming the others would follow.

"Whoa, wait professor!" Andi cried out. The professor turned around. "You expect an expedition to stop all that? This isn't a dig, or even an adventure. It's a quest! A dangerous quest with dangers never even conceived from which we may not return. I forbid my brother to be subjected to such a life-threatening ordeal! You haven't even told us your plan!"

The professor paused and smiled. "My dear, I cannot convey everything I have planned, not yet at least. I am asking for your trust. I cannot promise we will win, or even that we will all make it home alive. However, when you are faced with such evil and decide to do nothing to prevent it, are you not as wicked as the evil before you?" The professor leaned on his cane and let out a sigh. "I am just as afraid as all of you, but I am old and there are more years behind me than in front. I have been quite successful as a professor and inventor. I have lived a life of privilege because of my work. As it says in that wretched biography written about me, I have made life simpler for the common Citadel citizen and have been hailed as one of the greatest minds in Citadel's history, but none of that compares to the challenge of stopping this evil! What does my life, or your life, or anyone's life mean if we do nothing and let this evil break free? It could destroy everything and everyone we hold dear!"

Nikola Belladon took off his hat, wiped the sweat from his face, and took a large breath. Andi was shocked at how old he looked. "I am sorry to have placed this burden on you, but I am desperate. No one will listen to me. You and the team I have assembled are all I could muster! I am asking you to join me. Join me and together we can try to do the right thing and stop the apocalypse before us." The professor let out a heavy sigh. "But if you do not want to, I will not beg. The shuttle back to the Parnia leaves in thirty minutes. I will not be upset if any of you decide to go home, back to your normal lives." The professor turned around and left the three standing a moment alone.

For several seconds Andi, Glut, and Dean stood motionless and silent, trying to process everything that had been dropped in front of them. What they all thought was a normal expedition to dig ancient artifacts was really something much bigger, grander, and most of all, much more dangerous. Their silent reveries were broken when Dean took a step towards the professor. Andi and Glut stared at Dean intensely. He turned to look at them.

"I don't know about you guys, but after the shit we just saw, there is no way I can go back to my... normal life." Dean's voice was filled with determination, short and gruff. Andi and Glut made no indication to move in either direction, and Dean threw up his hands, "You guys stay here, but I am going to try to make a difference - Hell, maybe when all this is said and done they'll make a statue for me!" Dean turned and followed the professor.

Andi turned towards her brother, "We can't really be considering this, are we? Or are we foolish not to?"

Glut looked at his sister, his face awash with different emotions. Andi gave him a look of exasperation, waiting for him to say something as she anxiously thumbed her pendant. Glut watched her rub at her necklace and a tear formed in his right eye. One of the few memories he had of his mother was her telling him about the Maker, the creator of all things, how he hammered out all life and balanced it so that each being could live and survive. Taking a deep breath and tensing his shoulders, he looked above Andi's head and said, "The key to unlocking the truth is in the planet."

Glut left Andi standing there, shocked and speechless. Her eyes stung, a flood of old memories of her father and mother consumed her. The barren empty feeling she felt, when she realized her parents were not coming back tied her stomach in knots. Andi was pretty sure she was not going to be able to stand much longer. She looked at her brother walking away, and the memory of her parents walking out the door perfectly replayed in her head. She expected the knots to get worse, but what she felt instead was the opposite. She felt steadfast and resolved. She would not let history repeat itself. She took a step forward and walked towards danger.

Echo from the Past

-Countless Millennia ago

There was always pain, but no day as painful as the long-ago day that changed all of creation: the day I fell to the surface of Aurelia. The war was close to won.

The Ethereal, mortal enemy of The Fallen, were all but defeated. We had taken so much from them: The Spiraling Tower of Himmel, the Diamond Mountains of Surga, even the Fortress of Azure on the fields of Elysium fell to our might.

There was but one last refuge for the Ethereal, one last place for them to hide--the most sacred of planets, Aurelia. Only the Ethereal would dare foul this holiest of place with their presence. Arrogant and brash, we knew the war would be won on Aurelia. After gathering our forces, we attacked.

The battle for Aurelia took centuries. On that last day, when all was but over, our Master, the leader of The Fallen, struck down his equal; the lady Arcadia, first ArchEthereal. After the death of the Maker's first child, everything changed. We didn't just lose the battle, we soon lost the war. I was one of the first to feel the acrimonious wrath of the leaderless Ethereal. Battered and left for dead, I fell. Fell from grace and all that I knew, I fell. And I kept falling.

For days I lay, broken and forgotten, feeling the planet beneath me crumble and groan. Together, we would die. From my place on the ground, I could see the battle rage on in the heavens, I watched as my brothers and sisters murdered one another, fighting for their beliefs, until the last of my kind were either dead or captured... The conflict that had raged on for almost a millennium was now done. It was over, we had lost. The Fallen were no more, and I was alone.

I owe my survival to a single human child. She found me mangled, while searching for any food left on her dead husk of a planet. She saw me as the answer to an unheard prayer to the Maker. Send us a deliverer to save us from our decline. This poor girl nursed me to health. For weeks she hid me in a cave, bringing me food, despite her obvious destitution.

"My little angel" she called me.

William F. James

Inevitably, the Ethereal came looking for me, they were nothing if not thorough. My wounds were healing, but I was defenseless against their strength. For the first time since that young girl found me, I spoke to her. I asked her if I could live within her, to stay hidden from my enemies.

The ignorance of man is something I could never comprehend. That sad, ignorant girl didn't even think, she simply answered yes. As if I asked her if she wanted to continue breathing. I hid inside that child and watched as she grew from girl to woman. I was always there, and she knew it too. I think she found comfort knowing she was never alone. Not a day went by when I didn't want to snap the necks of her entire family, so pathetic, so filled with faith that one day the Maker would come and make their lives better for the sacrifices and adversity they had endured. If they only knew their daughter harbored one of the creatures that brought their planet's annihilation.

In the years that passed while I was hidden, the family wandered the barren, desolate lands searching for sustenance. Once in a great while they would find a poor soul or two that had survived the apocalypse, but these additions never lasted long. Pain and tragedy thrived; trust was a thing of the pass. Too many times outsiders would try to cheat, steal, and kill for the little resources the family had, even while they offered it freely to those in need. In those years, every single moment of every single day drove me to the brink of insanity. I was frozen, isolated, and powerless, unable to do anything but watch and feel the presence of my enemies searching for me.

Only once did I break my fast and kill. My vessel was cornered by a man who was unhinged by loneliness, so filled with carnal rage and lust it disgusted even me. In his eyes I saw my human body go limp as I manifested my true form. I ripped his heart from his chest and fed it to him. Blood spilled down his chin as life drained from his body. For the first time since my fall, I felt the acute awareness of my true potential and basked in the sweet delight of bloodshed. It was euphoria.

The pursuit made me hungry, I craved the satisfaction of the hunt, but I had drawn attention to myself. Ethereal began to materialize in my immediate area. They had felt my presence and were drawn to me. I had to return to the recesses of my vessel's mind and hide once more.

Years passed in the constant monotony of searching for food and shelter. It was difficult to perceive the passage of time, every day was the same. I sometimes wondered if my vessel even remembered I was inside of her. After the incident, she never made any indication to suggest either way, but I could hear her thoughts. There were times I even knew what she was thinking before she did. The familiarity one can have with another so different astounds me still. Her mind was too young to remember life before the war. She never knew any existence beyond the barren wasteland. Her parents instilled in her a sense of civilization as best they could, but one can never truly grasp something as complex as culture without experiencing it for oneself. Sometimes, I would show her parts of my world as she slept, colorful dreams to combat the desolate bleakness that was her life.

On a day, inextinguishable from the rest, I realized it had been some time since I had felt the presence of the Ethereal. It felt as though they had stopped looking for me, they had gone. I was certain it was a trick and for months I waited, straining to feel them. I slipped from my vessel's skin, trying to bait them, but they wouldn't return. Had they given up on finding me? Was I absolved of my sins, to live without punishment?

I kept my vessel for longer than I should have. Time is disinterested, if not unkind. We watched as her planet perished. First her mother, then her father, her brothers, and then the strangers passed. She yearned for death. She wouldn't eat or move without my persuasion. It was challenging to feel safe without my shield, and I wasn't ready to dismiss her. I wasn't ready to let go of my constant companion. I held onto her too long…

…and then she was like me; we were truly alone…

William F. James

A Shriek

Chapter Two

From the first scroll of Zakarael, chapter 4 verse 12-13:
"...do not be surprised at the fiery trial when it comes upon you to test you, as though something strange were happening to you. But rejoice insofar as you share in sufferings with the Maker, that you may also rejoice and be glad when his glory is revealed."
From the first scroll of Zakarael, chapter 21 verse 16:
"Have you not heard what the young and innocent are saying?" asked the Maker "Listen! For through their lips can prophets be made!"

The professor had spoken from the heart, and he knew he had done his best to persuade the three to join his expedition. The anticipation was building inside of him the further he walked away without an answer. The trepidation he felt was very unsettling, his fear cried out and told him to run back and plead again. But he did not turn back and face them. Nikola knew it had to be their decision. He did not want to pressure them into joining. It had to be of their own free will. Dean and Andi were right when they spoke of the dangers, this was no academic expedition. It was in fact going to be very perilous. They would be facing an unknown threat with many unknown variables, something the professor wasn't very fond of. He was an organized man his entire life, he always had a plan. But as much as the professor wanted to prepare, he knew he had no clue what he was leading his people into. All he knew for sure was that the danger was real, and he was the only person capable of stopping it.

Oh Nikola, is that hubris? He asked himself in his head, *or is it divine providence?*

The professor's self-doubt quickly dissolved when he heard two pairs of large footsteps following behind. *Two out of three isn't bad,* he thought, *but I had hoped Andi was going to join. She would have been a great asset.*

Nikola Belladon smiled widely when a third pair of footsteps fluttered quickly across the stone road. Andi panted and caught her breath, the sound of her footsteps soon steadied. For the briefest of moments, the professor turned slightly and gave her an encouraging smile, but she avoided his gaze and pursed her lips. *Her stubbornness is as strong as her father's.* He momentarily smiled and closed his eyes picturing Andi's father's stern crossed face. A new image overpowered the stubborn look of Giatros to one of him smiling brightly, holding up a very young Andi, kissing her on the cheek. It filled the professor with hope. Though his good friend and colleague may be gone, there was still a part of him here now, walking beside.

As they neared the central forum, they saw maybe one hundred people spread out in an area that would typically bustle with thousands of people, performers, and street merchants. Crates of every size filled the plaza. Each crate was labeled with the University's distinct district emblem: the infinite shield of knowledge. Supplies were scattered on long tables. Andi and Glut recognized much of the excavating equipment from previous digs. More noticeable was the considerable amount of armor and weapons, including tesla rifles and plasma swords, more commonly known as "Plaz Swords."

The professor led them through the numerous tables and crates towards the other end of the forum. In a long line was a column of some of the largest vehicles any of them had ever seen. Decades ago, when the professor was a far younger man and King Magnus was still alive, Nikola became one of the most famous men in the Citadel, thanks to his Steam Powered Wagon. All steam powered technology the Citadel now took for granted stemmed from Belladon's original design. A substantial portion of the professor's wealth came from the design and sales of these steam powered devices.

Professor Belladon stopped near the front of the column, "As you can see, I have procured the latest and most advanced models of my S.P.W.s. We have nearly twenty Mark VII streamlined *Charioteers* equipped with crew cabins and we have more than two times as many Mark V *Ironhorses* with large cargo carrying capacity."

Andi and Glut were in awe of the vehicles. Dean marveled at the chance to see a Mark VII's engine up close.

Dean walked up and touched part of the closest Charioteer, running his hands down a large pipe breaking off from the boiler and heading back towards the crew cabin. He climbed up the ladder between the crew cabin and the small cockpit for the driver. "These are real beauties, professor!" he yelled from the driver's seat.

The professor smiled, enjoying Dean's enthusiasm, "Pull the yellow lever, my boy!"

Dean did as he was told, and the entire roof of the driver's cabin opened up as glass slid down, opening the cockpit to the outside.

"It's a convertible!" Dean's smile was contagious, "Oh, I can't wait to drive one of these! Professor, this is amazing!"

The professor beamed, and signaled for Dean to come down, "All in due time, let's get going. There is still more to see!"

Glut was admiring the long line of Steam powered wagons when he noticed an odd one near the end. "Professor is that a Mark III down there?"

"YES! AND IF ANY OF YOU GO NEAR IT I WILL KICK YOU OUT OF THIS EXPEDITION AND REVOKE YOUR DIPLOMAS OR YOUR ABILITY TO GET ONE!" yelled the professor abruptly. "Under no circumstances do you go near it. Do you understand me?"

The Three of them, wide eyed and shocked, nodded in unison.

The professor's anger was gone a moment later and he smiled, "Very good, now come along, there is more to show you. Time is of the essence!"

The professor continued the tour. Near the edge of the column, several of the Mark V's were hitched to very long trailers covered in tarps. Dean made multiple attempts to sneak a peek underneath the green plastic and was reprimanded by the professor each time. Numerous people who appeared to be a part of the professor's team were busy organizing items and sorting through the crates. As they surveyed the area, the professor was approached at least three times by different people asking how he wanted things prepared.

"Professor Belladon, your tea?" A medium built young man held out a large mug. "Forgive the mug, but it was the smallest container I could find!"

The professor took the mug and sipped gently. "Thank you, Steven, this is a fine brew, very lovely indeed." The professor turned, "You all remember Steven?"

Andi and Dean nodded simultaneously. Glut, however, could hardly muster an expression. He kicked some dirt with his shoe, then belted out an awkwardly loud and tense "YEP."

Andi could hear the disdain in her brother's voice, but she ignored it. She knew Glut didn't always have such disdain towards Steven. Glut was actually quite fond of him when the previous year's expedition began. During that time, the group was excavating a progenitor temple site and Glut looked up to Steven. Everyone thought of Glut as Andi's kid brother, but Steven made a point to make him feel included; he even called him Garrett.

Everything changed after the discovery. It happened towards the end of the dig. Everyone was overworked and exhausted but coming up short. Some of the group took it out on Glut, insinuating he wasn't pulling his weight. Steven tried to cheer him up, and convinced him to call it a night, "Forget those jerks, and go get some rest. Tomorrow's a new day!" Tomorrow was a new day, Glut had accidently slept in. When he awoke, he felt strange. He stumbled out of his tent and immediately emptied the contents of his stomach. No one seemed to care, or even take notice. They were all too busy congratulating Steven. As Glut walked towards the group, he pulled off his shirt and wiped off his mouth, "What's going on?" That morning Steven had found numerous artifacts in an area Glut had already dug through. Alongside the relics, Steven also found several ancient manuscripts and sacred scrolls. The professor was thrilled, everyone was, and though nobody said it, he knew what they were all thinking: "Glut doesn't belong here."

The whole experience left Glut feeling betrayed and confused, and to compound the feeling, Steven completely shut Glut out. He thought perhaps Steven's sudden success had gone to his head. Andi repeatedly assured her brother he was being overly sensitive and jealous. Despite his sister's brush off, Glut couldn't help believing deep down something was not right about the whole ordeal. From that point forward, everything Steven said or did agitated Glut immensely. Especially Steven's tendency to miraculously appear with the professor's favorite hot brewed tea.

"Andrastii, it's been too long," Andi and Steven shared a quick embrace which was interrupted by a voice that rang like a delicate bell.

"Oh, professor!" This particular bell made Andi's skin crawl.

As Leora bobbed towards the group, her red hair remained perfectly in place. Draped over one arm was her tool coat, and attached to the other was a tall, muscular man wearing a tan leather jacket with large buttons. He didn't seem to mind being dragged about.

"Hello everyone! Look who I found just standing around!"

"Oh, forgive me, Thaddeus! I didn't mean to keep you waiting," Steven gestured for the large man to step forward.

"Professor, this is Thaddeus, the founder and commander of the Equinauts. He was recommended to me by Colonel Jaster. He and his men are the best armed protectors outside of the Citadel Army."

"Oh, yes. Thaddeus it's good to finally meet you in person." said the professor reaching out his hand. "But, I must say I am confused by the gift I received from you earlier today." He reached into his pocket and pulled out two small wood carved dice. "I am afraid I do not quite understand."

"They're symbolic of life and death" answered Thaddeus, accepting the professor's hand and shaking it firmly. "Life is the only true currency we own and every day we gamble against death. Hiring the Equinauts increases your odds of winning that bet."

The professor smiled and nodded, he appreciated the thought behind the gift. Obviously, Thaddeus was more than just a man searching for the next fight.

Andi stood rooted, mouth agape. Thaddeus was herculean, in stature and bearing. He was the most handsome man she'd ever seen. His gaze made her blush, and her jaw snapped shut. Andi was unsure how to handle such attention. In an attempt to seem unfazed by her star struck emotions, she forced out a question. "What is an Equinaut? I've never heard of them."

"My dear girl—" The professor pushed a button on his tall top hat, and down swung a monocle through which he peered at Thaddeus while searching for the precise words to use, "Well, an Equinaut... The Equinauts are Mercenaries cavalry men who get-"

"Mercenaries? Cavalry!?" Glut hissed tactlessly remembering the sign at the Crossroad station. "You hired Mercenaries, professor!? The Steward has outlawed all armed horsemen because of the black rider massacres. How do you know these aren't the killers themselves?"

"If they were the killers, do you think you've just placed yourself in a prudent position?" Professor Belladon gave Glut a moment to realize his mistake. "The Equinauts are a group of men founded by Thaddeus to protect innocents. They've risked their lives countless times protecting innocents stuck in crossfire during the Citadel War on the Slavine. Plus, many of their horses are not black."

"Ask yourself if we are to be trusted once I save your life, child. You are lucky your guardian has enlisted our help," Thaddeus's voice was gruff, but the words spoken were precise and fluid.

Andi could hear education in his accent, and conceit in his tone.

Thaddeus' deep guffaw did nothing to ease Glut's alarm.

"After witnessing the Mountain's demonic transformation, my men and I are equipped to confront any threat to the city," Thaddeus said more seriously, extending his hand toward the professor.

"Not just the city, Thaddeus, the entire planet!" the professor met his reach enthusiastically.

"Oh, of course, sir!" Thaddeus' professionalism allowed Andi only a glimpse of a puzzled frown.

As the professor made introductions, Thaddeus internally assessed his new charges. Glut was young, perhaps too young to be on an expedition like this, but Thaddeus recognized the potential for great strength, if not some arrogance in the kid. Dean, though brave, was not a fighter. Thaddeus's instinct told him not to trust Dean, and an instinct tested by battle was rarely wrong. Andi perplexed him. He wasn't sure where to place her categorically, as an asset or a burden, but his initial interest meant he would have to be cold to her. Then there was Leora. He was sure they were strangers, but at first sight he felt the strongest sensation of déjà vu. She wasn't just easy on the eyes, she felt like home. In spite of her obvious lack of experience, he admired her enthusiasm and could tell she had a lot of heart.

"Professor, half our men went on a mission in the Aedunic territory, but my remaining men are ready to go, just give the word. "

The professor made to place his hand on Thaddeus' shoulder, but settled instead on his forearm, "Fifty or one hundred, I'm confident in your abilities. I am glad you and your men are here."

Thaddeus stood tall. The sight was impressive. "There is still a lot of university gear to be packed and placed for the journey. My men will start there. I see you've acquired more horses for our expedition. It will be advantageous to have extra mounts for each of us. Your foresight will be rewarded when we travel twice as far on a single rest."

"Extra mounts were a cautionary measure, I've spared no expense acquiring the horses, they are the very best. And yes, please order your men to begin!" the professor inhaled deeply "The sooner we commence, the less likely the Citadel will notice our movements. Time is of the essence!"

"Thaddeus," cooed Leora, "I've never ridden a real horse before. Is there any chance you could teach me?"

Thaddeus turned to Leora, he couldn't help but smile. "I am sure we can arrange something."

"Thank you, thank you!" replied Leora with a genuine smile on her face, "I can write this down in my journal as the first real thing I've learned!"

"A journal?" asked the professor.

"Yes, my father asked me to keep one while I'm away. You see, we both enjoy learning new information, and after we've learned something new we always share it with one another. My only difficulty is retaining it all in my head." Leora spoke quickly. "It's incredibly frustrating, I wish my memory was better. He knows this about me, which is why he bought me the journal, isn't that a thoughtful gift?"

Andi rolled her eyes and turned her head slightly, so no one could hear her, "Maybe if you stopped talking so much you could keep something put in your head, trollop".

"What a splendid idea, I keep one myself," stated the professor, "my brain is always thinking up something new to invent or to enhance."

Thaddeus gave a small laugh, "Stick with me kid and you'll have that journal filled in no time."

Thaddeus wrapped his arm jovially around Leora's shoulders, and the two marched off, but not before the professor made sure Thaddeus and his men knew not to go near the Mark III wagon.

Andi's curiosity about the wagon was not as large as her displeasure of Leora, "I keep a journal, I've never ridden a real horse before. Ugh, could she be any more fake!?" Andi seethed as she watched Thaddeus move his arm from Leora's shoulders to her waist.

Fortunately for Andi, only Glut overheard her jealous remarks. When he raised his eyebrow, she felt a little ashamed.

"With this many men, we'll surely be noticed by the Citadel. Won't the Steward be angry that you're spreading the truth about Diamin? Are we going to get in trouble too if the Citadel arrests these Equinauts?" asked Dean.

"Perhaps we will be noticed, but soon the Citadel will be the least of our worries," the professor stated darkly.

***

Glut's arms burned. In the course of merely an hour, he had probably moved more boxes than he had in his entire life. The professor was definitely preparing for a long trip. He sat down for a much-needed rest, exhaled deeply, and wiped away the sweat accumulating on his forehead. "After this, the expedition will be easy," he whispered to himself.

"Come on youngster, we need to get these boxes loaded," said a hardy voiced man who had arms the breadth of a horse's head.

"Youngster?! You don't look old enough to be ordering me around, maybe wide enough!" Glut spit, annoyed.

"Watch your tone with me, I'm forty-seven!" answered the man, smiling and wiping his own sweat off his forehead, "You have to eat red meat every day, for every meal, and you will never grow old!"

"Really?" asked Glut "I love bacon."

"No!" laughed the man, "I just have good blood. My father looks the same way. Seventy nine, doesn't look a day over thirty-five."

"Wow," Glut wasn't sure if he was being tricked.

"The name is Egon Kassidine, but most people just call me Wrench," the man was holding out his large hand.

"I am Glu…" Glut forced a small cough, "I'm Garret. Why do people call you Wrench?" His own hand was dwarfed in Wrench's, and Glut feared for his fingers during the firm handshake that followed.

Wrench smiled and pounded his chest with pride, "Because I can fix, build, or jury-rig anything you ask!"

"Oh, well you probably would like my friend Dean, he has a Mech degree," replied Glut.

"Dean, I know him, good lad!" replied Wrench, "Let's get going, if we don't load all of these boxes of Aeturnus coal onto the S.B.s, we'll be walking at the end of all this."

"S.B.s?"

"The steam boilers, mate" Wrench lifted a large box with little effort.

"Oh, never heard them being called that before," Glut opened one of the boxes and noticed they looked nothing like ordinary coal, they were more like silver jewels. "What's the difference between a piece of normal coal and an Aeturnus coal?"

"Aeturnus coals are very rare, very valuable, and can only be found near the Red Gates of Nornwihr. A single rock can power a wagon for a whole day"

"Nornwihr? The volcanic city? But isn't that in Slavine territory?" mused Glut.

Wrench nodded, "You're right, that's partially the reason it's so rare. It's a shame really. Those ignorant Slavine, they horde it, when coal is absolutely useless to them. They haven't any kind of steam powered machines, and their bodies are so thick that they don't need heat. I've also heard they don't even cook their food. They just let it rot and stink outside for days! Grotesque, that's what they are. To never know the taste of a perfectly seared steak smothered in butter and topped with strips of slow-cooked bacon is downright criminal!"

"Thanks a lot!" Glut snorted.

"What?" asked Wrench surprised, "You're not a Slav lover, are you?"

"No, you made me hungry with all this talk of bacon!" Glut smiled.

Wrench let out a hearty laugh and smacked Glut on his shoulder, sending him forward a few steps, "I like you, Garret. You're a funny kid!"

At the end of the following hour, Glut was officially physically and mentally exhausted. After loading the rest of the crates of Aeturnus coal, Wrench had somehow talked Glut into helping him take apart the assembly casing for the cylinder and piston that propels the wagons forward. Glut was not a mechanical person, so Wrench's lesson on how the steam powered wagons worked was tedious and uninteresting. Wrench explained in four different ways how the coal heats the water in the boiler, and the heated water becomes steam. Steam then pumps into one end of the cylinder and pushes the piston forward. A valve rod moves and the steam enters the other side of the cylinder, pushing the piston back to its original spot.

"This process repeats over and over again and that, my friend, is what causes motion," Wrench finished his long lecture on locomotion. He re-bolted the cover to the piston assembly and smiled at Glut, "Ah, we're finally done. Let's get some food, I am starving!"

Glut helped seal the last of the metal plates to the boiler, "No arguments from me."

Slapping Glut's shoulder, Wrench walked over and picked up a very large, very heavy wrench. The wrench was nearly the length of his entire arm. Glut looked on wondering what machine would ever need a wrench that big.

"That's huge!" remarked Glut. "Why would you need a tool that big?"

Glut was answered with a laugh, "You'd be surprised the uses I find for a tool like this." Wrench smiled and stroked the smooth edge of his tool and placed it behind his back into a custom made sleeve. "I call her Besty. She is my most trusted tool and the real reason I bare the name Wrench. It's a great story— remind me again and I'll tell you all about it."

Wrench led Glut to the opposite end of the forum where a table had been set displaying all sorts of delicious looking meals, including the very same butter-covered steaks Wrench had spoken about.

Glut grabbed a plate, "This looks amazing. I've never seen so much food at once. This is way better than the C.P.'s we get. I could get used to this!"

"Hah, that's doubtful. I've been here three days working on the Mark V's and VII's and I got to tell you, I am tired of eating Citadel army rations. It's sort of like chewing on a boot that was walked in all day and covered with mud! That butter-like substance is pure lard." Wrench made a face. "I would take a C.P. over any army ration."

After that description, Glut looked down at his serving with disgust. Wrench on the other hand was balancing several large juicy steaks on his plate "Eat up kid, you'll need the energy!"

Glut resented being called a kid and was nervous that it was becoming a regular thing.

"Where's the bacon?" asked Wrench in a booming voice at a small man in a white culinary outfit behind the table.

"We don't have any bacon" explained the small man softly.

"Steak without bacon, what are we, Slavine?" bellowed Wrench. The small man scurried away, frightened. Wrench looked down at Glut and winked.

Glut laughed. "You sound like you eat bacon all the time. My sister and I are lucky if we get bacon in our C.P.'s once a month."

"Kid, I eat bacon almost every day!" proclaimed Wrench enthusiastically, "Stick around, I'll show you how to get more food a day than you could from a week's worth of Citadel Provisions! Anything you can imagine lad, bacon, steak, potatoes, bread, and even fresh baked apple pie!"

"DEAL," Glut followed Wrench to a table, his mind dancing with food, distracting him from the day's aches and pains. He dived right into eating his steak. Wrench sat down next to him and placed Besty on the table. The ping from the large tool hitting the table caused Glut to jump slightly. Looking around the eating area, he recognized many of the faces from past Progenitor digs and excavations. He smiled and waved at them. The rest of the faces he did not recognize and assumed the ones he didn't belonged to the Equinaut Mercenaries. They sat together, and each wore a leather jacket in varying shades of dark brown.

"—So, then the Slavine plowed through the wall, coming through at full speed," chanted a charismatic voice that could woo any woman. The voice came from across the table, and sure enough, the man was surrounded by several captivated women from the university.

"And then??" prompted a brunette.

"I heard a Slavine can sprint faster than a horse," a blonde added enthusiastically.

The man speaking had dark hair and a funny, thin mustache with a small goatee. He waited until they were all looking at him, "Why yes, ladies, it's true. They can run faster than most and the way their shoulders lock in place allows them to smash through almost any solid object." He threw out his hands to startle the women, "So, there I was, face to face with this monster. He stood at least two feet taller than me, probably more, and his soulless eyes stared right into mine. The family I was protecting were all huddled behind me frightened, begging me to save them from the terrifying reptilian ape." The women all gasped and some fluttered their lashes. "I drew out my sword and pointed it directly at his monstrous face," the man held out his arm straight out re-enacting the pose and said, "YOU SHALL NOT TAKE THIS FAMILY!"

"Then the Slavine brute began to laugh, for the scrawny little man in front of him posed no real threat" mocked a voice behind the group.

The dark-haired man slowly turned to see who had interrupted him with such a defamatory statement. The new man had short, neatly trimmed black hair that neatly connected to his beard via perfectly sculpted sideburns. His face was stern and foreboding, one good look at him and even the most accomplished sword fighter would think twice before engaging him. He was tall and large. His broad shoulders and large upper arms made him look quite formidable. Someone whose bad side you would not want to be on.

The dark-haired man stood up and tried to look intimidating, but due to the size differences, there was no stance he could enact that would pull off the look he was trying to achieve, "I believe you owe me an apology. "

The large man leaned in very close and pierced the short man with incredibly defiant eyes, "It will be a very cold day in Bellows when you hear me say that!"

Hearing the tone in the larger man's voice caused some of the witnesses around them to gasp. Seconds became minutes as the two men stared at each other, by now the entire food area had gone silent. Everyone was focused on the stare down between the two men. Wrench whispered under his breath, "Hit him," hopping for a good old fashion kitchen brawl. Glut, on the other hand, was quite nervous. He couldn't help but notice how the women swooned staring at the men.

After an eternity the game of chicken was finally broken, "Gladthorn!" The short storyteller had broken the lull, "If I remember correctly, was it not you who lay unconscious in a villager's house for hours? I believe it was Thaddeus and I who saved you."

Gladthorn bit his lip and formed a half smile and laughed, "Oh, yes, Italicus" his face grew serious and his voice deepened, "I do have to point out though, it was hard to stay conscious after your misfired artillery blast caused an entire house to fall down on me." Gladthorn stretched out his hand.

Italicus walked over, grabbed Gladthorn's hand, and gruffly wrapped his other arm around Gladthorn's shoulder, "Ladies," smiled Italicus, "Let me introduce you to one of the last living Bloodhound Marshals. He is the heart of our merry band. He is the best damn scout and tracker the Equinauts, nay, the shard has ever seen!" He leaned in towards the women, "And if I might add the greatest lover in the history of love. That's right, I'm looking at you, pretty eyes," he nodded his head towards Gladthorn and raised his eye brows several times. "Don't you think so? Trust me, he is all man!"

Gladthorn shrugged humorously at his friend's comments until Italicus began pointing at something below the belt, "Nope, that's enough you can stop right there!" Gladthorn's very concerned look spurred everyone into a burst of laughter. Gladthorn waited for the laughter to die down and then leaned towards Italicus and in a serious tone said, "Thaddeus needs you, man."

Italicus gave a curt nod, walked back to his table and grabbed a roll.

"Well ladies, duty calls! I'll have to finish that story later." Italicus bowed and seductively stroked one of the women's cheeks. He reached over and kissed another girl on her forehead. "It pains me to part with you all, but I know it pains you more to watch me leave."

Gladthorn's smirk was awkward, he wondered if Italicus was really trying to flirt with the ladies or just keep himself entertained. Gladthorn reached his arm around Italicus' shoulder to lead him away, but not before asking him in a very loud voice, "Did you show them your pretty, pretty, feather. It's gold and he keeps it in his ear!"

Italicus froze in place.

Gladthorn reached into his pocket and pulled out a very large, gold carved feather. Italicus instinctively reached for it, but Gladthorn was too quick and placed it back into his pocket. Italicus dove for his friend's pocket only to be easily deflected.

The women around the table began to giggle. Italicus looked up at his friend with swollen, red cheeks and large wide eyes. Italicus was clearly embarrassed at Gladthorn's comment and ability to out maneuver him, but what was even more shocking was that he had made an actual joke. Gladthorn was largely known for his sense of duty, not for his comedic talent, for which as far as Italicus knew, was nearly non-existent. Everything made sense though when Italicus saw Thaddeus standing in the distance dying in laughter.

Embarrassing feather or not, the girls stood to watch Italicus leave with yearning eyes. The girl Italicus had kissed smiled dreamily, "He's so brave!" She elongated each word.

Glut looked up at Wrench. They were sharing the same expression. "Can you believe that guy?"

Wrench, who had already devoured one of his steaks, smiled, "That, my boy, is a man who is lying to himself, compensating for something tragic in his life," bits of gristle sprouted between his teeth.

"What makes you say that?"

"Because mate, I am in the same boat," replied Wrench, as he ripped into another steak. "He's either trying to get over a bad break-up, or some gal he desires won't give him the time of day."

Glut nodded, trying to look like he totally understood what Wrench was referring to. His thoughts rushed to Leora, and how he pined for her attention. He wondered if he was compensating for it somehow, and worried it was obvious to Wrench.

"There you are!" Andi closed in on their table, "I was looking everywhere for you!"

Glut looked up smiling but quickly frowned when he saw the look in his sister's eyes, "I've been helping get the vehicles ready to move out!"

"Oh really? You've been helping? You don't know the first thing about steam powered wagons," challenged Andi mockingly.

Glut was annoyed with his sister's quick judgment. "You're right, I don't, but *he* does," he answered, pointing a thumb towards Wrench. "This is Egon Kassadine. Egon, this is my sister Andrastii. He is going to show us how to get more food than C.P.'s"

Wrench's face went slightly red, "Of course I will! It's a pleasure, Lass. Please, everyone calls me Wrench." He stood to shake Andi's hand.

Andi's was astonished at the size of the man. He towered over her like she was a small child. "Pleasure to meet you," she sighed. Andi sat down beside them, flopped a heavy book down onto the table, and laid on top of it, head in her arms.

"What's wrong, sis?" asked Glut, slightly embarrassed by his sister's lack of etiquette.

Andi lifted her head slightly, "I don't know, we've only been here a few hours now and I'm utterly exhausted. The professor gave me list of books to read ranging from ancient church history, celestial understanding, and a very disturbing book about the Bloodstone cult."

"Blood cult?" asked Glut.

"The Bloodstone cult Garret, they're nasty business I tell ya," remarked Wrench before Andi could answer. "They are fanatics- been around since before the Citadel formed. Every generation or so they rise in numbers and become a sore for anyone who isn't a member." Wrench paused for a moment, "The last time I saw one was about twenty-five years ago.

"I don't understand, "mentioned Glut, "What makes them so bad?"

"Blood" spoke up Andi, "They believe that their god was cast out of the heavens and fell from grace upon the Bloodstone. It's the very center of their entire belief system. They believe that through the giving of member's blood, they will bring about their god's return. The problem is, they have tried over and over again and it never works."

Glut huffed, "Maybe because it's false?"

"Maybe, maybe not" answered Andi, "They believe it to be true and when it doesn't work they always blame one thing."

"What's that?"

"More blood lad. "Wrench looked at Glut disgusted, "Innocent blood."

Glut was taken back, "That's horrible!"

"What's worse is that if their god did return, the world would be burned, and all non-believers would be destroyed."

"Why in the world would the professor want you to read that?"

Wrench had lost interest in the sibling's conversation and continued to eat away at his steaks. Reaching over he began to thumb through some of the titles to the books Andi had placed on the table. "Bless the stars, that's a lot of reading!" remarked Wrench, "How can Belladon expect you to read so many."

Andi sighed, "That's only a few, I have over fifty on my list."

"How can anyone read so much and retain all that information?"

Glut let out a small laugh, "Are you kidding, she'll have them all read in a few days. This girl reads faster than anyone I know, and the sick part is, she will remember every word."

"Really?" asked Wrench, impressed.

"No, not really!" answered Andi, angrily.

"Is that so?" said Glut abruptly grabbing the book right from under her, "'The Maker and Death' by Father Gildum Battshaw. That's pretty deep, Andi." Glut opened the book and flipped through a couple of pages, "What was said on the 23rd page, 2nd paragraph?"

"It's a quote from the formation scroll, happy?" Andi stuck her tongue out at her brother.

"Ahhh, but what does it say?" asked Wrench, smiling as he glanced down at the page.

Andi let out a large sigh, "Fine, it says, at the birth of the universe the Maker saw the vastness of his creation and became lonely. The scrolls reopened, the master scroll was unrolled, it wielding life and death in its command. In his rush, the Maker breathed life into existence, but so too did he breathe death. This caused the Maker much agony. In his compassion, he bestowed upon Death limited powers. By protecting us with his own divine, one by one we shall leave this world and join the Maker in paradise."

"Whoa, not a single mistake," Wrench was astonished.

"Yeah, she's great with books, but she can't remember where she leaves anything," teased Glut.

"I'll level with you two," Wrench's loud voice was now hushed. "I'm not much of a, you know, umm, religious sort. I always saw nature as the real ruler of the world, and only put my stock in things I could see and feel. But now, after I saw those mountains transform, nothing has been the same. I'm not so certain about life and death and how the world really works anymore."

"It's made me rethink a lot myself," commented Andi. "Take comfort in knowing that Nature and the Divine are not really separate beings but are one and the same. The order of the universe is not left to random chance or circumstance. It's planned out and thorough."

"Aye, but what about..." Wrench was unsure how to ask, "umm, death. You've obviously read a lot. Where do you think we go? What truly happens to us?"

"Well, if the scrolls are to be believed, we go to be with the Maker. What that means, I am not sure. The prophets use the word Paradise a lot," answered Andi.

"But what do we do there? Just sit around and be happy? Are there things to build? Stuff to do? I don't think I could exist in a place where I wasn't using my hands, creating something," replied Wrench, a little lighter now.

"Well. several of the new age scrolls found in later Progenitor sites read that once with the Maker, we won't be idle. Inactivity breeds contempt. Cognitive beings can't just sit around and do nothing for eternity. I am sure there will be stuff for us to do," assured Andi.

Glut proposed, "If the Maker is real, why wouldn't he just tell us so? You know, speak to us?"

Andi looked at her brother with annoyance, not wanting to get into the same philosophical debate the two siblings had had many times before, "The scrolls say that we were made to be free. Beyond the divine in all of us, the greatest gift we have is our free will to choose right and wrong, to have faith in others and the world around us. Now imagine if the Maker spoke to us all directly. Seeing him in all his power and glory, we would no longer have faith. And without faith we would no longer have free will."

"Why wouldn't we?" asked Wrench.

"Some say that if a being of such phenomenal omnipotent power capable of creating and destroying the world made himself known, people would tremble in fear, paralyzed in awe. Civilization would collapse as we know it," recited Andi. She added "If the Maker is real, and truly loves us, he will respect our free will and allow us to have faith in him."

William F. James

Wrench's eyes were red-rimmed, "Thank you, Lass, there's definitely a lot I still need to confront. For as long as I can remember, I have always had a fear of death. The idea perplexes me. One second, we are thinking and feeling, interacting with loved ones, and then suddenly, in the blink of an eye, we're gone, done. Is this something we notice only on this side? Do we transfer straight to be with the Maker? Or is there nothing after death. We cease to be, gone forever? It frightens me. It gives me a real headache to think about such things."

"Any time you want someone to talk to, I love a good discussion," answered Andi with a half-smile. She loved putting her information to use. She pondered death herself. She really hadn't thought about it before and she soon brushed the idea out of her head. She was young and healthy. She wasn't going to die any time soon.

**

Nearly four hours had passed since Dean and his friends arrived in Diamin, and he was becoming increasingly listless. He tried to help with the packing but was rebuffed by several of the university employees. Dean couldn't help but feel slighted. He had risked a lot joining this expedition, particularly, pending its length, his job. Working at the manufacturing workshop was not his ideal job. In fact, he resented working there, but after five years at the university earning his degree in modern mechanical design, the best job he could find was manual labor, working with smelting machines.

To pass the time, Dean decided to explore the empty forum. He eventually found himself around the makeshift corral, where roughly one hundred heads of horses stood aimlessly confused by the lack of grass on the stone floor. Another forty or so mules and donkeys were also penned in the corral. Several of the horses approached Dean, looking to see if he had anything edible, like carrots or sugar cubes. He felt a little intimidated being in such close proximity to these large creatures. He had only been around a few horses in his life and being as short as he was didn't help. Even smaller donkeys seemed daunting to him.

"Amazing animals- aren't they?" asked a soft voice.

Dean turned around to find a petite woman in rider's pants standing in front of him. Her brown hair was pulled back in a very tight bun, but her smile softened Dean's surprise.

Dean produced his most striking smile and held out his hand in greeting, "I'm Dean!"

The woman giggled demurely, "I'm Kaitlyn, it's nice to meet you, Dean."

She glided past him and reached out her arm towards the nearest horse. Her fingers opened to reveal a sugar cube. The bay horse walked up and sniffed her hand, wiggled his lips and pulled in the small treat.

"I think he likes it," said Dean, cool and cordial.

"She."

"Oh, right, of course!" choked Dean, cheeks blushing.

Kaitlyn grinned, "It's alright, the horses and I pardon your lack of experience. These animals are much more forgiving than any human."

The horse gave a small guttural sound, begging for another treat. Kaitlyn slipped her another cube, but now her secret was revealed, and more horses trotted over for treats. Dean was unsure if she was serious or not, so he smiled in an attempt to appear informed.

"Between you and me, I haven't been around a lot of horses. Maybe you could show me some tricks!"

"Be careful! They will beg like they are starving, but don't listen. They're all a bunch of actors!" interrupted Thaddeus approaching the two.

Kaitlyn let out a small giggle at Thaddeus' very true comment about horses, "Oh, I know!" She said enthused, "but I don't mind the attention it gets me."

"They sure know how to pull at your heart strings!" Thaddeus agreed.

Dean felt annoyed and slightly jealous. It was obvious that Kaitlyn was charmed by Thaddeus. A moment later Leora appeared smiling.

"Which one will I be riding!?" she asked eagerly.

Thaddeus smiled, walked into the corral, and returned with a large Liver Chestnut gelding. His coat was short and shiny. He had tall white socks on three of his legs, and his coarse mane and tail were a rich copper color.

"This is Wooley. I know he doesn't look like it now, but during the winter, his coat grows long and thick. He is very head strong but won't spook at anything. He's very smooth under the saddle."

Leora and Kaitlyn both began to pet Wooley as Thaddeus carried over a saddle and set it on the horse's back. Kaitlyn took the long straps in her delicate hands.

"You know your way around the saddle?" asked Thaddeus as Kaitlyn adeptly finished cinching up the girth.

"My father owns a large breeding farm outside the city. He does a lot of sales with the Men of the Lakes. He's the only breeder with stock from the Akhal-Teken line." Kaitlyn rubbed her hand up and down Wooley's sturdy neck.

"Your father is Marcus Duvel?" asked Thaddeus.

Kaitlyn nodded.

"Do you see the bay warrior, between those two black Friesians? The one with his head held high, that's Egghead."

"Egghead!?" Kaitlyn was astonished, "not *the* Egghead, last of the great sons bred from the Lord Horses Niatross and Bucephala?"

"Lord Horses? What kind of name is Egghead?" scoffed Dean.

Thaddeus smiled, "you are not the first to ask me that. Kernes Ivana named him."

"Who?"

"Ivana is one of the chieftains of the Reieni, one of the Aedunic tribes that settled south of Nornwihr in the valley of Veamini. The Reieni are known as Equitons, keeper of the Lord Horse Legacy. My Equinauts are based on their teachings. Each Lord horse's offspring are unique and usually named after a physical attribute. Egghead has a slightly domed cranium and was born with a small white star on his forehead, so Ivana named him Ceannu which translates to Egghead in the common tongue."

"What makes him a Lord Horse?" asked Dean.

Kaitlyn smiled, "There are only two Lord Horses in existence. They were the first two horses the Maker created. Every century, Niatross and Bucephala descend from the north and bare sires and mares for the Reieni. These offspring are called Capallcurada Champion horses."

Until now, Leora had remained silent, "I never knew the myth of the Reieni Horse Lords was true." She started to walk towards the beautiful bay warrior, "I can't wait to see Egghead up close."

Thaddeus threw Leora a large carrot from his pocket, "Give him this and he will love you for life!"

"You guys are kidding, Lord Horses that have been around since the beginning of time? Next you will tell me Hellhorses are real!" Dean chuckled, and Thaddeus shot him a dismissive look.

Kaitlyn completely ignored Dean's comment, "You are very lucky, once a Capallcurada chooses his companion, they are bonded for life."

"Egghead found me when I was only fourteen years old. The bonding ceremony was a few hours later and we haven't been apart since. He was the best man at my wedding," smiled Thaddeus.

"Oh, I didn't know you were married," replied Kaitlyn.

Thaddeus frowned, "Well, I'm not anymore."

Kaitlyn looked up and saw the pain in his eyes. Gently she offered, "I am so sorry."

Thaddeus nodded and immediately changed the subject, "Several of these mounts were bought from your father. He's especially perceptive when it comes to horses.

Kaitlyn didn't want to upset Thaddeus any further, so she indulged him with small talk, "Yes, he's gifted. My father only breeds his stallions with the best mares in the shard." said Kaitlyn, slightly too loud.

"May I ask a favor of you?" inquired Thaddeus, while placing Leora into the saddle.

"Of course," said Kaitlyn, matching the stirrup length to properly hold Leora's foot.

"I need someone experienced to oversee the horses while we are on this expedition. We will be traveling a good way and I need someone to make sure none of our mounts are over-taxed. Could you monitor their use and rotate them out when needed?"

Kaitlyn gave a sad smile, "I can do that, and I want to, but the professor has already given me a list of duties."

Thaddeus returned the smile, "No worries, consider yourself relieved! I will let the professor know you have been recruited by me. Welcome to the Equinauts!" congratulated Thaddeus, leading Wooley away with Leora on top.

Kaitlyn beamed and surprised Dean with a hug.

"I'm so excited! It's been so long since I have had a chance to be around horses!" She grabbed Dean's hand and pulled him along, "Come on, let me teach you!"

Kaitlyn pulled on him and he followed, smiling a large grin.

Dean thought he had been forgotten, but now followed Kaitlyn's lead. He gave Kaitlyn's hand a squeeze and thought to himself, *maybe this expedition won't be boring after all!*

***

Leora stood there, rattled and confused, staring at Wooley, hoping he would inspire her in some way. When no inspiration came to her she looked down at her journal. She had written many notes that Thaddeus had given her about being around a horse. He had been teaching her how to properly place the saddle on the horses' back when he was called away by the professor.

Leora looked up at the unharnessed saddle still lying on top of Wooly's back. It seemed like an impossible task of straps, loops, and hooks. She looked around for a familiar face to help her with the saddle, but everyone seemed to be busy. Leora reread her notes on how to take the saddle off. *Maybe if I do this backwards I can figure it out on my own,* she thought to herself.

Leora was standing at Wooley's side and reached under, grabbing the strap that she was guessing was the girth. She pulled it around the horse's waist, but it didn't quiet reach. Embarrassed at her own inexperience, she looked around hoping no one was watching her. She bent back over to look for a longer strap but there wasn't one. Leora leaned into Wooley and tried to pull the girth up tighter to the buckle, but it still wasn't enough.

"If this doesn't reach now, how did it before!?" she asked Wooley in frustration. Leora pulled the girth up with all her might, until it just reached the first latch.

"It's because he is bloating out his stomach." Leora was surprised by a voice she recognized. "The horse doesn't want you to make the girth very tight. Smart horses know how to play the inexperienced. Can I help you with that?"

Leora shook her head, "No! I am quite capable of doing and learning a great many new things, father! And if you are here to talk me out of going on this expedition, you have come for nothing. I am going and that's that!"

A very large and built man was now standing by Leora's side, "I thought we had agreed together you could, why would I change my mind now? I just wanted to stop by and see my only daughter off."

Leora looked up at her father, his eyes as brown as his full beard and shoulder length hair, "I am sorry father, I just assumed you were here to talk me out of this. You've been so protective in years past. You never let me go on any of the school trips."

Leora's father placed a hand around her shoulder, "What else was I to do? It was just me and you." He smiled warmly at his daughter, "It seems like only a few years ago you were just my little girl, but now you are a woman capable of making her own choices. All I care about is that you are home in time for your birthday!"

"That's months away!" affirmed Leora confidently.

"I am so sorry, Leora!" called Thaddeus, taking long strides towards the two, "The professor is getting a little frantic about leaving. How about I get Wooley re-saddled and I'll teach you once we make camp for the night." Thaddeus looked up at Leora's father who stood out like a sore thumb from the rest of the people in the forum, "Hello, I don't believe we've been introduced?"

Leora tried forming a full smile, her cheeks slightly blushed and her hair seemed to glow in the sunlight, "I'm sorry, this is my father, most people call him Lantheron. He was just about to leave!"

Lantheron looked down at his daughter. He heard the tone in her voice and realized right away she was smitten with this man.

Thaddeus held out his hand, "Lantheron, that's a very Aedunic name, unforgiveable, I believe."

Leora's father nodded and looked into Thaddeus' eyes sternly.

Leora giggled slightly, "That's not his real name, it's just what people call him. His real name is—"

Wooley let out a groan and his whole body shook. The saddle was now hanging sideways. Leora grunted in frustration, "That was tight a moment ago!"

Thaddeus laughed, realizing quickly that Wooley had played Leora. Thaddeus stopped laughing mid breath when he saw the look Lantheron was giving him. Thaddeus could now feel the tension in the air. Puzzled at Lantheron's harsh look and the awkward silence, "I am Thaddeus."

Leora's father's facial expression completely changed, he looked almost surprised to hear Thaddeus' name, "Thaddeus, Thaddeus PenRuger? Mercenary that used to live in KeyStone?"

"Yes, I did long time ago. I am sorry have we met?"

Lantheron shook his head, "No, but I have heard of you."

"Only good things I hope," commented Thaddeus smiling awkwardly, and holding out his hand again.

Lantheron looked down at Thaddeus' hand and then at Leora. Her face was now fully blushed and she stared at him pleadingly. *Take his hand* she urged with her eyes, bobbing her head slightly. Lantheron hesitated for only a moment before taking Thaddeus' hand.

"It was nice meeting you" chirped Lantheron robotically.

He hugged Leora tightly, "Be safe Leora, and be home before your birthday!" Lantheron turned and walked off at a brisk pace.

"Birthday?" asked Thaddeus, confused.

Leora shrugged her shoulders, "He's always been big on them."

***

The moment the last of the gear and provisions were packed, the professor yelled for everyone to enter their steam powered wagons, "Come now, time is of the essence!"

Andi ran to the professor, Dean and Glut following close behind. "Professor, where should we go? We haven't been assigned a wagon!"

"Bless the Maker, I totally forgot. You three are in my personal wagon, it's that blue one-half way down the line, the Mark II *Luxury Palace*. And let me tell you, despite its age, it's been fully modernized, upgraded, and fitted with a fantastic lighting system I invented! I call them propane candles. They haven't hit the market yet! Very good for reading, I dare say, and I think we will have a lot of time to read! Yes! Yes!" said the professor.

"Couldn't you have just upgraded it with the new light companion the Inventorii created?" Glut asked innocently.

The professor looked up at Glut with a perturbed face and muttered under his breath, "Damn ignorant inventorii."

They hurried down the line of wagons. Glut turned to ask the professor a question, only to see he was headed in the opposite direction. "Professor- aren't you coming with us?"

The professor turned back, "For now I prefer to use my horse! Do not fret my young lad, I will rejoin you in the wagon when I tire of the saddle!"

Glut nodded and hurried towards the line of wagons. In front of him, he recognized the back side of his very large and broad new friend. He called out, "Wrench, would you like to ride with Andi, Dean, and me? We have an open seat in our wagon!"

Wrench motioned to a second man almost identical to himself in size. "Garret! I want you to meet my brother, Martin Kassidine, you can call him Bolt though, everyone does."

Glut stopped briefly, "Bolt Kassidine!? The famous undefeated steam racer, Bolt Kassidine? You hold the fastest recorded lap, 2.5 miles in 40 seconds at The Lynthian Grand track! You sir are a legend."

Bolt smiled, "Two hundred and twenty-three miles per hour on a small four wheeled steam powered Chariot built by my brother Wrench!"

"Wow. Are you coming with us?"

"Nah, I am afraid my brother has a business to run," answered Wrench apprehensively. "He was just seein' me off."

Thaddeus's voice thundered over the bustle, "You heard the man, time is of the essence! Board up!"

"Well, I'll see you later, Wrench, there's a seat waiting for you if you want it," Glut held out his hand to Bolt. "It was an honor to meet you."

"Thank you, Garret," smiled Wrench. "I'm sure I'll join you guys at some point. One of the Mark V's is giving us problems, so I'll be there for now, in case it acts up."

"Good kid," Bolt said as Glut walked away.

"He's got potential, smart head on his shoulders," Wrench hugged his brother. "Are you sure you're ok with this? I can still back out."

"No, brother go, go. We owe the professor a lot. He needs you, I'll be fine, and the business is doing well."

Wrench looked at his brother firmly, "Do you have enough cash saved up? I don't want the Coiriúil family trying to rough you up for more money, so I paid Don Marone for three months of protection. Don't let Coiriúil's goons lean on you, you got that? I know what a push over you can be."

"Ha, we both know I'm bigger than you!" teased Bolt.

"I have a quarter inch on you but keep telling yourself that little brother and maybe it will be true one day," laughed Wrench, hugging Bolt.

At the head of the column, Italicus stood to the right of Thaddeus. They watched the professor mount his horse.

"That is a fine steed you have!"

The professor beamed despite himself. He was astride a perfectly coated Bay Appaloosa with a beautiful white blanket draped upon its rear. "Why, thank you, Thaddeus. Poncho and I have been through many journeys together. He has a backbone made of stone and has never failed me! Have you ordered everyone's weapons to be stored in the crates until we get out of the Citadel?"

Thaddeus nodded, "Yes, all weapons have been stored, only I and Italicus are armed with our plaz swords." Professor Belladon face was not pleased with what he was hearing, "Precautionary is all. "defended Thaddeus." We don't want to be totally defenseless. We will store them just before we arrive at the Great Gate."

"Very well." The professor looked down the long line of steam powered wagons, carts, and animals that were lining up behind them. His eyes locked onto the Mark III in the rear of the column, he was watching two Equinauts riding past it. "You are sure your men know not to go near the Mark III?"

Thaddeus took a large breath, "Yes, just like the other fifty times you have asked. Everyone knows not to go near it. Whatever you're keeping in there it must be dangerous."

"Or valuable!" remarked Italicus smiling.

A shudder clearly vibrated down the professor's back, Thaddeus could see Italicus' humorous comment did not sit well with him. Whatever was actually in the wagon scared the professor, Thaddeus was sure of that. "Please do not fret, there are no Verrator's among the Equinauts. We stand by our code of ethics."

"Ah, Verrator," remarked the professor amused at the allusion Which would make me Bailitheoir? The poor horse was betrayed by the one person closest to him. For you to betray me as Verrator did Bailitheoir, one must first trust you."

Thaddeus was slightly taken aback, but his charisma pierced through the sting of the professor's comment, "You trust us enough to protect not just your life, but the lives of all your men. Isn't that the purest, most intimate form of trust?"

"Very true "agreed the professor, "Let us hope that my trust in you will not lead me and my men to the same ending as Bailitheoir."

"My men and I will give our lives to protect the innocent."

William F. James

The professor smiled and bowed his head in acknowledgement. He took a deep breath and allowed the air slowly out of his lungs. He adjusted his top hat and mumbled a short, nearly silent prayer to himself. The professor reached into his pocket for his watch but instead found the dice that Thaddeus had sent him earlier as symbol of life and death. He stared at them for only a moment before dropping them back into his pocket and turned his focus onward, and spoke, "Thaddeus are you a betting man?"

Italicus snorted at the question and shot Thaddeus a smug look.

Thaddeus bit his bottom lip and pointed at Italicus, daring his friend to make a brash comment. Once he knew Italicus was going to be quiet, he looked up and smiled at the professor, "I have been known to take a bet from time to time, when I've felt lucky."

The professors' look was of resolve. He touched his hat, and his monocle swung up to the meet the brim, "I have never believed in luck, and I've been cautious with chance, but we stand here together taking the first of many steps towards a virtuous and perilous enterprise. It's unknown whether we will fail or succeed."

"Then there isn't much else we can do except trust in ourselves and pray for some divine providence," assured Thaddeus.

The professor smiled, "Oh, quite right." He paused and leaned down from his saddle, closer to Thaddeus, "Let's take this gamble now, you and I, and all those who follow us. We let fly the dice of chance and let them lie where they lay."

Italicus winked at the two men "Let's hope fortune smiles on us all." He motioned his hand in a dice throw.

Thaddeus shook his head sarcastically at his friend.

The professor smiled at Italicus' gesture and sat straight in the saddle, firmly grasping Poncho's reins. "It will take almost six hours just to travel to the edge of the Citadel, the sun is high now, but it will be dark by the time we reach the eastern road of Contúirt and the fields of Braum."

"We will make good time as long as we aren't stopped," added Thaddeus.

The professor nodded, "Quite right." He sighed deeply and closed his eyes, "Thaddeus, the time has come."

Both men mounted their horses, and at Thaddeus's signal Italicus lifted his right hand and yelled "EQUINAUTS! MOVE OUT!"

A loud chug of air and steam echoed off the deserted buildings of the forum as the wheels of the Mark V and VII's began to move forward. A collective clank of over one hundred horses' hooves drum-rolled and overpowered the high-pitched mechanical noises of the many steam powered wagons. The collective mood seemed charged and excited as the Expedition took their first steps away from the lifeless forum and out into the equally barren road and countryside of Diamin. Their excitement of adventure waned slightly passing through the vast emptiness. The destitution weighed on every soul as they traveled through one-fifth of the Citadel. They passed through cities, villages, and countryside, void of all forms of human life. Crumbling and forgotten, an entire kingdom of man became subservient to nature's will.

As the expedition neared the edge of Diamin, they moved towards the very populated Theme of Lynthia. They approached the internal wall system of the Citadel, marking the ancient borders of the old Kingdoms. The internal walls, standing at only several hundred feet tall, were tiny when compared to the vast heights of the Horizon. Built at the same time as its larger brother, the internal wall was seen as simply precautionary. In the unlikely scenario that the Horizon wall was ever breached, each Theme would be able to mount a proper defense against the besiegers. In the modern Citadel under the Steward, the internal walls were an easy means to keep the populace contained. Almost all transit between the Themes was done by shuttles, or through very limited gatehouse access.

Guard duty along the Gloriamarus, 'the little wall,' was considered punishment duty for disobedient soldiers, or the last easy post for older ones before retirement. Nothing, absolutely nothing, ever happened along the Gloriusmarus in the 'Silent Zone,' a rather Macomb nickname the soldiers had given to Diamin. So, it was a huge surprise to the sleeping guard, Amaro, when he was awoken to an entire convoy approaching his post. Unsure if this was an attack or just people caught on the wrong side of the border, Amaro began to panic tripping over himself.

"Ha- Halt!" he squeaked shaking slightly.

"The first peril of our journey!" joked, Italicus, as he held up his fist, signaling the column to halt. "Behold the low-paid, brainless grunt!"

Thaddeus shook his head and laughed. "Would you like me to handle this professor?"

"That's quite alright, Thaddeus. I got this, how do you think I got all this equipment into Diamin in the first place." The professor winked, kicked his horse and trotted to the guard.

Thaddeus and Italicus watched as the two men spoke. Without warning, more guards appeared.

William F. James

"What is the old man saying?" asked Italicus.

Thaddeus shrugged, "Beats me, let's hope it works, otherwise this will be one of our shortest jobs yet. We could use the money and I don't want to lose any more men to Finnius."

"Hey, It doesn't matter how short the mission is," Italicus paused for dramatic effect, "I'm keeping the security deposit!"

Thaddeus snorted. Time seemed to slow as they waited for the professor. Eventually he galloped back, but the professor's face displayed no sign of how the conversation went. He stopped in front of Thaddeus. The professor looked to his right and surveyed the unplowed and nearly decayed fields surrounding the area.

"Just look at this travesty. All those fields lay dead and wasted! The last Slavine war was fought over farming land in the northern area of Walderheim. How many more people have to die before the Steward stops denying this evil threat exists?"

"Professor," Thaddeus interrupted, "What did the guard say? Can we pass?"

The professor grinned, "Last time there were only two, but all five of those guards will be receiving their very own steam powered wagons. Small Mark IV's of course, courtesy of the General Lord Ram Corporation, the very same ghouls who made a great fortune off of my patents!" The professor chuckled, "ONWARD HO!" Thaddeus and Italicus were disconcerted over the professor's eccentric behavior. They looked at each other and wondered what they had gotten themselves into.

The barren land of Diamin had proven easy to cross for the caravan of wagons, which had been able to utilize both sides of the road, but in the county of Gantis, things became complicated. Gantis was Lynthia's nexus of agricultural and food processing. Delivery wagons constantly traveled the roads carrying goods for the rest of Citadel. The roads became more congested about half way through the county because the annual Agro Expo was just beginning. Farmers, ranchers, and other agricultural experts were all eager to see the newest inventions in farming equipment.

The livestock competitions and animal shows were an important component of the expo. The events included horse jumping and racing, hog catching, and the Dairy Show, where the best farms of Lynthia presented their prized cows. Milk and cheese were among the Citadel's most sought after products. The finalists of this show would later compete in the Grand Dairy Show hosted by the Steward himself in the courtyard of Citadel Proper. It was widely rumored that the Steward had a bizarre obsession with drinking milk and demanded it constantly.

The Expo filled Gantis with thousands of people. The Expedition had to slow their pace as they passed alongside its grounds. Tents and small buildings littered the area and the smell of animal waste filled everyone's noses. Leading the column, Thaddeus observed a small boy whose face was bright red, with tears in his eyes. He was desperately trying to pull a stubborn calf across their path. Thaddeus motioned to Italicus, "Go help the boy!"

Italicus slid from his horse and walked over to the young lad, "Here kid, let me help." He positioned himself behind the calf and gave a hardy push, but the calf did not want to move. Italicus thought for a second, walked back to his horse and pulled out a small bowl and filled it with oats. He held his hand to the cow's face and she began to eat. He pulled back and the calf took a step forward, wanting more. "Here, take this and bribe her forward."

"Thanks, mister, this calf and his mother are about to win the dairy show!" The young boy smiled brightly and led his calf away.

Italicus returned to his spot beside Thaddeus and the two shared a knowing smile.

It took a little longer than the professor had hoped to reach the eastern edge of the Citadel. The head of the convoy summited a hill and saw the first signs of the Shadow Realm. The Shadow Realms were areas of the Citadel built right up against the Horizon Wall. Standing at a height of about three thousand feet, the shadow the wall casted was quite large. There are some neighborhoods and areas that receive only a few hours of light each day. These dark towns are notoriously dangerous. It is said that many thieves, smugglers, and other riffraff that want to evade the law could be found in the shadow's protection.

Thaddeus looked through a small pair of binoculars he kept in his saddle bag, "We should make it through the shadow at a decent pace. There doesn't seem to be any traffic on the road ahead."

"It's not the traffic I worry about." warned Italicus, remembering days past when he was on the run from the law. It seemed so long ago, almost a different life, but seeing the shadow area always reminded him of a past he'd rather forget. "I know the kind of scum that likes to use the Shadow Realm to make a coin or two."

"I think in a caravan of this size, we'll be ok," assured Thaddeus. "Plus, the Citadel keeps a pretty large guard contingent near any of the Great Gates."

"I don't put my faith in those buffoons. Do you know how many times they could have arrested me and had no, ummm, they're just idiots, ok…" Italicus finished quickly at Leora's advance on Wooley. He made room for her to fit between himself and Thaddeus.

William F. James

Coming around the hill, Thaddeus was still using his binoculars and whistled at the sight of the Horizon wall and at one of the five Great Gate houses. Leora was acknowledging Italicus, thanking him for moving his horse over. She had not realized that Thaddeus was using his binoculars.

Leora smiled and beamed over at Thaddeus thinking he was whistling at her. Feeling he was being watched, Thaddeus lowered the binoculars and looked over at Leora, he had not realized she was now riding next to him. The flabbergasted look he gave Leora's extremely flattered face gave her pause, he was not whistling at her but at something else. She looked off towards the horizon to see the Horizon wall in the distance. Slightly embarrassed, "Other than its size, what is so impressive about a large wall?"

Italicus gasped at such a question, "Are you kidding? The Horizon wall has thousands of miles of tunnels and rooms inside of it, allowing soldiers the ability to move quickly and protected from harm if there is ever a siege. Once, at a tavern, an old drunken veteran informed me that there are entire areas hidden inside the wall where people still loyal to the crown can be found."

Leora stared at Italicus, trying to see if she was being played, "Really?"

"Stop it," remarked Thaddeus. "Those are rumors, nothing more. And I wasn't talking about the wall. I was talking about the Great Gate house! There are only five of them along the Grand Wall, each unique, and a masterpiece of engineering!"

Italicus shook his head. He knew how much his commander was into military design and architecture. "It's just a gate house."

"Just a gate house?" exclaimed Thaddeus. "Look at it, it stands nearly five hundred feet taller than the wall, the only structures in the entire shard that can boast that. Each of these gate houses is an entire military fortress in itself, capable of housing an entire army of soldiers. The Western Gate of Parnia is said to be cursed by the last mage of the court to keep its secrets hidden from the Steward. The North-Eastern Lythia Gate is said to have an entire manufacturing plant inside of it."

"Isn't there one with a museum at its base?" asked Leora.

Thaddeus nodded, "This is the one, actually. It had a very extensive collection of weapons and armor from before the crown."

Leora listened and nodded, "My father promised he would take me to see this gate years ago, when I was a little girl. He never did, but I've always been fascinated by history."

"It's not often you hear beautiful, young women such as yourself in awe of antiquated military structures," mused Italicus.

Leora gave a half smile. Her cheeks were windblown, and she twisted a piece of her long red hair slightly between her fingers, "It was just my Dad and me growing up, my mother died during childbirth, so I was kind of raised without female intervention." She had a hard time saying it out loud.

"Nothing wrong in that, all five of the Great Gates are truly mesmerizing. Each one of them unique in style and the design has hundreds of platforms equipped with all forms of Tesla ballistae and catapults. The Eastern *Great Gate* is especially a sight to see. Located at the very top of the gate are antique rope-and-tension rock throwers from the time of the early Kings, they are practically ancient! I would love to get my hands on one!" Thaddeus remarked in childlike enthusiasm.

"Thaddeus!" yelled the professor riding up on poncho, "Let us do one last check of everything before we enter the Shadow.

Though Thaddeus, Leora, and Italicus had been in the midst of a conversation, when Thaddeus heard the professor speaking, he immediately paused, "Sure thing professor!" He leaned towards Leora, "Care to join me?" He knew it was unprofessional, but he couldn't help himself.

Leora smiled brightly "Please!"

"Italicus, you now have point!" ordered Thaddeus, officially placing Italicus in charge.

Italicus nodded, "Your order, my will."

***

An abrupt stop woke Andi. She had slept leaning against one of the wagon's rear windows and it left her feeling a bit dizzy. As she regained focus, Andi peered through the glass. It surprised her to see how dark it had become. She wasn't sure of the time, but was certain she couldn't have been asleep for too long. Andi unlatched the wagon's right passenger window and stuck her head outside. A small gust of wind blew through her hair and she saw that they had entered into the Horizon's giant shadow. For the first time in her life, Andi saw how the walls could be considered imprisoning rather than protective.

Torch lights shone along the roadway and each level of the South Eastern Great Gate glowed brightly. Andi figured it wouldn't be much longer before they were outside of the city, and she felt eager to discover what lay on the other side.

"Why have we stopped?" Andi asked as she leaned back in her seat. Glut and Dean were too engaged in their own conversation to hear her and didn't answer. Andi rolled her eyes and rested her head against the wall of the wagon. Though the professor hadn't mentioned anything, she was beginning to feel that the sooner they left the Citadel, the sooner she would find her parents. Andi reached inside of her backpack and slipped out one of her father's scrolls.

Andi tried to see the scroll with fresh eyes, but it was too hard to concentrate with so much talking. Dean was clamoring over some girl he'd just met while with the horses in Diamin. Listening about Dean's new infatuation totally annoyed her. *How can he on go and on about someone he's only just met*, she thought. "One should concern themselves with more serious matters," she mumbled softly.

Glut turned on his sister, eyes narrowed, "Did you say something, Andi?" He felt that Andi's snarky comments and strange behavior hindered his ability to develop meaningful friendships.

A commotion outside caught their attention. The professor, Thaddeus, and Leora trotted by on their horses. Because they were smiling and seemed to be in good spirits, Glut and Dean quickly went back to discussing Kaitlyn. Andi remained frozen, staring out the window. She couldn't look away from Thaddeus; her eyes ran up his back, and over his wide, muscular shoulders. His leather jacket was pulled tight over his breadth, and he was so perfect at commanding his steed. He had an aura of confidence that Andi found intoxicating. She watched until he was too small to see. Andi imagined him teaching her how to ride a horse, perhaps riding double in the saddle with his arms around her.

"I think you're right, Dean" she interrupted. "It's high time we all learn more about horses."

***

Several hours passed, but the expedition still hadn't moved through the Eastern Gate. Andi stepped out of the wagon only to be immediately ushered back in by a patrolling Equinaut who refused to answer why they had stopped. Dean's ceaseless chatter about Kaitlyn furthered Andi's frustration. She couldn't have been more relieved when finally, the long line began to pass through the massive arches of the Great Gate.

The sun was setting in the western sky. Andi had her window and the top half of the wagon door fastened open, so she could enjoy the breeze. Molia's foothills were alive with poppies and wild flowers. Eventually, the expedition made its way through the flat plains of Braum. As far as the eye could see, wheat fields graced the endless landscape. Ultimately, the wagon's constant emittance of steam thickened the air and lowered visibility.

Glancing at her compass, Andi saw that the expedition was heading northeast. Every Citadel citizen knew that beyond the southern river of Se'bide, lay the lands of the Vielwood forest, which acted as a natural boundary between Citadel and Slavine territory. If you listened closely, the sounds of crickets and birds could be heard. Looking toward the south, Andi noticed the red tipped peaks of the Mountains deep within the horizon. Even at this distance, it scared her.

She rubbed her pendant with her thumb, "How are we going to survive this? Maker, help us!" whispered Andi.

"Pretty intimidating, isn't it?" asked a bodiless voice outside the wagon.

The out of body voice in the fog startled Andi. The loud thud of her skull hitting the window's frame was the preamble to an even louder groan.

"Ugh!?" exclaimed Andi, grabbing her crown.

Self-consciously she turned to Glut and Dean, but they were lost in slumber. Andi squinted into the thick steam, and a horse head with a beautiful black mane and metal armor glistening off the setting sun materialized. Behind it rode a hulking figure still obstructed by thick steam. As it drew closer, Andi was relieved and then sheepish to realize the figure was Thaddeus. His jacket followed a rectangular pattern across his chest and stomach. His black leather gloves were plated in iron around the knuckles. He sported the thinnest and most compact Tesla power pack Andi had ever seen, but despite its streamlined look, the power pack was still bulky and awkward to wear.

"Ha! I am so sorry, I didn't mean to frighten you!" called Thaddeus.

Andi bristled up. "You didn't! The wagon hit a bump," she said in her most matter of fact voice.

"Andi, right?" asked Thaddeus. "Leora has told me a lot about you."

"Oh, I'm sure." answered Andi coldly.

Thaddeus was taken aback, "She spoke very highly of you!" He turned to ride forward, but Andi called out.

"What do you think of the professor's plan?" asked Andi, hoping to keep Thaddeus' attention.

Thaddeus slowed down and remained close to the wagon, so he could answer, "The professor is being quite cautious at the moment, he is unsure of who to trust. I admire that, trust is something that must be earned."

Andi wasn't fully listening, she was distracted by Thaddeus' eyes, hooded by long lashes, they were hypnotizing. "So, what's it like protecting people? Always being on the move?"

Thaddeus gave a somber smile, "As with all pursuits, it has its ups and downs. It's certainly not the most comfortable life." Thaddeus let out a small sigh, "There were days during the war…Do you want to know?"

Andi would have agreed to anything he asked.

"We were hired to help protect Mystique, a neutral village not far from here. The conflict had pushed pretty far south, and this village of a couple thousand people was stuck between two massive armies. Despite their neutrality, both armies declared the village was theirs and claimed that the villagers were engaging with the enemy. Many innocents died. We tried to keep them safe, but supplies began to run low once the Slavine burned their only bridge. We held out for months, barely eating anything. Emaciated and discouraged, some of my men began eating their own boot leather. It was grim.

"After the fifth moon, the Citadel and Slavine armies tired of harassing one another and engaged in full battle. Neither side cared whether these villagers lived or died. We sent out carriers warning both sides if they came near the village, we would fire upon them. The battle lasted well over a week. On the fourth day, the Slavine tried to plow through the Citadel line using the village for cover. I don't think the Slavine considered us as a threat. They were by no means prepared for the resistance they were met with. When they couldn't push through, they began bombarding with catapults, many of the buildings began to crumble and burn. Italicus and I were bunkered with a family in a farm house, these two kids. They were so small, starving with swollen bellies. The flames closed around us, and I ordered Italicus to get the family to safety, but it was too late, the fire was out of control. A beam collapsed and half the building crumbled, the family was trapped in the debris."

Andi gasped, "That's horrifying."

"Out of nowhere, a Slavine brute broke through the wall of the farm house, I fought him while Italicus tried to free the family. We successfully pushed the Slavine back, but Italicus was only able to pull the father and children from the burning wreckage. We never found their mother" recounted Thaddeus.

Andi teared up, "Those poor kids, you need a mother."

Thaddeus met her gaze and recognized something more in her eyes than compassion for the villagers. "Aye," he said solemnly. "Days later, the battle was over. It was a stalemate and both sides retreated from the area. Before we left, we helped clear the wreckage and bury the dead. When we got to the farm house, we heard the strangest sound. It was like a cow mooing. We shifted the debris, and the noise got louder. At the bottom of the collapsed roof was the mother, she was alive! The moment those kids..." Thaddeus paused for a second, clearing his throat, "The moment those kids saw their mother... they thought she was gone forever. This is why the Equinauts do what we do."

For minutes Thaddeus rode silently, keeping pace with Andi's wagon.

"Have you ever killed anyone?" she asked.

The question made Thaddeus uncomfortable, not for his answer, but for the reaction he knew Andi might feel.

As gently as he could, "Andrastii, I'm a soldier."

"I understand, but I guess what I meant to ask was if there was ever a time you killed someone and regretted it after?" asked Andi. Once the words left her lips she considered it herself, *would I regret it?*

"Have you heard the myth of the Blessed Paladin?" asked Thaddeus as he pulled a silverfish gold medallion from the collar of his jacket and offered it to Andi. "This appeared to me the day my father died, the same thing happened when his father died and so on for countless of generations."

Andi shook her head and inspected the coin. The edges were marked with bronze words in a language Andi didn't recognize. Two wings sprouted from a circle engraved with a horseshoe laurel and below each wing was a beehive and an anvil.

"A beehive…"

Thaddeus couldn't make out what Andi had just said under her breath, "Beg your pardon?"

Andi heard Thaddeus voice, but she could not peel her eyes off of the beehive symbol. "That's so strange," Andi looked up after several long seconds of silence and grabbed her pendant. "We have the same symbol. "

She reached out and handed it to Thaddeus. Thaddeus squinted with his eyes and held it up to the light. "It's almost the same! Where did you find this?"

"My father made it for me a long time ago."

Andi looked back down still holding Thaddeus' medallion. The longer she stared at it, the heavier her eyes felt. She bit down on her bottom lip. "You said it appeared to you? What do you mean? Did someone give it to you?"

Thaddeus face contorted slightly to match with Andi's, nodded, "No, it appeared in front of me and dropped to my feet the day my father died. It's a family blessing, or maybe a curse. I know it to be enchanted." Thaddeus reached out to reclaim his winged charm, wanting to compare the two symbols side by side.

"Enchanted…" scoffed Andi handing him back his medallion.

Thaddeus ignored her snarky comment. "Where did you father get this?"

Andi took a small breath, "He made it, he made two actually and to make things stranger, the second pendant was an anvil."

"Does it do anything?" asked Thaddeus very matter of fact.

Andi laughed for a moment until she could see the seriousness in Thaddeus' face. "It, um, reminds me of my father? It was the last thing he gave me before my parents went missing."

"So it's really not enchanted?"

"No of course not." remarked Andi, beside herself that she would be asked such a silly question. "Why, is yours really enchanted?"

"Yes, it is. "answered Thaddeus seriously, "this medallion was blessed thousands of years ago by the Maker himself, and that the wearer is protected from most mortal harm. There's a single disadvantage though. It records every death I and my lineage have caused. It reminds me to stay true."

"Stay true to what?" asked Andi, not fully believing him. Despite how handsome the man was, hearing this crazy story of magic medallion was very off putting. "How does it remind you?"

Thaddeus paused, "Not every night but when I sleep, the medallion takes me through every kill and death I or my family have ever witnessed. It forces me to watch the life drain from their eyes."

Andi shook, and a chill ran down her spine. She looked up at Thaddeus who had a smile on his face.

"It may sound gruesome—" Thaddeus was immediately interrupted.

"How can you smile after telling me a story like that? It seems quite cold, almost sadistic. How could you make something like that up!" Andi recoiled and shuttered.

Thaddeus narrowed his eyes and looked at Andi very angrily. It was at that moment Andi realized he believed everything he had said to her. That he carried a great burden and had already endured a lifetime of pain. "I did not make anything up!"

Andi could not fully believe him. She had not completely yet come to grasp with the vision of the demons. This Supernatural, magic, and voodoo nonsense was hard to fully come to terms with. She still wasn't sure is she believed Thaddeus, but she knew now not to question his beliefs. "So tell me, do you take pleasure reliving your past glories, PenRuger!?"

He was surprised at the use of his last name, "You've heard of me?"

"Only in rumor," Andi's voice dripped with disgust "It's said that the PenRugers come from a long line of warriors and generals. It is also rumored that your father went mad, sided with the Slavine, and slaughtered women and children at Crakatoin."

"THAT IS A LIE!" bellowed Thaddeus, waking Dean and Glut. "My father was framed!" He threw his necklace back into the wagon.

"I thought the professor brought you along because you were most educated. Didn't you study Progenitor?"

Andi nodded, though it was partly a lie. She was fluent in it but never formally studied the language, only their culture.

"Read the border. That Medallion is a judge!" Thaddeus calmed as Andi studied the medal. "The myth of the blessed Paladin says that thousands of years ago, one of my ancestors was a Paladin in charge of protecting a small village when an epic red evil dealing in dark, arcane magic returned to the land. Some versions say the evil came in the form of a most powerful necromancer, others say it was a fierce and deadly stone mammoth. My ancestor was not strong enough to defeat it and was mortally wounded. He prayed for help and The Maker appeared before him. He found my predecessor to be pure of heart and soul. The Maker blessed this medallion and stated that it would give him the power to defeat the evil."

The longer she held the medallion the stranger Andi felt, *perhaps there was something to what he is saying?* "Does it really work?" asked Andi, "Did he stop the evil?"

"I don't know. Some say he was unable to defeat the evil and died because of it. Others say he destroyed the evil and the Maker took him up into the heavens. All we do know is that after his death, the medallion found his son, as it has for generations. My family quickly discovered that the Medallion had drawbacks. The dreams are a constant, it reads your soul and judges you if you kill unjustly. As long as it remains this silverfish gold, I have remained pure and just to my cause. The Maker is pleased I have defended the defenseless and brought justice to those who have been wronged. Like I mentioned earlier, the Medallion is a curse and a blessing. If I ever chose to kill in cold blood, I would lose my gifts and suffer greatly. That is how I know my father was framed."

"What exactly would it do to you?" asked Andi, now embarrassed.

"I am not sure exactly, it could be physical or mental. I only know the suffering would be severe."

Andi looked it over, the medallion was beautiful, but the longer she held it the heavier it felt. She turned it over and realized half of it was gone. "Where's the back?"

Thaddeus nodded, "Sometime ago, one of my line broke it. My grandfather was convinced if he could find the other half, the gifts would increase. He wasted most of his life searching for it. I don't put much stock in it."

Andi's thoughts were interrupted by a scream. Thaddeus turned his head forward, kicked his horse on its side, and dashed toward the noise leaving with Andi's pendant and his own medallion behind.

William F. James

Andi looked out the carriage's window and tried to see where the scream was coming from, but the steam from everyone's wagons filled the air and clouded her vision. Thaddeus was nothing more than small black shade getting smaller the further he went. Andi felt a sudden rush of dizziness. Her heart began to race and the world around her began to go silent. Her arms felt shaky and soon she felt drowsy. All she wanted to do was go to sleep. Her brain was slowly shutting down and so too was her eyesight. Andi slipped her head back into the cabin.

Dean began to snicker, and Glut had a hard time forming words.

"Steven better be careful, looks like you have a new love interest, Andi" Glut teased.

"What! Steven—ugh! No, Shut up!" shouted Andi her voice unnaturally low then high. "Besides, I think Leora already-"

Glut and Dean began to giggle slightly like teasing school children. Andi never finished her sentence, she suddenly collapsed.

"ANDI!" yelled Glut concerned rushing to her side and grabbing her limp body, "What's wrong!? ANDI!?"

Dean grabbed her arm and formed his fingers around Andi's wrist to see if there was a pulse.

"OUCH SON OF BIT- "yelled Dean dropping Andi's arm. "THAT'S HOT!"

Andi suddenly opened her eyes and jumped up. She felt odd and strange, but better than before. She looked at her brother and then at Dean unsure of why they were so close to her and why they had confused and panicked looks. She remembered that she was holding something in her hand and was about to look down, when a loud scream was heard nearby. Andi, forgetting about the Medallion, closed her window and latched the door. She was surprised to see both Dean and Glut brandished smug looks. Andi thought they looked ill.

"Are you ok?" What happened???" asked Glut, concerned.

Andi had no idea what he was talking about and shook her head, "Shouldn't you be more concerned with the screams?"

A thud quieted the boys, it sounded as if something had fallen onto the roof of their wagon.

Andi dropped the medallion into her pocket and reopened her window. It was dark, the steam dimmed what little light came from the rest of the column. Andi stepped onto her seat, stretching to see what had caused the noise when a second thud occurred inches from her face. She felt something warm splatter on her cheeks. The driver of the wagon had suddenly fallen face first right in front her. It took her several stunned moments to realize blood was coming out of the driver's neck and mouth. The dead man's chest began to glow. A bright light emerged from a giant open wound. Andi was suspended in shock. She heard viscera squish and followed two arms up from the deep cavity. Something was bent over the driver, searching in his chest. The black form noticed Andi, and two eyes flashed green.

Andi half-ducked half-fell back inside. The wagon began to bumpily roll from the trail.

"Is that blood? Andi?" Glut leaned forward and took Andi's face in his hands, searching for lacerations.

Andi tried to form words, but all that came out were unsteady breaths. Andi's eyes widened in freight, and she gasped, "Close the window!" Dean spun around, but it was too late. The green-eyed creature leaned down from above, and pierced a blade straight through Dean's right shoulder. It wasn't a plasma blade, but one made of genuine steel. Dean let out a shriek of agony. His cries were deafening. The creature twisted the blade and Dean crumbled to the floor. Glut tried to wrestle the window closed onto the creature, but its force was far too strong. It struck Glut square in the face and sent him flying to the back corner of the wagon. Andi was huddled between the seats, and she felt her side burn, her pocket was glowing.

The creature withdrew its sword from Dean's lifeless body and pulled. In a single motion, it ripped the entire ceiling from the wagon and tossed it aside. Andi peered through her hands and cried out to the Maker. The creature was almost manlike, but giant. Its black cloak was old and brittle and stunk of rotted flesh. It sunk into the cabin, floating off the ground, stretched its left arm towards Glut, and rushed forward. Glut's field of view was filled with the image of a Raven, the symbol of the Slavine.

Suddenly, an orange glow permeated the cabin, and cut through the steam. The creature turned on Andi. She held up a Plaz sword as steadily as she could. The creature swung downwards upon her. Andi turned her face away and used the sword to block the creature's descent. The two swords collided brilliantly. The old steel blade sparked against the electrical current of the plasma sword and the creature pulled back in surprise.

Andi sprung up and thrusted her sword towards the creature, but inexperienced as she was, she over extended her arms and toppled onto the seat. She felt the creature's green eyes boring into the back of her skull. A muffled animalistic laugh could be heard through its cloaked face. The creature raised its sword and prepared to thrust it into Andi's back. Andi cried for help, she knew her end was near. The creature answered her call callously, and plunged the sword into her spine, blood poured from her lips. She felt every muscle convulse, rejecting the pain searing through her. Her body slowly started to shut down. The creature wailed, a shrill shriek, and Andi used the last of her strength to lift her face. She saw Glut jump onto the creature's back, he was grunting loudly. Andi was helpless. She desperately wanted to save her brother but had nothing left.

"Maker, Ethereal and all, please give..." she coughed blood, trying to force air into her collapsed lungs "...me strength!"

Darkness crept over Andi's eyes, she faded from life. In her final conscious moment, Andi's eyes flickered as she violently gasped for air.

She heard a voice whisper:

"Awaken!"

Echo from the Past

So many years had elapsed hiding from the Ethereal, safely hidden inside the consciousness of my vessel, focused solely on avoiding detection. I was sure they would search until my capture. I never allowed myself to believe that one day I would be free. When I achieved abandonment, finally out waited their investigation, I was forced to face an ugly realization: my master was either captured or dead. In exile, I outlived my purpose.

My vessel had endured much. With the loss of her family, loss of any semblance of life, she was more than content with her demise, she wished for it. I considered telling her the truth, trusting that anger would give her reason to exist. I could tell her that my kind were to blame for the death of her planet. That we killed so many that I was unsure if I had even fought in the battle. If I had, I took more than a billion lives, in all forms, animals, people, trees, sentient and non-sentient, I was not biased. If her world was still alive and had not been ravaged by The Fallen, her people would have called her beautiful. She was tall and fit, her hair, never combed nor cut, reached below her knees, and even disheveled, it glowed brightly.

I almost showed her my nature, but instead, I felt sorrow for my vessel. Had she been born a generation earlier, she would have lived a full life, had a family of her own, and enjoyed what simple beauty life had to offer, music, culture, love.

When her family was still alive, they would travel great distances searching for food, but now that she was alone, traveling far from shelter was too dangerous. Though even without threat, she refused to trek further than a day's walk from the place we had buried her tribe.

Most days she meditated. She would remain motionless for hours, keeping her mind blank. I wondered whether she did it because she knew it irritated me. Walking outside the makeshift shelter of broken buildings, there was a nip in the air, winter was on its way. This planet's winters would easily fall well below freezing. Many years ago there was plenty of debris and wood to burn, now there wasn't much that hadn't been burnt for heat already. The area was becoming truly barren.

One evening, as the cold of winter began to set, a commotion outside roused her from her silent stoicism. She could hear human voices, there were people outside. She remained still, and couldn't decide whether or not she wanted them to notice her hovel. After a moment's hesitation, she broke off a piece of her wall and added it to her fire, welcoming the inevitable confrontation. She had no fear, she welcomed death. She closed her eyes and listened to the growing noise. Five large men pushed their way into her small shelter. It was dark, but she recognized the look of hunger and desire in their eyes. For several long seconds they stared at my vessel, surprised at her relaxed position. Then one of the men spoke.

"We're not going to hurt you. Do you need water?"

A blind rage overtook my vessel. She was ready to die, and once again, the universe had denied her. She was finished waiting. In that instant, her strength shone, and she was determined never to ask for anything, ever again. From now on, she would take.

"Angel," she commanded. "These are yours."

She put up no fight. She graciously, desperately allowed me control of her body. The five men were surprised when they saw my eyes begin to glow through my vessel's. The dark shelter was illuminated by a bright and blinding light. They had no understanding of what was about to happen. If they did, they would have run. With delight, I allowed myself to indulge, biting, ripping, and tearing these men apart with my vessel's small body. They pleaded for mercy, their cries of pain only heightened my hunger. It was over far too quickly, I was hardly able to enjoy myself.

I looked upon my work, their flesh tattered and torn all around me. I watched their souls rise out of their bodies and disappear into the veil, wasted. I walked outside, hungry for more, but neither I nor my vessel were prepared for what we were about to see. More than a hundred people were gathered, men, women, children, even the elderly. We didn't know this many people still existed. I rose above, floating in the air to take in their numbers. They began to fall to their knees, bowing before me, all of them begging for forgiveness and mercy. I was fully prepared to slice them to pieces, and feast, but a voice inside of me cried out, my vessel said two words that would change not just our relationship, but everything that was to come.

"Use them."

At that moment I had realized that she...she had been hearing my thoughts all along. All of the evil, gruesome, beautiful, and horrible thoughts. Not once had she thought to force me out, not once had she even been repulsed... She knew me, and she loved me. Together, we would use these peoples, preying upon their fear. They believed us to be a god and to them, we were.

We welcomed them to the beginning of a whole new era…

Thaddeus PenRuger

Chapter Three

From the first scroll of Zakarael, chapter 53 verse 6:
"Like sheep, so many have gone astray; Ambition and hubris have turned the faithless to follow in his own way, contrary to the Maker's purpose. Strike down these heathens of old, for the Maker has no room for them."
From the first scroll of Zakarael, chapter 6 verse 11:
"Death is the night which swallows the soul, but true love can conquer all."

- 72 Hours before the expedition's departure:

"Dear friends, as we gather here in the garden of *Sanctus*, we lay our dear Alana PenRuger to her final place of rest. Go in peace, sweet Alana, and do not weep, for no life truly perishes. The dead shall rise high above and meet the Maker, master and creator of all life, in paradise. Through our hearts and minds, memories of you shall continue to guide us. Blessed be the Maker, so say we all."

Alana's eulogy haunted Thaddeus. The words played over and over again in his mind, he couldn't shake them. A piece of him had been buried that day. Lying on his cot, he relived the hardest moments of his existence, his heart breaking. Thaddeus' tent was dimly lit by a single candle on the bed stand beside him. He reached for his jacket and pulled out a small, thin silver tin. Thaddeus was hesitant to open it. For years the box rested inside the chest pocket of his jacket, closest to his heart. Thaddeus feared he might somehow lose one of the last reminders of a life he could no longer live.

Thaddeus inhaled deeply, and gently opened the box. Nestled inside was a radiant ringlet of red hair. He tenderly reached inside, placed the box on his cot, and held the lock of hair for a moment, it felt like silk. Thaddeus closed his eyes, pressed the hair against his face, and gently guided it under his nose. As he inhaled the sweet scent that still lingered, his eyes began to swell. Fat tears rolled down his cheeks.

"I miss you so much, my love," mouthed Thaddeus, in the candle-lit darkness. Her perfume brought him back to sleepy mornings together in bed, he always woke before her. He'd lightly trace her delicate brow, sweeping her beautiful red tendrils from her face. Her mouth would stretch into a smile, and he knew she was awake. She'd peek out from under her curled lashes, brilliant blue contrasting against her smooth creamy skin, the softest Thaddeus had ever encountered. She'd burrow into his side, and he'd get a face full of her coiled red hair.

"I'm so sorry, my lamb, I've failed you. I should have been there to protect you."

Thaddeus set the lock of hair on his chest and picked up the box. Painted on the inside of its lid was a portrait of his wife. He brought it to his lips and kissed its rim. For the briefest of moments, Thaddeus allowed himself to imagine a life in which Alana had survived.

"Sir, permission to enter?" asked a voice outside the tent.

Thaddeus' mind snapped to the present. He carefully nestled the red lock of hair back into the box, and placed it on his night stand. "Come in."

Thaddeus rose and watched as his best friend and second-in-command entered his tent. Italicus' face was twisted into his usual goofy smile, and a plumed gold feather rested behind his right ear. "Thaddeus, I have to let you know, it's pretty bad out-"

Thaddeus let out a loud snort, "Are you really going to be wearing that all the time?"

Italicus beamed, lifting his head higher, posing it. "It saved my life, brings me luck!"

Thaddeus had no Idea why Italicus kept wearing that gaudy feather. He nearly replied with a witty retort about Italicus' ridiculousness wearing it, but decided not to. Instead, he motioned for his second in command to take a seat. Italicus, feeling Thaddeus' vibe sat down next to his friend and commander, but made sure he sat so that the feather was clearly in sight.

Thaddeus couldn't help but stare at the shiny yellow feather, "My friend, stop wearing that thing. It's bad, just awful. Your own reflection would laugh at you."

Italicus rolled his eyes and ignored Thaddeus' attempt at humor. "Gladthorn just brought me the latest scout report. Three Marshals broke off from the main posse and were searching for us twenty miles up, but got nowhere near the bluff. As of right now, the path to the camp remains hidden."

"That's the third time this week they have come back and searched this area," remarked Thaddeus, simultaneously relieved and annoyed. "The Marshals don't give up easily, do they?"

Italicus let out a loud clipped laugh "Have you met Gladthorn? The whole lot of them are mini versions of our master scout! All duty-bound zealots who will carry out the law, justified or not."

"Do you remember how rigid Gladthorn was in the beginning? So overwhelmed with all that Marshal Discipline, I honestly thought he didn't know how to relax." Thaddeus allowed himself a moment to reminisce.

"He drove all of us crazy back then! Everything was by the code. Do you remember that time we sent him into that tavern in Basadur disguised as a slaver looking for that young kidnapped girl— what was her name?"

"Salinia."

Italicus snapped his fingers. "That's it. So Gladthorn is there pretending to drink. When a very attractive companion of the tavern approached and threw herself at him. His body locked up so tight, you'd think he'd never been touched by a woman before!" Italicus began to laugh.

"Oh, I remember!" added Thaddeus, trying to hold his smile back, "He looked almost scared to move, and then she bit his ear and invited him upstairs…"

Italicus roared with laughter and tried to speak, "Thank you ma'am, but I do not require privacy. This chair and table are quite adequate for me."

Thaddeus couldn't help but laugh at Italicus' laughter.

"And then," said Thaddeus gleefully, "she slapped him across the face, and the whole bar went silent and she called him—"

Italicus joined in, "—a perverted freak!"

"I am so glad," Italicus winked so Thaddeus would know he chose his wording purposefully, "we broke Gladthorn of his Marshal rigidity!"

"That rigidity did save our lives," Thaddeus reminded. "It was that zealous adherence to the law that forced Gladthorn to challenge Malus and disband the Bloodhounds."

Italicus recoiled slightly, remembering how much trouble the Bloodhounds had caused years ago when the Equinauts were newly formed. "If they gave half of the energy and resources they wasted on us to finding the real bad guys, we would be home free by now."

Thaddeus nodded.

Italicus looked about Thaddeus' tent. He had forgotten how large it was. It had been well over a year since they had needed the long-term tents. The war had kept them busy and on the move. Italicus' eyes fell upon Thaddeus' desk, heavily littered in parchments and scrolls, "A little light reading?"

"I have been trying to find a pattern."

"Any luck?"

Thaddeus shook his head gravely as Italicus walked over and shuffled through several sheets of paper. He grabbed a wanted poster picturing a dark rider astride a black horse. Rumors of a group of black riders had started to swirl through the shard for several months, to which Thaddeus and the other Equinauts had paid no mind, busy keeping people safe amongst the crossfires of war. The poster read, "Wanted for the massacre and destruction of two family farms along the road to Bythinia."

"Did this just come in?"

Thaddeus nodded again. "Gladthorn's contacts have been keeping us informed. These black riders are being reported everywhere. Two weeks ago, they slaughtered a merchant leading a herd of mustangs to the City of Del, every man and horse. A week ago, a whole clan of Aedunic families were slaughtered on the northern border, and last week piles of human and horse bodies were found near Braum. Of course, the Citadel and the Marshals were quick to assign blame to us."

"Well they do think we kidnapped and tried to kill the Slavine Chamberlain."

Italicus looked at a marked up map hanging on the tent's canvas. "Based on my experience relocating high value items for those of great resources, I'd say these attacks make no sense. They aren't stealing for wealth. Could these psychopaths be from a cult like the Bloodstones and kill for the fun of it? Even then, why travel from Del to the northwestern edge of the shard, and a week later travel east near Braum? They'd have cantered their horses into the grave."

"Gladthorn saw nearly one hundred of them," responded Thaddeus. "Perhaps they're broken into groups to cause maximum damage?"

"WHY? Other than destroying our good name, what is their purpose? What is their goa—" Italicus caught sight of the silver box on Thaddeus' nightstand. "Oh. Are you alright? I didn't know you were still carrying that thing around with you."

Thaddeus stared at his hands in his lap. "It hasn't got any easier."

Italicus was silent for a moment. "Bless the Maker Thaddeus, I'm sorry. I forgot. It's tomorrow isn't it?"

Thaddeus nodded. "Nine years, and it still feels like yesterday."

Italicus placed a hand on his friend's shoulder. "I wish I could have met her."

Thaddeus let out a scoff. "I'm glad you didn't, you would have fallen in love with her. Everyone did. She was gorgeous, had the most infectious smile. She was so kind, but I'll be damned if she wasn't the sassiest woman on the shard. I used to tease her that she was more stubborn than a donkey's ass. Then she would look at me so seriously and ask me 'Does it hurt?'"

"Does what hurt?" asked Italicus confused.

Thaddeus smirked, "usually there was an added word at the end. Her father hated me, still does. He blames me. But when we first dated, Alana and I broke one of his chairs while doing something he wouldn't approve of."

Italicus bit his bottom lip, "Thaddeus, you dog!"

"Shut up. " Thaddeus cheeks glowed red, "So, trying to get on his good side, I built the exact chair myself. It took me weeks, Alana teased me the whole time saying I wasn't a carpenter. So, I brought it over to her father and he sat in it--and it immediately collapsed. That didn't help things, so I tried to build it again, and again. Until finally, Alana looked at me as I sat in the rubble of the fifth chair and she said to me, 'does it hurt being so stubborn?' Well, after that, anytime I did anything remotely wrong she would respond to me asking me 'Does it hurt?'"

Italicus slapped the side of his leg, "Wow, she really did know you!"

"A year or so later she told me that was one of the moments when she knew she loved me and wanted to spend the rest of her life with me." Thaddeus choked on his words, it had been so long since he had spoken so freely about Alana.

Italicus gave his friend a warm smile, "Are you going to go see her? The Garden is only about an hour's ride from here."

Thaddeus frowned, his face turned red from shame. "I can't." He shook his head with contempt for himself. "I haven't been there in years. Besides, the men here need me. If I don't get us through this rough patch, it'll end the Equinauts."

"Thaddeus, I can handle it for a few hours."

"No!" That was the end of it. "Now, was there anything else?"

Italicus gulped. "Well I hate to pour on more weight, but It's pretty bad out there. Morale is low, and by low, I mean the men could be kicked in the ass and that would be the highlight of their day. I don't know how much longer we can continue on hardtack bread alone. We need to do something, quickly or more will follow that little Verrator prick Finnius Ridge, the insubordinate little shit."

"We've lost half our men this week," interjected Thaddeus seriously. "We're down to fifty. We can't spare any more. Have the men no faith in me?"

"We have a lot of things stacked up against us, that's all. Our resources are extremely low. Thanks to the cease fire that we helped escort," Italicus spat on the ground at the memory of the mission that lead the Equinauts to this disastrous position, "We are criminals in both the Kingdom and Citadel territory. We were chased halfway across the shard by Independent Marshals who thought we kidnapped the Slavine's royal chamberlain and those black riders we encountered are slaughtering innocents. So now, not even the independent villages will trust us. I think it's downright narcissistic to think you're the reason the men are leaving." By Thaddeus' expression, Italicus could tell he may have said too much. "Regardless, with empty stomachs, they aren't thinking straight. Some would follow a Slavine if he promised them food."

"Perhaps they would do better under a Slavine," Thaddeus spewed with a hard, short laugh. "At least at half strength we can raise the ration level back to normal."

"Right- You do realize a full ration of hardtack is still hardtack?"

"You're right, but what can I do?" Thaddeus' shoulders slumped. "It's not good, my friend, any of this. Forgive me, I don't know how to deal with it all, and I'm bloody pissed that so many of our men would follow that arrogant bastard on such a fool's errand." Thaddeus let out a huge sigh. "I guess any starving man would sell his soul if he was promised food and gold."

"So, what? You forgive them?"

"Forgive, yes. Forget, never. As far as Finnius is concerned, he is as dead to me as Verrator's horse. Betrayal and mutiny can never be forgiven, I will never tolerate it!"

"Well, we need to think of something. Otherwise, we may have another mutiny on our hands."

Thaddeus thought for a moment. "Perhaps a distraction is in order?"

***

In an obscure part of a forest, hidden by a tall bluff and -wide river, just southwest of the Citadel along the Aedunic border, the sounds of flesh pounding flesh bounced off the restless trees. Loud, thunderous voices emanated from a boisterous crowd which surrounded two men entangled in a wrestling match. The cheers were so loud in a meadow usually quiet and tranquil, that all wildlife had run, frightened. The men had been fighting for the better part of half an hour and neither showed signs of letting up.

The grim atmosphere that had impregnated the camp was gone. Wrestling was a favorite pastime for the Equinauts. Zapp watched the spectacle for a while, but with no sign of the match ending, he lost interest and wondered away. The camp was mostly barren. The few who had decided against watching the brawl preoccupied themselves with small projects.

One of them was Kazah. Zapp noticed him tinkering with his Tesla pack. He was impressed with how mechanically savvy Kazah had become in such a short time. The steam powered trinkets that the average Citadel Citizen took for granted fascinated him. As a former slave of the Slavine, steam technology was a foreign mistress and he was determined to learn her language and unlock her secrets. The Equinauts were lucky to have Kazah. It was rare to escape the Slavine and live to tell about it.

Another Equinaut not watching the brawl was a particularly stunning warrior princess named Fryda. She was an Aedunic woman, tall, as they are, with a buff warrior's physique. She practiced with two sword swings against several hay filled dummies.

Niles, Zapp's best friend, was a burly man with a high forehead and short blonde hair. He hailed from the independent realm near the City of Del. He was busy pounding away on an anvil, shaping new steel shoes for the horses.

Zapp's stomach let out a low growl. Normally, the smell of delicious foods would have permeated the main camp area, but food was scarce. They had been hiding form the Marshals far too long without proper planning, stuck in an obscure part of the forest. No jobs meant no gold, and no gold meant no food. Over the past two weeks, everyone had been eating half rations of hardtack bread biscuits. It was more of a tasteless brick than bread.

"If it isn't my dear friend, Charles Jackson!" yelled a man to Zapp's left.

Zapp turned. The man was standing next to an obnoxiously large, custom-built, steam powered wagon which read: *The Amazing Kauf Bannister and His Legendary Mechanical Designs* in tall script. The wagon was made of the finest bronze, accented in jade green. Despite its size, the wagon had a streamlined rounded look, and each part of the wagon seemed to have a different function to it. Kauf was a renowned inventor who had been forced out of the Citadel Inventorii because his designs were considered too radical. Most knew him because of a food cooling box he had invented, but what caused his removal from the Inventorii was a suction system for removing dirt and garbage. It was a novel Idea, but the C.C.C., *Citadel Cleaning Corp.*, was one of the largest businesses in the Citadel and didn't want the competition. The company also employed numerous Citadel citizens who happened to have formed one of the largest unions. A device like that could potentially have harmed the Citadel economy. When Kauf wouldn't back down, insisting "Progress can never be stopped," the Steward himself asked for his letter of resignation. His refusal to quit made him unemployable in most of the Citadel.

Zapp approached the tall man sporting short black hair and expensive, if baggy clothes. "Hey Kauf!"

Bannister smiled, "Why, bless the Maker. I haven't seen you in months!"

"What are you doing out here?"

Kauf shook Zapp's hand. "There's a rumor circulating that not all is well with the Equinauts. I had to make sure for myself that those rumors weren't true."

Zapp shrugged. "Unfortunately, the rumors are true. We've had some issues, specifically with the ceasefire between the Citadel and the Slavine, and then there's the false claim we kidnapped the Slavine Chamberlain."

Kauf nodded somberly. "I heard the treaty had been signed, but shouldn't the ceasefire be a happy thing? The war is over, and no more men are dying." Kauf tapped a knob on the side of his wagon and a long robotic arm holding a small porcelain cup and saucer emerged. A second arm poured steaming water into it, and a third produced a tray with tea leaves, sugar cubes, and milk. Zapp stood, mouth agape. He was too mesmerized by his friend's invention to answer. Kauf smiled, he craved this sort of reaction. "How do you take your tea?" he asked cheekily.

Zapp raised his hand slightly, he was about to reject the offer until he heard his stomach growl. "No, thank y— with milk." He handed Kauf the tin mug from his belt, distracted by the contraption, trying to figure out how it worked.

Kauf reached into the front pocket of his coat, pulled out a small stirring spoon, and readied their tea. "Well, Zapp, do you have anything else to add?"

Zapp snapped out of his daze and looked at his friend as he tried to gather his thoughts. "Right, the ceasefire is good, but Kauf, the treaty labels all Equinauts and other hireling groups as outlaws of the state. Both states, actually."

"What do you expect from a man like the Steward? If you ask me, it was he who killed the king during *the Night of Blood*," scoffed Kauf.

Zapp gave his friend a half smile. "You are not the first to think that. But I reckon this particular part of the treaty has more of a Slavine influence."

Kauf shook his head. "It is such a shame that fortune has frowned upon you. All the people you Equinauts have saved should count for something!"

A new voice entered the conversation. "It's not just the Steward! We were set up and betrayed by that fat Slavine bastard!"

Kauf and Zapp turned to see an angry Kazah.

"I said that!" Zapp defended himself.

"Who is the bastard?" asked Kauf, confused.

"The Slavine Chamberlain, we had an ordeal with him that set all this craziness off. We sent letters to King Hugh of the Slavine, but we've yet to hear a response."

"Trying to reason with the Slavine Monarchy is pointless," spat Kazah. "The Slavine may appear barbarian, even naïve, but they are astute in the ways of political subterfuge. They're as evil and conniving as any Citadel councilman!"

"If anyone would know, it'd be you, Kaz. You have more reason than most to hate the Slavine," remarked Zapp, hoping Kazah would open up more about his time with the Slavine.

"Interesting, would you care to elaborate?" prompted Kauf.

Kazah looked at Kauf with an unmoving face. "It's personal."

"I'm sorry," Kauf mumbled, hiding behind his tea.

Kazah turned and stalked off.

"What happened there?" muttered Kauf, once Kazah was out of hearing range.

Zapp shrugged his shoulders, "I shouldn't have--It's not my place to say."

"Come on, Zapp, don't leave me hanging!"

"The only person who knows everything is Thaddeus. But he lets details slip sometimes, and people talk. Kaz used to be enslaved by the Slavine."

"You're not serious! How on Elisia did he manage to get out past the blunkers?"

"Shhh! Keep it down!" hushed Zapp through gritted teeth. "Like I said, only Thaddeus knows the full truth. Rumor is, there's a trail of bodies in Kazah's past. We know he killed, Slavine, but some of the rumors say he also killed humans as well--males, females, even children, just to flee the Kingdom. Whatever the story really is, it doesn't matter. He's an Equinaut now."

"Do you really think they'd *let* a man escape?" asked Kauf, ever cynical. "I'd sleep with one eye open if I were you."

"Stop it, Kauf. Not everything needs to be a conspiracy. Besides, no man is better with a sword than me," bragged Zapp in a cocky tone.

"Ha!" laughed Kauf, "What of Thaddeus then, does he not count? To be fair, many villages of the Independent realms say he is more god than man!"

Zapp laughed. "Who knows what Thaddeus really is."

"Zapp!" squawked a harsh and angry voice. "Excuse me, but where on the shard is the new shipment of steel ingots? I still need to forge 12 more pairs of shoes!"

"I'm working on it, Niles, you'll have your ingots soon!" answered Zapp defensively, "I don't even know why you took Thomas' job."

Niles ignored Zapp's comment, "Not soon enough. When Thomas left, he took his coal forge with him. I am forced to heat each shoe one by one!"

"I'm doing the best I can! I got it, ok?" assured Zapp rudely.

Niles glared, "Whatever you say, Hellsie!" He stormed off towards his anvil.

"'Hellsie?" asked Kauf.

"Short for Hellhorse" Zapp folded his arms and sighed. "No one believes that I saw a huge lacerated heart pulled from the chest cavity of a living man missing half his body."

"You think the heart was Bailitheoir's? Verrator's Bailitheoir?"

Zapp nodded.

Kauf looked to his friend and wasn't sure if Zapp was serious or making a queer joke. He decided to change the subject. "What's happened to Barrus? Is he dead?"

"No, not dead."

"Then why are you being asked for supplies? Barrus is the quartermaster, no?"

"He was, but he's gone now, along with forty-nine others. They 've been leaving sporadically to follow the crook Finnius Lindon Ridge."

"Follow him? You mean defect? How could they leave Thaddeus?"

"You mean besides everything else that happened? Sorry, that was low, it wasn't Thaddeus' fault. In fact, if it weren't for him, we would probably be all dead or arrested for crimes we didn't commit."

"So why did they leave?"

Zapp took a sip of his tea and savored its amazing flavor. He wasn't sure if the tea was actually amazing or if anything would taste this way after so many days eating hardtack. "Two days ago, we were visited by a Kern."

"Which Kern?" asked Kauf? "There are so many among the Aedunic tribes."

"Oh, no one big," mocked Zapp, "just the Chieftain of the entire Triviattii tribe, the largest and most powerful of the Aedunic nation. How he even found us here behind the bluff is remarkable. He rode into camp with about a hundred of his personal guard. At first, we thought the Marshals had found us. It was unnerving to us all, but we were prepared to defend ourselves if need be. Teslas give us the advantage, of course."

"I've heard it takes three full powered blasts from a Tesla to take down one Triviattii warrior," stated Kauf matter-of-factly.

Zapp rolled his eyes, "Aedunic propaganda."

"Was the Kern looking for a fight?" asked Kauf.

"Thank the great lady Arcadia, no!" Zapp sighed, remembering the tense event in his mind. "He was here to offer us a job."

Kauf noticed his friend's grave look. "But that's good, isn't it?"

Zapp shook his head, "The Kern brought with him some sort of mystic soothsayer, for hours he danced around, chanting and swaying. He started some sort of fire in the gathering tent and inhaled this green smoke. Thaddeus was not pleased. By the time the soothsayer started talking, Thaddeus was over everything Aedunic."

"It was Seric, wasn't it?" asked Kauf.

"How did you know?"

Kauf laughed "That old fool was born an actor. Don't get me wrong, he is good, and his predictions are top notch, but his over the top showmanship ruins any credibility," answered Kauf. "So, what did Seric tell Thaddeus?"

Zapp acted disgusted, "That crazy twit tried to tell Thaddeus that the savior of the world was Finnius Ridge."

"Seric said that!? Save us from what?"

"He didn't really say. He was in some sort of mystic trance. He pointed at Fin and said 'Take note, this person is the savior of our world.'"

Kauf let out an oof. "I'm sure Thaddeus did not take that well."

"To add insult to injury, Finnius informed the entire room that the Equinauts would stop at nothing to fulfill the Kern's contract. Thaddeus was pissed. Finnius is hard headed and ambitious. He convinced half of us to follow him into Aedunic Territory with promises of food, coin, and glory."

"What a blow to your outfit."

Zapp finished his tea. "Thaddeus is doing the best he can under the circumstances. It doesn't seem to matter how many walk away, he refuses to give up. It's been rough though. Thaddeus put on a wrestling match today, just to give us something to do."

"Hey, who doesn't love a good match?" remarked Kauf enthusiastically. "Is that where everybody is? Can we go and watch?"

***

"Aye! Get him, Thad!"

"Don't let him show you up, Italicus!"

The two men brawled while being cheered on by their comrades and brothers in arms. Everyone's stomachs were grumbling, and no one was looking forward to their half sheet of hardtack bread, but the wrestling match had been a good distraction for most of the day. The matches had lead up in rank. The top officers in the company were the last to compete against one another. Thaddeus had experience and size over Italicus, who was much thinner, but Italicus was slightly younger and definitely more flexible.

Completely winded, Thaddeus rasped, "Do you give up yet?"

Italicus, on his back, with Thaddeus' arm pressing into his neck, managed to turn his face enough to make eye contact with Thaddeus. He raised his black brows and winked. Or possibly blinked, his left eye was swollen shut. He forced his face into a smug smile. "I have you right where I want you!" The two played to the crowd, urging them into a frenzy.

Thaddeus laughed, "Not this time Ital—" Before Thaddeus could finish, Italicus managed to twist his body and wrap a leg around part of Thaddeus' arm and chest, pushing him off balance, sending both men into a barrel roll, tussling and grunting until they slammed into the side of a horse wagon. Italicus landed on top, struggling to keep Thaddeus pinned.

"Looks like the tides have turned, *old* friend! Concede!" commanded Italicus joyfully.

Thaddeus moved impossibly fast for his hulking frame. In moments Thaddeus had Italicus flat on his back.

"Time to fold," stated Thaddeus, applying pressure to Italicus' neck.

"Alright, I surrender, you win!" Italicus panted heavily, all joy and pride gone from his voice. "I really thought I had you this time."

The crowd cheered at their reigning champion. Some sported looks of dismay as they passed money to the hands of those who placed their bets on Thaddeus.

"Maybe next time," Thaddeus held out his hand to help Italicus up. "I will admit, you had me worried for a moment!"

Italicus reluctantly took Thaddeus' hand, his ego was slightly bruised. For a fleeting moment, he thought after years of trying he had finally beaten Thaddeus at wrestling.

Both men smiled at the crowd.

"Drinks are on me!" yelled Thaddeus to the people around him. "It's the only thing we have a surplus off." he said under his breath. The throng of spectators cheered louder for this. He turned and looked over at Italicus, "Give it up, you lost! A deal is a deal!" Thaddeus grabbed the feather and slung his arm over Italicus' shoulder. Leading him out of the wrestling arena he poked at Italicus' swollen eye with the tip of the golden feather. "Between losing this and that swollen cut, you actually look like a man, perhaps a person of the female persuasion will look your way for once!"

"Har… Har… leave the wit and levity to the master!"

"And who might that be?" Thaddeus faked wonder.

"The one and only," Italicus bowed his head and threw out his hand in the manner of a decadent well-bred Lord, "and be careful with that. I'm going to win it back!"

Thaddeus was about to mock Italicus' gesture when a voice rang from the crowd.

"Thaddeus! A great match!"

Thaddeus spun around, "Kauf! Well, by the Maker, if it isn't Kauf the Magnanimous! You got my letter?"

Kauf threw his head back and laughed, "I'm no longer 'Kauf the Magnanimous.' They now call me 'The Amazing Kauf!'" Kauf looked down at Thaddeus' hand, "What is that?"

"Just a trinket Italicus believes saved his life, "Thaddeus held up the golden feather. "What brings you to our camp?"

Kauf's face dropped. "I've heard of your troubles. Zapp filled me in about Finnius. It's hard to imagine, harder still to believe."

"Verrator Shit!" remarked Thaddeus, spitting on the ground in contempt. "I cannot blame the men though. You can only eat hardtack for so long before you go soft. It was the first opportunity we had to leave this forsaken area and get away from the Marshal's pursuit. They don't have jurisdiction in Aedunic lands." Thaddeus gestured for Kauf to sit down on a nearby fallen tree, "Perhaps I should have taken the job, but every fiber of my being steered me away. Aedunic politics are much more complicated than those of the Slavine or even the Citadel." Thaddeus shook his head, recalling memories of the Kern's visit. "Ugh, and that mystic with his smoke fueled dancing predictions and omens." Thaddeus' voice turned into a mocking tone, "Treveri's voice, Treveri's wisdom, Treveri's spear dick, reveal to me your wisdom."

Kauf laughed at Thaddeus' spot on impression of the old Searer Seric.

Thaddeus smiled wanly. "I felt if I took that job, I would be leading my men to their ruin," Thaddeus looked around at the bleak conditions of the map, "and that is saying something. We'll see how they do under Finnius, I hope they survive."

Kauf leaned forward, "Don't let it eat away at you. As you have always told me, man's free will is our greatest asset. Those men made the choice to follow Finn into a chaotic mission, they know the consequences. They will pay for their mutiny once they meet the Maker. We all will."

Thaddeus clicked his tongue, "I don't remember you being the religious sort. In fact, as I recall, you're quite the opposite."

Kauf tensed, "I wasn't, until recently, that is. Something is coming, Thaddeus. Everything points to it."

"Points to what?" asked Thaddeus, concerned by the look on Kauf's face. "What signs have you seen?"

Kauf frowned. Despite witnessing the miracles and signs himself, he still struggled to believe them. The only thing he felt for certain was absolute determination. He felt compelled to find Thaddeus, and let him know what he had seen and found. The look of skepticism written across Thaddeus' face reinforced Kauf's own doubts, but after a year's journey, this was Kauf's moment. This was his purpose, perhaps even his destiny, and he was not going to let his doubts stop him.

"Thaddeus, I have seen many. They began about a year ago. I was diagnosed with a terminal illness of the lungs by a Citadel doctor. All those nights smoking cigars and drinking brandy in my workshop inventing the next great thing for the Steward's tyrannical state finally caught up to me."

Thaddeus interrupted, "You're ill!? Why am I just now hearing this, Kauf?"

Kauf leaned backwards slightly and raised his hands in defense, "Settle down, I'm ok. I was, but now I'm not."

"You said terminally. How do you go from there to ok?"

"I will tell you. I was in the city of Del, looking for a particular doctor who had experience with problems with lungs. My reputation preceded me, and I was taken before the Senate of Del. Those pompous merchant senators are just as arrogant as the Steward they supposedly hate. They all but commanded me to work for them, they dream of starting a technology race with the Citadel. You know me. I hate the idea of being used for my genius. Add to that to the stress of my illness, my temper blew. I told those pretentious jackasses where they could shove it."

Thaddeus shook his head, "What does this have to do with your recovery?"

"Right, sorry, I found the doctor. He tested me and informed me there was nothing he could do. I was dying, and I had only days, maybe a week left. Defeated and fearing my fate, I parked my wagon outside the city and waited for the inevitable. Those days were very dark for me. I couldn't eat and I barely slept, when I did sleep I had ghastly dreams of a creature stalking me. Death, I had presumed. On the fourth day, I was beginning to cough blood and couldn't stop sweating and shivering. I was dying, Thaddeus, of this I have no doubt. On the seventh day, I awoke from another frightful dream, I felt compelled to leave and head west. For a moment, I thought maybe I just wanted to die alone, far away from the city. The further west I traveled, the more I began to feel different, almost content. I found myself in the Blue Forest. You know of the creature that dwells there. The creature's soul called to me in my dreams. It led me to the river Yardén. I felt compelled to strip my clothes and descend into the water. I floated for hours, drifting in the current. I was eventually swept away. I remember being pulled down by some invisible force. I was completely submerged, but I did not fear the water. I knew I would lose my breath and I would drown, but I was not afraid. Hours later I woke on the river's bank, dazed and confused. I arose as a new man, a man without illness," Kauf turned and looked at Thaddeus with serene eyes. Thaddeus felt suddenly envious of Kauf's content demeanor.

Thaddeus rubbed his chin, and crossed his arms tensely. He felt slightly uncomfortable sitting next to Kauf and hearing his miraculous story. "Your story sounds farfetched, my friend, but I will concede that you do seem to have an aura of confidence that I have never before seen from you."

"Thaddeus, I have purpose in my life again. I took my act to the independent villages. During the performances, I heard awful rumors. They say the Fortress of Ka'yatoluan is inhabited, that two dark evils are working together towards something nefarious. I saw the Tower of Emorragia bleed from its cracks." Kauf inhaled deeply, preparing himself for his next sentences. Thaddeus could feel the weight of his friend's words. "The Steward's great secret has been revealed and the Citadel will never be the same. All of these things were foretold in the Scrolls but even this pale in comparison to the secret of your own destiny, Thaddeus."

Thaddeus was unsure if Kauf was playing him or if Kauf's genius had twisted his mind and turned it dark. "What secret? My destiny? I am not following you, Kauf."

"You, Thaddeus" Kauf declared! "You are the secret! The scrolls read that a messenger will sneak passed the arms, and find the leader of the Maker: his Constabularius."

"Wait, what?" asked Thaddeus, stubbornly. "You can't honestly believe that. The Maker has a leader, and you think it's me?"

Kauf placed his hand on Thaddeus' shoulder and answered with great conviction, "You are the Constabularius, I am sure of it! There is no doubt in my mind or soul."

Thaddeus had known Kauf for most of his life. He wanted to believe his friend, but surely, he had gone mad! He stared at Kauf, trying to see some sign, any indication that his friend was crazy.

Though the more he thought and stared at Kauf, the more Thaddeus couldn't accept that his friend's mind had finally snapped. He also couldn't believe what Kauf was saying was true, "I believe that you believe it. But—"

Kauf interrupted, "You know what I say is true! Deep down in your heart, you know I am right. Your lineage directly connects you to the Maker. Look at your medallion, feel it burn hot!"

Thaddeus was still struggling with the concept, "Man cannot lead the Maker! Even if all you say is true, it would not be a man like me."

Kauf paid no attention to Thaddeus' doubt. "Listen to me, he can, and you are. Forces older than time and creation are converging. If nothing is done to stop these forces, an eternal war of fire and hate will consume everything. It's your destiny to stop it."

"Kauf-- "Thaddeus placed his hand on his friend's shoulder, "I honestly don't understand what you are telling me. But I know for a fact that I am not the mythical Constabul-- "

"BUT YOU ARE!" Kauf knocked away Thaddeus' arm and spoke with a fierce confidence, "Your journey will begin when you receive a message through your weapons!"

"A message though our-- "

Zapp approached and saluted Thaddeus with his right fist on his chest, "Sir, that big eared Merchant Quart has arrived, but he will not exchange anything on credit until he speaks to you personally."

Thaddeus sat silently for a moment. *As usual, duty called at the worst times.* "Kauf, don't move, I will be right back."

Kauf frowned. This was it, he had done his part, his purpose was now fulfilled. "I am afraid my involvement in this has come to an end, Thaddeus. I was sent here to give you this message and to get you through to the next part of your destiny. My wagon is large and all the food in it is yours, my gift to you, Constabularius."

"Kauf, I can't—"

"Nonsense. You cannot deny me this. I know why I was chosen. I have been in your debt since you saved me from those corrupt Citadel officers. I owe you my life. Please take my surplus of food and goods and know that you and your men are blessed."

Thaddeus' pride demanded that he not take food from Kauf, but what good is pride when men are starving? Thaddeus relented and thanked Kauf for his more than generous gift. "Very well, Zapp, help Kauf unload his supplies. I will deal with the stubborn double-talking Quart."

Thaddeus turned to leave, but a hand on his arm stopped him.

Kauf's face was earnest and solemn. He placed a small object in Thaddeus' huge hand, "This is for you, personally, I know of tomorrow. Please take it."

Thaddeus was near his limit. He looked down and stared at the item in his hand. It was a small stone carved into a figure of an Ethereal, one of the Maker's first creations. The Ethereal served and helped in the creation of the universe. The carved stone was of one of the Seven Arch Ethereal, Rahmiel, the bringer of light and the keeper of the dead. In Rahmiel's hand he held the decaying rose, symbolizing the death of a loved one. Figurines like these were called zeichens and were meant to be left on the graves or headstones of loved ones lost.

Thaddeus' eyes swelled.

"It's only an hour's ride from here," Kauf sweetly prompted his friend.

Thaddeus fingered the figurine, took a large breath, and nodded. Thaddeus tried to say thank you, but his voice had left him. Kauf bowed. He knew what Thaddeus was trying to say. He turned and led Zapp towards his wagon.

Zapp helped Kauf unload enough rations for at least two weeks of good eating.

"How do you have so much food, Kauf?" asked Zapp.

"Let's just say I was told you were all going to need it."

"Told by whom?"

Kauf laughed, "You wouldn't believe me if I told you. Can I ask you something Zapp? Have you ever been to Diamin before?"

"The Diamin Theme? No, never been there myself, actually."

"I doubt many have in a long time," muttered Kauf, slightly under his breath. "I was there recently. I was drawn to the temple of Arcadia."

"Oh, like by a premonition?" asked Zapp, letting out a chuckle.

Kauf immediately nodded, "I know you are not a believer my friend, but trust me when I say you will be soon."

Zapp held out his hands defensively. He had not meant to mock Kauf. "Didn't you hear me tell you about the lacerated heart?"

Kauf smiled, still unsure how serious Zapp was about his story. The two finished moving the crates of food in silence.

"I must go if I am to make it to the village before nightfall. But first, take this." Kauf handed Zapp a small wooden box and proceeded to mount his wagon.

"A puzzle box?" It was very old, the paint was faded, and in many spots the original wood showed through. "How do I open it?"

"I found it in the temple with the Ziechen I gave to Thaddeus. It was built for you. Keep it safe."

"Built for me? This box has to be ancient, made way before I was born."

"This box can only be opened by the person it was made for, and you, Charles Jackson are that person. You'll figure that out in time. Use it to unlock a heart!" Kauf ended with a wink. He activated the wagon's engine, steam bellowed out of the small stack in the rear, and the engine purred to life.

***

The day continued, the sun heavy in the sky. Thaddeus finished with the Merchant Qaurt and helped move the needed supplies of horse feed and steel ingots. For the first time in a very long time, the aroma of decent food filled the air. Its nourishment refueled the hearts, minds, and stomachs of the camp. Thaddeus could still see anger in some of his men's eyes, or perhaps fear. He noticed it when they thought he wasn't around.

Italicus found Thaddeus leaning up against the corner post of a tent staring at the zeichen of Rahmiel.

"Penny for your thoughts?"

Thaddeus raised his eyebrows and sighed, "a gift from Kauf." He held the figurine out to Italicus.

"Wow, what a kick in the pants," jested Italicus, lamely. "I've never thought of Kauf as the sentimental type. Have you given any more thought to visiting the Garden?"

"It's been nearly five years since I was last there. I don't know if I can go back."

"I understand. Maybe this will help," offered Italicus, gesturing to the stone. "Have you ever placed a zeichen before?"

"No, never."

"Well maybe you should. Some find it really helpful. It might give you some closure."

Thaddeus took in a deep breath, "Perhaps you're right."

Kazah and Niles walked by, they nodded politely to Thaddeus and Italicus, but the dejection in their eyes was obvious. "Make one bold decision and suddenly everyone hates you," scoffed Thaddeus.

"Come on Thad, it's not just the one…"

"Tell me, what else did I do wrong?"

"You could have let him die." Italicus' voice dropped, "Maybe then we wouldn't have this curse on us."

The man Italicus was referring to was a man no Equinaut could ever forget. Five weeks ago, the war between the Citadel and the Slavine was still raging. From time to time, the Equinauts were hired by the Slavine or the Citadel to keep trade routes or communication lines safe. Sometimes, they were hired to escort important messengers across enemy lines. It had been a lucrative adventure ensuring the safety of the diplomats as they traveled the vast stone arteries of the shard.

The Equinauts quickly learned that accepting work from both sides invited certain issues. Whenever anything went wrong, the Equinauts would be accused of playing one side or the other. The Slavine especially seemed to have a natural propensity towards distrust. Rumor of employing a former slave didn't help things either. There had been some bureaucratic backlash, but Thaddeus and his men didn't much care for politics on either side. They were present to protect the innocent and make an honest coin.

On one moonlit night, the Equinauts were approached by their usual broker for the Kingdom. A rather small Slavine named Laskin. He appeared with a smile, which usually meant he had been paid up front. Laskin claimed that he had been hired by the crown, and a peace treaty was now in the works. The war would soon be over, he proclaimed, and all that was needed was the signature of the Steward. King Hugh, regent of the Slavine Kingdom had personally asked that Thaddeus and his men to be hired to escort his Royal Chamberlain to the Citadel.

The number of times the Equinauts had actually entered the Kingdom could be counted on one hand. The borders were staunchly guarded by Blunkers, which were retired Slavine soldiers armed with giant wooden clubs with metal spikes near the tip. They were paid very handsomely to capture fleeing slaves and to keep the free humans out. Equinauts had always wondered what free human would ever want to travel into Slavine Territory. The risk of being captured and becoming a slave was too high to even attempt such a foolish endeavor.

A small military contingent of the King's royal division met the Equinauts at the border to escort them through the kingdom. Thaddeus had reservations anytime Laskin offered them a job, many of them turning out to be more dangerous or morally amiss than had been originally let on. Thaddeus questioned how truthful the mission was, but the weasel Slavine knew how to manipulate Thaddeus. With peace on the line, an end to the fighting gave Thaddeus no choice but to accept. The moment they entered the Slavine Kingdom through the Marilamanussa Valley, a wary Thaddeus knew something was amiss. This was more than just a diplomatic protection detail. His eyes were constantly turning to the horizon, he felt like the Equinauts had become prey.

The royal division left them at the gates of Orbarrow. The Equinauts cautiously rode through the large bronzed square doors, uncertain of what they would find inside. They gazed at the fortifications with respect and scorn, many of the Equinauts remarking that despite how small the walls and gatehouse were compared to the Citadel, the Slavine still managed to make their capital city seem formidable and intimidating. It would take a grand army to breach the walls.

This had been the first time anyone in the Equinauts, other than Kazah, had been inside the heavily guarded city. Thaddeus' first impressions were troubling. While some streets appeared as normal as any other city Thaddeus had traveled through, the horrors the Slavine committed against their human slaves were flaunted in obscene and graphic ways on many others.

They met their contact in a large square near Xenophon, the old slave market entrance. Kazah purposefully made sure he stayed far away from that area. His memories were still haunted, being sold on the Grand Stage as a child. The Equinauts were met by a frail man, very much in need of food. Despite his frame, he was dressed in the bright colors of a royal slave. The moment the man caught sight of the Equinauts, he began a loud and upbeat tune on a trumpet. The fanfare they received was alarming and confusing. They soon realized it wasn't for them. A gold encrusted litter borne on the shoulders of slaves turned the corner and into view. The trumpeter declared the arrival of Lord Translon, the King's royal chamberlain.

The emburdened slaves dropped to one knee, and an engraved, ornate golden door swung out. Two more emaciated slaves rushed to place steps and roll out a plush carpet. After taking far too long, the Royal Chamberlain finally exited his carriage, to a subtle gasp from the Equinauts. He was not a monstrous brute with painted scales, but was in fact a very ugly, misshapen man.

Upon seeing the man they were to escort, Italicus and several other officers were quick to question the legitimacy of their mission. None had heard of a human holding such a high title within the Slavine regime. The Slavine's extreme prejudice towards humans was well documented. Slavine were raised to believe in their own superiority in all ways. They were larger and stronger, their skins were thicker and harder, and their existence was divinely inspired. They were created by the brother Gods Degei and Turaka for a dual purpose: to conquer and rule.

Humans and Slavine had been raging war against one another for thousands of years. This last war between the Slavine Kingdom and the Citadel was simply the most current in a long list of conflicts between the two species.

Equally, human children were raised on scary and horrible stories of brute, ape-reptilian creatures who rule a vast kingdom of human slaves. It was known that Slavine children were raised to hate and despise humans, and that they wouldn't hesitate to snatch you up if you failed to finish your chores or stayed up too late after bedtime.

Despite all the prejudice, Kazah claimed that while he was a slave, there were a small number of wealthy humans living freely within the Slavine territory. Even with Kazah's claims, Thaddeus and the Equinauts still could not believe what they saw. The Royal Chamberlain was second in power, directly under the King.

Translon was quite bald and extremely hefty, or at least that was the illusion he gave standing next to the near skeletal slave who had announced his arrival. He addressed the Equinauts with toxic distain. He spoke more like a scaled skin Slavine than a soft skinned man. When Thaddeus gifted him with the traditional dice given to people as a symbolic promise of protection, Translon recoiled and sneered in contempt at such trivial objects being handed to him. His eyes turned to scorn and he ridiculed Thaddeus for not giving him the proper respect to his station and demanded to be addressed as Sire or Lord.

When Translon finally, and begrudgingly, mounted the large draft horse his slaves had provided, Thaddeus led the Royal Chamberlain and his men out of the city. Translon stayed near the rear of the escort while they traveled through the Slavine kingdom. That was fine by Thaddeus and the rest of the Equinauts. The only person who seemed to be able to get along with the man was Finnius Ridge. They shared a common trait, they excreted the essence of hubris, a superiority complex that was far exceeded any talents they actually possessed.

The feeling of being hunted still had not left Thaddeus' gut. He knew he had to get out of the Kingdom and rid them of this Chamberlain as quickly as possible. Turning south, Thaddeus decided to take the shortest, if more difficult path, from Orbarrow to the Citadel. The Equinauts followed south and then west around the perimeter of Lake Superion, traveling down the major Slavine road, the Maladinuck. Breaking off near the city of Violetrose, they turned southwest and moved through Kolanus Dirge. its path would take them straight through the border forest of Veilwood forest and into Citadel territory.

It was along this uneven, rocky path that the Equinauts encountered their next surprise, a disturbing site along the road. A small massacre of humans, Slavine, and horses lay shredded across the road. From what was left of the bodies and debris around them, Kazah was pretty certain that the bodies were a squad of Blunkers, though oddly none of the human skulls had been bashed. Many of them seemed to have been ripped off by sheer force.

Translon rolled his eyes and showed no emotion towards the horrific sight or even the slightest care that the victims were human or Slavine. He kicked his horse forward, ordering the Equinauts to follow suit. By the end of the day, five more massacre sights were discovered along the road. The Equinaut scout master Gladthorn, a former Marshal and Bloodhound member, inspected the bodies. Every site was the same, the victims and their horses' wounds were combinations of large sharp lances and vicious animal attack.

At the end of the road, the men were reluctant to enter the forest. Veilwood had a very dark and nasty reputation of holding horrors and creatures too formidable for most to survive against. Sightings of forest elementals were common occurrences in the independent cities along the forest's border. Despite their fear, the Equinaut's trust in Thaddeus was greater than any supernatural rumor, so they started into the forest without question. Only Translon rejected, roaring loudly about his adamant dissent. When the man did not get his way, he stopped his horse and would not move a step further. He was certain whatever attacked those Blunkers was also hiding in the forest. Thaddeus reminded the chamberlain that his safe passage was their top priority, but that the Equinauts would be entering the forest and it was impossible to protect someone who refused to stay with them. Within minutes of trekking through trees, Translon had slithered back into his place at the rear of the column.

It took them several days to navigate through Veilwood forest, and between walls of trees surrounding them and under the dense shade of the canopy, Thaddeus's sensation that they were being hunted gradually abated. Gladthorn tirelessly scouted the forest ahead of the column and made sure they stayed clear of any dangers lurking about. The task was momentous due to the sheer number of creatures and obstacles in the forest. Thankfully, on the beginning of the third day, the sun's bright rays pushed through the thick trees and the Equinauts emerged from the forest unscathed from any unnatural horrors.

Sadly, even with the sun shining and the birds singing, Thaddeus felt the moment he led the column out of the forest the familiar tingle on the back of his neck. The sensation of being hunted had returned. The air exiting the forest smelled putrid and the morning fog began to hug the road tightly. It was not until Italicus' horse Moose nearly tripped to the ground that they realize that they were riding through another massacre. Sudden wind pushed the fog aside to reveal mounds of limbs and viscera lining the road. Dead humans and horses intermingled together. From the number of bodies, it was clearly not another Blunker party. From the broken axels and wooden shards, it was determined this was a merchant trying to sneak through the forest with illegal Citadel goods. From Gladthorn's count, nearly thirty horses were slain, the majority of them in a large single pile. From the weapons on the ground, the merchant had hired an armed group of mercenaries to protect his illegal convoy, but by the looks of it they did little to stop who or what attacked them. Thaddeus ordered his men to investigate the piles in the slight hope that maybe there was a survivor hiding among the dead. Translon impatiently urged Thaddeus to move on, once again showing little to no attention or concern to the death around him.

The bodies had been left for days according to signs of decay. There were clear signs of animal scavenging, and by the size of the gouging and teeth marks left in several of the dead men's thighs, massive quadrupedal boar lizards had crawled from their rocky homes to feast upon the dead. Boar lizards are very passive, but very dangerous creatures. A typical adult boar lizard stands nearly four feet in height, from the ground to the top of their massive head. Scavengers mostly, but when provoked, they were dreadfully persistent in pursuit. Their bodies are impervious to most steel weapons. They have hard scales along their back from snout to tail. Leaving only their soft underbelly and thick penetrative tusks exposed.

Sure enough, as they continued to survey the remains, the boar lizards quietly reemerged from the rocky shrubbery and continued their feast.

Zapp and Niles efficiently scoured piles of flesh looking for any indication of the cause or perpetrator of the massacre. Zapp noticed a stone lodged inside a severed arm, but upon it's retrieval, Zapp and Niles were surprised to realize it was the lower canine tooth from a horse's mouth. The two men stared at it intently, it was strange to them. The wound was fresh, but the tooth looked ancient, like it was beginning to fossilize. What kind of enemy uses old bones to tip their spears?

Zapp sent Niles to show Thaddeus when Translon rode by sneering at him with disdain, Finnius Ridge riding by his side.

Zapp ignored Translon. His ears had caught the sound of something thumping. He turned towards the pile of bodies and listened, *thump da thump*. It sounded like a large heart beat to him. Zapp leaned in closer, the heart beat had stopped. It was silent. Zapp began to wonder if he really had heard anything at all. He turned away when the pile of bodies suddenly moaned. Zapp jumped and grabbed at his chest. Breathing heavily, he called out he may have found someone. He dug away body parts until he came to a man in a long black duster, missing the entirety of his left half. By all rights, the man should be dead. He did not have a heart pumping blood through his body, yet he showed signs of life. His face was badly wounded and his skin seemed more like pale plaster. Pieces of the man's forehead were chipped away. Black blood flowed down, soaking his eye. Zapp, out of instinct, leaned down and reached to feel for a pulse, when the black dressed man gripped his arm.

"BAILITHEOIR!" gasped the man frantically. "DEMON horse." He gulped air, choking on his own black blood. His arm was flopping around, the man was trying to move. He reached towards his left. To Zapp's dismay, the man reached into his own chest cavity and pulled out a heart. It was far larger than any man's and it was severely damaged. "Can't control–turn on us—the heart! Must find–fight—D-ma…ggghh–needs—death PenRuger mu—"

The half man's sentence was cut short when a torch was thrown and the pile of bodies erupted into flames. Zapp leaped out of the way before the flames could touch him. Translon was towering above on his draft horse, unapologetically. Zapp pulled out his Plaz sword and aimed it at the Chamberlain. He was about to strike when Thaddeus ordered him to drop his sword.

Thaddeus demanded a reason from Translon.

"The boar lizards moved. I thought they were going to attack," the fat man claimed through his teeth.

An anguished cry came from the flames. A boar lizard's tusks were tangled in the rib cage of a horse and the beast was burning alive. At his cry for help, his brethren charged the pack of Equinauts.

The Equinauts formed a defensive ring to fight, and Thaddeus ordered Translon in the protected center, but Translon, fearing for his life, dashed away on his horse, pursued by a pair of boar lizards. For miles the royal chamberlain galloped away fleeing, but the boar lizards did not let up. They followed the man until his large draft horse collapsed from exhaustion under his weight. Thrown from his ride, Translon ran from the path. Thaddeus and Zapp found him injured from his fall, struggling to hoist himself onto a tree's lowest branch with the two boar lizards circling for the kill.

Afterward, the Equinauts were tired and many of them had injuries. They blamed Translon for the unexpected lizard attack. Translon set himself down on a tree trunk and demanded preferential medical attention for the cuts and bruises he incurred fleeing. When Edryss approached to wrap his minor wounds, Translon insisted Italicus hold his elaborate and ornate coat, lest it get dusty on the ground. Italicus noticed an unsealed scroll in the pocket. The word Equinauts clearly written on it, he began to read from it out loud. The document was not a peace treaty, but a ceasefire agreement. At first it was hailed happily, an end to the hostilities meant an end to the death and suffering of so many. But as Italicus read on everyone's smiles turned, each word made them angrier. The treaty stipulated that all mercenary groups and in specific, the Equinauts, that had helped in the war must disband or be considered outlaws by both Kingdoms. In that moment, faced with the thought of becoming criminals for no fault of their own, turned even the most righteous Equinauts from their principles. They all screamed for the man's death. It was only Edryss who stood with Thaddeus' protests, preventing the ungracious man from being murdered on the spot.

The men's cries were silenced by two short blasts from a warning horn. Immediately, the men remounted, leaving Translon half bandaged on the tree trunk. In the distance, along the road in the direction of the massacre site, he could see the clear signs of a dust trail rising. Moments later, the form of a cantering horse with a very large man came into view. It was Gladthorn and he was riding as fast as his horse Spyder could carry him. The dust trail was far too large for a single horse to make. Gladthorn was being chased.

Tanslon laughed strangely, in an almost joyfully manor. To everyone's surprise, Gladthorn was being chased by over twenty black dressed riders armed with enormous harpoon lances that appeared too heavy to actually be carried by a man on a horse. The mystery of the large, sharp wounds had been solved. The Equinauts did not wait for the black riders to come to them, they charged to cover their master scout. In a tight delta formation, the horsemen fired their teslas at the black riders, taking several down at long range. The black riders were not fazed by the fact that several comrades had been taken out, they simply closed in and continued their charge. As the gap between the riders lessened, low, unnatural, animalistic cries thundered from the black riders' mouths.

Thaddeus ordered shields and Plaz swords out. The black riders lowered their harpoon lances readying them to impale the first line of Equinauts. Italicus blew a loud horn, the delta formation immediately broke at the center and wrapped around the sides of the black riders. Only the lances on the enemy's flanks had any chance of striking an Equinaut.

Two Equinauts were dismounted, but not killed, and the Equinauts managed to take down several more black riders. Breaking the delta formation and swinging along the sides of the charging black riders allowed the Equinauts to fully surround the riders, limiting their ability to use their long lances. The black riders dropped their lances and pulled out steel swords. The fighting was fierce, the black riders seemed to have overwhelming strength. It was impossible for the Equinauts to win a fight one on one. They began teaming up and engaging the black riders in pairs.

They fought for several disjointed charges, seemingly at a stalemate. The black riders were outnumbered but managed to keep the Equinauts at bay. Translon, still sitting, continued to laugh awkwardly. As a pair of Equinauts fell to the ground, throats slashed by a single sword strike, he began to slur insults at the Equinauts.

Exhausted, and entangled in their second fight of the day, the Equinauts' parries were losing their effectiveness. Not a single black rider had fallen, five more Equinauts were dead and at least ten were injured. The sound of intense fighting continued when a loud trumpet call pushed through the sounds. A very large contingent of Marshals from the Independent realms came cantering towards them.

Translon had somehow managed to hobble towards the fighting. Many of his bandages had fallen off. He was furious, insulting Thaddeus and his men, threatening them with their lives for the poor treatment he had received. Probably from the blood loss, the Royal Chamberlain collapsed to the ground.

The fighting with the black riders suddenly stopped and without in provocation, signal, or sound, the black riders moved as a single unit and broke through the Equinaut line. By the time the marshals had made it to the fighting, the black riders had already fled. Thaddeus considered going after them, but his men were tired and he had injured men. The Marshals, unsure of who was attacking who, kept their distance with their own Teslas aimed at the Equinauts. Thaddeus sheathed his Plaz sword and began to ride over to the Marshal line when Translon sprung from the ground. He began crying for aid and help, holding up his royal seal necklace. He claimed that he had been kidnapped by the Equinauts, who were going to sell him to the black riders but were double crossed. Thaddeus tried to defend and rebuke Translon's remarks. The leading Marshal had never heard of the Equinauts, he had no clue of their reputation. What he did recognize though was the un-fakable seal of the Slavine Royal Family. He ordered for Thaddeus and his men to stand down immediately.

Thaddeus for a moment was dumbfounded, how did everything get so turned around and why was Translon doing this? Was he that awful of a human? The Marshal could see the internal conflict going on inside of Thaddeus, and ordered him again to surrender their weapons. Translon urged the Marshal to fire, and when he didn't, began to yell and order him to obey his command as the Royal Chamberlain to the Slavine Kingdom. Thaddeus knew he couldn't surrender to the Marshals. Once Translon's treaty was signed by the Steward, the Equinauts would become outlaws. He also knew he couldn't fight the Marshals, they were not his enemy. The leading Marshal could see Thaddeus had made up his mind and when he saw Thaddeus grip his rains tighter he knew his choice was not surrender. The Marshals opened fire on the Equinauts, Thaddeus ordered a retreat.

The Marshals pursued them for over a week. Thaddeus lead them on a merry chase around the southern parts of the Shard between the Castiel Mountains and Citadel. Gladthorn knew what tactics the Marshals would use and it allowed the Equinauts to stay one step ahead of them. It was not until they reached Aedunic territory in the west that the Marshals cut off pursuit.

Once they knew the Marshals had stopped pursuing them, they made camp in a small clearing near the Aedunic southern border. Who were those black riders? And why did they attack? No one had an answer. Gladthorn reported that he found nearly one hundred black riders wandering in the woods like they were searching for something. They made their way to the massacre sight and began to sift through the pile of bodies. Gladthorn tried to sneak up on them to discover what they were looking for, but one of them spotted him and alerted the others. The next thing he knew he was being chased by a large number of them. He never figured out what they were looking for, though Zapp, to the disbelief of most claimed he knew what.

"It's the hellhorse."

Zapp tried to explain and to tell them about how he found the half alive man in the black rider outfit, and how he pulled a large laceraa Horse's tooth in the one dead men's arm. Of course, no one believed him.

Italicus didn't blame Thaddeus for their predicament, who would have thought the Marshals would suddenly show up and Translon would betray them? But perhaps a small act of evil, like killing the Chamberlain or at least letting him die, would have been better for everyone.

Thaddeus stared down Italicus with fury in his eyes, "You know I would never take an innocent life."

"I know. You asked and I gave you an honest answer," Italicus tried to back pedal. "You could have at least left him to die. His wounds were serious enough." remarked Italicus, "The man was such a sloth, so vulgar and rude. Do you think the shard would have missed him?"

"I did the right thing. Life is precious. All life." Thaddeus' voice was severe. "You would do well to remember that."

"What about our lives, Thaddeus? Your choices have consequences, and saving that man has affected all of our lives! Sometimes you have to get your hands dirty for the greater good!"

"You know I don't believe that. As men, we must always strive to do the right thing, no matter the consequences."

"Thaddeus, you could have left Translon to die. He killed himself when he decided to attack a sounder of boar lizards!" yelled Italicus. "We wouldn't be starving, and we wouldn't be without half our men."

"Doing nothing by choice, when I had the means and ability to save him, is the same as me killing him!" yelled Thaddeus, unable to control his rage.

Their tiff was beginning to draw attention. The men knew better than to continue their conversation in front of their company.

***

"Focus," whispered Edryss through clenched teeth. A blast of light erupted from the tip of her Tesla rifle, nearly hitting the bullseye on the target. "Damn it!" she muttered, brushing a lock of long thick dark hair away from her eyes.

A large colossus of a man stepped next to her and placed his large, almost giant size hand on her right shoulder. "Don't worry, you almost had it. It's difficult to accurately shoot a Tesla over a hundred yards away! But you'll be a sniper one day."

The moment she heard the man's voice, her frustration evaporated into embarrassment. Edryss forced herself to hold back a smile. She didn't want Gladthorn to see how much she enjoyed his company. Edryss instead pursed her lips and spoke in a sassy voice, "Well, we all can't have the natural talent of a Bloodhound now can we? You make it look so damn easy!"

"I assure you, it's not." Gladthorn drew his rifle from his tesla pack and brought it eyelevel so quickly and naturally that Edryss knew she could never rival his speed. A blue beam flew to the target, hitting its center exactly. Edryss raised a thin black brow, her large eyes focused directly at Gladthorn.

"Wow, really, you just do that right in front of me." Edryss cocked her hip and placed her free hand on it, "You're not helping your case, Mr. Thorn."

Gladthorn recoiled slightly. Mr. Thorn was a nickname Edryss used when she was mad or being sassy. Glad wasn't sure how serious she was and made a low and hardy attempt at a laugh. He turned his face towards Edryss and smiled charmingly, "It took me a very long time to be able to do that." The twisted smile on Edryss' face told him she didn't believe him. Gladthorn cleared his throat, "On my third day as a cadet in the Marshal Program they took us to the firing range. With no instruction, our drill instructor had us fire low powered rifles for three hours. At the end of the day, Marshal Oraculi said to me, 'son, of all the cadets I have taught, you are by far the worst at the rifle. You have no natural talent.' I felt devastated when he told me that. All I wanted since I was a boy was to join the Marshals and become an elite Bloodhound, and in that moment I saw my dreams shatter."

Edryss' heart broke slightly, she could see the pain Gladthorn was experiencing talking about his past, something that he rarely did with anyone. She reached up and touched his large, muscular shoulder and squeezed it tightly. "But you did become a Bloodhound."

Gladthorn's stern and confident posture melted at her touch, "A life's dream fulfilled and destroyed. Malum's leadership corrupted and twisted the Bloodhounds." his voice cracked slightly, he cleared his throat again. "Five hundred years of service and Gladthorn Jones brought it down in a single day."

"I've heard the stories" remarked Edryss, happy to see Gladthorn open up to her. "You did what was right, you saved thousands of lives. Including Italicus and Thaddeus."

Gladthorn turned his face away, "The rumors you have heard do not compare to the horrors of the truth. I too hold blame for the atrocities my blood brothers caused."

"That's not true. You didn't realize the crimes you investigated were being faked by Malum and the Cavalla syndicate. The innocents you put away you honestly thought were criminals and many of them were! Just not for the crimes you put them away for."

"Malum and the Syndicate may have used me to investigate and arrest rival gang members and their political enemies, but it doesn't matter. They were innocent of the crimes I arrested them for!"

Edryss felt slightly lost. She didn't know how to comfort Gladthorn, "They used your values and principles against you." She touched his hand, "You are the most honest, courageous, most disciplined man I have ever met! What happened all those years ago, it wasn't your fault, you aren't to blame!"

"YES!" yelled Gladthorn in contempt for himself, "I am to blame, three innocent people that I put away hung for murders they didn't commit!"

Gladthorn turned and faced away from Edryss, realizing how open he had just become with her. He was ashamed of his past and didn't want to have to share the pain with her. Edryss reached out, stroked his face and pulled him by the chin towards her. The weight and pain in his eyes was great. "You know you can always tell me anything."

Gladthorn's rage and anger left him. He pressed his cheek against her hand, if he could have melted into it he would have. "I know, thank you. But I didn't tell you that to talk about my past. After Oraculi's scorn, I went back to the range. Orcauli was there waiting for me. He knew I would be back and that's when he told me natural talent will only get you so far, men who have it never become great. Greatness is about practice, determination, and repetition. You have to be able to handle this rifle in your sleep, dreams and nightmares. From that day on, I practiced harder, better, and faster than any other recruit and once I became a Marshal and a Bloodhound, I practiced even harder. Now I can do things like this."

Edryss rolled her eyes slightly, she knew Gladthorn was about to show off. Staring at Edryss and standing sideways down range, he held his gun straight out with one arm. He fired eight shots at eight different targets, several of them were nearly one hundred yards away. His eyes never left Edryss', not even to look to see if his eight shots had hit their targets. He could tell by her smile that he had.

"Now you are just showing off Mr. Jones. "Mocked Edryss, keeping her eyes fixed to his, "Do you do that for all the women you talk to."

Gladthorn's cheeks turned red and his bright white teeth shined through his sheepishly boyish grin, "Only the important ones who have stolen my heart."

Breaking his stare, Gladthorn quickly used his peripherals looking left to right to make sure no one else was nearby. He leaned in and kissed Edryss forcefully on the lips, a rush and surge of electricity passed through them.

The urge to go further sung through Edryss' body, it wanted more, needed more. But fraternization between Equinauts was expressly forbidden. Knowing how much trouble they would be in and that at any moment someone could easily show up through the trees, she resisted her urge and pushed off of his chest breaking the kiss. Gladthorn opened his eyes and frowned, Edryss licked her lips seductively.

"Mm, Gladthorn Deon Jones" Edryss brought her hands to her chest and spoke in a very low husky tone, "you are going to be the death of me. I love you!"

Leaning forward Gladthorn kissed Edryss' cheek softly, "I know!"

Edryss smirked and punched Gladthorn in the arm, "You know, now do you? Is that how you were raised?"

"My mother did teach--" Gladthorn's usually low voice cracked slightly, "Oh, I'm sorry, I didn't mean to…"

"It's ok. You don't have to protect me. You can talk about your mother. I lost mine a long time ago."

"I know, I still feel bad to do so. I never want to be the cause of pain." assured Gladthorn softly, grabbing her right hand and holding it firmly in his own. "I love you too much."

"I know!" Edryss smiled fiendishly, bashing her eyes together. She stared at her hand dwarfed in his.

It took a moment for Gladthorn to realize what she had said. "HAHA!" he mocked back at her, "I guess we were raised the same way.

He gripped her arm tighter. He could feel his heart beat through his chest. There was never a moment near Edryss that he did not feel like his heart would burst through his chest. "When we tire of being Equinauts, I will—"

"I love it when you hold my hands." remarked Edryss, trying to change the subject. "Can I ask you a question?"

"Of course."

"The other day, I saw you talking to Finnius, why didn't you go with him? I've never seen you turn down a mission before."

Gladthorn rubbed his smooth, bald head, "He asked me to join him, begged practically. It didn't feel right, something was off. Finn's ego is way too large to properly command. To jump at a job solely for fame and money is reckless. I don't know, it just left a bad taste in my mouth. I fear he would become a more corrupt leader than Malum was with the Bloodhounds."

"Maybe if he had a person with your conviction by his side. "

"No, I am loyal to Thaddeus and his code! For so long I dreamed of being a Bloodhound. To be a hero, a guardian, a shield for people who can't protect themselves. Now I see my dream was misplaced, the Marshals maybe the law in the independent realms, but the Equinauts, Thaddeus, Italicus, they are the true heroes."

Edryss hugged the man tightly and whispered "And so are you!"

***

After dinner, Thaddeus ordered his assemblage to gather for an evening fire talk. Every Equinaut knew they had to be of top physique, but these infrequent seminars focused on strengthening the mind and soul.

"Our Spiritual essence guides our morality. A man's character is based not only on his actions, but by his heart. Equinauts who have pledged to protect others must stay vigilant, in both heart and mind!

"Be watchful, stand firm in faith, and be strong. Let all that you do be done through loyalty." Thaddeus paused briefly. This struck the soldiers. Usually, Thaddeus made it through the entire talk without skipping a beat.

Thaddeus looked around at the men and women who comprised his family, meeting each offered gaze, gauging their temperament.

"Brothers and sisters, there is something I need to get off my chest. I know many of you worry about our future. I know you were confused, even angry when I allowed The Chamberlain to live. But you know this is our way! We are men and women of character. We were hired to escort him safely! Yes, we were helping him in hurting us, assisting in our own demise, but The Maker will provide! He has never let us down before and will not let us down ever, as long as we stay true! As I look around, I see loyal Equinauts. I would trust my life with each and every one of you. You all have proven yourself worthy of the title, for we are the Knights of our Maker! We must fortify ourselves, this ceasefire between the Citadel and the Slavine means jobs will become few. The convoys traveling between the realms will need less protection, and our coin will soon begin to dwindle. But I have faith that the Maker will provide for us! There will always be people in need of protection, and our hearts will follow!" Thaddeus' passion was palpable, and the silence that followed deafening.

"What of the treaty declaring us and all mercenaries criminals? Both sides have ordered their soldiers to arrest us or kill us," yelled a voice from the crowd.

"And the Marshals too!" yelled another soldier.

Thaddeus nodded and gave the crowd a charismatic smile, "We will prevail! Finding proper work will be hard. We will head north and remain within the realm of the Northwestern lakes near Veamini."

"There's no coin in the west!" yelled a woman. Several grunted in agreement, "How will we survive?"

"Do not fret. Something worthy of our name will emerge! We will see hands filled with coin soon enough!" declared Thaddeus confidently.

Despite Thaddeus' desperate assurances, the crowd dispersed, more upset and worried than when they had arrived. Italicus was the last to leave.

"I think I made things worse," said Thaddeus miserably.

Italicus was matter of fact, he knew better than to try to smooth things over, "Yeah I think you did, but don't beat yourself up. Right now, you could give them the entire contents of the Steward's treasury and they would still be upset, just give them time."

"Perhaps…"

Several moments of silence passed between the two.

"I got Egghead all saddled up for you."

Thaddeus peered up.

"Go, it will do you some good to get away from here."

"Perhaps."

"Go!" demanded Italicus. "Go and see her!"

***

The hour's ride to the Garden of Sanctum took minutes for Thaddeus. His anxiety warped time. The narrow road was dimly lit by torches tied with blue ribbons, symbolizing loss and grief. The garden was dedicated by the third king of the Citadel, Lucius Gerald Magnus Theodus II, over thirty generations ago. The King sanctified the Garden as one of the holiest sites in Elisia. Hundreds of thousands of souls rest within its hallowed grounds, but Thaddeus cared for only one.

The arched entrance gate to the garden was sculpted from marble and accented in gilded gold. Two giant gargoyles stood as sentries, forever tasked with guarding the sacred grounds. Thaddeus dismounted, took up a torch, and placed it in a sconce attached to Egghead's saddle. The two tentatively passed under the archway. The garden was more of a labyrinth than a cemetery. So many tombstones and graves were scattered about the massive complex that a person could easily get lost. There are myths regarding the young who never found their way out. They spend an eternity living among the dead, forever lost.

Despite the years that had passed since Thaddeus had visited the Garden, the route he needed to take was carved deeply into his memory. The path was less than a mile in length, but the short walk seemed longer than the ride from the camp. Each step left Thaddeus' feet heavier, his shoes were slowly turning to stone. Thaddeus grasped the Zeichen, squeezing it slightly, hoping to find some strength in it. The garden was in its natural state of gloom. There were countless monuments, many of which stood at Thaddeus' knee. Some were so delicately chiseled that erosion left them smooth. A few were almost a story high, carved into amazing shapes, depicting characters from the shard's mythology.

Thaddeus was filled with dread and overcome with sorrow. He moved past a large mausoleum and turned the final corner, and his heart broke all over again. Even in the darkness he knew what was lying before him. Thaddeus dropped the Zeichen and let Egghead's reins fall to the ground, all remaining strength in his body drained. Under the weeping branches of a small willow tree lay a row of plaques and memoriam. Among them was a pure white piece of marble stone that glowed like moonlight. Thaddeus could not make out the words, but he knew them perfectly.

Here Lies Alana Mary PenRuger
Daughter of Joshua Loft
Beloved Wife, Taken Before Her Time

Thaddeus approached the stone from the side. He tried not to step over anyone's grave out of respect.

"Hey Lana, I am sorry it's been so long," Thaddeus said softly, "but the pain hasn't gotten any lighter since you left. Not a day has gone by that I haven't missed you. I even miss your Shepard's pie. It has been a very trying time recently. I feel like the world is stacked against me, the Equinauts are in serious distress *and* we have been branded outlaws by the recent peace treaty. We saved innumerable lives, and this is how the universe repays us. It's too much."

Thaddeus stared at the stone, his eyes tracing Alana's name over and over again, "None of that matters though, I would give it all up, every life I have saved, every good deed I have ever done, only to hold you once more, to hear your voice again..." Thaddeus wept... "Oh, your voice, my love, I can barely remember it. I remember things you have said to me, but I can't hear your voice. How could I forget?" His words dissolved into sobs. What little composure he had was totally gone. He collapsed against the tombstone. Thaddeus was exhausted, but fought hard to stay conscious. This was not a place he wanted to fall asleep. Eventually, whispering to Alana, Thaddeus gave into the urge and closed his eyes.

The sun crested above the horizon, its powerful rays slipped between the boughs upon Thaddeus' forehead. His consciousness was slow to regain. Part of him wanted to drift back into one of the few dreamless sleeps he had ever had, but he felt a presence close in on him. A small guttural nicker indicated that it was only Egghead. Thaddeus gradually opened his eyes. An inch from his face was Egghead's nose. He was standing on the grave next to Alana's.

"Hey buddy, how long was I out for?" Thaddeus watched Egghead throw his head up into the sky towards the sun. Thaddeus smiled, "Good point, the sun wasn't there when we started this, was it?"

Egghead let out another nicker, and dropped something heavy from his mouth. It was the Zeichen. Egghead had grabbed it while Thaddeus slept.

"So, you're in on this conspiracy too then? Everyone wants me to perform the ceremony."

Egghead nudged Thaddeus in the chest, and shook his head, messing up his mane and forelock.

"Fine, you win Eggers, I'll do it" Thaddeus patted Egghead's nose.

Thaddeus knelt in front of Alana's tombstone, he felt awkward being on the actual grave, but, he was determined to do this right. "Oh Maker, blessed are the dead for they now reside with you, may you watch and care for them as you will me when I pass through the veil of this life." Thaddeus took a large breath. New tears ran down his face, "Blessed is the Lady Arcadia, for she commandeth the Arch Ethereal Rahmiel, keeper of the dead that ensures all souls will reach thee. Oh Maker, with this Zeichen I give you dominion over Alana's safety, I invoke the Lady Arcadia to ensure this be done, so let it be done, so say we all." Thaddeus kissed the figurine and placed it on the ridge of Alana's tombstone. Thaddeus ducked when a fierce thunderclap punctuated the ritual. When he looked up, the sky was clear.

"Goodbye, my love. I promise to see you again." Thaddeus mounted Egghead and steered him towards the Garden's gates. Thaddeus contemplated the rite he had performed, and for the briefest of moments, he felt like something or someone was staring at him. During that pause, his mind jumped to a memory of Alana cooking and singing out the open window. Thaddeus smiled, he remembered her voice, her beautiful, angelic voice, and for the first time in nine years, he felt almost whole again.

***

The obstacles facing the Equinauts hadn't lessened, but to Thaddeus, they seemed smaller and easier to tackle. Everyone noticed the change in their leader, his aura radiated confidence and optimism, it was contagious.

"You seem better." Italicus sipped from a steaming mug of herbal tea.

"I feel better, I didn't think I could, but Italicus, I remember…"

"You remember what?"

Thaddeus' smile wrinkled his eyes, "Everything." He walked off towards the blacksmith's area.

Thaddeus spent most of the day teaching Niles, the Equinauts' new blacksmith and horseshoer, how to properly trim and nail a shoe onto a horse. He reveled in the physicality of the task.

"The first thing you have to do is clear out dead sole from the foot. We use this hoof knife right here, it has only one sharp side and it's bent so that we can cut out anything dead." Thaddeus, held the front left hoof between his knees which were protected by a pair of thick leather chaps. He took the hoof knife in one hand and began to cut through the bottom of the foot, around the outside heel, around the hoof's toe and back to the inside heel. "Once we have this cut out, we can see the new sole underneath. Do you see this line around the edge of the outside wall of the hoof? That's a pretty good marker to show how much toe and wall we need to nip out to shorten the hoof."

Niles contemplated the move, "If that line is more of a guideline, then how can you tell how much to nip off?"

"There are several other things you have to take into account. How the horse stands, his confirmation, whether his ankles run short or long, and how much heel the hoof has. I know it's a lot, but once you have trimmed enough horses, you will eventually gain the eye. It'll become second nature. Don't worry, I'll be around to help you out."

"Thaddeus! Come quickly!" Gladthorn shouted from a distance.

Thaddeus placed the hoof down and ran to the center of camp. Standing there was a man who was too small and scrawny to be threatening.

Gladthorn nudged the scrawny man forward, nocking the butt of his tesla rifle into the man's back, "We found him walking straight through the middle of the camp."

"How did he get past our guards?" Thaddeus asked Gladthorn.

The scrawny man held up his hand and tried to speak, "Sir, I have a message for—"

"You don't speak!" Gladthorn interrupted the small man. "I don't know, but I found him walking straight through the armory tent like he owned the place."

"THE ARMORY!" Thaddeus's mind flashed Kauf's prophecy, "The messenger will sneak through the weapons."

Thaddeus shrugged off the superstition and approached him, "How did you get so far into my camp?" Thaddeus questioned the man in his most commanding voice.

The slim man bowed his head in the old ways of greetings, "I walked, if you must know."

"You simply walked right in, past the sentries and through everyone else!?"

The man nodded. "Forgive me, but I am on an urgent mission. I am looking for a man named Thaddeus, son of Uther PenRuger."

"I am whom you seek."

"Maker and Ethereal be praised. I am Steven. I work for Professor Nikola Belladon at the University of Citadel. We are in urgent need of your services. Countless lives are in jeopardy!"

"You're asking to hire us?" asked Thaddeus cautiously.

"Please, forgive me for intruding like this," pleaded Steven, "but I was afraid of being turned away. It is of the utmost urgency that you agree." Steven reached into his pocket and handed Thaddeus a scroll. "I've been authorized to guarantee this job will pay your highest fee! Will you come?"

***

The sun sank until only the outline of the western mountain range was illuminated. Perhaps their luck was beginning to change. With the arrival of this Steven fellow, the Marshals had for some reason left the area and headed north, taking the path towards Veamini. Thaddeus was thankful for the end of the day. The Equinauts may have shrunk to fifty men, but their camp was set up for a hundred. It took all day to pack and prepare to leave for the Citadel. Thaddeus finished his lesson with Niles, helping him nail shoes onto the final six horses. Thaddeus returned to his cot, replaying the events of the past few days: the Kern and that blasted mystic, Finnius and his mutiny, Kauf showing up unexpectedly with food, visiting Alana's grave, and Steven with the promise of work. After several minutes of contemplating, Thaddeus couldn't help but smile. He had promised his crew that the Maker would provide, and out of sheer providence, a man showed up with a job. Thaddeus hoped it wasn't too good to be true. The coincidence of Kauf's prophecy coming true exactly as he said troubled Thaddeus slightly. Though he thought prophecies were nonsense in principle, this felt different. Thaddeus sensed that this job was meant to be. Thaddeus noticed the silver ornate box with Alana's hair on the bed stand. It was the first time he had ever forgotten to return the box his chest pocket. He kissed the tips of his fingers and placed them on the box.

He felt oddly content. "Good night, Alana. I love you."

Thaddeus pulled the pungent fur blanket over his shoulders. His body ached from his night spent slumped in the garden, it didn't take long to find sleep. For most of his life, Thaddeus hated dreaming. Last night's dreamless sleep was the best in recent memory. His abhorrence stemmed from the Medallion. His current dream was the worst.

There was nothing but blackness, void of creation, shapeless. But then, an essence was sharply felt. The essence was powerful and strong, but ultimately lonely. Climactically, a patterned green and blue sphere materialized. The sphere cleft until only pieces remain.

Then, a scream pierced the quiet tranquil air. It was a screech so unnatural that it made Thaddues' heart pound and his skin crawl. Pure, unadulterated fear pulsed through his body. Thaddeus found himself standing right in front of the Mighty Gates of Astronomicus, located in the Great Bazaar of the Citadel. All around him appeared bodies of innocents, strewn lifeless, limbs akimbo, complete and thorough carnage. Thaddeus felt sick, and utterly despondent. His lips parted, but no scream issued forth. The contents of his stomach wrenched inside of him. As a veteran of countless battles and campaigns, he knew the gory and unnerving sight of the dead at his feet, but he had never felt so culpable. The dead eyes of children stared, but none were as bad as the accusing looks of their mothers, butchered, bereft of life.

William F. James

Thaddeus covered his face with his hands and screamed silently into them, the horrific carnage too much for him to handle. Upon his emotional and physical upheaval, he discerned he was back at camp, looking off towards the southern mountains. They were burning, like a saffron pyre. Through the smoke and the flames he saw creatures, abominations, and demons pouring from the mountains. Atop monstrosities they galloped straight towards him. Inhuman howls and blood crazed screams emanated from each of the mouths of thousands of creatures--booming, blaring, deafening. A group of black riders barreled towards him, yelling and screaming incomprehensible, unnatural demonic sounds. Leading the charge was a rider upon a pitch-black horse with glowing eyes, blue flames pierced through its nose. It was an unholy beast with flesh and muscle missing. A large, deep, unhealed scar was cut down the neck of the beast. The very tissue around the scar pulsed and out of the tissue was the clear sound of a thousand dead equine souls. Thaddeus knew what he saw, all true horsemen would. The rider was astride Bailitheoir, the Hellhorse.

Fearing the horse, Thaddeus ran. But he wasn't running. He was paralyzed. Desperately fighting, trying to get away, every muscle in his body rejected his orders, and there they were nearly upon him! There was nothing left to do. Thaddeus closed his eyes and waited for the inevitable. He waited…he waited…but nothing happened. He opened one eye, he opened both eyes. All of the demons had vanished, including the Hellhorse and there he was, gazing upon the broken sphere. It became red, every crack oozing copious thick blood. Thaddeus was startled by the sensation of a faint breath against his neck. He spun around, fists raised, ready to attack, believing it to be a demonic creature. But instead, his heart sunk far below his chest and he felt his knees buckle. He could not believe who was standing in front of him.

Thaddeus' lips trembled. He barely managed to mouth the word, "Alana…"

Thaddeus' body shook with each beat of his heart. This could not be his Alana, she was dead and gone. This could not be her. Thaddeus tried to turn his head, but no force could have broken his gaze. The woman before him slowly approached, her stride gliding on air.

Instinct continued to yell at him, there was not a chance this was his wife, but every fiber of his being told him whoever or whatever was in front of him surely was his beloved. Thaddeus' mind continued to bounce between belief and doubt. As she moved closer, Thaddeus' doubt increased. If this was Alana, she was not as he remembered. In fact, her body seemed to flicker between the woman he loved and something else, the outline of her body blurred blue.

"Hello, Thad," she spoke, her voice was angelic, every syllable a song. Despite his doubt, hearing her voice destroyed any ability for Thaddeus to question. He quivered. Her voice, how he missed it. Her perfect hair glowed, every tendril floating mid-air. She emitted an aura of superiority. Thaddeus swelled as he gazed into her eyes. For over nine years, he dreamt of this moment, to be standing in front of his wife, to see her, to hear her, to feel her lips upon his. It was not as he had imagined. So many emotions swam within him, but the brightest one was guilt.

"Why?"

Alana closed her eyes and lowered her head. She concentrated and slowly came into focus. "It's been a long time, I have missed you so much!" her whisper was warm. Alana stepped forward and softly palmed his face, Thaddeus felt himself retract.

"No, not after what I have done!"

Alana's blink took a lifetime. "My Thaddeus, it's not your fault."

Thaddeus' face burned red. He tried to say I love you, but instead shouted, "Yes! Alana, if I had not left your side, if I had not been forming the Equinauts, the universe wouldn't have taken you!" His words echoed over, and over, and over again in the distance. Thaddeus' knees finally gave out, he tensed his body, wracked with sobs. His voice flowed hushed, "I found you, lying in the middle of the house, still warm! I tried to save you, Alana. The medallion should have saved you!" Thaddeus searched for his wife through swollen eyes, defeated. Alana pressed her body against his. His head rested against her stomach.

"It's alright, Thaddeus. It was my time to go. The future holds so much more for you!" Thaddeus reached up, and pulled her onto his lap.

Thaddeus couldn't speak, but knew his thoughts were heard "The future is nothing. I have no future. My only life is here, raising a family with you! To have children of our own, to grow old together! You were taken from me. If not for this damned medallion keeping me alive, I would have joined you sooner!"

"No!" A cacophony in a single sound, Alana brought their foreheads together. "Mine was only ever a reflection of your light. The Maker blessed us, though it was only fleeting, and we must cherish it. But now you must move forward!"

Alana's eyes filled his field of view. It was as if nothing had ever existed outside of her stare. "I can't move on. And I won't. You are my life." Thaddeus felt rage bubble up and consume him. "Who did this to you?"

Alana stood, shrinking, smaller by the moment. "Why does this matter?"

"It matters, Alana! Tell me! I will avenge your death! You deserve justice!"

A sudden bang filled his ears "Goodbye, my love!" the sweetest whisper.

"Don't go! Tell me who it was!" Thaddeus reached for Alana.

"I won't Thad, it's not important." It was unclear whether she was getting smaller or farther away.

"TELL ME WHO!" Thaddeus was desperate, uncontrollable.

Alana sighed and in that moment, she was with him, and he could see in the reflection of her eyes the name of her killer.

"No." The word slipped through Thaddeus' gritted teeth. A second bang, closer. Alana pushed against Thaddeus' chest and again began to drift away, "PLEASE, DON'T LEAVE ME!"

Alana mouthed something, her perfect lips making shapes that Thaddeus could only stare at without comprehension. A third bang and Alana vanished from sight. The banging rang inside Thaddeus, shattering his mind. The violent howling and screaming returned.

Through the roars, one voice tolls above the rest, "SON OF UTHOR, BRING ME MY VESSEL!!!!!"

Thaddeus awoke, alert and grounded. "What in Elisia." The following hours brought no sleep. His mind raced feverishly, and one word surfaced to his mind: Lockburn.

Echo from the Past

For the first time in so many years, my vessel and I were not hungry or scared. We were to be a god to these simple, pathetic people. They had seen my power and were in awe of it. My vessel was right, use them, bend them to our will. They took us away, carried on their backs with a litter created out of the debris around them. They chanted songs of worship devoted to the Maker. If only they knew. The Fallen's true purpose. Why we had killed so many. Perhaps if they had, they wouldn't have given themselves freely to us. My vessel doubted the assumption. For years our minds had been mixed. I asked her why she had never spoken to me before. Her reply was simple and powerful, she had no need to until now. Even I could understand the value in that.

Our worshipers carried us for miles. They brought us to an encampment where a thousand more of them festered in shanties. The camp smelled of rot and the people smelled worse, it was truly a horrific site. To me and my vessel, it was beautiful, for it was now ours. We would rule this pitiful group of survivors.

Our arrival was announced, and many ran to the gate to see their new god. The litter bearers lowered us to the ground and we stood to address our people. They fell to their knees, giving thanks and worshiping. A few stood, demanding proof we were all powerful. One man shouted out, asking not for proof of my divinity, but for dedication of my love for these people, a promise to be a steward of them. I asked him his name, it was Jude. Immediately my vessel spoke to me. Kill him. Her pleasure in the thought delighted me. I would not disappoint my pet. Slowly, my hands rose to the heavens, and I called upon the power of the Celestials. Absolute power snaked around my arms and into my hands, lightning and thunder danced to my will. The mortals quaked in fear, the man who stood against me put his face to the dirt and begged forgiveness. There was no forgiveness this day, he should have been grateful for the purpose I bestowed upon him in death.

"RISE!" My voice echoed through the camp like a hurricane from the East.

The small man rose, the crowd shied away from him. I smiled at the obedience. I would reward him, it would be quick. I could feel my vessel laugh and I could not help but join in. I released the energy from my hands, and it charged towards the man. It reached him before he could scream. He was completely and utterly obliterated into fine dust, even his soul was fragmented.

My people were silent.

"Worship me. Follow me. I promise you, your lives will forever be changed. Deny me, deny my godhood, and I will judge you more harshly and more quickly than Jude."

After that, our position was sealed. These people were fully in our grasp.

In the years that followed, what was a barely inhabitable squabble of huts slowly grew into something more worthy of my presence. A large temple ascended from the ashes and debris. A temple, where I could leave my vessel safely and occupy a chamber, Sanctum Sanctorum. A room protected from the eyes of celestial beings. Still, I feared if I used too much energy I would rouse the attention of the Ethereal.

Our destruction on Aurelia was incomplete. I was dismayed to learn of other survivors. In time, I adopted them into my care. It was a delicate process, pruning my herd. I struggled with some, not all are swayed by great acts of power. Free will was a gift the Maker had given his creations. While usually bendable to the will of the stronger, sometimes free will cannot be broken. Certain men refused to accept me as their god. If I lived without fear of discovery by the Ethereal, I could have easily smitten the creatures, but alas it was safer to cull them to the north than to obliterate them completely. I had to use my powers sparingly, and I couldn't allow their disbelief to infect the rest of my people.

In my youthful pride, I postponed their demise to a later date, when my follower's army would stamp out all who dared deny me. Their power grew stronger with each passing generation. They dedicated their lives to me on Aurelia, and their souls to me after.

I was on the course of total victory; of this I had no doubt. The power of souls was too intoxicating to ignore, too alluring to give up. Every plan was thought out, every strategy weighed and calculated.

If I had known the consequence of waiting, that this was the first steps towards the end, the first seed of discontent between me and my vessel, I would have vanquished the entire northern encampment of heathens myself and be damned if the Ethereal found out.

No one could have predicted a new god falling out of the sky.

Gladthorn Deon Jones

Chapter Four

From the first scroll of Zakarael, chapter 2 verse 8:
*"...and then evil shall be revealed; awaken thy spirit for which the
Maker has prepared and protect the brightness of thy soul."*

- Day One: Several hours before the first demon attack:

·"Finally! I thought that guard would never let us pass!"
remarked Leora, re-buttoning her numerous vest pockets.

Italicus cradled his bruised left cheek. "Well you know Leora,
it would have helped if you had told me about the weapon you were
carrying. I thought the man was trying to grope you!"

"It was just a 'pat down,'" laughed Leora, pushing her dark
red hair behind her back so she could get the last of the buttons
snapped. "When they asked me to disclose all my dangerous weapons I
had assumed the small blade of a letter opener wouldn't qualify as
dangerous."

Italicus turned on his heels and looked back at Leora
incredulously. "It was a letter opener? That's what they held us up
over? The guards patted you down eight times over a letter opener?"

Leora held up the sheathed blade of a small, simple, non-
ornate letter opener. "I've learned long ago men will find any excuse
to, you know." Leora motioned carelessly to her chest. "But thank you
for standing up for me when you thought he was groping me. It's
comforting to know I am in the presence of such polite gentlemen."

Thaddeus approached astride Egghead, his face heavy. The
professor, furious over the delay, had reprimanded Thaddeus sharply
over the importance of the mission.

Leora smiled at Thaddeus, pretended to refasten the final
button on her vest, and peered up at Italicus. "I told you I could handle
it myself." She glanced at Thaddeus and smirked, "I'm used to men
trying to touch me."

Thaddeus' stern face was unwavering. "Leora, let this be a
warning, if you continue to engage in such careless, flippant behavior,
your journey ends here and now. I won't tolerate it."

"There's no need to be so serious." rebuffed Leora, unsure
why Thaddeus was upset with her. It was her first mistake. "It wasn't
my fault, they were looking for any reason to touch—"

"Don't be childish, this is a serious issue!" snapped Thaddeus, unwilling to hear Leora's explanation. "By not properly disclosing your weapons to a Citadel Guard, you endangered the safety of my second in command. Your arrogance could have jeopardized this entire expedition!"

Italicus inhaled, puffing up his chest, "And we can't afford to lose our handsome and noble second in command, now can we?" After a moment he added, "Don't be so hard on her Thaddeus, it wasn't really her fault. They stopped her over a stupid letter ope—"

Thaddeus glared at Italicus.

"Glare at me all you want," growled Italicus, in no mood for Thaddeus' temper, "You're angry, but it's not because of us!"

Thaddeus did not acknowledge Italicus' comment.

The longer the silence stretched the more upset Leora became.

Italicus tried to get Thaddeus to speak. "I hope the professor didn't give up any more wagons to those vulgar guards!"

"He did."

"How many this time?"

"You don't want to know." Leora was visibly shaken, she knew it wasn't entirely her fault. Those guards had eyeballed her the moment she arrived at the gate. She knew before they even spoke that she was going to be asked for a random search, but she honestly didn't know it was going to lead to eight different pat downs and hours of delay over a simple letter opener. "I…I'm sorry. I didn't know a letter opener needed to be registered."

Thaddeus pointed to the small letter opener with a wooden hilt hanging between Leora's breasts, "You're lucky the guards let you keep that thing! I expect next time you won't presume to know better than direct orders from a superior!"

Thaddeus gave a slight nod to Italicus, and the two men trotted to the head of the expedition. Leora slumped in her saddle as others from the expedition rode passed her. She felt humiliated and confused. "What orders?"

"I won't be surprised if those particular wagons come out of our part of the gold," sneered Italicus.

"You're not innocent, Italicus," declared Thaddeus, firmly. "In the future, don't involve yourself with civilian matters, and next time a Citadel guard asks you for your name, don't give it to them. We're 'outlaws,' now, remember?"

Italicus waved the warning off, and Thaddeus watched him trot off on his large, warm blood horse, Moose.

"Hey!" called Thaddeus. Italicus knew better than to ignore Thaddeus when he used that tone, "Did you ever hear back from your contact in the Citadel?"

Italicus shook his head, "Don't worry Thad, if I hear anything about a Lockburn you'll be the first to know. Unless it's a civilian matter."

Thaddeus gave Italicus an unimpressed stare and nodded.

**

Gladthorn mounted Spyder, his muscular but short black horse. Edryss teased the large man for riding such a small steed, as she often did. Gladthorn ignored the comment, he knew It was in good fun, and besides, his was one of the best horses outside of Egghead and Moose. Gladthorn smiled and pulled down the brim of his worn leather hat. With a well-placed tilt of his chin, he could hide most of his face in that way. Now that the Expedition had gotten through the Citadel, the Equinauts were able to re-equip their swords and tesla packs.

Miles from the Citadel, the horizon wall still loomed behind, and the whole eastern shard beckoned ahead. Gladthorn wondered what thrills and horrors they were now heading towards. His brain was still reeling from the crazy and unnatural visions all had experienced in the heart of the Diamin theme. He looked down at Edryss who had left her jacket's front cover open since strapping on her tesla pack. "You're unbuttoned, you know. Would you like some help? I do know that jacket pretty well."

Edryss glared and prayed no one nearby was listening. "You mind yourself, now," she said harshly, before adding in a hushed tone, "Besides, you only know how to unbutton it."

"What was that?" asked Gladthorn, lifting a hand hand to his ear.

"Stop it!" snapped Edryss, holding back a smile. "You heard me damn good and well enough, Mr. Thorn."

Gladthorn winked, despite the edge in Edryss' voice, and urged Spyder forward, heading for the front of the column to begin scouting the area ahead.

Before he could get far, Italicus trotted up on his horse Moose. "Gladthorn, Thaddeus wants around the clock scouting reports. If you have to, take Edryss and a few extras with you. Use the professor's people as couriers if needed. Keep sending reports, changing course with this large of a column is no small task."

Gladthorn saluted. "What has Thaddeus worried?"

"We encountered a small family heading back towards the Citadel. They made mention of Marshals stopping traffic several miles ahead and searching through their valuables. They said the treasure of Motany Bay was stolen."

"There is no treasure of Motany Bay, it's a myth."

"It may have been believed a myth," Italicus held up his finger and smiled charmingly. "That was until I foun—"

Gladthorn's mind raced trying to piece together why the Marshals would be using Malus' corrupt tactics. Instead of smiling at his boasts like Italicus expected, the Equinaut's master scout clenched his fists tightly.

"We have to do something!" spat Gladthorn suddenly, "That's a trick Malus used with the Bloodhounds to extort people's property. Why are they doing that here?"

"Does it matter? It's best we find an alternate route," interrupted Edryss, suddenly on his left. "We should steer clear of any Marshal activity, you don't pull on a sleeping wolf's tail."

Italicus shuttered, as a child he had a very real and dreaded fear of wolves. A fear he never overcame as an adult. He managed to hide the fear well, always insuring that any mission or encounter that had anything to do with wolves he always seemed to be needed elsewhere. "Honestly, why would anyone with half a brain want to pull on a flea-bitten beast's tail?"

Edryss was about to express that her comment was just an Idiom but Italicus did not want a conversation about wolves to continue, just thinking about them made him apprehensive. Throwing a quick salute, he urged Moose forward, he had not made it five strides when Edryss called out to him.

"Where is your feather, sir? I thought it looked good on you!"

Italicus pulled on his reins and twisted around, his face wide eyed and partially annoyed, "He has you in on this too?"

Edryss placed her hand on her chest and faked innocence, "In on what, sir?"

Gladthorn placed his face into his hand and tried to hide his laugh. Edryss couldn't help but snicker as well. Italicus knew this was Thaddeus' doing, he rolled his eyes and bit his bottom lip. He threw his hand towards the two, "Oh, wait till I get my feather back!" Gladthorn, unhappy with their ambivalence, forged ahead and began scouting, leaving Edryss to recruit the necessary extras. Scouting is primarily a solitary endeavor, a job that afforded Gladthorn many hours of solace for which he was grateful. He was a very private man, holding onto much regret for his past misdeeds. Gladthorn hid his burden well behind layers of duty, honor, a rigid code of conduct, and a slowly forming sense of humor. His emotional weight began with his father's legacy and the ways through which he strived to live up to it, but his true heaviness accrued when he was forced into disbanding the Bloodhounds. That was by far the hardest thing he had ever had to do, but he did so to preserve the honor of the group.

The Bloodhounds were once a great organization, made up of the best of the best Marshals. People throughout the independent realms looked up to them as defenders and guardians of the law. Once Gladthorn discovered deep corruption within its ranks, he knew that it was his responsibility to put a stop to the wrongdoing in penance for his service, albeit unknowing, to the corruption. Unfortunately for many of their victims, the deeds were done and there was no recompense, no turning back. His only path was to prevent further wrongs and save those who could be saved. The Bloodhounds did not go quietly into the night. Gladthorn had to force his will, which lead to many engagements with former brothers-in-arms. He tried to spare as many as he could, but some, like Malus, were too stubborn to walk away.

After disbanding the Bloodhounds, Gladthorn wandered the shard looking for honest work, a broken man without a cause or a friend. He found work as a cook for a rundown crossroad tavern. He was unsurprised when Thaddeus appeared in his doorway on a gloomy winter's night. Gladthorn knew a night would come when he would pay for his misdeeds. If Thaddeus had come to exact revenge and kill him, he was ready to accept his judgment. Instead, Thaddeus offered Gladthorn a position among his Equinauts as his Master Scout. Gladthorn could not tell if the tall, blonde man was serious or only luring him into letting his guard down. He could not see how Thaddeus, or his men could accept him. He had hunted them tirelessly, made their lives absolutely miserable, and forced them to jump from town to town for well over a year. As he was in all his cases, Gladthorn had been utterly determined to arrest and capture the nefarious criminal and alleged murderer Italicus at any cost. Gladthorn and his team worked tirelessly to capture the Equinauts until only Thaddeus and Italicus remained free. To Gladthorn's great surprise and embarrassment, Thaddeus and Italicus managed to corner him alone. He knew his only way out was to fight. Then Italicus and Thaddeus revealed themselves unarmed, and in fact offered themselves freely under the condition Gladthorn free their captured men.

Gladthorn agreed to the exchange. The men and women he captured were not wanted by the law, his warrant was for Italicus. Capturing and bringing in Thaddeus who had a large bounty on his head was only a perk. However, their selfless surrender caused Gladthorn to begin to question the details of the men's warrants. When he returned with the prisoners, Gladthorn's eyes were truly opened to Malus' corruption. Thaddeus and Italicus were quickly marked for execution. Malus claimed their overwhelming guilt made a trial pointless. Gladthorn's conscious itched, a trial was the right of every person, no matter how apparently guilty they were. Bloodhounds were the best of the best from the Marshals, and the Marshals' sole purpose was to uphold the law, the law that no man should be above. How could they agree to skip a fair trial? More importantly, if the men were so guilty, why were they skipping the trial? He began to worry if his prisoners were to face the executioner's axe for crimes they did not commit. How many others would face the same fate without a trial? Once Gladthorn determined that Malus' actions were wrong, he arranged for Italicus and Thaddeus' escape, hours before their appointment with the executioner. Malus showed his true colors after that, it was then Gladthorn realized how deep the corruption went, and the true reason he wanted Italicus and Thaddeus dead.

"Gladthorn!"

Edryss cantered along the small cow trail leading Niles, a young new recruit named Akash, and two nervous looking men from the professor's expedition.

"How could you tell I left the main road?" asked Gladthorn, genuinely curious.

Edyrss pointed towards the recruit, "Mr. Akash was able to deduce that."

Gladthorn smiled. Akash, with another man, had only recently joined the Equinauts just before everything went sour. Gladthorn had not had a chance to really get to know the two new men. "Perhaps you were meant to be a scout? What say you?" asked Gladthorn. "You're an Independent, right? From what town do you hail?"

"I would be honored to be taught by a former Bloodhound. I am from Lankar, sir." His voice was soft and low, but confident.

"Lankar!? Really?" gasped Niles. Lankar was a mixed city of Aedunic tribes and Non Citadelians known for its extreme isolation. "You didn't happen to know Briana Hawk, champion of the Chalice of the Warrior?"

Akash nodded with a slight annoyance in his face, "Yes sir, my mother."

"You're a Greyhawk?"

Akash nodded.

"We have a celebrity in our midst," remarked Edryss smiling, "Rookie celebrity!"

Akash's dark cheeks burned sepia, he had always been in the shadow of his mother, a great Warrior with Aedunic fierceness and the discipline of civilized man. She was the first woman to win the Chalice of the Warrior competition. He had tried to compete in the competition himself, as was his birthright, or so his mother had told him since his birth, but Akash did not win the chalice. His adventure there lead him into a chaotic journey of political subterfuge, kidnapping, and murder.

"I am not here under her title, but only under my own name."

Niles spoke soothingly, "That's all anyone can ask of you, R.C."

Akash groaned, knowing the nickname would stick. "Do we really have to call me that?"

"Of course not, R.C.," answered Edryss, "We don't *have* to."

Gladthorn shushed them, jumped off Spyder and snuck his way into a thick bush. Edryss dismounted Faith gracefully and whispered, "Stay here!" before slipping though the same branches herself.

She found Gladthorn lying on his stomach, peering through the scope of his rifle. "What's the matter?"

"This is where that family told Thaddeus the Marshals were. It's an ideal location for a check point." Gladthorn nodded north to show Edyrss what he meant. "See the small river? It runs along the north side of the road and then cuts through there at that small bridge. The river is just large enough to prevent a wagon from going through it, so they have to use the bridge. Perfect spot for a checkpoint."

"But I don't see any signs of the Marshals."

"That's what has me worried."

"Maybe they were wrong about the place?"

Gladthorn was not going to accept that. "No, I have to find—" Edryss touched his large hand and squeezed it.

"No, you don't. I know what you're thinking."

"How could you possibly--"

"You fear the Marshals have become corrupt and will follow the same path as the Bloodhounds," Edryss took a deep breath, "and you believe that their actions are a reflection on you, and it's your responsibility to fix it."

Gladthorn averted his eyes from Edryss' gaze, confirming her statement.

"I forget how well you know me."

Gladthorn laid his gun on the ground and leaned over. He was about to kiss Edryss when something bright reflected off the ground below them. Gladthorn slid forward and grabbed it. It was a small, curved piece of metal that he immediately recognized. "This is part of a Marshal's uniform jacket. They had to have been here!"

Edryss noticed something else in the debri near where the metal piece had been lying. She retrieved it and sighed deeply, "Oh Great Arcadia, look at this!"

Edryss held up a severed finger. The blood was fresh. Edryss recognized the look in Gladthorn's eyes. She knew there was no talking him out of it, he was going to go after them.

The two exited the bush.

"What did you find?" asked Niles.

"The Marshals were there, but obviously have moved on."

Niles smiled, "That's great, right?"

Edryss shook her head. "We found a finger."

Niles recoiled as Gladthorn walked past them, eyes firmly set. "Does that mean…?"

Edryss noddded, "Pretty much."

Akash was confused, "Mean what?"

Niles frowned, "Let's hope your sword work is as good as your mom's."

Gladthorn addressed the two men from the professor's side of the expedition, who had been quietly and nervously watching the events unfold. "I need you two to head back now and tell Thaddeus that there are no Marshal checkpoints up to the small bridge. We believe they were here recently and have moved on to the east. The four of us will continue to scout ahead."

The two men looked relieved, and repeated Gladthorn's message before riding off.

"What now?" asked Niles.

Gladthorn mounted Spyder. "We continue east."

Gladthorn led the four at a trying pace. The cow trail's terrain changed for the worse, and it began to turn south, away from the road the Expedition was taking. A series of footsteps had been spotted, the shape and design consistent with boots usually worn by Marshals. Gladthorn believed a struggle or at least an argument had occurred. He was certain they would catch up to the Marshal group that had maimed the man. That was two hours ago.

The ascending cow path had become less than a path, and the ground grew rougher to navigate. The trees and bushes were so densely packed that they needed to be hacked back just to pass.

"Come on, keep moving!" Gladthorn urged again.

"Gladthorn, we can't keep going this way, "pleaded Edryss. "Every mile we follow this trail, the further we get from the column. We need to turn back."

"Just a little further!"

The trees suddenly parted, and the riders found themselves on top of a small bluff; they had gone as far as they could. The slope in front of them was too steep for a horse to descend without falling. The height of the bluff gave a decent view of the surrounding area. To the north were the large open farm fields of Braum, and to the south stood densely packed trees scattered in a chaotic pattern of clumps.

"Glad, I don't see any sign of the Marshals," observed Edryss. "I don't think they were ever here."

"No! They're nearby, I can feel it."

"No Gladthorn, they're not!" argued Edryss softly. "It's time to get back to the column."

"I too think its time to get back to the column," offered Niles. "For all we know, the Marshals doubled back and are giving Thaddeus and the others problems."

Gladthorn took a deep breath and looked harshly at Akash, "Well what say you, junior scout."

Akash knew Gladthorn was offering him a chance to earn favor, "Well to be honest—"

The branches behind Gladthorn shifted, and Akash saw the subtle glint of steel. To the others' surprise, Akash grabbed his Tesla rifle, aimed it at Gladthorn and fired.

***

Never in a thousand years did Dean ever think he would be reading a book about horses and enjoying it. Horses were one of the least mechanical things he could think of. He knew if he wanted a shot at being the least bit interesting to Kaitlyn, he would have to learn as much as he could about these four-legged creatures. Feeling that his search was nearly hopeless, Dean thanked the Maker when he found someone with a book on the subject. How many people carry a book on horses in the middle of an expedition? His luck turned when he was introduced to a surprisingly friendly Equinaut, Balin. Balin had a saddle bag stuffed with books on various subjects and was more than willing to trade Dean for one of two of the mechanical books he had brought with him. It was a fascinating read, the lore about the creation of horses went far deeper than he had expected. He wasn't sure how much of it he actually believed, but as he read each word he saw the beautiful face of Kaitlyn in his mind.

Glut and Andi were also thankful when Dean found a book to read. Now more than five minutes could pass without Dean speaking. Every word out of his mouth was about Kaitlyn and horses. Andi hoped this wasn't any indication on how the Expedition was going to go. Forming relationships almost always ended with people feeling awkward around the loving couple or worse, the couple would break up and suddenly need everyone to cater to their need for "space" from one another. It didn't help that Andi was plagued with jealous thoughts whenever Dean would go off on a tangent about this woman he had just met. *What does that Kaitlyn have that I don't? It's not like I want Dean,* Andi reasoned with herself, *but we've known each other for ages, why wasn't he ever obsessing over me like this? He doesn't even like horses! Were his eyes always so thoughtful? His cheekbones weren't that high before, were they?*

"Listen to this," announced Dean. Glut sluggishly turned away from his window watching, rolling his eyes slightly before meeting Dean's gaze.

"The book claims that the Maker created the original two horses during the first day of creation. He named them Niatross and Bucephala and honored them with the title Lord Horses, giving them many responsibilities in the heavens. He commanded them to spread their seed, for inside them were all the breeds of horses creation would need. It is believed that all horses can trace their lineage back to this first pair."

"How did they create these breeds?" asked Andi. "Did they birth them specifically, or did they change over time?"

Glut shushed his sister down, "Not this again."

Glut was met by a cold stare from his sister.

"It doesn't say, not in these pages at least." He continued, "Horses were created to be companions of humankind and all other sentient creatures. They were a special gift from the Maker so that no one would ever have to be alone in life."

"That's sweet," interrupted Andi, her voice a pitch higher than normal.

Dean was unaffected and continued without missing a beat, "When mankind and all life was still in its infancy, the Maker instructed if you felt worthy of a companion, to find a clear hill on a full moon's night and recite the Pledge of the Bonded."

"Does it say what the pledge is?" asked Andi.

Dean frowned and shook his head, "With the pledge cited and your heart measured you would then be greeted by the two Lord Horses and with them would be your Sahakaru. A sahakaru is the perfect companion, a mutualistic symbiotic partner that will stay with you your entire life."

"I never had that kind of a bond with an animal. I mean maybe with our cat?" pondered Andi.

"Are you kidding me?" Glut smirked and shook his head. "That filthy feline would sell us to slavery for a bowl of tuna and then not even eat it!"

Andi giggled and shrugged. "It's still the closest thing we've had to a Sahakaru! Go on, Dean," She added demurely.

"As with all mutualistic relationships, one cannot truly survive without the other. This was the Golden Age for horses and for a time no person young or old, rich or poor knew loneliness and no horse knew suffering or hunger. It was not to last though, as civilization began to form men and women lost their need for equine companion. Many neglected their Sahakura for the petty wants, needs, and desires that come from living in a city. Others saw their Sahakura as a means of free labor. Men traded their companions for coin, or rented them to farms and smiths, or to those whose hearts were measured unjust on the hill. The divine bond between man and horse was diminished into nothing more than tenuous concord between man and slave. Many horses died of neglect or starvation. Despite these harsh conditions, their hearts could not be broken, and they stood by their bonded's side.

"The two Lord horses pleaded with mankind not to forget their Sahakaru. When they were met with deaf and self-indulgent ears, Niatross and Bucephala pleaded with the Maker to intervene. Realizing that men and women had forsaken their special gift, the Maker reached out and found the most noble among the human race. He asked one man and one woman to give up something of theirs. He plucked the sternums out of their chests and placed it around the hearts of all horses to protect them from human's neglect. The Maker wept and said to all creation, "I am sorry. When I created the equine heart, I created the strongest force in nature. Nothing can bend the will of the horse, and man has shown only the most worthy among you deserve to receive the gift of the bond.""

Dean turned the page and read in silence, after a few sentences he began again. "It gets better. As centuries passed, fewer and fewer humans were bonded, while the number of horses bred annually increased steadily. Horses were no longer companions, but beasts of burden, spending their entire lives working fields and other labor-intensive jobs, never knowing peace or love. Horses were still suffering and Niatross and Bucephala knew they had to do something. They returned to the ascended realm and looked for the Maker to beg his intervention once more, but the throne chair was empty, the Maker was not to be found. The Lord Horses stood alone at the Balcony of Eternity and saw all of creation, and they wept for their children. Arcadia, the first Ethereal, heard their cries and told them she could not help the living, but could command Rahmiel, the keeper of the dead, to create Asvaya' Aegeria, a place between the corporeal world and the ascended realm, a special place for all the past and future horses' souls. Here they would be allowed to live eternity in paradise. Niatross and Bucephala were thankful and understood their deep debt to Arcadia.

"The Lord Horses entered the infinite pasture for the first time and smiled at their children running, hollering, and playing with lost stall mates. Soon after, the Lord Horses noticed the bonded humans who had proven themselves kind and loyal were there as well. Despite this happiness, Nitatross and Bucephala never fully forgave mankind. Gathering all of their children together, they declared their first law that never would a horse leave Asvaya' Aegeria and never would another human enter the Equine Kingdom. The bonded humans already in the realm were rounded up and forced to become slaves for the Royal Chevals. The Sahakarus were furious and demanded the humans' freedom. They claimed the bonded were the best of humanity, not the ones who caused so many other horses pain. Niatross and Bucephala were not convinced, and the Sahakarus were outnumbered by the herds of horses that had never experienced the bond, or who were abused by their companions.

"This first law remained unbroken for a thousand years. When the war in the heavens broke out between the Ethereal and the Fallen, both sides urged the Lord Horses to join them, but Niatross and Bucephala were determined to remain neutral. 'This was not an equine matter!'"

Andi straightened, "I didn't realize horses were such a part of our theology. If the Lord Horses were divine, how did they not realize that in enslaving the bonded they were doing exactly the thing they said was wrong? I would assume that Niatross and Bucephala would be above such irrationality."

Glut sighed. "Professor Belladon told me years ago, 'If you stare long enough at evil and allow it to flourish, you yourself will become a reflection of that evil.' The Lord Horses were so focused on the worst of humanity they forgot to see the best. They became what they hated."

"How did Thaddeus bond with his horse?" Dean wondered out loud. He thumbed through several pages quickly and began to read again.

"Nothing was allowed to change within Asvaya' Aegeria without the Lord Horses' consent. They greeted each equine soul as it entered into the Infinite Pasture and ensured the new arrival understood the first law. For a time, Niatross and Bucephala found peace in the fact that all horses now had a home to return to. They did not see their laws and actions as contradictory to the promises of Asvaya' Aegeria. The love the two shared for each other never weakened during their many millennia long lives. Feeling secure in their Kingdom, they eventually decided to have more children of their own. Perhaps due to their iron will, they could not have foreseen the effects Arcadia's blessing would have."

"Oh, I think I know where this is going!" interrupted Andi.

"Shut up! Let him continue!"

"The blessing the Lord Horses received from Arcadia carried over into their offspring. These were the first foals to be born in Asvaya' Aegeria. These children did not live, nor did they die, nor were they normal horses. They were Capallcurada, Champion horses with gifted power from Arcadia's original blessing. The blessing manifested itself differently in every Capallcurada born. Halki the Grey was the first of this new royal lineage. Halki's parents quickly realized that he was extremely intelligent, very headstrong and incredibly compassionate. For centuries Halki was content to learn as much as he could about anything and everything. After learning all he felt possible, Halki walked the edge at the Infinite Pasture's entrance. For the first time he saw the world of man, beautiful in its capricious nature, majestic though mercurial. There was so much life happening all at once. Instantly he became intrigued by this strange and splendid world. For the next half-century, he gazed upon the corporeal realm and dreamed of knowing what the corporeal world was like, to truly be alive."

A half snort escaped Glut.

Dean continued, unmoved by the outburst. "Halki followed melodic laughter to a young girl living on a hill top farm. In all his existence he had never been moved by a song such as this. Halki returned daily, growing more intrigued and attached to the headstrong, but compassionate human. Halki observed the relationship between the woman and her pony, and longed to be alive, to share the kind of bond horses and humans were meant to have. To preserve his heart, he left the world's edge."

"One day, Halki heard the young woman's voice crying out, mangled with pain. Halki ran to the edge to see the woman in distress, crying over the body of her small pony. Halki begged his parents to meet and welcome this pony's soul in the Infinite Pasture. The pony was named Twinkle and had been struck down by a lone lightning bolt. The girl's name was Carissa, and Twinkle spoke at great length of how special she was. Twinkle and Halki became friends and for months they watched Carissa. It broke Twinkle's heart to see Carissa in such pain, she was alone in the world. When they saw Carissa and her family being attacked by a roaming gang of thugs, Twinkle begged Halki to intervene. Halki was bound by his land's law, but in his desperation to help the woman he had come to love, Halki leaped from the edge and fell from paradise."

"Halki defended Carissa and her family the best he could, fiercely attacking the bandits without thought or care for himself. Within Asvaya' Aegeria there was no pain, so Halki was unprepared for the searing sensation that overtook him when his haunch was sliced by a mortal man. He fell to the ground, unable to move. The bandits were about to kill him, but Carissa grabbed a discarded sword and stood between Halki and the bandits. She raised the sword and threatened to kill anyone who got near the horse. The bandits laughed, but behind them the skies swirled black and the wind rolled like thunder. The clouds parted, and a bright light flashed. Out of the light Halki's parents appeared, flanked by hordes of Halki's kind. The sudden appearance of descending horses scared the bandits and they fled. Carissa did not lower her sword, she could see the anger in the Lord Horses as they approached. 'You will not harm him!' Carissa declared."

"So, let me guess," interrupted Andi again, "Seeing the brave young woman stand up and defend Halki, the Lord Horses saw that some of mankind had redeemed themselves and were worthy of the bond?"

Dean skimmed ahead and nodded. "Pretty much. They allowed their children, if they so chose, to descend to our realm and be bond with a worthy human."

Andi pondered for a moment, and then asked Dean if he believed any of it.

"I'm not sure. But they say once a century Niatross and Bucephala descend to the valley of Veamini to the tribe of the Reieni and allow their children to find their bonded companions, so there's one way to find out."

"Who says?"

Dean smiled, "Kaitlyn for one." And then knowing she wouldn't be as quick to dismiss it, he added, "Thaddeus too. Thaddeus' horse Egghead is supposed to be a Capallcurada."

Andi wasn't sure what to think. Thaddeus had sounded so educated when he spoke. How could he really believe this mythological story to be true? *Does he also believe planets are real?* The thought made Andi smile at the absurdity of it. She then remembered the gossiping women she had overhead in the Citadel earlier in the day.

"Does this book have anything about a Hellhorse?" asked Andi.

Dean flipped back to the table of contents and nodded. "Yeah, one called Bailitheoir, it's near the end."

Andi held out her hands for the old book. "Here it is, born a Capallcurada, he was considered one of the greatest sons of Niatross and Bucephala. Of all their foals, Bailitheoir excelled at all he attempted and surpassed all obstacles he encountered. Halki the Grey mentored Bailitheoir and did his best to protect his charge from their parents warped anger towards humankind. Halki's protection could only go so far, as the Lord Horses ruled the kingdom strictly. Being that Bailitheoir was the strongest, bravest, fastest, and most capable of the Capallcurada bloodline, Niatross and Bucephala felt both pride and fear towards him. In an unfavorable decree, they ruled Bailitheoir would not be able to choose his bonded companion. Bailitheoir's parents wanted to ensure he was partnered with the best mankind had to offer. Niatross and Bucephala searched high and low throughout all of creation until they discovered a great warrior called Verrator. Verrator was the Citadel's first great champion and hero after Gideon PenRuger helped unite the Five Kingdoms of man. Verrator learned at a young age that he was a gifted swordsman and he loved the accolades and attention it brought him. He picked a fight with a large man in a bar, and unwittingly defeated the leader of a large gang extorting money from poor villages nearby. Verrator was hailed as a hero. Once he tasted that admiration and worship, his thirst was never quenched. Verrator used his sword to protect the innocent and defend the weak, and quickly became known as Gideon's successor.

"So, he's only fighting for the glory?" Andi looked disgusted. "Why are people so vain?"

"That's not too bad, good is still being done. He's still a hero, right?

Dean shrugged.

Andi continued, "Niatross and Bucephala saw the greatness of Verrator and the love and admiration the people had towards him. They offered him Bailitheoir's bond. Bailitheoir knew in his heart that this man was not his Sahakura, he did not see the greatness in Verrator that his parents did. Bailtheoir begged not to be bonded with the man Verrator.

"It's like being forced to marry someone you don't love," remarked Andi with a frown.

"Bailitheoir's pleas were ignored, the decision was made, he had no choice. Bailitheoir and his parents descended to the realm of man to a fanfare of a celebration. Verrator was not going to let a good chance at more admiration go to waste. Families from across the new Citadel traveled to see the bonding ceremony. There was singing, dancing, and speaking, Verattor's own speech lasting the longest as he recounted each of his great achievements, and spoke of the even greater achievements his future held."

"After their bonding, Verrator and Bailitheoir became the greatest heroes in the history of creation, or at least so claimed Verrator at every town and tavern they visited. He spread stories of his single-handed victory over a small Slavine army, or his heroic capture of the raiding parties of Aedunic warriors. The fame and fortune Verrator received was so great, he was simply known as the Hero. There wasn't a person on the shard who had not heard of Verrator and his magnificent horse. As Verrator's adventures continued, the myth behind him grew to unimaginable heights. The number of enemies grew, two Slavine attackers became twenty, a boar lizard encounter became a tangle with a giant dragon. People believed Verrator an invincible god.

"Soon Verrator came to believe in his own exaggerations and his ego grew far beyond that of a normal man. He took on more dangerous missions and charged into overwhelming enemy numbers without batting an eye. Bailitheoir was dumbfounded, how could this man not realize how close he had come to death? But Verrator was either greatly confident in his horse's abilities or was unaware the lengths he went to keep them alive.

William F. James

"During the early reign of King Theodus, the first great war between the Slavine and the newly united Five Kingdoms of Man broke out. The Slavine had invaded Citadel territory and pushed fast towards the heart of the land of man. They were determined not to let the humans finish the Great Wall. The frightened people begged Verrator to join the war and defeat the Slavine. Verrator agreed on the condition he would command the forming Citadel army. Verrator was obliged and hailed victor before even reaching his new army. The troops beamed, seeing Verrator as an undefeated god; there was no way they could lose.

"Verrator ordered his men to march straight to the Slavine camp and attack it. The camp was three days march, and Verrator pushed his men tirelessly to maintain the element of surprise. By the end of the third day the soldiers were exhausted, but Verrator did not notice or care, he only saw glory for himself. He signaled for battle lines and ordered the charge. Despite their superior numbers, the exhausted human soldiers were slaughtered and surrounded by the larger Slavine. Verrator cursed his men's inept skills and lack of discipline. The human army was nearly routed, and Verrator's officers implored him to call for a retreat, but Verrator was certain all that was needed to win the battle was for him to join the fight. Without hesitation, he kicked Bailitheoir forward.

"The two fought as hard as they could, but the Slavine were too organized and the humans were too tired. Soon Verrator and Bailitheoir found themselves alone on the battlefield, their troops dead or deserted. Verrator turned Bailitheoir to flee, but it was too late, they were surrounded. Verrator became hysteric at their eminent defeat. Slavine war horns sounded, and Slavine soldiers moved to converge on the two.

"It is not known what Verrator thought during this time, but he jumped to the ground and began grabbing the dead, shaking them, perhaps hoping someone was still alive and could help them, but they were alone in a sea of death. Only a few cries of the few mortally wounded broke the eerie silence of the battlefield. The last moans of the damned wailed, severed arms and broken bodies reached out to Verrator and Bailitheoir for help. Frightened for life and reputation, Verrator knew he had only one option. He fled the battlefield, he knew he had to be the first back to the Citadel. Leaping onto Bailitheoir, Verrator aimed his horse West and cantered off the battlefield leaving his vanquished army behind him.

Racing through the woods, Verrator continued to beat and kick his horse forward. His mind so focused on what to tell the King, how to spin the whole battle to his favor. Little did Verrator know, but the Slavine force was far larger than expected. And the entire area was saturated with their kind. He barely made it several miles before realizing that there was no place he could go. Every road was blocked, and every inch of the forest was being roamed by patrols. Staying out of sight the best they could, it was only a matter of time before they were caught. Late into the night, a patrol had gotten a quick glimpse of the two. Verrator commanded Bailitheoir to flee as fast as he could. Approaching a hill, the two came to a complete stop, at the top of the hill were the torches of another Slavine patrol.

Verrator realized he had slim chances at survival, he dismounted Bailitheoir and led him into a small thicket of trees. The closer the Slavine approached the more certain Verrator was of his own capture and death. He was out of options, except for one. Without remorse or apology, Verrator slit Bailitheoir's throat. In his anger and desperation, the dagger slid deep into the flesh of his Sahakura. He slit Bailitheoir's throat and continued up the side of his neck, the horse cried out and wailed in pain. He felt as his heart inside of him begin to tear. He had been betrayed by the one he was told to trust beyond all others. The horse fell to his knees and Verrator guided him down so that Bailitheoir would lay on top of him, to cover his body so he could hide from the Slavine patrols.

Andi finished reading the last of the page and looked up from the book. Her face seemed twisted, she was angry and sad, "How could he have done that to Bailitheoir."

"Hubris." answered her brother who had been intently listening once he heard about the war.

Andi turned the page the next section read 'Bailitheoir - the dreaded Hellhorse'

"Bailitheoir's life force drained from him, he could feel death's icy grip. He had been betrayed, and the divine bond between them was breaking. Bailitheoir cried out in anger and condemnation towards his parents, they had chosen poorly for him. Verrator, covered in his horse's blood, could feel Bailitheoir struggle. Afraid he would be found if Bailitheoir kept struggling, Verrator pierced Bailitheoir's heart, breaking his sternum. Even that was not enough to bring the great horse down.

"Why have you betrayed me beast?"

Verrator stabbed Bailitheoir's heart again and again, and with every thrust great pain shot through Bailitheoir's body. Rage swept through the horse's being. He was the greatest of the Capallcurada, lying in pool of his own blood, slain by his companion. With retreating strength, Bailitheoir twisted his mangled neck and bit down on the arm that had stabbed him. Verrator shrieked in pain, forgetting his desire to hide. Bailitheoir pulled with all his remaining might, and tore flesh from bone, ripping the arm from Verrator's body. With the dagger still clutched in Verrator's torn hand, Bailtheoir whipped his head around and swung Verrator's own arm. The dagger slashed and cut Verrator's head and neck. Bailitheoir kept swinging until Verrator's face and neck were as lacerated Bailitheoir's heart was."

"Shit," uttered Dean.

"I guess the moral is that Bailitheoir's parents are as flawed as we are?" responded Glut. "Because they chose Verrator. It's a dark myth."

Without looking up, Andi said, "It gets darker. According to the book, when you are bonded with a Capallcurda, you are essentially balancing nature. It is the original will of the Maker for horses to become companions with humans, it is written into the base code of existence. Because there are only a few Sahakaru in our realm, each for only the span of a human lifetime, each bond is greater than the bonds of the past. Breaking the bond disturbs nature and disrupts the balance. When Verrator betrayed Bailitheoir, he began a stream of entropy in nature. Nature demands balance and Verrator would be punished for his deed."

"Good!" Glut dropped his palm into the armrest of his seat hard. "He should be punished!"

Andi frowned. "But Bailtheoir didn't leave it to nature. Bailitheoir's last act of anger killed Verrator. By nature's scale, Bailitheoir was the betrayer."

Dean's mouth dropped open. "That's not right!"

"Nature punished Bailitheoir."

"How?" asked Glut.

"It doesn't say. The Slavine ran once the weather began to change violently. According to this book, Bailitheoir was in agonizing pain, every joint bent and every pore in his skin began to burn, and his hooves began to melt. He cried out once more to his parents for help. The book gives two versions here, one says his cries for help were ignored, the other says his parents descended from Asvaya' Aegeria and made a deal with nature. Either way the results are the same, Bailitheoir was transformed into a Black Reaper, an unholy, unnatural creature who would take the anger, pain, and wrath he felt and turn it on the living. He would become judge, jury, and executioner to all who abused or betrayed their companion. He was tasked with escorting the souls of the abused and murdered to the Infinite Pasture."

"That's kind of nice, he becomes the guardian to abused horses."

Andi shook her head, "No, Bailitheoir was consumed in anger, his feelings of betrayal now centered on his parents, he blamed them for pairing him with Verrator and for cursing him as a Hellhorse. Instead of protecting horses, he slaughtered them. His unquenchable rage turned on humans as well. He saw them all as extensions of Verrator. Instead of escorting the souls to the Infinite Pasture he absorbed them into the very wound that sealed betrayal. With every Equine soul he collected, Bailitheoir became more powerful and more dangerous. He began to slaughter all life sans discrimination."

"Something had to have stopped him or he would still be around," said Glut. When he saw the look on his sister's face he added, "if it were real, of course."

"Niatross and Bucephala could not allow him to end so many lives and absorb so many souls. They descended from the heavens with all the Capallcurda with their bonded slaves and fought Bailitheoir. They could not kill him, but they managed to steal his lacerated heart and wove a powerful spell into it. Whoever controls the lacerated heart becomes bonded with Bailitheoir and commands him. They buried his body in the depths of the Castiel mountain range where no light would ever reach and placed his heart in a volcanic cave near Norhwirh."

"Well, no one is going to get the heart there," concluded Glut. "Not even the reptilian bastards can stand the extreme heat of the lava."

"The book says that even though Bailitheoir is trapped within the mountain, his rage has yet to be quelled and his essence has a far reach that still absorbs many of the souls of horses who die. His power increases with every soul absorbed and if he were to ever escape he would become a plague upon the living."

"Wow. What a twisted story," sighed Dean, "Why do people like horses so much if that is their legacy?"

***

Akash's tesla beam shot right passed Gladthorn, the tree behind him exploded in a brilliant explosion. A loud thud came moments later as a body spilled onto the ground. Niles and Edryss took fighting posture on their horses. The man was armed, a dagger in his hand, and a tesla pack strapped to his back. Gladthorn never looked back at the exploding tree or the fallen man on the ground. He knew that this was the Marshals, and that it was too simple, too easy. There was more danger out there. Gladthorn felt subtle anger flare inside him. He perused the bluff and trees around them, noting the lack of wildlife. No birds chirped, and no squirrels scratched.

Edryss nodded at Akash and dropped to the ground to check the fallen man for a pulse. Nothing.

Edryss turned and looked at Gladthorn who had been sitting on top of Spyder, remaining nearly completely stoic. Her knowledge of Glathorn told her the danger was far from gone. Gladthorn had subtle external signs that only she and maybe a few others knew about. The lower he brought the brim of his hat the more certain he was of impending danger.

Edryss remounted Faith as they all backed against the bluff, scanning the trees for the rest of the Marshals, readying themselves for a surge, all but Gladthorn, who had the most experience in tactical strategy. He faced the bluff.

"DUCK!" ordered Gladthorn in a low, fierce roar, reaching out and yanking Edryss' arm down hard.

Gladthorn's shout and training saved their lives. At his signal, the Equinauts had flattened themselves in their saddles as streams of light flew over them and into the trees burning everything in their path.

"Stay down!" yelled Gladthorn, letting go of Edryss. "To the path! Snipes down the bluff!"

Three more shots fired encouraging the group to follow his orders.

Edryss was horrified to look back and see Gladthorn on the cusp of the bluff making a rude gesture to the snipers below. Gladthorn listened for the humming of tesla guns preparing discharges and readied his shield on the opposite side of his horse.

Edryss hissed, "Come!" to Niles, and they dismounted and shimmied up to the edge on their bellies, tesla rifles hot. The humming stopped, and three oversized beams of energy surged at Gladthorn who yelled and swung his glowing shield around to absorb the bursts of kinetic energy in a wild figure eight. Short bursts of light followed, pelting Gladthorn high and low, giving him less than enough time to block them. Somehow, he moved his shield with impossible speed and precision, performing acrobatics that would have impressed even the most obstinately apathetic audience. Aiming at the trees from which the shots came, Edryss and Niles fired steadily until the treeline was flaming, and the screams following their energy foray turned to death rattles. Once the spray of beams ended, the Equinauts backed away from the bluff, and Gladthorn gave his brothers-in-arms a grateful look.

Edryss spoke in a shrill and deliberate voice, "Gladthorn Jones! Of all the stupid, pig-headed, needlessly reckless things to do! What were you thinking, taunting them like that!? You could be dead!"

"I was hoping you'd have my back. And you did. Besides, I could have handled them on my own once I figured their positions."

"You cocky fool!"

Gladthorn's eyes widened and he drew his rifle at the path behind her. Fear crossed Edryss' face as she spun around, her anger forgotten in a flash. There was no one on the path, and she turned back on Gladthorn who merely smirked and mouthed the word cocky back at her with a wink. Akash was breathing heavily, despite being the only one who hadn't engaged in the scuffle. What he'd seen was almost unnatural. *How could a man so large be so fast?* For the first time ever, he wondered if he'd met someone who could have bested his mother in her prime.

"Treventor's beard and holy Arcadia! How did you do that? That was incredible, impossible even."

"Practice!" shrugged Gladthorn, his large mouth forming a foolish, prideful grin.

Edryss swung a leg over faith and shot Akash a dark look. "Don't encourage him!"

Gladthorn grinned wider at Akash who asked, "Do we head back to the column and alert Thaddeus of the attack?"

"NO!" Yelled Gladthorn, his face immediately stone cold and determined. "I have to deal with the Marshals. We will push forward. I know what they will do next. We need to get off this bluff and continue east, or they'll only—"

"Gladthorn!" barked Edryss. "Stop. We're going back to the Column."

Gladthorn rose up, practically standing in his stirrups. "No, we are not."

Edryss was unmoved. "Yes, we are."

"I am your superior!"

"YOU ARE NOT ABOVE THE CODE!" roared Edryss. "The code clearly states if number of foes is unknown, do not engage! Return to the main group! I let you push it this far, but you're not going to endanger our lives again when we have no idea what we're up against!"

Gladthorn turned away to grapple with Edryss' reasoning, wracking his mind for a contrary rule.

Finally, "Very well." Gladthorn turned Spyder towards the path, "R.C., you'll bring the man you killed to Thad—"

Gladthorn could not finish his statement. The man was gone, only a trail of blood leading into the brush remained. "How long has he been gone? Did anyone see him leave?"

"I swear he was dead." said Edryss. "I checked him, you saw me do it."

"We can't go back, not that way," declared Gladthorn, becoming increasingly agitated, "We need to attempt the bluff."

"Wait, what? We can't," said Edryss, "There's no way our horses can make it. It's too steep."

The wind suddenly changed and Gladthorn instinctively reached for his sword. "Oh shit!"

The brush around them ruptured as a dozen or so armed men rushed swiftly into the open area against the bluff. The horses reared at the sudden sound and movement. Niles' horse nearest the path turned and galloped off, with its eyes rolled back. Niles tried to reassert himself, but his horse was too frightened by the surprise attack.

Akash and Edryss closed the gap between their horses, activated their swords and began to swing, defending themselves. Gladthorn, separated from Edryss and Akash, pulled out his rifle and opened fire. Within seconds, several enemies were lying on the ground dead, their chests and heads smoldering from pinpoint Tesla blasts.

The attackers attempted to rush Gladthorn but were kept at bay with short Tesla blasts. To Gladthorn's horror, Edryss was overwhelmed and thrown off her horse. Though he could no longer see Edryss, He knew she would activate her shield and could protect herself. Akash was still swinging his plaz, but now his attackers knew to stay just out of reach as they taunted him. Gladthorn tried to push Spyder towards Edryss' last position but he couldn't get an opening. He jumped off his saddle and began firing repeatedly into the fray.

Despite her prowess, Edryss was having trouble with her last standing attacker. He was trained and proficient. He waited for Edryss to make a move. Frustrated, she swung feinting an attack, hoping her opponent would take the bait, but he didn't. It left her open and he took advantage, swinging for her legs, forcing Edryss back towards the ledge. Gladthorn was blinded by his concern for Edryss, and he missed the second wave of men barreling through the trees, aiming their charge at him. The new enemies pushed him back towards Spyder. Gladthorn fought valiantly, gutting two men easily. The remaining four attacked in practiced unison. Gladthorn was forced to lift his sword to block one blade, his shield to deflect another, swing his shield to smash the third man off balance, and duck to avoid the fourth blade.

The attackers regrouped, and Gladthorn adopted a battle stance. "ATTACK ME, YOU CORRUPT COWARDS! YOU DON'T DESERVE TO WEAR THOSE BADGES!"

"Oh Gladthorn, virtuous to a fault." Said a raspy voice that sent shivers down Gladthorn's back. "Perhaps that's why you were one of our best."

The four attackers split to allow a man with a bad limp to stumble forward. He wore a long, brown Marshal's coat. His hair and beard were brown and matted. A thick scar down his right cheek and jaw glistened transparent in the sun, his bent nose showed years of abuse and neglect. In place of his right hand, a dagger was lashed to an ugly stump.

"It also made you the most susceptible to manipulation. During your time as a Bloodhound, you captured me more innocents than any other. You were relentless in justice, my justice of course. You know, the people you brought in sold me everything they had for freedom or else became slaves. The troublesome ones were executed. Can you sleep at night knowing your actions led to so many lives ruined or lost? I may have pulled the bowstring, but you were my arrow."

"You live," Gladthorn said gravely, eyes glued to the scars he had inflicted. "How? I left you dead in a pool of blood, mine and yours."

"You may have thought me dead, but I was quite alive. My slaves found me and feared retribution from my men. They healed me as best they could. Now I am scarred, though no less powerful, and fate has most conveniently delivered you to me. Revenge, Gladthorn, is what I seek. The reaper I have become, with only one name on my list." The scared and shriveled man let out a raspy laugh. "I have come not to just destroy the man, but to the kill the soul as well."

Gladthorn felt his heart beat fast, pumping blood to his arms and legs. He felt a rush of adrenaline and he knew to take advantage of it he must act fast. "I stopped you once, Malus, and I will stop you again! I will not die here today."

Gladthorn rushed forward, sword ablaze, and Malus smiled, revealing how few teeth he had left. The man made no move to defend himself. Malus reached into his coat, and unsheathed a Kentic Dagger, pulsing with energy.

Malus threw the dagger down at Gladthorn's feet and the kinetic energy released power stored within the dagger. It exploded in blinding light and sent Gladthorn flying backwards into the air and over the bluff's edge.

***

Thaddeus heard the unsteady approach of Leora's horse Wooly. She gave him a meek smile, around her eyes looked a little red and her brows were knit together.

"Are you really mad at me?" Judging by the stern look on his face, Thaddeus' defenses were up.

"I'm not your father, Leora."

Tears welled in Leora's eyes.

Thaddeus felt a wave of remorse. "Listen, I'm sorry. I shouldn't have yelled at you like that in front of everyone, it wasn't professional. I'm just trying my best to protect everyone on this expedition, and every obstacle increases our chance of failure."

Thaddeus tossed Leora a small linen handkerchief. She wiped at the corners of her eyes and stared down at the perfect embroidery of his initials.

Leora bit at her lower lip lightly, "It's like I said earlier, I only had my father, and he did the best he could, but I seem to get into trouble more than the average girl."

"I certainly wouldn't call you average." Thaddeus kicked himself internally. He couldn't seem to act like a normal adult around Leora.

"I wouldn't know. I don't really have any friends to compare myself to. My father thought it was best to always keep moving, I've lived in almost all of the themes."

"He must have had some influence, they don't usually allow for moves between themes. What about your mother, did she travel with you at all?" asked Thaddeus. "I bet you got your looks from her." Another comment across the line, another kick.

"Um, maybe. I'm not too sure." Leora lowered her gaze for a moment, pushing to remember things her father had told her as a young child. "My mother died during childbirth. My father barely speaks of her. I barely know anything of mother beyond her name, Naomi. I asked once if she looked like me, but my father only insisted that I was unique." Leora's shoulders lifted in a small shrug, and she looked up at Thaddeus through her long lashes.

Thaddeus was surprised by the sudden lightness of his stomach "I think that sums you up perfectly. May I ask you a question?"

Leora grinned, "You already have, several actually."

Thaddeus' lips twitched up at her playful jibe. "Of course. Umm, I just, I wanted to ask, how old you are?"

Leora bit at her bottom lip again and smiled, "How old do you think I am?"

"If I knew, I wouldn't be asking, would I?" Thaddeus felt a little guilt at how much he was enjoying this banter.

"Well when you've figured it out, let me know and I'll tell you if you're right. How old are you, Thaddeus?"

"Ha, nice try, when you figure it out, let me know!" replied Thaddeus with boyish mirth.

"Thaddeus, we need to talk."

Turning his head to his right, Thaddeus saw the professor trotting towards him. The professor cocked his head when the two made eye contact. Thaddeus immediately realized the smile on his face and quickly dropped the boyish grin. "What did I do wrong now?"

"I deserved that, I apologize for my anger earlier. As you know, time is of the essence, but once I heard the reason we were delayed I regretted my outburst. It was not your fault, nor was it hers." The professor half smiled and nodded once towards Leora. "The Citadel, especially the cogs, have become a haven for abusers of power. The Constables of old never would have condoned such treatment of Citadel Citizens."

Leora shrugged, "It's alright professor, like I told Italicus, I am used to men trying to touch me."

"It pains me to know that, no woman should have to be used to such assaults. You have my sincere apology." The professor took off his top hat and bowed as best he could while astride a horse. "Though my dear, if you would be so kind, I would like to discuss something with Thaddeus."

Leora nodded and urged Wooley forward. Thaddeus reached out and touched her arm.

"Here!" he said, handing her a golden feather. "Give this to Italicus and ask him how he got it. It will be a good entry for your journal."

As Leora cantered away, the professor spoke quietly. "I am glad you've taken her under your wing. I couldn't be more pleased, I feel you'll make a splendid mentor to her. She's going to be a remarkable woman one day. Yes, I have very high expectations for her!"

"I couldn't agree more. Leora is—"

"Special?"

Thaddeus nodded. "I was leaning towards unique. I feel like she has lived a lifetime and yet is still a raw cadet. I can't pinpoint it, but there's something so familiar about her."

"Don't mention this to anyone, but I didn't have a reason to invite her on this expedition. Leora was the last person I asked after hiring you and the Equinauts. She's completely inexperienced and has never been on any of my previous digs, but the universe just spoke to me. I had to invite her!" remarked the professor, contemplating his actions. "Inviting Leora was an absolute, she is a bright beacon in an often-un-navigable world."

Ahead, Italicus stretched his arms out and Leora laughed deeply. Thaddeus smiled, pretty certain he knew where they were in Italicus' story. "She is definitely a breath of fresh air," he said, softly. "I have been studying your proposed route. The village Karlotan along the east coast of Lake Superion is deep within Slaving territory. I passed through there once before. It's just a destitute fishing village."

"It's not what is there now, but what was once there I am more concerned with. However, I'd like—"

"It seems the timing of the recent cease fire has finally become fortuitous. Marilamanussa Valley has reopened, and we can bribe guards to get papers to enter the kingdom. The wagons can go through the valley and be inspected by customs while most of my men carry anything that wouldn't be approved through an old smuggler path and meet you on the road to Violetrose."

The professor nodded but did not look Thaddeus in the face. "That is a very good plan."

"But?"

"But I am afraid things have changed slightly, we are still going to Karlotan, but we must get there through Veilwood."

Thaddeus pulled back on Egghead's reins and brought his horse to stop. The professor followed suit. "Veilwood! You never said anything about Veilwood before! Veilwood is a bad idea, the wildlife alone is reason enough to stay clear, and the way through is rough and perilous."

"We don't have a choice. Dinnela and Souza have made a potential discovery and it warrants an investigation."

"What kind of discovery?"

The professor frowned. "I am afraid I do not wish to divulge that information yet."

Thaddeus sighed, annoyed, and shook his head, "You do not wish, very well. Whatever this discovery is, it must be more valuable than the risk of Veilwood, and if it's valuable, it means it's dangerous to obtain. I know you are hiding something in that Mark III. The Equinauts will do as hired and protect this expedition to the best of our abilities from the facts you have given us." Thaddeus lifted his arm and pointed his index finger sternly only inches from the professor's face. "But I will not let my men or your own be needlessly killed on a fool's errand. If I find you have left anything out that jeopardizes our safety beyond reasonable expectation, I will knock your old frail ass to the ground."

The professor thought for a moment and nodded, "I respect your concern for your men, PenRuger. You certainly are not like your father."

"Whatever you think you know about my father is false." It was difficult for Thaddeus to keep his voice steady. "Uthor PenRuger was a good and honest man!"

"I know, Thaddeus," The professor offered, as gently as he could. "He would be very proud of you." Thaddeus was taken aback. He wondered how the professor knew his father.

Steven suddenly approached, running on foot, "Professor, I have your tea!"

"My goodness Steven, you do me such great honor, but where is your horse?"

"Oh, dear lord, no, no horses, professor, not again, not after last time. They are beautiful, but terrifying beasts!" stated Steven, handling the oversized mug which had become known as 'the professor's tea cup.'

"Oh yes, I nearly forgot about that unfortunate oat incident, how is that knee of yours?"

"I hardly notice it." Steven forced a smile. In reality the pain was excruciating, but he kept pace with the professor.

***

While riding his titian spotted paint horse, Face, Zapp fiddled around with the puzzle box Kauf had given him. He'd found no luck in solving the secret to the strange gadget.

"Zapp!" A strong female voice interrupted his thoughts. "I need to talk to you!"

"Fryda, how can I help you?"

A large, black draft horse named Shilo carried the Aedunic warrior to Zapp. "What's that around your face?"

Zapp moved the red bandana covering his mouth and nose to under his chin. "It helps with my allergies. The fields of Braum are filled with tiny things that make me sneeze."

Fryda grimaced and held up her hand to quiet him. "Burrus and I had an arrangement, and since you are the new quarter master I was hoping we might as well?"

"I think I know what you're referring to. Kazah had a similar arrangement with Burrus, trading Slavine china for Aeturnus coal. He's always tinkering with that damn tesla pack. If he isn't careful it's going to blow up on him one day."

Fryda leaned in towards Zapp, "Before I tell you, you promise to keep it a secret?"

"My lips are sealed."

"I've been collecting Citadel Girl dolls and sending them to my niece back home, but my sister and I don't see eye to eye on many things. Specifically, she sees me as a traitor to leave the tribe to fight with Thaddeus."

"Fryda, I didn't realize you were such a softy! I suppose I could squeeze that into my busy schedule."

Fryda decided to let Zapp's comment slide without rebuttal. "He would send the gifts to another woman in the village, Notia, who would "give" them to my niece. She doesn't have much. Her father died when she was very young and my sister struggles. Those dolls are one of the few things she has to look forward to."

Fryda handed Zapp a list. "Here are the dolls Burrus has already gotten for me. if you tell a soul, I will rip out your heart and leave it for vultures!"

Zapp threw Fryda a wink, "Don't worry princess, mum's the word!"

Fryda and Zapp sat straight in their saddles and saluted as Thaddeus passed by quickly.

"Where is Thaddeus going?" asked Fryda. "Think everything's ok?"

Zapp noticed Fryda's fingers tracing the hilt of the sword on her hip. "If it were important the horns would be blowing. Did you hear the professor chewing Thaddeus out earlier back at the Great Gate? The professor was furious and said some outrageous things. For a moment I thought Thaddeus was going to slug the man."

"Niles mentioned it earlier," remarked Fryda thoughtfully. "Despite his age, the man does have a fire about him. I bet he has a tale to tell!"

Zapp could hear interest in Fryda's voice and rolled his eyes.

***

Half of Gladthorn's body felt cold and wet, the other half stiff and crisp. Movement was nearly impossible, and his head whirled. Each attempt to sit left the man wobbling and tumbling back into thick mud. A face appeared in the forefront of Gladthorn's mind, a face so different from that in his memories. Malus was far from the handsome and charismatic man he once was as the corrupt leader of the Bloodhounds. Gladthorn had a hard time believing he had survived their final battle as it had been one of the most difficult of his life. Malus was a torn meat sack by the time the fight was over. There was no way he could have survived those wounds no matter what medical attention he received. Using the butt of his rifle, Gladthorn managed to stand up.

The area around him was quiet, there were no signs of fighting. Gladthorn wondered how long he had been out cold. He looked up at the sun and tried to remember where it was before the attack, estimating it could only have been about an hour. Gladthorn unsteadily retrieved his hat from where it had fallen and shrugged his way out of his tesla pack, which he had landed on and smashed. A damaged tesla pack was unpredictable and could as easily kill its user as his target. Afraid to call out, in case Malus or his men were still near, Gladthorn attempted the bluff. It was extremely steep, and with every foot of progress, the heavier his aching body felt. He feared what he would find at the top of the bluff, Edryss' face pushed Malus' aside in his mind's eye.

At the edge, Gladthorn chanced a peek onto the small summit. To his angst and relief, Edryss' body was not lying on the ground, and neither was Akash's. Signs of the fight were certainly there, but all the soldiers' bodies had been moved. Judging by the heavy tracks left leading west, Malus didn't care if he was followed. In fact, Gladthorn was certain that was what Malus wanted.

Gladthorn considered rushing back to the column, he knew Thaddeus would send a decent rescue, but Gladthorn feared how long it would take to find them without a horse. Malus wouldn't wait long. If he suspected Gladthorn was not going to show, he would kill Akash and Edryss and move on. Gladthorn swept through the area for any other clues. *Perhaps Edryss managed to escape?* He found a plaz sword a few feet within the forest, but it most likely belonged to Niles, dropped when his horse went berserk. There were no signs of Edryss or Akash. Malus must have taken them.

The tracks were clearly left for him to follow. It almost insulted Gladthorn that Malus was making it so easy. *Why though? What is his plan? Could he possibly know how important Edryss is?* The harder he thought about it, the harsher his headache became. Malus turned and travelled south, until the tips of the southern mountain range were clearly visible through the trees.

Gladthorn quietly picked through the forest alongside Malus' trail. He knew that Malus and his men were waiting for him, but still hoped that the trees would provide enough cover to keep his approach hidden. The ground became rocky, allowing only the strongest and hardiest flora to survive, making hiding increasingly difficult.

A scream startled Gladthorn from the other side of the tree cluster he was in. The scream grew louder and more intense. Gladthorn knew the scream didn't belong to Edryss, but someone was being hurt or attacked, and it sounded like a small woman or child. Gladthorn ignited his plaz sword as he neared the edge of a rocky outcrop. Wary of another trap, he assessed the scene before him. A man dressed similarly to Malus' soldiers held a tall brunette from behind, pinning her slender arms behind her back. Another man touched and fondled her, intermittently tearing her clothes. Her chest was exposed, her skirt nearly in ribbons, and they had taken her shoes. "STOP IT!" screamed the woman, struggling to break free, and kicking the man in front of her. He slapped her hard in the face, though her feeble kicks couldn't have hurt him. She screamed again.

A third man stepped out from the forest. "You'll stop screaming if you don't want this same fate for your boy."

Gladthorn's blood boiled, but he wasn't sure how many men were still in the forest.

"You can have her first Jon. You're so small she won't notice you poking around!"

The man's wheezing cough at his own tasteless joke was interrupted by Gladthorn's sword through his throat. The second man fell almost as quickly.

"I'll kill her!" The third man held the woman in front of him, but now with a dagger to her throat. "Just go away, man! I'll do it, I will kill her. You make one move and I will slit her throat!"

"You aren't going to kill her." This was not the first time, nor would it be the last that someone thought they could use a human shield and get away with it.

"I WILL!" yelled the man desperately, pressing the iron flat under the woman's chin.

Gladthorn spoke calmly and moved slowly. "If you kill her, you lose your shield. You will be dead moments after that. In fact, if you don't let her go, you are already dead. Your body just hasn't accepted it yet."

The man was slow to understand the threat. The words only made him angrier, he pushed the blade into her neck, blood began to trickle slightly onto the blade. "PUT THE SWORD DOWN!" "Alright, I believe you. I don't want anyone else to get hurt. I'm gonna just put my sword down right in front of you and back away from it, ok?"

The man looked wildly from side to side, looking for an escape. "Just put it down right there man, not another step!"

"I'm gonna give it to you, right here. It's ok."

Gladthorn nodded and deactivated the plaz sword. It immediately began to cool and retract itself into the blade's handle. He bowed over to place the weapon at the woman's feet, but then swept up and activated the sword. The blade formed perfectly back into shape between the woman's legs and into the attacker's crotch. Letting go of the grip in mid air, he knew once the sword was fully formed it would still be there. He reached up and grabbed the man's arm away from the woman before he could slice her throat. Gladthorn pushed the woman aside and grabbed the sword still piercing the man's genitals and followed through.

The man gasped and looked down at his broken body, the glimmer in his eyes began to fade, "You killed me!"

The woman ran for the tree line towards her child's sobs.

Gladthorn followed to see the young boy's hands were tied harshly to a branch. The mother fell upon him, showering him with tears and kisses, and then fumbled with the knots, shaking too severely to untie him. While untying the boy, and searching the bodies, Gladthorn learned that the woman was named Annette and her son was Jareb II. Annette's husband, Jareb the first, was a struggling farmer, their crops had been overrun with pests, and their flock of sheep had nearly been wiped out from the lack of food. Their annual ten wagon loads of grains, vegetables, and wool were gone. They barely managed to scrape together a single wagon load of wool to be sold in the Citadel textile district. When they heard that a checkpoint had been established confiscating goods from travelers, Annette's husband tried to circumvent it but was found anyway by Malus' men.

"We were tied and taken to see a man with a blade for a hand. He said my husband had broken the law and would be killed. He was wrong, but we were denied our right to a trial."

"His name is Malus. I can see nothing has changed."

Taking a large breath, Gladthorn looked down at the young boy, who had just asked his mother what she meant by sentenced without a trial. Jareb began to cry. Kneeling, Gladthorn touched the young boys shoulder, "I will find your father and bring him back to you, I swear!"

Annette's sobs increased, and she threw her hands around Gladthorn's neck, "You truly are a righteous man!"

"A righteous man has no rules." sung the boy.

Gladthorn looked at the boy, "Where did you hear that?"

The boy shrugged.

"The man, "answered Annette, "Malus was singing it earlier."

Gladthorn led the pair to the path he had taken and told them to keep following it until they found the main road.

"Please!" cried the little boy in farewell. "Save my dad!"

***

"She is awake." Edryss gulped fresh air once the thick canvas bag was pulled off her head. She scanned the rocky terrain and tried to guess how far south they'd travelled based on the height of the mountains. This camp was erected against the bottom of several large boulders near a fork in a path. By the size of the camp, Edryss guessed it had been made for a large number. Several men were scouring through personal belongings, jumping from one cot to the next, probably cots of men she had killed. Darkness blocked her view, the coat of the man with one hand. She had seen him attack Gladthorn, wondering if he was dead, she saw no signs of him here. The man knelt in front of her. He had an apple pierced through on his dagger, and he took a few bites before speaking, juice dipping down his chin and onto the scar across his throat.

"Welcome back to the land of the living, my dear. I hope you find your bindings comfortable. We spare no luxury for friends of the righteous man."

Edryss pulled against the ropes binding her hands and feet together behind her. With some effort, she was able to struggle into a sitting position.

"Good girl. Very good." mocked the deformed man. "You deserve a taste!" He offered her the apple on his dagger. Instead, she turned her head and spat.

Malus slapped Edryss across the face with his good hand, and then offered Edryss the apple again. Edress hardened her lips, and Malus motioned to his men.

Akash, similarly bound, was half carried, half dragged into Edryss' view. His lefteye was swollen shut. One of Malus' men kicked him in the gut. Aksah brought his knees to his chest as well as he could, bound as he was.

Malus offered Edryss the apple again, and reluctantly she took a bite, chewed, and swallowed. It tasted like sand in her mouth. "Good girl! Good little girl, friend of the righteous man!" The man began to sing, almost gleefully. "A Righteous man without any rules, when he breaks them who does he fool?

Edryss feared they had been captured by a mad man. A soldier appeared through the brush marching straight for the deformed man. He saluted and bowed. "Regent Malus, he took the bait."

Malus smiled, "Very good! It's a very good day, indeed."

"Malus?" Edryss asked. "I thought you were dead."

"*I thought you were dead,*" Malus mocked. "Do I look dead? Do I look like the sort of man who dies?" Malus held out his hands and posed. "No, I'm too important to die. I have too much to do. You want to see death, though? Today, the righteous man has felt my sting. He will soon realize that in the end, all good men become, well become like me I suppose. To be fair, most die before they get here. It's not easy to be me." He took another juicy bite of the apple and sung the same verse from earlier, "Righteous man without any rules, when he breaks them who does he fool?""

Edryss glared at Malus, "Gladthorn will never be like you!"

"She speaks his name! Hmm, yes, it seems we have struck a chord." Edryss realized her mistake, and tried to turn away from Malus, but was stopped by his dagger. Malus' smile grew devious and treacherous once he saw the fire in her eyes. "This is even more opportunistic than I had expected, the second verse may have already arrived."

Malus placed his blade against Edryss' cheek and sensuously lead the blade down the defined line of her jaw to her chin. He pricked her cheek and held his blade to catch the small stream of blood. He licked it and savored it.

"It seems we have a winner! Change of plans boys, our sting today will be ten times as potent with her." Malus leaned and placed his lips against Edryss' ear and sang, "Heavens will cry as true love dies when a righteous man has no rules."

Edryss bucked forward, teeth bared, aiming for the pearlescent scar across Malus' throat, but Malus avoided the bite, and smiled wickedly.

"Yes, yes, I like you too." Malus lowered his dagger and split the seam at Edryss' crotch. He slashed at her jacket carelessly leaving little beads of blood in a random pattern and yanked one sleeve off her shoulder and threw it aside. "Very pretty, very, very, pretty." He turned to walk away but stopped at the pleased chuckles of his men. He looked back and added, "No one is to touch her, yet. I need the righteous man thinking the worst, but I'll not have any more of you idiots killed by this whore because you were thinking with your tiny battering rams!"

The men grumbled assent.

***

Gladthorn pushed on through the rough and rocky terrain. He had not seen a single person since freeing the young woman and boy, though he was certain he was going in the right direction. Sticking to the trees and the large rocks that moved along the path allowed Gladthorn some protection. Ahead, the path forked, west and southeast. Climbing to get a higher view, he approached the edge cautiously. To his surprise, he found remnants of a camp below him. From the look of the smothered fire, it had been recently occupied. Looking southeast he saw denser forest, but to the west was an open field of rocks and dirt, and far down the path was a small dust cloud, before sparse trees and rocks like the ones he hid in now. He was sure the dust cloud was Malus' men, forcing him out of hiding. Gladthorn was about to leave in pursuit when he noticed something familiar lying on the ground. Closer inspection confirmed his fears. The sleeve of a tan leather jacket, one he knew well. It was slashed and dotted with blood, and Edryss' shirt sleeve was still inside it. He thought back to Annette, and Malus' wretched men. He clenched the jacket sleeve tightly and held it to his face, trying to hold back angry tears.

Gladthorn kneeled for a moment and bowed his head. He knelt in silence and prayed for Edryss' safety. "Thank thee, oh Maker. Allow me purity of mind, and strength of arm. Help me vanquish the unrighteous and save the innocents, but most of all, please Maker, protect Edryss. Allow me this and I will be forever your instrument! So, say we all!""

Gladthorn rose to a soft rumble from the mountains and smiled. He turned west.

Edryss had no idea where she was being taken, they had replaced the bag over her head and untied her feet. She was cold in her torn clothes, shivered, and swayed dangerously. She was astride a horse, her hands still bound. An arm wrapped around her, someone was squeezing her, instinct for warmth forced her to move closer. For a brief moment she thought it was Gladthorn. "Don't you worry, my dear." It was Malus. "This will be all over soon, and you and the righteous man will be free to leave, changed forever by the force of my sting."

"What in Bellows does that even mean? You are mad, Malus. The only thing changing today is that you will die."

Malus laughed, "Perhaps, my pretty, but not before my sting!"

"You are wrong. "rebuked Edryss upset she even spoke, "There is nothing you can do to change that man! He is the best man I have ever met."

"By the great dark one, he found a copy of himself in you, didn't he?" mocked Malus holding Edryss even tighter. "Or are you just trying to live up to his impossible code?"

Malus was met with silence.

"Let me tell you a secret. All men have a breaking point. A righteous man still possesses the same darkness that we all house inside. He may hide it, he may deny it, but when he is pushed, he will break, and the man we all knew will be as deformed inside as I am outside. Your righteous man just needs a little push. You'll see."

"Regent Malus, horsemen are nearing the area."

Malus sighed, "It looks like your friends are looking for you. Was our righteous man a part of this group?"

"No, sir, they seemed to be searching, not chasing. Your righteous man has disappeared. Our lookouts at the plain's edge are dead."

Malus laughed. "Never matter, we are still on track. Spread out and find him, but do not harm him. He's mine alone! I will sting him today!"

"Yes, sir!" the man grabbed the jacket and rode off. Edryss could hear the hooves get further and further away when BLAST, ZAPP, and BOOM echoed in their ears. The man riding the horse was shot from a tesla bolt from a thick brush of trees. He fell to the ground few strides later.

Malus laughed, "HE IS HERE! Oh, I knew he couldn't let that scout go." He leaned in and pushed his head against the cloth bag over Edryss' head. "See, a righteous man will risk anything and everything to do what is right. Not what is necessary!"

Gladthorn pulled back into the woods, he had no choice but to kill the scout before he had turned the bend and been covered by the winding path of rocks and uneven terrain. The forested area was dark and dank. By the soft soil and thick brush, it was obviously a low lend area for the local rain water to gather.

Gladthorn's decision to fall back was correct. He was now running for his life, the immediate area around the edge of the forest erupted in a bright fury of explosions. Two of Malus' men were armed with antique Citadel Tesla Packs, and those packs had only one setting 'BOOM.' The forest edge was an inferno.

Malus laughed, "Enough boys! I am positive that with your shitty aims you didn't manage to actually hit him. He will fall back for only a moment." He grabbed Edryss by the arm and started to lead her away, "Prepare the other guests for his arrival!"

The constant smell of smoldering embers of burnt wood filled and burnt his nose. Gladthorn's lungs rejected the smoke. The long way around the dense forest was further than Gladthorn had anticipated, he tired of coughing. Next, he tried to find an area where he could flank Malus and his men without being seen. The task ended up being impossible, Malus had chosen his spot well.

Sneaking from large rock to large rock, Gladthorn was surprised at how quiet it was. Malus' tactics in the past had always been loud and in the opponent's face. *What is his game?* He wondered. Sliding around the side of another large rock, Gladthorn traversed it with his back against the cold stone. His eyes quickly moving right to left ensuring no one was watching him, so worried about being seen from a far he forgot to look forward and stumbled. Gladthorn had just tripped and fallen on top of one of Malus' men. From the frightened look on his face, the man was equally as surprised as Gladthorn. The two struggled. The man tried to pull his rifle out of his tesla pack but Gladthorn had the upper position and quickly the upper hand as well. He squeezed the man's windpipe just long and hard enough to render the man unconscious. Peering around the rock he was certain no one else had seen the encounter. To the distance in the north, Gladthorn spotted Akash tied to a very large boulder with no signs of any guards.

Malus had been able to plan every detail for his revenge, he was completely certain that Gladthorn would play right into his hands. The only detail he could not control was the exact time the righteous man would show up. In his gut Malus knew he was already here, but he needed proof before moving on to the next stage.

"I will sting him today my pretty girl," Malus added quietly to Edryss.

Edryss heard the other man trot away as Malus stopped their horse and guided her off of it and pulled her by a rope around her waist to a wall of stone. Malus licked his lips with only half a tongue and admire Edryss' natural beauty with a carnal lust. Had she known what Malus was doing she would not have stood so sedately against the rock, but the bag over her head prevented her from seeing. Her torn and slashed clothing only increased Malus' perverted appetite. He moved slightly closer, Edryss recoiled at the proximity.

A hand touched Edryss' shoulder and squeezed it so gently that again she thought maybe it was Glad. But the hand soon slipped down over her collarbones and hovered over her right breast. Edryss tried to break away, but her body suddenly flinched in pain. The cold steel of Malus' blade sat against her bare skin. He had pointed it into her stomach, the more she struggled, the more she cut herself. "Gladthorn will come, and he will kill you."

Malus' tongue ran along Edyrss' neck. "I am counting on it."

The next few minutes were some of the darkest of Edryss' life. Every touch, poke, and twist made Edryss' soul feel tainted. Shallow cuts scored her stomach as she squirmed. At least the pain distracted her.

"Maybe I will keep you for myself," whispered Malus, tearing her clothes further. "You'd like that wouldn't you? Say you would."

Edryss gritted her teeth and prepared a response that did not begin with *I would*, when one of Malus' men returned. Malus loosened his grip and the man stopped, frozen.

"Come. It's not like this is the first time you've seen me dance with a woman before." The perimeter scout bowed so low, his hood fell forward, a gesture of sincere apology. He held it until Malus acknowledge it. The man approached closer but did not salute or speak.

"What is the report?" Malus barked impatiently.

The man cleared his throat. "No sign of him."

Malus closed his eyes, feigning disappointment. "Will he ever learn to play by the rules?" Malus released his grasp on Edryss' body, but not her rope. She collapsed to the ground and adopted the fetal position trying to put pressure on her bleeding stomach. Malus nodded at one of his three bodyguards that had been with him the entire time. He and another guard ran off.

There was silence for several long seconds. Malus rubbed the scar along his jaw and smiled at the guard. "In the grand scheme of things, I guess it doesn't matter. We have his love. The verse is clear. The only question is whether he feels for you as you so clearly do for him. *Heavens will cry, and true love dies, when a righteous man has no rules.* Funny thing about songs. People don't realize the power they hold. There is another verse, you know, it's my very favorite. *All will suffer, his pain will be great. Has her death jeopardized and destroyed his fate?*"

Malus laughed sadistically and examined Edryss lying at his feet, the bag still on her head. She was quivering and held her legs tightly to her stomach. Malus spats. "It's a shame the righteous man did not come. Your death will at least amuse me for the moment and hurt him forever."

Malus reached down with his good hand, grabbed Edryss by the fabric around her neck and lifted her to a standing position. "Edwin! Fire on the prisoner."

A guard who had been sitting nearby hidden from plain sight stood up from behind a smaller boulder that had been blocking him from view. Edwin aimed his rifle at Akash. Three shots were fired in quick succession. Akash screamed and fell to the ground. His bonds broken, and Edwin and the third bodyguard were dead, their blood soaking into the ground.

Malus ducked and dodged the next set of shots. He reached down and grabbed Edryss by the scruff of her neck and twirled her in front of him. "Well done Gladthorn. At first, I thought you were one of my men, but you forgot to salute."

"I would never salute sucha fetid piece of congealed monkey vomit."

Malus nearly laughed, "Not exactly what a righteous man would normally say! But it does have some grit in it!"

Gladthorn ripped off the cloak he was wearing. "Give her to me now Malus and I will let you live."

Malus laughed and held his flesh infused bladed arm to Edryss' throat, "This is why I will always win! A righteous man is predictable. You are predictable, Gladthorn Jones!"

Gladthorn glared confidently and pulled out his Plaz hilt. His thumb smashed the button and activated it, a stream of molten hot plasma formed into a two-sided blade with a devastatingly dangerous long tip. Gladthorn pointed the tip straight at Malus' face "I killed you once Malus. "

Malus was about to mock Gladthorn when Edryss suddenly smashed his foot and tried to push him backwards.

"Kill him!" yelled Malus struggling to hold Edryss who began to fight the moment she heard his name get called out. Gladthorn made a move towards Malus but the two large body guards appeared from the other side of several large rocks and charged straight for him.

Gladthorn moved swiftly and determined, his sword flew with such precision he killed the first attacker in seconds. Seeing how dangerous the man was, the second attacker turned and fled.

A bright beam of light flew through the air and smacked the retreating attacker in the back. Gladthorn spun to see Malus' bladed arm wrapped around Edryss' neck and a Marshal standard Tesla revolver in the other. Gladthorn immediately recognized it, it was the same gun Malus had always carried with him. The gun was very powerful short range but weak at long. Each shot was held in a capacitor, which meant that Malus had seven or eight shots left if it was fully loaded.

"You didn't have to kill him." yelled Gladthorn

Malus looked at Gladthorn like his statement was the dumbest thing he had ever heard a man utter, "Of course I did! Can't have a coward in my ranks, I have a reputation to uphold."

"Your reputation died the night I killed you!" remarked Gladthorn, "You are nothing more than an echo of your former self. A forgotten, bad memory from the people you have harmed."

Malus pointed his gun at Gladthorn, "But a memory is still a memory." he fired his tesla revolver.

Gladthorn leaped from his spot.

Malus began to retreat, he continued to fire and drug Edryss with him.

Edryss fought against Malus, "Unless you kill him, he wont stop coming after you."

"Don't you listen, dearie? I am not trying to kill him, not yet at least"

Edryss stumbled several times, she could not see where the man was taking her. Malus continued to fire his revolver. The sounds of rock breaking caused Edryss to freeze.

"That should hold him for a moment." Malus looked around the area. "Oh, this is it!" hooted Malus dropping Edryss to the ground. "The time I have been waiting for. Are you ready for your part?"

Edryss was furious, "Go to hell!"

Malus kicked Edryss in the side, "Not everything I do is directed towards you, dearie!"

Malus paused and spoke again, "Well, are you?"

"Yes, as long as you promise to free my family." respond a voice that trembled with fear and pain.

Edryss was shocked, "Who else is here?"

"You will find out soon enough!" Sneered Malus, "No actually dearie, you may not. Your last moments are nigh and the last sight you will see is that fabric of that bag. Gladthorn, the righteous man, he will never choose you. Love is something he doesn't understand, because love is war, love is darkness, love is cruelty. To love or be loved is to have pain to see the darkness and a righteous man shuns the darkness."

Edryss wrenched in pain, her stomach wounds were agonizing, "You are mad!"

Edryss gasped. "Glad!?" She began to cry.

"Oh, there you are! Good sport!" shouted Malus watching Gladthorn make his way over the rocks that Malus had knocked down.

Gladthorn made his way over the debris and stormed towards Malus. The clothes he was wearing were ripped and torn, and his face was sweaty and bloody. The look in his eyes was dangerous and stern, Malus took half a step back out of sheer instinct.

"It's time for the end now isn't it?"

"It's time for you to die!" roared Gladthorn pointing his sword straight out almost within striking distance.

Malus raised his pistol and began to aim it at Gladthorn but instead changed directions and pointed at a man whose arms were bound tightly together. "Oh, I see you recognize Jareb."

"I saved his family from your men."

Jareb's face twisted and smiled, "Are they safe?"

Gladthorn nodded, "Yes, they are."

"Oh, woopie dippity doo." mocked Malus, "It doesn't matter, you won a small battle. I am about to win the war between us."

Malus knelt down, keeping his good arm with the pistol pointed at Jareb and reached for Edryss, yanking her up and placing his flesh blade around her neck. "Here it is. The end, the fall of the titan. Make your choice and live with it. You can only save one, the love intrest or the innocent father. You vowed to save him, right? I knew your righteousness couldn't resist that. Why else did I make it so easy to save that mother and son? I knew you would make an incredibly moving vow to risk all life and limb to save him." Malus snickered, "I have orchestrated everything to this moment, this singular and greatest of moments, the moment when a righteous man must actually choose to follow the darkness or light?"

"You are delusional. "Roared Gladthorn, "All this for me!"

"Of course, all for you!" hissed Malus, "You maimed me and ruined my life! Now choose! Save the father or save the woman you love. Save one or let me kill both?"

"I knew the darkness had consumed you, but I never realized how much it had until now." Gladthorn started to walk forward.

Malus sneered, "Darkness always wins, don't you know? The light, if that's what you want to call it, will always be extinguished. All life becomes dark in the end. I and people like me, the powerful, the ambitious, are willing to do anything to succeed. We will always win!"

"Not today!"

Malus laughed and held Edyrss tighter the closer Gladthorn moved, "Oh yes, today will be my greatest victory!"

"Save the father Gladthorn!" urged Edryss

Malus pushed his blade into Edryss' neck, "Shut up wench. Honestly, other than the body what do you see in her?"

Gladthorn bit his lip, tears in his eyes. He moved between Malus' pistol and the father. He turned his back to his enemy and activated his plaz sword and begun to undo the ropes tied to Jareb. "Thank you so much! You are a good and honorable man! My family, I thought I would never see them again."

"You will." replied Gladthorn his voice coursed.

"Ah yes!" remarked Malus, "Just as I knew you would. Love is meaningless to a righteous man when innocents are around. Remember this dearie, he had several chances to kill me and save you but chose to save others instead. How is that love?" Malus began to laugh and laugh, so excited to finally be at this point. "Now once you have freed Jareb you will turn and watch me slit your loves throat."

Gladthorn closed his eyes and pictured Edryss' face, his heart rushed to feel the love he had for her. The unmistakable fact that he had never loved someone so strongly or powerfully and he never fully showed it, his heart began to ache at the thought this was the last time he would feel such emotion. "I am sorry." he whispered coarsely.

The young father did not understand the apology until it was too late. Malus suddenly gasped in pain. A man's face barreled into his own nearly headbutting eachother. The face Jareb was wearing was the same terrified and shocked look as Malus. Both had not expected Gladthorn to make this move. As instantly as the initial shove, both men cringed in agonizing pain as a sword pierced through their touching chest cavities.

Malus, so surprised, dropped Edyrss to the ground. He chuckled for a long moment and gasped for air, "You, wow- you crossed it. I never thought you--you of all people would cross it so easily. You did it, you actually did it! Which means I did it? Funny, I didn't expect it to hurt so much."

Malus and Jareb keeled over in pain, as Gladthorn pulled his blade out of both of them.

"GLAD!?" asked Edryss lying on the ground scared at the sounds she was hearing.

"I am coming." declared Gladthorn.

Edryss waited patiently, someone was rummaging for something around her. She was confused, *was there someone else with Gladthorn?* Malus moaned and gasped, scaring Edryss. She did not know he was lying and dying mere feet from her. A large hand grabbed her. Edryss struggled until she heard his voice. "Darkness never wins, but sometimes the light has to get dirty. Your death will save so many others from your cruelty."

Malus attempted to laugh, but only choked on his own blood. But through gasps and coughs, he managed to say, "Beware the righteous man when he has no rules, when he breaks them who does he fool?"

"Say all you want. Your death ends this whole charade."

Malus' smile curled up like a mischevious feline and he reached out his hand towards Gladthorn like a lover would, "My death only makes my soul greater!" he coughed several more times before his body went limp.

Gladthorn freed Edryss from her bindings and took off her bag. She gasped at the sight of Jareb and Malus dead on the ground. "Gladthorn, what did you do? What about his family? You promised." She stared at the body of Jareb and teared up, "Why?"

"He may have been innocent at first, "Gladthorn pointed at a dagger lying near the father's body, "The moment he took up arms for Malus, he chose his side, Edryss. I will not apologize for saving you. We didn't have time for diplomacy."

"Maybe he didn't get the chance to choose! Malus had his family! What choice is that!?"

"MALUS HAD MY FAMILY!" Gladthorn roared, anger and fear flashing in his eyes. He sunk to the ground and held his face in his hands. "I saw what he had done to you Edryss. I saw it. The man tried to kill me." Gladthorn lied, "Malus knew it would tear me up to have to kill him, but they would have kept you, I couldn't let them. I couldn't let them have you. I had to save you, no matter what."

"No matter what?" asked Edryss, unsure if the story she was being told was true. "You would break the code of the Equinauts and the Marshal's Creed and kill an innocent to save me?"

"No code, no creed, no rules will stop me from saving you." Declared Gladthorn, "But I didn't have to, Jareb attacked me first."

No rules will stop me, the words echoed in Edryss' mind. *A righteous man who has no rules, when he breaks them who does he fool.* She wondered if she understood why now. A man with obligation can't be impartial. When he is pushed, he will break. Edryss hated that Malus had planted this seed of doubt in her.

Leaning down over Jareb's body, Gladthorn held his hand over the man's head, "Rest in peace, I saved your family. They are safe." Gladthorn practically whispered through his hand. "I saved his, and I saved mine."

Edryss crawled to where he was kneeling and rested her forehead against his. *Malus knew how to break him, but I don't know how to fix him.*

Akash stumbled into the small clearing. "I almost lost you guys, but I heard yelling, thank the Maker."

Gladthorn stood up, his face like stone. "There are Equinauts somewhere nearby, a search and rescue. We need to find them and get back."

Gladthorn hugged Edryss and held her turning her head away from the carnage, "I did and will always do what I have to, to save you! I love you!"

Edryss' body shuttered slightly, and she managed to turn her head enough to see the bodies lying there in the periphery. "I love you too." she whispered back. For the first time ever though, Edryss wondered if she truly meant it.

***

-An Hour before the first demon attack:

Thaddeus rode up and down the column just to ensure everything was still in proper order. Niles' report of the ambush had caused a ruckus, and the decision to send a large search party had been contested. The professor loathed losing so many of his guards. Gladthorn and the others' return had set the column mostly back at ease.

The fields of Braum had slowly consumed the scenery. In the distance to the north, a harrowing reminder of darker times stood in plain sight, the ancient tower of Emorragia, a relic from the shard's middle age before the unification of the five kingdoms. Thaddeus was quite familiar with the tower and its layout from dreams of a long-ago ancestor of his who vanquished a sinister evil.

The further east they moved, the fewer people they passed. As the Expedition neared the Slavine Kingdom, Thaddeus knew they'd have to be much more careful. A human convoy this large moving towards the Slavine border unannounced could ignite another war, and while war was part of the Equinauts' currency, Thaddeus wasn't prepared to carry the burden of causing one.

Thaddeus galloped to the head of the column. His mind raced and struggled to focus on the journey ahead. He repeated Gladthorn's story in his head over and over, something seemed off. Thaddeus was there the day Gladthorn killed Malus for the first time, and he too was sure the man was dead. *So how did he return? And why now?* Thaddeus tried to focus his thoughts, but every time he began down a path of reasoning, niggling thoughts would distract him. Thoughts of Leora.

Eventually he gave in. *Why her?* She was not the strong and independent type that normally captured his attention. She was so inexperienced! Leora's naivety was outright, yet he was entirely charmed. She was unique. Her potential seemed limitless. Somehow, she reminded Thaddeus of himself, but an old version of himself, before he was laden with the medallion. As a young man, Thaddeus felt insecure, unsure of his future, but it was Alana who realized his great potential and helped him become the man he was today. Thaddeus briefly fanaticized that perhaps he could do for Leora what his wife had done for him. Thaddeus was stunned when he realized that for the first time in his life, he was allowing someone other than his late wife to capture his heart.

His new muse appeared alongside him, interrupting his reverie. It flattered him that she preferred to ride close and engage him in conversation.

"You owe me several pages in my journal. I had scribbled half of Italicus' story before I realized he's full of it! Larister the Bird King!? Was I supposed to believe all that?"

Thaddeus laughed. "What if I told you most of it was true?"

Leora shook her head, beaming. "I may be gullible, I did show you this right?" Leora grabbed the front of her jacket and opened it. "You see all these empty pockets and hangers? I didn't bring a bag with me because I misinterpreted the meaning of 'on your person.' So, we've established I'm naive at times, but even with that being said, there is no way I can believe that story to be true!"

"You don't have to believe it, but if I were you, I'd scribble down the second half. I was there for most of it, and I can vouch that never in my life have I seen something so amazing." Thaddeus trailed his arm through the sky playfully, "Italicus soaring majestically through the sky, the only time in that man's life where he was he truly in his element."

Leora raised an eyebrow and looked at Thaddeus skeptically, "Soared!?"

"Yes, soared!" Thaddeus grinned and spoke dramatically, "Through the sky, landing on and killing Larister. He saved all the birds."

Leora shook her head and laughed, she still did not fully believe their story. Thaddeus felt content. Leora looked stunning with dusk's sun upon her face, illuminating her above all else. The passage of time ceased as the two spoke. For Thaddeus, it was refreshing to hear someone so passionate about life and learning new things. Thaddeus usually had difficulty talking at length with others, but Leora was exceptional. With her, he was at ease. He felt safe, like he was free to be himself.

For a good portion of their conversation, Leora talked about Andi, who Thaddeus remembered meeting that morning, the girl with the blonde bob. Leora admired her and expressed hope that through the course of the expedition they would become close friends. Thaddeus made a mental note of this, he thought perhaps speaking to Andi would give him better insight on Leora.

Leora paused and noticed Thaddeus' smile, "So, is there someone special in your life right now?" she asked, pushing Wooly a little closer to Egghead.

"No," Thaddeus sighed, relieved by the way Leora asked the question. "My work is grueling, it affords me little time for a personal life. We're often gone for weeks, sometimes months at a time. And If I did have someone, I couldn't imagine bringing her along, it's far too dangerous." Thaddeus had decided earlier in the day not to bring up Alana, it was too soon in their budding relationship to discuss such personal matters.

Leora grinned. "What if you found a woman equal in strength and heart? Would you bring her along?"

"Perhaps." Thaddeus felt uncomfortable, the question reminded him of something Alana asked him once. He gave Leora a large goofy smile, and then cocked his head in confusion. For the briefest of moments, he thought he noticed Leora's hair begin to glow. Thaddeus closed his eyes and shook his head slightly. When he opened them everything was back to normal.

"What?" asked Leora.

Thaddeus wasn't sure if he should say something. "Nothing, I've been riding too long."

Leora smirked and ignored Thaddeus' momentary confusion. "Well, Thaddeus PenRuger, you let me know when you find that woman of equal stature." And she trotted away.

As night's darkness slowly kissed the convoy, Thaddeus remained vigilant, patrolling up and down through heavy steam clouds. Fortunately, the reports from Gladthorn's scouts remained constant, safe and clear. However, Thaddeus knew not to be lulled into a false sense of security. Malus, a marshal, or the entire Slavine army could suddenly appear anywhere at any time.

"How are we going to survive this? Maker help us!" He realized the voice belonged to Andi, the girl Leora had been raving about. Thaddeus thought this would be an opportune time to talk. *Maybe she'd put in a good word about him to Leora.*

"Pretty intimidating, isn't it?" answered Thaddeus, riding Egghead towards the voice.

Andi enthusiastically badgered Thaddeus with a multitude of questions. At first, the deluge made him feel a little defensive. *She must think I'm not good enough for Leora.* He knew it was important to make a good impression and chose his words carefully. Thaddeus normally wouldn't speak of such personal things with strangers, but surprisingly, a rarely felt trust grew between the two. Thaddeus had completely opened up to Andi when she questioned him about his father. This girl really puzzled him. He didn't understand why she tried so hard to draw him in only to push against him so fervently. He reminded himself to remain guarded around Andi and wondered what about her garnered such blind respect from Leora.

Abruptly, a scream pierced through the air. Thaddeus feared it sounded like Leora. Without hesitation, Thaddeus and his horse bolted off towards the scream, leaving Andi and his medallion behind. At full gallop, Thaddeus reached down for his horn and blew it loudly, caught his breath, and shouted. "Equinauts, FORM UP!"

Within seconds, the nearest members of the Equinauts — Faramal, Gladthorn, Fryda, and Edryss— gathered behind Thaddeus. The five cantered swiftly towards the front of the column, where they could see a fight erupting. Their fellow Equinauts were engaged with great creatures shrouded in black cloaks. They could see the professor's men cowering under their wagons. There was blood mixing with the dirt road, erubescent muck beneath everyone's feet.

"Fryda, Faramal, help Kaz. Edryss, fetch reinforcements, get to the med wagon, and tell them to come too. Don't engage! Gladthorn, help the injured, move them safely inside the wagons!" Like extensions of himself, the Equinaut members obeyed Thaddeus' commands nimbly.

From ahead came another scream, Thaddeus saw Leora's hair glowing brighter than her Plaz sword. She had dismounted and was fighting off two cloaked creatures on foot.

Thaddeus was temporarily frozen, the sight of Leora's hair burning like the sun had him stunned. *It has to be the glow of the sword reflecting off her red hair.* Swinging the great sword before her, Leora managed to clumsily defend herself.

She wasn't going to last much longer, Thaddeus could see even at this distance that her right leg was trembling from an injury. Thaddeus urged Egghead forward and flew towards her, surprising even himself at the speed of Egghead's gallop. He dropped his reins, drew his Tesla rifle, and began firing bright blue beams of energy directly at where he thought the cloaked creatures' chest were located.

Five Tesla bolts hit their target with stunning accuracy, but the creatures didn't fall. All Thaddeus had succeeded in doing was turning their attention away from Leora. Angry, one of the shrouded creatures rushed towards their new attacker.

Thaddeus leapt from Egghead's saddle, landing feet first onto the ground and fired an extended stream of light from his Tesla rifle at one of the creatures. Unbelievably, the creature continued towards him, the Tesla had no effect. Thaddeus tried one more time, firing at the creature's head. Despite a perfect shot, it advanced unimpaired. Thaddeus unhooked, threw down his rifle, and unsheathed his plasma sword.

The cloaked creature rushed towards Thaddeus. As it approached he was dumbfounded by the sheer height of the creature towering over him by several feet. Thaddeus looked up, searching for the creature's eyes under its dark hood, but within, Thaddeus' gaze was met with nothing but a cold abyss. The thought of facing a faceless beast was horribly unnerving. *What is this abomination of nature before me?*

Cold chills ran down Thaddeus' spine as the creature lept into the air striking its right hand down, swinging its cold, steel sword. Thaddeus dodged and rolled on the ground, springing back up quickly. Thaddeus flipped a switch on the hilt of sword, the rim of the hilt began to glow, molten rock began to take form in the shape of a double-sided blade.

Angered that it had missed Thaddeus' head, the creature readied itself for the next attack, positioning its blade for a quick strike to Thaddeus' side. It charged once more, this time letting out a blood curdling screech. Thaddeus' blood ran cold and felt his heart sink with the recognition of the sound. Since his dream of Alana, it had haunted him in his sleep.

Were these the creatures from my vision? Thaddeus' mind raced at the implications. Never had he nor the Equinauts faced such evil. A red-orange glow reflected off his face indicating Thaddeus' plasma sword had finished forming. He felt safer behind the glow of his sword.

Thaddeus' ancestral sword had fought in more battles and killed more opponents than the entire history of the Citadel army. Simply known throughout the shard as *Gladius,* it has become a symbol of justices and protection. Though it was originally designed to be a two-handed sword, Thaddeus easily held it in his right hand.

The cloaked creature swung to its left, trying to slice through Thaddeus' gut. Thaddeus moved away and used his sword to block the blade. The creature let out another roar and swung forcefully towards Thaddeus' leg. Thaddeus jumped, missing the blade by mere inches. The creature tumbled forward several steps. Taking the opening, Thaddeus sliced at the creature's back. A loud, high-pitched squeal came from the creature's hood. Despite the pain from Thaddeus' strike, the creature spun and re-engaged him. Thaddeus adjusted a band on his wrist and thumbed a button. The length of his left arm glowed red and blue, his pack blew steam, a whistle sounded, and a blue energy shield formed around his left arm. As the creature lunged forward, Thaddeus lowered his hip, planted his right leg to absorb the hit, and used his shield to block the swing with an upward slash.

Thaddeus was only inches from the cloaked figure. He stared directly at where the creature's face should have been, and two menacing green eyes emerged from within the black abyss. With a mighty shove, Thaddeus pushed the creature off balance and thrusted his Plaz sword straight out, catching his opponent's arm. As the creature lunged to strike again, Thaddeus threw up his left arm, shielding himself in a defensive position. The creature's weapon struck his shield, generating an unnerving clang of clashing metal. With his full strength, Thaddeus rotated the blade away with his shield, its edge scraped along the grooves and the weapon toppled to the ground. Thaddeus didn't waste the opportunity. He quickly brought the shield back up for protection and rammed its pointed end towards the creature's face. He struck something hard, and the creature flailed backwards. Thaddeus leapt towards it and thrust his sword downward several times into the evil's flesh. The creature shrieked in pain as it clutched onto Thaddeus' shield and wouldn't release. It flailed violently around, desperately trying to throw Thaddeus off balance. Despite this, Thaddeus managed to land several more blows as the creature screeched louder and louder. Thaddeus saw another creature approach his 3 and prepared to face two foes, but the second creature grabbed its brother and began to pull him away. The pair vanished into thin air before him.

Thaddeus chased after the creatures, but they were gone. He howled in anger.

"Where did they go?" he demanded. Each of his men were in shock from the impossibility they had just encountered and fell silent.

Edryss found the group panting and staring into space. Italicus, the professor, and a small group of bloodied Equinauts followed her. It was at this point that Thaddeus realized the entire expedition must have been ambushed by these malicious creatures.

"Report!" demanded Thaddeus. Edryss and Italicus shared a look, unsure how to explain that they had lost their opponent mid-fight.

"Speak, one of you, or be parted from this world forever." Thaddeus' eyes bulged with intensity.

"Settle down, it's alright now!" consoled Italicus, trying to calm his friend, but the rage in Thaddeus' eyes did not calm. "Man, I always forget to let that temper of yours cool after a good fight, you really should talk to someone about it!" Italicus laughed nervously.

Thaddeus understood what he meant and took several deep, calming breaths.

Italicus spoke as Thaddeus composed himself. "We were ambushed from the rear. Robed creatures came out of nowhere. So far, we've seen two of the professor's people dead, gutted by a steel sword." Italicus paused, but Thaddeus could tell there was more.

"Go on, tell me everything you know!"

Faramal took two steps forward. "It was of Slavine origin, I saw the raven on one of their cloak sleeves."

Thaddeus looked at Faramal, "You're telling me the Slavine possess these creatures!? How is that possible?" Thaddeus looked to the others. "Did anyone else happen to see the insignia?"

The group maintained their silence, and Faramal felt betrayed.

"It was Slavine, I know it!" Faramal's tone was confident, but his hands were trembling.

"Let's not be ridiculous, Faramal. Do you honestly think the *Slavine* could have something like this up their sleeves?" sneered Italicus. "Furthermore, if they had these creatures in their arsenal, why the bloody hell would they have agreed to a cease fire?"

Faramal turned on Italicus, and said icily, "I know what I saw!"

Thaddeus stepped between the two, "Faramal, no one is denying what you saw, but when you're faced with two explanations, the simpler one is usually correct. There has got to be a simpler solution than the Slavine controlling an otherworldly foe such as this. For now, go and see if Kaz needs any help!" Faramal looked like he was about to protest. "That's an order, Faramal. GO!"

Faramal gave Thaddeus a quick salute, turned, and disappeared into the smog.

"Did you see a Slavine insignia?" Thaddeus faced Italicus expectantly.

"Hell no. Faramal is crazy! It's clear that his deep-rooted hatred of the Slavine has warped his mind. And great move, by the way, sending him to help Kaz. He's the one person who hates the Slavine more! We don't need them spreading paranoid delusions!"

Thaddeus shook his head, "Yeah, well I don't care to think about that at the moment, we've got enough to deal with. Go on and finish your damn report, Italicus."

Italicus bristled. "The creatures let out deafening screeches. Thaddeus, I don't know what we're up against. We found their victims, torn apart. I saw one of them clawing at this guy, his chest was completely dug out and I'm not sure what it was or how it got there, but he pulled out of it this bright orb. I've never seen such brilliant light in entire my life; it was like the sun, hard to even look at. As soon as he had it, the creature vanished. The others continued the attack. Thad, our Tesla rifles had no effect on them."

Thaddeus sighed deeply. None of the past half hour made any sense. *An orb like the sun,* he repeated in his head, trying to contemplate what Italicus had said. "Our rifles may not work, but the Plaz swords do. Pull out the reserves and make sure every member of the professor's team has one. We'll start basic training tomorrow. If they come back, I want to be ready! First, we must tend to the wounded and prepare a pyre so that we may burn the dead."

Italicus started away but turned back. "I don't know that we have enough Plaz swords to give to everyone."

Thaddeus nodded. "Do what you can."

Italicus saluted Thaddeus and hurried off to perform his duties.

Thaddeus walked to Edryss and placed a hand on her shoulder. "You did good, Edryss. Though I thought the medic insisted you not over exert yourself."

Edryss forced a smile, which looked more like a gaging reflex. "The cuts weren't really so deep. Having that bag over my head really screwed up my perception. All I could feel was pain and bleeding, but I couldn't tell how much. I thought I was dying to be honest."

Thaddeus squeezed Edryss' shoulders warmly. "Not with Gladthorn around!"

Edryss wasn't sure what Thaddeus meant. *Does he know about me and Glad?* Edryss ignored the comment. "Luckily, only one of the slashes needed stitches. I'm good, sir. I have seen you continue to fight with worse injuries."

"Maybe so," acknowledged Thaddeus, "and I prefer you do in cases of life or death, but the Equinauts are only as strong as our weakest member, so fight if you must, but healing is more important. Be honest. Do you need to rest?"

"No, sir."

"Alright. Please go help Italicus arm the civilians." Edryss bowed her head and set off.

Until now, Thaddeus had ignored the professor, who was busy helping the wounded who had been hiding under the wagons. He was disheveled, his top hat was partially sunken in and his eyes were bloodshot. Gladthorn was beside him, tending a wounded man's arm.

Gladthorn turned and noticed the professor staring at a lifeless body.

"One of those…creatures tore a nasty hole in his chest. I tried to stop the bleeding, but the wound was just too big."

Gladthorn rested a hand on the professor's shoulder. "For what it's worth, sir, he was brave till the very end. He pushed right through the pain, even while I tried to bandage him up. I've seen strong and brave men lose control over that much of pain."

The professor met Gladthorn's gaze and smiled as tears rolled down his cheeks. "Thank you." And then more softly he added, "Poor Souza."

The professor was beside himself, his heart ached for Souza and for the others dead or in pain. *What have I brought on these people?* The professor hobbled towards Thaddeus' position. Italicus had returned and was speaking.

"We barely have any extra Plazes to hand out, we will need to find more. Without our Tesla rifles range advantage--"

"Keep everyone who is not cleaning up inside the wagons," ordered Thaddeus, ignoring Italicus' statement of the obvious, "and make sure everyone's wagon has at least one sword."

Italicus saluted and walked away, nodding at the professor as he walked by. Thaddeus was scanning for Leora when the professor called his name.

"Thaddeus…UMPH!!"

The professor suddenly found himself lying on the ground cradling a very painful jaw. Everyone in the immediate area froze and looked at Thaddeus and the professor.

"What were those creatures!?" roared Thaddeus with a force of anger few had seen from a person before. "You knew these creatures were out there, didn't you! I told you if I found out you were lying or hiding information pertinent to our safety I would knock you on your old, wrinkled ass!"

"Mission accomplished, I would say," commented the professor, struggling to get up. He cradled his left cheek, already reddening. Thaddeus helped him up "I know this looks bad, but believe me when I say this attack was as much of a surprise to me as--"

"Thaddeus! Professor!" yelled Italicus. "Come quickly!"

Thaddeus helped the professor through the muck and over to Italicus, who was kneeling down over something black and green. "Get a load of this. The creature you fought left behind some nasty residue. Do you have any idea what the hell they are and where they came from?"

"Unfortunately, I do. I fear what we are dealing with are Shrieks, foot soldiers of the demonic force. It is their purpose to collect the souls of their victims."

Thaddeus sighed in frustration and rubbed his chin. "The demonic force. So, you did know about them."

"Souls?" asked Italicus. "Why do they want souls?"

"That is a very good question, but one for which I am afraid I don't have the answer." The professor leaned on his cane, surveying the damage before them. "I believe if we can get to Veilwood, we will find answers there." The professor peered up at Thaddeus, "Believe me, I did not know the enemy had found a way to ascended through the red aura. I fear this is entirely my fault. I have completely underestimated them."

"You ensured us those creatures couldn't cross into our realm," growled Thaddeus. Finished with the professor's dishonesty, he grabbed the professor's arm firmly.

A sudden bright blue light filled Thaddeus' field of vision and the word *Anipidem* repeated itself over and over in his mind, followed finally by two more words: *Bailitheoir* and *Dumak*. He was left with a vision of a lacerated heart covered in blood, and absolute sorrow filled Thaddeus' body. He shook violently.

The professor held steady against Thaddeus' shaking body, afraid the Equinaut was seizing. "Are you ok, my boy?"

Thaddeus blinked, trying to refocus his eyes. "I'm…I'm fine" He shook his head. "Professor, you owe me an explanation about everything you know and everything you think you know! We must better prepare ourselves!"

"On this, we agree."

Thaddeus' anger subsided slightly when he noticed Leora walking towards them, dragging her right foot slightly. He started to go to her, but the professor pulled him back down and asked gravely, "Until we can gather more information, can I trust you to keep this demonic creature theory to ourselves? We wouldn't want to scare everyone any more than they already are."

Thaddeus considered the professor's proposal, and eventually agreed. The professor walked away as Leora limped to Thaddeus, blood from a bad gash trickling down her calf. Her hair was disheveled and dark, with no hint of its previous glow. Her face was sweaty, and she was completely covered in dirt and mud. "What were those things?"

Thaddeus pushed aside the torn fabric around her leg and inspected her wound. "I'm not sure what they were," he mumbled. Thaddeus looked up and for a brief moment he unconsciously reached for the left pocket on the front of his jacket, ensuring the small tin was still there.

"Thaddeus?"

It took a moment for Thaddeus to return to reality. "Sorry, for a moment I could have sworn…just some déjà vu or…it's nothing, I'm sorry"

"What? You can't pass off that look as nothing."

Thaddeus gave a half smile. "I just thought for a moment, has your hair lightened at all?"

"My hair?" Leora laughed, wide eyed. She pulled a lock of it in front of her face and flicked it away, "I mean, we have been in the sun a lot, so maybe."

Thaddeus' ears burned red, "Well, it looks like you will have a great entry for your journal, and a battle scar to boot. The blade cut smoothly through your skin, the muscles should heal just fine."

Leora was paying no attention to Thaddeus' words. As soon as he had dropped his gaze to look at her wound, Leora had franticly began parting her hair, scouring through it, looking for changes. Her face twitched at the sight of strands that were slightly lighter than the rest. *Why is my hair doing this*?

"What, um, blade?" scoffed Leora trying to piece together what Thaddeus had just said. "It wasn't a blade! The horse, uh, Wooley got spooked when the creatures appeared, and he threw me to the ground."

"Wooly doesn't normally spook like that. I'm sorry you got hurt, but honestly, you're lucky to be alive. Here, I'll clean it so it doesn't get infected." Thaddeus produced a small bottle from his pocket.

"Do you always carry alcohol on you?" Leora asked at the smell.

"Indeed, I do. Being an Equinaut is tough work, you never know when you might need to clean a wound."

He held her leg steady with one hand and she grasped his shoulders, preparing for pain.

Thaddeus stood up after binding Leora's wound with a clean cloth. "So, you're telling me you held off two creatures, without getting nicked at all? That's pretty impressive. Those creatures were brutal!"

Leora smiled broadly. "It was pretty scary, and stressful! But what else is a girl to do when her knight on faithful steed doesn't show up to save her?" she joked, sliding her arm through his.

Thaddeus remembered what Leora had said earlier about finding an equal in battle, now he felt red creeping up his neck and couldn't look Leora in the face. "I'm sorry I wasn't there."

Leora smiled, stared at Thaddeus, and spoke from the heart, "But you came. You don't need to be sorry. You were there when I needed you. That's what matters, right?"

Her voice was almost melodic, it seemed to sing to Thaddeus. He tried to smile but the pride in him kept him from it. *Should have been there. I am where I need to be to protect the ones I lov--* Thaddeus couldn't finish his thought. He startled himself once he realized he had been gazing into Leora's eyes, unsure of how long it had been. Leora's smile was seductive.

"Leora, I don't know how to say this, but I can't help but—" Thaddeus paused, he cocked his head curiously and reached out his hand towards Leora's face.

Leora sighed and swooned. She thought he was going to stroke her cheek, but his hand went past her head and reached towards her hair.

"No!" she cried out once she realized he was reaching for a lock of hair that was still slightly glowing.

The moment Thaddeus touched the lock of hair he dropped to his knees, dragging Leora down with him. His head exploded with searing pain, and all he could hear was a high pitched whine. He gripped his head, trying to block out the noise and groaned. The pain was so great he felt like his skull was going to crack and cave in on him.

"Thaddeus! What's wrong? Are you ok?" Leora screamed. "HELP! SOMEONE, COME QUICK!"

Over the noise, Thaddeus heard a voice. He couldn't tell if it was coming from beside him or within him. A deep, booming, musical voice, repeating the word: "Awaken!" "Awaken!" "AWAKEN!"

William F. James

Echo from the Past

War was always a favorite pastime of mine. The carnage, the hatred, the sheer fear and total destruction that comes with it. The heathens to the north built higher walls and carved out countless arrows, a pathetic attempt. My holy army was protected by the power of my godhood. My vessel and I blessed each and every blade, we sanctified every piece of armor, each soldier was totally committed to his cause, willing to die for his god. When the heathen army met us on a small plain south of their quarters, they were slaughtered by the thousands. They fought tooth and nail, determined to defend their free will.

Had I known though, the numbers they would call upon, things would have gone differently. Many of the survivors from The Fallen attack had found refuge in the northern mountains. I still am appalled at how many survived the attack, so many souls that should have been collected. They called for reinforcements from encampments we had yet to encounter. How our scouts could have missed so many.... Mid battle they swarmed like ants to rotten fruit. They attacked the left and center rear of the army, striking at our soldiers' backs. A panic soon set in, a rout was certain. The entire centerline was in collapse when a man of faith stepped in and rallied our holy soldiers. He turned the tide of battle. Aaron was his name, commander of the right flank. Out of the chaos, my army proved victorious, the surviving heathens bowed before my vessel and began to worship us. I forgave them their transgressions, a choice my vessel made. I was ready to enjoy the wrath of destruction that they deserved, but my vessel was right. Sparing the rod and granting forgiveness showed the heathen's allies the mercifulness of our nature, and they too joined our holy cause without a fight.

Aaron the commander, who had saved our divine army from ruin, was appointed commander in chief of our holy armed forces. His first act was to relocate all separate encampments to the temple Oppidan. I dared not leave these creatures alone. In isolation they would return to their old ways. They needed daily reminders of my power.

Years passed, and my vessel remained beautiful. Once she had reached maturity she hadn't aged a day. The temple site was slowly becoming a city in its own right. It's strange how the human mind works. My worshipers knew the power that I wielded, yet they prayed and begged for the most insignificant things. I did not want to listen. How pathetic to ask a god for help? But my vessel, she truly understood manipulation. Absolute fear cannot wholly rule, only obedience through hope of redemption can a god truly rule absolutely.

So what did my little pets ask for? They demanded the city be named. I knew not what to name it, nor did I care for such trifles. My vessel, always thinking, suggested one almost immediately. In a ceremony more grand than anything these people had ever seen, my vessel and I dedicated the city with the blood of one hundred heathens. In that blood we scrolled the name of the city on the temple walls. Leistung und Zerstörung, Power and Destruction: Leistörung.

Long ago, before creation occurred, I witnessed the spark, the initial conception of the universe. I, for one, am sure the Maker did bestow a conscious upon it. In my many millennia, I have come to believe that the universe has its own mind and soul and that it hates me. On the surface of Aurelia, when all was but won, when The Fallen's victory was assured, the universe somehow allowed our defeat. Once again, the universe strikes out at me, jealous of my success, jealous of my perseverance. Of all days, it occurred on the day of Leisöstrung's dedication. Nearly a million people witnessed, down on their knees, worshiping me, a god!

In the distance, a star seemed to fall from the heavens. Many took it as a sign of my divinity. In that pivotal moment, when all of my subjects were murmuring in awe, I felt a presence, a strong, defined presence that I hadn't sensed in over a millennia. I reached out with my mind. I could feel nothing but power, no consciousness. Such power, such strength could only be wielded by a god. I had to find it, it had to be mine!

For days I dwelled in my Sanctum Sanctorum, trying to pinpoint the location of the descended power. My vessel presided without me. Without power, she still knew how to handle herself as a god. When the Sanctum Sanctorum was constructed, I left her alone for hours, but now I left her for weeks, meditating on the new essence, trying to understand its power. If I had only known the consequences of my actions, or perhaps had been less absorbed in my quest, much would have turned out differently. But, as I have come to learn, great power isn't always taken by another, but from within.

Professor Nikola Belladon

Chapter Five

From the first scroll of Zakarael, chapter 3 verse 19:
"...And this shall be the condemnation of the living; with light, so too comes darkness."

From the first scroll of Zakarael, chapter 13 verse 4:
"Rejoice! As Husband and Wife, two souls unite as one; let thy fountain be blessed, for in this sacred embrace, new life shall transcend both flesh and bone."

-Seven days prior to the Expedition:

With the support of his cane, Professor Nikola Belladon hastily hobbled through the halls of Citadel University's main building. Though he was running late for an important meeting, he was determined not to slip on the freshly polished marbled floors. Typically, before his morning class began, the professor would leisurely peruse the Mmain hall's stunning stained glass windows, sip his tea, and admire its craftsmanship. But, today there was little time and nothing to see. The sun's blinding rays pierced through the glass and obscured the professor's vision. The professor tittered. He could tell it was going to be one of *those* days. He withdrew a scroll from his tattered leather satchel and held it above his brow to shield his eyes. The monocle adhered to the professor's top hat bounced wildly as he scurried through the kaleidoscope of light and particles of dust. Close behind were two of the professor's assistants. Each carried an armful of scrolls and appeared frazzled.

At the toll of a bell, hundreds of students flooded the hall. Soon they plastered the walls, making a clear path for the frantic professor and his embarrassed minions. "I said, get out of the way! Please, move!" insisted the professor. The students were flabbergasted. None had ever witnessed Professor Belladon act in such a way. The normally composed atmosphere of the university was rattled by noise and commotion.

Most of the students stared in silence, but a few chucked jibes at the old man scurrying right down the middle of the hallway. "Stop sneering at me! I did say please, now didn't I?" Two students stood still, preoccupied in an intimate embrace. The professor plowed between them without any hesitation or consideration, "Really people, kissing at this hour!"

As the professor turned a tight corner, he noticed several young students in a classroom working on a mechanical arm. The professor halted to take a closer look. His abrupt stop caused his small entourage to stumble and spill their scrolls.

"Dean, what are you doing here?"

From his position on the floor, Dean adjusted the arm's spring mechanism. "Professor Belladon!" Dean nodded hello at the professor while concentrated on his work, "I just stopped by to help. They needed some assistance getting the torque right."

The mechanical arm looked like a very intricate piece of technology. Gears, wires, and tubes flowed in and out of its casing and connected to a small steam engine with a single piston. The professor bent to marvel the invention up close, "you know, if you lowered your steam pressure there, you could allow for..."

"Professor, we're *late*!" yelled one of the professor's assistants, retrieving the last of the fallen scrolls.

"Right, right! Dean, sadly I must go, but do come by my office later."

Dean nodded politely, "I look forward to it, Professor Belladon!"

The professor wiped his forehead with a small cloth and hurried away. Several hallways later, he and his assistants arrived at two large bronze doors which displayed the Universities' insignia, the infinity symbol representing the continual pursuit of knowledge. Deiz, the professor's executive assistant and aspiring professor himself stood impatient at the door nearby.

"Professor, you are so very late, I've run out of excuses!"

The professor leaned on his cane, and gulped for air, "I appreciate that Deiz, I really do."

"Professor, are you sure you don't want me in there with you?" Deiz's voice was calm, but his expression betrayed his worry. "I hope you know I am willing to verify everything!"

The professor smiled warmly at his protégé, "Thank you, Deiz, but I fear this may not end well, and I'd rather not drag you down with me."

"Even more reason for me to be in there!"

"No! That's final! You are married now. You have a beautiful wife to think about. If your dream is to teach at this university, then its best you stay clear from this!" The professor turned, "Dineela and Souza, the same goes for you two. Hand me everything you have and go wait in my office!"

The professor haphazardly accepted the two armfuls of scrolls, "It's certainly better to be over prepared, isn't it?"

"Good luck, sir," replied Deiz with a strained smile.

The three watched as the professor took a moment to gather his thoughts. His breathing was still elevated and he looked completely disheveled. Belladon shouldered open the doors and walked into the grand auditorium. Adorning the north wall of the spacious room was a great stained glass window depicting the University, the King's Plateau, and each of the five Themes. Below the pattern was an inscription of the University's motto, *"All of life can be reduced to its smallest part."* The professor hated everything it stood for. While the school preached conformity, he always strived to instill in his students free-thought and innovation.

This wasn't the first time Professor Belladon had received a summons to the auditorium. Usually, he was invited there to promote his latest invention, like the original steam powered wagon, but unfortunately today wasn't one of those days. He walked up to a small wooden podium, let down his satchel, and gingerly unrolled a scroll.

"Professor Belladon, you are late to these proceedings," sneered a podgy, middle-aged man dressed in a black robe. The man sat on a small chair behind a red conference table. He appeared rather aggravated.

"Yes sir, please forgive the infraction, Head Chancellor Marinus," replied the professor.

Several long, awkward minutes passed in silence as the professor organized his scrolls. The five members of the university's hierarchy scowled.

Chancellor Marinus cleared his throat noisily, and sunk deeper into his seat, the small spaces under his arm rests bulged with stomach fat. "Professor, anytime would be great, we have other business to attend to today!"

The professor nodded and adjusted his monocle. "Ladies and gentleman of the Circle, I've been called here today to defend my spending of university time and resources. I would like to discuss and substantiate a most pressing matter. A discovery of epic proportions has recently been made just south of the Castiel Mountains. I am afraid I have--"

The Chancellor interrupted, "Professor, our time is valuable, and you presume to waste it. It's well known there is nothing beyond the Castiel Mountain range."

"While that was widely thought to be true, I can ensure you it is no longer the case," argued the professor passionately. "The undeniable truth is that there *is* something beyond the mountain range and I am afraid its threat is beyond our comprehension!"

Three members of the Circle chuckled. Marinus raised a chubby hand to quiet the laughter. A female member began to speak, "Come now Professor Belladon, how can you expect us to believe such a claim!"

The professor straightened and spoke darkly, "because I have witnessed it for myself, Madam. I have proof! As several Progenitor Scrolls foretell, an apocalypse is coming. There is an evil force among us, and if we do not act soon, it will wipe every life form on every shard!"

Next to the plump Chancellor sat Madam Minister Erna Northeim. She appeared old and frail, but her voice was strong. "Every shard? My dear, you mean wipe out all life forms on *the* shard.., correct Professor Belladon?"

The professor huffed. "No Madam Minister, I mean *every* shard, beginning with our own! Everything will be destroyed. All-OF-CREATION! I am unsure how you could possibly have misunderstood me."

The Circle tittered condescendingly, the Chancellor's double chins bounced with every laugh. "There is no life beyond our shard," insisted a gray-haired man sitting next to Marinus. "Do you really take the Progenitor Scrolls that literally? Those people were basically savages. It's a miracle that they could even write!"

"That is hearsay! My research indicates that the Progenitors were more technologically advanced than we are today!" The professor stood firm in his beliefs.

The fifth circle member broke his silence, "That's ludicrous!"

"The Progenitor Scrolls also make mention of an orb which man could walk all the way around," argued Marinus, "are we to ignore all science that disprove that as well?"

"Orb? No, no, no, it's called a planet!" the professor's voice was soft.

More laughter arose from the circle, and the professor's face grew red with frustration. "It makes perfect sense. What explanation can you provide for the variation of culture and language of the people living on this shard? There is an entire tribe in the Aedunic Nation that has no resemblance to us physically! Furthermore, this tribe worships a cat! No other group can claim that! Can you truly believe that this divergence arose from a single race? Can't you see the most reasonable explanation for these anomalies is that we were once a whole planet and over time were separated from the other land masses? We are one of many shards, and I am certain—"

"Enough!" barked Chancellor Marinus. "Professor Belladon, while my fellow Circle members and I value your numerous inventions and past discoveries, your recent behavior concerns us deeply. These allegations of yours are unfounded and downright foolish. The Board has spoken. We feel that it is in the best interest of the University that you take a leave of absence. Your funding will be suspended during this time, but your salary will remain intact."

"No. I will not be silenced, and I will not be pushed out!" the professor continued rigidly, "I have proof. If you would only—"

Chancellor Marinus shook his head, leaned forward and smirked. "When the University first heard of your discovery, we sent professor Akroyd to validate your claim."

The Chancellor's smirk confused Professor Belladon. Professor Akroyd was one of the professor's closest and dearest friends. They joined the university at the same time and had led many expeditions together, and the professor had even saved Akroyd's life once. If anyone would back him up, it would be professor Akroyd. The snide tone with which the Chancellor spoke caused a cold sweat to form behind the professor's neck.

As if on cue, the side door of the auditorium swung open, and in walked professor Akroyd, draped in a black velvet robe. His expression was austere, and his posture was uncharacteristically stiff.

"Ah, professor Akroyd, what perfect timing. Please reiterate to the Circle and Professor Belladon what you found beyond the Castiel Mountain range?" asked the Chancellor.

Akroyd's voice was low and quiet, "Nothing."

"Could you please repeat that, professor Akroyd?" The Chancellor's voice dripped honey.

"There is nothing beyond the mountain range. It is my professional opinion that Professor Belladon's discovery is a complete fabrication," Akroyd noted, little louder.

"Unbelievable," sighed the professor, realizing defeat.

"You have forced our hand, Professor Belladon." sung the Chancellor "The Circle cannot tolerate this type of behavior. We refuse to stand by idly while you tarnish this University's reputation!".

The professor stood stunned. He could feel a migraine beginning in his left temple. He knew the Circle would be slow to accept such a monstrous threat, but he was astounded that his colleague would be willing to lie.

"Your resistance is understandable. A threat of this magnitude is difficult to face, but as our shard's academic leaders, a responsibility I know none of you take lightly, you're swift and immediate attention is more than necessary. Without action, the end…" It was at this moment the professor realized that the Circle was not in denial, and his friend was not lying to them. Akroyd was conspiring *with* them, to cover up the signs.

"Why are you doing this? Your adamancy in deceiving the shard will only hurt its people." The members of the Circle sat, emotionless.

"This meeting is adjourned, professor, thank you for your contribution. Your leave of absence shall begin next week after the student's finals. You will be notified when you've been approved to return."

As the Circle members left the auditorium, Chancellor Marinus approached the professor. "I sincerely hope you get some rest professor. These delusions of yours are quite worrisome. Listen, why don't you swing by my office in a few weeks when you've cooled down, we'll have lunch and discuss next steps."

"That's doubtful."

"Now Belladon, why is that?"

Professor Belladon began to gather up his scrolls and spoke matter of fact, "Because Marinus, by then, you'll be dead."

***

-Several hours later. Professor Belladon's office:

"What to do, what to do?" exclaimed the professor, walking back and forth in front of his desk. His assistants Dineela and Souza sat in chairs against the wall.

"We could appeal before the Steward? He has the final say in anything that happens inside the Citadel."

"Thank you, Dineela, but that won't work. We don't have enough time to deal with the bureaucracy of Citadel Proper. To organize a meeting with the Steward would take months. Plus, we have all seen the phenomena Diamin Theme. he is more than likely a leader of the conspiracy."

"Well we can't do nothing! Who else is there?"

Anxiety overwhelmed the professor. He never would have predicted that his best friend would turn on him so viciously. He agreed they had a moral obligation to address this threat, but he was running out of allies.

"I'll start a petition, I know everyone will sign to have you returned from your leave" Souza offered.

"No dear, that is the least of our problems." The professor's chest tightened. In a fit of rage, he swiped the ink well from his desk and hurled it against the wall. It shattered and black tears ran down the stone, staining the mortar. Dineela and Souza jumped in surprise. This was perhaps the single most important discovery in the history of the shard, and the lack of support from his friend and the University made Professor Belladon feel vulnerable and insecure.

Dineela tried to calm the professor, "I have been scouring the ancient scrolls of your archive, and some make reference to the end times, when true evil re-emerges into existence. They say a syndicate will emerge from the darkness to spread light. They are followers of the Maker, and will be led by the lineage of the God Slayer, the Constabularius."

"The Consta…what does that mean?" Souza looked to the professor who chuckled.

"My dear lad, the Constabularius is a tale as old as time. The Constabularius is a title given to the leader of the Maker's forces. This person is the purest essence of what is good, his or her values are unwavering. They strive to do what is right and defend against evil."

"So, we just have to find them and then the Constabularius will fix all this, right?"

"Not as far as I know. I've never found mention of who the God Slayer is, much less a record of his or her lineage."

The crew sat in a ponderous silence, broken by Steven's entrance with a tea pot and four porcelain cups balanced on a wooden platter.

"I thought you might be in need of some liquid comfort," he poured a cup and handed it to the professor. The amenity calmed him down immediately. Upon offering the second cup to Souza, Steven tripped over a short stack of books, and dropped the tea, platter and all. The piping hot liquid splashed against the wall, and the porcelain dishes shattered. "Oh, professor, I'm so sorry, I'll clean this mess up right away, and steam more tea."

The group began gathering the broken china, and mopping up the spilt tea, as the professor sipped, lost in thought.

"Stop! Stop! Stop what you're doing! I know what to do!"

***

-Six days prior to the expedition:

A deep rumbling broke the silence, and the professor's cheeks turned slightly red. "Forgive me. I forgot to have breakfast this morning." He was accompanied by his right-hand man Deiz, on the second floor balcony of an unused ward of the university academic building. Some years ago, a group of students were granted the ample balcony for a study area, and since then the students had run an under the table independent café. There read a sign hanging over the door, *Fon McCloud's Serenity Café*. Enclosing the ledge was a giant glass birdcage with green moss growing at its joints. Located at its center sat an ornate fountain topped with a statue of the late King Magnus, the Citadel's last king. Coffee tables and chairs surrounded the fountain. A stocked kitchenette was set up within the building.

"Thank you for joining me Deiz. I am sure you and your wife had better things to do today."

Deiz stared down at his menu, "No worries, professor. I am always at your service."

The professor grinned. "I hear the students have an appreciation for noodles and melted cheese."

Deiz found the dish on the menu. It was the cheapest item listed, "That sounds perfect, what about you?"

The two were interrupted by a waitress with short brown hair, "Hi, my name is Valissa, I'll be serving you today. Are you guys ready to order?"

The professor motioned to Deiz, "Go ahead, you order first."

"Alright, I will have the noodles and cheese."

"Anything to drink with that?"

Deiz smiled sheepishly, and waved at his bag, "I brought water."

The young waitress wrote down the order and looked at the professor. "So, how's my favorite professor doing today?" She smiled brightly, "Your usual?"

"My sweet Valissa, I'm feeling a little adventurous today. I think I'd like to try that new carbonated drink everyone is talking about, but drop a few cherries in it, will you dear?"

Valissa giggled, "You got it, Bell!"

Deiz watched the professor's eye follow Valissa as she walked away.

The professor looked up and saw Deiz's face was a bit askew. He was trying to hold back a laugh.

Realizing he had been caught staring, the professor scoffed, and then laughed lightly.

"I didn't realize you frequented here," stated Deiz, still trying to contain his smile.

"It's a capital little hideaway. It's one of the few places where I feel…" Ever distractible, the professor stared as a couple walked past their table. "That's odd."

"What is?" asked Deiz

The professor tilted his head to the left, "Those two. I have been coming up here for years, and never have I seen another professor step a foot in this place. You know, the University has tried to shut the Café down several times."

Deiz leaned back in his chair. "No, I didn't."

"They tried to keep it hush, but for years we've had meetings on the subject. The University has made up several excuses, 'It's not up to health code,' 'It's a safety hazard,' et cetera but that's all hogwash. The reality is the powers that be don't like the students congregating in a private space. 'Too much liberty leads to rebellion.'"

"I find it very interesting that professors Dinkly and Sherbert randomly show up here today. I'd be willing to bet the Circle sent them to keep an eye on me, to make sure I don't cause a scene before my leave begins."

"Or, maybe they just like it here? You know, it is possible they come on days you don't."

"My dear Deiz, you give people far too much credit. Dinkly and Sherbert are diehard Circle men. they are up to something, I'm sure of it. We'll tread carefully."

"Professor, don't you think you're being just a tad paranoid? I'm sure most of the faculty would agree that what the Circle did was completely unjustified!"

"Have you not been noticing the changes in people lately? Darkness is forming around us. You need to be careful in whom you place trust."

After several minutes of silence the professor started again, "May I ask you something personal? Where do you think our souls go when we die?"

Deiz inhaled, perplexed, "Well, first you'd have to assume we have souls."

"Okay, let's assume we do."

"Then I would hope our souls go somewhere peaceful," said Deiz simply. Professor Belladon raised an eyebrow, waiting for more.

"Well what do you think professor?"

The professor smiled seriously, "I believe that our souls are the most precious gift bestowed upon us, whether it's by the Maker or by nature itself. I am not sure where we go, but I like to think there is more to existence than all of this." The professor opened his arms, indicating the space around them, and nearly hit Valissa, who had just appeared with a package in her hand.

"Your drink will be right up, but here, professor, someone left this for you."

"Thank you, Valissa," answered the professor fondly.

Valissa handed him the leather sleeve and walked away.

The professor broke the seal and opened the package. He began reading a long scroll, "Very good indeed, the General Lord Ram Corporation has agreed to loan me as many Mark V's and VII's as I want." He handed the letter over to Deiz.

Deiz skimmed through the typed words, "Holy Arcadia professor, forty-five Mark VII's! Really? Those things are incredibly expensive and they are just giving them to you?"

The professor sneered, "I dare say they have little choice in the matter, as I am the inventor of those infernal contraptions, and though I don't own the company anymore, I made sure there were provisions in there to meet my needs."

"I have never understood why you sold your company to Lord Ram. He is the most rude, vile, egotistical fat man I have ever seen in my life." Deiz laid the letter on to the table and looked at the professor with angst, "Why him? Why did you ensure he would become one of the richest men in the Citadel?"

"He was already one of the richest men when I sold it to him," rebutted the professor, feeling quite old remembering the long ago day he had no choice but to give Lord Ram his company, "but the reasons are my own. Maybe one day I will tell you, but today is not that day. I need you to look at this." He pulled a scroll from his satchel and handed it to Deiz. "Let me know what you think."

Deiz didn't have to read far to understand the implications of the words. "So, you really are going through with your plan?"

The professor nodded and was about to answer when Valissa returned with the drink and noodles. The professor took the glass and smiled, he inspected the new carbonated drink closely. She paused at their table, waiting to see his reaction.

The professor took a tentative sip. It was cold and sweet, and he could feel the individual bubbles bursting on his tongue.

"Well, what do you think professor?"

The professor looked up at Valissa, "It's spectacular!" He was about to smile when suddenly a loud, uncontrollable burp erupted from his mouth. The professor was mortified, "My goodness, please excuse me!"

Valissa laughed. "No worries professor, the Carbonator affects everyone like that."

The professor's face burned red with embarrassment. She touched his shoulder and winked, "Let me know if there's anything else I can getcha, Bell."

The professor tried to say thank you, but the moment he opened his mouth, another burp escaped. He clapped his hands over his mouth and nodded. Valissa patted his shoulder and looked over at Deiz, "Enjoy your noodle melt!" before walking away to serve another table.

Deiz continued to read the scroll in his hands, "Professor, are you really sure this is the best course of action?"

The professor took another sip of his fizzy drink.

"An expedition?" asked Deiz in a harsh whisper. "How is an expedition going to challenge the horde of creatures we saw on the mountain range?! I'm going to be honest with you, I have a bad feeling about this."

The professor raised his index finger for a moment and took another sip from his drink, "I have some concerns about it myself. Regardless of whether this is the best course of action, it seems to be our only choice." He scanned the room right and left to make sure no one else was listening in, and spoke more quietly, "I'm certain whatever is controlling those abominations is searching for something on Elisia. I think this shard is the key to something much bigger!"

Deiz looked puzzled, "how could you possibly know that?"

The professor revealed a tiny scroll from his shirt pocket, "Dineela has been translating the Progenitor Scrolls we recovered from our last expedition. This one predicts that an evil entity will escape from the lonely stone, a small rock island in Lake Superion."

"The lonely stone?" asked Deiz. "There is a rock island in the middle of the lake? When will this evil be released?"

There was a twinkle in Belladon's eye, "I don't know, but I must find out!"

"You seem too excited about this."

"How could I not be? Don't get me wrong, those creatures scare me to death. But look at it like this, a unique opportunity has been presented to us, it's a chance for a true adventure, a chance to destroy evil and become heroes. Even greater, LEGENDS!" The professor slurped down some more of his drink. "You know, or at least die trying."

Deiz let out a heavy sigh, "Very well, I will start the paperwork with the university Quartermaster. I am not hopeful I'll be able to get everything approved before your leave."

The professor's eyes flashed, "No, no paper work! The Circle of ministers cannot get word of this!" He leaned in closer, "I have suspicions that the Circle members are already being controlled by this evil power!"

"How is that possible? I thought those creatures only inhabited the area south of the mountain range?"

The professor's face grew defensive, "Listen, what I witnessed the other day was not normal. I cannot say for sure how the creatures have infiltrated our University, but I guarantee you I'm going to find out! Something big is coming. Our only chance of survival is to foil this dark scheme before it breaks the veil separating our shard from their legions of—"

"Demons?"

"Yes, exactly!" The professor's hurried whisper had grown into a small hoarse yell, "Demons!"

"Someone sounds excited!"

At the sound of the new voice, the professor and Deiz jumped. It came from an attractive woman with wavy brown hair. Thankfully it was only Libby, Deiz's wife.

"Bless the Maker, you scared us, Libby!" hissed Deiz.

Libby smiled, "Oh lighten up, you're being way too serious. What are you up to anyway?"

"The professor has decided to embark on one last expedition before he takes his sabbatical," answered Deiz.

"How exciting professor! Your students must be lining up to go! I bet they're really going to miss you. Deiz told me all about it, taking a year to study the ancient Aedunic ruins sounds fascinating."

The professor cocked his head slightly confused, but when he saw the look of terror on Deiz's face he understood the meaning, "Oh yes, the Aedunic ruins, quite fascinating indeed. There's still so much to do before we leave!" The professor's voice was slightly strained, "I'm sure you two have something special cooked up for this evening, so I won't keep Deiz from you too much longer. We just need to finalize the expedition's security before he goes. I was thinking of hiring the—"

"Security?" interrupted Libby. "Why would you need security?"

The professor frowned slightly, wondering how she could not have heard of the recent dangers outside the Horizon wall. "Well, there has been many reports of merchants being attacked by men on horseback dressed in black and there--."

"I am sorry professor, but we should really get going," chimed Deiz. He stood up and pulled some coins from his money pouch.

"Put that away Deiz, I already told you the meal was on me!" insisted the professor.

"Thank you, sir, I will start preparations for the expedition first thing tomorrow morning."

Just then, Valissa appeared with a small paper box "Did you want your noodles and melted Cheese to go?"

Deiz started leading Libby away, "No, that's alright, the professor can have it. I know his stomach is empty, we really must be going now."

"Is he ok?" inquired Valissa.

The professor inspected the melted cheese with his fork, "He's juggling a lot right now."

Valissa smiled, "want some company?"

"You are always welcome at my table."

As Valissa sat opposite him, the professor noticed Dinkly and Sherbert leaving the cafe. The professor's mind raced with questions.

"Is everything alright, Bell?" Valissa noticed the concerned look on the professor's face.

He thought for a moment, "Valissa, how would you like to go on an adventure?"

***

-Five days prior to the expedition:

"Have you finished translating that scroll?" asked Souza, organizing some papers the professor needed for the expedition.

"Almost done," replied Dineela.

Souza walked towards her and leaned over her shoulder, "What have you got so far?"

Dineela felt the warmth of his body against her back. She glanced left and noticed his face was mere inches from her own. Her chest filled with static, and she held her breath.

Souza caught her staring up at him, "What? Do I have something stuck in my teeth?"

Dineela laughed and turned slightly red, "No, you're fine."

"So?" prompted Souza.

"Oh, right. Um, it's ancient. I think it may have been written during the barren period between the Progenitors and the early settlements. It describes a time when gods roamed the lands, two gods to be exact. These gods rescued the Progenitors from a great calamity."

"Gods? Really?" Souza sat back, and Dineela turned to face him, I thought there was only the Maker?"

"Well, their definition of God could be totally different from ours, though they use the same word. After the great calamity, the entire shard had to have been barren and dead. With nothing to eat and no place to live, the few survivors were probably scared and looking for any sign. I imagine the idea of these gods gave them the hope to move forward."

"Does the scroll describe these gods?"

Dineela took a small breath, "The scroll is badly cracked. I can only decipher detail about one of the gods. This god was the Blood Stone God, a genocidal maniac who ruled through absolute fear. There are many examples of torture, beheading, flogging, even cannibalism in its name. Despite all of these atrocities, people worshipped this god zealously."

"Cool, how twisted! So, what happened to the gods?"

"The information is fragmented, but it appears the two gods and their holy armies engaged in fierce battle over a tangible object of power."

"Who won? Does it say what the object was?"

"I don't know, we're missing parts of the page," replied Dineela. "The only thing I can piece together is that the battle, or part of the battle, occurred over the fields of Braum and into Veilwood Forest."

"How can you know that?"

"Because it says the battle was fought under an old, giant metal Chi-Ro, it was described as a warped metal beam that stands high in the sky. Now, do you know of any other mysterious warped metal beam?"

"Ok you got me there. Wow, a war between two gods. It must have been an epic battle. I wish we knew who won."

Dineela glanced up and down the scroll, in search of a specific passage. "There is a vague reference.., it says the defeated god was 'held,' but I'm not sure if that means that god was killed or just confined."

Dineela's mind raced with possibilities. For many years, she had thought the scrolls she'd been translating were fables, created by an uncivilized group of people, but lately she was realizing otherwise.

"Dineela?"

Dineela basked in her reverie a moment longer, then looked up and batted her eyelashes, "Yes?"

"You ok? I lost you for a second there."

"Do you know the story of The Blessed Paladin?"

Souza nodded, "Yeah, it's the one about the courageous Paladin named Gideon who defeated the wicked mammoth."

"What if the mammoth wasn't destroyed, but was imprisoned?"

Souza pondered the premise for a moment. "So, you think that the mammoth is really a god?"

"Yeah, well, think about it. When reading the story of The Blessed Paladin, I always assumed that the mammoth was killed, but the Paladin was blessed by the Maker because his soul was pure and good. If he were *truly* pure, he wouldn't have been capable of destroying another life. He would have instead chosen to imprison his enemy."

"That's kind of a stretch, Dineela."

Deiz entered the professor's office, "Hey, how's it going? Have you guys found anything yet?"

Dineela smiled brightly, "I think I may have found our Constabularius!"

***

-Four days prior to the expedition:

"I am one lucky woman!" exclaimed Libby, enjoying a scrumptious slice of steak seasoned to perfection. "How were you able to get us a table at the White Marble Plaza?"

Deiz smiled coyly, "I'm very important, they're lucky to have us." In truth he'd been tutoring the manager's son, and bartered a few lessons in exchange for a special dinner."

Libby set down her silverware, and pursed her lips in a tight smile "What's the occasion?"

Deiz looked sheepish. "Does a husband need a reason to do something nice for his wife?"

"Usually that means you have done something wrong and are seeking forgiveness. Are you trying to butter me up?"

"Not at all," confessed Deiz. "I just, I don't know how long I'll be gone on this expedition and I wanted to do something special."

Libby raised her eyebrows, but her lips maintained their smile.

"Honest! I swear!"

"Well, I appreciate it." She leaned in for a quick kiss. "It was very thoughtful of you to bring me to one of the fanciest restaurants in the Citadel."

A waiter returned to the table. His uniform was a black three piece suit. "May I offer you some wine while you enjoy your evening meal? Might I suggest our local Malbec?"

"Yes, please, bring us your best!" Libby blushed. Only the extremely privileged had actual waiters serving them.

"Very good, sir!" The waiter reappeared after a moment with an open bottle and tipped some into Deiz's glass. At the taste of dark fruit Deiz smiled, and the waiter filled their goblets.

"May I ask you something?" asked Deiz.

"Anything."

"Have you noticed anyone on campus acting oddly lately? I'm not sure what it is, but I've observed a few professors behaving quite strangely."

"Like who?" asked Libby.

"Like Dr. Oren and professor Kane. This morning I saw them roaming the halls dragging these over-sized burlap sacks. They were completely disheveled, and completely expressionless. It was extremely unsettling."

"My goodness, are they alright do you think?"

"I was going to ask, but they didn't look approachable."

"Weird. You know, what if they were let go? Bless the Maker, both at once. I hope I'm not next! I've only been teaching for a year. That would completely ruin our plans," Libby was working herself into a panic.

"No, no, don't be foolish. The Circle loves you. That's not it. I can't explain it, but I have this strange suspicion that some of the faculty is involved in something sinister."

"Well, I haven't noticed anything myself, I think someone has been spending too much time with a certain professor."

Deiz shrugged and sipped his wine. "You're probably right."

***

-Three days prior to the expedition:

Deiz rose from bed feeling anxious and quickly dressed. Libby woke when he sat on the edge of the bed to put on his socks and boots.

"Hey there, Constance," teased Libby, rubbing sleep from her eyes. "What are you doing up so early?"

"I promised the professor I'd meet him back at McCloud's. We need to prepare."

"Ugh, he takes up so much of your time. I hardly see you anymore."

"I know, but remember, it's only temporary. When I become a professor, things will slow down."

"And once that happens, we'll move closer to the university and start a family." Libby repeated the plan, as if saying it could ensure it would happen.

"Yes, but let's not get too excited. We still have to wait and see if our paperwork gets approved."

Libby shrugged off Deiz's worried comment, "I told you not to worry about the papers. My father's buddy is the principle C.O.G. in Lynthia. We'll definitely be approved."

"I hope so." Deiz finished tying his laces, and stretched to his wife for a kiss goodbye. She pulled him onto the bed, boots and all. "Libby, I have to go!" he managed, in between kisses.

"He's about to have you for weeks, he can wait." Libby whispered and then nibbled Deiz's ear playfully. To punctuate her point, she rolled over and straddled her husband. With very little hesitation, Deiz decided he could afford to be a little late.

***

McCloud's Café was quiet. Only a few students were having breakfast and fewer still were studying.

"I wonder where Valissa is today," the professor pondered aloud.

"Isn't she a little young for you?" smirked Deiz.

The professor made a face. He was glad for the joke. Deiz was one of the few people who felt comfortable teasing him. "Let's focus now. Who on the list has agreed to join us?"

"Almost everyone said yes."

"Splendid. What about Wrench, has he confirmed?"

"Wrench?" asked Deiz.

"Egon Kassidine. He's the best damn mechanic I've ever met, we *must* have him!"

Deiz glanced down the list. "Yes, Egon was a yes."

"Very good news," the professor nodded. "And who so far has declined?"

"Only two who said no. Ummm, Oliver Knight and Margret Pierce."

"Interesting, they're the only religious scholars on campus."

Deiz bent closer to the professor, "They didn't just refuse, they adamantly demanded to know who was planning such an expedition. Professor Pierce became furious when I refused to say. I had to quickly vacate her office because she was about to throw a chair at me. It's no secret whose man I am. it won't be long until she figures out I work for you."

"Most peculiar," replied the professor. "See, the Margret I know is a kindhearted soul. The very thought of her engaging in such violent behavior furthers my suspension that things are not as they should be."

The professor thought for a moment, "I think it is time we finalize security."

"Do you really think it wise, professor? Hiring armed strangers seems unnecessarily risky. How can we trust them?"

"I understand your concern, but we haven't many options. Aside from possibly Wrench, none of us are trained in combat. We're all eggheads. What will we do if we come face to face with a foe, throw a book at them?"

"Then, let's get ahold of some weapons and arm ourselves!" said Deiz passionately.

"I don't know Deiz, just the rumors of these black riders and massacres are enough to convince me to hire extra security. Let me think about it."

When the men finished brunch, they walked down the café's spiral metal staircase to the first floor of the school building.

"Well professor, if there isn't anything else, I will ensure that your contact inside the provision office meets every need you require of him."

"Very good Deiz, just remember to be careful!"

Deiz gave a half smile, "I will, professor."

The two exited the abandoned college building and walked north following a stone path towards the main campus.

The professor wanted to ask Deiz why he felt the need to keep secrets from Libby, but didn't know how to ask without offending him. Professor Belladon valued his relationship with Deiz greatly, it was beyond mentoring, he considered Deiz a true comrade. As they turned the corner and passed through the gates of the main campus, they entered the shade of a very old giant oak. The professor was stunned. The tree appeared to be dying. *This just can't be* he thought to himself. Only yesterday the tree was healthy and strong.

The professor stared at the thinning branches when something hard whacked him from behind. His knees buckled, and he fell to the ground. The professor looked up and saw a small, black robed figure jump onto Deiz's back and repeatedly punch him in the face. Deiz lifted his arms, trying to block the blows, but was unsuccessful. Trying to lift himself up, the professor was stopped by a severe pain in his back. He rolled several feet down a small grassy knoll. Professor Belladon pulled down his monocle in hopes of identifying the attackers, but its glass had shattered during the scuffle. He crawled up the hill and noticed Deiz in a fetal position. Two small people dressed in black were kicking him. The professor charged towards them. He jabbed the bottom of his cane into the gut one attacker, and then thrusted its handle into the face of the other. Each fell to the ground and squirmed. One landed on the path and blood ran between the stones. Belladon offered his hand to help Deiz up, but he had pounced onto the attacker lying in the grass. The professor watched as Deiz threw punch after punch, but somehow the person managed to overpower him and they rolled in the grass, entangled. The professor moved to help Deiz, but instead took the full force of a massive blow to his left temple. He crumbled to the ground. For several minutes the world was a blur, he was expecting to be struck again, but no hits landed. Slowly the world focused, and he found himself staring up at Steven.

"Bless the Maker, Steven! Help, please!"

Steven smiled, "They're not going to bother you now, are you alright? Who was that? I saw you two being attacked, so I intervened."

"How on Elisia did you do that?"

Steven helped the professor to his feet and motioned to a large rock that had been removed from the path.

"That was incredibly brave of you, Steven. I'm impressed, but more so, I am grateful." The professor chuckled and grasped Steven's hand in both of his.

They walked towards Deiz who was using a tree for support, holding the side of his head while cradling his stomach. Under him laid two black lumps on the ground, seemingly lifeless.

The professor jabbed his cane into one of the attackers, "Are they dead?"

Steven stared at the two bodies and spoke unemotionally, "They might be, I hit them both really hard in the head."

"Steven, I'm not sure how you managed to knock them out so quickly, but thank you, I owe you one," remarked Deiz, catching his breath.

"Don't worry about it. I'm just glad I got here in time." Steven turned to the professor, "Should I go inform campus security?"

"That won't be necessary Steven, not just yet," the professor kneeled next to the attackers to take a closer look. Both faces were obscured by black, cloth masks. The professor pulled off one of the masks, and gasped in shock. It was Minister Erna Nordheim, her skin was pale and wrinkled.

Deiz shook his head, "That's not possible. There's no way this frail old woman overpowered us."

"I was under the presumption that this woman could barely walk, much less attack two men!" The professor pulled off the other mask to reveal a much younger woman staring blankly. "My goodness, It's Valissa!"

"None of this makes any sense, why would she attack us?" asked Deiz.

"Perhaps she didn't have a choice?" answered Steven after several seconds of silence.

"You think someone made her do this?" Deiz shuddered at the implications. "What could they threaten her with that she'd be willing to hurt us?"

The professor spoke stoically. He was still staring at Valissa studying her, "She was forced against her will."

"How would someone force her to do something like this? Look at her skin, perhaps she was sick and delusional?"

"No, Deiz, she was not sick, this skin decay is not natural…" The professor's voice trailed off as his mind raced over the possibilities until he remembered something he read from a Progenitor Scroll. "They didn't do this. They were only vessels I surmise." The professor reached down and closed Valissa's lifeless eyes.

"Vessels? What does that even mean?"

The professor turned north and stared at the Citadel Proper. The Castle could be perfectly seen perching on its mountain plateau. "What it means, Deiz, is that my suspicions were correct. Our enemy has already begun its attack upon the shard. It's been happening for some time now, under our very noses. Like a cancer it has crept its way in slowly, eating away at our society. Our decadence and conformity made us all easy targets!"

Steven looked at the professor, concern obvious on his face, "You don't really think they can travel freely beyond the mountains?"

"No," stated the professor coldly, "If they could, they would have overrun us. But perhaps a small minority might have infiltrated this region. If we do not act swiftly, this evil will devour indiscriminately, no one will be spared. It must be stopped!"

Deiz was shaking, "Professor, I'm sorry. I don't know how much of this I can take. You're really starting to freak me out."

"Maker's balls Deiz, you should be afraid!" yelled the professor turning slightly red after using such a vulgar slur. "Now you know what we're up against. Let that fear power you! If we do not engage with urgency, everything we cherish will be destroyed," the professor's voice was hoarse.

Deiz stared down at Valissa. Just yesterday her face was like porcelain, pale and smooth. Now it appeared cracked, decayed. The professor stroked her cheek. A bit of skin flayed off and floated to the ground. The wound was brittle and dry, black stagnant blood began to slowly drip from her nose. The sight filled the professor's eyes with tears.

"I'm afraid I am to blame for this. She wouldn't have been chosen if not for me. Akroyd, Erna, Valissa, all gone because of me. I shouldn't have involved them." The professor dripped wet tears into Valissa's hair.

"Shouldn't have involved them?" demanded Steven, confused. "You saw evil and you wanted to stop it! Don't blame yourself. Blame the people who turned a blind eye, who have stalled your research, who have hindered your actions!"

The professor began to stand when Valissa reached out and grabbed his arm, startling him. Her yellow skin began to glow pink, and her wounds began to bleed normally. Clean red blood flowed down her cheek. She clenched her teeth, "Bell, it's coming back, I can't fight it!" She looked scared, like a child.

The professor stared deep into her eyes. "It's going to be ok sweetie, I am right here. You can't fight what?"

"*Him*!" sobbed Valissa, "He wants contr—" Valissa blanched, she could hardly get the words out. "He wants control, Bell".

"Who?" Deiz stepped in closer. "Who is he?"

"Stone bathed in the blood of a g--" Valissa abruptly turned and looked at Deiz, her eyes widened and tears streamed down her temples, "Everyone you love and care about..." She groaned and choked, "They're coming for her..."

"Coming for whom, Valissa?" Her body trembled slightly, the professor held her tighter. "You're doing well. Just hold on a little longer, you're going to be ok." The professor spoke trying to sound soothing, in almost a whisper. He stroked Valissa's hair.

Valissa struggled but her skin began to turn pale again and her blood started to flow black. She moaned loudly. The pain was so great, her whole body began to tense, her joints started to pop and bend in the wrong directions. She stared directly at Deiz, "YOU! YOU MUST GO NOW!" Valissa cocked her head sideways and spoke in a low dark demonic voice, "She will join or she will die."

Looking up at the professor, she reached up and stroked his cheek, "Goodbye, Bell!" Valissa's unnaturally cocked arm pulled out a small dagger from her robe and stabbed herself in the stomach. She trembled for several moments gasping for hair. The professor screeched in horror as her lifeless body collapsed against him. The professor lifted his head. Steven's face was frozen in shock, while Deiz was already running in the distance.

Steven barely was able to speak, "Where is he going?"

The professor sprung up, his face as wet with tears as his clothes were with the blood of Valissa, but his eyes filled with determination, "Come along Steven, we must hurry after him. Hopefully we'll get to Libby in time."

***

-The sun setting on the first night of the expedition, near the fields of Braum: Mark III Wagon: Forbidden

The professor dismounted Poncho and loosely wrapped his reins around a pipe connected to the single Mark III in the expedition. Looking to his left and then to his right, the professor reached into his jacket and pulled out a key. Unlocking the door, he opened it just enough for him to fit in sideways. Shutting it behind himself quickly.

The inside of the Mark III was spartan except for a few long tables and chairs. Most of the tables had scrolls, parchments, and old brittle books. The professor reached down, grabbed one, and began reading. Moments later, the door near the other end of the wagon opened.

"PROFESSOR!?" spoke Dineela, startled, "I am sorry, I was using the facilities. I didn't know you were coming?"

"It's quite alright," assured the professor, "Where is Souza? I don't want anyone to be alone in here as long as its locked up."

Dineela shrugged and frowned slightly, "He was getting a little crazy cooped up in here. He went for a walk. He said he needed to 'stretch his legs.' To be honest, I think he walked up to the front of the column to get a glimpse of Leora, he has a crush on her."

"Oh? I thought you two were...nevermind."

Dineela blushed and looked away embarrassed. The momentary silence was awkward, "I wasn't expecting you, professor. Our checkup isn't for another few hours."

"Thaddeus and his men returned from saving their scouts from an ambush."

Dineela nodded, "was it the Marshals? That's what the rumors are saying."

The professor cocked his head, "It was something like that. How is our guest?"

"Sleeping, for now. It's a blessing, the pain and torture is getting worse." Dineela's stance collapsed, she looked awkwardly at the professor like a child at a parent who didn't want to be there. "Are we sure this is the right way?"

The professor closed the book in his hand and sighed, "As much as it pains me, we have little choice in the matter."

Dineela reluctantly nodded, "It's just not right. She wants to die."

"IT!" corrected the professor harshly, "It's no longer a she. It's no longer human."

"What if it's both?" asked Dineela, "What if we are becoming no better than what we are--"

The professor slammed the book onto the table, "Enough Dineela, I will not debate you once more! Whatever that thing is in the forward compartment, it and its kind have killed innocents, including people we cared about. DIEZ, LIBBY! Don't forget about that. Our loved one's blood is on its hands!"

"Right." replied Dineela still struggling with what they were doing.

"Now, have you gotten any more information out of it?"

Dineela shrugged slightly, "Bits and pieces, nothing concrete. It's only as it's going in and out of control does there seem to be a moment when anything useful is told. A few names were said. My only guess is that they too have been corrupted, for the lack of a better word. I wrote the names down in--"

The professor seemed frustrated, "We are out of the Citadel now, names aren't going to help us. Has it talked anything more on the blood stone? Where in Veilwood is it? What does the stone have to do with anything or how to stop the creatures on the other side of the mountains?"

"Maybe? It did repeat the word shriek, over and over again. Followed by souls, need more souls."

The professor was confused, "What do souls have to do with anything?"

"I don't know." answered Dineela, reaching over and grabbing a scroll, "Souza found this passage about a creature called a Shriek, a deadly scavenger. According to the scroll, millions were created from the leftovers of the dead and became a foot soldier for a great evil."

"A great evil. I used to enjoy the cryptic nature of these scrolls and parchments. I love puzzles, but why does everything they say have to be so vague! Is this the evil we are dealing with now? Or some greater evil we will have to deal with later" remarked the professor, annoyed.

A loud, unimaginable scream suddenly roared through the Mark III's rear chamber. The professor's feet almost gave out, falling onto his cane for balance. Dineela grabbed her ears, the pain was horrible. The cry was coming from the front chamber. Rushing towards the front of the wagon, the professor entered the front compartment. A single, large table was riveted to the thick metal floor. Strands of rope and chains dangled off the table and down to the floor, securing the creature strapped to the table.

"THEY'RE HERE!" roared the creature in an unnaturally low voice, "COLLECT, COLLECT THEM ALL!"

"Who is here?" asked the professor, harshly looking down at the creature with pure disgust.

"LEGION!" answered the creature filled with rage and disgust.

"What is Legion?"

The creature did not respond, thrashing about, struggling against its chains.

"Tell me!" yelled the professor, "Tell me now! What is Legion? Where in Veilwood is the Bloodstone! What is its importance?!"

The creature began to laugh and spat at the professor. Furious, Belladon swung his cane down onto the creature's forehead, slamming it onto the metal table and leaving a nasty gash. Dineela cried out in shock and empathy.

"The dark lady, the bright blinding light," yelled the Creature in a higher voice filled with sadness and pain, "She is there!"

"Who is she?"

"YOUR DEATH!" roared the creature.

The professor smashed the creature's head again. "TELL ME!"

The creature's face softened and looked pleadingly at the professor, gasping for air. "She is the answer you seek, find the dark lady and the bright blinding light!"

"WE ARE UNDER ATTACK! WE ARE UNDER ATTACK!" yelled a voice from the outside.

The professor looked over at Dineela with fearful eyes. The creature began to cry. Belladon reached, leaned down and stroked its head softly. The creature recoiled, frightened it was going to be hit again. Seeing the utter fear in the creature's eyes he leaned down and kissed the side of its temple. "Thank you and I am so, so, sorry!"

The creature started to whimper like it was going to cry, without warning or hesitation is struck out forward trying to bite the professor's face. "HAHAHAHA!"

Startled, the professor stumbled backwards. Dineela rushed to his side and grabbed him, keeping him from falling. Once he regained his composure he moved to strike the creature again, but Dineela grabbed him by the arm.

"Please, don't!" she pleaded, "look!"

The creature was not scowling or laughing, it was crying.

The professor was confused he felt rage and compassion inside of him. He was distraught.

"TAKE COVER!" yelled someone outside.

The professor sighed, "I better go find out what is happening." Turning to leave, the professor only made it several steps when he suddenly felt a hand around his wrist. The creature had somehow slipped its arm out of the chain and leather straps.

"Please, KILL ME!"

"I am sorry, but I cannot."

The creature let go of the professor's wrist and reached towards its stomach trying to rip the skin from its own body.

"No, stop it!" yelled Dineela, wrestling with the creature's hand trying to place it back into its strap.

Once the creature figured out it was not going to kill itself, it gave up and began to cry uncontrollably. The professor's heart broke. He could not take anymore, he turned and left the front chamber, the creature still pleading to die.

"PLEASE, KILL ME! PLEASE, KILL ME, BELL!"

***

The professor mounted Poncho and looked for signs of danger. It was quiet where he was until the sounds of a horse cantering were clearly heard. An Equinaut on the other side of the wagon flew by with his rifle drawn. The professor urged Poncho forward and headed after the Equinaut.

Poncho was no match for the speed of the short, black horse ahead of him. He followed the rider past the wagons. A sudden burst of steam from the last wagon momentarily blinded the professor and scared the line of pack animals carrying gear and mounts for the Equinauts. The animals were balking, blocking the professor's path. They could sense the upset up ahead. He pulled back on his reins, and Poncho responded immediately. Night was rapidly approaching and the temperature had begun to drop. Belladon saw an opening and was about to lunge forward when a vicious howl made his skin crawl. A paralyzing shiver ran down his back. Something was inches away from him, breathing on his neck, he was sure of it. Fighting every instinct, he forced his head around to see what it was, but in the fog he could see nothing. The professor kicked his horse's side, trying to urge him forward, but Poncho stubbornly refused to move. Belladon had broken one of the first rules of riding. He began to panic, and his horse sensed it.

The bushes to the left of them began to aggressively shake, and a guttural moan loomed within the foliage. He could feel Poncho bristling below him, and his jaw hurt from how tightly his teeth were clenched. The horse couldn't take it anymore. He was spooked, and reared up. Belladon flipped backwards into a large puddle of mud. Wet and afraid, he listened as Poncho raced away. The professor couldn't pick himself up. He had pulled a muscle in his right side.

"That's the last time I tell anyone you have a backbone of STONE! You're a yellowbelly coward!" As he yelled, his right side throbbed with pain. He wiped the mud from his face with the sleeve of his shirt, but his vision was still blurry. Belladon managed to roll on his left side and hoist himself up onto his knees. Staring ahead into the smog, he saw movement, reached out, and felt cloth.

"Please, help me up!" pleaded the professor through his teeth, blinking mud from his eyes. There was no reply, only a heavy breathing. Straining, he lifted his chin. It took only half a second for him to wish he hadn't. Towering over him was a terrifying creature. Demonic, green eyes glowed beneath a thin black veil. The professor dropped the cloth, fell backwards into the mud and scrambled to put distance between himself and the thing before him. The creature swooped down and screeched in the professor's face. A large sword swung forward and the professor dropped flat on the ground, barely missing the blade. The creature hovered close, and drew its hand up, ready to stab down into the man. The professor kicked the demon with both his legs, sending it to the ground. He saw it rise up, and then up more, off the ground, floating in the air. It charged for him from above. Professor Belladon closed his eyes and waited for the inevitable, listening to the whistling sound that only comes from the swing of a sword. Death was coming for him, but nothing happened. His next sensation was a breath of hot air on his face. He opened his eyes to see Poncho nuzzling his cheek. Looking up, he realized he was now surrounded by several Equinauts.

"Professor, are you ok?" asked Italicus, hand outstretched.

The professor took his hand and stood up. "Did you kill it?"

"Edryss managed to wound it. She grazed its shoulder with her Plaz sword, and it flew off back into the brush."

"Aren't you injured?" asked the professor looking up at Edryss in an almost hero like admiration.

Edryss smirked and nodded.

"Well, thank you my dear, you are far stronger a person than me. Thank you, everyone. I didn't think I was going to make it. You guys are worth every penny I am spending. Could someone please get my water canteen and a rag? I need to clean the dirt from my eyes."

Zapp retrieved the items and brought them over to the professor. "Those were some nasty creatures!"

"Indeed. Thank you, very much!" Belladon poured some water onto the rag and wiped at his eyes, "Ah, that's so much better!"

Zapp helped the professor back up onto Poncho. "So, how many more of those horrid things are there?" he asked.

"About a dozen have been reported," responded Zapp.

"I hate to interrupt, but Thaddeus needs our help near the front of the column," urged Edryss. "We have to go, now!"

The group of riders set off, but they didn't get far. A group of creatures had several other members of the expedition surrounded. Most of them were cowering behind a Mark VII wagon that had tipped over. Niles, the farrier in training, was holding off about three of the demons using a long metal rod normally used to prop up a tent.

"Prepare the Teslas!" yelled Italicus.

"Niles, take cover," screamed Edryss.

Zapp warmed up his machine, "Let's show these devils how we play."

Italicus yelled fire, and the night's sky lit with bright neon beams of blue and red light. Most of the Equinauts hit their marks, but the Teslas had no effect.

The creatures began to circle Niles, who was crouched down with his hands over his head.

"Plasma swords OUT!" ordered Italicus.

The Equinauts charged forward with their blazing orange Plaz swords drawn. Before they could attack, the black-clothed creatures vanished into the woods. Italicus and his fellow mercenaries stopped just short of trampling Niles.

Niles slowly rose from the ground. He looked up and smiled meekly, "Boy, am I glad you guys showed up! What the hell were those things?"

"What happened to your sword?" asked Zapp.

Niles pointed to the ground. His plasma sword's hilt was in pieces and the blade, which was once liquid hot metal, was now a hard metallic pool. "When I activated my sword, they swiped at it with their massive claws. This is all that's left."

Several members of the professor's team were moaning in pain. They were seriously injured.

"Zapp!" ordered Italicus. "Stay here, and guard the wounded!"

Zapp dismounted, "Yes, sir!"

The professor approached on Poncho and jumped down to help. He was walking towards the wagon when he noticed Wrench crawling out from under it, covered in dirt and blood. "Wrench, my goodness, are you ok!?"

"Yes, it's not my blood. Lynette was hurt really bad."

"Goodness gracious, where is she?"

Before Wrench could respond, Italicus butted in, "Professor, we need to go. Thaddeus needs us!"

"Very well, be safe" said Professor Belladon to Italicus.

"No, professor, you need to come with us!"

"Is that really necessary? I need to take care of my friend. She's been injured."

"Yes, in fact, it's an order. We almost lost you once, and keeping you alive is a top priority!" declared Italicus firmly.

"Go on, professor, I will take care of Lynette." Wrench began to tear cloth from his shirt and wrap it around Lynette's wound. The professor was at a loss for words, he simply hugged the giant man.

"Let's go!" shouted Italicus.

Professor Belladon mounted Poncho, and waved back to Wrench. He couldn't help it, his eyes were fixed on Wrench's blood-stained shirt. Had organizing this expedition been a mistake? His tears blew off his cheeks as he urged Poncho forward.

Italicus and the rest of the Equinauts galloped towards the front of the column. The professor followed behind them in a less enthusiastic trot. The professor was stunned by the time he reached the head of the column. He had passed nearly a dozen of his people, injured. A large moan brought the professor's attention to his left where he saw a large bald headed man dashing between bodies lying on the ground. The Equinaut scout, Gladthorn, who looked almost as injured as the others, was bandaging an injured man.

The professor quickly approached the ad hoc triage. "Let me help!" he called out to Gladthorn.

"Start with him," ordered Gladthorn, pointing at a body lying to the left of the row of injured.

The professor was thankful to see many of the wounds were not life threatening. He moved from body to body, bandaging wounds where he could, and offering words of comfort where he couldn't. He stopped abruptly when a boy on the ground caught his eye. In that moment, all the blood in his body went cold, his stomach sank to his feet, and his heart cracked in pain. Lying before him was the lifeless body of Souza.

Gladthorn looked up to see the shock and pain on the professor's face. "One of those creatures tore a nasty hole in his chest, I tried to stop the bleeding, but the wound was just too big."

The professor's whole body shook. He wanted to cry out in anger and pain. *Why Souza? Why? Damn it, Maker! Why Him?* The professor knelt to stroke Souza's face.

"Poor Dineela," he whispered softly.

Gladthorn approached the professor and touched his shoulder gently. "For what it's worth sir, he was brave till the very end. He pushed right through the pain, even while I tried to bandage him up. I've seen men lose control over that much of pain." The professor didn't acknowledge Gladthorn's comment. He remained crouched down, motionless. His stomach was in knots, his gut cried for him to call a retreat. No more death, but he knew it was too late to turn back. With a heavy heart he turned away from Souza, knowing his death was not going to be the last, nor was it the first.

***

-Four days until the Expedition leaves, right after the attack on campus:

Deiz ran as fast as he could. Never in his entire life had he run with such determination. Nothing was going to stop him. The hardest part was getting through the college's shuttle station. He pushed his way through the line, and jumped on the shuttle headed for his neighborhood. He would have traveled the whole way on foot, but he knew no one could outrun the transit shuttle.

Eighteen dreadful minutes later the shuttle doors opened. Deiz bulldozed his way through an entire crowd of people, and ran for several blocks. The nastiest cramps formed around the sides of his torso, but he pushed himself onward. By the time Deiz made it up the stairs to the door of his apartment, his back and underarms were drenched in sweat. His mind was riddled with anxiety. All he could think about was his wife Libby, and if she was okay. After fumbling with his house key, he opened the door to his apartment. Deiz felt nauseous. Their entire apartment was trashed. Furniture was turned over. Paintings hung slashed on the walls, and dishes were smashed on the wooden floor. Obviously, there had been a massive struggle. Deiz stepped on tiny pieces of broken glass throughout the apartment, in search of his wife.

"Libby, where are you?"

As he made his way through the hallway that led to their bedroom, something caught his attention. Scattered all over the floor were broken pieces of melon-sized egg shells. He peered closer and noticed that a blue, yolky membrane clung inside every shell. Deiz kicked them to the side, and made his way further down the hallway. To his right, the bathroom door hung open. The body of a man was lying dead on the white tile floor. The man had a massive chest wound and a black mark on the side of his neck. It was a plus sign surrounded by a horseshoe, inside of a triangle, with a circle around it. At the very center was a white rock covered in red. Deiz had never known anyone with a tattoo, let alone seen a symbol like that. He had no clue what it could mean.

He walked past the bathroom and rushed to the last door in the hallway, his bedroom. Deiz tried to open the door, but it wouldn't budge. There was something in the way. He pushed with all his might and the door began to give a little. Deiz squeezed himself through. Another male body was stuck between the door and the bed. He too had the odd symbol tattooed on his neck.

Inside the bedroom everything was in chaos, the dresser drawers were open, and clothes had been flung everywhere. The bed was in complete shambles and the walls bore scorch marks, like from a fire or an explosion.

Deiz called out to Libby again, but there was no sign of her. A slight creak in the wooden panels of the closet door alerted to him someone was hiding inside. Deiz slowly walked over to the closest doors, his heart pounding. He found a piece of broken wood and picked it up. Until today, it had been part of the frame surrounding the large mirror attached to their dresser. With the make-shift weapon in hand, Deiz quickly swung the closet doors open. There, sitting inside, was Libby in a pool of blood. She had her face between her legs and her clothes were shredded.

"Libby?" asked Deiz softly.

She raised her head. Her face was bruised, bloody, and swollen. Deiz could hardly recognize her. He dropped to his knees and wrapped his arms around her. "Bless the Maker, you're alive!"

Her body shook uncontrollably and her breathing was erratic.

Deiz tried to soothe her, "I'm here baby, I am right here. Everything is going to be ok. We need to get you to a hospital."

"NOOOOO!"

Deiz jumped in fright. She sounded different. Her voice was gravelly and demon-like.

"GOOOOO! Get away from me!" she cried out frantically, trying to push him away.

"Libby, what's wrong with you?"

"It's in me, Maker help us, it's in me!"

Deiz was frightened, "What do you mean? What's in you?"

"I thought I had stopped them in time. They were chanting something awful, something dark! It wanted inside of me, it said I had to say yes. I had to let him in. Oh Deiz, the pain! The pain was so bad, my whole body burned." Libby was panting, speaking faster and faster, crazed and confused. "I had to say yes, I didn't have a choice. The pain, it had to stop. It had to! Once I said yes, I saw an opening. I killed them, I killed them both! To stop him from entering me, I killed them both with this!" She revealed a small blade. It was the letter opener Diez kept on his desk.

"You did what you had to. They're dead now. Nothing can hurt you," consoled Deiz. "Whatever it was, it didn't find you, you are ok, baby!"

Libby hugged Deiz tightly and then pushed him away and screamed at the top of her lungs, "BUT HE FOUND ME!"

Deiz crawled closer to his wife and hugged her once more, "It's ok, whatever it was, it's gone now. There's no one here, nothing can hurt you!"

Libby rested her head on Deiz's shoulder. She could feel every breath her husband took.

Suddenly, she grabbed him tightly, and lifted her face towards Deiz's ear. She wrapped one arm around his face covering his mouth. Deiz struggled against her but he could not break her bond. She began to lick Deiz's cheek erotically, like she was tasting something sweet. Deiz tried to pull away, disgusted and confused. Libby's tongue touched the rim of his ear, she blew softly into it, giggled and moaned. She finally whispered slowly but passionately, "hhhheeeee's ssssttttiiiillllll hhhheeeerrreeeee."

Deiz panicked and fought to break away from his wife when a sharp pain pierced his neck. He felt the warmth of blood flowing down his shoulder, and gasped for breath. Libby pushed Deiz onto his back, straddled him, and then pulled his head forward by his hair. Her face was twisted and her skin appeared jaundiced.

"Your soul is useless!" she screamed.

Deiz was losing consciousness and could hardly speak, "ppplllease Libby, it's me."

Libby exposed the dagger in her hand, and repeatedly stabbed him in the chest. She laughed and panted like a whore, becoming more aroused as blood spattered from her husband's body.

The amorous laughter became cries of overwhelming sadness and shock. Libby's skin returned to normal as she let the dagger drop from her hand. She slid off his body and backed into the corner of their room, hyperventilating.

Just then, she heard a voice coming from the hallway.

"Deiz! Are you here!?" It was Professor Belladon. He peered through the small opening of the bedroom door, and slid through it.

"I didn't mean to, something came over me" Libby managed between sobs.

"It's alright Libby, I know it wasn't you, everything will be fine."

"FINE!? It can't be fine, I just killed my husband!" Libby suddenly grabbed her head with both hands and started to scream in pain, "It's coming back, GO AWAY!"

"Fight it Libby, you must!" pleaded the professor.

"I can't!" yelled Libby, "It's too strong!"

"Fight it!"

Libby looked up at the professor, part of her skin started to change again. She ran towards the window and vaulted through, shattering the glass. "NOOOOO!" yelled the professor.

Professor Belladon sprinted over to the jagged opening and looked down, expecting that a fourteenth story drop would be fatal, but there was no evidence of her remains. Libby had completely vanished.

"Professor?" asked a voice behind him, "What on Elisia happened here?"

William F. James

The professor turned towards Steven and began to cry, overwhelmed with emotion.

"Professor, what are we going to do?"

The professor knelt at Diez's side, his protégée. Losing him was like losing a son.

Steven watched as the professor's face went from complete sorrow to absolute anger and resolve. "We are going to stop this evil from killing anyone else. The first thing we must do is locate the Constabularius." The professor stepped over Deiz's body and left the room. Steven was still processing what had happened when he heard the professor call out from the hallway.

"Come along Steven, we are going to find ourselves a God Slayer!"

Echo from the Past

Power is a most provocative seductress. Mine was a beautiful, terrible, delicious addiction. The ability to control all around you, the rush, the high you get from having dominion over all, that life and death of millions are solely in your hands. It's the purest forms of ecstasy. I had all that once in the city of Leisöstrung, my city, my domain.

Ever ambitious, thirst for power could never be quenched. I spent far too long in my Sanctum Sanctorum, searching for the descended power, so sure that it was the key to absolute dominance. I knew without a doubt that the power, that energy, was calling out to me. It haunted by my every thought. It had to be mine, it had to be mine!

I spent weeks focusing my mental state, searching for its exact position. I sent out countless numbers of expeditions, so sure that I had pinpointed the power I sought. With each failure, my vessel warned me a god must be absolute and never wrong, never to make a mistake, for a mistake would only breed contempt and questioning. It was the first time I ignored my vessel advice. She was right. My worshippers began to question me. If I had only listened, but nothing mattered- only the power.

My vessel asked me to leave my Sanctum Sanctorum, suggesting I take my own form, a feat I had not undertaken since our beginning. Holding form required so much energy and concentration, possession of a host was so much easier. I think she was planning to kill me. Why else ask me to take form? I was certain she had no clue how to kill an ascended being like me, but for a lifetime we had shared thoughts. Perhaps she had gleaned from my own mind how, or perhaps she was more cunning than I knew.

Fate kept me from finding out. I missed the signs. Had I not been so intently focused on finding the power, I would have seen this new threat coming. A bright flash of light engulfed the entire city and then the barren fields of dust that had finally been showing signs of regrowth were covered in darkness. We saw the black forms of a million men and creatures outside our walls. An army had appeared out of thin air and they were ready for an attack.

The bells rang and the alarms signaled. My holy warriors rushed to prepare themselves for the coming onslaught. My vessel and I remerged together, but part of her mind was cut off to me, like she was forcibly forming a mental door. It troubled me greatly, but we had more pressing concerns. Energy pooled in my hands, and I fought the tide cascading against my walls. Thousands perished.

My vessel and I laughed at the pitiful attempts this army made at gaining the walls. My holy warriors had nothing to do but watch their god destroy their enemies, proving the absolute power I wielded, solidifying their love and worship. They would never doubt me again.

I was sure this enemy army would soon retreat, but they sent forth wave after wave of charges against my walls, each of them failed. That was part of his plan. He sent his men to their deaths, to find my location.

In a swirl of smoke and light, a figure appeared in my temple. He was not an Ethereal, nor was he Fallen, he was a man. He was the first of his kind a man with magic- a man with power.

This gorgeous regal man claimed to be my better and assured me he would take my city, my worshipers, and my power away from me. My vessel and I laughed at the thought. The man mumbled some words and pure energy leapt from his hands and struck me to the ground. The pain was excruciating, not since my fall from grace had I felt such pain. It made me angry. I returned his attack, and we fought for hours on top of the temple. My worshippers watched the light show from the ground, unsure of what they were witnessing.

The new threat's army then started their real attack, their real siege, letting loose thousands of catapults and ballistae, destroying the mighty walls my people had built.

The fight was brought to Leisöstrung's streets. All of my people, my men, my women, and my children stood their grounds to fight for their god and their lives. I could hear their prayers, their cries for help. They spoke my name, faithful to the end. I ignored them. My fight was with one man.

How a simple mortal could wield such power, how he could match my own power vexed me so, until I realized: the descended power, he had it. The realization that I had been right about the locations of the power, my worshipers just weren't fast enough. That was why they couldn't find it, it was constantly moving within him! He used it to gather an army.

The fighting outside raged on both sides fought valiantly convinced that the heavens were behind their cause. Aaron desperately tried to form a blockade before the temple grounds, but soon they were over run. He ran with all his might to the top of the temple.

The magic man was relentless in his attacks and I could not stop him. The pain was great and overwhelming. My vessel and I tried over and over again to stand up and fight, but his power was too strong. We could not break the magical shield he protected himself with. He looked aside and laughed at the sight of the temple guards losing the entrance. His men swarmed around the grounds and would soon make their way to the top so they could witness the death of a god. He offered my vessel and I a quick death and a quick death for my worshipers that would not bow before him. I could not let him beat me. I could not lose all I had made! My vessel and I agreed that if this was to be our last day, then all would burn!

Italicus

Chapter Six

From the first scroll of Zakarael, chapter 8 verse 17:
"If your brother sins against you, go and tell him his fault. For nothing is hidden that will not be made manifest, nor is anything secret that will not be known and come to light."

Wrench recounted the vicious attack of those dark hooded creatures in his mind, his heart still racing. He felt ashamed for hiding beneath a wagon during the attack, but hopefully his lack of courage would save the lives of Lynette and the others he had grabbed and pulled under. A phrase continually repeated in his mind: *Thank the Maker for the Equinauts*. Had it not been for the timely arrival of Niles, he was positive the creature would easily have killed everyone nearby.

Wrench and Zapp carried the last of the wounded to a modified Mark V Ironhorse steam powered wagon that had been converted into a simple medical facility. The man Wrench was carrying was unconscious with a bad laceration on his forehead. Though when he looked down Wrench didn't see a man. His mind was not focused on the present. This was his fourth sprint with an injured comrade in his arms. The image in his mind that he couldn't shake was that of Lynette. She was the first person he and Zapp had rushed to the Medical wagon and the most severe. He couldn't shake the desperate and hopeless feeling he had holding the poor woman in his arms, her breaths sounding shallower with every step he took. When they arrived at the medical wagon, Lynette and the rest of the wounded they had carried were still alive, but barely. Inside, they tried to assist the medics as best they could. Zapp had some battlefield training but had never before put those skills to use.

Soon they realized they were inevitably getting in the way more than helping, so the two left their wounded to the few skilled medics the professor had convinced to join the expedition.

"Do you think everything is ok now?" asked Wrench, stepping down out of the medical wagon. "Are those bloody creatures gone?"

Zapp was unsure, "I would like to think so. It's been almost an hour since the last sighting."

"What do you think they were?"

Zapp shrugged his shoulders. "Who the bellows knows-Honestly, I don't think I want to find out either."

A cold shiver travelled down Wrench's back. "Neither do I."

The men sat on a long narrow crate, breathing heavily, watching the steady line of injured slowly trickling in.

"I'm just glad we got that girl to the medwag before this lot. I didn't think she was going to make it. She lost a lot of blood".

"Lynette is a trooper. If anyone can, she'll pull through," answered Wrench. He wanted to believe what he was saying. "No thanks to me."

"Don't be so hard on yourself, you had the sense to pull them under the wagon, it was the safest place to be."

"Never in my life have I been in situation where I couldn't protect myself," bellowed Wrench with a false sounding bravado, "I mean look at me lad, I am huge! But those creatures, they were bigger and stronger! There was nothing I could do. I was helpless as a child."

"Against them, we're all children. Besides, regardless of your size, fighting's not all about strength, there is so much more to it. You have to use your wits with your strengths. Plus, you need a weapon, not just your bare fists." Zapp grabbed one of Wrench's hands, "Damn, these hands are huge. *You* might not need a weapon." Zapp handed Wrench his Plasma sword hilt, "Here, turn it on."

Wrench looked at the device. He had never held one before. It was small in his hands, and he fumbled over the button to activate it. The blade ignited out of the hilt. The metal was solid and liquid at the same time. It glowed red and slightly orange but resembled dark steel, "Now what?" Wrench asked.

"Swing at me!" said Zapp, light heartedly.

"Hit you?" asked Wrench, "I'll kill you, no!"

"You won't even touch me, I promise you!" Zapp winked as he rose from the crate.

Wrench wanted to laugh, but he held it in. Zapp was standing in front of him, hands hanging loose at his sides, his eyes closed. Wrench stood, and hesitated for a moment, staring down at Zapp's relaxed body. Then he swung down with the sword. Zapp never flinched or gave any indication at all that he was going to move out of the way. The side of the blade was nearly upon him and still Zapp did not move. The plasma whistled through the air where Zap had been standing. Wrench blinked in disbelief that a man could move that fast. Zapp had tilted his body slightly to the left and lowered his head missing the blade by a half inch.

Zapp opened his eyes and smiled, "Try it again."

Wrench stood still, eyes wide.

"Come on, don't be chicken!"

Wrench shook his head and swung again. Zapp bent backwards and missed the blade once more.

"My one-legged grandmother could swing better than you," teased Zapp.

Smiling, Wrench swung and again, Zapp dodged it. Determined, he stepped sideways and lunged the sword forward. Sparks flew as the sword contacted with a tree. Circling, Zapp smacked Wrench on the rear and laughed.

Wrench was not accustomed to losing. He swung as hard as he could, trying to catch Zapp, who reached behind his jacket and pulled out a large plasma dagger. As Wrench's sword swung by, Zap caught it with his dagger. He dropped to one knee and spun in place, knocking Wrench off balance and onto the ground.

Wrench was now lying in the dirt on his back. He could not believe that he was staring up at the stars. Suddenly, a funny little face was blocking his view.

Zapp smiled, "See my friend, it's not about strength, it's about reading your enemy, anticipating his movement. I waited to get you so frustrated that you over extended, it's one way a smaller man can defeat a large, stronger man."

Zapp helped Wrench up.

"Can you teach me how to do that?" asked Wrench.

Zapp smiled, "You will be my greatest, and largest student!"

The men's laughter was brief. Glut appeared out of the fog, practically dragging Dean, both were covered in blood.

"Garret!" yelled Wrench, "Maker's beard, are you ok? Where is your sister?"

Zapp swung Dean's limp body over his shoulder and rushed him into the medical wagon. Glut's eyes were frozen open, he looked like he was about to faint. He tried to answer Wrench but couldn't force sound from his mouth. Wrench understood that something was very wrong.

"Where is she? I'll go get her!"

Glut grabbed Wrench by the arm. For several long seconds Glut simply stared up at his tall, large friend and shook his head minutely back and forth. When he finally spoke, it was a soft whisper choked with tears, "I don't... I don't quite understand what just happened."

Zapp stepped down from the medical wagon, "We were attacked by some form of creature."

Wrench nodded, "They caught us with our knickers down."

Glut was still staring off into space, still in shock.

"Where are you hurt?" asked Wrench.

Glut shook his head, "It's umm, not my blood. Its Dean's and it's ummm," he gulped. "It's Andi's."

Wrench's eyes filled with tears, "I am so sorry, my boy!"

A high-pitched whinny echoed off the wagons. Glut hid behind Wrench, clutching his large arm. "It's ok, Garret, it's just a horse. Why don't you go into the medical wagon where it's safe, huh?"

Wrench led Glut into the medical wagon and set him in a chair next to Dean. It was unclear whether Dean was alive or dead. He was at least unconscious and looked white, as though he'd lost a lot of blood.

Zapp sat back down on the long, narrow crate and tinkered with his puzzle box.

"What's inside?" asked Wrench, walking down the wagon's steps.

"I don't know, the person who gave it to me said I would save a heart with it. Not really sure what that's supposed to mean- could be anything."

Moments later Glut exited the wagon, his face pale. Wrench and Zapp feared the worse.

"Is Dean ok?" asked Zapp, tentatively.

"He's alive, but barely. They ummm, they…" Glut cleared his throat. "They lost Lynnette, uh, lost… she lost too much blood. There was nothing they could do," Glut answered softly past a lump in his throat, "I um, I'd never seen a dead person before. It was not what I thought it would be. It was a lot worse."

Wrench and Zapp were at a loss for words. Wrench in particular felt like he had failed.

Glut started to speak steadily in a low voice, his heart pounding in his chest, "Those creatures, they came out of nowhere. One killed our driver, then it forced its way into the wagon. It almost killed Dean, stabbed… it stabbed Andi, with a sword. Why? The nicest, smartest person I know. Why, she never did anything to deserve that." Glut's shock was growing into anger. "We will… I will kill every single last one of them, THOSE BASTARDS!"

Glut continued to mouth a few more words, but no sound came out. His eyes rolled up into his head and he collapsed to the ground. Wrench leaped off the crate, scooped Glut off the ground, and carried him back into the medical wagon. A medic handed Glut a serum to drink, something to calm him.

When Wrench returned, he and Zapp headed to the overturned wagon. They joined with some others to upright it. Zapp looked around and slapped the side of his leg, "He did it to me again. Ugh, I really need to find my horse. Who knows where he's wondered off to?"

"I'll help you find him," offered Wrench, glad for something to do.

"I'm sure all we have to do is find the closest mare." The annoyance and frustration in Zapp's voice was clearly heard. "Face will be there, whispering sweet nothings in her ear. He was gelded at an early age, but he keeps thinking he's still a stinking stallion."

The two looked for signs of Face, but all they found was evidence of the attack. Blood mixed with the dirt trails and people limping to the medical wagon.

"This is worse than the Blue Forest," reckoned Zapp in frustration.

"The Blue Forest?" asked Wrench, "How's this like a myth?"

"No, it's fact. It's just northwest of the city of Del. A small valley, south of Mount Procidengratia," answered Zapp.

"You're pulling my leg, lad"

"I am not. During the war we were escorting a convoy for the Citadel, and the Slavine wanted to raid the convoy really, really badly. It was a hundred of us against two thousand Slavine soldiers. Outnumbered, Thaddeus ordered us to go around the west of Del, you know, use the city as cover. What he didn't realize was that those damn Dellian Senators, so consumed with staying neutral, would do nothing when two thousand Slavine soldiers showed up at their walls. We had to find a place to hide. We ended up in the valley, and that's when we saw it. An entire forest vibrantly green, the trees were luscious and thick, a quiet river flowed through the middle, it is true paradise!"

"See there Zapp, you mean you found the *green* forest."

Zapp smiled "No, everything – and when I say everything, I mean *everything* – every tree, every leaf, every blade of grass, gave off this aura of pure blue energy. I cannot use words to adequately describe the beauty of this place."

Confused, Wrench asked "Ok, let's pretend you're right, how on Elisia is right now reminding you of that?"

Zapp's face grew serious, "Something lives in the Blue Forest, something unnatural, something powerful. We realized this on the second night camped there. We were settled near a river and I was on guard duty. A bright figure in blue appeared at the river bank. At first, I thought all the energy was playing tricks on my eyes, but I saw it. Its eyes, its fingernails, parts of its skin were black as the night sky. It reached out for me and I think it growled. I was overcome with anger and sorrow. I was sure I was done for, when suddenly an arrow came flying through the air and struck the creature from behind. The arrow was shot by the Slavine. They had found us and were attacking. I don't know if they meant to hit that creature or not, but it turned on them. Thaddeus ordered a quick retreat out of the forest. I was one of the last to leave. Two thousand Slavine went up against this creature. I am pretty sure there were no survivors."

"It didn't attack you though?"

"No, it didn't. Perhaps two thousand Slavine was enough for one night, or maybe it wasn't planning to attack anyone until it was struck. I don't know for sure, I just know that was the first time I saw something beyond normal, it scared me to death. But at least then we all got away safely. Now though, here are these unnatural, dangerous creatures who are attacking us, killing us. I hate to say it, but I'm down right scared. How can anyone wrap their minds around crap like this?"

Wrench shrugged his shoulders, "I'm a mechanic, not a philosopher. I just know I want to stay alive, and if I can, stop this evil. I think of my brother. I'm happy to do this for him and for people like him. When good men do nothing to stop evil, the evil has already won. If this evil is escaping the mountains, then we are their only chance."

Zapp smiled, "You know Wrench, you may be a philosopher yet!"

***

Life had changed. it was no longer as it seemed to be. The world and universe were in chaos. Thaddeus tried to focus himself, but his head was throbbing and the ground was spinning out of control. He tried to stand up straight, but that just made things worse. He was pretty sure he was close to retching.

At least the pain in his head was subsiding. The pain had been debilitating. It cried out a word. The only word that seemed to matter:

"AWAKEN."

A voice in his head that was both familiar and strange.

"Thaddeus, are you ok?" The question broke Thaddeus' trance. His head was still ringing and spinning, sight had yet to fully return. At the sound of the voice, Thaddeus tried to stand up straight, his legs wobbled, and he reached out for support nearby.

"I am fine, I think. Everything keeps spinning. Oh Please!" Thaddeus made a very unnatural grunt or cry, "Come on now ground, stop spinning." Vision was slowly returning. Shadows becoming colorful blurs.

"You're fine, is that so? Are you sure?" Thaddeus recognized this high-pitched voice. *But it couldn't be.* "Then would you care to explain?" The voice was slightly too high and ended with a "humph."

Thaddeus felt like the spinning in his head was starting to slow, he tried very hard to focus in on the direction of her voice. He was sure he could hear her breathing, the voice had to be leaning on the same support he was. It struck Thaddeus as odd that the voice was so close to him. In fact, it made him a little claustrophobic. Why was she hovering over him? She was too close. Thaddeus, for a moment, felt his headache settling. He let out a huge sigh, then the pain came rushing back and light-headedness started to take over. Thaddeus was going to fall, he was sure of it. He leaned heavily on whatever it was that was supporting him. The support wasn't firm though, it began to move as he placed more weight on it. Thaddeus suddenly realized his support wasn't as reliable as he had hoped. In fact, he was now having a hard time holding on at all. Thaddeus' right knee was about to give out and he reached out with both hands towards his support, grasping clumsily trying to get a better grip. A sudden spasm of pain erupted from the side of his face. Thaddeus wasn't sure what caused that pain, but it snapped him back to reality and his eyes began to see more clearly a tall, red wall. Thaddeus focused on his hand that was stretched out in front of him, and beyond his hand was Leora.

Leora's face was fixed in shock, her eyes wide open, her lips gaped slightly. "Usually, a woman gets dinner before this."

Thaddeus was still disorientated and Leora's words made no sense to him. For a brief second, he smiled, trying to force his brain to comprehend what was happening, and several moments passed as the two stared at one another. Thaddeus realized that he wasn't alone with Leora. The professor and several others surrounded him. Their faces were a mix of confusion and concern.

Thaddeus' eyes quickly opened and his face turned as red as Leora's hair once he realized where his hands were. Lifting his hand from Leora, Thaddeus looked around, "What?"

"What happened?" asked the professor. "You screamed out in pain and fell to the floor."

Thaddeus dusted himself off and gave a sheepish smile to Leora, "I'm not sure. The last thing I remember was talking and a sudden intense pain." Thaddeus grabbed at his head, "It was consuming. I've never felt that kind of pain before."

The professor placed his hand on Thaddeus' back, "Let's get you to one of the medwags, hmm? You should rest for a bit."

Thaddeus bristled at the thought. "No!" His voice was firm. "There was something else, a voice, and maybe images." Thaddeus grew frustrated, "They're fading. A bright orb of light, a blood-soaked stone and a voice, a voice that said—"

"Awaken?"

Everyone jumped at the surprise of hearing a strong voice emanating from behind the closest wagon. A slender, dark figure was obscured in the fog and slowly walked towards them.

Thaddeus exclaimed, "Yes, exactly!"

"Wait! Did, did you say the word awaken?" asked the professor.

"Yes, I did. I heard it, in my head, just before I died! Well, before I should have died!" shouted the voice, walking from the shadow of the steam powered wagon. The figure walked into the light, it was Andi. Her shirt was ripped across the middle and her vest stained red with blood, her short blonde hair was completely disheveled and her eyes burned with fire. Lifting her shirt, she revealed her fit, flat stomach, and to the left of the belly button was a scar, 3 to 4 inches in width. Thaddeus' own experience told him it was a large knife or sword wound.

The group looked at Andi with disbelief, "It's true! I was stabbed, I was bleeding to death. I could feel life slowly fading from my body. I remember how cold I felt and I couldn't breathe, and all these colors were whirling around me and suddenly—"

"A blazing hot pain shot through your excruciatingly cold body and then no pain at all?" finished Thaddeus.

Andi's eyes bulged in disbelief. Thaddeus understood what she barely understood herself, "Yes, exactly."

Thaddeus walked up to Andi and reached into her pocket, pulling out his medallion. "That's exactly how I feel, just before I am healed by this!" He raised his medallion, its wings still glowed a slight orangish color.

"What is that?" asked Leora.

"It's a family heirloom, and it's very powerful. It heals me if I am ever mortally wounded! In the thousands of years it's been in my family, it has never once healed anyone outside our line." Thaddeus stared intensely down at Andi, studying her, hoping to find some answers.

"May I see the medallion?" The professor asked, fascinated, rubbing his chin.

Thaddeus handed it to him. The professor's monocle swung down from his top hat, and he began to inspect the medallion. "I need some light." remarked the professor moving towards a lantern hanging off one of the nearby wagons. "Yes, marvelous workmanship. Progenitor in origin, late dark age. I am simply guessing here, but perhaps you two were meant to find each other? Yes, it has to be. Why else would there be a connection like this?" The professor babbled on enthusiastically while analyzing the medallion, reading the ancient words.

"Maybe they are brother and sister! Right? What else could it be?" Leora offered, a little too loudly.

Thaddeus was completely captivated by Andi at the moment. He stared at her unblinkingly. The very idea of the medallion healing another person was unheard of. Maker knows he tried desperately to get the Medallion to work on dying friends and family, including his wife Alana.

Andi felt uneasy, she was not sure how to take Thaddeus' intense staring. She was confused enough as it was having no idea why he was so fixated on her.

"Thaddeus," the professor called out waving him to come over.

Thaddeus hesitated to move. His eyes were still fixated on Andi.

"Thaddeus?"

Turning away, Thaddeus left Andi and walked towards the professor.

Leora was distraught. She too had no clue to the reason why Thaddeus couldn't take his eyes off Andi. When Thaddeus finally began to walk away, Leora tried to get his attention but Thaddeus' mind was not in the here and now. "Thaddeus, what's wrong? What does this all mean?" Thaddeus ignored her questions. Leora wasn't even sure if he had heard her.

Andi recounted her story for the third or fourth time, the sudden noise on the roof, the creature ripping something out of the driver's chest, Dean getting stabbed, followed by herself getting stabbed and feeling her body failing, her life slowly being extinguished, how she died and then had somehow not died, feeling a spreading burning hot pain and the abrupt word awaken. Following the attack, Glut rushed Dean to the medical wagon. That's when she came here, looking for the professor, hoping he had an answer to how she came back to life.

Of course, the professor wished he had answers, but he was as baffled as anyone else. Thaddeus and Andi pondered the word and meaning behind it. The professor admitted that he too had heard the call. Leora tried desperately to be part of the conversation, but eventually understood she had nothing to offer and trudged away feeling the nasty tinge of jealousy. It was not often she was ignored.

Steven marched up to the group and presented the professor with a cup of tea. His calm demeanor and goofy smile perplexed everyone. He was acting as if there had been no attack, and he was unfazed by Andi's near-death experience. Steven was bouncing around, offering to fetch a cup for anyone else, when he stopped stiff, eyes locked on Thaddeus' still glowing medallion. At once, his eyes rolled up under into his head and he fell to the ground, completely unconscious.

People ran towards Steven but stopped when a new voice emerged from the shadows. The voice was shrilled and coarse.

"ANDI!?" the voice yelled, "You are dead- I left your body in the wagon. You had no pulse!"

It was Glut. He walked into the light, his face twisted in anger, surprise, and extreme sadness. It was obvious he had been crying to the point of running out of tears, his red eyes seemed dry and aching. For a moment, he stared at his sister, unsure if that was actually her. It had to be a trick, or one of those horrible creatures in disguise. This couldn't be Andi. He wanted to believe it was his sister, but she had no pulse, she was dead. Her blood covered most of the wagon floor.

Andi could see her brother's hesitation. "It's really me."

"You can't be! My sister is DEAD!" yelled Glut dashing away, back into the darkness, crying.

***

When the next morning broke, there was a layer of dew on the plants and trees. It was only a few hours after the attack. The professor was slow to rise, overwhelmed with emotions and second guesses, a form of survivor's guilt heavy on his heart. He was not prepared to encounter such resistance so early on. His heart knew to expect the unexpected. He hated to admit it, but the shriek attack did not surprise him as much as it should have. After encountering the phenomenon in Diamin, he had to expect some sort of demon attack. He had ruffled too many feathers to travel unnoticed. What the professor was unprepared for, though he knew it was an eventuality, was the loss of life.

In his younger years, the professor had ventured out with the citadel army and had seen the carnage war brought. Many of those deaths were nameless – soldiers he did not know. He was able to separate himself from the event, not take it personally. The deaths of Deniz, Souza, and other team members rendered him unable to separate himself from sorrow and guilt.

Sitting up silently, wallowing in self-pity, he mulled over his decisions. He wondered whether this expedition really had a chance of succeeding. He was torn between doing the right thing and the easy thing. Of course he wished he could pack everyone up and send them home before any more tragedy befell them.

"Professor?" called Thaddeus, standing outside the professor's tent. "Are you awake?"

"Yes." answered the professor, clearing his throat. "Come in, ah Thaddeus." Thaddeus was still wearing his full armor and uniform jacket. "My dear boy, when do you sleep?"

"No rest for the wicked. Post battle nerves keep me up. There's plenty to do and staying busy helps keep my mind off the ones we lost." answered Thaddeus, matter of fact. As he entered the tent, he glanced at several scrolls and books on the table, including one that read 'the story of Gideon the Paladin."

"Ah yes, I suppose we each have our own rituals to deal with these nerves. I myself have always had success in separating from the emotions entirely, but lately it has proven more and more difficult," replied the professor, his red eyes and nose obvious. "How do you fare this morning?"

"To be frank, I could be better. In place of sleep, I helped fell several trees for fire wood and boy if my face isn't sore from that slap Leora gave me."

"I thought it looked a little red," smiled the professor. "The same could be said for my cheek as well."

Thaddeus bit his bottom lip, "Sorry about that."

The professor shrugged, "You are a man of your word, my cheek can speak to that. What can I do for you?"

"We built a pyre for those we lost. I thought maybe you would want to lead the service, offer some words for the dead, and give counsel to the living. Afterwards, Edryss is presenting a mandatory crash course on weapons to your people."

The professor nodded, "This isn't your first time dealing with death."

Thaddeus frowned slightly, "No death is easy, but we find comfort in that their struggles are over. It's the survivors that must live on with the loss."

"Quite right," whispered the professor, deep in thought. "I don't want to lose anyone else. Do we have enough swords for everyone?"

"We have enough plasma swords to equip half of your number."

"That won't do, we'll need to find more."

"I know a place. We are about two hours south of a village named Mystique. They will have enough swords to purchase," Thaddeus said. "Plus, it may be a good place to stop before we enter Veilwood. If there is the slightest chance there is a demon/Slavine connection, we need to make sure our defenses are in order before entering their territory."

"Quite right, Thaddeus. Quite right."

***

"I died, right there." whispered Andi staring at a dark red stain in the upholstery of the professor's wagon. The idea of dying and coming back didn't quite seem possible, even for a person who had experienced it. It had only been a few short hours, but to Andi it already felt like it was a lifetime ago. She knelt and touched the stain with her finger. To her surprise it was still wet. A heavy, dreadful reminder of how recent it really was.

"You are- were dead."

Andi turned to see her brother Glut standing behind her.

"I held your lifeless body in my hands." Glut's voice trembled, "I begged and begged the Maker to bring you back, but nothing happened. Your body did not move. It was limp in my arms. How, how are you alive?"

Andi turned towards her brother. Glut was hesitant and scared. He still wasn't convinced this was really Andi standing next to him. Andi reached out and grabbed Glut by his collar. He was about to fight back when he realized Andi was hugging him and crying. "Does it matter? Thaddeus' med-"Andi paused hearing the words out loud made it even more unreal. "Thaddeus' medallion, it's magical or has some kind of power. I don't know how it works or how it's even real, but he left it with me when he rushed to fight off those creatures and it healed me. I don't understand how or why, but I am here, aren't I? I am never going to leav-"

"Andi!?" yelled Glut, suddenly feeling his sister's weight fall upon him. He looked up and saw a lifeless look upon his sister's face. Glut's heart began to race and he thought for a moment he was going to hyperventilate. He heard hoof steps on the other side of the wagon. Glut laid his sister on the ground of the wagon and moved to open the opposite door. A tan colored horse rode by, "Was that Thaddeus? He will know what to do." Glut spoke out loud to himself.

Glut opened the door, it was Thaddeus. Glut was about to yell out his name when he eerily heard his sister's voice.

"Oh, there it is" said Andi reaching underneath the seat and pulling out a book, "I have to finish reading up on the history of the Bloodstone cult before the professor asks."

Glut was in shock, he wasn't sure what was happening. What was wrong with his sister, was this even his sister anymore?

"What!?" responded Andi several seconds later, noticing Glut's stare.

"What is wrong with you?" asked Glut very concerned, "You stopped talking midsentence and collapsed. Something isn't-"

"I did?" remarked Andi. Unaware any of it had happened, she felt unnerved. "Are you sure? I don't remember anything like that. Perhaps I am just tired? I did die and come back."

Andi walked out the opposite door and headed towards the front of the column.

Glut stood like a statue, he wasn't sure what to say, he didn't understand why Andi wasn't more concerned.

***

The ceremony to honor the lost was somber. The professor took to the small, crude wooden platform and delivered a thoughtful eulogy, naming each victim by their full title and recounting fond memories of them. Their bodies were escorted to the front of the assembly one by one, each had their moment to be honored. Lynette's and Souza's moments, in particular, were difficult for the professor. Thaddeus was quite impressed with the professor's words. Despite the obvious pain he felt for the loss of his friends and colleagues his words focused on reassuring his people and not himself. Thaddeus knew the challenges of standing before your men, pushing your own grief away to be strong for your people. The professor's long-winded speech showed his love and connection to every member on the expedition.

After the service, every non-Equinaut was ordered to partake in weapons training. They gathered near the wagons. Edryss, fully armored, stood behind the wagons. Her tan, buttoned jacket covered the straps of her Tesla power pack.

Edryss approached Thaddeus haltingly, "Sir, permission to speak freely?"

"Granted, what's on your mind? Are your wounds hurting you?"

"No, they're fine." Edryss' cheeks were bright red, brightening her dark complexion. "Do I have to do this? I've never spoken in front of so many!"

Thaddeus laughed. "You fought those creatures last night with a belly wound and I have seen you jump in front of twenty charging Slavine soldiers without hesitation. But you are afraid of this?" Thaddeus placed a hand on her shoulder, "Don't worry, Edryss. You will be fine! You are among the best Equinauts I have ever had the honor of serving with. You know these weapons better than most."

"Gladthorn said he'd do it," pleaded Edryss.

"Nonsense, you will be amazing. Now go," encouraged Thaddeus.

"What about Zapp? He is excellent with the sword, don't tell him I said that, but shouldn't he be teaching this part?"

Thaddeus laughed, but Edryss stood rooted. "Do I have to make it an order?"

Edyrss exhaled slowly, "Actually sir, it might make things easier."

The smile fell from Thaddeus' face and his voice became stern, "Edryss Salisbury, you are ordered to teach and train those people how to properly use our weapons to the very best of your ability!"

"YES SIR!" acknowledged Edryss saluting. She abruptly spun away from Thaddeus and marched around the wagon in front of the crowd, which quieted. Every pair of eyes stared directly at her. The crowd was larger than she expected. Edryss tried to focus on familiar faces. Leora had her journal open ready to take notes, and the brother and sister were nearby. To calm herself, Edryss took several deep, slow breaths, but this only made her lightheaded. She swallowed her trepidation and clenched her fists tightly, holding on to her nerves.

"Many of you have never held a weapon in your lives. Well, that will change, really soon!" yelled Edryss, as she pulled her rifle from the back of her tesla pack. "This is a tesla rifle. It is standard issue for the Citadel guard and for the Equinauts. We currently don't have enough packs for all of you, but that does not mean you don't need to learn about this weapon!"

"Why, if we aren't going to use it?" yelled a man from the crowd. The sudden interruption caused Edryss to falter slightly with her words.

"Because, you never know when you may be needed to use one." Edryss looked out over their heads. She was losing them. She began again, stronger, "In battle things change constantly, any one of you may be called to wear one of these!"

The same voice called out, "Well, I for one did not sign up to become a soldier!"

"Sir, what is your name!?" Edryss stared him down as the crowd buzzed around him.

"Copernicus," yelled the man.

"Well, Copernicus!" Edryss' voice was loud and cold, her confidence returned, "*I for one*, did not plan on encountering these 'Shriek' demon creatures. Now, either you will learn to defend yourself or you become their next victim! The choice is yours. I will not waste my time teaching people who don't want to be taught!"

The crowd hushed, and Copernicus bowed his head, refusing to look Edryss in the eye. Seeing the crowd was hers, she continued her presentation.

"Let me demonstrate the Tesla's power." Edryss shot a branch off a nearby tree. The branch burst into flames and fell to the ground. "This is a range weapon, powered by our packs. The packs are powered by Clastine crystals, or CC's. These weapons have several intensities, stun, blast, pulse, and beam. The most common intensity, and probably the only setting you will use, is blast. It fires a bolt of energy. It's perfectly balanced between range, power, and rate of fire. If you find yourself in a very tight spot, and your enemies are clustered together, pulse will fire a large sphere of energy that can hit multiple targets. Pulse is high power, medium range, and the rate of fire is dramatically lower than blaster shot. Only use the beam setting when you are being attacked by a large number of enemies. It'll eat your power up pretty quickly. Never ever cross your beam with someone else's beam, it will cause feedback and the packs will explode!"

Murmurs came from the crowd, many were apprehensive.

"This is what most of you will be given." Edryss held out a sword hilt with no blade. She flinched her thumb, and suddenly molten hot metal sprung from the hilt of the sword. The molten hot metal appeared to be in a state of liquid and solid at the exact same time. It glowed red and orange.

"This is a plasma sword, more commonly called a Plaz. These swords are filled with molten metal. The Lithic crystal inside keeps the metal hot and the many lodestones inside this hilt keep the molten rock in form. The moment the outside layer hits the air it will be cool to the touch, despite their glow." Edryss touched the blade with her hand. Several of the audience members gasped, expecting her hand to burn. "As you can see, the blade is cool to the touch, but trust me the inner layer is still superheated. BE CAREFUL! The edges are extremely sharp, but can be brittle. Every time the edge is broken, intense heat escapes, melting and burning anything it touches. However, moments later the missing edge will re-solidify and it will become hard and sharp again. This sword is almost the perfect weapon and no armor can stand long against it!"

Edryss broke the university members into groups and led them in battle stances. With the help of Gladthorn and several other Equinauts, she taught several proper positions to use a sword in combat, and several more defensive positions. If their foe weren't so formidable, it would have been laughable seeing them flail their swords up in the air, including Copernicus, who obviously had never held a sword before in his life.

"Remember, if you use the same move more than twice in a fight, your enemy will learn to use it against you! Change up your attacks, do not allow your opponent to predict your next move!" yelled Edryss to her group of university members.

It was a slow process, with a steep learning curve, but the Equinauts knew any amount of experience would save lives in the future.

***

The expedition turned north and headed for the village of Mystique. A year had passed since the Equinauts had saved the village in the war between the Citadel and the Slavine. Much of the small forested area that hugged the northern road still bore the scars of the conflict. Trees were torn down or leaning against each other, and the ground was still scorched in countless areas. Despite the carnage, there were clear and definitive signs of regeneration. Large patches of the forest were slowly growing back, like small green sprouts that seemed to whisper hope. At a particularly wide section of road, the village had placed large stone markers, each marker representing a life lost. Bronze represented fallen Slavine, silver represented fallen Citadel soldiers, and gold represented a fallen civilian.

Leora sat astride Wooley. She felt much more comfortable on him than she had the day before, but she could feel her legs, especially her inner thighs and lower calves becoming very sore. She began to wonder how people traveled long distances on horseback without losing all sensation in their legs. For most of the day, she rode with several Equinauts Thaddeus had introduced her to. Zapp and Fryda were kind, but Leora was upset that Thaddeus left her with them. Zapp fumbled over most of his words. Leora was unsure if he had formed a single sentence in the hours that had passed between them. Fryda though, was fascinating. She was a warrior woman from a unique and strong culture. Leora knew very little of the ways of the Aedunic. Littler still how an Aedunic woman could leave her tribe and join a mercenary group.

Fryda relished in telling Leora the story of her tribe and how she became an Equinaut, "...he approached my Kern and stood there defiantly."

"Has your hair gotten lighter?" asked Zapp, interrupting Fryda's story.

"No!" snapped Leora, "Why does everyone think that!"

"Because it..." Zapp stopped speaking when he saw the death glare Leora was giving hm.

Leora looked back to Fryda, "What were you saying? Kern and who?"

Fryda smiled "You can't stop this story from coming out, Charles."

"Its Zapp!" muttered Charles, "And I most certainly can try! I hate this story!"

"As I was telling you, Charles 'Zapp' Jackson approached my Kern," continued Fryda. Leora gave her a confused look when she used the word 'Kern.' "Aedunic for chieftain!" Leora nodded that she understood. "So, Zapp, standing defiant to a man who was at least two feet taller than he, looked him straight in the eye and began to profess his undying love, and demanded to be allowed to marry me. Whenever a man not of our tribe asks to be betrothed to a woman, he has to prove himself through sword combat. Not to the death, mind you, just enough to prove he can defend his family."

Zapp's face was turning red.

"Aw, that's so sweet," cooed Leora.

Fryda was smiling, "It was! Zapp is one of the best swordsmen. He defeated the Kern in six rounds of combat. At the end of the ceremony, you're supposed to recite a passage." Fryda looked over at Zapp who was hiding his face in his hands, shaking his head, "But the darn idiot was so gung ho, trying to prove himself to Thaddeus, he wasn't listening. When the Kern asked for the name of the woman he wished to wed, he blanked. He couldn't remember my name!"

Leora clapped her hand over her mouth and tried to hold in her laughter, which came out in several small snorts, "He didn't!"

Fryda nodded, "So there is Thaddeus, Italicus, and about ten other Equinauts, all jumping up and down behind the Kern trying to get Zapp's attention without being noticed, each of them mouthing my name or trying to make a letter with their hands and arms. Italicus even yelled out, 'man I would love to eat a FRIED piece of chicken.'"

Leora tried to keep her laughter in check. She looked at Zapp, "So did you get the hint?"

Zapp lifted his head from his hands, "It gets worse!"

Fryda continued, "So Zapp, after a very long awkward pause, finally looks back up to the Kern and says the name *Franda*."

"Franda!?" Leora looked astonished, "Is that even a name?"

"Yes, so the Kern brought him the only woman in our tribe named Franda, a seventy-eight year old midwife with no teeth."

"NO!" screamed Leora, laughing outright now.

"Yes, and Zapp was so confused and so scared of insulting the tribe, the two were married that day and are still married!"

"I question the legitimacy of that marriage. I do not ever remember saying I do, and he never asked if anyone wished to object. I know that to be one hundred percent truth," exclaimed Zapp seriously.

"So then how did you get to leave your tribe?" asked Leora.

"Well Thaddeus had to wait an extra month, but this time Niles was the suitor and won the right to marry me," answered Fryda.

"So, you're married to Niles?"

"You could say that, but only in the sense that my Kern thinks I am. In every other way, I am not."

"So, then you to haven't.., aaaah, you know, consummated the marriage?" winked Leora.

"Those two? Hahaha, Niles is scared straight of her," mocked Zapp. "He's afraid she'll break him."

"This is so going into my journal. This story is way too good to keep unwritten! *'How Fryda became an Equinaut and Charles, Zapp's story of true love!'*"

"I hate you," teased Zapp staring at Fryda. "You should be the one upset! You could have had all this!" He used his arms and hands to show off his manly physique before trotting away from the abuse.

The girls rode together until Fryda left in a scouting party ahead of the expedition. Leora found her way to the front of the column where Thaddeus and Italicus rode. They were recounting the horrible fighting that occurred in the village, how much suffering both sides had caused. Leora could not believe the Citadel would take part in death upon innocents.

The expedition followed the road further north, across the only bridge in the immediate area that provided enough strength to support their loaded wagons. Thaddeus remembered the bridge well. Several prolonged skirmishes between the town and Slavine had occurred over control of this bridge. When the Slavine finally realized the Equinauts were entrenched in the town's protection, they destroyed their side of the bridge, effectively cutting off all major supplies into the village. After the siege ended, both the Citadel and the Slavine army left, and the Equinauts helped rebuild the bridge, allowing for trade to resume. On the village's side of the river, the ground was fairly flat with only a few slight humps. It was perfect for farming.

Thaddeus purposefully took the route that passed through the Callan farm, the family which Thaddeus and Italicus held during the first actual attack on the town. Thaddeus smiled at how vital and lush the farm appeared compared to when he had last seen it. As soon as Thaddeus laid eyes on the house, two children ran towards him.

"THADDEUS! ITALICUS! You came back!"

Thaddeus threw his arm up and out, with two fingers raised, signaling the expedition to slow its pace. He and Italicus turned their horses off the road to talk to the kids.

"Hey kids! Man, you guys have gotten big!" Italicus beamed.

"ITY!" yelled the little girl, using her nickname for Italicus. She was so excited to see him, the two had bonded during the siege. Italicus had protected the kids when the Slavine tore through their house. When all hope was lost at finding her mother, Italicus stayed with the children as much as he could. It was a miracle that they had found their mother days later in the rubble of their house, still alive. The little girl looked up at Italicus and tilted her head strangely, "That feather is silly, Ity! Why are you wearing it in your ear?"

Italicus, wide eyed and furious, threw his head towards Thaddeus who had burst into laughter. Italicus stared deathly at him.

"Don't look at me!" defended Thaddeus between gulps of air and laughter. "How could I possibly have gotten them in on it as well?"

"Are you here to stay?" asked the little boy.

"Well Caleb, it's only for the day and maybe the night," answered Thaddeus.

"Will you eat dinner with us?" asked the little girl.

"I think that can be arranged." Leora appeared on Wooley. Thaddeus and Italicus looked at her, surprised she would speak for them. "What, how can you think of saying no to that pretty little face!?" The little girl giggled at the compliment.

Out of the house came the children's parents.

"Hail Thaddeus!" said the father. "It's been too long, my friend!"

"Aye, Callan," replied Thaddeus.

"What brings you back to Mystique?"

"Nothing big,protection detail," answered Thaddeus, not wanting to alarm Callan with the full truth. "Is it possible we could use your southern field for camp tonight?"

Callan smiled and spoke with sincere gratitude, "Anything for the saviors of our village!"

Thaddeus nodded, "Your graciousness is appreciated. How has the village fared?"

"Many of the old families have been collaborating. Mayor Carlissian has worked hard quelling the old feuds. Much of the village square is rebuilt. The Mayor has tried to balance the reconstruction effort between housing and commerce. We have begun trade with several nearby neutral villages, which has helped in securing building materials. Everyone will be so pleased that you're here!"

"Looks like things are getting better. If anyone deserves a run of good luck, it's Mystique!" replied Thaddeus.

The professor trotted upon poncho, "Thaddeus, might we speak?"

"Professor Belladon, meet Callan and Gloria Überleben and their little ones, Caleb and Mara," introduced Thaddeus. "Callan and Gloria have agreed to allow us their southern field to camp."

"Thank you, sir." The professor removed his top hat and nodded his head, "You are assisting a noble cause, I assure you."

"Professor Belladon?" asked Gloria, eyes wide.

"Why, yes. I beg your pardon, have we met?"

Gloria looked uncomfortable, on the verge of tears. Callan showed no emotion, "I think you need to come into the house, before you are seen. Come now, quickly!"

"Italicus lead the column around the hill," ordered Thaddeus. "Stay in formation while I speak with Callan."

Italicus nodded and saluted, "Your order, my will!"

Callan ushered Thaddeus and the professor into his house, as Gloria scampered about, drawing the curtains.

"Please, sit." signaled Callan, his face betraying fear and despair.

"What's the matter?" asked Thaddeus, confused.

"Forgive me, Thaddeus. I don't say this lightly, but it may be best if you and the Equinauts take the professor and leave the village!" stated Callan softly, but seriously.

"It's not possible," started Thaddeus, "We need supplies."

"Then I will go get them. No need for you to enter the village!" said Callan, passionately standing up.

Thaddeus was beyond confused, "Callan, what's happened?"

Callan slowly sunk back into his seat, "I am sorry, Thaddeus, but for the last few weeks black riders have ridden up and down the countryside killing anyone or anything they come across. We didn't know where the Equinauts were and the Marshals have not been seen in this area for some time. We sent a message to the Steward for help and they sent us a small contingent of soldiers."

Thaddeus sighed, "We have had some dealings with these black riders, they are formidable, but they can be defeated."

"The black riders aren't our only concern. For the first time since the war, we have had Slavine patrols."

"That's understandable," interrupted the professor. "This village is on the Slavine border. It seems only natural that they would like to patrol it."

"The only time Slavine enter Veilwood is for war." Callan shook his head, "No, this isn't normal border patrol. There's something more to it."

"What do you mean?" asked Thaddeus.

"They are changing people!" whispered Gloria unexpectedly. "The people in town are different now. Mark my words. There is something foul, something evil happening here!"

Thaddeus and the professor looked to Gloria, then back to Callan who was now looking intensely down at his feet.

"What my wife said is true," stated Callan cautiously.

"How are people changing?" asked Thaddeus.

"I really wish I could tell you, Thaddeus." Callan took a deep breath, "Believe me when I tell you something isn't right, and it has something to do with the Citadel Soldiers. Everything seemed fine when they arrived, but after two days of trying to chase down the black riders, they returned different."

"But what does that have to do with Professor Belladon?" asked Thaddeus.

"They want him!" declared Gloria.

"Who? Who wants him?" asked Thaddeus.

"The soldiers!" insisted Gloria.

The professor shook his head, "It's only been a day since we left, I would have thought the university would take more time in indicting me."

"A day?" Callan looked at the professor strangely. "The soldiers have been whispering your name for weeks now, three at the very least!"

"Professor?" asked Thaddeus, annoyed that Belladon was once again hiding something.

"Honestly, I am as confused as you are," answered the professor. "It's been only a matter of days since I decided to act on this expedition."

"Could it be for something unconnected to the expedition?" asked Thaddeus.

The professor thought for a moment, "I did discover the phenomenon in the mountains about a month ago."

Thaddeus' face was stoic, "But if that's the reason…"

"Then the corruption goes higher than we thought." finished the professor solemnly.

"Well, we had better head into the village." stated Thaddeus, rising from his chair.

The professor was mortified, "You can't be serious!"

Thaddeus looked directly at the professor, "We need those weapons no matter what!"

"Your presence will be known immediately. The soldiers will take you captive, or worse, they'll try killing you!" proclaimed Callan, standing up as well.

"They'll be forced to confront us. Better a foe in the open than one in the shadows," acknowledged Thaddeus. "Callan, are you still willing to allow us use of your field?"

"What's ours is yours, Thaddeus."

The professor rubbed his chin and thought for a moment. Eventually he looked up, "I'm coming with you."

***

Thaddeus decided to keep Callan's warning tight to his chest. The Equinauts were greatly disappointed when Thaddeus ordered everyone to wait in the field while he and Italicus secured the supplies. They wanted to visit their friends in the village. Thaddeus ordered the wagons in a protective circle around their camp and asked that no tents be erected.

"Sir?" asked Edryss, approaching Thaddeus. "Circle formation with no tents erected, are we expecting trouble?"

Thaddeus finished tying the girth on his saddle, then smiled and winked, "You know me, Edryss. I love spending the night under the stars."

Edryss knew Thaddeus was purposefully acting evasively, "Very good, sir. While we are, enjoying the stars, I will ensure we are able to leave rapidly if needed."

Thaddeus laughed to himself, "Are you expecting trouble, Edryss?"

Edryss smiled, "Always, sir!"

"Are we ready professor?" asked Thaddeus, now sitting astride Egghead.

"Almost!" yelled Professor Belladon, sorting through a saddle bag. He left only the essentials inside. "Poncho, my boy, what have we gotten ourselves into?"

The professor had severe reservations about Thaddeus' plan to enter the village, knowing there could be a trap waiting for them. When they left Callan's house, the last words spoken were a plea, "Turn around and forget about this village!" *Perhaps we are acting rashly,* thought the professor

"Edryss, you're in command while Italicus, the professor, and I are gone," stated Thaddeus. "Do not allow anyone to leave camp!"

Edryss saluted, "Your order, my will!"

Thaddeus returned the salute, "Thank you, Edryss." He urged Egghead forward.

"You're welcome, sir." Edryss held her salute, "Just don't be surprised if the men are pissed at you when you return!"

Italicus rode up to them on Moose, "You will learn this one day, if the men aren't pissed at their leader," He wore a large grin on his face, "then you're doing something wrong!"

As the trio rode into the village, Thaddeus and Italicus immediately noticed how much of the village had returned to as it was before the war. Life was getting back to normal for the small village. Though, not everything was the same. Several of the streets were all newly named. One read, Thaddeus Road, while another was PenRuger Way. The deeper into the village they road, the more extravagant the names got, The Great Thaddeus Drive, Noble Thaddeus Street, and Fabulous Thaddeus Lane.

Italicus couldn't help but smile brightly. He knew how much Thaddeus hated being in the spotlight for this type of attention. He was about to make a witty comment about where his road was when the professor spoke.

"If every road is now named Thaddeus, I'd hate to be the mailman."

Italicus burst out in laughter, while Thaddeus' face turned red.

Near the center of the village was a long, narrow, rectangular forum centered among buildings made of wood and clay, freshly painted. Inside the forum stood the only building made of stone. It was the temple built for the Maker, which also acted as city hall, and sometimes as a place for protection. A crowd was forming behind the men. Many of the villagers rushed to see Thaddeus and Italicus, giving thanks and praise. They owed so much to the Equinauts. It seemed like half the village was now standing in the forum, insistently yelling to Thaddeus and Italicus on how the town had prospered since they left.

"You seem to be quite popular here," commented the professor, slightly overwhelmed at the festive crowd,perusing every detail of the village, searching for signs or clues of an ambush.

"It does seem that way." Thaddeus smiled at the familiar faces, trying to greet as many people as possible.

Two men walked through the crowd, and many of the villagers made room for them to pass.

"Well, if it isn't No-Brains and Do-Nothing!" Thaddeus smiled at the men approaching.

Both had blonde hair, and both wore very expensive clothing. They approached the Equinauts and exchanged handshakes.

"Are we ever going to live down those names?" asked the taller of the two.

"Well, you did earn them fair and square. Your family feud really complicated defending the village effectively" Thaddeus' face scrunched comically.

"You're right, we were wrong," the shorter one sighed. "But, with the help of Mayor Carlissian, we have done a lot to put those old feuds aside and help rebuild the village."

"Well that's good to hear, *Randoll and Lister*" said Thaddeus. The men smiled brightly at his acknowledgement of their names.

"Thaddeus, Italicus!" called a man marching down the steps of the temple. The crowd quieted at the mayor's voice, "We did not expect to see you back so soon! We're honored to host you here in Mystique. We all owe so much to you both!"

"Thank you, Mayor. The village looks amazing and I have heard it has a lot to do with you!" complimented Thaddeus.

"I wish I could take credit, but it belongs to the people of Mystique, and for the generous help of Randoll and Lister. We have all worked long and hard together to rebuild! Most of the houses have been renovated and we will soon be done with the Forum. Then we will be working on a wall to protect ourselves," pointed out Mayor Carlissian as he stroked the lapels of his pristine, blue suit.

"A prudent decision," answered Italicus. "Any chance I could see the plans?"

The Mayor looked unsure.

"That would probably be wise. This oaf may not look smart, but he has a keen eye for fortifications" supplied Thaddeus.

"Oh, of course, thank you! Perhaps later, when the sun isn't so bright? Please, please come with us. The village has something we would like to show you," ordered the mayor, and the crowd buzzed with excitement.

The men followed Mayor Carlissian towards a tall fountain. Thaddeus and Italicus both remembered a simple, unremarkable fountain being in the forum. During the siege it had become one of the most important areas. Several large skirmishes were fought on the forum streets over control of the fountain. Without it, the village would have died from dehydration and been overtaken by the Slavine.

"Blatherin Crickets!" muttered the professor wide eyed and surprised.

Thaddeus and Italicus glanced at each other with the same look of awe. The fountain was by no means simple or unremarkable now. It was large and ornate, made of marble. Large, cascading rings went down multiple levels into a large pool that went several feet into the ground. Inside the rings at the very center of the fountain was a marble statue of a gorgeous woman standing on a pedestal, wearing a very elaborate gown. The professor was impressed and admired the detailing, the dress was just superb. The craftsmanship had seemed to capture the essence of a person perfectly. There seemed not to be a single flaw until the professor looked at the bare skin of the statue along the arms and neck. The white marble texture seemed off, more porcelain than stone. The face itself was covered by a blindfold and wavy bangs. The only clear feature was her lips and they were frowning. The arms were extending upwards, holding an oval sapphire over her head. The blue jewel acted as a prism for the sun, surrounding the fountain in dancing blue light. The professor had never seen something so beautiful outside of the Citadel Proper. Next to the fountain stood something equally tall, but sheathed in a cream linen cloth.

"This is amazing." remarked Thaddeus, he turned and looked at Randoll and Lister, "Which one of you coughed up enough money to build this?"

"The center piece was just delivered and finished a few days ago! It was a gift," answered the Mayor, "a gift from the Steward and the Citadel to make amends for all the destruction their war caused us."

"That is one hell of a gift," remarked Italicus, "you could have rebuilt the city twice over for the cost of this fountain."

The professor nodded in agreement.

"Quite." The mayor dropped his smile for but a moment, obviously annoyed at Italicus' comment. He approached the sheathed object, his smile now anew. "Please forgive this Thaddeus, it's not quite finished. We weren't expecting to see you so soon." The mayor grabbed ahold of the sheet. "I hope you appreciate our memento."

The mayor gave a mighty pull, revealing a marble statue depicting a horse at full gallop with a rider wearing a Tesla pack, rifle drawn. The statue stood on a pedestal with a plaque that read:
Triumph! Thank you, Thaddeus, and the Equinauts for saving our homes and our lives.
Battle of Mystique
The carved face on the statue seemed to be a blend of Italicus' and Thaddeus' faces with maybe Gladthorn's shoulders and Fryda's arms. Thaddeus and Italicus were dumbfounded. The professor could see they struggled to find words and could not help but let out a small chuckle, despite his wariness. The entire village waited breathlessly for their response.

Thaddeus was uncertain how he felt, staring at the statue. He, of course, had never fought for tribute or adulation, nor, to his knowledge, had his men. "It's humbling to see such love and gratitude from you all. On behalf of myself and the Equinauts, thank you!" said Thaddeus genuinely.

The crowd's cheering was disrupted by angry shouts as several armed men violently pushed their way towards Thaddeus.

"ARREST THAT MAN! By the order of the Steward of the Citadel," ordered the lead man. He was dressed in the manner of a Citadel soldier.

Thaddeus' heart sank. He had hoped the three of them could travel in and out of the village before trouble arose. Thaddeus looked over at the professor, who blanched. He cursed under his breath. He knew there would be fanfare upon his and Italicus' return, but he did not expect it to be such an event. As the soldiers approached, Thaddeus found a small glimmer of hope that trouble could be averted.

"Colonel Jaster!?" yelled Thaddeus, surprised and relieved. The colonel was an old, dear friend of Thaddeus' father. But the colonel didn't even look at Thaddeus. His eyes were fixed solely on the professor.

"Nikola Belladon is wanted for the murder of Deniz Insigno, and theft of University property!" The Colonel looked at his men and nodded. Two of them approached the professor and Poncho, but stopped at the sight of Thaddeus's large plaz sword pointed at them.

"You have no jurisdiction here in a neutral, *independent* village!" hollered Thaddeus. Beside him, Italicus had drawn his rifle and pointed it at the soldiers. The town's people were frozen in a tight circle around the men, afraid to move and call attention to themselves.

Colonel Jaster looked at Thaddeus for the first time, and a cold, unnatural aura emanated from his eyes. "Go ahead and fire. Start a fight right in the middle of the street, surrounded by your precious innocents. You do make it easy for us, PenRuger. We should arrest you two as traitors to the Citadel!"

Thaddeus gave the colonel a questioning look. This was not the man he had known for most of his life.

"On whose authority do you enter this neutral village?" asked the professor.

"On the only authority of significance, that matter on this forsaken Shard. The authority of the Steward Cromwell and the Citadel throne! Give yourself up now, or be killed," ordered Jaster. "Seize these men, and remember, the Steward didn't specify dead or alive."

Two of the soldiers started towards the professor, and the others drew their rifles. Italicus looked to Thaddeus, hoping for orders, unsure if he should begin firing at the guards.

Thaddeus searched desperately for a way out that didn't involve bloodshed. At this range, several villagers were sure to be caught in the crosshairs of their weapons, not to mention the probability that at least one of their horses would spook and charge through the small crowd, injuring many. His only option was to surrender and fight their way free from the squad of soldiers on the road. He didn't like it, but he raised both hands and nodded to Italicus to do the same.

A flash of light spirited across the sky over the Soldiers heads. Many of the villagers in the crowd ducked in fright, looking for where the beam of light originated.

"Get out of here!" yelled Randoll, surrounded by four men, each armed with very crude and bulky versions of tesla packs.

Four more men accompanied Lister, equipped with the same type of gear on the other side of the crowd. "We don't want any citas in here!"

Thaddeus was both relieved and horrified that these two men now had heavily armed bodyguards. Colonel Jaster's face contorted with rage. It bore no resemblance to the man he knew so well.

For a very brief moment, Thaddeus was sure the colonel would refuse to let down and there would be a bloodbath on the streets. "Colonel, please, you cannot win this fight," pleaded Thaddeus.

The colonel looked at him fiercely, and then, for the briefest of moments, his face contorted and he struggled to hold on to his anger. His eyes softened.

"Very well," stated the colonel, and he looked over at the professor. "Mark my words. As long as you are in this village, you are safe. But the moment you leave its border, you are mine, professor!"

The colonel turned abruptly and led his men from the village forum. Lister, Randoll, and their men followed closely behind them, to ensure they actually left.

"That went better than expected," mused Italicus.

"Good gracious!" yelled the mayor. "Why did they want to take him? We will not harbor a criminal."

"Mayor Carlissian," Thaddeus held his hand out towards the professor, "this is none other than Professor Belladon, the Inventor of, well, Maker knows, everything!"

"I think he invented inventing," said Italicus jokingly.

The professor smiled meekly, still stunned from the encounter with the guards, "Ahh, I don't know that I am old enough to invent inventing, but I suppose I can't help but tinker."

"What are you planning to do with the professor, considering Colonel Jaster is out there?" asked the Mayor.

Thaddeus thought for a moment, "I am not sure yet, but don't worry. As long as Lister and Randoll have their men here, I don't think he will bother you. I am not entirely certain he is doing the Steward's work right now."

"The colonel and his men were the ones who brought us the last piece of the fountain. He wasn't that serious then." The Mayor still looked frightened, "Look at these people, Thaddeus. They are scared. What should I do?"

"Give them a reason not to be."

The mayor thought for a moment, then turned towards the crowd and raised his arms, "This is the famous Professor Belladon. In his honor, and for our Equinaut saviors, I declare a feast is in order for tonight!"

The crowd let out a loud and happy cheer. Within seconds, they began to scatter, anxious to do their part in preparation for this last-minute celebration.

"Thaddeus, do you really think we should be attending a feast?" asked the professor. "What if the colonel comes back with more men? I think we should get our supplies and move on."

"We will take the colonel at his word. The moment you leave the territory of Mystique, they will grab you regardless of the repercussions." Thaddeus sounded confident.

"We should rush out of here, surely they wouldn't follow us into Slavine territory," argued the professor.

"It's probably too late for that now. The colonel's company is probably comprised of twenty-five to forty men. If the colonel does what I expect him to do, the road to the north will already be blocked. He will then send some his men to the south and take the bridge." Thaddeus rubbed at his chin, "He will force us to strike first near the bridge while trying to flee."

"He'll wait for us to engage?" asked the professor

Italicus butted in, "If this is political, and not- I can't believe I am using this word, 'supernatural,' he wants us to strike first. He gains the grounds to call us the aggressors. We are already outlawed by the treaty. If we attack, then he won't have to worry about jurisdiction. If it's," Italicus paused again, trying to get the word out, "supernatural, then he will wait for us to be vulnerable and then he will attack. Either way, we will have to be patient."

"But Thaddeus, time is of the essence! We must get going, we cannot be delayed! The longer we are in this village, the higher the likelihood of those creatures finding a way through the mountains!"

"He knows professor," answered Italicus calmly, "But right now, Colonel Jaster has us trapped."

***

Leora could feel her muscles getting sore. Her eyes stung from sweat. Edryss had almost instantaneously become one of the most hated people in camp, organizing another round of mandatory weapons training.

Leora's arm was failing. She could barely keep her sword in the proper position. It was sinking down her left side.

"Never let your sword drop! It is a clear sign to your opponent that you are tiring. Plus, it limits your ability to counter your opponent's next attack, like so!" Edryss swung at Leora, who had become her personal pet project.

Edryss worked Leora tirelessly, making her swing and thrust over and over again, deflecting attacks, and showing her how to throw an opponent off balance. Edryss was impressed how much of a beating the poor girl could take, but everyone had their limits and Leora had begun to approach hers. Edryss swung her own blade down towards Leora, who tried to bring her own up to the proper position to block, but was unable to deflect Edryss' attack. Her sword flew from her hands. Leora gave Edryss a look of defeat. Edryss returned that look with a frontal kick to the chest, sending Leora to the ground.

Leora sprung back up, adrenaline running, and fury in her eyes.

"What in Bellows was that for? You already disarmed me! That hurt!"

"Good, maybe you will remember that pain when you tire again. If this was a real fight, that pain would be tenfold greater, with a sword through your gut!" asserted Edryss in a commanding voice.

"I am tired and I have done everything you have asked of me! A real fight won't last for hours and hours," shrieked Leora.

Edryss was unmoved, "I have been in battles that lasted days. In this very village the war lasted months, and the battles lasted weeks. The Slavine sent a charge every two hours for at least five days straight. I barely slept. I was fighting tooth and nail every moment, trying to keep innocents from being slaughtered. So, yes, a fight can last for days if it has to, and the moment you let your guard down, you're dead, and so are the people you are protecting!"

Leora was at her wits' end and didn't care what Edryss had done or how right she might have been, "I don't care! I'm not doing this anymore!"

"You have to get up. We are not done. We could be attacked this very night. You don't know! You have to be prepared." Edryss spoke in short, clipped sentences.

Leora threw her hands into the air, "So be it, if they attack, let them come. I am so exhausted, they can kill me first!"

Beside them, Zapp had been helping a small group, teaching them the prudence of reading your opponent before engaging in a full offensive attack.

Zapp rushed to Leora and Edryss once he heard the small fight they were having, "Whoa ladies, calm down!"

"Stay out of this Zapp, this girl needs to learn from her mistakes," ordered Edryss.

Leora gave Edryss a deathly stare.

"Perhaps," said Zapp diplomatically, "but maybe it's time to switch groups, let me give Leora a stab, she might do better in my capable hands."

Edryss snorted loudly, "Your capable hands! You mean wandering hands. I've seen how you teach women and trust me Leora would kick your ass the moment your hands wandered too low."

Leora smiled brightly at the compliment, and then gave Zapp a cold look.

Zapp held his hands up in protest, surprised at how quickly Leora changed from being upset with Edryss to taking her side against him. "I was only trying to help, I meant nothing by it."

Edryss' stare was unchanging.

"Really, honest! It was an innocent suggestion. I didn't want to see you two fighting," babbled Zapp, avoiding Leora's eyes as he turned and walked off towards his group.

"What was that all about?" asked Leora.

"Just keeping the politics down," answered Edryss. "Zapp is a great guy, and he is amazing with the sword, but he's had his eye on you since the moment you arrived."

"Really?" asked Leora blushing slightly.

"Yeah, but you're Thaddeus', if anyone's. Everyone knows that,"

Leora's cheeks turned a deeper shade of red, "No, I'm not. Am I? Me? Did he say something to you?"

"No, he didn't. It's mostly just gossip but trust me, in all the years I have been with Thaddeus, he has never looked at anyone the way he looks at you."

Leora was unsure how to take such news.

"I'm sorry I kicked you," Edryss offered. "I just don't want anything to happen to you. You have skill. You just need to be taught how to hone that skill properly. Talent alone will get you killed. Discipline and practice will ensure you survive an attack every time"

Leora nodded and was about to speak when Edryss lashed out with her blade. Leora lifted her sword, deflecting Edryss' blow just in time. Leora let out a veracious scream of frustration. With all the strength she could muster, she pushed Edryss' blade away. Edryss was surprised by Leora's reaction and was even more surprised when she suddenly found herself on the defensive. Leora's face was filled with rage. Her eyes were firm and confident. She lashed out, swinging her blade with precision, feinting and thrusting perfectly. Edryss struggled to parry and deflect, and somehow Leora increased her rate of attack. Blocking low and to her left, Edryss knew where Leora would strike next, but Leora feigned her low strike and went for Edryss' stomach. In jumping backwards to miss the blade, Edryss left herself exposed. Leora planted and kicked, her right foot landed perfectly on Edryss' stomach.

Edryss fell to the ground and immediately the tip of Leora's blade was inches from her neck. Edryss took a very large breath. For a brief moment she was uncertain if she would get another. The look on Leora's face was unnerving. This wasn't the innocent, inexperienced girl she had just been training.

"Where the Bellows did that come from?" yelled Edryss. "The only other person I've seen use that move is Thaddeus."

Leora's eyes suddenly softened, "Bless the Maker, what did I do?" she exclaimed, reaching out her hand to help Edryss up.

"That was some of the best damn sword fighting I have ever seen! How did you do that?" asked Edryss. "You were playing me the whole time, weren't you!"

"No!" pleaded Leora. Her face was bright red and she was panting heavily. "It wasn't, I mean I don't..." She took several more breaths and shook her head, "I don't understand."

Edryss felt confused and concerned, "It's ok Leora, calm down, it's alright!"

"It's not alright!" yelled Leora, panicking. She looked to Edryss, her brow furrowed, only to find Edryss staring slightly to the left of her.

"What!?"

Edryss pointed, "Your hair. Right there, it just got brighter!"

"No! Not again!" Leora shrilled to herself, trying to pull that particular part of her hair up to her face to see, "Why is it doing this?"

"I don't understand, how did your hair do that?" Edryss took the section from Leora and held it against her crown, comparing it.

Leora's eyes filled with tears, "I don't know- it just happens. Please don't tell anyone! Promise me you won't!"

Edryss patted Leora's shoulder awkwardly. "Ok, I promise. With blade skills like that, I'd promise you anything. Who would ever want to get you angry?"

Leora gave Edryss a weak smile.

Edryss was about to ask Leora more questions when Gladthorn approached. Leora spun away from him, wiping her face with her sleeve. Gladthorn gave Edryss a knowing look. He assumed Leora was worn out from training.

"How does your group fare?" asked Edryss.

Gladthorn smiled warmly at Edryss, he was happy to be near her. "Decent enough, Andi and her brother are learning the blade as well as any beginner, Dean will probably be better with daggers than a full blade."

"Perhaps Italicus should take over with him," suggested Edryss.

"My thoughts, exactly," agreed Gladthorn, grabbing Edyrss' hands and bringing them to his lips, "but I did not come all the way out here to talk business."

"Oh, is that so!?" mocked Edryss. "My, my, what has Gladthorn Jones come up with this time."

Gladthorn's large smile was infectious, "Well you know, it's hot out, but there's a pretty decent breeze. Perfect for picnic, wouldn't you say?"

Leora recomposed herself and turned towards Edryss, who glanced back at her, "Men."

Leora looked at Edryss, confused.

"They think all they have to do is be spontaneous with a nice idea and women will drop everything for them," Edryss smirked sarcastically.

Leora giggled slightly, "It would work on me."

Gladthorn chuckled and smiled at Leora, "Smart lady."

"I agree, Leora is, special." Edryss winked, "I don't think I can, Thaddeus put me in charge."

Gladthorn's smile turned to a frown and he began to pout slightly, "We will be back before he returns. It's just a small picnic."

Edryss closed her eyes and took a large slow breath, "Fine, let me clean up first."

Gladthorn clapped his hands together and began to walk backwards, "I'll just go and pick up the food then." Before he turned around, he gave Edryss another large, warm smile.

"Is that the look Thaddeus gives me?" asked Leora innocently. "I want my man to smile at me like Gladthorn smiles at you."

Edryss smiled, "Trust me, there is only one Gladthorn Jones," she adjusted her hair, "and he is all mine!" She gave Leora a wink, and walked off.

***

From Thaddeus' point of view, the village seemed to be in a worse state of chaos now than they were when the Slavine had attacked. Everyone was running around, placing decorations, setting tables, and preparing food for the upcoming feast. It was a sight to behold, so many working towards one purpose. Thaddeus had a hard time getting Sherridon, the owner of the village's private armory *Grenade and Me,* to stop for a minute and sell him the much needed Plaz swords. The professor was having a similar hardship attempting to convince the *Tager-mart* General Store owner to sell him goods instead of cooking a fat pig roast. Italicus, employing some charm on Meg, the owner of the *Foxhead Corner,* had a very easy time getting the extra bales of hay needed for the horses and pack animals. After gathering the needed supplies, Thaddeus, Italicus, and the professor borrowed a cart and headed back to Callan's farm.

"So," Thaddeus looked at Italicus with a goofy smile on his face.

"So, what?" asked Italicus, which broadened Thaddeus' grin?

"How's Meg?" prompted Thaddeus.

"Who is Meg?" asked the professor, intrigued.

"Meg is a very single, very attractive woman who is, by far, the largest klutz on the entire shard, and she has somehow caught the Italicus love train spell," jested Thaddeus.

"Oh," laughed the professor, "Do tell, my boy! A good story will do wonders for my spirit."

"A gentleman doesn't kiss and tell," remarked Italicus, innocently.

"But you," the professor paused for dramatic effect, "are no gentleman"

Thaddeus laughed loudly, "Ouch!"

Italicus, for a moment, was unsure what to say. He didn't realize the professor could be so snarky. He just shook his head and tried to hold in a smile until he could think of a good retort, but all he managed was, "I hate you both!"

Thaddeus poked at Italicus, "Well go on, we're all ears".

"Fine," said Italicus, faking an exasperated voice, "I was charming, debonair, I was one smooth cat. You know- my normal self." Italicus let out a hardy laugh, "Meg, working hard in her shop, had her back to the door, wearing a particularly tight red apron. I walked in and said 'hey baby, hail to the king.'" The two men looked at him confused.

"It's an inside joke I have with her. She turned and saw me, and it was like love itself was being created. Her eyes were so deep, her lips were so moist, we made love in the hay. It was passionate, it was amazing. It was—".

Thaddeus interrupted, "You crashed and burned, didn't you?"

Italicus' pride was hurt, "What!? HOW DARE YOU! How can you say that! I did no such thing, it was perfect love, it was," Italicus threw his hands up in the air and sucked in a sharp breath. "Yeah, I failed miserably." Italicus faked a laughed, "she barely even looked at me, like I was a perfect stranger!"

The professor and Thaddeus laughed hysterically.

"I'd like to see you two do better!" mocked Italicus.

"Hand it over!" insisted Thaddeus.

Italicus looked down at the horn of his saddle, "I don't have the slightest idea what you're talking about. I misplaced it, lost it actually."

Thaddeus snapped his fingers and opened his hand out, "Deal is a deal."

"Fine." grumbled Italiucs, pulling the gold feather from his inner jacket pocket, "I've really got to stop betting with you, my precious!"

Italicus handed Thaddeus the feather reluctantly, "THANK YOU!" he said with gusto.

The professor, confused, asked about the feather and its importance. Thaddeus was all too happy to share Italicus' great flight through the air.

During the story, a large thunderclap echoed in the sky. Suddenly, the clouds grew dark and hid the sun. A strange and eerie fog rolled in.

It was strange to see the contrast in weather so clearly. "That's puzzling," said the professor, still smiling.

"No worries, professor," Italicus pointed towards the direction of the river. "The fog comes and goes. It rolls off the river every now and then. It saved our bacon during the first engagement with the Slavine."

"I am not sure about this fog, Italicus. It seems off," remarked Thaddeus.

The men arrived back at camp just as the professor finished telling a particularly funny story involving himself, a woman, a dog, and a lot of motor oil.

It didn't take long for Thaddeus to gather his troupes and inform everyone of what had happened inside the village with Colonel Jaster, and what that meant for their current position. Thaddeus was disappointed with several members of his team, including Gladthorn and Edryss, who had ignored his orders to stay put while he was gone. Thaddeus understood their desire to see friends with whom they shared such hardship during the war, but orders were orders, and they would be punished upon their return. What Thaddeus had not thought to do was restrict people coming into the camp. Many of Mystique's villagers showed up to visit, bearing gifts of thanks.

Thaddues' gut had turned. Something was amiss. He was so sure of it. He realized what was wrong once he heard the Equinauts gossip about their encounters with villagers. Everyone who had visited with a villager seemed to share the same story. Their friends had developed some peculiar personality traits. Several Equinauts were reporting that they watched the mild-mannered people with whom they had lived for half a year suddenly behave un-characteristically. They would lash out at loved ones or enact random acts of violence on inanimate objects without provocation. Despite the random outbursts, what really struck Thaddeus as odd was how well Lister and Randoll were treating each other. After spending months with their constant bickering and antagonizing, it seemed impossible that they could be getting along so famously. Following the discord with Colonel Jaster, he knew something was amiss.

***

Glut's arms were tired, but not nearly as tired as the day before, moving all those boxes with Wrench. Training with the swords was hard and had lasted a good part of the day, Gladthorn had been his instructor. He was a decent teacher. Glut had been very interested to learn how to properly use a blade for many years now. Today of all days though, his mind just wasn't fully into it. He was worried for his sister. He kept a keen eye on her the entire day. He knew she would faint or die, or whatever it was that she does now. He had to make sure if it happened again he was nearby for her. Gladthorn could easily tell his mind was someplace else. That only meant Glut got worked longer and harder. It made things far more difficult than Glut had foreseen. Watching his sister was in vain, she never once fainted or died. There was one point he thought his sister was about to go down while practicing in a field of flowers near the Callan's house, but whatever spell of weakness that came over her stopped once she fell to her knees. Gladthorn, thinking Andi was just tired, called the practice to the end.

Glut was now sitting near the edge of the circle of wagons. He chose his spot specifically so he could see Andi reading her book in the shade of a wagon and still have an eye out for when the professor returned.

The professor arrived with Thaddeus and Italicus in good spirits, the three were laughing when Glut ran up to them.

"Professor, please. I need to speak with you?"

"Of course, my boy" said the professor smiling until he saw the look on Glut's face, "Will you give me a minute, all this riding, I need to find a privy."

Glut nodded and waited near one of two Mark V's that had been converted into bathroom facilities including showers. The professor was still tightening his belt when he walked down the small step ladder attached to the side of the wagon. Glut stood up and began to approach him when he stopped to the sound of yelling. He looked around and saw Dineela rushing passed him.

"Professor, come quickly!"

"What is the matter?" asked the professor, concerned, "Why aren't you in the wag-"

Dineela didn't have to say a word. The professor understood. The two dashed the way Dineela had come.

Glut reached out towards the two as they ran passed him, "professor!?"

Glut turned and ran. He didn't catch up to them until the professor was at the steps of the Mark III wagon. "Professor, please. I need to speak with you!"

The professor had the door part way open. He turned and looked at Glut. He was angry that he was followed, "GO AWAY! No one is allowed near this wagon!"

"Wait, please it's Andi. I need to talk to you about her!"

A loud, unnatural scream came from inside the wagon, "There are more important things here than your sibling problems!" yelled the professor slamming the door shut, leaving Glut scared, mad, and curious what the professor was hiding in the wagon.

***

Thunder rolled in the distance, but the sporadic lightning never spread to the village. The temperature dropped, and the wind whipped. It was as if the weather wanted to evolve into a rainstorm, but a celestial force was keeping it at bay. Andi and Leora felt cold, they had borrowed dresses from Gloria, but lacked proper jackets to wear over them. The ladies were agitated. Thaddeus had chosen to attend the feast alone. Andi was escorted by the professor. Leora, not wanting to be left behind, convinced Italicus to take her.

The forum was transformed. It was impressive, decorated in vibrant red and blue flowers, every torch light wrapped with ribbons and bows, long wooden tables draped with beautiful cloths and dotted with glowing gold candelabras. They opened the feast with a passionate, if heartfelt, prayer to the Maker lead by the mayor, who then invited Thaddeus and the professor to break the wishbone of the largest roasted pig they had cooked, a tradition to bring good luck and spread thanks for the sacrifice of the animals they would enjoy. The smell of the fresh food was thrilling. Everyone smiled, laughed, and sang, many danced to the rustic, upbeat music. It was a needed reprieve from the stress of their journey.

Leora was having a hard time in her dress. Callan's wife was short and petite. The dress was meant to be tea length, but Leora's height made it cut off just below her knees, and the normal waistline rose, creating an empire waist, causing Leora's bust to be pushed together and up. It was uncomfortable constantly adjusting the way the fabric swooped between her shoulders, attempting to maintain modesty. Despite her wardrobe problems, Leora sat at the head table. She was enjoying a well-seasoned roasted pork drizzled with a thick balsamic vinaigrette.

Andi and the professor sat opposite Leora, a few seats down the table. Andi couldn't make out what Leora was saying, but could see that her smile was bright, and she was enjoying her dish. Andi stared jealously. *At least she isn't Thaddeus' date. She's going to rip that dress the way she's squeezed into it. Is her hair lighter?*

"What are you staring so intently at?" The professor followed her gaze, and then leaned in close, "Oh, her? Why are you so worked up at Leora? She's a sweet young woman, really."

Andi bristled, "Yeah! Sweet, young, and just perfect. *Really*, tell me, professor, how was she able to hold off two shrieks, with barely a mark on her while I got killed by one? It's because you're right, she's just *perfect.*"

The professor was momentarily thrown off guard, uncertain how to comfort one who had died and come back. He starred at the person before him, who had so long been under his care, realizing for the first time that she was closer to a woman than she was to the little girl whose protection had fallen to him.

"Andrastii, you have nothing to be jealous over. First, I am very, very thankful for whatever power saved your life. And second, you are a remarkable young woman who has already accomplished so much!" The professor reached for his cup, took a large sip and quickly spat it out, "My god, what is this retched concoction?" it took him several seconds to compose himself from the nasty, bitter drink. He could see Andi was still upset, "Andi, few women and even fewer at your age can say they have graduated from college. You are head strong and street smart! Count your blessings my dear, you will find you have many."

The professor's compliments didn't make it past Andi's ears. Her eyes never broke from Leora, "I mean, where did she come from? Honestly professor, it's like she just appeared one day out of the blue. I never, ever saw her on campus *or* in the undergraduate program. Leora is nothing but a giant beacon. People all seem to love her and want to be near her. You would think I would have noticed her before, she's only a year behind me."

"There's an explanation behind every occurrence, no matter how bizarre it might seem."

Andi turned on the professor, with her lips pursed. This sounded suspiciously like he was defending Leora. "You have an explanation for this? Then spill it."

After a moment, the professor stroked his chin, "It's not my place to tell."

Andi was surprised that he actually might have the answer, "Please, professor, you know you can tell me anything. I won't say a word to anyone, I promise!" The words rushed from Andi's lips in a single unbroken line.

The professor felt an obligation to Andi. Further, he hoped sharing this information might help Andi soften towards Leora. He knew Leora wanted badly to befriend Andi.

"Very well, but you can't breathe a word to anyone, including Leora. Do you understand me!" demanded the professor, speaking firmly, and pointing his finger at Andi. "Her father came to see me about a year ago. He asked me if I would help him test Leora into college so she could start further ahead than normal."

"That's very unlike you, professor. You don't normally bend the rules for anyone," pushed Andi, but not too harshly. She was desperate for more information.

The professor shrugged his shoulders, "Normally, yes, I would agree with you, but there is more to the story than that. Her father is someone of importance who is trying to keep a low profile. Even then, I was going to refuse, but when I finally met Leora I just couldn't say no. There is something about her that I can't quite put my finger on."

This was not what Andi had wanted to hear, "And what does that mean?"

The professor frowned, "I am sorry, Andi, that's really all I can divulge. Leora herself doesn't fully know her family's history, I am afraid." He lifted his hand and pointed at Andi with his index finger, "Remember, you are not to say a word to anyone, especially not to her."

"Yeah, yeah, I know." Andi's voice trailed off and she returned to staring at Leora. *So, her father is special and she is too. Great.* At this moment, Andi felt her first tinge of sympathy for Leora: *She doesn't look happy anymore.*

Tonight was, by far, one of the worst dates Leora had ever been on. Not that she had gone on many herself, but on the few she had, at least the dates had tried to talk to her. Leora tried to laugh and kept up a fake smile to keep the appearance of having a good time.

"I have never seen such a feast before!" she offered, smiling at Italicus.

"Yes, it's very nice" slurred Italicus half-heartedly, his eyes focused on Meg who was wearing a fetching emerald gown and talking to several people across the forum.

Leora sneered at Italicus' disinterest. Looking across the table, Leora watched Thaddeus chat with the mayor and his wife. She wondered if Thaddeus was going to ask her to dance before the night was over. Further down the table, Andi and the professor were laughing and smiling. After emptying her plate, Leora walked towards a table nearby that had all sorts of sweets and desserts tastefully arranged. On her way, Leora was approached by a young man. He looked fewer than sixteen years old. Leora could tell right away he was nervous and unsure of himself.

"Hi, I am Lucian. My friends," Leora could see a gaggle of kids staring at her, "challenged me to ask the prettiest girl to dance." His face was bright red, "Would, umm, would you care to," His voice shrunk until she couldn't hear him at all.

Leora smiled brightly at the chance for something fun to do, "I would love to, Lucian!" She grabbed his hand led him to the wooden dance floor. Lucian mouthed some words, his face giddy, as the kids at the far table showed expressions of shock and disbelief.

Leora could tell Lucian was still nervous. The song was slower than the previous ones the band played, "It's ok, take your time and find the beat," she encouraged.

Lucian looked down at his feet sheepishly, "I am not much of a dancer."

"I'll let you on a little secret," Leora smiled and placed her lips near the young man's ears, "Neither am I!" She looked up and noticed that Thaddeus was still sitting at the table with the mayor and his wife but his face was turned to the dance floor, watching her, "But when you find the right partner, dancing is easy. It's just meant to be fun!"

Andi gave up obsessing over Leora once she started dancing with the young boy. The professor had been talking about the past and the many governesses that had come and gone through Andi and Glut's life.

Andi gave the professor a half smile, "You know I can never thank you enough for what you did for my brother and me. I feel like we were pretty ungrateful." Andi felt her cheeks burn.

"It was an honor as a godfather to be able to do it, my dear," answered the professor sincerely.

Andi choked on her drink, those words were not what she expected, "Godfather?" she asked, "I didn't know you were our godfather. How did you even know my parents that well?"

"Oh my, Andi, do you really not remember? It pains me how much that affliction affected your childhood. After all these years I thought you knew! Your mother and I are cousins! I introduced your mother and father." He paused to let it sink in. "I do miss them so! I forget how young you two were. Providing for you and Glut was the least I could do for them, and for you and your brother."

"Affliction!?" Andi looked at him completely confused, "What affliction are you talking about?"

The professor's heart skipped a beat. He realized that this was not the time or place for a conversation about the past. His eyes opened slightly larger than normal, looking around, trying to find something to help him escape. Without thinking it through, he took a quick sip of the contents in his cup, forgetting the bitterness. He nearly choked on the contents. He coughed several times, "You know one of my biggest regrets?" he asked trying to change the subject, "I wish I was able to spend more time with the both of you rather than leaving you in the hands of women like Governess Prumfley."

Andi's head was spinning, she was in disbelief that she was actually related to the professor and didn't understand what he meant by affliction. All these years she saw herself as a burden to the busy man who barely showed up. Though the mention of one of her last governesses roused her slightly and she answered in monotone, "Old Fatty Prum, we hated that woman."

The professor nodded and smiled, "She was so course and abrupt with everyone, she almost made me lose my temper during her hiring interview," the professor laughed, "but you two had gone through so many other governesses I thought some grit might have been what you needed."

"Thank you," said Andi abruptly.

"For what?" asked the professor?

"For just everything, professor. I know I have said this before, but thank you for taking care of us, paying for our education, inviting us on this expedition."

The professor removed his top hat, revealing a slightly bald head. He rubbed his forehead and placed his hat back on, "I don't know if you should be thanking me Andi. Recently I've realized it was selfish on my part to allow you and your brother to come along on a journey so dangerous. I thought it would be safer to have you with—"

"It *was* wrong of you, Mr. Belladon,"

Both Andi and the professor jumped at the sudden closeness of the man.

"Akroyd, what in the heavens are you doing here?" asked Nikola Belladon, shocked.

"I am here to show you reason! You steal university property, and falsely lead university members on a fool's expedition, and expect no repercussion?" Akroyd's voice and demeanor seemed strange to both Professor Belladon and Andi.

"How can he steal university property? He's leading an expedition *for* the university!" declared Andi, in Belladon's defense.

"Well, my dear, I am afraid he is partially correct on that matter. I was forced into a sabbatical by the Circle of Ministers. They wouldn't believe my warnings on the danger of the evil you saw in the mountains," the professor looked at Andi, embarrassed.

"They can't do that to you!" yelled Andi. The people around them began to stare.

"Nikola, old friend," pleaded professor Akroyd, "Come back to the Citadel. We know you didn't kill Deniz."

"Old friend," The professor felt stung, "how dare you say that to me? You, you're not my friend. Lying to the Circle about nothing happening in Diamin, the entire Theme is deserted! You are not Ray Akroyd! The man I know, the man whose life I saved so many years ago, would never turn his back on his *old friend*!"

"I am sorry you feel that way. Look how far you have fallen. You were once the university's best professor." Akroyd's face was twisted and covered with contempt. "What has happened to you?"

"It is not I who has fallen. It is you, Akroyd! I know what you really are, or what's inside my former friend. I will stop you!" Professor Belladon stood from his chair. "Andi, my dear, they are playing an excellent song, would you care to join me in a dance?"

Andi nodded and took the professor's extended hand. Akroyd grabbed the professor's other arm and pulled the professor face level. "Your foolish expedition is doomed, your deaths are certain."

"We will see about that!" The professor ripped his arm away, turned, and walked away to the dance floor.

***

Thaddeus had never been a fan of large social functions, especially now when he was one of the guests of honor. Everyone seemed to want a chance to talk with him, and several women offered to dance. He was having a difficult time finding polite ways to turn down the constant advances.

"Are you enjoying yourself?" asked Randoll, Lister following close behind.

"Quite so, amazing feast!" lied Thaddeus.

"Have you tried the Cherawaberry cake? Lady Ellis did a spectacular job!" insisted Lister.

"Not yet, but the night is young," Thaddeus tried to speak diplomatically. "You will have to forgive me. It still seems so strange to see you both next to each other and not trying to kill one another."

"It's been a long road!" exclaimed Randoll.

"Quite long!" added Lister.

Randoll laughed. "Now we are inseparable!"

"Best of friends!" replied Lister.

The contrast was unnerving. "Well, that's good to hear!" He held up his glass, "To good friends!"

Thaddeus and the two wealthy men raised their glasses.

Randoll and Lister continued to talk and Thaddeus half listened to them. His eyes were scanning the forum's perimeter. Throughout the night he was sure he had seen faces of the Citadel soldiers peeking out from nearby alley ways and buildings. Thaddeus was convinced something foul was afoot, he was just uncertain how or when it would rear its ugly head.

***

Italicus hadn't noticed Leora had left her seat. He looked around and saw her dancing with some young kid, smile on her face and dark red hair flowing with the unending breeze. Italicus took the chance to approach Meg, who had been talking to several people by the fountain and statue, but now stood alone with a plate in hand, eating a small pastry. Italicus took this chance to approach her.

"Hi Meg, I have to ask, you seemed so abrupt and off at the store, did I do something to offend you? Did you not get any of the letters I sent you?"

Meg's brown eyes seemed darker to Italicus and she was tense, very unlike the playful, clumsy, delightful woman he remembered. "No. Leave me alone, please," demanded Meg, her voice high but stony.

"Well whatever I did, or didn't do, I just want to say--" Italicus was forced to stop. Meg had rolled her eyes, turned, and started to walk away from him, mid apology. Italicus was shocked. Meg was not this type of person. He grabbed her arm to stop her from leaving, it was ice cold to the touch, "Meg, please let me apolog—"

Italicus fell to the ground. A fist from nowhere had struck him hard on the cheek. He jumped back up to find himself surrounded by four large men that he didn't recognize.

"Whoa, wait fellas, I was simply apologizing to the woman, I'm not even sure what I'm apologizing for, since she won't tell me, but I was apologizing nonetheless. So, we are all good right?" Italicus threw his hands up in a non-threatening gesture. The look on the men's faces were still extremely angry, "Meg, you're ok, right? Let them know I meant no trouble."

Meg stood, silent and motionless. A bright light filled the night sky, and illuminated her, followed by darkness, and a roll of thunder. For a brief moment, the four men seemed disorientated and Meg grabbed her head. She looked up at Italicus and smiled brightly.

"Italicus! Oh, my Italicus, it's really you!" her voice danced up and down, just as Italicus had always remembered it. She ran to him and hugged him tightly, "I'm so glad you are here, you have to help, something is happe—"

A new flash in the sky lit up the forum. Suddenly Meg pushed, struggling to free herself from Italicus' arms, her face stoic once more.

Italicus was so confused, "What the Bellows just happened?" he asked out loud.

The four men took a step forward. Italicus knew he was in trouble, and he wished he had his Tesla pack with him, "Come on guys, we can settle this like civilized men, we are not Slavine, right?"

The man closest to Italicus threw the first punch, just missing Italicus' head. Not waiting for the next swing, Italicus kicked out at the man in front of him and swung his right fist into the face of the man who had missed him. All four men began swinging and punching, several villagers began screaming at the sight of the fight.

Thaddeus was engaged in conversation with several villagers at his table, retelling their adventurous stories from the war. Thaddeus was somewhat relieved when he noticed the commotion. Now he was no longer on edge, here was the problem, right in front of him. He excused himself from the conversation. From the dance floor, the professor and Andi noticed Thaddeus abruptly leave the table and march off, and finally noticed the commotion themselves.

Thaddeus approached the ornate fountain. He was about to push through the crowd when they saw Italicus fly backwards, smashing right into the Equinaut statue, causing it to fall off its pedestal and hit the ground with a piercing crack.

"Perhaps we should find out what is happening" remarked the professor.

Andi nodded and began to follow the professor when she started to stumble. The professor still holding her hand turned just in time to see Andi's eyes roll into the back of her head and fall. He was barely able to catch her in time. "ANDI!"

Thaddeus spun around when he heard the professor's cry and looked confused to see Andi lying on the ground. He reached for his Medallion assuming it was about to begin to glow and heat up, but nothing happened. He started to move back towards the dance floor when a bright blue flash of light enveloped the entire forum. For a moment, everyone held their breath, the villagers were speechless, Randoll and Lister helped Italicus to his feet.

Italicus rubbed the side of his face. "Thank you. I am not sure what I did to deserve that!"

"IT'S RUINED!" yelled the mayor, "What, what have you done?"

Lister looked at the mayor, "It's ok, we can repair it!"

"What, with your lousy stonemasons? Look at the half-assed job they already did!" yelled Randoll furiously.

Lister turned to look at his friend. Unsure where the animosity and anger came from, Thaddeus watched as something began to change in Lister. A darkness was awakening inside of him.

Randoll looked furious, like the darkness had consumed him already. Thaddeus' gut began to turn, he knew there was about to be a major problem. The whole area began to feel tense, like the air was getting heavy. Italicus was standing between the two men cradling his head unaware of the tension rising around him.

Lister arched his shoulders and stood as tall as he could, "What is wrong with you, Randoll?!"

Randoll was copying Lister's pose, "What's wrong with me? It's that I have been friends with a dirty-blooded piece of garbage, and I can't take the smell anymore!"

Lister, the fury evident in his eyes, tackled Randoll to the ground and landed punch after punch into Randoll's head, chest, and arms. Thaddeus looked on in shock as he witnessed the villagers of Mystique begin to change. Nearly a quarter of them began to laugh in unison, the exact same laugh, breath for breath. The laugh was low and unnatural. Thaddeus reached for Italicus and started to step backwards away from the group and towards the dance floor. One by one the villagers fell to the power of the invisible darkness swirling around the forum. The statue inside the rings of the fountain began to cry and moan. It struggled to break its marble prison. The intensity of the situation increased with another bright blue flash of light. This time though, it was followed by an agonizing scream from the fountain. Men, women, and children of Mystique began to indiscriminately fight with life and limb. Thaddeus wasn't sure how to stop them without hurting them. It was obvious they were in some sort of haze. He felt guilty for wishing for more than small talk.

Echo from the Past

Twice in my life I have seen death at my doorstep, and each time I felt the same wonderment. The Maker ensured his corporeal creatures had souls, a tether to the ascended realm, but he never spoke about what would happen if an ascended creature should die. Where do we go? Is there anything after this? We always thought we were eternal, that was until the war. Perhaps the Maker never foresaw his ascended creations needing another path, never thought there would be war in the heavens.

My vessel and I faced that moment together. My temple was now glutted with unclean heathens who denied my status as a god. My city was burning, and my people cried out in terror as they were slaughtered by the invading army. From my knees, I could see my private courtyard fill with men who wished to see the death of me. I had not the energy to strike down a single one of them.

The magic man laughed cruelly and stared at me like I was pitiful and unimportant, no better than a bug to be squashed. For the first time I wondered whether that was how I looked to the billions of lives I had extinguished. Did I show them the same utterly disinterested contempt that this man showed me now? He sent out a surge of energy from his hands. The energy stream fractured into every color of light, each bringing another degree of pain. Pain was not a normal sensation for an ascended being. I felt it when I fell from grace. The pain from my wound. The pain seeing my brethren lose the war. I felt it now.

Every pore in my vessel's skin stung, burning from within. The pain was unbearable. I could feel my vessel's body began to breach. Her tendons pulled and her joints groaned. Gurgling gasps escaped her lips pulled tight. I tried to pull the pain into me so that my vessel would not suffer, but it was futile, we shared the same pain. The usurper asked for our surrender once more. I would never give up, never give in to something as unworthy as him, but my vessel, she was beginning to break. I assumed she was as strong willed as I was, but I was wrong. The mental door she had formed was where her weakness was coming from. What was in it? I had to know.

The magic man could see the suffering he was causing on us, and he began to laugh, delighted in the pain he caused. He snapped his fingers, and the heathens around him began to separate. They brought forth Aaron, bloodied and bruised. The magic man spoke to his followers.

"See what happens when you stand against Duth Dumak Arazeg the Necromancer!" Aaron looked straight towards me, his eyes still confident and sure, he prayed. I could hear his thoughts, let me die. Dumak raised his arm and prepared to kill Aaron, energy sprang to life in his palm. I prepared to watch one of my most faithful die for no reason other than following me willfully.

Suddenly, I moved forward. I was caught off guard. My vessel, who just moments ago was on the verge of giving up, of letting the man kill us, suddenly took total control of her body, tapping into a strength I had never before witnessed. I could do nothing. I was merely an observer. She raced towards Dumak who was unprepared for the sudden attack. She grabbed his energy filled hand and forced it into his own chest. Dumak's body began to shake violently, but another thing happened, something amazing, something marvelous. The energy, the descended power Dumak had tapped into began to flow through both of us. It ignited something inside myself and my vessel. I recognized that power, I knew it, it felt so familiar. We used the power to lash out at our enemies. Lightning bolts of pure energy flew from our body.

Dumak struggled to gain his composure, still shocked with pain. Aaron, who was still kneeling between Dumak and ourselves pulled out a small dagger from his boot and began to stab Dumak over and over again. We giggled at the sight. Blood spilled onto the ground, and the heathens were in a panic. Dumak cried out in pain. He muttered some foreign words and he and his army vanished in a brilliant flash of light.

I looked down upon my city from the top of my temple, and cried out in a voice that echoed for miles and miles in every direction, "YOUR GOD IS VICTORIOUS!" My followers looked up towards the sky and cheered and praised me, through the pain within them and the soot around them. I felt anew, so much power flowing through me, I lifted my vessel's arms towards the heavens and I made it rain. I now had control over nature itself.

Dumak left us with much death and more carnage. We healed as many people as we could, beginning with Aaron. I would have let the weak and injured die, but my vessel reasoned that this was a time for compassion. Our people had just gone through a great trial of faith and should be rewarded.

My people rebuilt their city and strengthened its walls. Soon, pilgrims from far off places began to migrate to the city, their stories were all the same--a mighty army appeared at their encampments and demanded total subjugation. The encampments that said no were burnt to the ground. We allowed these migrants into our city as long as they vowed their life and souls to their true god.

William F. James

A side effect occurred with this newfound power, it was too much for myself or my vessel to contain separately, which meant I could not leave her. It pained me. If I was going to find this Dumak and his heathen army, I needed to go to my Sanctum Sanctorum and reach out into the veil of the void. I grabbed a stone from my temple courtyard, and transformed the rock into a seele stone, a stone with the ability to absorb energy from the ascended realm. I transferred our new excess energy into the stone and kept it upon my alter. Of all things I have done in my existence, I regret this the most. Before long, I had stored enough strength in the stone to kill an ascended creature. I should have realized the possible consequences of my actions.

Leora Adriana

Chapter Seven

From the first scroll of Zakarael, chapter19 verse 19:
"It will become a sign and a witness to the Maker of hosts in the land.
For they will cry to the Maker because of oppressors, and He
will send them a Savior and a Champion, and He will deliver
them...."

Night blanketed the tight cluster of steam powered wagons on Callan's southern field. Throughout the camp, the professor's name was collectively called upon in distain. Those who had volunteered did so without the knowledge that they would be spending their waking hours in combat training. Tired and sore, they gathered about small campfires to share stories and commiserate with one another about their aches and pains. The smell of amazing foods from the village's impromptu feast lingered like a plague, torturing everyone's stomachs. Complaints about dinner, led by Wrench, ran rampant. Some of the Equinauts laughed at the spectacle Wrench was causing. He obviously didn't know that any dinner was better than another night of Hardtack bread.

Faramal sat near a small fire with his best friend Kaz. Faramal brooded over the previous night's demon attack. He was convinced of the Slavine's connection with the demons. To him it was obvious.

"They just don't get it. The Slavine are weeds that must be exterminated," implored Faramal, slamming his fist into the palm of his hand.

Kaz nodded his head and stared into the fire's embers, "You know that. I know that. But the rest of these people, they just don't get it. They know the Slavine are dangerous, but they have no concept of their barbaric cruelty. I have felt the task master's razor-sharp whip against my bare skin. I have seen the contempt they have for humans!"

Faramal stood up, "How are they are so blind? We must make them see the truth!"

Faramal and Kaz spent their night visiting each campfire, spurring rumors of Slavine involvement and the likelihood they had made an alliance with the demons. The Equinauts brushed off Faramal and Kaz's claims. Their hate for the Slavine was widely known. The university members, however, blissfully soaked in every word they said.

"They are practically one and the same! Both Have an errant disregard for the sanctity of life," was Faramal's reply to anyone who would challenge his accusation.

"Trust me, the only good Slavine is a dead Slavine" insisted Faramal to one campfire group.

Zapp, Niles, and Fryda rolled their eyes at Faramal and Kaz. Glut and Wrench followed suit.

"What about the Human Slavine? They better off dead too?" asked Zapp. Kazah stiffened, which prompted the modification, "Present company excluded, of course."

"Any Human Slavine that isn't actively trying to escape or kill their Slavine masters deserves death just the same!" replied Faramal defiantly. Kaz nodded his head in approval.

"Get out of here, Faramal," replied Zapp, tiredly. "Go find more willing ears, there are none among us."

Faramal eyed Zapp, "Watch yourself, I out rank you, Charles."

Zapp stood, "Get out of here, unless you want me to challenge that ranking"

"In a duel, experience wins over unpracticed talent," spat Faramal.

Zapp shook his head, "It may, we can test it out if you keep harassing us with unfounded and idiotic rumors of Slavine-demon alliances. We don't even know if these demons are really demons."

Faramal clenched his fists, "Fine, don't believe me, but when the Slavine come to kill us all, don't say I didn't warn you." And with that he stormed away.

"Someone's knickers are in a tight wad!" Wrench finishing the last bite from his plate, "What is wrong with him?"

"We all would like to know that," replied Fryda, poking a stick into the fire, "he is a great warrior, highly honorable, but his hatred for the Slavine is more of a mystery than Kazah's"

"At least with Kazah, with what little bit you know of him, you can understand his hatred. Banishment is a pretty tough thing to go through. But Faramal, who knows what's happened to him," supplied Niles.

"I heard Kaz wasn't banished," spoke Fryda in a low tone, "I heard that he was a slave. That he killed his master and escaped!"

"You really think so?" asked Glut, "That he's a murderer?"

"I don't think killing one Slavine, especially if he was mistreated, makes him a murderer.," stated Zapp.

Wrench cocked his head, "Isn't slavery, in itself, being mistreated?"

"Perhaps," Zapp paused, "but and I am just thinking out loud here, does the act of holding slaves alone merit murder? At what point is it ok to take a life when it isn't directly self-defense?"

After a moment, Fryda spoke, "It's definitely self-defense. Even in the best of conditions, slavery is a prison that kills you slowly. If it is true that he killed his master, he was acting out of self-defense. Besides, we've killed Slavine in battle. Does that make us murderers?"

Nobody was willing to answer the question. Everyone sat around the campfire, silently contemplating.

"I wonder how the feast is going?" asked Zapp trying to change the topic of conversation.

"I don't want to know!" lamented Wrench, his stomach growling and his mind filled with images of perfectly roasted pork wrapped in bacon, "The feast is in honor of the professor and the Equinauts, why aren't we there eating?"

Glut let out a small chuckle, Wrench looked over at the small friend "And what's so funny?"

"You wonder why you're not at the feast? It's because they want food for the rest of the village!" teased Glut, "Not just your stomach, Wrench!"

Wrench snickered slightly and looked at the others around the fire, "The wee lad does have a point."

Zapp nodded and smiled, "I believe I overheard the professor say an entire wagon of food was dedicated just for you Wrench!"

"REALLY?" asked Wrench, looking quite excited at the possibility.

Zapp smirked and very dryly said, "No."

Wrench frowned, "Well, I think someone should suggest that to him. A full stomach Wrench is a happier, more efficient Wrench!"

Niles spoke up, "When are you ever full?"

Everyone around the fire laughed.

"Well, I still want to know who was brave enough to keep me from food!?" bellowed Wrench, boasting mightily.

Fryda spoke up "It was Thaddeus who made the decision to-"

"Well then, Thaddeus, beware the power of a man's empty stomach!" teased Wrench "I'll eat his horse then!"

Nobody laughed, the looks given to him by the Equinauts around the fire told Wrench he had gone a little too far.

"If Thaddeus tells us to stay put in camp, I guarantee you there is a very good reason" stated Fryda, staring into the campfire's flames. "I would follow that man to the depths of Bellows if he ordered us to!"

Zapp and Niles both nodded, they too would follow wherever Thaddeus lead.

Everyone ate the small portion of food they had been allotted for the night in silence. Niles was the first to finish and was still hungry, "I wouldn't worry and think too much about the feast, it'll just get your stomach going," Niles stood up and looked towards the village, inhaling deeply. Even at this distance, the feast's aromas could be found swirling in the wind. Niles subconsciously licked his lips, "All the foods they cooked, the roasted chicken, pork, juicy steaks, pounds and pounds of bacon!"

A large growl was clearly heard…

"Good job Niles!" joked Glut, "You got Wrench hungry. Again"

Everyone laughed, Wrench winked at Glut, "It's not really that hard to do."

Fryda put down her plate, "He's not the only one, this isn't enough to keep a warrior fed!"

"I agree." added Zapp.

Wrench leaned back and picked up a very large, leather bag. He reached deep inside of its bowels. After several failed attempts at finding what he was looking for, he bent over and placed his massive head inside.

Glut laughed at the sight of the large man partially inside the small bag, "What do you have in there?" He reached a crossed and grabbed the bag away from Wrench.

Wrench was startled and gave Glut a look of sheer shock. He reached for the bag, but Glut was too fast and moved it from his reach. Wrench stood up and gave Glut a ferociously angry look. Glut never flinched, he was not intimidated by his large friend's size.

Glut looked inside the bag, his eyes gasped at the sight. Lifting his head he gave Wrench a perplexed look. He couldn't believe what he had seen. Beads of sweat began to form on the top of Wrench's forehead. Despite the worried look, he kept his angry eyes firmly locked on Glut's. Everyone else sat in silence, frozen, unsure what was about to happen. No one had ever seen Wrench look so angry before.

After several intense moments of silence, Glut began to giggle. The giggle quickly grew to a chuckle and right into a large, hardy laugh. Fryda, Zapp, and Niles looked at each other, completely lost at was happening.

The longer Glut laughed, the heavier Wrench's breathing got. Zapp was sure he was about to see the poor kid's head bashed in. Wrench took a step forward and knelt down, his eyes never looking away from Glut's. Wrench clenched his fists together and popped his knuckles. He reached down and placed his hand into the bag that Glut was holding. Wrench's large hands scurried inside for a few seconds.

"It's right there." replied Glut, pointing towards the back of the bag.

Wrench bit his bottom lip slightly. He then proceeded to pull out a partially eaten turkey leg wrapped in paper.

Wrench began to rise and ferociously, yet softly, yelled, "MINE!"

Glut started to laugh again, and after taking a massive bite out of the turkey leg, Wrench joined in.

Zapp looked up at the turkey leg, back down to the bag, then back up to the turkey leg and once more back down to the bag, "Wait, WHAT!!! You have food in there!?"

Niles licked his lips, "Ummm, Wrench, what else do you have stuffed in that bag? You wouldn't happen to have a pie in there? I have been craving a warm, freshly baked pie"

"What kind of pie?" asked Fryda, smiling. Her head filled with the image of a warm baked pie, freshly cooked.

"Any pie as long as it's fresh" interjected Zapp, licking his lips.

Glut looked down at his feet for a moment, "Well…"

Wrench let out a large cough and grunt.

Glut looked up and stared very intently at his friend, nodding down towards the bag.

Wrench's eyes widen in sheer terror and shook his head no over and over again.

"Wait, what is this?" asked Niles, who had been quietly watching Glut and Wrench silently communicate to one another.

"What's what?" asked Zapp, who looked at Niles confused and then at Glut and Wrench.

"Maker's beard, you do, don't you?" exclaimed Zapp completely shocked and surprised.

Wrench's face was no longer stern, he now had the look of sheer terror and he was slowly trying to reach down to grab his bag while still holding on to his turkey leg.

Zapp was quick, grabbing the bag and pulling it to his position around the camp fire, "You DOOO!!! You have an entire baked pie in here." Zapp took a huge wiff, "Cherawaberries, this is a Cherawaberry pie! How did you get a fresh Cherawaberry pie?"

Wrench stood over him and ripped the pie from Zapp's hand and held it like a baby, "If you must know, I uh, I nicked it off of Lady Callan's window sill!"

Everyone in the circle began to laugh.

"Wrench!" yelled Fryda, "That's not very honorable. I know you're not an Equinaut, but while we are protecting you we don't steal from our hosts!"

Wrench turned slightly red, "I wouldn't have, but she would only sell me a fully cooked turkey, steamed carrots, and a half a pound of bacon." Wrench held out his hands, waving his turkey leg around and looking at his friends like his logic was completely obvious. "Honestly, bacon and turkey, but not a pie to go with it? Was she trying to starve me or something?"

Zapp and Niles locked eyes and squinted, trying to see if the other understood Wrench's logic for stealing. "You have all that in your bag?"

Glut shook his head, "At one point maybe, but not now."

"You ate all that food already today and your're still hungry???" said Zapp amazed, "do you even have a stomach or does it just fall right through you?"

Wrench sat back down, staring at the ground for a moment. For the first time he looked slightly embarrassed, his eyes staring at the group like a sad, guilty puppy, "You're not going to make me give it back, are you?"

Zapp, Niles, and Fryda looked at each other in silence. They weren't sure what to do.

Fryda knew the right thing was for him to take it back, but when her eyes locked back onto the pie, her moral compass quickly went askew. "Well, nothing we can do about it now. But next time, NO STEALING!!!" stated Fryda firmly in a warrior's voice, "You got that?" she waited for Wrench to acknowledge her.

Wrench nodded.

"Good, now that that is settled, you are going to share right?" asked Fryda smacking her large lips together.

The look Wrench gave her was utter shock and worrisome. Obviously, the thought had not occurred to him and he subconsciously pulled the pie closer to his chest. Standing up slowly, Wrench looked at every hungry face around the camp fire. His worrisome look was slowly changed and he began to grin brightly, everyone else copied the same goofy grin. Zapp, Fryda and Niles were excited, thinking Wrench had relented about sharing and they reached for their plates.

Glut on the other hand knew something was afoot, stood up, and reached for the pie, "Don't."

Once Wrench knew Glut had figured his plan out, he had no choice but to act. Being such a hefty, brawny, and massive man, no one would have thought Wrench would be particularly fast. But without warning, Wrench began to sprint away from the campfire, turkey leg in one hand and a pie in the other.

Niles and Fryda were frozen in place trying to understand what they were seeing.

Zapp on the other hand jumped up, "GET THE PIE!"

He chased after Wrench. The rest of the group, including Glut, were close behind, all wanting a piece of the Cherawaberry goodness.

Zapp thought about whistling for Face to help chase after Wrench. He couldn't believe how fast he was running, "I hope Thaddeus and Italicus don't have to chase after their food!"

***

Chaos erupted in the village forum. The peaceful feast was now a brawling match for every single grudge and slight the villagers had ever felt. Like a pot of boiling water, uncontrollable carnal rage bubbled up to fill each villager. The more they fought, the more intense the fury inside them became. Thaddeus could not believe what he was seeing, dodging several punches and kicks aimed at him. How could these normally peaceful, nonviolent villagers, who just a year ago could barely defend themselves, be brawling like crazed maniacs? Chairs and dishes were being thrown, and food was flying everywhere! Several villagers ripped torch lights from the ground and were using them as long, fiery lances, stabbing and bashing everything and everyone they saw. Fires soon burned all around the forum.

"Oh dear, oh dear," mumbled the professor, taking several steps back while holding his cane like a sword. He had placed himself between Andi and several crazed villagers. The feast had been going so well, the food had been delicious and the professor had enjoyed the opportunity to spend some quality time with Andi. There had was no way they could have predicted how quickly things would turn for the worse. "Stay back! I am warning you, I will not let you harm my godchild!"

Three villagers awkwardly slithered towards the professor and Andi. They stared at Andi's lifeless body like it was a roasted pork from early this evening.

The professor swung his cane several times through the air, pain seemed to be the only thing the villagers understood. No amount of pleading or talking was getting through to them. The tallest of the three made a dash towards the professor, aiming for Andi. Professor Belladon swung with his cane, smashing the villager's face and sending him to the ground. A loud snap and crack from the villager's jaw bone was clearly heard. The professor smiled slightly, he didn't want to hurt anyone but he felt good knowing he was capable of defending himself if he had to. Despite the break and the sheer amount of pain the taller villager had to be in, he pulled himself unnaturally back up to his feet. The professor was not going to wait for the villager to fully recover, he swung his cane. He swung it again and again until the villager no longer had a face or skull.

The two other villagers began to move forward now, "AAHHHHHHH" roared the professor defiantly, "I WILL TAKE YOUR HEADS OFF TOO!!!"

The two villagers roared back, the noises from their mouths sounded far more creature-like than human. The sound was quite unnerving to the professor. He unconsciously took a step backwards, stepping on Andi's left hand. "Sorry!" he whispered. When Andi did not react, his heart sank.

The professor looked up just in time to see the two villagers make their move. He lifted his cane up and waited for them to get into range. Hoping he could recreate the last attack, he swung for the villager's face on his right, but was stopped when the other villager grabbed his cane and ripped it from his hands. Scared and defenseless, the professor moved backwards, tripping and falling on top of Andi. Having no other option, he placed his whole body over his godchild, hoping he could protect her for a moment longer. The professor squeezed Andi as tightly as possible, squeezed his eyes shut and waited for the pain.

Four pairs of hands grabbed him by the back of his jacket and pulled him up. The professor hoped it was Thaddeus and Italicus. He opened his eyes to see the driveling, hungered looks of one of the villagers. "GREAT SCOTT!" screamed the professor trying to break their grasp. The villagers clawed at him, trying to take bites out of his neck.

"PROFESSOR!" yelled Thaddeus, rushing towards him and Andi. Italicus was several steps behind him. It took seconds for his rescuers to reach him, but it felt like minutes. The villager's attacks were relentless, he had claw marks across his face and his clothes were tattered.

The professor fell to his knees, Thaddeus and Italicus did quick work to the professor's attackers. They were lying in a pool of black and red blood. The forum was still in chaos with people were fighting each other, but for now the immediate danger was gone. The professor's concern immediately went to Andi.

"What happened to Andi, professor?" asked Thaddeus. "Was she struck by someone or something?"

"No!" barked the professor, he was patting her body down in a frantic and strange manner. "Where is it? She promised to never let go!"

Thaddeus searched the area, "Where is Leora?"

The professor didn't answer, he was still searching through Andi's clothes.

Italicus knelt down next to the professor and Andi's body, "What are you looking for, professor?"

"A family heirloom! It has to be here!"

Thaddeus continued his search, there was no sign of her, "Can't this wait!?" yelled Thaddeus, annoyed the professor was more concerned with an object than with a person. "She is hurt. We need to get her out of here and find Leora. Once we are safe then you can find your valuable heirloom!"

"NO!!! I HAVE TO FIND IT!" yelled the professor passionately, paying no attention to Thaddeus' anger.

The professor's yell carried across the forum, attracting more villages towards them. Thaddeus tapped Italicus' shoulder and the two charged their attackers. Fighting against out of control opponent is easy work for a disciplined fighter. The villagers' attacks were over extended leaving them vulnerable. It took only several minutes for the two Equinauts to put down a dozen villagers.

One of the buildings on fire came crashing down onto the forum's streets. Debris flew past Italicus, just missing his face. "This is getting ridiculous. We need to get out of here!"

Thaddeus nodded he agreed.

"WHERE IS IT ANDI!" Giving up that it was on her person. The professor was on his hands and knees looking on the ground. "It has to be here!"

Thaddeus was appalled that the professor was still searching for whatever this object was. "Damn it Belladon, I was just beginning to think you were a good person. That this whole expedition was a truly selfless act by a good man, but this is the last straw! We are getting Andi out of here and I swear whatever treasure or fortune you thought you would find out here will be pyrrhic for you."

Thaddeus was about to reach down and grab Andi when the professor grabbed him by the front of the jacket. Thaddeus' first instinct was to defend himself, "No, don't touch her. Her father he made her an amulet. A pendent. It will help her."

"Help her what?" asked Italicus standing next to them quite confused.

The professor was still holding onto Thaddeus's jacket, "When Andi was a child, she was afflicted with these sleeping spells. Her heart slows down to a single beat per minute. Her father and I never figured out why or how, sometimes she was afflicted for minutes, or hours at first. Then it became days, weeks, and then months. No doctor could diagnose her. We had some luck with a few flowers from the Aedunic realm. Then we found this ore, and as long as she is near it, she will stay awake." The professor let go of Thaddeus, "I have to find that pendant, its missing. Without it I have no clue when, or if, she will wake up. "

"Forgive me professor. I misjudged you." Thaddeus unzipped his jacket and pulled out a chain with a pendant on the end of it. "I think this is what you are looking for!"

"Oh, thank Arcadia, that's it!" yelled the professor, "But how did you have it?"

"Long story, just use it." ordered Thaddeus, "we have to find Leora and get out of here."

Leora had no idea what exactly was happening. Dancing with Lucian one moment, and the next the kid was attacking her. At first she thought the kid had just gone crazy, but when everyone around the dance floor began brawling she knew something worse was happening. She was having trouble defending herself. She didn't want to hurt him.

"Please, stop!" yelled Leora panicking, kicking him away from her.

"I am coming, Leora!" yelled Thaddeus, running to her position.

Lucian screamed something unintelligible and lunged at Leora. Thaddeus rushed towards her and managed to place himself in between her and Lucian. There was a loud crack as Lucian's jaw broke from Thaddeus' sudden right hook. The impact left Lucian lying on the ground, unconscious.

"You killed him!" Leora stepped back in horror.

Thaddeus shook his head, "No, but he will be in pain when he wakes up. Come on, let's get going!"

Thaddeus was relieved when he saw Andi awake. The professor and Italicus were leading her to his position. "Good to see you awake."

Andi shook her head, she honestly had no clue what he meant or what the hell was happening.

"Why is everyone fighting?"

"No time to explain." Thaddeus grabbed Andi by the hand, and lead everyone down the forum.

"This way everyone!" ordered Thaddeus, "Keep moving, don't stop for anything." Thaddeus ducked just before a flying plate nearly smacked him in the head, "And keep your heads down!"

The deeper they moved through the forum, the more difficult it became to move. Villagers with crazed, uncontrollably hungry looks were running amok. Thaddeus and Italicus braced themselves against the oncoming charge.

"I told you we should have brought our swords!" yelled Italicus, blocking a large male villager from getting through to the professor and the girls.

"You're right!" bellowed Thaddeus, holding back two villagers himself. "Remind me about this the next time we have a feast in our honor!"

Nearing the edge of the forum, both Thaddeus and Andi let out cries of pain and grabbed at their chests.

"Stop! Help! I'm burning up!" screamed Andi, clawing at her dress, searching for a wound.

Thaddeus grunted, the pain was great. He pulled out his medallion, and it was glowing bright gold.

Andi did not understand, "Why is it glowing? Are you hurt?"

"I don't know, it's reacting to some—" Thaddeus didn't get to finish his sentence.

The entire forum went quiet. The villagers were still fighting, but all sound seemed to disappear. Everyone found themselves taking very large breaths, gasping for air. It didn't matter how much you gulped in, it wasn't enough.

Thaddeus tried to yell, but nothing was coming out. With no oxygen to feed them, the fires all over the forum were dying, each torch extinguished. From the darkness, a low, deep sound echoed between the buildings. A single voice seemed to rock the foundation of the village, it began to laugh, a terrible, mean, nasty laugh. After the laughter, words, "Daevaentala has risen. Your doom, revived!

Italicus looked to Thaddeus, asking for direction. But Thaddeus was engrossed in his own pain, he was leaning against a wall, doubled over.

"My time is nigh! The day cometh that you would pay for the sins of your fathers' against me! Your death will pass, forgotten, and the power of the gods will be mine!" A new sound emerged and grew, like glass shattering. A bright blue flash blinded everyone.

A loud sound like a train rumbling in the sky roared overhead. Air suddenly returned, Leora felt her ears pop from the radical pressure change.

"What in Bellows was that!?" gasped Leora hoarsely, tears running down her face.

Andi was on the ground, "I felt like my heart was about to be ripped out of me!" Andi looked right at Thaddeus, "What did you do? What was that?!"

Thaddeus was breathing deeply trying to catch his breath, "I don't, I'm sorry, I don't know."

The professor was bent over, his hands on his knees, "You heard the voice Andi, sins of his fathers'. This could be the creature leading the demons."

Andi opened her mouth to respond when high pitch squeals erupted, multiplying in echoes off of every building in the forum. Shrieks began pouring out of alley ways, the very same alley ways in which Thaddeus knew he had seen the Citadel soldiers hiding. The shrieks charged and attacked the villagers who were too occupied with each other to notice the threat descending.

"We've really got to go. Like, now!" yelled Italicus.

Thaddeus yanked the nearest torch pole from the ground. This was no longer a village brawl, it was a full-fledged demon attack, and he had the professor and the girls to protect. Swinging the unlit pole around, he bashed anyone who charged at him. The shrieks were keeping their distance, attacking nearby villagers who were too focused on their personal fights to see the coming demons.

As they neared the exit, an enormously large shriek leapt into their path. Thaddeus swung at it with his pole, which did nothing to the shriek, who ripped it from Thaddeus' hands.

"RUN!" yelled Thaddeus, pointing towards a dark alley way, partially consumed by the smoke of the reignited fires. Lightning struck again and again, causing many of the buildings to the north to catch fire, which spread easily among the wooden structures. It was quickly consuming the entire village.

"This way! This will lead us to the next street!" Italicus led the group into the alley. He was running as fast as he could until he had no more room to run. Italicus' heart dropped when he realized this alley was a dead end, and there was no way out.

"That wasn't here a year ago!" Italicus backtracked, "Turn around it's a dead end!" But it was too late. The others were following behind him, and the shriek was following behind them. It now blocked the entrance of the alley way.

The smoke was getting heavy, and everyone was coughing uncontrollably. Two more howls could be heard. The shrieks had brought friends. They were slowly floating towards the group, taking their time. Their prey had nowhere to run, trapped. The crumbling, crackling sound of fire was nearing their channel.

"Thaddeus, what do we do?" asked Andi. The fear was evident in her voice.

"I'll charge them, you guys make a break for it!" yelled Italicus.

Thaddeus was about to protest when the shrieks pushed their way through the smoke and revealed themselves. The quintet stepped back, now pressed against the wall. The shrieks stopped a few strides from them, allowing a person to emerge from between them.

Relieved and confused, Italicus yelled, "Meg, what are you doing?"

The fire to her left cast a dark shadow to half of Meg's face, she turned her head unnaturally, almost horizontally, to her right, "You think a simple villager could control such evil?" the voice emanated from her mouth, but wasn't hers. It was dark, male, the same voice they had heard in the forum. "She is but a puppet to her master!"

"Her master? Are you the leader to the evil we have seen outside the mountain range?" Thaddeus moved in front of the girls and the professor, acting as a shield.

"You know nothing! Those demons and their whore, they are insignificant. For I am the Harbinger that is to come! I am the instrument of creation's destruction! All will cower before my might, good and evil alike, all will know who I am. Bow to me now, PenRuger!"

"Bow to whom?" asked Thaddeus, standing his ground.

Meg's body stretched until she towered over Thaddeus, "You forget me so soon? I am the Daevaentala! The mammoth of your past, I am Duth Dumak Arazeg! Put your nose to the dirt, and maybe I will kill you quickly."

***

Edryss and Gladthorn could not believe how long they slept. Gladthorn had taken her to a clearing in the wooded area north of Mystique. The Ador river snaked across the wooded area, its waters heated from the sun's rays. Several large trees umbrellaed over the shore and water. The locals around Mystique placed several rope swings along lower hanging branches, it was the perfect spot for picnic.

"When we retire, this is where I want to build our house!" Edryss sang happily, "Against the water, I want to wake up each morning to the sound of that beautiful brook and your loud snores."

"Snores?" laughed Gladthorn rubbing his chin and smiling, "I don't snore."

Edryss held in a laugh, causing her to let out a small snort, "Right, that's from a squirrel in your pocket?"

Gladthorn smirked and drank from a cup filled with red wine.

"Explain to me this?" asked Edryss, holding tightly to Gladthorn's hands.

"What's that, my sweet?" asked Gladthorn, bringing her small fingers to his lips.

"It's so peaceful out here, why did we have to bring our tesla packs with us?"

Gladthorn laughed, "Probably shouldn't have. They're a kind of reminder that moments like these are to be treasured because we don't know when, or if, there will be a next time. Plus, you know Thaddeus and Italicus, 'always ready, at a moment's notice,' and its one less thing they can use against us. It's so late, there is no way our absence wasn't noticed."

"Was it worth it?" Edyrss smiled, staring at the setting sun, whimsically.

"A single moment with you is worth any trouble I may get into!" Gladthorn leaned over and kissed Edryss' neck.

"I can't believe you remembered about that small brook!" giggled Edryss.

"How could I forget, it was the first time you told me you loved me, one of the best days of my life!" Gladthorn laid back on the blanket, his hands behind his head. "I just wish the weather had held up!"

"Hush, you!" Edryss sunk down and snuggled into his side, her head resting on his broad chest, "It could have rained the entire time, it wouldn't have mattered!"

Gladthorn bent forward and kissed Edryss' crown. He breathed in, smelling her hair, "Maker help me, I don't know how I am going to resist you when we get back to camp."

"Oh, I'll make you resist, Gladthorn Jones, -with a quick slap across the face and knee in your... potatoes!" laughed Edryss and looked down at Gladthorn's face. She didn't want to show it, but ever since Malus, she worried about Gladthorn. "Why did you kill the father?"

Gladthorn's smile dropped and his face became stoic. Edryss could not tell if he was upset by her asking. "I did what I had to do, what I will always do, anything I have to do to protect you! Heavens may hang in the balance and I will always choose you!"

"But you were supposed to save him. The code, the bloodhounds, being an Equinaut, does that mean nothing to you?"

"It means nothing if it means I would lose you!" stated Gladthorn unemotionally. "For years I have watched the pain and burden Thaddeus carries for the murder of his wife. A murder he can't even avenge or bring to justice. I don't ever want to deal with that amount of pain. I hold so much against myself. I don't know if I could keep living if-"

"If you had to deal with the pain?" interrupted Edryss, miffed. "That's kind of selfish."

"Selfish?" Gladthorn's stoic face and voice turned slightly, she had greatly insulted him. "Why would you even bring this up today, Edryss? You know why I did it. What do you want me to say? I don't know if I could keep living without you! You are the reason I deal with the pain and burden of my past. You are the light around which my whole world revolves. My code, my discipline, I used to use it to keep myself centered to be a greater man. Now I use my discipline so that I don't climb the highest tree or the tallest mountain and declare to the world my love for you. I know how important it is for you to be an Equinaut and helping people who can't help themselves. I could never take that away from you. Because if I did, then I would be selfish."

Gladthorn waited for Edryss to say something. Instead of speaking, she swung her leg over Gladthorn and pushed herself up, hands on his chest. As she bent to kiss him, her hair fell around his head, closing them in with a shiny black hair curtain so that the whole world consisted only of their faces. Their eyes, their lips, and that little spot where their noses touched.

"I love you Edryss!"

"I love you too, Mr. Jones," answered Edryss, unbuttoning the buttons of his tan leather jacket.

***

The smell of singed wood woke Edryss. She sat up disoriented, unsure of how much time had passed. She turned to look at Gladthorn, who was snoring deeply, and shook him awake.

"What's burning?" he asked sleepily. It was at this point that they noticed just how much smoke filled the sky, obscuring the stars. Edryss and Gladthorn knew there must be trouble. They got up and ran as fast as they could. The closer they got to the source of the smoke, the more certain they were it wasn't a large campfire. The whole village must be in flames. If that was indeed the case, they knew the Equinauts were going to be right in the middle of the rescue efforts.

As they reached the peak of a hill, they saw destruction and fire. "What happened? I don't see any white smoke, are they not trying to put out the flames?"

Gladthorn scowled at the sight of the fire, it reminded him of a village Malus had burned to the ground, "I don't know."

Once they reached the edge of the city, neither of them were prepared for the carnage. Bodies were strewn in pieces everywhere, their chests ripped open. Edryss and Gladthorn were horrified at the sight.

"What happened here?" asked Edryss, under her breath while igniting her Plaz sword.

"These are too similar to the wounds from last night. Keep your eyes peeled for shrieks," said Gladthorn with anger and disgust in his voice. "These are villagers. I don't see any Equinauts or anyone from the university team!"

The two crept swiftly towards the commotion, following profane screams and yells. As they approached the forum they were ambushed.

Five soldiers dressed in Citadel armor with a blood-soaked stone painted on their chest barreled towards them from nearby buildings, swords drawn and charging fast. Edryss and Gladthorn, though confused, ran straight for their attackers, limiting the impact strength of their charge. The well trained Equinauts activated their hard-light shields just before coming into contact with the guards. They smashed their shields into their opponent's chests, sending the guards flying to the ground.

"What the hell? I am a Citadel citizen, stand down!" yelled Gladthorn, but the guards   seemed fixed on one purpose: to kill Gladthorn and Edryss. As blow after blow fell, the two blocked, hiding behind their shields.

"I don't think they care!" yelled Edryss, thrusting with her shield, throwing off balance one of her attacker, "Permission to defend myself?"

"Granted!" answered Gladthorn.

Blood spilled onto the dirt. Edryss and Gladthorn used their swords in a deadly and accurate fashion. Three of the five soldiers were dead on the floor before they had time to react to Gladthorn and Edryss' change in stance.

Out of the smoke emerged a man dressed in full armor. Gladthorn looked to him, confused, "Colonel Jaster? What is the meaning of this? Your men attacked us!"

The colonel's head cocked and he ran his hand along his blade's shaft, "Fear not, young man, they've obviously made a mistake. They were meant to kill you!" The voice was not the colonel's.

"I've got these two, take him down!" yelled Edryss, charging the remaining guards.

Gladthorn hesitated. Killing his own brethren, a man he knew no less, was much different from killing a Slavine soldier or a bandit. The Colonel smashed into Gladthorn's shield with great force, breaking Gladthorn from his momentary reverie. The colonel raised his sword and struck down at Gladthorn. Completely surprised by the speed with which the colonel moved, Gladthorn dodged the colonel's strikes by scant inches. Swinging his own sword, Gladthorn met with nothing but air. The colonel jumped out of the way with ease. They continued to fight, swing and deflecting, one blow and then another. They were evenly matched, despite the great age and size disparity.

Edryss felt exhausted, and by the time she had finished off the last of the guards she could feel her legs shaking, struggling to catch her breath. *I am glad Leora isn't here to see this.* She watched Gladthorn and the colonel continue their rapacious fight. Two alpha male animals pounding on each other for leadership of the pack.

The two slammed into one another, shield against shield. Toiling to overpower the other, grunts and steel clangs echoed off the nearby buildings. Gladthorn pushed with all his might, but somehow the colonel seemed to be stronger. Gladthorn could feel his footing begin to give out. He knew he had mere seconds before he could be thrown to the ground. Pulling back his sword, Gladthorn leapt from the ground and thrust his sword over his own shield and that of the colonel's. He aimed his blade downwards, towards the colonel's face. The colonel, unprepared for such a desperate and unwonted move, turned his head in time to miss the blade, but not by enough to miss the hilt of Gladthorn's sword which smashed into his forehead. The colonel collapsed to the ground and Gladthorn fell atop him.

Gladthorn's sword was trapped underneath of the colonel, so he pushed his forearm into the colonel's throat while Edryss kicked the colonel's own sword from his hand.

"Gladthorn, please wait…" choked out the colonel. Gladthorn was shocked to hear his normal voice. Color flooded into the colonel's skin.

"It's inside of me, in my head! It's constantly scratching at me, forcing me to give in, to obey its words. You must kill me, before it takes over again, but more so, you must destroy that!"

Gladthorn had no idea what the colonel meant.

"You must destroy it, only a few of us are actually corrupted and possessed. The rest of the villagers are being manipulated."

Gladthorn frowned, "I don't understand."

The fighting in the forum began to pour into the street around Gladthorn and Edryss. Hundreds of villagers, covered in blood and wounds, many of their faces swollen beyond recognition, continued to beat and fight one another. Several of them, people they recognized, ran and crawled viciously towards them. Edryss held them off as best she could, trying not to hurt them beyond the injuries they had already sustained.

"We have to do something," yelled Edryss, punching a poor villager in the gut, "Please, stay down!"

The fighting continued to stretch further down the street. Edryss and Gladthorn began retreating backwards, Gladthorn dragged the colonel with them.

"STOP IT!" yelled Edryss, scared and confused watching friends and loved ones screaming, punching, and kicking one another. "Why are you doing this? We don't want to hurt you!"

Gladthorn had had enough. He activated his sword and held it at the ready. He was not going to allow Edryss to be hurt by these villagers, friends or not. He began swinging at anyone who dared to get close, several villagers lay at his feet, disemboweled.

"Gladthorn, don't hurt them!" yelled Edryss, horrified.

The colonel grabbed Gladthorn's pant leg and pointed towards the forum. Gladthorn looked out and saw a large gem atop of the ornate fountain. The gem was in the hands of the woman statue near the northern edge of the forum. It was several hundred yards away, but it was glowing and easily seen even at this distance.

"It's, it's what causing the villagers to strike out at one another! Destroy it. Hurry!"

Gladthorn threw his sword to the ground, and drew his rifle.

"You need to get closer! There is no way you can hit that!" yelled Edryss, kicking and pushing at her attackers.

Gladthorn found his sights and took a breath. He fired his Tesla rifle, and the shot was true and sure. He hit his mark perfectly, and the sapphire shattered. A bright flash of blue light blinded everyone. The villagers dropped onto the ground crying, exhausted, bloody, and in pain.

"Nice shot!" said Edryss, shocked.

"Did you really doubt me?" asked Gladthorn, throwing a wink at Edryss.

"AAAAHHHHHHH" A blood curdling scream in the distance, followed by cries of pain and crying. The statue holding the gem was moving.

"What in Bellows is happening here?"

"It's coming back. I can feel it." The colonel yelled.

Gladthorn hooked his rifle back on his pack and retrieved his sword.

"There, there are others like me," said the colonel, who was visibly struggling. "They can't be helped. Kill them. They must die. They can't be left to finish his work."

"What work? Whose work?" asked Edryss.

The colonel was beginning to shake, his body wracked with trembles, "He will betray her. She thinks he is her servant but…"

Gladthorn frowned, "Colonel, I don't understand."

"I don't ha… have much time," Colonel Jaster pulled out a key from his pocket, "this is ta… to my pur… urse wag…" The colonel's head rolled sideways, his skin grew dark, and a sadistic smile was forming on the colonel's face. "Death to PenRuger and all his allies."

Gladthorn did not hesitate a second time. He plunged his sword down into the chest of the colonel, whose face went from smile to shock. His body tensed up and then went limp.

***

"You forget me so soon? I am the Daevaentala! The mammoth of your past, I am Duth Dumak Arazeg! Put your nose to the dirt, and maybe I will kill you quickly."

Thaddeus took a step forward, putting space between himself and the others, "You want me. I will bow, I am yours, if you will let the others go."

"You presumptuous child, you will—"

Whatever Meg's body was about to say was lost as the fire beside them roared and the building was consumed and collapsed into a pile of rubble, embers, and smoke. As it crumbled, it leaned, directly over Meg and the shrieks. Italicus rushed forward, looking for a way to escape through the wreckage. Hope for survival was lost seconds later when loud, high pitched howls pierced through the smoke and dust. The shrieks were moving, unaffected by the fall.

There was no way out, there was no place to run, and they had no weapons with which to defend themselves.

"What are we going to do?" asked Leora, coughing.

"I am going to throw myself at the shrieks, try to buy you enough time to slip past them!" Thaddeus shoved the girls towards the building that still stood, to their right.

"You can't," yelled Leora.

"I'm not leaving you," insisted Andi.

"He can, and you will," Italicus said firmly, taking both girls' hands.

The shrieks were still not visible through the thick, black smoke, but the sound was getting louder, and they were getting closer. The howls pushed through their ears and reverberated into their very souls. They had mere seconds left before the shrieks would descend upon them and surely rip them to shreds.

"Run on the count of three!" said Thaddeus.

"One!"

"Two!"

"Three!"

As Thaddeus charged for the shrieks, a bright, orange light pierced through the smoke and dust in front of him. There were screams of pain, and then nothing. Through the smoke a figure was visible, illuminated by the ignited blade at its side.

It was Meg. She stood swaying, completely covered in ash and soot. Her gown was ripped and she fell to her knees. There was a very large gash on her forehead, blood running down her face and neck.

"Meg!" yelled Italicus, running to her and gathering her in his arms.

"Go. Now!" Meg dropped the Plaz and tried to push Italicus from her, "Before I hurt you!"

"You aren't going to hurt me!" replied Italicus, holding her tightly.

"I will, Italicus. I will kill you. The voice in my head is too strong. So go!!" Meg broke away from Italicus and stood.

"What are you talking about?" asked Italicus.

Meg began convulsing, her body was bending in unnatural ways, her skin was turning grey "I'm sorry. I'm so sorry."

Thaddeus grabbed Italicus' shoulder, "We've got to go, now!"

Italicus shook Thaddeus off violently, and looked at Meg with pleading eyes "You can fight it. I'm not leaving you!" Italicus grabbed Meg and hugged her to his chest, "Come on, fight it!"

Meg saw the conviction in Italicus' eyes, and was determined not to disappoint him, "I'm trying!" she yelled, and Italicus could feel her whole body tense, "You do not have control over me, demon!" The convulsing was beginning to slow.

"That's it Meg, you've got it!" cooed Italicus, looking into Meg's eyes. He could tell she was fighting with all her might. Her face was trembling, eyes red, and her heart was beating so hard he could feel it through her back.

"I control my own BODY!" she screamed, tears flowing freely, mixing with blood.

Meg's body began to relax and her pulse was slowing. The grey tint was slowly leaving her, and she smiled weakly at Italicus! "Hail to the King."

"Hail to the King, baby! You did it!" repeated Italicus louder, tears flowing down his own cheeks!

"I did it!" screamed Meg, pushing back from Italicus. The giant smile on her face faded as she realized a shadow stood over them.

"No mortal can break my bond!" bellowed a dark, inhuman voice from the shadow.

Meg began to cough, and blood poured from her mouth. Looking down in fright, Italicus could see claws protruding from Meg's chest, blood spilling out of the wounds.

"NOOOOOO!" yelled Italicus in horror. Meg looked up at Italicus, and with her final moment of life she smiled, and lifted her hand to touch Italicus' cheek. Then she was ripped from his arms and went flying into the smoke. Italicus lunged to grab her, but was halted by the shriek that killed her. The normally green eyes of the shriek glowed bright red.

It held out its bony hand pointed at Italicus, "Your friends have abandoned you. Even PenRuger has fled like a child. You are alone, and now you will die alone *Italicus*!"

Italicus was too tired to fight. He closed his eyes and waited for the inevitable, hoping it would be over quickly. Instead, he heard a large thud before him and opened his eyes. Standing over him was Thaddeus, armed with Meg's Plaz sword.

"Thought you left!" gulped Italicus, tears still wet on his face.

"You thought wrong, brother." Thaddeus helped his friend up, "Let's get going, there are more shrieks on the way."

Italicus wanted to protest. He wanted to find Meg. He knew there was no chance she was alive, but it felt wrong to leave her. Several howls in the distance assured him that if he wanted to survive they would need to go now.

They rushed from the alley way, and caught up to the girls and professor who were surveying the slaughter. The entire forum was littered with dead bodies.

"I want to go home," gasped Leora crying. Andi pulled her into a hug and rubbed her back. Andi met Thaddeus' gaze, and to him, she seemed years older than the young woman he had met earlier this week.

"Bless the Maker." whispered the professor.

Thaddeus and Italicus looked out over their friends. Every single one of them with holes carved deep into their chests. Their deaths looked worse than when the Slavine had plowed through during the war. *Was this why we saved them? So they would be killed a year later?*

Thaddeus was furious. *Someone will pay for the loss of life that occurred here.*

Loud howls filled the forum. The group looked to the north, where appeared five shrieks and a small corps of Citadel guards.

"Run!" ordered Thaddeus, "The stable! Go!!"

The professor could feel the ache in his legs, he had not run so fast in his entire life and he was repeating in his head, *Why did this adventure come now? I am so old.* At that moment, he felt his legs lift from the ground as Thaddeus unceremoniously picked him up and threw him over his shoulder.

Andi glanced back to see the shrieks and guards getting closer. Blue beams shot past them, the guards were firing their teslas.

"We're almost there!" yelled Italicus dodging an incoming tesla blast.

Shot after shot came at the group, the scene lit up like it was day.

The howling shrieks flew forward, picking up speed. Italicus threw open the stable door, Andi and Leora ran through, followed by Thaddeus and the professor. Thaddeus set the professor down apologetically. The professor excused him with a wave of his hand, then hobbled over and collapsed on a hay bale. Italicus was the last one in, slamming the door on the shrieks without a moment to spare. Thaddeus and Italicus braced the door with a heavy beam. The group sat in silence as the shrieks pounded on the door, waiting to see if it would hold.

Once they were sure it would, Andi huffed, "Thank god they are piss poor shots! I can't believe we're still alive!"

"I don't think they really wanted to hit us," replied the professor, breathing heavily.

"Care to explain that, professor?" asked Italicus. "Do you think they want us locked up in this stable?"

The professor shook his head, "No, that's not what I am trying to say."

Leora interrupted, "What the professor *means* is if those guards are possessed like those we have seen so far, they are fighting whoever, or whatever, is in them."

Andi scoffed, "That's ridiculous."

The professor cleared his throat and dusted off his top hat. He stretched the lapels of his jacket to clean off his monocle, "Actually, that is what I was trying to say."

Andi began to speak when the pounding against the door suddenly stopped.

"We can't just sit here and wait for them to get in! What do we do?" asked Andi in a panic.

"We can use the horses to escape, right?" asked Leora.

Thaddeus scanned the stable for anything they could use. Leora pressed her head to the door, listening to the outside. She was still breathing heavily. Thaddeus could see she was scared. She wrinkled her nose slightly and looked to him. He smiled, forgetting their dire circumstance for a moment. Once again Thaddeus was struck by the strangest of sensations. Leora smiled awkwardly in response, then she blushed and soon her face was as red as her hair. Thaddeus shook himself from his daydream, where Leora's crown seemed to glow.

"The door and the rest of this stable was built with Ironwood, some of the hardest wood around. It was constructed specifically to prevent wild horses from kicking holes in the walls, so I'm willing to bet those shrieks won't be able to break in." Italicus reasoned calmly.

Three curt knocks on the door startled the group, the guards had caught up with the shrieks, "This is an Officer Guard of the Citadel. With authority bestowed upon me by the Steward of the Citadel, I order you to open this door!"

Andi and Leora exchanged looks of panic. The guard repeated his order. The group of guards started pounding on the door, and the shrieks began their battle howl, deep, but rising.

The professor stood up, "Ironwood can take over 3,500 pounds of force, I doubt the shrieks can muster that."

Andi let out a sigh of relief, which was interrupted by the sound of wood cracking under stress. With bated breath, the group eyed the stable door in fright. Several planks began to splinter and the shrieks' monstrous claws penetrated through the Ironwood.

Italicus groaned, and the professor muttered, "I do so hate it when I am wrong."

***

Zapp was in heaven. The chase had been enduring and he couldn't believe how fast and how long that large man could run, but he finally caught Wrench and his delicious Cherawaberry pie that he had stolen from Mrs. Callan's window sill. Muffled sounds of a man gagged and tied to a wheel of a wagon were loudly heard. Wrench was trying to break free from his bonds.

"Don't worry Wrench, we will save you a piece." replied Zapp, laughing slightly.

Niles, Glut, and Fryda all laughed at Zapp's comment.

Glut took a large bite of his slice. The pie was amazing, it tasted so good, "We hope there is a piece left!"

"Man guys that smells amazing!" replied Dean, walking up with Kaitlyn, who was helping hold Dean up. His wound was still bandaged around his chest and shoulder.

The pie eating group looked up in fright, like they had been caught with their hands in the cookie jar. Niles wiped the Cherawaberry jam that was all over his face, trying to hide the evidence. Wrench stared at Dean with wide open eyes, and then back at his almost half eaten pie. Dean decided to ignore the fact that Wrench was gagged and tied to a wheel. He knew Wrench from working in the Mech industry. He was a legend, able to fix or make anything you asked. But what was more legend than Wrench's ability to fix, was his gluttony to food. How he managed to stay so large and fit despite how much he ate was a mystery to all who knew him.

"Can we have a piece?" asked Kaitlyn, softly blinking her eyes several times flirtatiously.

Glut grabbed the pie pan and starred at it intently and then lifted his face to see Zapp, Fryda, and Niles all with the same frightened and unsure look on their faces.

Glut started to move the pie pan in a gesture of offering to his friends, he was sure he heard Zapp whisper "No, don't do it," which made Glut hesitate slightly, but in the end he offered his friends a piece. The moment Dean took the pan from Glut's hand, Wrench began to shake and his muffled voice was getting louder.

"There is still plenty to go around." replied Glut hoping he was still right.

After everyone had enjoyed their piece of pie and breaking one piece into several small pieces so everyone could enjoy one more taste of its delicious goodness, they left three pieces for Wrench.

"Who is going to let him go?" asked Dean

Everyone yelled at about the same time, "Not me!"

"We take straws?" asked Glut

Hesitantly, everyone agreed that was the fairest way of choosing. Kaitlyn grabbed some long hay pieces from an eating horse and broke it into equal pieces, except for one. Each person took a straw, letting out a huge sigh, till only Zapp and Glut were left. Glut pulled the second to last straw. It was by far the shortest.

"FINE!" said Glut exasperated, "Make the kid do it, brave mercenaries you all are!" Grabbing the pie pan he walked over to Wrench, who looked up at his supposed friend with evil eyes, "I tried to tell you to share before you ran off, be proud it took me and three professional mercenaries to take you down and tie you up."

Wrench was unmoved by Glut's comment.

"I am going to let your gag out now and then I will feed you your pieces, that way you won't punch me, you got it?" asked Glut.

Wrench thought about for a moment and shook his head yes.

Glut slowly untied the gag.

"GARRET KIMBALL!!! When I get out of this you're going to regret telling them abou--"

Wrench was not able to finish his threat. Glut stuck a huge piece of pie into his mouth, followed by another and another.

Everyone behind Glut laughed softly, not wanting to antagonize Wrench any more than he already was, but it was quite the sight to see Glut feeding Wrench food.

"TO ARMS! TO ARMS!"

"To arms? What for?" asked Zapp, already on his feet.

"The Northern part of the camp is being charged by human and Slavine brutes!" yelled Faramal, "Kazah is forming a battle line as we speak, I can't find Gladthorn or Edyrss anywhere."

Zapp hoped Faramal was overreacting, but the look in Faramal's eyes made it obvious that he was indeed telling the truth.

Zapp pulled on his tesla pack "Then the chain says you're in command, Faramal, and I am your second, what are your orders?"

Faramal looked thankfully at Zapp, he had expected more of a fight from him, "I think the best course is to reinforce Kazah's line and then build a line on the wings to prevent flanking."

"I will see it done" replied Zapp, saluting.

Zapp turned to the rest, "You heard our commander! Move!"

Dean stood, and Kaitlyn had to catch him from falling, "We're under attack?"

The bellows of a large horn echoed through the sky.

"That, son, is a Slavine war horn. Yes, now move! Grab a sword or anything that can be used as a weapon and form up on the other side of the camp. Be ready as a reserve line. I know you're injured but we are probably going to need all the help we can get!"

Dean nodded and headed towards his wagon to retrieve his sword, Kaitlyn at his side. Niles and Fryda were already running towards their gear, leaving Glut alone with Wrench.

Glut looked over at Wrench and gave him a half smile. He could feel his stomach in knots. He was scared about the camp being attacked, but Glut was even more afraid of untying Wrench, who was giving him the evil glare. Untying the knot slowly, once it became lose Wrench jumped up to his feet. Glut coward slightly, he knew Wrench would want retaliation so he grabbed the pie tin and presented it to Wrench. Crumbs fell onto Glut's head the giant man was eating the last piece of the pie quickly. Wrench reached down and easily picked up Glut. Glut was sure he was going to get punched. Instead the large man held him between his arms and began running forward.

"Come along little lad, we have Slavine to fight!"

***

The stable door was fracturing, and it became apparent that there was nothing Thaddeus, or anyone, could do to stop them from breaking in.

"Everyone, jump on a horse, we need to get to Callan's farm and the camp!" yelled Thaddeus, shoring up the door with additional beams.

To their luck, this particular stable was used as a remount station for the Citadel's foreign territory mail services, which ensured a constant communication line between the Citadel and the Slavine. Many of the remounts in the stable were already saddled and ready to go the moment a Citadel mail officer arrived.

Thaddeus swung himself onto a large, black horse. "Not a word to Egghead!" he said to Italicus, who mounted a second black Percheron.

Thaddeus was about to break open the door when Leora let out a resounding, "Wait!"

"We can't leave the rest of the horses in here, the shrieks will kill them!"

Andi shook her head and made a rude noise, "Damn it, Leora! We don't have time!"

"No, she's right!" replied Thaddeus "Open their stall doors!"

Within minutes, Thaddeus lead the way, slicing the wood beam and kicking what was left of the door open. Seventeen horses rushed from the door, each running full speed, five of which carried people. The shrieks balked, momentarily confused by the rush of horses. Rushing by with their only plasma sword, Thaddeus swung with all his might, slicing downward. He managed to kill one of the shrieks, slicing it in half as they rode by.

Thaddeus looked back to see the shriek fall to the ground and the remaining shrieks and Citadel guards turn to chase after them. But the horses were much faster than either.

As the cadre neared Callan's farm, they were shocked to see the camp being attacked by shrieks, Citadel guards and Slavine brutes. Thaddeus threw up a fist, signaling a stop.

"Well I guess Faramal was right about Slavine involvement," said Italicus, slapping his thigh in frustration.

"But Citadel soldiers too, working with the Slavine?" challenged the professor astonished, "Something isn't right!"

"They're all possessed aren't they?" asked Leora, "Look at their scales? They are nearly white!"

Andi nodded, "Leora has to be right, Slavine are supposed to be green.

"No need to worry about that now! We must get to Callan's house. I left them a pretty good cache of weapons a year ago. Let's hope that they still have them." ordered Thaddeus, already leading them to Callan's.

Inside the house, they found Callan and his family taking cover in a closet with a single, cold plazma sword, "Is the fighting over?" asked Callan, who was attempting to shield his wife and kids with his small body.

"I'm afraid not, the village is not safe," answered Thaddeus, hoping he wouldn't have to expand on that. "Do you still have those weapons I left you?"

Callan nodded. "They're in there," motioning to a large chest at the foot of his bed.

"Perfect," exclaimed Thaddeus, grabbing one of the two tesla packs inside the closet. "We will return these to you when we've won," he assured Callan

Italicus took the other pack. Leora, Andi and the professor took Plaz swords.

"Ok, here's the plan. We ambush the shrieks that were on our tail, then we find the far left flank of the attacking line and we charge that. Hopefully, that will allow the camp's line to fold one end onto the other, and send those bastards retreating!"

Thaddeus adjusted the straps on his tesla pack and neared the door, but instead of exiting, he knelt down, and signaled for the others to do the same.

"Colonel Jaster is dead! Damn PenRuger and his men, he was a valuable internal asset in the Citadel!" The bodiless voice floated in through the open window.

Thaddeus inched the door open to reveal professor Akroyd engaging in some form of conversation with a shriek, though they couldn't hear the shriek's half. Thaddeus thought on his feet and dashed out the door, leaving the rest looking at him confusedly and struggling to keep up with him. Thaddeus leapt form the house, plaz drawn, and quickly killed the creature with a thrust into his hood. The creature wiggled slightly and then collapsed. Thaddeus turned around and pointed his sword right at Akroyd.

Akroyd looked at Thaddeus sadistically with a sideways head tilt, "By the Runes of Cloisester, PenRuger, I will rip your soul right out of your body!"

"Yeah, we'll see about that," mocked Thaddeus, as Akroyd was surrounded by the group. The man hissed. Realizing he was in a no win situation he leaped towards Thaddeus hoping to kill him before he himself was. Thaddeus had no intentions of killing the man. With a quick step to the right Thaddeus moved out of Akroyd's leap and knocked the possessed professor on the back of his head with the butt of tesla.

Akroyd awoke, unsure how long he had been unconscious. He realized he was tied to a chair, inside a rustic farm house.

"He's coming to!" yelled Leora.

"What, what's happened?" asked Akroyd. His skin lacked the grey hue that it had a few minutes ago, his color, and voice returned to him. In a flash, everything came to him, "Maker's beard, the darkness, how did you defeat it?"

"It's gone for now, but it will return, and you will have to fight it!" replied Professor Belladon to his friend, "Now tell us, do you know anything that could help us?"

"I'm, I'm not sure. There were men in robes, they kidnapped me, they performed some kind of dark progenitor ritual. I recognized some of the words, you were always better than me with progenitor."

Belladon smiled at his old friend and prompted, "Go on."

"Corruption. That word was used a lot. Mind, soul, and Dumak!"

"We heard that from Meg, Dumak, it's a name. Who or what is Dumak?" asked Thaddeus, standing behind the professor.

"It's a who, a very dark, old who."

"Why is he controlling people?" asked the professor. "Is he leading this demon attack on the shard?"

"I know he commands many of the shrieks," answered Akroyd.

"What do you mean by 'many of?'" asked Italicus. "We saw him speak through you, through Meg, through a damn shriek!"

"Why are the demons here?" asked the professor.

Akroyd began to tremble and tears welled in his eyes, "They, they put something in me. Something evil and foreign. It doesn't want to be…it wants to break free, and escape. But Dumak, Dumak uses it for his own purposes. She doesn't realize what he is doing."

"She?" asked Thaddeus

"The demons seek an ancient prison, the one who put this all in motion. Raised the mammoth from his ancient grave! Seeks to free the Prime Evil."

"How many evils are we up against?" Italicus threw his hands up in the air in mock defeat! "Who the hell the one is it the she or the he?"

"I am sorry, I don't know." answered Akroyd, ashamed "I just know Dumak is very powerful."

"What is the Prime Evil?" asked the professor.

"I don't know that either, other than it was imprisoned at the beginning of the Barren Age."

"What do you mean the Barren Age? What is that?" asked Italicus.

The professor straightened, "Despite the much more common use of the Citadel calendar, the academics in the university needed to come up with a way to measure dates beyond the founding of the Five Kingdoms of Civilized man. There were four ages before ours. We are in the fifth, which has not been named yet. The Barren Age refers to the third age. Ask me later and I will explain to you the others."

Akroyd looked up at Thaddeus, "I do know this, Dumak knows you, Thaddeus. He hates you with a passion. PenRuger is always on his mind! He is determined to kill you and end your family's line," Akroyd clenched his teeth, he was struggling to speak. "It's coming back. I am sorry, I am so sorry. Got to fight it…"

"How can we stop him?" asked the professor, grasping Akroyd's hands.

Akroyd looked up at his friend, Nikola, like he should already know. The only word Akroyd was able to get out was "Gideon."

The color drained from Akroyd's face, and his body began to twitch and contort. Malice came into his eyes and he said, "You cannot stop the evil that is coming! All will burn! We are Legion!"

Thaddeus stepped forward and punched Akroyd across the face, knocking him out cold.

***

Thaddeus left Akroyd tied up and unconscious, Callan's plaz pointed at him. Thaddeus then lead Italicus, the professor, Andi, and Leora in a charge on the left flank of the attacking line, praying that he wasn't lining up the little trained trio for slaughter. Thaddeus was amazed at how well the professor and the girls held their own in the fight. Leaving Italicus to lead and protect their charges, Thaddeus cut and killed his way through the enemy line to meet up with Faramal, who was commanding this area of the fight.

"It's great to see you, sir!" shouted Faramal, visibly relieved

"Where is Gladthorn?" demanded Thaddeus, fearing the worst.

"Setting up a Citadel war wagon to fortify our center!"

"Casualties?"

"Several Equinauts injured, but no deaths yet. We were able to form a line faster than they could charge us!" answered Faramal.

"Small blessing!"

"Yes, sir!" said Faramal saluting, passing command back to Thaddeus. "I think the enemy is about to break after your charge from behind! Zapp is commanding on our left flank, he is holding steady despite shrieks, but sir, there is something else."

"What is it?" asked Thaddeus, accepting his salute.

"Reports of Mystique villagers as a part of the attacking army, how can this be true?" asked Faramal.

"It's true. I'll explain after the battle!" Thaddeus fired several shots from his tesla at a Citadel guard, "Once they break, push this flank forward, roll into the center, and kill these bastards from behind!"

"Your will, my command!" replied Faramal, galloping off to fulfill his orders.

***

To the professor's most adamant disagreement, Thaddeus ordered him away from the battle and to stay inside the protective ring of steam powered wagons. Sitting on top of one of the Mark VII's he had a panoramic view of the action. The professor was quite impressed at the disciplined nature of the Equinaut tactics. As a Mercenary group, he would have expected them to fight more chaotically. Instead, though they fought in three lines, two fighters deep. The soldier in front would fight with their plaz sword and tesla shield while the other used their rifle. Like clockwork, every five minutes the two would switch. It was an ingenious way to keep your fighters fresh. Not everyone was an Equinaut, though. Many of those on the university team fought as well.

Right behind the center line of the fight was a Citadel war wagon that one of the Equinauts had found. It acted as an anchor with thick plated armor and plenty of slits on the side for tesla rifles. Despite the clear advantage, the off colored Slavine fought fiercely through the Equinaut line several times, almost making it to the war wagon. Not a single university member was found on the left line. The professor was shocked when he counted nearly half of the Equinauts could be found on the left holding back a mixture of Citadel soldiers, Mystique villagers and shrieks. The right line was where Thaddeus had stationed himself, with the majority of the university members and what seemed to the professor as the core officers of his squad.

"That's what he is doing!" remarked the professor once he understood Thaddeus' tactic. "He kept his most reliable in the center and left to keep the enemy in place. With mass of numbers, plus his best fighters, he is going to force the enemy back and then come down onto the enemy's center and left from behind! YAHOO, those bastards won't know what hit them!" Looking to his left and then to the right he remembered he was the only person sitting on the roof of the wagon.

The professor was amazed how far Thaddeus' voice carried, even with all the noises that came from the fighting, his voice still pierced through, "HOLD THE LINE!!!" he yelled, urging the fighters along the right line on, "Let them have an inch, take a foot in kind!" How Thaddeus was able to move along the line and still be able to get into the thick of the fight was quite astonishing and impressive to the professor.

The sound of wood cracking and buildings falling began to overpower the sounds of the fighting. With no one in the village to stop or slow the flames near and around the forum, it didn't take long for the entirety of Mystique to be become engulfed. The flames were so intense that they rose high into the night sky, illuminating the entire area in a fire orange glow.

"They did it!" yelled the professor, shaking his arm and cane into the air. The right line had done it. They had broken through the enemy and forced them to retreat. Once Thaddeus was sure the enemy was truly fleeing, he turned his entire line to come down on to the backs of the off-colored Slavine. Rotating and falling like a domino, Thaddeus stayed on the top end to ensure the fleeing enemies didn't turn back and attack.

Overjoyed, the professor thanked the Maker. He was confident that the battle would soon be over.

The enemy's center began to crumble. University members who did not take part of the battle but was charged with the defense of the wagons cheered! The professor was about to climb down off the wagon when something in the distance caught his eye and a strange noise entered his ears.

The sound that came next was utterly unfathomable. A low, loud, rumble from the north pulsed through the entire region. A second rumble rippled through moments later, followed by another, and another. The incomprehensible rumble increased in speed. The professor could feel a rhythm, one and two, repeated over and over again. He could feel his spine vibrate with each pass. The louder it got, the greater the professor began to fear it. "What the dickens is causing it?"

The battle slowed slightly as more began to feel the rumbles. The professor's eyes glowed red, not from the flames of the fire burning in the village, but from a perverse aura of something evil in the distance. Cast in the shadows of the fire were nearly twenty horsemen dressed in black, leather dusters with square collars.

The horseman in the lead wore a dark cavalier hat. He pulled back on his reins, causing his mount to rear up. His horse's massive front legs thrashing about in the air. Even from this distance, the professor could see that the lead horse was a freakish abomination, a stain to the living. A reaper had arrived, there was no denying it. The professor knew the tales. What he thought was ancient superstition had just taken breath into reality. Unmistakable was its unholy and aberrant features. Flesh and muscle were missing around its chest, the white of cartilage and bone was seen in full clarity, it had red glowing eyes and a blood-soaked mane. The professor didn't want to believe what he saw was true. The truth of knowing that something so incredibly scary and evil existed was terrifying. Even at this distance he could see the large, open, beating wound pulsating down the horse's neck. he knew there was no denying it. Bailitheoir the undead reaper, Bailitheoir the hell horse had arrived, ridden by a master strong enough to control its lacerated heart.

"Professor!" yelled Kaitlyn, scrambling up the side of the wagon, trying to reach the professor. "Do you see it? It can't be! Bailitheoir is real! My father told me stories of him, the embodiment of revenge. He is a creature unable to die, with an endless thirst to kill all men, an unholy collector of the slain equine, capable of absorbing their souls into his own!"

The professor reached out with his hand and helped Caitlyn onto the roof of the wagon, "Yes, I know the tails myself. I just pray that everything I have heard of the reaper horse is not true."

The master and rider of Bailitheoir raised its sword and charged straight for the battle lines. The men behind the dark rider moved in perfect precision. The professor watched helplessly as the deathly cavalry charged closer to the folding right line of Thaddeus'.

"THADDEUS! THADDEUS! LOOK OUT!" yelled the professor. His attempts to warn Thaddeus or anyone fighting in the battle were futile. His voice wasn't powerful enough to break through all of the other sounds. The professor held his breath while Caitlyn grabbed his arm and squeezed tightly, burying her head in his chest. The horsemen were nearly upon the right line. The professor's heart stopped, it was almost too late. But by the will of the Maker, an Equinaut grabbed Thaddeus' arm and pointed towards the horsemen.

Thaddeus turned and activated his shield, "SHIELDS! ORBIS SITUATION!" he yelled.

The professor and Caitlyn continued to watch in apprehension, an orb of light appeared in the hand of Beilitheoir's rider. "What is, how is that--"the professor had no words to describe the scientific impossibility of what he saw. He had no understanding what that orb of light was. He realized his lack of understanding scared him more than demons.

When the rider threw that orb of light towards Thaddeus, the professor had no clue what would happen. An eternity passed in the short amount of time it took for the orb to leave the rider's hand and hit Thaddeus. Thaddeus raised his shield to deflect the projectile, but little did he know, the shield was useless. The explosion that occurred was violent and bright. Only from the professor's position on the wagon could he see Thaddeus' body fly backwards into the air and descend back to the ground. Shocked and horrified, the professor and Caitlyn waited with bated breath for Thaddeus to get up. The longer they waited, the more tense they felt.

The momentum the expedition had in the battle was lost. The dark riders, armed with harpoon-like lances, plowed through the line and pushed the right flank back. Soon, the center and left lines began to break. Thirty seconds later, all three lines were in full retreat. Equinauts and university members were running as fast as they could into the protective circle of the steam powered wagons. The scene had become chaos and the professor and Caitlyn were rushing down off the roof of the wagon. Thaddeus' body was being carried in by Zapp and Niles. To the professor's relief, the man was still breathing, but he was badly burned down the entirety of the right side of his body. The pain he must have been feeling was unimaginable, but despite the pain, he was still yelling and issuing orders.

"Thaddeus," Called out the professor, rushing towards Thaddeus, when he suddenly felt something hard hit him in the back of the skull. The world around him went dark.

***

Inside Andi's body she could feel abnormal energy rushing through her, she felt powerful and untouchable. The medallion of Thaddeus' was healing his burns and at the same time giving her something as well. The power was euphoric. She wondered if this is what Thaddeus felt all the time? *Perhaps this is why he was so confident and determined, who wouldn't be if this is how you felt!* Andi had been stationed on the right line during the battle. She was nearby Thaddeus when the demonic horses and riders charged at them. Where they came from and how they were so powerful was beyond her understanding. When she heard the call to retreat and run back to the camp, she grabbed her brother's hand and ran as fast as she could.

The circular formation provided a limited amount of protection, but to the expedition at this moment, it was a castle. Andi and Glut were positioned between the space of two wagons with half a dozen of others trying to keep the enemy from breaking inside of the enclosure. Without enough space to maneuver, the enemy cavalry's advantage was severely diminished.

Nearly all of the villagers who had engaged in the battle were lying dead on Callan's field. The handful that remained were now charging Andi and Glut's position. Andi raised her sword to block a blow coming from a villager with a large sickle. Deflecting the blow, she waited for the villager to swing again. Angry for missing, the raging villager swung as hard as he could. Over extending his throw, he left himself vulnerable and Andi didn't hesitate to thrust her sword into the man's gut. Wrenching in pain, the man fell to the ground. Looking down at the dying man, Andi suddenly recalled the question she had asked Thaddeus. *Was there ever a time you killed someone and regretted it after? Would I regret it?* Andi realized she now understood. A good person will always regret having to kill, but will always do so to defend themselves, loved ones, or innocents. When she stabbed the sickle wielding villager in the chest, she did so to ease his pain and to ensure he didn't get back up and hurt anyone else.

It didn't take much longer for the others in Andi's area to finish off the crazed villagers. Taking a moment to breathe, she looked around the enclosure of wagons. There wasn't a single breach yet, but the fighting was intense in several areas. Thaddeus was hobbling, barely able to move from the burns. He was issuing orders and moving men around to the areas that needed reinforcement. She thought about rushing over to help, but a presence nearby forced her to turn around. The leader of the dark riders rode by, it was the first clear sight she had truly seen. Whatever confidence and courage she felt from the medallion's energy was gone. The rider and horse were a perfect match for each other. A gruesome duo of darkness, Andi recalled the wanted poster she had seen by the C.O.G. officer when they first left the Citadel and the strangers talking of a demonic man in black slaughtering innocents along the trade roads. Andi gasped when she finally saw the open wound across the dark horses neck. It came down along its side and then around its jugular. It wasn't the wound itself that was the most shocking, it was the inside of the wound. It was beating, pulsating, and glowing. Inside you could feel and see hundreds, if not thousands of horses. Their slaughtered souls resided inside an eternal prison.

Andi wasn't sure if it was her gasp that caught the rider's attention or if he had already decided. When she saw the reins on the horse get tighter, she knew he was going to turn and charge her area. Sword drawn, he cantered straight for them. Glut took several steps back, unsure what to do. The four Equinauts, scared but trained, activated their shields and held their swords straight out like spears. If they had known what was coming at them, they would have ran. But it was single man and rider. Childs play for four trained soldiers.

The carnage that Andi and her brother witnessed at the hands of the dark horse was gruesome and grotesque. The viciousness of the horse, how could it have so much hate inside of it? The soldiers dashed forward trying to force the horse and rider back. The dark rider began to laugh. He let go of his reins and sheathed his sword. Unsure of what he was doing, the four Equinauts thought for a moment he was going to surrender. Bailitheoir sang an unnatural guttural cry and reached out with its mouth, grabbing one of the Equinauts by their arm and breaking it. Still biting down on the arm, he swung his head sideways and ripped it from the man's body. The poor soldier wailed in pain. Bailitheoir turned on point and kicked out with its rear feet, right into the man's chest. He went flying backwards and landed near Andi and Glut. To their horror, the man's chest was caved in, he was dead. Angry, the three other Equinauts swung with their swords, not a single blade managed to touch the horse. Swinging and rearing so lightning fast, Bailitheoir struck out with its front legs, striking one soldier in the head. He then charged the other two and trampled them. With no Equinauts to protect them, Andi and Glut fled as fast as they could.

The dark rider grinned and laughed at the carnage his horse left behind. Dismounting, the dark rider reached to his belt and unhooked a large, beating heart. He held it up to his face, "Do as I command, kill all who stand in your way, but find me the one they call Professor Belladon. Remember though, PenRuger is mine!"

Bailitheoir's eyes glowed and he shook its head while making a low, guttural sound. The rider was annoyed, "Do not use that tone with me HORSE! I don't care if there are a hundred horse souls for you to collect!" The horse made a louder guttural sound, "NO, YOU WILL DO AS I SAY! I CONTROL YOUR HEART!" Angered, Bailitheoir growled and stomped his front foot in protest. "I don't care about you reaching Asvaya' Aegeria and bringing the Horse Lords to their knees. I am your master! I raised you from your earthly sleep. I made your body physical once more!" The rider pushed the tattered heart into the forehead of Bailitheoir, "You have no option, no free will, and no ability to deny me. Now go find the man I seek and kill all who get in your way!"

Bailitheoir knew he had no choice but to obey, lowered his head, bowed, and cantered off in search for this Professor Belladon.

***

When the battle first began, Faramal had asked Wrench to lead the medic squad. Due to his massive size and strength he could easily swoop in, grab any of the wounded, and get them out of the danger. With the battle turning against them, it was an all hands on deck situation. They needed everyone capable of holding a sword in the fight. When Zapp handed Wrench a plaz sword, it looked incredibly small in his hands. In fact, his index finger was so large that he covered the area where the thumb would go, which was also where the switch was to activate the blade. Wrench fumbled with the hilt, he was adamant to do it himself, always wanting to be self-sufficient. Wrench tried on his own to turn on his blade, almost gutting himself in the stomach when he nearly dropped the sword hilt through his fingers. When Zapp realized his massive friend couldn't turn on his own sword, he teased only slightly and did it for him.

Wrench had been in some bar brawls and even a few fights in the alleyways, but none of that compared to the life and death situation happening right now. Being the largest man in the expedition, he acted as a rallying point for the expedition members in the immediate area. The fighting was intense for the first few moments, but the speed and accuracy of the lead Equinauts, including Zapp, Niles, and Fryda, made quick work against the shrieks and Citadel guards that attacked their area.

Wrench was able to get a few blows in against the enemy, but the sword still felt awkward and small in his hands. It made fighting far more difficult, he nearly dropped it twice and sliced part of Zapp's hair off. Instead of continuing to fumble around and maybe hurt someone, he decided to stay back and let the professionals do their work. Looking around and staring at the nearby areas of fighting, Wrench silently said a prayer not to let the enemy break through. Loud, frightful screams from behind him confirmed his prayers were not answered. To his amazement, a black horse was viciously chasing people, biting and kicking anyone in sight.

"What the devil?" exclaimed Wrench pointing at the horse, his stomach turning in knots when he realized that horse could not be alive with the wounds it had. "Bloody balls," Then he saw blue flames exit the horse's nostrils, "it's a freaking Hell Horse!"

"HELP!" yelled a familiar voice to Wrench.

On his right he looked and saw Andi and Glut running from one of the black riders. "I'll be damned if I will let you hurt Garret and his sister!" Wrench yelled before charging towards them. He held his sword in an aggressive fashion, but it didn't feel right to him. He dropped the sword, reached behind his back, and pulled out his giant wrench 'Besty.' "I am going to clobber that guy!"

Andi pulled against Glut's hand, he was starting to slow. "Come on, we have to keep running!"

"I can't!" exclaimed Glut, through breaths he grabbed his stomach with his free arm. "It hurts so badly!"

Andi tried to urge her brother further. She looked back and cried out. The black rider was still chasing after them. His large caviler hat and shoulder length hair covered most of his face, but Andi could clearly see his grin. He was enjoying the chase. "Come on Glut! Please, we have to get to Thaddeus or Italicus!"

Glut was breathing heavily, the world felt dim, his body was shaking. He was certain he would either be fainting or puking at any moment. He didn't dare look back, he knew the sight was not going to be nice. Only from the urging and prompting from his sister did he force himself to keep moving.

It didn't really matter how fast Glut and his sister moved, the dark rider was gaining. When Andi finally realized there was no chance of getting away, she threw herself in front of her brother. Igniting her sword.

The dark rider pulled out his steel sword and pointed it at Andi, "Your soul is mine, child." He swung down but stopped. His eyes betrayed his feeling of foreboding, he threw his left arm out towards Andi with his palm pointing at her. It began to glow slightly. "The Morustranconatra, you actually exist? NO! You will ruin everything I have worked towards. You must die before she finds out!"

The dark rider swung with his sword.

"NO!" yelled Wrench leaping in front of Andi. He growled and stared down the black rider, who was momentarily shocked at the size of the man. He spoke in a low voice that cracked with his accent as he approached the last words in his sentence, "If you want them you will have to go through me, LADDY!"

The black rider merely laughed and charged Wrench, striking and swinging his steel sword. Wrench was able to block each blow. The black rider was fast and strong, every time Wrench moved to strike, the black rider would react swiftly and defend himself. Wrench was beginning to get frustrated, he wanted to hurt this man very badly. The black rider swung with his sword and punched with his free hand. He swung again. Wrench had no choice but to block it, but it allowed the black rider to kick him in the knee. Wrench fell to one leg. The black rider started to laugh again and swung down, aiming for his opponent's head. Wrench just barely moved in time to miss contact with the blade. The black rider was not prepared for a man of such size to move so quickly. Furious, Wrench swung Besty with all his might, smashing it clear into his opponent's face.

The force from Wrench's hit was great, the dark rider's cheek crumbled and the skin was torn off. He fell to the ground. Wrench roared in victory over his opponent and turned to look at Andi and Glut. Andi smiled, "Thank- "

Andi's smile fell. She looked upon Wrench with utter fear. Before she could speak, before Wrench could realize what was happening, he felt the cold sting of steel rush through his lower back. He turned quickly, spinning so fast and with such force that he ripped the sword out of the dark rider's grip. Wrench gasped not from the pain, but from the fright he saw. The dark rider's face was partially missing, his jaw bone was clear as can be and it was cracked and chipped., pieces of flesh hung off of him.

"My God, what are you?" asked Wrench.

The dark rider laughed and spoke hoarsely, "I am God, I am death, your demise! I am Duth Dumak Arazeg!" Dumak punched Wrench across the face again and again. "You will not stop me." he kicked him in the gut and punched again. "I will have my revenge on PenRuger." Wrench tried to raise his arms, but his body would not listen, he felt himself get weaker and weaker and fell to his knees. Dumak grabbed Wrench by his chin, laughed, and forced him to stare into his face, "Your soul and body will make an excellent host." Dumak grinned, the very sight of seeing muscle spasms was revolting to Wrench. Bodily fluids escaped from Dumak's opened cheek, hanging and threatening to spill onto Wrench's face.

"Kill me!" gasped Wrench, "Get it over with!"

"No," answered Dumak, "You will live, for now. And when I come back, you will become part of me, part of my corrupted army."

"I will never!"

"HA HA Ha-" laughed Dumak, mockingly, "Many have claimed that, all have succumbed." Dumak punched Wrench in the face, sending him to the ground. Dumak wiped his hand on his duster, cleaning Wrench particles off of him, and pulled his sword out of Wrench's back, "I am done playing with you."

Dumak turned to kill Andi, but she nor her brother were where he had left them. Furious, Dumak roared in anger for a moment, but he then realized the only place the kids would run to, "PENRUGER!" yelled Dumak, far louder than any mortal man could. The fighting in the immediate area ceased. "FACE ME NOW, YOUR TIME IS NIGH! I AM GIDEON'S BANE!"

***

The pain that Thaddeus felt only pushed him to keep going. He had been burned before. but this was beyond anything he had ever experienced. His memory of the events leading to the retreat back to the steam powered wagons was hazy. When he saw the dark riders charge towards the rear of the right line, he was more concerned with the horses and the harpoon lances than the bright orb in the leader's hand. When the orb bounced off his shield and hit the ground near his feet, he was not prepared for the powerful explosion and shockwave.

Thaddeus' next moment of consciousness was being carried by Niles and Zapp. He was confused, *why am I being carried? Why is everyone running?*

Thaddeus struggled, he didn't want to be carried.

"Don't move, Thaddeus!" barked Zapp in serious tone, "You're hurt pretty badly."

"I am fine! I don't feel--" Thaddeus tried to pull away, but his body would not fully listen. His right side seemed sluggish. *What was wrong? What happened?*

Thaddeus tried to lower his neck to look down at his body, but even that felt stiff.

"Thaddeus, don't look, it's pretty bad!" remarked Niles while holding Thaddeus' legs.

Thaddeus strained, but when he finally managed to lift his right arm enough to see it, his stomach turned sour and he nearly choked on his own vomit. His entire right hand and arm was burned severely, his leather jacket was melted to his skin. It was only then that Thaddeus realized he was burned so badly that his nerves must have been destroyed.

The wound looked grotesque. Seeing your own skin and body charred is not a sight most people would calmly accept. Thaddeus was reluctantly thankful, he knew his ancestral medallion was going to heal him, but he also knew the cost. Healing was not a painless process. Imagine feeling someone cutting your arm very slowly and very deep. You can feel your skin and every muscle fiber being torn apart by the blade. Now imagine that same process in reverse. The healing pain was going to be severe. He had time though. The Medallion worked in stages, focusing on the brain, the heart, and other vital organs before healing wounds like burnt skin.

Out of pure instinct, Thaddeus patted his chest with his left arm, ensuring the tin containing his wife's hair was still in his pocket and intact. To his relief it was still there, though he feared it may have melted.

Thaddeus could hear people yelling and screaming, he knew he was needed. The initial chaos from the retreat was slowly growing into a monster that couldn't be stopped. Everyone was in a panic, out to save themselves rather than working together to save everybody. Thaddeus began issuing orders to start forming defensive pockets between the wagons.

When the pain began to manifest, itself it felt more like pins and needles. His right arm and legs were asleep and were slowly waking up, but the pain didn't stop there. It continued to increase in intensity. Thaddeus did his best to push through the pain, but he knew he didn't have long before it would become so severe he would lose consciousness.

"Where is my telsa pack?" asked Thaddeus

Zapp waited for Niles to let go of Thaddeus' legs before helping him prop himself up against a metal crate. "We had to cut you out of it, some of the strap melted to you!"

Niles pointed towards the nearest Mark VII, "I saw Edryss place it in that wagon"

"Thaddeus!" cried out the professor. Zapp, Niles, and Thaddeus turned just in time to see the professor fall to ground, his head hit by flying debris from nearby fighting. Several of the corrupted villagers had begun to hail the area between the two nearest wagons with anything they could get their hands on. Zapp rushed to the professor's side and checked him for wounds. His head was gashed, but it wasn't severe.

"Take him to the nearest wagon and take out those villagers!" yelled Thaddeus through his teeth as the pain increased. He looked up at Niles and urged him to go help Zapp.

Fryda came running up, passing by Zapp and Niles as they carried the professor away. She looked down, worried, but relieved the man was still alive and continued to Thaddeus, "Report, sir!"

Thaddeus nodded slowly while leaning against a very large metal crate for support.

Fryda saluted and waited several seconds for Thaddeus to return it, but he was not able to use his right arm. She knew Thaddeus had been hurt but did not realize how bad it was, "The defenses are holding, no reports of any breaches." she paused and deliberately diverted her eyes away from Thaddeus' wounds.

Thaddeus could tell she had more to say, "And?"

Still not wanting to look, "The enemy cavalry is holding back, they are the same black riders we fought before. They are circling and letting the ground forces do the fighting."

"Probably waiting for--"

"PENRUGER!" yelled a menacing voice from inside the wagon formation, "FACE ME NOW, YOUR TIME IS NIGH! I AM GIDEON'S BANE!"

Thaddeus hobbled to turn around. A black rider was standing on the other side of the wagon formation holding a blood-soaked sword in his hand. A large body was lying next to him, motionless.

"Oh Taranis, is that Wrench!" remarked Fryda, gasping.

Thaddeus reached for his sword hilt but fumbled it with his fingers, dropping it to the ground "Son of a--"

Thaddeus cursed and awkwardly bent down, though it was excruciatingly painful. Before he could grab his sword Fryda had beaten him to it. "No, sir, you are not healed yet. I'll handle this.

"No!" he yelled in anger, "This is my fight!"

"No, sir, I won't let you!" argued Fryda.

"Give me my sword Fryda! THAT'S AN ORDER!"

Fryda was hesitant. it was against her character to disobey.

"Give it to me now, soldier!" demanded Thaddeus, limping closer to her.

Thaddeus should not have moved. If he had stood still and stayed firm, Fryda would have given up the sword, but seeing him falter in his step and the pain it caused him, she knew she couldn't. Activating Thaddeus' Gladius, she pointed it directly at his face. "I am sorry!" she whispered before swinging the sword and thrusting the blade into the top of the metal crate. Sparks and hot metal lit up the immediate area. "If you can pull this out, join me!"

Thaddeus was wide eyed and red, not even Finnius' mutiny caused him such anger and shock. Fryda ran off and left him there. Thaddeus reached out and tried to free his sword, but he had no strength and the harder he tried, the more pain he felt. He had no choice but to wait for the Medallion to heal him.

***

Fryda could feel her heart racing, every single drop of her blood coursing through her veins. She charged straight for the black rider. The closer she got, the more rage she felt, the clearer her head was, and stronger was her lust for his blood.

There was no way Dumak could have missed such a large and intimidating warrior come charging straight for him. He bared his teeth, the loose skin across the left side of his mouth flapping around. He raised his sword into position and spat some blood onto the ground. "YOU ARE NOT PENRUGER!"

Fryda was unphased by the grotesque and unnatural state of the Black Rider. She activated her right-handed sword and raised it above her head. Feeling the pureness of her people's blood rage, she roared defiantly, "My name is Fryda and by Treveri's Spear I will be your DOOOOM!" She leaped into the air. Dumak raised his sword to block her attack. Fryda rejoiced at his move, the moment their blades met she activated the switch on her left-handed sword hilt. Dumak had no ability to block the attack, Fryda's second blade pierced through the black leather duster and into his chest.

Dumak was shocked at what had happened, he looked down at the hot, scorching blade protruding inside of him. He could feel his internal organs begin to boil, the pain was great. Fryda relished in her victory and kicked out, smashing her foot into Dumak's chest. Dumak fell backwards and onto the ground. Fryda roared again and kicked Dumak in the side.

"Gideon's Bane, HA!"

Fryda looked down at Wrench's body, he was soaking in a large pool of his own blood. She reached down to see if there was a pulse when a shadow over came her. She twisted in time to block Dumak's blade. To her horror and surprise, Dumak was standing in front of her. The wound she caused him was clearly seen. Light from behind them shone through the whole. "What are you?"

Dumak swung with his sword, Fryda blocked again, "You say you're my doom you Aedunic whore, but I will be your annihilation." He swung once more, this time harder and faster, Fryda just barely blocked his attack "I am the one who will corrupt your everlasting soul. You will become an unclean stain on your family's legacy, Aedunic!" Dumak swung away, forcing Fryda to open herself and kicked out with his left leg. Fryda cried out in pain when Dumak's foot came into contact with her knee and she nearly fell to the ground. Dumak raised his sword and swung downward as Fryda reached out with both blades. They struggled against one another, his blade against the both of hers. Dumak pushed down with all his might, he could see Fryda's strength begin to falter. "And when I kill PenRuger I will become your God and Reaper!" Dumak laughed sadistically, "Caomhnoir will not be willing to ferry you to Neamh!"

Fryda, lashed, closed her eyes and urged her body to call upon more of her people's blood rage, *Taranis, deliverer of our people, give me strength!* Fryda's heart began to pound harder through her chest. She opened her eyes and locked them into Dumak's dead ones. Despite the massive amount of force pushing against her, Fryda lifted her body with mighty legs and stood up.

Dumak, surprised by her sudden strength, took several steps back as he readied his sword. Fryda closed her eyes and kept them closed, she gave herself willingly to Taranis' gift. The speed and agility the large warrior showed was almost too fast for Dumak. He could barely keep up with blow after blow from Fryda's blades. "If this is the best you have, I will have your entrails scattered across the ground soon. I'll use your stomach as a shit bag for my horse!"

Dumak was not moved by her awkward use of his stomach. What he was concerned with was her skill and ability. He had not counted on such a formidable warrior before engaging PenRuger. He had not wanted to waste so much time or energy, but this warrior princess was leaving him no choice. He blocked several more incredibly fast swings, purposely waiting for her to get very close. "You fought well, time to die!" Dumak's left hand began to glow, a new orb of light formed in his hand. Fryda had no time to react, the orb fell from Dumak's hands and fell to the ground. The explosion was powerful, but not as strong as the one Thaddeus had been hit with. Fryda was sent flying backwards slamming hard to the ground and sliding several yards.

Fryda was in tremendous pain, her body ached all over. She struggled to get up, but she was unable. She tried to use her swords as leverage and stumbled back down. Dumak was slowly approaching her, she struggled backwards, crawling on her back. Dumak began to laugh, "Let go, your struggles are over! Let me bring you peace!"

Fryda raised her swords but Dumak easily knocked them out of her hand. He knelt down and dropped his sword. He grabbed Fryda by her jacket and brought her face close to his own. "Your soul will be harvested. Your strength will bring me closer to my ascension." Dumak pulled out a dagger and started to push it into Fryda's flesh. Fryda struggled, her mind begged for her arms to work. She prayed to Taranis and the Maker for strength that did not come. The pain was horrible as the dagger moved deeper.

The pain settled for a moment, the dagger was no longer going deeper. A bright flash flew across her eyes and Dumak fell backwards. Fryda looked to her far left. From a wagon, she could see the silhouette of a man wearing a large top hat. It was the professor.

Dumak rose in anger, but when he saw who it was that had hit him he laughed, "BAILITHEOIR! THE PROFESSOR! BRING HIM BEFORE ME!"

***

The loud, panting breaths of a creature beyond life and death sped past several expedition members as they fought off corrupted Citadel soldiers. Had they known or understood that they had just had their lives spared they would have been on their knees thanking the Maker. Death from a hHell Horse is one of the worst ways for any mortal to die. The foul hooves of the undead pounded against the ground, its fierce, foreboding red eyes searched the battlefield for the one called Belladon.

As he searched for his target an all too familiar pain struck Bailitheoir, the pain started near the top of his neck and ran down almost half way, then around his jugular--the last gift from Verrator, his former bonded companion. The wound begged to be fed. It had become a bottomless, ravenous void whose appetite could only be quenched with taste of equine souls.

A cherry wood colored horse was trotting along the perimeter of the steam powered machines, it was pulling a small wooden wagon. The legs of a person lying down dangled off its edge. The rider was a tall, pale skinned redhead urging the cherry wood horse forward. Bailitheoir pushed the lust away and tried to ignore such an easy target. He knew that horse's soul would ease the pain and rage he felt burning through his veins. Dumak's orders were to find the man named Belladon, but the intoxicating poison pulsing through him could not be resisted.

Barely changing his stride, Bailitheoir turned and dashed towards the cherry wood colored horse.

Leora urged Wooly forward, her voice cracked. She was extremely nervous, the fighting had been scary enough but this seemed even scarier. She felt completely out of her element as she had never driven a horse connected to a wagon before. How she somehow became the appointed driver was a series of mistakes and misunderstandings. Now she was tasked with shuttling the seriously wounded straight to the medical wagon. She knew time was important for the injured but feared losing control. Wooly was the first to sense the danger and he automatically began to pick up his pace, when Leora pulled on him to slow down he resisted the prompting.

"What are you doing?" asked Leora, "Please, I don't--"

Wooly suddenly surged forward from a trot to a full canter. Leora was beginning to panic, she wasn't sure how to get Wooly to listen to her. A prompting from inside her head told Leora to look to her left. She didn't have to look far, the moment she saw the danger out of the corner of her eye she loosened up her reins and urged wooly to go even faster. The wagon bounced and shook over every bump and Leora prayed that the man would not fall out.

William F. James

Bailitheoir was gaining on them, no matter how fast Wooly tried to run, the Hell Horse was faster. Once Bailitheoir had caught up to Wooly and was now running neck to neck with him, he threw his mouth open and dashed right for Wooly. Leora pulled the reins hard to the right, Wooly for first time since sensing the danger listened and veered off course, Bailitheoir's teeth just missing the skin of Wooly's neck.

Leora pulled to the right out of necessity and had not looked what was on her right. A single tree branch stood in the way and while Wooly was short enough to run under it, Leora took the branch in the gut. She grunted and cried out, hanging onto the tree branch for dear life. When she lost her grip and began to fall, she closed her eyes and waited for the inevitable thud. Leora opened her eyes seconds later not a thud, but to the sound of galloping. She was riding a horse, though the saddle felt off, she assumed Wooly had returned for her. Feeling relieved she leaned forward and hugged the neck of the horse. Instead of seeing the cherry wood coat of Wooly, what she saw instead was the rotting flesh and pulsating wound of the Hell Horse. Inside the wound she saw the souls of every horse Bailitheoir had ever slain and all of them whinnying and crying out in torment. Leora screamed and sat up, Bailitheoir began to buck, rearing and jumping around trying to get Leora off of his back. He turned his neck nearly 180 degrees trying to bite and get ahold of Leora's legs.

Bailitheoir cantered as fast as he could, leading her around the entire inner perimeter of the wagon formation. Leora screamed for help the entire time, several tried to stop the Hell Horse.

"Get out of the way!" she yelled, "No, move!"

Those who were quick enough managed to jump out of the way, but a few poor souls were trampled and injured.

"SORRY!"

Bailitheoir picked up a burst a speed and then suddenly ground all four of his hooves into the ground coming to a complete stop. Every single Equinant, even the most experienced with horses would not have been able to stay on the saddle. Leora flew high through the air, for a brief moment her mind flickered to Italicus and she wondered if this was how he felt flying. The moment came and went, seconds later she slammed into the ground and skidded through the dirt, hitting every root and rock along her path.

Feeling like every part of her body was in pain Leora struggled to move and slowly sat up. When she did, she felt the hot breath of the creature she had been riding. She looked up and screamed as loudly as she could.

Bailitheoir reared up and threw his front legs forward. Leora leaned back and covered her face. A low rumble and an even lower cry caught the Hell Horses' attention. A large bay horse cantering faster than Bailitheoir had with Leora rammed right into Bailitheoir's side.

Leora peaked through her arms to see Egghead standing over her, staring down Bailitheoir.

Furious, but slightly shocked, Bailitheoir leaped back up, the horse was about to dash forward when he stopped in his tracks. Leora watched but didn't realize that Bailitheoir recognized that Egghead was one of his brothers. It was the first Capallcurada Bailitheoir had seen since his family had banished him to the mountain prison and stole his lacerated heart. All horses sired by the Lord Horses have a telepathic connection. Egghead and Bailitheoir spoke for only a moment, he was surprised at what Egghead had to say. For a moment, he even thought of taking his offer, but Verrator's gift was constantly begging to be fed and a Capallcurada would be a powerful soul to feast upon.

Egghead knew his words would fall on deaf ears and he didn't wait for Bailitheoir to attack. Leora gasped at how fierce and terrifying it was to see two animals trying to kill the other. Leora was frozen in place, she had no clue what to do. A hand touched her shoulder and she jumped.

"It's ok Leora, it's me, Kaitlyn."

Kaitlyn held out her hand, Leora grabbed it and stood up. Kaitlyn had Wooly in her other hand. The horse's eyes were locked to the fight between Egghead and Bailitheoir.

"Come on, let's get going," remarked Kaitlyn patting Wooly on the neck. The horse was visibly shaking in fear and was on the verge of bolting backwards. "Get on, I don't know how much longer Wooly will stay this close to the fighting."

The two girls got on Wooly's back no more than a second before the horse bolted straight into a full a gallop. They left the two the horses fighting and prayed that Egghead would be victorious. Wooly kept running until he was at the other end of the formation. Kaitlyn lead him to an area of supply boxes, using it to block his view of the chaos around him.

"Hopefully, not seeing will calm him down," remarked Kaitlyn very concerned, "If he keeps acting upset he could make himself colic and that is the last thing we need."

Leora had heard of the word colic but she wasn't entirely sure what it meant, she was about to ask Kaitlyn when her mind suddenly snapped to Egghead. "We must find Thaddeus!" pleaded Leora, "He would want to help Egghead."

"Right." Kaitlyn nodded until she noticed something different about Leora, "Great Arcadia, is your hair glowing?"

Leora eyes widened and she looked frightened, "No! Of course not! What a silly thing to say!"

There was no denying it, Kaitlyn was looking right at it. Leora's dark red hair begun to glow brightly. Kaitlyn was somewhat frightened when out of nowhere, the boxes around them began fly and fall in every direction. Egghead's and Bailitheoir's fight had followed them. Leora and Kaitlyn fell to the ground and covered their heads. Crates fell all around them. Egghead squealed, spun, and launched his rear feet right into Bailitheoir's side. The Hell Horse fell to the ground, but was back up moments later. Wooly had been struck by several crates and was just now able to get himself up. Unfortunately for him, he was now standing next to Bailitheoir. Panicking, Wooly turned to gallop away, but Bailitheoir was not going to let him go. Teeth bare, Bailitheoir reached out and bit down over Wooly's neck. Wooly hollered and whinnied in pain, he tried desperately to break Bailitheoir's grip but there was nothing he could do. The Hell Horse positioned himself so that he could break his victims neck. Wooly collapsed to his knees, he had used the last of his energy. He was giving up to the inevitable. Yards away, Egghead was cantering the best he could through the large crates scattered among the area. It slowed him down too much, there was no way he could make it in time.

Bailitheoir bit down even harder and blood was flowing from Wooly's wounds. Though Wooly could not speak, the pain and fear in his eyes was evident. He was not ready nor did he want to die, but he had nothing left in him. He could no longer resist. Wooly hollered a low, unnatural cry for help. Bailitheoir's eyes began to glow an unholy red, he was beginning to drain and accept Wooly's soul into himself.

"Stop it!" yelled Kaitlyn rushing up to them, "Stop that right now!"

Leora was shocked, "Kaitlyn, what are you doing?"

Kaitlyn didn't respond. She was holding a very large bucket, she ran right up to Wooly and Bailitheoir and hurled the contents of the bucket right at them. Leora wondered what was in the bucket, to her surprise it looked like just water. Bailithoir's head was soaked and the horse released its grip from Wooly. The Hell Horse shook his head about. Kaitlyn positioned herself between Wooly and Bailitheoir.

"YOU WILL NOT HARM THIS HORSE!" she yelled with her hands stretched out.

Bailitheoir roared a loud, high-pitched cry that nearly popped Kaitlyn's ears. Despite the pain, her resolve was unmoved. She stared the Hell Horse down with absolute surety that he would not harm Wooly again. Bailitheoir dashed forward, mouth open, ready to strike out and kill this human girl.

"I forgive you."

The words Bailitheoir heard did not come from his ears. No, they came from his mind. The Hell Horse stopped several strides away from the girl, who still had not moved from her spot, her defiant look still in place. *What is the meaning of this?* He thought in his head, never in his entire life had he heard a human in his mind without them holding his heart in their hands. It was a gift only reserved for the truly worthy and the ones who were supposed to be bonded together. Despite his bonding to Verrator, they never had the gift. He never heard or felt the man's thoughts. If he had, then maybe he would have known that Verrator was going to betray him, maybe then he wouldn't be cursed to the Lacerated heart.

Bailitheoir allowed himself a moment to consider the possibility that after so many centuries, he may have found the person he was supposed to be bonded to. Kaitlyn must have felt something too, she was overwhelmed not with words but emotions. She could feel the rage and anger swirling inside of Bailitheoir, but most of all she could feel the hunger of the wound and the torment of all the Equine souls.

"You don't have to do this! Please, don't do this. This horse has been a kind and gentle horse all its life. His compatriots try to protect life not take it. Please!"

Bailitheoir, for the first time in forever, felt remorse and guilt for his actions. He could see the pain it was causing the human girl in front of him. He took several slow, soft steps and placed his forehead against Kaitlyn's. It was at that moment Bailitheoir realized how wrong he was.

The rhythmic sound of his heartbeat repeated inside his head and he heard his new master's call. "BAILITHEOIR! THE PROFESSOR! BRING HIM BEFORE ME!"

He could not resist, he was cursed to his lacerated heart. But as he left, he realized he was now leaving a part of himself with the young girl, a connection that could never be broken.

***

Thaddeus watched in trepidation as the black rider nearly killed Fryda. He felt hopeless, he tried yelling for others for help but the fighting and chaos between the wagons was increasing. When a bolt of energy clearly from a tesla pack slammed into the chest of the black rider, Thaddeus hobbled around to see where it had come from. What a shot the professor had just made, even Gladthorn would have been proud. For a moment, he thought maybe they had found a break and this unholy man was dead. Luck was not quite on the Equinauts' side. The Black Rider rose from the ground, seemingly unhurt, despite a large hole along the right side of his chest. Fryda, on the other hand, struggled to get up.

Thaddeus' guardian instincts kicked in, he knew he had to protect Fryda, but the burn damage along his right side was still throbbing in extreme pain. *The medallion was certainly taking its time,* he thought in his head, annoyed. He knew the medallion was still working, he could feel it healing him, but it was healing far slower than ever before. Andi's face appeared in Thaddeus' mind, he wondered if her connection to the medallion was slowing the healing process.

Thaddeus knew he had no choice, he had to try to do something. Standing around watching others fight his battle went against his entire being. He reached out with his right hand for his sword, still stuck in the metal crate thanks to Fryda. Any movement using his right side caused Thaddeus a great amount of displeasure, but he did realize that his movement was less sluggish, it almost felt normal.

He grabbed the hilt of his sword firmly and began to pull with all his might. Pain of the worst kind circulated through his body, every pore along his arm burned like fire. He pulled and pulled and even with all the strength he could muster, the blade did not budge.

Defeated, he kicked the metal crate in anger, hurting his left foot. *Ugh!* Thaddeus nearly let go of the hilt and gave up when an idea suddenly snapped in his head. "Such an idiot." He said to himself with distain. With the click of his thumb, the blade deactivated and was reabsorbed into the hilt, freeing it from the crate.

Thaddeus turned to face the black rider, only to see Edryss had already engaged him while Fryda crawled away to safety. Thaddeus was determined not to let another friend be hurt by this black rider. He attempted to walk, but the burns down the right side of his leg were still severe. Despite the injuries, he struggled through the intense, sharp pain of every step.

"Thaddeus!" yelled Leora running up to him, "Egghead has been fighting the Hell--" she gasped at the sight of his burned face, "What happened?"

"Not important, it will heal." answered Thaddeus gruffly while still attempting to walk.

Seeing how bad Thaddeus was burned she thought there would have been other Equinauts with him, "Where is everyone?"

Thaddeus pointed towards Edryss fighting the black rider. Leora gasped seeing Fryda crawling towards a large hulking body that could only be Wrench. "This is my fight."

Leora looked at the man like he was quite mad, "Your fight?" Leora paused. She nearly gasped once she realized what he was attempting to do. "Wait, you're not that thickheaded." she placed herself in front of him. "You aren't going out there to fight, are you?"

"I don't have a choice!" remarked Thaddeus, sternly pushing past her.

Leora grabbed ahold of his jacket and easily swung him around, "No, you don't! Not in this condition!"

"Let go of me, Leora!"

Leora face was unmoved, "No!"

Thaddeus's face was equally unmoved, the two stood face to face both unwilling to give.

Edryss was holding her own against the black rider, but Thaddeus could tell by her stance she was fighting defensively. He tried to push Leora to the side but couldn't.

"You're not going out there until you are healed more."

Thaddeus stared at her wide eyed and pointed his finger at her, "THAT COULD TAKE HOURS!"

Leora yelled back with equal intensity, "THEN YOU WILL WAIT!"

Thaddeus clenched his wrist tightly, his anger and rage was extremely high, had Leora been an Equinaut he would have discharged her right there for insubordination. But Leora wasn't an Equinaut, he technically had no authority over her except for being her protector. This time though she was trying to protect him. Thaddeus' anger began to subside. It confused him, the longer he stared at Leora the less mad he got. Her eyes seemed to pierce straight through him, almost a familiarity to them.

Leora could feel something as well, it puzzled her too. It felt almost natural for her to be this close to Thaddeus. The change in Thaddeus' eyes was almost instantaneous to her own that they both felt the same thing at the same time. For the first time since meeting Thaddeus, she saw pain in his eyes. Not a physical pain, but a deep sorrow or burden that he couldn't let go of. She could feel her heart break for him. Thaddeus suddenly leaned in towards her, Leora's pulse began to race and she held her breath. She couldn't believe what was about to happen, but it felt so natural, almost even inspired, that fate had brought them together at this one moment.

Thaddeus whispered into her ear, "Leora…"

"Yes, Thaddeus?" asked Leora with affection in her eyes, her lips intently waiting in apprehension.

Thaddeus leaned in slightly, Leora closed her eyes, "Forgive me."

Leora kept her eyes closed for several more seconds thinking Thaddeus was still going to kiss her, but when she finally lifted one eye lid to peek, she saw Thaddeus had already hobbled several yards away with his sword activated. "I, uh, WHAT!" Leora could not believe herself, he had left her there. "THADDEUS PENRUGER!! I can't believe you! When I, when you!! UGH, DOES IT HURT BEING SO FOOLHARDY!!!!"

Thaddeus immediately regretted his actions but nothing was going to stop him from protecting his people. Leora's words though stopped him in his tracks, had she said almost anything else it would not have even affected him. He stopped walking for only a few seconds thinking of the past long gone. He looked at Leora with his peripherals, she was stomping the ground angrily, still shouting insults towards him. He couldn't help but smile at her zealous behavior.

The Black rider began to laugh a horrific unnatural cackle, Thaddeus refocused his attention to the fight. Edryss was cradling her left arm, she had been injured and the black rider was taking complete advantage of it. Thaddeus whistled in the air and seconds later, Egghead came galloping to his side.

"I need you buddy, I am still not fully healed."

Egghead snorted several times and stomped his foot before placing his head into Thaddeus chest. "Don't worry Eggers, I will be ok, he can't hurt me as long as you are with me." Thaddeus had to try several times to mount his horse. His body was not ready for such a task. Once he was on, he urged Egghead forward, straight into a gallop. With his sword Gladius activated, Thaddeus and Egghead charged straight towards Gideon's Bane.

Echo from the Past

The war in the heavens lasted over a thousand years. I played my part well. I slaughtered and killed billions in the name of The Fallen and the most holy of quests. The Ethereal stood for everything that was wrong with the world, the status quo. I was one of the Great One's lieutenants. I commanded countless battles with over a million Fallen soldiers at my command. I waged war and battled across solar systems. But this war, the war against Duth Dumak Arazeg, was by far the hardest I had ever waged. His insane ability to warp himself and his armies into the veil was troubling. Aaron, the head of my holy army, marched half across this infernal planet chasing after Dumak. I was losing men by the thousands each week to attrition. Dumak proved to be a coward, never facing my army in battle, but his strategy was sound. I was losing men far too fast. At this rate, I would have no army left if I kept chasing him. I ordered Aaron and his men back to the city.

From my temple's balcony, I watched my men return. Staring up towards the sky, I remembered how much time had passed since I set this planet ablaze. I was constantly ashamed at how many humans did not die in my inferno, but now it was a blessing. I needed these worshipers as much as they needed their god. Still, human resilience always surprised me. Of all of the Maker's creations, they are hardest to eradicate. Like rats, they can survive anything and they breed faster than rabbits.

Many of the survivors of The Fallen's attack inhabited the mountainous area to the north. The most populated survival camps could be found there, an area Aaron had urged to annex for many years. There were camps to the south, but they were fewer and further between. Scouts reported that more and more northern camps were falling to Dumak. His number of followers and soldiers were swelling mightily. Soon, Dumak's army would out number mine. I needed to take the southern camps.

Sometimes, when focusing on a point directly in front of you, a temporary blindness ensues. When I ordered Aaron to take half the army to conquer the south, my vessel argued with me. She believed taking the southern camps was pointless and a waste of time. We need to directly attack and destroy Dumak before he takes all of the north, or we should build up the city's defenses to withstand any attack. I relented. I don't know why I relented, and I shouldn't have, but I trusted her judgment more than I realized.

A direct assault against Dumak was out of the question. He would have my armies marching back and forth once more. We had to make him come to us. We ordered Aaron to begin fortifying the walls.

I retreated to my Sanctum Sanctorum and reached out to the veil to monitor Dumak. Months passed by, our walls got taller and thicker. Dumak's army grew larger. Dribs and drabs of survivors who managed to escape Dumak's wrath made their way to my city. Many of these survivors spread the tales of Dumak's evil, ruthless nature, killing entire camps who said no to joining him, massacres to prove his power to other nearby camps. The man was audacious, you had to give him that. Beside him, I looked absolutely domestic. The humans rushed to me for protection, singing praises all the while.

Each day I spent part of my time with my vessel, ensuring my holy army and city were properly preparing for war, and the rest I spent in my Sanctum Sanctorum. I alone monitored Dumak. His conquest of the north was near complete. Aaron's scouts reported only a handful of camps remained independent. Dumak's army swelled to outnumber my army six to one.

Word came that Dumak had begun his decent into the southern camps. I cursed myself for listening to my vessel. Within her mind, we fought. I took my anger at myself out on her, and she ousted me from her body. I had no choice but to retreat to my Sanctum Sanctorum. To my surprise, my vessel followed me in, and we argued well into the night. The fight turned from war strategy inward, and she reminded me of all the times she faced hardship during our early years and asked why I did not manifest myself to help. I chided her, reminding her of her place, she would be nothing without me. She would be weak, powerless, and empty. Together, we created an empire. My vessel was not coy, she knew I needed her as much as she needed me. The arguing went on for hours and I began to strain, keeping my form. I asked her to let me return within her so that I could rest. She agreed, but under one condition. I assumed I would have to give up something important, but her request was odd and one which I did not understand the purpose of.. She wanted to know my name.

My name? Why did she need to know my name? I was first angel and then I became god; that was all that needed to be known or said. Why did she want my name?

The doors to the Sanctum Sanctorum opened, it was Aaron. Only he would dare enter the Sanctum Sanctorum, he alone knew of my vessel and my duality. Our argument stopped when he reported that Dumak's army had begun to march towards the southern encampments. I was furious and about to reignite the argument with my vessel when Aaron urged us to come and see something miraculous outside. After re-merging with my vessel, we rushed to the balcony overlooking the city. From the south came a multitude of people, a mass chaos of men, women, and children, pulling wagons and carts, fleeing Dumak's wrath. Over four hundred thousand people now stood at my doorstep.

My vessel nudged me in her mind, pointing out that we didn't have to conquer the south after all. She had no way to know that so many would flee and head our way, but I let her have this small victory. Despite this huge influx of people, Dumak's army still outnumbered us greatly.

The great multitude of new followers saw me stand before them in my temple, many bowed before me. I could hear their prayers of hope and thankfulness. They asked for forgiveness and protection. Aaron opened the city's great gates and slowly began moving my new followers in.

Once more, the skies opened up and the universe proved to me its unwillingness to allow me to succeed. Something fell that was meant to remain locked away inside the Void, never to see the light of existence until the end of days. This falling star would shape not just the immediate future, but all futures to come. Spiraling out of control, the forgotten object fell near the city. It was a massive and stunning crystal, nearly ten feet tall, a prism of multiple colors and more raw power than the universe itself. I retrieved it, and running my hands down its serene surface, could sense something ancient and powerful inside.

What it was, I did not know, but I knew it had to be mine.

Most of all, I knew it was something that Dumak would want.

Duth Dumak Arazeg

Chapter Eight

From the first scroll of Zakarael, chapter 10 verse13:
"Therefore, don't be afraid of them, since there is nothing covered that won't be uncovered and nothing hidden that won't be made known. For all things are corrected by The Light and they are revealed, and everything that reveals is light."

Thaddeus and Egghead charged the black rider. With his sword drawn, he swung down at the mysterious, darkly dressed man. Their swords collided with such force that an echo of metal on metal reverberated throughout the battlefield. It was a signal to both sides that the real fight had begun. A battle Dumak had been waiting over a thousand years to happen. Thaddeus swung again, rolling his right shoulder as best as he could and swung downward, hoping to slice off the black rider's arm. The attack did not work. Frustrated that he had been deflected, Thaddeus kicked out with his leg using his height advantage on top of Egghead.

Dumak fell to the ground.

Thaddeus mockingly laughed, "This is Gideon's Bane? You were the mammoth of old?" Thaddeus spat on the ground in contempt, "The fabled stories of your prowess have been greatly exaggerated!"

Dumak, still lying on the ground, began to laugh, "Mock what you don't understand boy, I am Duth Dumak Arazeg, I am the eternal nightmare, the mammoth of destruction. I will take great delight when I tear your flesh off your bone and watch it rot in the sun!"

Thaddeus rolled his eyes, "Ha, idle threats coming from a man lying in the mud, you have to defeat me first."

Dumak rose from the wet dirt without using his arms or legs, "You are wrong PenRuger, I am no man. No, not anymore. I am greater than you, more powerful than you, I am unstoppable. Life is a hindrance, death an annoyance, and the only true absolute is power."

Dumak whistled and vanished, a black blur passed between him and Thaddeus. Egghead took several steps back, he knew immediately what the blur was. Sensing his agitation, Thaddeus patted Egghead's neck. "What is it buddy? What do you see or know?"

Egghead abruptly dashed forward as a blur ran past them. The high-pitched noise of a sword slicing through the air could be clearly heard. Dumak laughed fiendishly. Thaddeus tried to focus on the source, but the laughter was coming from everywhere at once. Another blur swooshed by, this time Egghead spun on his haunches. Another mocking laugh from Dumak. Seconds later, another blur swooped past, and then another, and another. They were happening way too fast for Thaddeus to react, he was at the mercy of his horse. He had complete confidence that Egghead would keep him safe, but it still bothered him that he could not see his enemy coming.

"FIGHT ME! DO YOU HAVE NO HONOR!?"

Dumak's laugh grew louder, "Honor is but a fool's shield, it will bring you no comfort when you are dead!"

Thaddeus leaned his head down and whispered to Egghead, "This time buddy, don't move, let them come."

Egghead snorted and stomped his back foot.

"No, it's not stupid, trust me."

Thaddeus closed his eyes and waited for the next blur. As the air to his right moved, Thaddeus swung his right arm up the best he could and deflected a blow from Dumak's sword. Activating his shield at the same moment, he swung his left arm behind him, smashing it into the face of Dumak who had not expected Thaddeus to go on the offensive.

Dismounted from his horse, Dumak fell to the ground. Thaddeus leaped from Egghead and swung with his sword. Dumak rolled out of the way and sprung back up to his feet. He roared with anger and frustration, charging at Thaddeus. Thaddeus met him halfway, sword and shield ready. The two men fought with such speed that to anyone watching, it appeared as if their arms had disappeared.

Edryss turned her head to glance at the fighting between the black rider and Thaddeus. Her body shuttered as she had never known fear, nor had she seen true evil until this black rider. She was thankful she made it out of the encounter alive. Edryss knew that her left arm was dislocated, it was completely limp, but she was unable to do anything about it. Using her right arm, she helped Fryda drag the large body of the mechanic, Wrench. They were still unsure if the man was dead or alive, all they knew was once Thaddeus and Egghead joined the fight, this would be their only chance to get him away to safety. If he was alive, he would need medical attention immediately and probably a blood partner.

"I have never faced such an opponent before," Fryda said, a slight tinge of shame in her voice. She was breathing heavily, her body bruised and cut. "Not even if Treveri left Neamh could we stop such an abomination to nature!"

Edryss, who understood all too well the skill and power the black rider possessed, nodded in agreement. She was speechless, her brain was still reeling from the fact that for the second time in the past forty-eight hours, she had been certain that she was going to die. Malus had whittled down her confidence. She had been abused physically, and mentally raped by him. This black rider though, he was ten times worse than Malus. He toyed with her, he allowed her to get close. The moment she was close enough for a killing blow he would push her back. Even when Edryss managed to get the upper hand, a sword thrust through the chest, left arm, and lower neck, none could bring the man down. None of her strikes even slowed him down, he mocked her in the most disparaging ways.

When Thaddeus joined the fighting, he ordered her away and for the first time in her life, Edryss actually backed away from a fight. Her mind split between feeling ashamed and relieved to make it out alive. She prayed for Thaddeus to win, *if he was to die for my failure...* She pushed the thought out of her mind.

Where is Gladthorn, she wondered to herself and began to worry.

They continued to drag Wrench's body all the way to the medical wagon. It took six medics to carry the hefty man up the stairs and into the wagon. Wrench's massive size made it hard for the medics to feel for a pulse. Still unsure if he was dead or alive they placed him in a cot and began to inspect him.

As the two women were forced to leave the medical wagon, Leora ran up to them panting.

Fryda quickly saw the poor redhead was in distress, "Leora, are you ok?"

Leora nodded, "Yes, I just need to get some supplies for Kaitlyn. Wooly was attacked by that dreadful demonic horse. He is bleeding badly, and we can't stop it."

"FRYDA!" yelled Zapp, hobbling towards them from between the nearest wagon. He had gash along his forehead and his jacket was torn in several areas, "We are outnumbered, the horsemen are trying to push in- your husband needs you!"

The voice of Niles was clearly heard over the combat, "ZAPP, DID YOU REALLY!?"

Fryda rolled her eyes and allowed herself a small laugh, "I never thought marriage would be like this."

Edryss allowed herself to laugh slightly as well, she had almost forgotten about the fighting around the encampment. Edryss grabbed her sword and activated her shield, "I'll come too."

"Oh, no you don't!" said Fryda sternly, "Your arm isn't fixed yet. You stay here!"

Edryss wanted to argue but knew better than to argue with an Aedunic woman, "Kill one of those bastards for me."

Fryda nodded and followed Zapp back towards the front of the wagon. Fryda's blood-cry howling above the rest of the fighting.

Edryss deactivated her shield and gasped in pain.

Leora turned and grabbed Edryss' arm, "Let me take a look at-
-"

"AH, YOU WILL DIE A THOUSAND CURSES FOR THAT PEN RUGER!!!"

Leora and Edryss' attention turned to the center of the formation where Dumak and Thaddeus were still fighting with the same vigor and fierceness as before. Thaddeus' body was moving more freely, his burns healing. Dumak staggered, gripping his left forearm, Thaddeus had obviously struck him. Angered, Dumak charged and spun, striking Thaddeus's shield. Thaddeus slid across the ground by the brute force of Dumak's hit. Not letting Dumak have an inch, Thaddeus rushed back to his position and attacked once more.

As fierce and hard as the two men were fighting, Egghead and Bailitheoir were equally entangled in a fight to the death. Both of them kicking and striking out at each other, each and every blow a death strike if contact was made. It was obvious to anyone watching the two colossal horses fight that Bailitheoir was oozing with rage and anger. He had one purpose and one purpose only--to kill. It was a singular, unrelenting desire, a hunger that had to be quenched at all costs. Despite the obvious single mindedness of Bailitheoir's vendetta, when Dumak was struggling, he would break off from attacking Egghead and head straight for Thaddeus.

Bailitheoir would throw everything into the attack, forcing Thaddeus to dodge Bailitheoir's massive hooves, razor sharp teeth, and blue flaming nostrils. Dumak of course would attack as well, taking advantage of the situation. Dumak's attacks nearly worked had it not been for the timely arrival of Egghead.

Leora cheered as she watched Egghead spin and kick both back legs into Dumak's chest.

Dumak flew backwards, "KILL THAT HORSE!" he demanded in a fit of rage.

Bailitheoir turned his attention away from Thaddeus and cantered towards Egghead.

"The lacerated heart, that's the key to stopping the Hell Horse", said a voice from behind Edryss and Leora.

"What did you say, Dean?" asked Leora, "The heart?"

"That's what Dumak has hanging off the back of his belt," Dean pointed towards it, "Without, it he can't control the Hell Horse."

Edryss spoke next, "What are you doing here? Your wound hasn't healed."

"I am fine, I am just helping Kaitlyn." stated Dean annoyed, "But if that is Bailitheoir, his heart is the key to it. Whoever controls the heart controls the horse."

"Then we must get it!" said Leora confidently like it was already a done deal.

"Easier said than done, even if you managed to get the heart, if you're not strong enough, Bailitheoir might be able to control you!"

"Do we have a choice?" asked Edryss

Leora shook her head, "No, we do not."

Dumak continued to fight Thaddeus, forming a sphere of energy in his left hand and hurling it at Thaddeus. Knowing the danger now, Thaddeus leaped out of the way, rolling on the ground. It took Dumak several seconds to form another sphere of energy. He threw it, hoping to kill Thaddeus before he was able to rise. The sphere was slightly short of its target and it threw Thaddeus backwards. Thaddeus flew in the air, slammed into the muddy ground and slid right into several large crates. Thaddeus was slow to move, he was completely encompassed by supplies and a very large crate had fallen on his legs. While he struggled to get up, Dumak began to laugh manically and slowly approached. A third sphere was forming in his hand.

"Who is lying in the mud now? As much as I hate to admit it," remarked Dumak, speaking with a very repulsed tone in his voice, "Gideon was at least a worthy opponent. Strong, unyielding, he had a sense of nobility about him despite his orphan upbringing. Something that the Maker, or the Celestials at least, thought important. You, PenRuger, you are a pail and unworthy successor of that infernal medallion. Oh, how the years of breeding has weakened your bond."

Thaddeus was still struggling to get up, the crate was way too heavy for him to move in his awkward position, he had no leverage.

"Please, stop struggling, let your last moments be peaceful. Don't feel upset, it was your destiny to die at my hand. It was written in the stars long ago that I would utterly destroy the PenRuger bloodline."

Thaddeus was not going to go down so easily. Pushing backwards as hard as he could, he managed to move the crate behind him just enough. A loud whistle and wine began to rise, it was a warning to Dumak. One that he didn't listen to. A focused beam of pure energy shot through the crate in front of Thaddeus and right into Dumak's chest.

Dumak wailed in pain and fell to his knees, "DAMN YOU PENRUGER! WHEN I AM DONE WITH YOU, I WILL NOT JUST KILL YOU, BUT EVERYONE HERE. THE PROFESSOR WAS WRONG TO TAKE ONE OF MY KINDER! MOST OF ALL NOW, THE DARK LADY MUST NEVER KNOW OF THE MORUSTRANCONATRA'S EXISTANCE!"

Dean ran off with supplies for Kaitlyn while Leora and Edryss watched in suspense as Thaddeus was thrown into the air, slamming into the box of crates, "We have to do something, he is killing Thaddeus!"

"I can't, my arm is of no use." remarked Edryss, her voice cracking and unsure.

Leora could see the fear and angst in Edryss' eyes, "We have to do something!"

Edryss, looking at Leora with a mixture of shame and pride, "Take my gear!" She handed Leora her sword.

"I can't. "

"Yes, you can," Edryss began unsnapping her jacket, taking off her Tesla pack. "Whatever you did or whatever you tapped into while we were practicing, use it!"

Leora grabbed the sword hilt out of Edryss' hand and activated the blade, the cool orange glow lit her fiery red hair. Tears of fear fell from her eyes.

Thaddeus kept firing focused beams of energy, his Tesla pack wailing, filling the immediate area with steam. Dumak tried to push closer to Thaddeus' position, but Thaddeus kept him at bay.

"ENOUGH OF THIS!" roared Dumak in defiance, "This expedition, this fool's errand stops here and now! You have no understanding of the primordial forces working against you. I, Dumak, will stand on top of you all! Creation as you know it is at an end, the world will burn in my light!"

Dumak rose from the ground, sparks of dark red light began to emanate from his body. The flickering lights became swirls of energy. Dumak was becoming one giant sphere of power. "This was not the moment I wanted, but with your death it will be worth it."

Thaddeus had destroyed enough of the crate on his legs to be able to move it and he began to stand. He tried to fire his weapon, but his pack was overheating, "Fight me, Dumak!" he roared in defiance.

"No, it is time for you to die! You were a fool to think you could stand up against me!" Dumak threw his arms out and the energy around him grew. The moment it came into contact with the ground, the earth began to tremble. The energy was destroying anything and everything it touched, but Thaddeus stood defiant in his spot. He kept checking the gauges on his gun, hoping his Tesla pack would cool down. *Come on, you can do it. Come on, don't fail me now.* Thaddeus began to feel the heat from the sphere and shuffled backwards away from it. He smacked the side of his rifle, trying to get it to activate. His hair began to stand as the energy pulled him towards it. Every few seconds Thaddeus instinctively kept shuffling away from the growing sphere. Further and further back he was pushed, the sphere showing no signs of slowing.

"COOL DOWN DAMN YOU!" he yelled at his Tesla pack. The energy field was still growing. Thaddeus moved back another step and walked right into the crates he had just freed himself from. He looked to his left and then to his right, realizing that he had just trapped himself. There was no place to go, his only hope was his pack cooling down in time.

The heat against him rose and Thaddeus' body began to burn, his chest was on fire. He reached for the tin box inside his jacket and threw it behind him away from the energy field. Thaddeus feared this was the end, he wondered what the medallion would do without an heir. *Would it go to Andi?* The heat became so unbearable that Thaddeus could feel his legs begin to buckle, he would fall into the energy. All hope left Thaddeus and his last thoughts, the last image he saw in his head was his wife. "I am sorry Alana," he whispered, "I failed you." His legs began to collapse and fall towards the energy sphere.

Dumak could see and sense Thaddeus had given up. The feeling of victory swelled in him, thousands of years of suffering and now his revenge was complete. Dumak joyfully laughed until suddenly, he began to choke. His energy abruptly stopped, and he fell to the ground. Dumak landed face first into the mud, his back was on fire. The light of the pulse beam dimmed.

Thaddeus' knees gave way, he was ready for death. Believing he was going to be consumed by the sphere of energy, he was surprised when his knees hit the ground. To his surprise, the burning energy had stopped. He was even more surprised to see Leora now standing in front of him in the distance, wearing a Tesla pack.

Thaddeus's emotions were a jumbled mess. He had been ready to die with no chance of escape. Now, somehow, he had survived, and he was saved by the last person he had expected. As he sorted his emotions, only one thought kept repeating in his mind, *PROTECT HER!*

"Get out of here!" Thaddeus ordered at the top of his lungs, trying to get up.

Leora was about to yell back something defiant when Dumak rose once more and attacked her.

"YOU WILL DIE HORRIBLY FOR THAT, GIRL!"

Leora fumbled with her left hand but she managed to activate the hard-light shield in time to deflect Dumak's sword. Leora lifted hers and swung back.

"DUMAK, YOU BASTARD, FACE ME!" yelled Thaddeus, he tried to run but his legs were still wobbly. "YOU COWARD ATTACK ME!"

Dumak threw himself into his next swing and knocked Leora to the ground.

"Humph," gasped Leora, as she struck the ground hard, the back of her head smacking into a rock. The world around Leora went dark.

Dumak smiled fiendishly and glanced back at Thaddeus. He could see the determination in his eyes as hobbled. "Perhaps this is better. I will make him watch as I drain the life from your body, girl!"

Dumak hurled his balls of energy at Thaddeus, forcing him to jump out of the way. Dumak stopped his attack when his peripherals caught a strange, familiar red glow. He turned his head forward to see Leora standing in front of him, her red hair floating and glowing in piercing light. "Balance has been broken, your secret is known. " her voice was great and echoed with power.

"YOU KNOW NOTHING!" interrupted Dumak, furious.

Leora didn't finish or clarify her statement, she charged at Dumak, swinging with her sword. Dumak brought up his own and easily defended himself. The evil man laughed, expecting more from his opponent. Dumak's smile fell as Leora swung again and again, she moved at such speed and precision that Dumak could not keep up. With every swing Leora swung, the power and force increased like she was building energy inside of her, like something new was awakening. Dumak began to retreat, for the first time this night he feared he couldn't win. Leora swung down and feinted her attack. Dumak gasped, he realized his mistake but there was nothing he could do. The sudden and sharp pain was intense. Leora sliced his right arm off near his elbow.

Thaddeus was still rushing towards them. Dumak looked down at his severed arm. Wide eyed and fearing for his life, Dumak screamed. Energy flew from his other appendage. The energy wasn't concentrated like the balls of energy, it was unruly and spead out like a spider's web.

"NO!" yelled Thaddeus, reaching his arm out into empty air. Leora was too close. She tried to dodge the attack but was struck in the chest. Her whole body began to convulse and shake. Her eyes rolled into the back of her head and she collapsed to the ground.

"Your doom has been postponed long enough, PenRuger." Dumak spun and readied himself for Thaddeus' attack.

Thaddeus stopped approaching and stared at the deformed and rotting man, "Your arm is on the ground, you have holes in your chest, and your face looks like you lost a fight with a cheese grater. What possess a man to let himself be so completely seduced to darkness and evil?"

"POWER, PENRUGER. " Dumak threw out his hands as if he was the ultimate power in the universe, "The only thing in all of creation that truly matters!"

"Not even life, the very essence that makes you sentient?"

Dumak rolled his eyes, "You are truly daft, life with end is meaningless. Only everlasting life has true meaning and life everlasting is only for those willing to take power."

"You possess such power?" Thaddeus shook his head, "You barely have enough power to defeat me. An innocent, inexperienced redhead just severed your arm. The hubris you find in your own so-called power is laughable, contemptible even."

"YOU DARE MOCK DUMAK! The power I wield is unmatched, no single force on this shard can match me and when I kill that blonde brat no single force in all of creation will match my power."

Thaddeus' face remained stoic, despite the astonishment he was witnessing around him, "I am not so sure about that, there is one single force that can!"

"HA, WHO?" mocked Dumak," The man who is covered in mud and burns"

"No, not me!" remarked Thaddeus, "I may be from a long line of warriors, generals, and heroes, and this medallion may give me an advantage over most men, but that's not where my greatest strength and power comes from. A power stronger than you will ever be!"

"And what great power is that?"

Thaddeus smiled, "One simple word, EQUINAUTS!"

Dumak was puzzled, he didn't understand.

"FIRE NOW!!!"

Dumak's body lit up, not from his own power, but from nearly forty men with Teslas firing at him at once. Shot after shot Dumak's body began to crumble. Dumak was taken completely by surprised. He had not noticed that all the black riders, demons, and corrupted villagers had been killed. To his even larger astonishment, the redheaded girl appeared next to him. She crawled underneath the fire of the Teslas. Her clothes were clearly burned to the point of indecency, but the flesh around her was not hurt. She reached up and grabbed the netting containing the large lacerated heart from Dumak's belt. There was nothing Dumak could do to stop her, his body was crumbling.

"NO!" yelled Dumak, "NOT THIS WAY!"

Leora crawled away as fast as she could in the mud trying to get away from Dumak, the large lacerated heart netting in her mouth.

Dumak's body broke in half, his upper body separating from his waist, and the shots fired from the Equinauts slowed, only a few still had clear shot at him lying on the ground.

"Cease fire," ordered Thaddeus as he began to approach the remnants of Dumak's body.

Dumak was not ready to die. He bit what remained of his bottom lip and yelled. His voice cracking in desperation and shame, "Ollpheist, I need you."

Moments later, there was a flash of light and loud popping sound. A large, horrific creature in the shape of a man appeared in front of Dumak. The creature was rotting, its flesh was wet and deformed, bones and scales scattered among its arms and legs. Large, thick bones protruded around his rib cage. Its face was nearly gone, only a few pockets of decayed flesh over exposed muscle and bone remained. Its eyes glowed fiercely red and it snarled at the humans around him. It reached down and grabbed Dumak's upper body and disappeared in the same manner as it arrived. The clear sound of a pop reverberated in everyone's ears.

Bailitheoir stopped fighting the moment the horrific demon creature appeared, he watched in horror as another rider betrayed him and left him on the battlefield. What little feeling he had left went numb, *why is it so easy to betray me?* He thought in his head.

Egghead could feel the change in his brother and stopped fighting as well. He approached Bailitheoir and placed his nose against his adversary. Bailitheoir pulled back at first. Verrator's gift still begged for substance, in the moment he wanted nothing more than to take Egghead's soul, to feed the wound and stop his madness for a time. He resisted when surprisingly another yearning appeared, deep down in the core of his being. He felt something that was more than this horrific existence. He felt an urge, a voice singing to him to let go.

Once Dumak had disappeared, Thaddeus ran to Leora. She was still crawling away fearing the danger. "Leora, its ok, Dumak is gone. You are safe."

Leora was hesitant, she was still in-flight mode. A shadow overtook the position in front of her, she looked up and saw Thaddeus' hand. His skin looked smooth and healed, but the sleeve of his jacket was burnt and ruined. Leora's body was shivering and shaking, the adrenaline coursing through her veins was beginning to subside.

Thaddeus knelt down next to her and touched her shoulder, "You did great, Leora. You can relax now." Leora remained silent and wrapped her arm around Thaddeus' leg and hugged it tightly. He began to unbutton the upper straps to the broken Tesla Leora was wearing and took it off of her.

Leora's grip around Thaddeus' leg went tighter. He gingerly took the pack off of her back. Holding the Tesla in his hands, he noticed the straps were nearly gone. They had melted away and large crisp pieces of Leora's dress had fused together. "My God, Leora! Where are you burned?"

Leora had no idea what Thaddeus was talking about, she felt no pain. She rolled onto her back and sat up.

She dropped the netting from her mouth, catching the large, lacerated heart in her hands. Only then realizing most of the top of her outfit had been burned away. Despite the singes and ash around the edges of the outfit's cloth, her skin was as smooth as it had ever been. Neither a single scorch mark nor burn could be found.

Thaddeus pulled off the remnants of his jacket and wrapped it around Leora before she could act bashful at being so revealed. Thaddeus' jacket so burnt and melted as well that he only managed to cover the important areas of Leora's chest. "Where are you burned?" Thaddeus reached out and touched Leora's stomach in disbelief, but thankful she wasn't hurt. He looked at her in complete shock. "Did you feel yourself being healed?"

Leora shook her head.

"Then how are you not burned?"

She shrugged. Leora didn't have an answer for him.

The battle of Callan's Field was over, the town of Mystique was a burnt pile of ash and its inhabitance littered the area dead, lifeless. The surviving expedition members were physically and emotionally tired, many sitting in the very place they had been fighting. A silence filled the camp, no one wanted to move and disturb the sorrow-filled peace that had crept its way into the camp. Thaddeus sat on the ground with Leora leaning against him, every time he started to get up Leora would hold him tighter. Leora was frightened, she had no understanding of what fully transpired after Dumak's energy hit her. Vague memories of the fight popped in her head, but the memories felt foreign to her. Thaddeus did not see or hear anything that Leora said to Dumak once she arose, he was not fully aware of the emotional turmoil Leora was feeling.

"Who am I?" asked Leora out loud, finishing a prayer to the Arcadia and the Maker.

"You are the one who saved my life and maybe everyone else!" answered Thaddeus, assuming the question was for him.

Leora was about to speak when she gasped in fright. The fear in Leora's eyes reminded Thaddeus of another great evil inside the camp. The deep beat of hoof steps approaching caught Thaddeus' ears. He looked up to see that Egghead and Bailitheoir were approaching him, walking side by side. Behind them, a large group of Equinauts and university members followed. They tranquility in the camp was gone. Egghead nuzzled his nose into Thaddeus' chest and pushed him towards Bailitheoir. The Hell Horse lowered its head in an act of submission towards Thaddeus. For a brief moment, a chill went down Thaddeus' back, he had never seen the horse up close. It was odd and disturbing to see a horse in such a deformed and decayed state. The sight of Verrator's gift was extremely disturbing, a long open wound that continued to beat. Thaddeus could almost feel the tortured essence of all the horses this Hellhorse had consumed. It was easy to see why this horse evoked such fear in the people who saw him. His eyes though, despite all of the terrifying grotesqueness, his eyes were soft and scared. Thaddeus' bond with Egghead and his lifetime experience with horses allowed him to see beyond the physical. All horses, from Capallcuradas to the smallest of yearlings, speak to humans all the time. You just have to know how to read them. Thaddeus could tell something had changed in this horse, he wanted to be free of his curse. Reaching his hand out, Thaddeus was about to touch Bailitheoir's forelock to offer it forgiveness when the crowd surrounding them now suddenly began to scream.

"IT'S A KILLER!"

"KILL IT!"

"PUT IT DOWN THADDEUS!"

Bailitheoir became agitated by the crowd. Thaddeus soothed him and held up his hand to quiet the crowd. He bent down and grabbed the netting holding Bailitheoir's heart. "You are connected to this and it tethers you to this world, correct?"

Bailitheoir stomped his foot and shook his massive head in the affirmative. "If I destroy the heart, will it allow you peace?"

Bailitheoir was unsure, Thaddeus looked over at Egghead, "What do you think?"

Thaddeus could sense that Egghead was unsure as well.

Thaddeus opened the netting and allowed the heart to fall into his hands. The moment his hands came into contact with it, his mind swirled with rapid images and feelings of the past. He saw everything that Bailitheoir saw and felt. To most the images would be too much to comprehend, but Thaddeus' medallion-cursed dreams were similar. Thaddeus' heart broke at this poor horse's life, he saw the Lord Horses force him to bond with Verrator, how the man used Bailitheoir for his own personal glory, and how he betrayed him in the end. Thaddeus winced at the sting of Verrator's blade, his betrayal and the curse that followed. A pit in Thaddeus' stomach formed and it grew bigger and bigger, the hunger he felt was so strong that he craved the flesh of anything. The hunger was so powerful it took over every feeling and instinct. "Verrator's gift." he whispered, Thaddeus had no comprehension until now how strong and constant the hunger was and how much strength it took to resist it.

Thaddeus snapped out of his trance, the rapid images were gone, but he awoke to a world in chaos. The weather had suddenly changed, the wind began to whip, and roar and the clouds circled around them. Everyone began to get scared, "It's the Hellhorse! HE IS CAUSING IT, KILL HIM!"

Thaddeus ignored the crowd, "I am so sorry, you deserve peace. " he said softly, "Will you let me give it to you?"

Bailitheoir lowered his head.

Thaddeus pulled out his dagger and was about to strike the heart when a loud voice yelled "NO!"

Dean appeared from the crowd, "You must let go of the heart, nature is unbalanced! You are already bonded! You cannot have two bonds. "

Thaddeus handed Leora the heart, placing it in the netting. The winds suddenly stopped, and nature returned to normal. "I don't want to bond with him, I want to give him peace. "

Several of the people in the crowd who had watched friends die in the most horrific ways were disgusted at the idea of letting the creature have peace.

"IT'S A DEMON LIKE THE OTHERS, IT MUST DIE!" yelled one man in the crowd.

Several of the university members filled with rage and hate dashed forward and began to stab Bailitheoir. The Hellhorse winced and hollered in pain, Thaddeus could see anger begin to reassert itself. Bailitheoir was losing control to the hunger. More people from the crowd ran forward, each wanting to take a piece of the horse. More blades pierced Bailitheoir's flesh.

Bailitheoir dropped to his knees. Egghead, angered, moved to attack the people, but Thaddeus stood in his way. "No, stop. I'll handle this." Thaddeus roared as loud as he could, "STOP!"

The crowd ceased their attack, Thaddeus' voiced thundered and echoed like a god from the sky. They turned to look at Thaddeus in fright. "Enough blood has been shed, back away from him now before--"

It was too late, Bailitheoir could no longer resist Verrator's gift, the hunger was too strong, and he tired of the pain humans had caused him. Flames from his nostrils shot out and he whinnied a hellish cry of anger. He kicked out with his back legs sending two men flying backwards. He threw his face to the left and burned everyone around him. Some of the crowd coward and began to retreat, others dashed forward hoping to kill the beast.

"Please, Bailitheoir, stop this!" pleaded Thaddeus.

His words were useless, Bailtheoir was gone, the Hellhorse had returned.

"Run! Run away you fools!" urged Thaddeus.

Bailitheoir grabbed and bit down on a man's arms and threw him into others. Rearing up, he kicked out again at two men behind him. One person in the crowd standing in front of the horse took the chance and stabbed him in the chest while the Hellhorse was focused with the two men behind him. Bailitheoir cried out in anger when the sword pierced his empty chest. He dashed forward and knocked the man down. Rearing up onto his hind legs the Hellhorse was about to smash his hooves into his attacker's face.

"Please, don't do this!" yelled Kaitlyn, emerging from the crowd, standing in front of the horse. "Please, they are scared, they don't understand. Forgive them and they may forgive you."

The hellhorse cried out and thrashed outward with his front legs high in the air, fire flamed from his nose and his hooves flew to the ground. The man covered his face and cried out in fear, but the hooves did not strike, landing inches from his face.

Bailitheoir walked over the man and threw his face into Kaitlyn's chest. "It's ok. I forgive you, its ok to let go."

Everyone backed away from Bailitheoir forming a large circle, Thaddeus and Leora approached with Bailitheoir' heart. Leora held out the heart for Kaitlyn to take.

She was hesitant.

Thaddeus smiled, "After thousands of years of pain, I think he found his bond partner. "

Kaitlyn teared up and was about to grab the heart.

"The next experience you will feel will be," Thaddeus paused to think of the right word, "different, maybe overwhelming at first. But it will pass."

Kaitlyn nodded. The moment she touched the heart she was filled with images of Bailitheoir's past, she saw and felt everything he had. She looked at Bailtheoir, who for the first time was ashamed of everything that had happened. Kaitlyn hugged his large and massive head, "You must let them go. I forgive you." She could feel Bailitheoir's hesitation, he feared what the wound would do to him. "I know it's scary, but you must. Every horse' soul you took also took a piece of you with it. To be whole again, you must let go. It's the only way for you to find peace."

The crowd gasped.

Kaitlyn feared it was because Bailitheoir was going to attack them again, she hugged his head harder and began to cry, "Please, please don't, just let them go, just let them go. I forgive you, let go."

Dean reached out and touched her shoulder, "Kaitlyn, look!"

Kaitlyn opened her eyes. Standing next to her was the disembodied soul of a horse, the very first horse Bailitheoir had slain and absorbed. It was transparent with a heavenly glow about it. It nuzzled its head into Kaitlyn, the sensation was warm and electric. The souls of horses turned, reached out, and rubbed the neck of Bailitheoir. A small sliver of the wound disappeared, and a speckle of grey appeared near his nose. The soul backed away, bowed before Bailitheoir, and ascended into the sky. Another soul appeared, followed by another and another, soon the entire area around the crowd was filled with the souls of Bailitheoir's victims.

"Good heavens look at this!" remarked the professor in awe, walking through the crowd escorted by Andi and Glut, who knew he would want to witness this, "Quite remarkable!"

Soul after soul repeated the ritual and little by little Bailitheoir was healed, his black, deformed face was healed, and his grey coat shined white. His red, black eyes were becoming blue and pure.

"Nya…!"

"NYAHAHA!"

"NYAHAHAHAHAHAHAHA!"

Everyone went quiet, the sound of something strange and unusual had arrived.

"Great Scott!" remarked the professor apprehensively, "What is that dreadful noise."

"NYAHAHAHA- Dreadful!?"

Kaitlyn suddenly screamed, Bailitheoir's heart vanished from her hands and the souls of the horses swirled and vanished back into the beating wound. Bailitheoir cried out in anger, a small creature appeared on its back holding the lacerated heart. Bailitheoir tried to rear up and send the creature flying off his back, but the creature held out the heart and commanded him to stop. Bailitheoir had released too many souls, he wasn't strong enough to overpower the creature's will. He had no choice but to obey.

"Nya- See Here Old Fleshie, my voice maybe rough and high, but the poets will cry. Of all creatures in the land, there will never be one like me that is so grand! Oh, Nyhehe! That was quite melodic wouldn't you say?"

No one was sure what they were staring at or listening to, but once Thaddeus saw the heart in the creature's hands he charged at it. "Stupid Fleshie." The creature snapped its fingers and Thaddeus rose and hung in the air, unable to move forward. Akash and two other Equinauts charged as well, the creature pointed his finger at three different spots and each spot exploded into large pillars of fire. "Nyahaha, Uh-Uh-Uh, I got the heart! Don't try to it away like a slutty slutty tart!"

"What are you?" asked the professor in shock and disgust.

"NYHA!" laughed the creature, "I am a messenger I am!"

"From?"

"The Dark Lady, the great and unholy she demon, general and leader of all the terror legions, collector of souls, destroyer of worlds, murderer of billions, the Fallen's reckoning, soon to be releaser of the Prime Evil, and so on and so on."

"What is this message?" asked the professor.

The creature, standing upon Bailitheoir's back holding the lacerated heart, danced slightly. The creature was small, with a deformed body, it looked impish and childish, sharp eyes, chin, and ears with a single, small horn protruding from its forehead. "Nyahaha, the Dark Lady is most displeased. Dumak revealed her hand too soon, he will be punished Nyahaha. Betrayal always comes with a price. GO BACK TO YOUR HORIZON! And the Mistress of Evil will forget about you. Continue on your path and she burn your souls and--"

The creature stopped speaking and stared at Andi, "The MORUSTRANCONATRA, you exist! Your father lied, told us you were dead! Oh, how happy the Domina will be! She will find you and you will be the instru--" The small creature's focus changed from Andi. It looked upon someone else. It appeared to almost recognize her and wondered why it was there, that it did and didn't belong. That person was Leora. Its face turned sideways, to the left, back to the right, and gasped with its long snake like tongue out. "Nyahaha- how are you a--"

"MY FATHER!" yelled Andi. Surprising everyone, she approached the creature, looking determined. "TELL ME WHAT YOU KNOW!"

Glut ran after his sister, "Andi, come back!"

"FIRE!" yelled Thaddeus, while still dangling helplessly in the air.

"NO, WAIT!" yelled Andi ducking her head.

Bolts of energy hit the small creature in the face and body. "Nyahaha, ouch that hurt!" A large bubble appeared around the creature and the horse. It was transparent but it glowed red. The Equinauts continued to fire but the shots were absorbed. Egghead charged the shield and slammed his front hooves into the bubble. His hooves did nothing, "Dumb horse Fleshie- you are no match for--"

Egghead turned on his haunches and fired both of his back legs into the bubble again and again. the creature laughed until the bubble suddenly shook. "NYA- HOW CAN YOU!?"

Egghead was not going to let his brother down. Bailitheoir was so close to having his curse lifted. He kicked the bubble over and over again. One of his back shoes broke from the impact and went soaring into the sky, forcing people to scatter. The bubble kept shaking and shaking until it suddenly cracked.

"ENOUGH, STUPID FLESHIES!" The creature's voice rose to levels that few creatures could reach. Everyone stopped firing and stared at the creature, wondering what it would do next. "A price must be paid for your transgressions. Listen to me and to what I say and maybe you will live one more day."

The tiny, annoying creature suddenly broke out in verse, confusing everyone.

"Continue to attack us with all your mortal might-
The Dark Lady's righteous wrath will you invite
Darkness has fallen across the land-
Deaths will come quickly by her swift hand
Demons rise, in legions they come-
All who oppose them will succumb
Creation dwindles, life we will consume –
The Fallen are coming and it will be you DOOM."

The creature bowed while still standing on the Hellhorse's back and then snapped his fingers softly. Out of that snap, a powerful shockwave of energy burst out of the sound, everyone including Egghead was sent flying backwards, falling to the ground, clasping their ears. Bailitheoir tried to resist the creature's control over him, but it was futile. Letting out a loud scream the Hellhorse tried to call for help, but nobody could hear him. Moments later the creature, along with Bailitheoir, disappeared in the blink of an eye, leaving only a high pitch noise ringing in everyone's ear.

***

The sun's rays pierced through the low hanging morning clouds, it was only as this new light appeared over the battlefield that everyone began to understand how horrible this battle really was. So many people were lying on the ground, dead and rotting. It was a sobering moment for everyone as they walked among the slain, looking for any chance of an injured survivor. There were none.

Failing to find survivors, the expedition prepared to burn the dead. The number of bodies was going to require great amounts of wood. Groups began falling any tree they could find in the immediate area.

Of any duty required of Italicus, this was by far the one he hated most. The Butcher's Bill, a crude name for the list of the dead and injured. It took most of the morning for him to compile the first list.

Thaddeus wept when Italicus entered his tent and presented him the Butcher's Bill. The professor's team was hit hard with over twenty of his men slain, twenty more severely injured, and three critical, not expecting to survive. Thaddeus knew he had failed them. It was his duty to ensure everyone in this expedition remained safe. At the bottom of the list, Thaddeus truly felt sick. The air from his lungs left him and he nearly began to cough and gasp. Written as clearly as Italicus' chicken scratch writing could be were six names Thaddeus recognized. "Six Equinauts!?"

"And three more critically injured," responded Italicus, his voice cracking from the sorrow he felt. "Gregor, Leah, and Arnos are in bad shape."

Thaddeus' eyes swelled, "Chances?"

Italicus looked away, "Maybe Leah, but she will be crippled, they have to take her left arm."

Thaddeus placed his head into his hand and slowly lifted his head, "A fifth. " mouthed Thaddeus, as he reread the name of each Equinaut who had passed. This was the largest loss of life that the Equinauts had ever occurred in one battle. Thaddeus smashed his fist onto the small, wooden table nearby, "DUMAK WILL PAY FOR THEIR DEATHS!"

Italicus saluted, he agreed and expected his commander and friend to make such a statement, "Your command, my will! So, say we all!"

"DAMN IT TO HELL!" yelled Thaddeus in fit of uncontrolled anger. He kicked one of the stools near him. It tore through the canvas as it soared through the sky, falling several yards away from the tent.

"I know it looks bad Thaddeus," remarked Italicus, trying to sound optimistic and help his friend, "But we won, didn't we? Didn't we just prove that these demons and such are not unstoppable? That we have a chance at beating them, that's a victory, right?"

Thaddeus folded the Butcher's Bill and placed it in the pocket of his ceremonial jacket, the only other jacket he had with him. It was blue rather than tan, had gold stitching and styling, and it only had large buttons down the right side. "Was this a victory, Italicus? If it was, it was pyrrhic at best. We lost a fifth of our company? AND FOR WHAT!? They attacked us, and we defended, we didn't gain anything. If you hadn't reached Gladthorn inside the Citadel war wagon and used that against the black riders we probably wouldn't have won."

Italicus beamed, "So your're saying I single handedly won this battle? Maybe all I need to do is challenge the whole demon horde? ITALICUS THE INVINCIBLE!"

"Italicus, the damn foolish. " Thaddeus took a very large breath and stared into oblivion for a moment, "Did you happen to find her?"

Italicus' smile dropped, "Yeah, I found Meg. She was near the alleyway, or what's left of the alleyway at least. I took her home. Her place was one of the few buildings that didn't catch on fire. Strange really, Meg was burned badly on her upper arm during the war, she has feared fire desperately ever since and her home is one of the few that survived on scathed."

Thaddeus hugged Italicus in away only best friends could, "Do you want help preparing her body for the--"

"No, I don't want her burned. "Said Italicus harshly.

Thaddeus shook his head and rolled his eyes, "I was going to say help burying her? We can get a few people to build a casket?"

"Oh, sorry," remarked Italicus sheepishly for his outburst, "I already made one. I just need to go through her closet and find the right outfit. She always wanted to look her best."

"I agree completely, I'll get some shovels and help you. "

Italicus shook his head, "Its ok Thaddeus, I need to do this myself."

Thaddeus nodded, "Of course, if you change your mind though."

"I'll let you know."

"Thaddeus?" called out a voice from outside his tent. The professor poked his head in, his hate was off, which made him look different. The top of his head was bandaged, forcing his hair to stick up wildly. "Pardon me, but may we come in?"

"Of course, professor"

Thaddeus squeezed Italicus' shoulder, "If you need help, let me know. Oh, and here." Thaddeus handed Italicus his golden feather. "I'll win this back later."

Italicus smiled and placed it in his ear, "Not a chance."

The professor walked in with Andi and Glut, both of them tried not to laugh at Italicus' accessory. Italicus acknowledged the professor and others before heading towards the exit.

"Thaddeus," spoke the professor, "I need to talk to you, but you have to promise not to hit me."

The tone in the professor's face was sarcastic sass for which Thaddeus appreciated. He nodded and offered him and the others a stool.

"HA! professor!" remarked Italicus about to push through the flap to the tent, "I tell you there isn't a day that goes by that I don't want to smack that handsome smile right off his face." Italicus gestured the idea wildly with his hands.

Thaddeus bit the bottom of his lip, this was not the time or place for humor, but even in the darkest of times Italicus will still try to make people laugh.

"Take your ugly ass feather and get out of here, will you?"

Italicus mimed being shot in the heart at Thaddeus' words.

Thaddeus smiled out of sheer annoyance.

Italicus pointed and beamed, "Yep, that's the one." Italicus made a slapping motion into the air "Smack it right off your smug face!"

Thaddeus threw an empty mug at his friend, Italicus dodged it and ran out of the tent echoing his last words, "right off your smug face."

"Forgive me professor, we all have different ways to deal with out grief and Italicus runs high until everything needed to be done is done. Then he falls harder than most, so let people know that we will keep the feather teasing down to a minimum. What can I do for you?"

"We need to talk. "

Andi noticed Thaddeus' friendly demeanor change.

"Yes, we do." remarked Thaddeus sternly. "I didn't expect you to walk into the lion's den so early to be fully honest."

The professor's cheeks went slightly red, "Yes, well, we must discuss what Dumak meant about Andi. "

"No!"

The professor was shocked at Thaddeus' interruption, "No? What do you mean no?"

"No!" Thaddeus sat back on his stool and crossed his arms, "We are going to be talking about what you have inside that Mark III wagon."

The professor went very quiet and looked at Thaddeus with an angry rage, "This is not the time."

"I already know what you have inside, it didn't take much to figure it out once Dumak told me we had one of his Kinder. Kinder is a western Aedunic word for children. Obviously Dumak sees the people he corrupts as part of him. They have some sort of mental connection to him, don't they? That is why they attacked us on the first night, wasn't it? Dumak wanted his pawn back and when he realized we could defend ourselves he had to attack us with a larger force!"

The professor lowered his face and remained silent on the matter.

"AM I CORRECT, PROFESSOR?"

The professor took a large breath and twerked his nose, he lifted his head and glanced at Andi and Glut. He then stared directly at Thaddeus "I am here for Andi, this not the place nor the time to be discus--"

"SIX EQUINAUTS ARE DEAD! Three more critically wounded and twenty of your own men are rotting in the sun, dead! NOW TELL ME THE TRUTH! Do you have a demon in that wagon?"

The professor stared in silences.

Thaddeus took a large breath, "I'll take your silence as an acknowledgement that I am correct. You do have a demon in the--"

Andi interrupted Thaddeus and looked at her godfather shocked, "PRFOESSOR?"

The professor was beginning to shiver, and his eyes filled with tears, "I didn't know."

Andi and Glut gasped

"You actually have one of those demons in the Mark III?" asked Glut.

"Good heavens, no!" defended the professor sighing, "It's not a demon. Several days before the expedition left, Deniz and I were attacked by black robed assailants. I thought for a moment I was going to die, but Steven intervened. One of the robed attackers was still alive and it was Valissa, the young waitress at the Mcloud Café'. I knew then something was wrong, she is one of the most delightful people I know. Then she started to change and revert to whatever corruption that was infecting her. Between transitions she began to tell us what the enemy was up to. Most of the useful information I have obtained has come from her. I didn't know they would come after her, I didn't even think or consider that was the reason for the first attack."

Thaddeus placed his finger in the professor's face, "That's part of the problem, professor. You didn't think! You may be a genius about technology, but strategist or military general you are not. As the appointed military leader of this expedition I demand no more secrets!"

"I get it, yes of course!" answered the professor, "My intentions were good, but the results were less than desirable, but right now we need to discuss Andi, "Belladon waited for Thaddeus to protest but he sat on his stool in silence, "because of the connection the two of you share. Whatever the enemy has planned may affect you both."

"Dumak was very adamant that he had to kill her, thank the Maker he failed."

"He almost did," added Glut looking very sad, "if Wrench hadn't arrived I don't think we would be here."

Thaddeus' eyes looked down at his jacket remembering the Butcher's Bill, "How is he? I don't remember seeing his name on the list. "

Andi and Glut looked down at their feet in sorrow.

"Expect that list to increase," the professor spoke gravely, "the medics are still working diligently to help all that were injured, but so many were hurt."

"I'll send any Equinaut with triage training over to help."

"They're already there Thaddeus, but back to Andi. Dumak was very convinced that Andi must die, but that horrid little creature saw her and was almost delighted to see her alive."

Andi sprung from her stool, "He said my father must have lied, that means they know something about what happened to our parents. We have to find them and figure out what they know!"

"Andi my girl, please sit," The professor reached and touched her arm gently, "If they did have your parents, they are probably, "He chose his word carefully, "gone. I hate saying this out loud to you, but why would the demons keep them alive?"

"Our father is alive!" yelled Andi, "I know it! He got away from the demons!"

"Maybe so." said Thaddeus trying to calm Andi down, "What we do know is that they have some sort of fascination with you and we need to figure out why?"

"Dumak called her, the MORUSTRANCONATRA. "The professor rubbed his forehead, "I can't translate it. The Progenitor language doesn't like spaces and they loved to make new words by stringing many words together. I've never seen this strain of words, the closest I can come up with is maybe one of the words means a jar."

"A jar?" remarked Thaddeus confused, "That is very vague and unhelpful."

"I might have a way of helping with that." Stated the professor, "The information we have gathered from Valissa, we know the demons have some sort of staging area or camp in Veilwood forest near some ruins believed to be where the Bloodstone cult originated."

"We thought maybe the Black Riders Dumak led were part of that cult or a similar one. I guess we were wrong."

"No, I don't think you were, Thaddeus. But I'll explain that latter. One piece of information we got from Valissa is that the enemy has an Urithum, it's a device that allows us to see Progenitor secrets written in code. I believe that will help us translate the word Dumak used, plus unlock many other secrets."

Thaddeus stood up and grabbed a map of Veilwood off one of his desks, "Veilwood forest alone is a treacherous and unforgiving place. Seeing how strong the enemy is here, I strongly think our original idea to go north is our best bet and bypass Veilwood completely."

The professor feared Thaddeus would say no, he was about to jump out of his stool, "Thaddeus you must understand."

"I do understand what you are telling me, professor!" he said in a commanding voice, "But from a military aspect you are asking us to take the fight to the demons, infiltrate their territory, and extract an object we aren't even certain is there. There could be thousands of demons there!"

The professor wrinkled his nose, "If Dumak had thousands of demons at his disposal, don't you think he would have used them?"

"Dumak isn't the leader," rebutted Thaddeus, "This Dark Lady rules the demons, and Dumak's own words showed that he has his own agenda. He didn't want her to find out. That's why the attack was limited to a few shrieks, people, and Slavine soldiers he had corrupted." Thaddeus took a large breath, "Plus, professor, we need to figure out what our current situation is, figure out what resources we lost and what we will need to carry on. We have to burn or bury the dead, we have to heal ourselves. Once that is done, only then will I begin to consider if we head north--"

The professor began to protest. "But we must--"

"AH!" interrupted Thaddeus using a stern voice, "Or if we head into Veilwood. Like I said, professor, I understand what you are saying to me, but I am not going to lead my men into a battle we cannot win."

Gladthorn walked into the tent and saluted, "Thaddeus, you had better come and see this. We found something."

Gladthorn lead the professor and Thaddeus to the war wagon that he and Edryss had taken from Colonel Jaster. A large number of people were standing around looking at intently, "Zapp, show them what we found."

"We were looking to see if the colonel had left us any supplies, what we found were these things." Zapp handed a strange oval rock with unique writing all around it. "They're everywhere sir, the entire cargo area, every nook and cranny. There has be a thousand of these rocks inside of the wagon."

"A thousand rocks!?" Thaddeus had absolutely no clue what he was holding, "Any idea, professor."

"I do not immediately recognize any of these words other than its Progenitor in origin." The professor held the oval rock up to the sun for more light, wishing he had his top hat and monocle with him. "Maybe if I had a Urithum, but as of right now I have no clue."

"Is that a non-subtle hint, professor?" asked Thaddeus

"No, it is not, just a matter of fact." Spoke the professor honestly, "I have faith in you Thaddeus, you are an honorable man, I will attempt to translate this writing the best I can with what I have. And I will respect whatever decision you make on our next course of action."

***

Leora kept to herself after the battle was over, she was embarrassed and currently had no way of rectifying her situation. The dress she had borrowed from Callan's wife was destroyed and burnt beyond use and Thaddeus' burnt jacket was just barely doing the job of covering her up. Once everyone had settled down from the chaos of earlier, Leora searched for the right wagon that was carrying her belongings. She really wanted a warm bath or shower to wash away the filth of the battle and night away, but she was willing to accept just a change of clothes.

Unfortunately, the theme of the nigh continued, Leora was met with another problem. Several wagons, including the one that had almost every belonging she had brought with her, had caught on fire. Every last piece of clothing she had was gone, all she had left was some of her tools and her journal.

Kicking the steel wheel of the wagon, Leora grumbled loudly.

Leora's last option was Callan's wife, *hopefully she has another outfit and will let me pay her for the loss of this dress?* Leora thought to herself as she approached the farmhouse. She knocked on the door, but no one came. She waited anxiously and knocked again. When she was still met with silence she slowly opened it and called out. She waited again for a response, Leora felt even more frustrated and was about to leave when she noticed something odd on the floor. She picked it up and brought it to her face. It was part of a severed finger, she abruptly screamed. Opening the door further, Leora was left in utter shock and horror. The entire Callan family was dead, their bodies ripped and shredded across the living room in the most horrible and gruesome ways imaginable. professor Akroyd, still tied to the chair, was dead as well.

Several more hours went by and Leora was still stuck in her burnt outfit. With nothing else to do, she grabbed an axe and helped log trees along the river. She purposefully made sure the trees she cut were away from everyone else. She was surprised how many trees were needed. With so many dead, a pit was being dug. The logs were to be soaked in oil and placed at the bottom of the pit and the bodies burned and given a proper service. Then the pit would be filled in with dirt.

Tired and sore, she handed her ax to someone else and headed for the food. She ate her dinner away from others, but close enough to watch Wooly. Kaitlyn and Dean had assembled a wall-less tent over the injured horse to keep him from boiling in the hot sun. Doing better, but the horse was not out of the woods, his blood loss was great, and his wounds could easily develop an infection. Kaitlyn was also greatly concerned with the horrific condition of an ailment called Founder. Leora had never heard such a term before, but Kaitlyn described it as when something internal causes the bone inside the hoof to move. It pulls on all of the ligaments and tendons along the leg and can be extremely painful, but there is nothing they can do to fix it. Some horses whose bones move slightly can live with it, others who have a more severe case can become crippled and have to be put down as a result.

Leora ate her food and wondered what she should do, her tent was destroyed in the fire as well. The sun was beginning to sneak behind the horizon and the temperature was falling. She shivered while leaning against the tree.

"Leora?" asked a voice coming from her side, "Why are you still in that dress?"

The redhead blushed and made an awkwardly funny face as Thaddeus approached, "All my clothes burned, this is all I have."

Thaddeus laughed, which only made Leora feel worse about her situation. She looked away, tearing up slightly, hoping Thaddeus would leave. Instead, his jacket was off and was now sitting, leaning against the tree as well. He held out his very regal looking blue jacket.

"I am sorry, I can't"

Thaddeus dropped the jacket in her lap, "Please"

She tried to hand it back to him, "No, I am ok."

"You saved my life. "responded Thaddeus admiringly, "It's the least I can do."

"I don't need it."

"It's cold and you are shaking, take my jacket."

Leora shook her head.

Thaddeus laughed, "What did you say to me last night, does it hurt being so stubborn?"

Leora attempted to hold in her laughter, but it came out in small, uncontrolled blurbs of noise, "Foolhardy is what I said, so you did hear me?"

Thaddeus spoke matter of fact, "I always hear what you have to say." He grabbed his jacket and held it so Leora could put her arms through.

"Then why didn't you listen?" she asked while putting the jacket on.

It was Thaddeus' turn to look away for a moment, "Perhaps I am foolhardy, but I knew I had to protect my people at all costs. I guess I didn't do a good job at that." Thaddeus' voice cracked, "I lost seven men now, two more may not make it through the night."

Leora grabbed Thaddeus' hand and held it tightly, "Did you do the best you could?"

Thaddeus nodded, "I'd like to think so, but no matter, people died on my--"

"People are going to die." Leora spoke with a unusual confidence, "There is nothing you are going to be able to do about it. No matter what you do, no matter how hard you try, Thaddeus PenRuger, you can't save everyone." She paused for a moment, the words she said felt right, but were not her own.

Thaddeus took in her words, she was correct, but Thaddeus knew he still had to try to save as many as you can, "Are you sure you haven't done this before?"

Leora's blue eyes stared at the last sliver of the day's light, "Yeah, never even left the Citadel. I just wanted to do something without my father. Professor Belladon's expeditions were known to be great, fun experiences and a way to see the world. I guess I chose the wrong one to be my first. I thought this would be a fun adventure and maybe I would find--"

Leora paused and looked away from Thaddeus, who waited over a minute for her to continue. "Find?"

Leora blushed, "Nothing, just a foolish girl's dream."

Thaddeus attempted a pleading smiled that looked goofier than pleading.

"You look pathetic, PenRuger, fine!" Leora leaned in, even though no one was around she didn't want anyone else to hear her. "I was hoping to find a dance partner."

"Dance partner?" asked Thaddeus confused, "This is the second time you have brought up dancing."

"It's stupid." she remarked, "When I was younger, my father had a woman friend who he would take dancing." Thaddeus looked at her in shock with his eyes open. Leora immediately knew what he was thinking. "NO, STOP IT! It wasn't like that, get your mind out of the gutter. It really was just dancing and dinner, my father was classically trained."

Thaddeus couldn't help but smirk, Leora tried to push him away but he was too heavy to move. Seeing how upset she was, Thaddeus apologized, "I am sorry, please go on."

Leora took a large breath and flicked her hair away from her face, her eyes filled with angered sass, "Like I was saying, I was always jealous that she would take him away from me once a week. When you move around as much as we did, he was the only person constant in my life. One of the nights I pleaded and pleaded to go with them. He finally relented. We lived in Lithia at the time and we took two long shuttle rides to the Gates of Astronimicus and then a boat ride to the foot of the mountain. I don't remember a lot of the platform ride up, but we entered the Citadel Proper late into the night. It was the first time I had seen the palace and the other mansions up close. We went to the South-C Club, the one with the dance floor that hangs off the mountain, there is not a greater view of the city in the entirety of the Citadel. We--"

Thaddeus interjected surprised, he tried several times to get Alana a seat there, "That's a very fancy, expensive, establishment."

Leora nodded, "We had dinner, it was very nice, and Clara was very sweet and polite to me. I really liked her, and I began to think as any little girl would that maybe she could be my mother. My father doesn't smile a lot, I think the pain of losing my real mother still weighs on him. I don't know if he will ever let go of that pain."

Thaddeus understood completely. Letting go of the pain feels like you are letting go of the person and losing them for a second time. He thought about telling Leora about Alana, but he wasn't ready to reveal that part of him yet. People who know you are a widow and your wife was murdered change. They feel sorry for you and pity you. Everything suddenly revolves around her death and it makes it monumentally harder than it already was to move on. "I can understand that it would be hard to deal with such a loss." He tried to say diplomatically.

"Yeah it is, but when I watched him dance, it was like the pain was lifted and gone. He and Clara staring into each other's eyes, gliding majestically on the dance floor. The world around you disappear and it's just you and your partner, a perfect moment in the music. I don't know, I guess I just wanted to feel what that was like." Leora's eyes swelled and she wiped the forming tears away, looking away. "Listen to me talk about dancing while sitting here surrounded by all this evil and death, it's just a silly girl's dream."

Thaddeus touched Leora's face softly and brought her gaze back to him. He smiled at her warmly, "It's not silly, in fact it's quite beautiful." He rose from ground, "Come with me, I have something to show you."

Thaddeus took Leora by the hand and lead her to his tent. As soon as they entered his tent, he offered her a seat and immediately went rummaging through a chest by his cot. He handed her a box that looked very old and extremely dusty.

"Please open this, it's yours now." He said while staring at the box very emotionally, "It was for an Equinaut who never got a chance to receive it." Leora started opening the box, eagerly wondering what was inside of it. Thaddeus stepped back, like the very idea of the box opening was wrong. "I'll, I'll be right back. I have something to show you from one of the Equinaut wagons."

It took Thaddeus almost fifteen minutes to return, he was holding a small but heavy wooden chest. As he entered the tent, it looked empty, "Leora?" he asked, afraid that she had run off.

"I am here." she declared walking around a small divider, "I was looking at it in the mirror, what do you think?"

Thaddeus stepped around and saw Leora, he was completely and overwhelmingly stunned. "Alana." he whispered out loud. Leora was wearing an Equinaut uniform, tight forming egg white riding pants, a white silk shirt with a unique gold and pearl beaded design around her chest and a perfectly fitting long, green, leather jacket with red and gold designs.

Leora blushed at the astonished look Thaddeus had, his bottom jaw dropping, "Do I look good in it? I can't believe how well it fits, just a little tight in a few areas."

"Not even Arcadia could match your beauty in that." responded Thaddeus.

Leora beamed, "Thank you so much! It feels so good to be in a proper outfit."

Thaddeus was still trying to cope at how beautiful Leora looked and close she was to Alana. *That's not your wife*, a cautious voice inside of him echoed, *Alana is dead, gone.*

Thaddeus tried to hide his emotions, "I am happy the outfit has found a good home and will no longer be collecting dust in my chest."

Leora sat on the stool. Thaddeus followed, never taking his eyes off her.

He sat down next to her, still holding the very heavy, small chest. Leora waited for Thaddeus to speak, but he was lost in his own thoughts.

"What's in the chest?" she asked feeling slightly uncomfortable in the silence.

"Beg your pard-- oh duh," Thaddeus fumbled with the chest and began to open it, "this was given to us from the city of Del for dealing with a problem they had a few years back. Something I am not at liberty to talk about because it would embarrass several of those grubby ass senators and break the contract we have with them. But this is a music box."

Thaddeus wound a small crank on the side, adjusted some of the levels, and it began to play a very slow, soothing melody. "They say it changes songs, but I have yet to figure how. But you said you like to dance." Thaddeus stood up and offered his hand, "I warn you I am not very good."

Leora took Thaddeus' hand smiling brightly, "We can learn together, if you would like?"

Thaddeus knew what he wanted to say, but the feelings felt right now were almost foreign to him. It had been so many years since he had felt anything remotely close to it. His heart had been torn and broken for so long that it felt almost wrong to feel anything else. The pain of losing Alana kept it from mending and he almost forgot what it was like to feel the potential of caring for someone again. Not wanting to lose the moment, "I would like nothing better!"

It was nearly morning before Thaddeus left his tent, allowing Leora to stay there and sleep on his cot. He would bunk with Italicus, who he knew always had a second cot with him. Italicus, sound asleep, never moved as Thaddeus snuck inside his tent. Thaddeus laid there trying to sleep but unable to, his mind remembering the night's events.

"Well good morning sunshine, I don't remember you being here when I went to bed." remarked Italicus, kicking Thaddeus' cot and waking him up. "Why aren't you in your tent?"

Thaddeus stretched and yawn, to Italicus' horror the man was smiling, "I let Leora take my cot, her tent--"

"Wasn't big enough for you, too?" mocked Italicus washing his face in a bowl of room temperature water and placing the gold feather between his head and right ear, "You dog, always with the redheads!"

Thaddeus' face scoured and he pointed at Italicus harshly, "Nothing happened, we talked and, " he mumbled his next word, embarrassed to admit it, "danced, the entire time."

"What was that?" asked Italicus cupping his ear, "Did you say DANCE!?" Italicus bowed regally and began to dance with an invisible partner, humming a melodic tune.

Thaddeus threw his pillow at him, "STOP IT, you ass! Her tent and clothes burned in one of the wagons. So, I gave her the uniform I never got to give to Alana."

Italicus stopped dancing, he realized then that this wasn't a joking manner, "Whoa, really!? You really do fancy her don't you?"

Thaddeus's face blushed, "Maybe, I am not sure. I just know she saved my life and when I am around her I feel, I feel," he looked up at his friend, searching for the right word, "I feel whole and that is something I haven't felt in a very long time."

Italicus pulled over a stool and sat next to his best friend, "Is there a chance you feel like this because Leora reminds you of Alana? I never met her, but if I was to picture her from what you have told me, Leora fits the bill pretty close."

Thaddeus shrugged, "Maybe she does remind me of Alana in some ways. "

"She is not Alana, Thaddeus, you do realize that?"

"I know that!" Thaddeus thought for a moment, "I think I do, I am not sure yet?"

"You need to be sure." Italicus wrapped his arm around Thaddeus' shoulder, "All kidding and teasing aside for a moment. As a friend who doesn't want to see you hurt, nor Leora for that matter, you need to be one hundred percent sure. She is a young, naïve woman with potential to be something great. Don't lead her on unless you know it's her that you have feelings for. Not who you hope she is."

Thaddeus took in Italicus' wise words, "Thank you, dad. "

Italicus rolled his eyes.

"No, you are right. I need to be sure, but like I said, nothing happened."

Italicus smiled and stood up, "Good, just promise me one more thing."

Thaddeus rose from the cot as well, "Of course, name it?"

"No matter what happens, you'll save the last dance for me!"

Thaddeus laughed, "Only if I get to wear the feather!"

Italicus let out a belly full of laughter, "Of course, buddy!"

***

Three weeks passed before the expedition finally left Mystique behind them. It took Fryda and her small squad of university members three days longer than expected to return from a neighboring village with the needed provisions to replace everything that was lost. Thaddeus and the professor worried when they had not returned on time.

Everyone was thankful to be leaving the horrors and deaths behind them. A monument was erected over the burial pit, parts of the Equinaut statue was used for it, which Thaddeus had thought fitting. Zapp and Niles spent two weeks chiseling a record of what had transpired and the names of everyone who had died. The professor was adamant that the last words written would be, *'Your deaths will be avenged.'*

Gladthorn and Edryss were thankful to be leaving the city behind, Thaddeus had been furious with them for leaving their posts. Many of the Equinauts were quick to remind them that if they had not found the Citadel war wagon, the battle may have been lost. While Thaddeus acknowledges that, they still broke a direct order. Thaddeus could think of no better punishment than three weeks of straight Hardtack bread and double guard duty. The only blessing was they were able to do it together, something neither Gladthorn nor Edryss would complain about. It was Thaddeus' way of thanking them for the wagon Gladthorn assured Edryss.

Eventually, the professor came fully clean to everyone about the secrets of the Mark III wagon. While many were disappointed or angry at the professor's decision, no one could say he did it with any sort of malice. The professor allowed Thaddeus to decide Valissa's fate. Valissa pleaded with Thaddeus to kill her or let her die, something Thaddeus could never do to an innocent life. He knew that this was one of those decisions that he himself couldn't just make.

Valissa was brought out of the Mark III and everyone was allowed to see her transform between the girl and the monster. They heard her cry and beg for life, they heard her yell and scream about killing them all and they also heard an innocent young woman beg to go home and see her mother. Frightened at the monster, many in the expedition cried out for her death, but Thaddeus who pleaded for life asked who among them was righteous enough to judge her and to be the one to deliver the killing blow? Thaddeus, despite his fear of the outcome allowed the decision to be made by everyone. They voted, and it was decided by a full majority that Valissa would live in the hopes of finding her a cure to her demonic corruption and to continue to receive intel on the enemy. Only a small number, including Dineela and the professor voted to let Valissa die, seeing that as the only humane thing left to do.

Thaddeus continued to sleep with Italicus while Leora slept in his tent, nearly every night the two spent together talking, joking, and dancing. Thaddeus didn't want the expedition to continue, he was happy for the first time in forever. Though despite how happy he was, Italicus' words of warning lingered in his head. As much as he enjoyed Leora, he knew he had to be sure what his feelings truly were.

On the last night before leaving the remains of Mystique, Leora became frustrated. After spending so much quality time, it felt obvious to her that Thaddeus liked her. *Why hasn't he tried to kiss me?* She asked herself since she had no one she could confide in. Feeling determined, she decided to try and make her own move. Thaddeus was unprepared for it, nearly panicked when it happened. Leora did not understand why Thaddeus would react like that. Insecure and emotionally hurt, Leora blamed herself and began to cry. Thaddeus tried to comfort her and explain why he panicked, but he still couldn't bring himself to tell her about Alana. His reassurances felt hollow and fake, Leora got angry and told Thaddeus off, leaving his tent.

Andi read everything she could on the Progenitors, she was determined to figure out why Dumak wants to kill her. More importantly, how does all of this connect to her parents? The more scrolls and books she read, the more she realized that a lot of it made absolutely no sense. It was her father's journal all over again. The scrolls were gibberish when translated literally. "This makes no sense!" yelled Andi in frustration, throwing a book across the professor's tent, "The cow's udders were soft and pliable with great amounts of steak. That's what the entire last sentence translates to, while the rest of the scroll goes in depth about the alignment of the stars and how they align into individual constellations. Especially about the constellation of the Dark Horse, it's very important to the Progenitors or perhaps they feared it. The words used are words that can also mean danger? Are they foretelling us about Bailitheoir?" It was usually after she finished her rant or asked her questions that she would realize her brother, nor the professor were around.

Glut tried for seven days straight to check on the status of Wrench, but the medics had quarantined the area. They feared the wounded could get infections from visitors. It frustrated Glut and for some reason no one would let him know how Wrench was doing.

Since he couldn't see Wrench, he decided he had a different mission. He did not possess the photographic memory of his sister and reading was never as easy as it was for Andi, but he was very good at listening. He followed Thaddeus as much as he could, determined to figure out the connection between Thaddeus and his sister. He asked Thaddeus as many questions as possible about the medallion and the PenRuger history. Thaddeus usually was never open to talk about his family's history and legacy, but he knew the concern Glut had for Andi, so he did the best he could. Thaddeus' understanding and knowledge of his family and the medallion was limited. His father was never around, he knew the basics and what his mother could tell him, which wasn't a lot. The answer to many of Glut's questions were" I don't know."

"Speak to Balin," He finally told Glut, "He was going to write a book on my family. The man loves to research history, he is brilliant. He probably knows more than I do now."

Balin was not a person Glut would have expected to be an Equinaut. The man was not a warrior or a fighter and in fact, the best word to describe him would be awkward. He wasn't very sure of himself and he overacted to compensate for it. Luckily for Glut, Balin was more than happy to talk about Thaddeus' lineage. "Gideon PenRuger was the first to receive the blessings of the PenRuger medallion. Some reject that it was blessed by the Maker, others say it was Arcadia, and a few believe it to be one of many objects the Maker created that contains divine magic, the highest form of magic there can be. Once this happens, we have the first bloodline that has a sprinkle of divine blood in them, otherwise, they wouldn't be able to interact with such high-level magic."

"Are you saying that my sister and I have divine blood in us?" asked Glut in disbelief.

"Perhaps, definitely your sister or she would not be able to be healed by it." answered Balin.

Glut could not comprehend that, "But how? And I thought the medallion only healed the first-born males."

Balin began to laugh, part of the answer was easy. His laughter annoyed Glut.

Balin pulled out a large scroll and unraveled it. It was a family tree of the PenRugers. "Why did it heal the first woman ever? I have no clue, but the blood is simple. The PenRuger linage has many off shoots, it's not like they stopped after one child. Many generations had several brothers and sisters that would also carry the divine gene. The medallion of course followed the first-born path. I bet your family may be related to them from a long time ago."

"What about this portion of the tree?" asked Glut, pointing at a bare area near the middle?

Balin's smile grew larger than it should, "That, my friend, is a mystery!" he waved his hands far too dramatically to be taken seriously. "That is Ambrosius PenRuger's family. "

"What happened to it?"

"Who knows, lost to history I guess, there are no records of Ambrosius or his son. There are dark rumors that swirl around Ambrosius, but none of them can be corroborated."

"Like what?"

"Well, most of the rumors say that Ambrosius was the first PenRuger to go mad or evil and that he was a vicious killer and necromancer. Supposedly, he kidnapped King Micromedex's daughter and raped her, the son of that sprung from her loins also inherited his fathers corrupted ways."

"Whoa, Really?"

"Maybe," remarked Balin, "the family history picks up about fifty years later with a man claiming to be Ambrosius' grandson."

"How do we know he was?" asked Glut.

Balin shrugged, "He had the medallion and it worked, I guess that's proof in itself."

"Can I take this and write it down for myself?" asked Glut, certain the family tree was the first clue to explain what happened to his sister. Balin nodded. Glut ran off with the scroll in hand, *who is Ambrosius PenRuger and what did he do?* Glut asked to himself.

***

Three weeks of the professor's ceaseless prodding was enough to convince Thaddeus to take the path through Veilwood forest. The small, dirt roads that led towards the forest and the Slavine border had become monotonous. Italicus wiped the sweat off of his neck, his shift leading the expedition seemed to go on forever. Small, muddy hill after small, muddy hill, only the calming sound of running water from the Se'bide River kept Italicus from going crazy. It had been almost two days since they had left Mystique. Many were apprehensive to start moving again, three weeks of no incidents was making some complacent. Thankfully, there hadn't been a single sighting of anything out of the norm, neither demon, nor possessed person since they left. The only event to occur was with a very territorial pack of wolves, an incident Italicus was thankful to have not been a part of.

Italicus scanned the horizon then peered into the brush lining their path, weary of a second encounter. A high-pitched wolf howled out in the distance. Italicus pulled back on Moose's reins, trying to determine the direction of the howl. He could feel a cold chill of a childhood fear shuttering down his back. "Eeerrrr wolves." he muttered under his breath, shaking his head. "Hate them! Hate them! Hate them!"

"Penny for your thoughts?" asked a voice, startling Italicus from his depressed perusing.

"Damn it, Edryss!" huffed Italicus, grabbing his chest. "You snuck up on me!"

"I am sorry, Sir," replied Edryss, smiling slightly and adjusting her black hair. "But I've been riding next to you for last five minutes."

"How are those stitches?" he asked stoically.

"Already healed and out. Thanks for asking, how are you doing?"

Answering that question was the last thing he wanted to do, so Italicus didn't even acknowledge her speaking. He stared ahead, stone faced. Like Thaddeus had predicted, once the expedition began to move again, Italicus' emotional state fell hard.

Edryss reached out and touched his shoulder, "Would you like to talk about it? Meg was my friend as well. She, she was special. What they did to her wasn't right. It was unholy."

Italicus sighed slightly and rubbed at his forehead, tiredly checking on the gold feather in his ear, "Thank you, Edryss, but I'm fine. You know me," he clapped his hand to his chest several times, "I am a rock. I am stone. I am, one cool dude."

"Well, cool dude," mocked Edryss gently, "if you wanna talk, all you gotta do is ask."

Edryss slowed her horse and waited for the column to catch up to her.

Once alone, Italicus didn't have to hold back his tears, he hated having to deal with such strong emotions. He quickly wiped his face and snorted his nose, trying to quickly hide any indication he had been upset. Cantering to meet him were Thaddeus and Gladthorn, returning from scouting.

"Well, it's exactly as we feared," said Thaddeus disappointedly, pulling back on his reins and turning Egghead around so he could walk with Italicus. "The further east we go, the rougher the terrain gets."

"Did you find a place to make camp?"

"The best we could find is about two miles up, where the river takes a sharp turn north for several miles and loops back bordering Veilwood. There is a nice spot where the river would be on two sides," answered Gladthorn, riding along Italicus' other side.

"It's not ideal, a risk we will have to take." stated Thaddeus, feeling the same frustration as Italicus. "The ground is by no means flat, but like Glad said, between the river on two sides and the forest edge, we will have some natural protection,".

"You fear we will be attacked tonight?" asked Italicus, "It's been three weeks and not a single sign of any demon or corrupted activity, maybe we showed them we are not to be trifled with?"

"Do you really believe that?"

Italicus let out a small 'ha' and shook his head, "So, you'll want us to keep the wagons in a tight circle formation like we did at the camp? We can keep the Mark VIIs closer to the path, less chance of them getting bogged down in this mud."

"Even that makes me nervous" asserted Gladthorn, "Perhaps we shouldn't push our luck. We could keep the VIIs along the path and form a U with the others?"

Thaddeus nodded and accepted the idea "Would be prudent, we shouldn't push our luck. Hopefully we will have another night without Situation."

"And if it doesn't?" prompted Gladthorn.

Thaddeus looked at Gladthorn sternly, "Then you and Edryss will be on guard."

"Your will, sir."

Supplied and ready for anything, everyone was in high spirits. As scary as the demons were, winning the battle on Callan's field shattered the idea that they were undefeatable. Despite the high hopes and winning attitudes, no one was happy once they saw the area in which they would be camping for the night. The ground was wet and unleveled, the whole area reeked of natural decay, and it bordered Veilwood forest. Every child from the Citadel grew up hearing spooky and horrifying tales of the unnatural occurrences in the Veilwood forest, and now they were camping along its ominous edge.

The night was cold. Torches and moonlight dimly illuminated patches of the camp, but within hours of nightfall, a thick fog came rolling in off of the river, dampening what little light there was. It became more and more difficult to see anything beyond the tip of your nose. Thaddeus placed Edryss in command for the night and reminded her of the precarious position she was in if she wanted to remain an officer. Edryss was tired. When she wasn't on guard duty, she was training the university team on how to fight and defend themselves. She was patrolling tonight on barely any sleep and prayed to the Maker for a little bit more energy.

Gladthorn approached, "All clear on the east side, no commotion on the river."

"Hopefully it stays like that." Edryss adjusted her leather jacket as a cool breeze came blowing by, billowing the fog around them. "Remember when I said yes to the picnic?" Gladthorn nodded.

"Well, I was wrong! Damn I am so tired!"

"I don't remember you saying no after the picnic. In fact, I remember a certain someone screaming ye--"

The night was so dark that there was no way anyone could see how flushed Edryss' cheeks were, she pushed Gladthorn away from her, "You finish that sentence Mr. Jones and I swear it will be the last time you hear me say yes!"

Gladthorn quickly closed his mouth. Like Edryss' cheeks, no one could see the large, goofy grin across his face.

Edryss yawned, "Maybe it's just that I am so worn out right now, or maybe it's the fog playing tricks on my eyes, but something seems amiss tonight."

"None of my scouts have reported any activity, it's a dead night tonight."

"Let's hope it stays like that."

Gladthorn looked around to make sure no one else was near but realized immediately the thought seemed silly since no one could see anything in this darkness. Feeling safe that no one would see them embrace, he wrapped his arms around Edryss.

"I know you feel like the walking dead. My eyelids feel like they're carrying weights, but I wouldn't take back what we did for anything." Gladthorn whispered. Edryss could barely see his face in the dark, but she could feel his face smiling against hers.

"Maker bless me!" whispered Edryss passionately embracing him back, "Why do I love you so?"

Their lips were sweet and soft to the touch as they kissed each other. Both of them longing for the other, how long the kiss lasted was lost to the darkness. The only thing they knew was that it wasn't long enough. Gladthorn continued to hold her and he nuzzled his nose against Edryss' cheek, "I don't want to let go. Do I have to?"

Edryss sighed, "Never, never let go of me!"

Gladthorn squeezed so tightly that both could feel their heart's drumbeats calling out to the other, after several seconds, their drumbeats became one, "Marry me?" asked Gladthorn. "I know we can't right now as Equinauts, but I can't wait any longer."

Edryss sighed and placed her finger on his mouth, "Gladthorn Deon Jones, I would want nothing more than to be your wif-"

"Shh!" Edryss cocked her ear outwards, pushing off of Gladthorn's chest. "Did you hear that?"

"I don't hear anything?" answered Gladthorn, "Is this your way of getting out of the question, its n-"

Gladthorn's ears picked up on what Edryss was hearing. It was less of a sound and more of a feeling, almost a buzzing, a little too low to fully hear but enough that your eardrums could feel it.

Edryss walked backwards into Gladthorn, instinctively grabbing his hand. She knew someone, or something, was out in the thick, dark fog. "I think it's hurt, it's moaning."

Gladthorn could feel it too, something was off, where was that noise coming from, "Yeah, or it's angry, and that's growling. I'll signal for more men."

"No, wait," whispered Edryss, who took several steps forward and continued to peer out into the thick folds of fog. Her eyes told her nothing was around her, but every other sense indicated otherwise.

"Damn the Maker, I see nothing!" grumbled Gladthorn, tugging on Edryss' hand. He felt helpless against this seemingly invisible foe. "We need to re-group and get some more torches lit."

"That's a good idea. We will alert the other guards and tell them to be..." Gladthorn didn't hear Edryss finish her sentence, the charcoal fog around them billowed and swirled black, and Edryss's fingers tightened around his palm and then yanked away. Gladthorn grasped wildly, searching the air around him. The fog thickened into a wall, which forcibly plowed past Gladthorn, pushing him to the ground.

"Edryss!!!" Gladthorn swept the floor with his arms and with each empty reach his heart shattered. He fired his Tesla into the air, a signal to all of the Equinauts that trouble had arisen.

"UNDER ATTACK!" bellowed Gladthorn, he looked to the air and saw his light-had joined at least eight other Tesla shots. The sky glowed blue and red, refracted in strange ways through the fog.

At the first sound, Italicus sprung out of bed, rubbing his eyes and automatically pulling on his tesla pack. "If this is a false alarm," he said through gritted teeth, half asleep.

Several loud screams from outside his tent broke Italicus' groggy trance. He rushed from his tent, Tesla rifle drawn, the power pack behind him was humming to life. Italicus tried to gauge the situation, but once again he found himself in complete chaos.

Equinauts and university members were running frantically in every direction. He followed their paths, but despite the genuine fear in people's faces, he saw no enemy, no threat. He grabbed the first Equinaut that passed him, "Zapp, what the bloody hell is happening?"

"I don't know, sir. We're under attack, maybe? Shadows, everyone is seeing shadows. We're surrounded, and Edryss has been taken, sir!"

"Edryss!?" Italicus looked around the camp, hoping to find Thaddeus or the professor. *Shadows? Shadows are attacking us? What the hell does that mean?* Italicus stopped dead in his tracks when he heard what had now become all too familiar of a sound. His heart froze as harsh howls echoed through the camp.

"SHRIEKS!" yelled Italicus. "PLAZ SWORDS OUT!"

Italicus ducked and rolled on the ground just as a shriek swung its steel blade. It had charged at him at from behind. Italicus could hear the whine of the sword pass over his head and sprung to his feet with his Plaz sword activated. The shriek swung and changed directions with tremendous speed. Italicus stumbled backward, the rusted steel blade just missing him again. Italicus activated his hard light-energy shield from his left arm, and he heard his pack hum with strain as the shriek swung its sword several more times, each blow absorbed by his shield.

Italicus fought back, but the shriek was able to defend itself, far more formidable than the previous demons he had encountered. A quick thrust forward caught the shriek by surprise and it hollered in anger. It charged up against Italicus and swung down with extreme force. Italicus fell to his knees, unable to get out from under the creature's constant blows. Italicus' left forearm was throbbing, and he was unsure how many more impacts his bones could take before breaking. He waited for the creature to swing down once more, and as the shriek retracted his sword, Italicus pushed his shield upward with his full strength to throw the creature off balance. A horrendous amount of pain shot through his forearm, but it worked. Italicus jumped to his feet and pushed his shield further, right into the shrouded face of the shriek and followed that by a straight and powerful thrust with his sword. The creature let out a cry of pain and began to convulse violently. Italicus pulled his blade out of the creature's stomach, preparing for a counter attack. The shroud around the wound began to burn from the intense heat of the sword. The shriek cradled its wound and began to retreat, but within seconds it collapsed to the ground.

Italicus approached the wounded entity. It wasn't quite dead. he watched as it tried to claw itself away from harm. Italicus took its fallen sword, and stabbed straight into the cloth of the creature, pinning it in place. He gave the Shriek a hardy kick, flipping it onto its back.

"This is our world!" Italicus had started the sentence whispering, and ended it shouting, his face contorted with rage, focused only on thoughts of Meg and how she was taken from him by a similar shriek. He plunged his Plaz sword right into the chest of the beast and repeated his stabbing until the creature was undeniably dead, then he swiftly removed the hands and head from the beast, ensuring that even if it could come back to life from that it would be useless.

On the other side of the camp, Glut and Andi were also awoken by the sudden commotion. They dressed quickly and jumped from their tent with their new Plaz swords drawn. They were met with expedition members running for their lives, being chased by dark, floating shadows. In the distance, they saw one man fall as the shadow overwhelmed him, he cried out in pain.

"What are we supposed to do?" Andi looked up at her brother, horrified.

A new sound pierced through their camp, a high frequency whine that grew louder with every agonizing second until both Andi and Glut clasped their ears from the tormenting pain. Andi followed Glut's terrified stare to the other side of the river, where a ball of pure white and yellow light emerged from the forest's edge. The light was so bright, it was as if a new sun was being born. Whatever it was, Andi could feel her stomach tying itself into knots and her heart pounding out of her chest. She knew beyond a doubt that that amazingly terrifying creature was here for only one thing, it was here for her.

Andi's first instinct was to run, but before she could react, a new high pitch ring erupted in her eardrums. Andi fell to her knees and began to flail, screaming in severe pain. She could feel her vocal cords yelling, but she couldn't hear her own voice. The pressure suddenly changed drastically as the aura of something powerful radiated from the bright light, encompassing the forest, then the river, and then the camp. Andi could see the form of a perfectly shaped woman begin to take shape in the center of the ball of energy. Beside the woman were four dark, humanoid beings whose eyes shone like rubies. From the forest entered a similar creature, shorter than the others, and with a prominent horn coming out of its crown. It offered the creature in the light something, and she produced a loud scream accompanied by a burst of purple energy which burst from the ball. It sent the smaller horned creature flying onto the ground.

"Whoa," whispered Andi, in shock. She immediately regretted it. The heavenly shaped woman inside the light looked straight at her. The gaze was so intense that Andi was unable to break it. She tried desperately to look away, to run, to hide, but the creature had her and was peering deep inside her, searching her very being, leaving in its wake a deep, dark feeling of despair within her soul.

The creature spoke in an unrecognizable tongue, but her order was clear: *retrieve the girl*. Its voice seemed to command the very heavens. Shockwaves of sound caused the nearby area to vibrate, and then shake. Every tree, branch, and root bent to the power.

The evil, red eyed creatures all bowed inward and vanished into thin air and the smaller, horned creature disappeared into a fog of dark smoke. Andi sank to the ground, released, but unconscious. In a panic, Glut shook her and slapped her with no response. He pulled his limp sister over his shoulder and ran into the camp, past shrieks and shadows, trying to escape the aura of light. Once he broke from its light, Andi woke up.

"What happened to you?" yelled Glut, tears streaming down his face.

"I don't know." Andi hugged her brother and wasn't sure who was holding up who. "Glut, we have to find Thaddeus and the professor!"

***

The professor hadn't slept a wink. His mind was racing, trying to interpret the unique runes they had discovered. There were hundreds of large, oval stones inside the Citadel war wagon that Gladthorn and Edryss had taken from the possessed Colonel Jaster in the village. The professor was confident these runes had to have important meaning. The writings were presumably ancient Progenitor, though he had yet to authenticate them. He struggled to translate the stones, they had few similarities to other Progenitor runes. The professor let out a long yawn. his body begged for sleep, but his mind would not relent. He had to keep working, he had to keep his eyes open. Every time he closed his eyes he saw professor Akroyd, slain in the chair they had tied him to.

Professor Belladon tried to focus, to push his guilt aside. *They possessed and corrupted Akroyd because of me. They targeted him because of the actions I took.* Hopelessness and dread consumed the professor. *Who else will die for this foolhardy quest? How much more blood would be on my hands?* He knew whatever evil power they were working against would return soon to try to stop their crusade. The professor wished for everything to go back to normal, to pick up the threads of his old life. The prestigious professor and brilliant inventor. Alas, he feared there are some wounds time cannot heal, some things you cannot come back from. Professor Belladon placed one of the large, oval rocks on the table next to his bunk, rubbing his eyes and giving out another hardy yawn.

"What mysteries do you hold?" asked the professor to the rock, "I dare say I am afraid of what you might be and if I find myself to be correct, you may be more dangerous than the combined armies of the Citadel and Slavine."

"Uh hum," said a voice from the entrance of the tent. "I am sorry to bother you, professor. I couldn't sleep, and when I saw light in your tent, I thought you wouldn't mind a nice cup of tea?"

"Ah Steven, yes! You always know when I am in need," smiled the professor, taking the large mug from Steven.

Steven looked at the rock, "Any luck on the translation?"

"I am afraid not, if these writings are Progenitor, they are the oldest form I have ever seen. So much of the rune does not make sense to me," admitted the professor, comforted by the hot tea.

"Professor may I ask you a question?"

"I always welcome questions, my boy."

"Do you believe in angels?"

The professor looked up at his young friend for a brief moment, "I am unsure how to answer that. If you had asked me that question a year ago, I would have told you, 'As a man of science and knowledge, I do not believe in the existence of celestial beings.'" The professor frowned.

"Why?" asked Steven

The professor rubbed his chin slightly, thinking, "Because there was no way to observe them. No way to measure them, but now we have seen creatures far beyond what any academic would say possible and if these creatures we have witnessed and encountered are demons or evil, then why wouldn't there be equally good creatures as well? Nature finds a way to balance itself, hm?"

"So, are you saying you do believe?" asked Steven

"The Maker's scrolls do make note of the first beings created in the moments leading to the creation of the universe, the ArchEthereal. So, perhaps they do exist."

Steven grabbed a chair and sat near the bunk, "Yes, I learned about them as a child. There were seven original ArchEthereal, and later the Maker created countless more."

Steven stood up from his chair and held up one of the stones, "Zakarael was the ArchEthereal in charge of keeping two of the greatest keys the Maker had. I remember a verse my mom taught me about the great beings of light..." Steven smiled, "She would read to me in secret when my father was away, he was never the religious sort. The verse always brought me comfort though, 'When the darkest hour is upon you, and survival is bleak, look to the two things which the Maker gave to guide us through the darkness!'"

"And what are those two things, my boy? I dare say they'd be helpful to us now."

"Probably the two greatest gifts the Maker bestowed upon us, hope and faith."

The professor smiled sagely, "Yes, of course." He took a sip of tea, and for a moment, his heart didn't feel as heavy. "Thank you, Steven. Sometimes I need to be reminded."

Steven stared down at his stone, flipping it around in his hands, embarrassed.

"It is late, perhaps we should try to sleep," said Steven, setting the stone down gently. "I'd better be going." Steven made it halfway to the canvas flap before spinning around and hurrying back. "Wait professor- look if you look at it this way. The writing could be up and down, in a continuous circle, not left to right. If you rotate the runes, we know this one. It's the Progenitor rune for spirit, or soul."

The professor grabbed the rock, "Maker's beard, you are absolutely right, why didn't I see that before?" Grabbing his quill, the professor began to write vigorously, many of the runes and corresponding words starting to make sense.

Steven smiled as he walked out of the tent and said, "Good night, professor"

Professor Belladon turned to say good night to Steven but he was gone. Only the flapping of the tent's entrance showed any signs he had once been there. The professor's hurried translating was soon interrupted by a deep yell, "Under Attack!"

***

With all of the carnage and death that occurred at Mystique, it was easy for many of the expedition members to feel like this was a hopeless cause. How can you fight against such a formidable foe? Through all the evil and darkness, though, rays of light still pierced through the veil, proving to all that miracles were on their side. One man in particular was a living embodiment of those miracles. Despite his horrific injuries, the largest man in the expedition, Wrench, was still alive. For over two weeks he laid on the small medical cot in an unresponsive coma. The medics, so certain he had no chance of survival, wrote him off. His internals were too far gone, Dumak's sword had pierced too many organs and his intestines were leaking fluids. They were certain the man would die from becoming septic.

Wrench's survival was a medical mystery. Perhaps it was his will to live, or perhaps it was divine providence, but on the fifteenth day around lunch time, his eyes opened. Sore and slightly incoherent, he reached out and grabbed the first medic who walked by and asked for three steaks with no less than four whole pies. When the medic told him, there was no way they could possibly let him eat so much in his condition. Wrench proceeded to hobble out of the medical wagon. It took nearly ten men and the promise of one small steak to get the man back into his cot.

Tonight, was the first night he had been allowed to leave the confines of the medical wagon. First, he looked for Glut, but when he was nowhere to be found, he looked for food. The medics though already warned the cooks not to let Wrench have too much and for it to be soft and easily digestible. When the cooks presented to him some oatmeal and pees, Wrench flew into an angry, furious rant. Knowing what the medics had told them, the cooks were not going to let Wrench intimidate them. Angered and disgusted, Wrench stormed out of the food wagon. After throwing the oatmeal across the wagon, Wrench marched, looking for the professor. On his way, he saw the floorboard removed from one of the Mark VII's.

"Bloody hell, I am unconscious for two weeks healing and they destroy all my work." Wrench bent down, his body aching in pain. He could feel the stitches pulling. Determined to see what was wrong with the wagon, Wrench defied everything the medics warned him not to do and proceeded to wiggle on his back to get underneath the floorboard.

Several minutes passed when he heard someone approach. Fearing it was a medic, Wrench froze and waited for the person to leave. Whoever it was decided to sit down, leaning against one of the wagon's large wheels.

"Bless my bagpipes, "mumbled Wrench under his breath until his nose cot a whiff of food. Despite the pain, he crawled closer and sniffed in the intoxicating aroma, his stomach growled, and his lips trembled. He smelled roasted chicken, sautéed onions, and cooked potatoes with white wine gravy.

Wrench moved closer but froze again when the man leaning against the wheel moved. He placed his plate of food on the ground next to his side and began to drink from a flask. Inches from Wrench's face were two large chicken legs, one large breast, and two potatoes. Reaching out, Wrench quickly took one of the legs gently but swiftly off the plate. Seconds later the man put down the flask and picked up his food.

"What the--"said the man, Wrench recognized it as the Equinaut Niles, Zapp's friend. "Where, I thought I grabbed two?"

Wrench devoured the leg. It had been so long since he had real food that it was almost like tasting chicken for the first time. He finished the leg, eating everything down to the bone. He tossed it away and looked at Niles with an almost animalistic look. He had to have more.

Wrench waited for Niles to put his plate back down, but he was too busy eating the chicken breast. Poking his head ever so slightly out of the bottom of the wagon, Wrench tried to grab something off the plate, but there was no way without being seen. Slowly descending back underneath the wagon, never taking his eyes off Nile's plate until he was fully covered by the wagon, he wiggled to where he threw the chicken leg bone and gingerly broke it in half. Positioning himself right behind Niles, Wrench threw one of the pieces of the chicken leg to his left, pinging it against the metal wheel of another wagon. Niles froze and looked to his left. Wrench reached from the right and grabbed one of the potatoes. Niles stared to his left for a moment longer and then started eating again. He twitched and counted the potatoes in his head, looking to his immediate left and right, thinking maybe he had dropped one of his potatoes. To his confusion, he couldn't find it. Hungry, he went back to eating.

Finishing Nile's butter-soaked potato, Wrench threw the other piece of his chicken leg, this time to the right. Again, Niles looks towards the noise, Wrench's massive arm reached from underneath the wagon and took the last chicken leg. Feeling bold, he reached for a second time for some of the sautéed onions as well.

Niles jumped and gasped when he looked down and saw his other chicken leg missing. Realizing something was up, Niles called out, "Zapp? is that you?"

He was met with no answer. Listening carefully, Niles picked up on a noise that sounded like lips smacking and a slight moan. He followed the noise and realized it was coming below the wagon. Unarmed, Niles was hesitant to look, but he had to know what it was. Peeking his head below the wagon, he was not prepared to see a massive man devouring a chicken leg.

"Wrench!? What are you doing under there?" asked Niles, still holding his plate of food. "I thought you were still confined to the medical wagon?"

Wrench poked his head out from underneath the wagon, his face covered in chicken grease and potatoes.

"What'd ya think I am doing, getting a tan?" mocked Wrench, laughing boisterously at his own joke and regretting it moments later. A sharp pain ran through his stomach, "So, is that for me?"

"What, uh- no." Niles exclaimed staring down at his plate. Wrench pleaded with his eyes, Niles sighed, "Well, I guess I owe you for that pie. All I have left is another potato, some onions and a cooked carrot?"

Wrench had his hand out before Niles finished his sentence, grabbing the plate and bringing to him under the wagon, "Thank ya, laddy."

"You don't mind if I sit against the wheel?" asked Niles, "I didn't want to disturb anyone's sleeping while I was going to chow down. Just got off guard duty, I am beat."

Wrench didn't say no, he was too busy eating.

"I'll have a full day tomorrow, pounding out new shoes for a quarter of the horses we have," Niles complained. "If I had known how much work went into horse shoeing, I never would have agreed to take over when Thomas left."

Wrench grunted to show he was still listening.

"I'm envious of Thomas, following Fin and all. They're doing a job in the Aedunic territory. Have you ever been out there, Wrench?" Niles didn't wait for Wrench to answer, "I have, back before I joined the Equinauts, back when I had a family. We lived in the independent city of Del. My father was a merchant and did major trade with many of the Eastern Aedunic tribes, selling them spices and boar lizard skins. I would take my wife on many of our trade missions. It really is one of the most beautiful areas in the entire shard, the greenest fields and the prettiest forests, with trees so tall and healthy they reach the heavens. With so many babbling brooks and rivers flowing through the entire area," he sighed deeply, "Ohhhh, the great lake Pezron'teara'laduel. I have seen the great lake, clearest of water. On a spring day, small breezes sweep down off the western mountains, making it perfect to sail on or just a simple picnic on its shores. Oh, if you ever get a chance to see the sunset off a boat on the great river, the most breathe taking sight."

"Why would you ever leave?" Wrench asked from underneath the wagon.

Niles was quiet for a moment, "She died during childbirth. She bled, nothing the midwives could do."

"And the baby?" asked Wrench with potato in his mouth.

Niles closed his eyes and shook his head, but Wrench couldn't see, "After, I was lost. I wasn't sure what to do. My life was over without Trista. I couldn't trade anymore, I just wandered. A year later I met Thaddeus and he gave me purpose, something to live for. I owe that man everyth—"

Wrench suddenly yanked Niles down to the ground. A deep thud resonated in Nile's ears as a shriek's sword connected with the wagon in the space that Niles had just occupied. The men scrambled underneath the wagon's floor, and Wrench yelled, "Kill it!"

"Kill it?" replied Niles, confused seeing Wrench for the first time, realizing how much mass the man had lost. He was still daunting but was obviously not at the size he was before his injuries.

"Yes! Kill it, now!" demanded Wrench, making a sword swing motion with his arms.

"I can't."

"Yes, you can, its ok to be scared, I am too. Now be a man and get him" argued Wrench, kindly and quickly.

"I can't," insisted Niles, visibly upset.

"I believe in you, laddy!" Wrench answered back.

"No! I don't have my sword on me. I left it in my tent. I was just trying to eat dinner! I didn't think I would need it!"

The wagon began to rock as the shriek was trying to knock it over.

"You don't have your sword?" exclaimed Wrench through gritted teeth.

"I don't have my sword!"

"How do you not have your sword?" Wrench exclaimed, trying to anchor the wagon down with his own weight, "That's like me not having my wrench!"

"Your bloody name is Wrench. You better have a wrench on you! My name is Niles, not PLAZ SWORD MAN!"

"You are a mercenary! What reason on earth would you not be armed, PLAZ SWORD MAN?"

"I was just EATING until you stole my food!" screamed Niles, pointing his finger at Wrench.

"Shhhh!" said Wrench softly, pointing up, "Is it gone?"

"I don't know, where would it go?"

Wrench jeered, "I don't know."

"What do you mean, you don't know?" Niles' eyes practically popped out of his skull, "You mean you weren't watching it?"

Now Wrench shoved a finger in Niles' face, "I was holding the wagon down, what the hell were *you* doing, boy?"

Niles slapped Wrench's hand away, "Don't you call me 'boy!'"

A large thump hit the side of the wagon and instantly the hooded cloak of a shriek was now laying face first in front of them, howling. Wrench yelled in fear and let swing a massive fist. The creature leapt out of the way and let out a hardy laugh, "You two sound like an old married couple, you do know that, right?" The shriek shrugged off its cloak to reveal that it was not a shriek, but a very amused human man.

"You should have seen your faces," laughed Zapp, who suddenly let out a cry of help, as his legs were swept out from under him by Wrench and he was pinned down by Niles.

***

Thaddeus forced his face muscles to relax enough to get out a whistle while waiting for his pack to warm up. By the time it beeped, Egghead was standing in front of him, waiting.

"Good boy," Thaddeus cooed, as he grabbed a handful of mane and threw himself on top of Egghead's bare back.

At the squeeze of Thaddeus' thighs, Egghead jumped straight into a gallop. Thaddeus threaded between expedition members, swinging away at the shrieks chasing them. Soon, shrieks charged directly at him. Even with Egghead's added height, Thaddeus was only on level ground with the creatures. He pounded his shield straight into the face of one shriek, two others came charging from Thaddeus' right, both swinging down their swords. Thaddeus managed to block both, but the force of two shrieks bearing down was too much. Thaddeus could feel his arm giving out, and the swords got closer to his face. They were inches away when Egghead spun and reared up, kicking out with his hind legs. He knocked both shrieks off balance. Thaddeus slid from his horse, stabbed one into the ground, and swung around to behead the other. Thaddeus struggled to remount with his shield and sword powered up, and his enemy took advantage of his discomposure.

The shriek swung and Thaddeus, realizing his mistake, squeezed his legs with all his might, signaling Egghead to move out of danger's way. The shriek raised its claw to slice Thaddeus' neck and face. Thaddeus braced himself for the coming pain, knowing his medallion would save him from the worst, but felt nothing. The shriek let out its own cry as a sword suddenly appeared through his shrouded face.

The shriek convulsed slightly and fell to the ground, dead. Standing behind it was a man without armor, wearing only a sleeping gown. Capernicus from the university was panting heavily.

"Thank you."

Sweat was pouring down Capernicus' beet red face, "Thank Edryss for being a good teacher." replied Capernicus through deep breaths.

"THADDEUS!" called a frantic voice. Poncho and the professor came into view, "We are being attacked by shrieks and shades!"

"We can name them later, professor." replied Thaddeus, whistling Egghead back to him.

"Please, come with me. Steven has been cornered by at least three of them!" The professor bounded off without turning back to see whether they were following him.

Thaddeus looked down at Capernicus, "Try to get everyone you can find out of the immediate area, the Equinauts will deal with these creatures!"

Thaddeus followed the professor to a very still clearing. He shot his rifle into the air to shed some light and saw several clumps on the ground that looked like bodies.

"Steven?" called out the professor, worried. There was a slight moan from the clumps.

Thaddeus held out his sword to illuminate three shrieks, whether unconscious or dead he couldn't be sure. Among them was a smaller body, Steven's.

"Maker, no!" gasped the professor. "Is he dead?"

"No, he's breathing," replied Thaddeus, surprised to see Steven's chest moving up and down. "How he managed this is anyone's guess. I don't think he was even issued a sword."

"HELP! Help us, it's after us!" Andi and Glut's screams arrived at the clearing shortly before they did.

"Where is it?" asked Thaddeus, searching the fog or a charging shriek. Andi and Glut spoke over each other, rambling incoherently about a creature made of light and four more creatures behind them. They sped through descriptions of how the light creature could control nature with its voice. It spoke in a foreign tongue that they somehow understood.

"Are you getting any of this?" Thaddeus asked the professor.

"I hope that I am mistaken, but I think the 'she' Akroyd and that small creature told us of is making herself known. " The professor shuddered, "I am afraid we are all in real danger."

No sooner had the words left his lips, the winds picked up and an unnatural breeze swept into the camp from the direction of the river. Everyone looked towards the water. For a moment, they each felt a curious sensation, as if a friend stood beside them. The feeling dissolved almost immediately, replaced by shock, then fear. An obscure, black figure whirled passed them. Thaddeus immediately recognized the familiar the blur. Everything that happened next lasted between heartbeats. Thaddeus tried to scream, tried to push the kids from its path, but he was too slow. The dark blur passed over the siblings, and while inside its darkness, Andi and Glut disappeared.

The familiar laugh of the creature from Mystique taunted them, "NYAHAHAHA!"

Out of the fog and shadow, Bailitheoir appeared, rearing up with the small creature holding its reins. Bailitheoir's white face glowed against the silhouette of its black and deformed body.

Egghead whinnied and cried out for his brother.

"BRING THEM BACK!" demanded Thaddeus furiously, pulling his rifle and firing repeatedly at the creature. The beams had no effect, bouncing off the small creature's body, "Stupid, foolish, Fleshie! Nyahaha, with a twist of my wrist and a conjuring trick, no words from me and you, lose the chick. I surrender now, before she knows, this is it, here it goes!"

The creature turned Bailitheoir on a dime and flew off to the north.

Thaddeus watched helplessly as the creature rode off. Thaddeus reached for his chest, it was burning. His medallion was glowing bright orange. Andi was tapping into the medallion, she wasn't safe. Without a second thought, Thaddeus spun Egghead around and pushed him into a full-fledged gallop, chasing the shadow and leaving the professor in his dust.

Egghead and Thaddeus ran as fast as they could, following Bailitheoir and the creature due north, straight out of the camp and into the open fields.

"Damn it, I can't see a damn thing," muttered Thaddeus to Egghead, "Follow him!"

Egghead turned sharply west at full speed. They had lost visual contact, but Egghead still had the creature's scent. Egghead followed the shadow through several more turns, some so quick, Thaddeus was unsure how Egghead was keeping up with the creature. After a straight stretch he was sure he could make out the dark shape in the distance. It was right front of them and getting larger. "That's it Egghead, just a little bit faster" said Thaddeus, urging on his friend and steed.

The small, annoying creature made another hard turn left, straight into one of the thick patches of woods nearby.

"Damn it!" yelled Thaddeus, frustrated at losing his prey.

Thaddeus stopped pushing and urging his horse forward, they had lost them. After several minutes waiting for a sign, Thaddeus was ready to go back to the camp. Egghead refused to go back, he was not going to give up on his brother. With his ears locked forward, he peered into the woods. They began twitching at an invisible force. Thaddeus realized that Egghead had found something.

"We're not giving up on your brother now, are we?" asked Thaddeus as Egghead grumbled and began to step into the dense woods.

Egghead sniffed the air and followed Bailitheoir's path into the woods. Thaddeus tried to peer through the brush and leaves of the trees, but it was almost impossible to see through the thicket. He listened carefully, but there was not a sound outside of Egghead's heavy hooves and labored breathing. They plowed further into the patch of woods. Thaddeus was forced to lie against Egghead's neck, trying to decrease their surface area and push deeper into the thick branches. Egghead was so focused on finding Bailitheoir he had no consideration for his rider.

Suddenly, the barrage of branches hitting, and scratching Thaddeus' face, shoulders, and legs stopped. Once Thaddeus realized Egghead was not moving forward any further, Thaddeus froze and listened to the night. He waited for some noise to reveal the creature's position. Minutes rolled by but the only thing both could hear was their own breathing. Thaddeus knew that if Egghead has stopped, and he could hear no movement at all, it meant that the creature had stopped as well. It had to be hiding nearby. Thaddeus unsheathed his Plaz sword and quietly looked around into the darkness. Not even moonlight could penetrate the brush and trees. The hair on Thaddeus' right cheek bristled, and without wasting time to look, he swung the handle of his sword straight out to his right, activating it mid swing. There was a small gasp of air, the crunching of branches followed by a thud, and then silence.

***

Dean found silence in the professor's wagon. His own tent was full of whatever argument Andi and Glut were having, and he had been frankly refused at Kaitlyn's tent. He layered the bench cushions to make himself a bed and found that it was actually more comfortable than his cot in the tent. He laid on the opposite side of where Andi had been killed, placing a pillow to hide the stain of blood. After a few hours of fitful sleep, Dean woke to the howls of shrieks and the frantic footsteps of people running.

Upon exiting the wagon, Dean was instantly noticed and charged by several shrieks. With no weapon to defend himself he ran as fast as he could. The shrieks were quickly closing the distance between them and with the whole camp in chaos. Dean had no clue where to run. Dodging between half collapsed tents, Dean narrowly avoided being trampled by a man on a horse as he rode by. Dean tripped over a burned-out campfire and fell to the ground with the howls and cries of the shrieks nearly upon him. When Dean looked up, he was relieved to see the shrieks had turned and charged the man on the horse.

Dean found his bearings and headed for Kaitlyn's tent. On his way, he searched for a weapon and cursed himself for not taking one of the Plaz swords they had gathered at Mystique. He knew his injury would prevent him from wielding a sword properly, but he felt naked with no weapon. When he neared the plot of land where Kaitlyn's tent was, Dean's heart sank. The entire tent lay flat on the ground.

"Kaitlyn?" Dean yelled, "Kaitlyn, are you there?"

There was no response, and not a single part of the tent was moving. Dean dove underneath the canvas and began to search for Kaitlyn, but there was no sign of her anywhere. Dean clumsily made his way through the maze of the collapsed canvas tent, taking a giant breath of fresh, cool air once he emerged from underneath the cloth. At her absence, he assured himself that no news is good news, and tried to focus on that as he made his way to check the paddock for the horses. If she was anywhere in the camp other than her tent, it would be there.

While dashing across camp, Dean was pursued by several more shrieks that had been pursuing other targets. But had decided to break off and pursue him. Perhaps they smelled the blood from his wound, making him look like the easier target. Dean weaved between the erected tents and around others fighting or running for their lives, being chased by their own shrieks or shadows.

A deafening howl stopped Dean in his tracks. A shadow of death loomed over him. He ducked, barely missing the blade meant to sever his head from his body.

Dean heard a human voice ring out, "Don't be a fool, bring that monster my way, why don't ya!" He looked up to see a rather large woman finishing off a shriek. Fryda, wielding two swords, split the creature in half at the hips.

Dean did as he was told and ran straight towards Fryda. The shriek chasing after Dean noticed Fryda standing next to his fallen comrade and flew off in retreat, not wanted to be Fryda's next victim.

"Where did it go?" asked Dean, panting heavily and kneeling on the ground.

"Treveii' beard it was a coward!" mocked Fryda, spitting at the dead shriek, "It didn't have the stomach to face me." Fryda sounded overly boastful to make up for her loss with Dumak.

Dean glanced at the dead shriek on the ground, "Do they even have stomachs?"

Fryda pointed down at the top half of the dead shriek, "You can find out for yourself?"

Fryda laughed at Dean's disgusted look and offered him the hilt of one of her swords, "Here, take this. I want it back when we're all done, though."

"I have to find Kaitlyn. She wasn't in her tent, but she may have run to the paddock. I need your help to find her."

Fryda smiled at his command, "You would make a good officer with that voice, but I am afraid I was ordered by Italicus to find Faramal and Kazah. We need to form a defense line around the Mark III wagon. I have to carry out my orders." She looked south where Faramal and Kaz were supposed to be on guard duty, "By the looks of it, they are going to need help ending those shrieks before they can start forming the defense line. Come with me."

"I can't, I have to find Kaitlyn," replied Dean firmly.

"You have to come with me, we need that defense line or the whole camp could be overrun." Fryda could tell she had scared Dean. Gently, she said "Tell you what, help me free Faramal and Kaz so they can rally a line, and I'll come and help you find Kaitlyn"

Dean reluctantly agreed, aware that he didn't actually have a choice in the matter, "Lead the way."

***

Kazah watched as a fellow Equinaut was stabbed in the thigh. He was unsure who it was, but he yelled out to the attacking shriek in a challenging manner, trying anything to lure the demons away from his brother-in-arms.

The southern end of the camp was being hit pretty hard. Over twenty shrieks had easily floated over the river's depth. They pushed their way through the defense line of steam powered wagons. Despite their seemingly limited communication, the shrieks worked as a team, as fingers of a hand. While several shrieks were attacking people, the majority of them were ignoring the humans all together. In coordination, they began to search through the camp systematically.

Kaz stumbled backwards, watching several shrieks coming straight for him. He glanced with his peripherals, Faramal was currently defending several injured university members and the dozen or so other Equinauts nearby were all doing about as well as he was. Everyone was engaged. The first shriek who reached Kazah sliced down with its blade. Kaz raised his shield above his head, blocking the blow. He shoved his sword forward, trying to get the creature to stop pressing down against his shield. Kaz could feel the strength and pressure of the shriek in his legs, he swung out again, and the shriek easily dodged the coming blade.

Struggling, Kazah's arm ached from holding up his shield and his legs began to shake. The shriek pressed down harder with its sword, letting out a triumphant cry. Kaz's whole body was shaking.

Kaz was pretty sure of what was going to happen next. The shriek was applying a tactic that the Slavine would use on Citadel soldiers. When in combat, a Slavine brute always had height and strength advantage. Using their greater might, they would force their human opponent into some form of strength contest, then, while locked in combat with one Slavine, a second Slavine would appear from the side and gut the unfortunate Citadel soldier who was too arrogant to back off. Kazah's fears were realized when the second shriek came charging from his right side, ready to thrust its blade into his gut.

Kazah had little choice, he pushed off with his left arm as hard as he could and swung his sword again towards the first shriek, throwing it off balance slightly. Kaz brought his shield down to a level position just in time to deflect the second charging shriek. The shriek in front of him was forced to step back to avoid the second shriek's trajectory.

The first shriek let out a cry of anger, regained its balance and focus, and waited for two others to form up with him.

Kaz had succeeded in avoiding death but had now placed himself in a more dangerous position. He contemplated retreat, but noticed his comrade moving his arms, trying to get up. He was still alive, and that meant Kaz couldn't leave him to die. Kaz took several steps forward, trying to put more space between his wounded and his fight. He took a defensive position and waited for his opponents to make the first move.

All three shrieks attacked at once, each with a different swing. One charged forward with a thrust, another came swinging low, going for his legs, and the third was trying at his neck. Kaz had milliseconds to react, there was no way he would be fast enough to move his sword or shield to stop the two of the blades, his only option was to chance a roll and slide on the ground. Waiting for the right moment, Kazah leaped, two of the blades missing him by inches, while the third blade grazed his upper right arm.

Kazah grunted in pain but jumped back to his feet. The shrieks were already ready for another attack. Kaz knew the odds of one human against three shrieks and was searching desperately for a way to cheat death. The shrieks slowly moved forward, one of them letting loose a blood curdling scream. Kaz shuffled back, trying to decide which shriek would attack first.

The center shriek lunged forward, Kazah blocked the blow with the sword. This distracted him long enough for the shriek on his left to hit him upside the head with its sword hilt. Kaz could feel his whole world begin to go black. They were cackling, laughing, only allowing him to live for as long as they wanted to play with him. They took turns slicing into his limbs as he squirmed and prayed for a swifter death.

"Aye! Over here, uglies!" yelled Fryda intimidatingly, "By Treverii's will, your deaths will bring him and my people glory!"

For a moment, Kaz felt nothing, the world was spinning, and he was bleeding badly. The shrieks stopped toying with him and readied themselves to be attacked by Fryda. They were distracted, and if Kaz could get up, he knew he could thrust his sword up into the belly of one of them. He tried to get up, but the pain was great, and his limbs shook violently. No matter how hard he tried, he couldn't do it, he felt useless. With no hope of rising on his own, Kazah pleaded with the only entity he knew and understood, "Turaka, allow me to get up." whispered Kazah, invoking the Slavine god. He felt ashamed to say name of the god whose people enslaved him for so long, but it was all he knew. Two of the three shrieks were engaged by Fryda and Dean, while the third held back, waiting for an opening to attack. Dean was swinging large and wide, Kaz quickly realized he would be an easy target for the third shriek to pick off. His over exaggerated motions left him vulnerable.

The third shriek was about to make its move but screamed in pain instead. A sword pierced its belly. Kazah twisted the blade and yanked it out. The shriek fell over, dead. Hobbling over, Kazah stabbed the shriek Dean was engaged with from behind as well.

"Thank you!" yelled Dean, "I swear, I was done for, I don't know how to fi—"

"Shut up and help, Dean!" roared Fryda, having trouble with her opponent.

Kaz jumped as high as he could and swung, trying to behead Fryda's shriek from behind. But his legs wouldn't work properly, and his sword got caught in the shriek's shoulder. Dean charged Fryda's shriek and swung up at the shocked demon. The creature turned its head to the left to see his other opponent. Dean's swing split his head open and Fryda finished him with a thrust to the gut. The scent of burning flesh filled their noses as Kaz set his foot against the still corpse and pulled mightily, releasing his sword. "Gratexcelsi" replied Kazah, his body shaking, "The greatest thanks, in my tongue."

"You're welcome." replied Dean, breathing hard, clenching his teeth from the pain in his shoulder. "I didn't know Slavine had a word for thank you."

Kaz had already walking away to help the Equinaut who he had protected.

Fryda called out to him, "Thaddeus wants a defense line formed to help protect the wounded and the Mark III. Get Faramal to help you."

Kaz wanted to argue but instead dutifully called back, "His will, our command. It will be done!"

***

Kaitlyn was too tired to fight any longer for her life, but for the life of the horses corralled in the small paddock, she forced herself to continue. At the first cries of attack, Kaitlyn rushed to the paddock to find two shrieks bent over horses, digging and clawing into their chests. More were chasing the innocent horses left in the shanty that had been erected for the night. Kaitlyn snuck up on one of the digging shrieks, picked up its discarded sword, and with her full weight, threw the sword into the middle of the shriek's back. In death, it let out a dreadful cry, warning the other shrieks of her position. She sprinted for the paddock and leapt over the small fence. The animals inside were running amok, stampeding in a tight circle in their blind effort to escape the chaos erupting around them. The shrieks followed her in, pushing their way through the chaos of running horses, slicing at them with their razor-sharp claws. Once Kaitlyn realized that coming into the paddock was making it worse for the horses, she had to get out. She managed to leap and jump onto the back of Wooley, who had run to her the moment he saw her. She prayed that he was in a condition to accept bareback riders and wouldn't pull his stitches along his wither. Squeezing with her legs and grabbing a handful of mane, Wooley obeyed her command and went straight into a gallop.

Wooley ran as fast and as hard as he could. The horse was probably cursing Kaitlyn's name, danger was always around Kaitlyn and Leora, now he had four shrieks chasing him. A few hundred feet away was a small patch of trees and Kaitlyn hoped it would provide some cover to fool the charging creatures. Passing through the first set of trees, Kaitlyn signaled for a hard right, dodging bushes and branches. She slowed, hoping that the shrieks had not seen the hard-right turn. She waited for some sign from the shrieks.

Only a soft breeze whistling through the trees could be heard, no branches snapping or brush being disturbed. Kaitlyn let out a sigh of relief, she had lost them. Turning Wooley, they headed back towards the camp. That was her first mistake, as she exited the trees. She looked to her right and out of the forest popped one of the shrieks. It let out a crying howl. Wooley didn't wait for a command. He went from walk to gallop in an instant. Kaitlyn leaned forward and wrapped her arms around Wooley's neck, unprepared for the sudden burst of speed. Wooley was running on pure instinct, not responding to any of the commands Kaitlyn was trying to give him. Kaitlyn closed her eyes in fright. A frantic, running horse could be just as dangerous as an attacking shriek. Wooley weaved in and out between wagons and tents, and when he almost ran over an Equinaut and shriek fighting, he reared, then bucked. Unable to hold on, Kaitlyn went flying over Wooley's neck and tumbled to the ground.

Kaitlyn cried out in pain as she rolled several feet, only coming to a stop when her back hit the wheel of a steam powered wagon. For several long seconds, her entire world spun in circles and she was pretty sure Wooley went running off without her. A loud howl jostled her world back into focus. Kaitlyn wasted no time in clambering into the wagon she had slammed into. She locked the door, pulled the shades, and tried desperately to quiet her breathing. Beside her were boxes stacked to the ceiling, each box was full to its brim. The wagon must have held hundreds, if not thousands of oval shaped rocks. The letters, C.M.P. were stamped on the sides of the boxes and plastered on the wagon's walls. Kaitlyn realized she was inside the Citadel Military Wagon that Gladthorn and Edryss had found in Mystique.

She could hear the shriek tearing around outside. Kaitlyn's heart was beating fast and the howls the shrieks made were by far the scariest thing she had ever heard.

"Please, Maker," she prayed, "just let it pass, just let it pass."

Kaitlyn's prayer went unanswered. A large shadow blocked what little light was coming from outside. The shriek howled once more and the door to the wagon began to shake violently. The boxes began to move on the shelves and the oval rocks banged against one another, some crashing to the floor. Kaitlyn pushed deeper into the wagon, moving boxes in front of her, blocking the path

"I don't want to die. Please, Maker, not today. I don't want to die! Save me! Oh, please, Maker, send someone to save me!" Kaitlyn fought to keep her tears and prayers quiet.

The wagon began to rock back and forth, Kaitlyn covered her head with her arms, but that wasn't enough to protect her from the cascade of oval stones that rained down on her

Kaitlyn could taste iron on her lips. A large gash on her forehead was spilling blood and she could feel the skin on her knuckles was split. She wiped her brow and tried to push the rocks aside. Some of the rocks began to give off a yellow aura, the glow reminding Kaitlyn of firebugs in the night sky. The shriek continued to rock the wagon as she tried to claw her way to the top of the rocks. The more stones she pushed aside, the brighter the yellow light got. When the glowing stones began to heat up and vibrate, Kaitlyn regretted choosing this wagon for shelter.

The wagon continued to rock, knocking more stones loose and preventing Kaitlyn from keeping steady. Her forehead bled profusely, the blood obscuring her vision, but she could clearly see the yellow light glowing brighter. She heard the shriek's claws digging into the thick, hard wood of the door, and she struggled to put more space between herself and the creature, climbing over the fallen stones and boxes. The door suddenly ripped open and the shriek's hood entered the wagon. Small, green eyes hideously glowed through the darkness, greedily taking in the light from the stones. The shriek moved further into the wagon and Kaitlyn froze, hoping dearly that it wouldn't notice her among the light. The shriek reached for the brightest glowing stone, which was very near her face. Kaitlyn felt the cold skin of its hands brush up against her cheek. Kaitlyn muffled her scream into a small groan, which the shriek completely ignored. Its green eyes fixated on the glowing stone. For several long seconds, there was silence in the wagon. Kaitlyn was sure she heard a sniffle come from the hooded creature, and then the shriek suddenly and violently let out a huge cry and howl. A blade pierced through its chest and it fell onto the pile of stones, dead.

"Kaitlyn?" asked a low gruff voice, "Kaitlyn, are you in there?"

"Dean, look. What is that?" asked a woman's voice.

Kaitlyn's heart leaped, "Yes, DEAN! Help! I'm in here!"

Dean and Fryda pulled the dead shriek back out the hole where the door was. Dean climbed into the wagon onto the stones and boxes to help Kaitlyn down. On her way out, Kaitlyn grabbed one of the brighter glowing stones. She showed it to Dean and Fryda and told her story of trying to save the horses and being chased by the shrieks.

"I thought I was going to die, but the creature seamed to forget I was even in the wagon." replied Kaitlyn, leaning on the wagon wheel for support, "I was sure it was over, and then all the stones started lighting up. It's over now, I survived and it's dead. I know its dead, but I feel like running far away."

"Your adrenaline is still running it will soon pass" replied Fryda, pushing a cloth against the weeping wound on Kaitlyn's forehead. "In my culture, we call it blood lust, the energy to protect yourself. It's a gift from the Treveii. Perhaps you have some Aedunic blood in you?"

"Well, I don't think I want this gift," remarked Kaitlyn still shaking, blood and tears running down her face, "It's a quite dreadful feeling."

Kaitlyn stood and was overcome by dizziness. She fainted, and Dean grabbed her limp body before she fell, but the pain in his shoulder wouldn't allow him to hold her, causing them to both hit the ground. During their descent, the glowing stone had fallen from Kaitlyn's fingers, hit the ground, and cracked open.

Dean's clumsy apology was interrupted by a bright burst of light from the stone. The light expanded out, and from the stone uncurled a small, scaled creature, who cried out a small version of a howl they had all learned to recognize.

"Shit." Fryda bent over, cut the sleeve from the dead shriek's cloak, and gathered the tiny thing in the cloth. "We need to get to the professor, *now*. Kaitlyn are you good to move?"

Kaitlyn looked up from her place on the ground, "They're eggs?" horror resonating in her voice. "We have hundreds of them. Oh, shit!"

"We thought the attack was for Valissa again, but could it may have been for these eggs?"

"Maybe?" said Fryda, "Grab the egg, and get a few of the glowing ones too. And don't drop them. Let's go!"

* * *

Andi's forehead felt like a hammer has smashed in her temple. She did not have the faintest clue on what happened or what was happening, everything was dark. Her world was moving and jostling about, she could hear breathing, but it wasn't normal, it seemed unnatural. Trying to get up, she realized she couldn't move, there was something holding her. The more time that passed she realized she was being carried. Andi tried to speak to call out to her brother, but nothing came out. Her eyes were open, but she saw nothing, she began to panic and struggled against what was holding her. The harder she tried to free herself the tighter her bonds got.

She could feel pressure tightening around her waist to the point of severe pain. Despite it, Andi was not ready to give up. She knew it was better to escape now before they reached their destination. Who would she meet, the demon who wants her alive, or the one that wants her dead? Andi kicked with all her might, the dark shadow around her broke slightly. What she saw was terrifying, the ground around her was wet and covered in the flesh of the dead. Skulls and bones were scattered and broken, the grass was dead and stained in blood and the trees were dead, burnt with red embers glowing inside their dead husks.

The dead, unholy scenery got even worse as it transformed from natural decay to an architecture that could only be describe as looney, maddening, unnatural. The wall that encircled the camp was made from every conceivable body part imaginable, the number of animals and people that died to make such a formidable wall was haunting. The creature carrying Andi turned to the left, allowing her a better sight of the camp. There were several small stone buildings that were on the brink of collapse. Boxes and crates were strung around in no particular order. Andi gasped as a massive, stone structure came into her view. It was old and had collapsed in many areas long ago. It was made of pure white stone similar to the Citadel. Columns littered the perimeter, only a few were still standing, the rest were broken or fallen over. Andi's first thought of the building was a temple, but to what or whom she had no idea. That is, until she saw something she never thought actually existed. Near the foot of the temple was giant, white stone covered in blood. It glowed unnaturally and gave Andi a sense of foreboding. There was no doubt in her mind. That was the blood stone, the marker where a god fell to ground.

Was this Dark Lady, the creature in the light, the god who fell? Asked Andi to herself?

Starring at the blood stone, Andi felt like she was being intently stared at. She turned her face and saw a wooden crate, and through a crack in the crate she saw two piercing eyes. The gaze of those eyes frightened Andi, the strength and determination she saw in them was terrifying. Moments later, the strength was gone. Several shrieks and tiny demons that Andi had never seen began to harass the crate. The eyes never looked away from Andi, but fear was now present where she had seen power, and hopeless had replaced determination.

For as long as Andi could, she never stopped looking at the eyes in the crate. The creature holding her turned once more and the crate left Andi's line of sight.

"Andi?" asked a terrified voice coming from Andi's right. The way she was hanging off the creature, she had no way of seeing that direction.

"Glut?" asked Andi, "Is that you?"

"What is happening?" asked Glut, "I can't move!"

"SILENCCCCE!" hissed one of the creatures.

The voice was terrifying, and the siblings did as they were told. Andi kept gazing when she saw something familiar, an object she never thought to see again. It was discarded against a crate, it looked old and torn but Andi was certain she knew what it was. "GLUT, LOOK! IT'S OUR FATHERS BAG!"

"SILENCE!" yelled the creature again, angrier than before.

Andi's heart raced, could her father have been here? Was he still here? So many questions and possibilities ran through her head. She started to struggle once more to be free, but the creature's grip was far too powerful. Suddenly, she felt the grip loosen and began to fall. Wooden walls grew around her as she fell into a large crate. She looked up to see what had been carrying her. It appeared to be a man, but he was deformed, decayed, parts of bone protruded out thicker than it should. Flesh, muscle, and skin were scattered among its face. Andi could not make out who it was, but for a brief moment thought about the possibility that her father had been corrupted, "Dad, is that you? It's me, Andi!"

The creature's eyes glowed red and it hissed at Andi, slamming the lid of the crate. She looked to her left and saw her brother slowly sitting up. She grabbed him and pulled him to her, hugging him tightly, beginning to cry. A shadow moved in the corner of the crate, causing the siblings to jump. A face appeared. It was Edryss.

"SSHHHH ITS OK GUYS, IT'S JUST ME!"

"Edryss!" both Andi and Glut yelled now leaning in the cramped crate, hugging her.

"What are we going to do?" asked Andi.

"I don't want to die!" remarked Glut, scared.

"You don't have to worry." Remarked Andi, "You aren't the one they want."

Glut looked at Andi like she was stupid, "Yeah, but that means they don't need me, why keep me alive? I'll be the first to die!"

Edryss kicked the side of the crate, the two siblings looked at her shocked, "Both of you calm down, neither of you are going to die. Right now, this very instant, Thaddeus and Gladthorn are moving mountains to find us and believe me when I tell you, soon the demons will cower when they hear the name Gladthorn Deon Jones, my fiancé!"

***

After a bitter and hard fight, the Equinauts had won. The demon forces were routed, scurrying with their tails tucked between their legs back across the river and into Veilwood forest. The expedition members cheered at their victory, though Italicus wasn't sure if it was an earned praise. The demon forces had been relentless in their attacks, throwing everything they had into the defensive line. Italicus was on the verge of ordering a strategic withdraw when suddenly, the demons lost steam. Or maybe their objective had been accomplished and they withdrew. Italicus feared it was the latter, though matter the reason, Italicus was as relieved as everyone else that the fighting was over.

Italicus bent down and spoke plainly to a young university man clenching his own wounded arm. "I am not going to lie to you. This is going to really hurt." He waited for the young man to acknowledge his warning. Italicus looked over at one of the medics who was handing Wrench some wrappings, "Get him something to bite down on. Wrench, I know you're still healing, but do you think you can hold him still for me?"

Wrench smiled and nodded, placing the wrappings he had gingerly on the ground.

Scrapping the side of his Plaz sword with a steel dagger, Italicus released the superheated metal and pressed it against the young man's wound. The man screamed, horrified at the amount of pain he felt. The heat melted his skin and sealed the wound. Had Wrench not been holding him down, he would have burnt more than just his arm.

"There, that wasn't so bad now, was it?"

"Thaddeus!?" yelled Fryda, looking for her commanding officer.

With no sign of Thaddeus, Fryda looked for Italicus. To her luck he was easy to find, he was wearing his gold feather in his ear and it reflected off the torches. She rushed towards him while dragging the professor by his arm.

"Good Heavens, Fryda!?" expressed the professor in a tiff. "What reason is there to drag me across the camp in such a fashion? I have far more to worry about right now. The demons have taken my Godchildren!"

Fryda knew what Kaitlyn and she had discovered was very important, so she ignored the professor's gruff. By the time Fryda was done recounting the events with the Citadel war wagon and how the small shriek had emerged from the stone egg, Italicus and the professor looked at each other gravely.

Italicus' face twisted in disgust, "Are we saying the demons are procreating, laying eggs!? Which ones are the males and how do they, you know," Italicus made a jabbing motion back and forth, "do it?"

The professor shook his head and lowered it slightly, "I do not think it's as simple as, or as grotesque as, demons having sex." He turned and looked in the direction of the war wagon, "I fear the process in which these demons are created and placed in these eggs is far more disturbing and unnatural than we can imagine."

"Treveri's spear tip." spoke Fryda in disgust and anguish, "More disturbing than demon sex???"

Italicus met the professor's gaze towards the war wagon, "I don't know what to fear the most, the demons returning for these stone eggs, or them hatching on us. Perhaps we should destroy them?"

"No." commanded the professor sternly "Any attempt to destroy them may awaken whatever is inside and what if it's more than just a shriek?"

"Then we leave it here!" yelled Fryda, "Safer than letting them hatch on us while we are unprepared or focused on another problem."

Italicus thought for a moment, "No, we can't abandon it and let them retake it. It may be the only bargaining chip we have to get our people back. Right now, let's keep this between us. Imagine the panic it would cause."

The professor and Fryda both nodded in agreement.

"Look who I found." announced Leora, walking up to the small group. Behind her was Thaddeus striding up on Egghead.

"Damn it, Thaddeus, where have you been?" Italicus folded his arms, "I thought they may have taken you as well."

"Was anyone else taken?"

Italicus shook his head, "Just Andi, Glut, and--"

"You mean Garrett?" interrupted Leora.

"Whose Garret?" asked Italicus confused?

Leora was taken aback by Italicus' question, "Andi's brother of course."

There was silence for a several seconds, "His name isn't Garrett, is it?" asked Thaddeus out loud.

Italicus shrugged, "I am not sure, I thought it was Glut or was it Grunt?"

"No, Grunt is definitely not right." remarked Thaddeus.

The professor tried to speak but was cut off.

"Yeah, I think it was Glut, but it can't be, what a horrible name. Oh, wait, I know." Italicus turned and yelled, "Hey Wrench!"

"What!?" replied Wrench, wrapping a wound.

"What is Andi's brother's name!?"

Wrench hesitated. He thought it was an unusual question, "GARRETT!"

"That's what I thought." remarked Leora smiling that she was right.

The professor tried to speak again, "No, no, its--"

"Well I feel bad now. "interrupted Thaddeus, frowning, "I've been calling him by the wrong name."

Italicus joined the frown, "I guess I have as well"

The professor stomped his foot down, "All of you quiet, it's not Garrett, he was born with the name Glut. He just hates it and lies about it" answered the professor, slightly annoyed that this was a concern right now. "We have to get Andi and GLUT back, including your own colleague, Edryss."

"What's the point professor," said Italicus stoically, "none of them have anything the Demons want or need, they are probably already dead."

"No, they could be used as leverage, "spoke Leora, "we have things they want, don't we?"

"Valissa, the war wagon, "answered the professor, "they may want to negotiate with us? Plus, that one creature said Andi was important to them, they won't just kill her"

"That's assuming it wasn't a demon loyal to Dumak. If it was, she is already dead." inserted Italicus.

"Then why take her? Why not kill Andi on the spot?" asked Leora, "Unless Dumak wants to do it himself?"

"Dear heavens." The professor began to tear up, "I have got to believe they are alive and the demons want to negotiate."

Italicus shook his head violently, "No, you are wrong professor. There will not be any negotiating! If the demons really want something, they will come and take it. We barely managed to hold them back, we didn't break them, they didn't retreat. They withdrew by choice. If they want something, the best we can do is delay them slightly. THEY ARE DEAD!"

Italicus' harsh words were met with silence. Kaitlyn, Dean, Gladthorn, and several others approached, confused at why Italicus was yelling.

Thaddeus began to smile, "They are alive I know this to be a fact. I have a pretty good idea of where they were taken as well."

Italicus looked up at his friend in shock, "How could you possibly know this?"

"If you know Thaddeus, then we must go now!" demanded Gladthorn, "I must save Edryss. We must go now, before they can regroup and prepare for our counter attack."

Leora placed her hand on Gladthorn's shoulder, "We will save her."

"Counter attack, is that wise?" asked the professor out loud, "I want everyone back, but do we have the men to pull it off? It may be wise to let them come to us to negotiate a swap, our people for the war wagon."

Italicus rolled his eyes, "There will be no negotiating, professor!"

Everyone began talking and arguing at the same time, "QUIET!" yelled Thaddeus, annoyed, rubbing his eyes with his thumb and middle finger. "I already told you, they are alive, and I know where they are being kept."

Italicus spoke, "Alright Thaddeus, spill the beans, tell us how you could possible know the impossible?"

"You wouldn't believe me if I told you, let me show you." muttered Thaddeus as he reached into his bag. "You all remember that annoying little rhyming demon that was astride Bailitheoir? Both of them just took Egghead and I on a merry chase for Maker knows how long. "

"BAILITHEOIR WAS HERE?" interrupted Kaitlyn breathlessly, "He is still alive?"

Thaddeus nodded, "I doubt the horse is in danger, he is too powerful to give up. So, Bailitheoir dragged Egghead and I through the woods. For a moment, I thought we lost them, but then I caught that little beast, I took his head. He's unlike any race I know. Look."

Thaddeus revealed a severed head, holding it aloft by a small horn protruding from its forehead. The smell assaulted the group, who were stuck between wanting to take a step back from the pungent aroma and wanting to step closer to examine its source. Below its horn were large, shiny eyelids, a pointed lizard-like nose, and a seemingly human smile, except for small fangs jutting out of both sides of his mouth. A thin, forked tongue lolled as Thaddeus gave the head a firm shake.

"Wake up, you!" commanded Thaddeus.

Italicus tilted his head confused, "Thaddeus, that's a head."

"I know that. "Answered Thaddeus, shaking the head even more violently, "Ah, wake up, you. Don't play possum with me!"

Leora approached Egghead and Thaddeus, "Thaddeus, did you get hit on the head?"

Thaddeus looked down at Leora, completely shocked at her question, "No, I did not get hit on the head. This head is just being stubborn. Aye, you have better wake up now, you hear!" the head remained lifeless. "So, help me if you don't wake up soon I will put you back in the--"

Suddenly, the pointed ears twitched forward, and the eyes flicked open. "Nya. No, not there, anywhere but there!"

The group let out a collective gasp. It was at that moment the head realized it wasn't alone with Thaddeus. The head stared at the group for several seconds before letting out a maniacal cackle that went from high to low and then broke straight into an animated rant.

"Nyah-ha-ha! So, these are the Fleshies you spoke of, HAHA! Fleshy, Fleshy, Fleshy, they all look very sketchy."

"EH!" roared Thaddeus, "No rhyming!"

The head used his eyes the best he could to look up at Thaddeus annoyed, smacking his lips. He wanted to protest but thought better of it. For a moment, the head looked back towards the group, confused. He began to stare at each person. When he got to Italicus he paused and began to laugh, "NYU-aha that is the girly man with the golden feather you spoke of. Honestly, I thought him to be prettier and perhaps a little taller. NYAHA!"

Italicus' jaw hit the ground, as he ran his hand self-consciously over the feather in his ear, "You even got a demon on it!?"

Thaddeus shrugged innocently, "It was a long ride back to camp, and it wouldn't shut up."

"So, what the hell is it? Shouldn't it be dead?" Kaitlyn had positioned herself halfway behind Dean.

The head's eyes focused on Kaitlyn, and his tongue wiggled in her direction, "Nya-he hee! So, you're the one who took and stole Bailtheoir's heart, what a floozy, what a tart! Nyha, I my dear am me, and I am very much free, so go and flee in terror, for I am on good behavior! In all the worlds and seas, there is in fact only one me. "The creature's voice went up and down and it sounded like the bodiless creature was trying to entertain the group with his rhymes. He looked at Leora with an almost longing face, "Talk and talk and what to say, Nyhaha, I only communicate with they! On my own but not alone, the voices I hear I can't condone."

"AYE, you!" yelled Thaddeus, shaking the head and pointing at it, "What did I just say about rhyming!?"

The creature smashed his teeth and lips together, trying to bite Thaddeus' finger, "Nyah, dumb Fleshie, take the fun out of life."

"Thaddeus," the professor prompted darkly.

"I know," said Thaddeus closing his eyes and sighing.

"Ha, you know nothing ugly flesh bag! In fact, you all know nothing!" hissed the head, smacking his lips, "I, on the other hand, know a lot, maybe even everything! I am not ssssure. Perhapsss I do, perhapsss I don't, but one thing I do know, isss that Ssshangri iss going to kill all of you, Nyah heh hem hem hem!"

"Thaddeus!?" said Italicus, even more seriously.

"*I know*" said Thaddeus, sighing deeper. "But listen," he lifted the head and turned it to face him, "Speak now, devil. Who in Bellows is Shangri?"

"NyaHa, Ha, Hell, she isn't from Bellows! No, no, far from it. The Evil, the great Evil, the one, the only, the Prime. Shangri's master, she knows the secrets of the prime, he is in Bellows niyah-he-he. And soon she will release him! But you, all of you, will be dead long before that. Shangri will exterminate you. She will kill all of you! Heee hee heee!" cackled the monstrous head. "That, of course, will not happen if you listen to me and make me Captain! NYAHAHA!"

"Stop ryhming!" Thaddeus shook the head until it was quiet, "Now, tell them what you told me or its back into that bag."

"Ni'uh, do what you will, ugly, stupid, Fleashie. I fear nothing! You've already taken my body, I have nothing left to lose, except to help you!" hissed the head bravely, but as Thaddeus motioned to return the head to his bag, it screeched, "No! Ssstop headhunter! I will ssspeak, I will talk! I will sing like a bird bawk bawk bawk!" Thaddeus continued to move the head towards the bag, "NOOO, No, Noooo!!!"

The creature's chin was sliding into the bag and he began to cry hysterically, "NOOOO! It smells ssso foul, stomach and bowl, pleassse don't put me back in that bag! I am a prince not a hag!"

"Manure bag?" asked Italicus, smiling widely.

Thaddeus nodded.

"PLEASE, I WILL TELL YOU ANYTHING, FLESHIE!" yelled the head.

"Tell them what you told me!" commanded Thaddeus, pulling the creature away from the bag, "and no more rhyming."

"Very well, headhunter," The head's eyes narrowed into slits and his voice changed to a less enthused tone. "Shangri, the last of the Fallen, she is powerful beyond corporeal measure."

"She is a celestial, isn't she?" asked the professor.

The creature tried to nod, but it came out more as a wiggle. He was unable to nod without a neck. She is not of this plane. She is the most powerful creature among the demon army. We are all hers to obey!"

"Why did she order an attack on us?" asked Thaddeus.

The head's face was a mix of anger and disgust, "You ordered an attack on yourselves when you defeated Dumak and stole the wagon. Nyahaha, stupid fleshies you are! She now knows you exist, she knows now the vessel was with you. Now she is taken. Dumak will kill her or Shangri will use her. But before that happens she will come after what you have stolen, what was not supposed to be revealed yet. The deformed man will pay for that, just as *all* in your army will pay for stealing it! Nyah ahah!"

"You lie!" roared Thaddeus, "We stole nothing!"

The professor coughed, "I do believe I know to what he is referring."

Thaddeus turned his gaze. The anger in his eyes was far more dreadful than the demon's head.

The professor cowered for a moment, "Don't look at me like that, I have hidden nothing from you. We just now discovered it while you were gone."

Thaddeus hesitated, but his eyes softened. He then nodded his acknowledgement.

The demon head gasped at the professor, "Whoa," he said through his teeth, "You say I am ugly!"

The professor began to bawk at the head's insult, but Thaddeus interrupted, "Why was Edryss taken?"

"You kill us and ask why we take prisoners?" said the head dumbfounded, "Shangri has taken notice of you all. She is no fool! You have defeated Dumak. She needs leverage against you fleshies. You are the only creatures on the shard to challenge her army. You poked at the hornet's nest. Edryss was an easy mark to take."

"You underestimate Edryss!" shouted Gladthorn shaking with anger.

"She is far stronger than you realize!" added Leora, angry as well.

The head looked at Leora and failed to conceal the strange look he had for her. The head stared at her for several long moments, and slowly it began to smile, its eyes darting back and forth between Thaddeus and Leora.

"Is it me, or is her hair darker?" tested the head, smacking his lips slightly "Niyah- he"

Leora was horrified, but the comment was ignored by everyone else.

The professor pressed the head for more information, "What do you know of Dumak? How can we kill him?"

The head looked to him with anger in his eyes and then back to Leora, "You can't, wrinkled old flesh bag, not without sacrificing."

"Sacrifice what??" asked Leora, her voice a pitch higher.

When the head did not speak, Thaddeus shook it and yelled, "Answer her!"

The head looked down ashamed, "Red Fleshie doesn't want to know the answer, it will eat away at her like a cancer!" Thaddeus shook the head, "Dumak the necromancer is Shangri's second in command and in power. You cannot simply kill him. No. No. No. That cost would be too great. Imprison him. Lock him away and SHUT THE GATE. That is the answer, the one I will only say, do what you want, make me pay! Nyeh."

"Why is he corrupting innocent villagers and Citadel citizens?" asked the professor.

The head wrinkled his scaly nose, like he had smelled something putrid, "Corrupt? Villagers? That- that- that's not part of Shangri's plan? If he is doing this on his own, Shangri would never condone."

"Great! Either Dumak is following his own lead or this *thing* knows absolutely nothing!" responded Italicus. "For all we know, it's the demons form of a court jester? Why else all this rhyming?"

"Which means he has no purpose here!" declared Leora loudly, "Finish it off, kill it!"

The head flicked his tongue, "Now that's simply not true! Don't be rude Red Fleshie! I know lotsss of very usseful thingsss."

"We have names you know!" Leora huffed in contempt, "Don't call me Red Fleshie."

"Nyah-HAHAHA I do, I have purpose! I know the only way to kill Dumak. By his own blood he must die, but the price, trust me is way too high. Lock him away, far away, back to the grave he must stay. Only then will you save those you care, and you will not live a life full of regret and despair." The head smiled at the attention this brought him, and then snickered, "Meh-he-he I know lotsss more! I know what Shangri is after, and once I'm reunited with my body, I will tell you where Shangri's camp is, where she has taken your friends. Deep! Deep, in the forest, it's easy to get lost, but I know the way! I, I can teach you!" The head taunted, "Your Fleshies are not so far away as you may think!"

"Your body- never! Teach us? You mean lead us. Once our people are back safely, I will consider the possibility of not cutting you further." expressed Thaddeus assuredly, making sure the head understood his threat.

"Eh, testy headhunter." answered the head, frowning. "Nyaha, telling you what I have means I have already betrayed Shangri. If I get caught, certain unending pain and suffering waits for me! No chance I am going back to that camp. I will tell you all you need to know, I will not go back to that camp no, no, no." The head smiled cruelly, hoping he had convinced Thaddeus he was not needed at the camp. "Nyaha, trust me fleshie you must. That is, if you want to reach your fleshie friends before they become dust! Nyahaha"

Thaddeus was in no mood to be toyed with, "You will tell me how to get there now, or I will bury your head so deep in a hole in a bag that will make manure smell like perfume!"

Echo from the Past

I knew the power inside the crystal was the bait necessary to lure Dumak to the city before he could finish the conquest of the southern encampments. I made sure the crystal's power radiated throughout the lands, there was no way he could resist its temptation.

Our armies were trained, equipped, and blessed. The walls were thickened and strengthened. There was nothing to do now but wait for Dumak. I thought it would only take days for him to arrive, but days became weeks. There was no sign of him or his armies. Scouts returned with reports of no movement to the south. With the threat seemingly gone, the number of southern immigrants to the city diminished. Dumak's delay allowed me time I had not foreseen, so I began studying the crystal. I had to figure out its secrets. Where did it come from? Why did it fall here of all places? What was in it? How could I make its power my own? I performed every spell, I used every piece of magic known to me, and nothing brought me any closer to understanding its mysteries.

As time wore on with still no sign of our enemy, my vessel began to feel the trepidation I had been hiding. The longer we waited for Dumak, the more skeptical I became at defeating him. The power we had accumulated in the seele stone, was it enough to kill Dumak? I was starting to have doubts. What if he had found another power source? Had the Void given up more of its secrets? Had other crystals of Celestial power fallen from the sky?

Feeling me worry was a sensation my vessel was not used to. I had always been her invincibility, the unbreakable strength in her life. It troubled her greatly. I was unsure how to reassure her, so I didn't. We stared at the crystal for hours. The silence was eventually broken when my vessel spoke. Her cunning amazed me. If she had been an ascended solider, she would have been a great general by the war's end.

Her question was simple, it showed her ignorance to the truths of the universe, but that allowed her to see what I couldn't. The answer to the problem with Dumak was staring me right in the face and I was oblivious.

"If we can't kill Dumak, can we imprison him?"

I dismissed her question until she reached out and touched the pristine, cold, smooth surface of the crystal. It was only then my mind finally connected the dots that my vessel had seen. If we can't kill Dumak, perhaps we could seal him in his own crystal prison.

We immediately set to work knowing it would take great ingenuity to build such a device. Finding a natural crystal of sufficient size and density would be impossible, so with the help of all the people, we began gathering every piece of crystal and glass inside the city. Only after depleting the entire city's content of glassware was I able to form an artificial crystal large enough to hold the likes of Dumak.

During the 5th week, a scout reported a large body of men thirty miles south of the city. I tried to tap into the veil, but the void gave no indication that Dumak was that close. I sent Aaron and his best men to scout out the area.

This marks my second great mistake. Days went by and there was no word from Aaron or his scouts. My vessel was agitated that I had sent Aaron, and the longer he was gone the more furious she became. I did not understand her anger. I needed to verify Dumak's position and I trusted no one more than Aaron. After a week of silence, Aaron rode back to the city's edge, bruised, bloody, and wounded. How he had held on to life could only be described as sheer will, the man should have been dead. Through shallow breaths he recounted how he was ambushed by Dumak himself, and that his scouts were obliterated before his eyes. Dumak tortured him for information, and when Aaron gave him nothing of value, he used him to send word to me. A simple message: Run. For I am coming.

Dumak was on his way, and I relished the chance to meet him in battle armed with the seele stone and with the crystal prison. I knew that this fight, that this war would be mine. I would be victorious.

With a heart filled with angst, my vessel uncharacteristically forced me out, telling me she had something important to do before Dumak arrived. I assumed her unease was for the coming battle, but with my mind so focused on the fallen crystal, I did not give her abruptness a second thought. I did not need her body to study it. I noticed stress cracks along the cCrystal's edges. It was beginning to break, and whatever was inside of it would soon be mine.

Scouts reported that a large army was marching our way. The numbers of men were too great for Dumak to transport all at once. Dumak's army created a dust cloud that filled the entire southern horizon. At one point, Dumak reached out through the void and made contact with me. The control over his powers was expanding. He asked for parley.

I entered my Sanctum Sanctorum and pierced through the veil and into the void. This was my third mistake. Dumak tried to fluster me, threatening me with great pain and suffering, and an even longer death if I did not surrender to him the crystal. I laughed at his threats and countered with my own.

"Kill yourself now, and spare me the trouble. Between my fortified city and my strengthened power you will be the one dying this day!"

Dumak warned against my hubris, "Beware, the strongest foundations can break if weakened from within!"

The war horns blew, and my city was alerted to Dumak's approaching army. We prepared for battle. I left my Sanctum Sanctorum, and met my vessel running from her personal chambers towards me. Her face red and her hair disheveled, but she wore a look of determination, bloodlust clearly written across her face. Her taste for battle impressed even me. We merged and delivered a rousing speech to my troops. The city bowed before us, worshipping and offering their lives.

For many hours, Dumak's army stood beyond my walls and did nothing, quite annoyingly. When the saffron sun kissed the horizon, Dumak began his siege. Thousands of heathens charged towards my walls, hundreds of catapults let loose their projectiles. Not a single stone hit the walls. Each one was destroyed by me mid-air. My soldiers of faith easily kept siege ladders and ropes off the walls. I laughed at the pitiful display. Horns alerted my army's commanders that the western gate had been breached, by who is still a mystery to me, but it proved Dumak's threat about moles was true. On the eastern front, Dumak unleashed a magical bravo that destroyed an entire section of wall. The explosion was so large and powerful that the entire temple shook. More horns sounded. My legion on the ground moved in place, trying to keep the surging army from venturing into the city.

My western forces were able to push the enemy back and managed to reclose the gate. They turned to reinforce their brothers, keeping the eastern hole contained. The battle was slow, and my faithful soldiers fought with everything they had. Night fell as the fight raged. To my surprise, the crystal began to emit even more power. A great beam of energy connected it to the heavens, providing light for my army. The fissures grew, and it was clear something was happening inside. Fearing the crystal and its power falling into my hands, Dumak decided he had no choice but to face me once and for all in the temple, leaving his army without a commander.

"You grotesque creature, you have no claim on what is rightfully mine! This whole world belongs to me!" cried Dumak, "I will destroy you from existence!"

My vessel and I ignored Dumak's arrogance. We didn't even give the upstart necromancer the courtesy of an acknowledgement. Calling upon the power of the heavens, we delivered the first blow.

Edryss

CHAPTER NINE

From the first scroll of Zakarael, chapter 94 verse16:

"For judgment will again be righteous, and the entire upright in heart will follow it. Who will stand up for me against evildoers? Who will take his stand for me against those who do wickedness? If the Maker had not been my help, my soul would soon have dwelt in the abode of silence...."

-Deep in the center of Veilwood Forest:

The pain was excruciating, unbearable. Every muscle and joint cried out as if a hundred daggers were piercing her body. She found solace only in sleep, but the mugginess and heat from the sun bearing down on her prison walls kept her awake. In dreams she was free, but in the world of the conscious, she was nothing but a forgotten prisoner in a crate too small for a full-grown woman to be in.

They left her to rot. In this, her life lost meaning and she was without worth. Unable to find the reprieve she desired, she sighed, dreaming today was beyond her grasp. The abandoned woman in the crate strived to stretch. Her neck was stiff, and she struggled in vain to find a more comfortable position, an impossible feat in such a confining space. She was able to extend her legs slightly and sit up or lay down in a tight fetal position. Her prison wouldn't allow anything else.

She felt along the scum and moldy stew-like residue on the ground, searching for her small stone. She ran her hand across the planked wood and felt the many indentations in the grimy, damp planks of wood. When she reached the center of the third plank, she pressed the stone against the wall and engraved an inch-long mark. At one time, the small, porous stone had been a large rock, but her daily habit had eroded it down to almost nothing. She leaned limply against her handiwork. It had been a long time since she last hoped for rescue or escape. Now, she simply prayed to die.

"Let me out of here!" yelled a voice the distance.

"Free us now, or when I am rescued, I will cut down each and every one of you." It had been a while since her captors had taken new prisoners. It was refreshing to hear the voice of a person. The first one had arrived late at night, two more arrived later. The demons celebrated their capture for many hours. Throughout the night the new prisoners screamed to be let go. She wondered if she had screamed like that her first few nights, she couldn't remember.

She pitied the new prisoners, new flesh and souls for the demons and their master.

"Poor things," she whispered to herself. Her voice was course, it cracked with each syllable. "At least they will die soon."

"SHUT UP, YOU!" yelled a brutal, guttural voice.

The small slit in the roof of her crate opened, rays of bright light shined down, blinding the woman and burning her pale, translucent skin. The woman peered through her fingers at a filthy creature with saggy, dark eyes, and a boar bird face with two horns coming out of his head.

"You're not—where is Lorux?"

"SHUT UP, FREAK!!!" cried the creature with distain, spitting into her crate.

The creature lifted a metal bucket. The woman closed her eyes and opened her mouth. On the days they remembered to feed her, thick, grey liquid was poured into the crate over the poor woman. She desperately tried to catch as much as she could in her mouth and hands.

"ROT ON THAT, YOU FILTH!" mocked the creature, sliding the lid closed, then he walked away laughing, "TOMORROW IS THE DAY WE SKIN YOU!"

The demon guards enjoyed playing their cruel games, laughing at the woman's expense. Terrorizing her was sweet nectar to them. Those words used to frighten the woman. She feared that one day it would come to pass. Now, she'd sometimes yell back, trying to goad them into realizing the threats. Even a painful death would be a victory. Eventually, many of the guards lost their enthusiasm. It's no fun playing with a toy that is broken. That was around the time they stopped feeding her every day. Despite all anger, rage, and evil inside the demon camp, one creature did show kindness to her, though he wasn't often around. A single horned demon with a Jinn-like smile that the other demons feared greatly would go out of his way to feed her slowly, allowing her to catch most of the food in her mouth. It had been many weeks since she had last seen him. She feared he had grown bored with her too and wouldn't return.

She sucked the food from her ripped and deteriorating clothing and returned to her routine, trying to push out the constant pain and soreness of her body. She tried to ignore the new prisoners' continued cries for help. Some days, when there wasn't a lot of commotion and the pain was not quite so bad, the woman in the crate swam in the ocean alongside a beautiful beach. Near the water's edge she would meet a magnificent white horse with a perfectly shaped black star on his forehead, and the two would ride for hours at a time.

Unfortunately, today was not one of those days.

"What do you mean she isn't here?" yelled a voice she didn't immediately recognize. It sounded unnatural and dark. Darker than the demons she was used to. "When you summoned me, you said she needed to speak to me!"

A new voice spoke, this voice was lower, angry, and melodic, "Do not raise your voice to me! I am doing what our master has commanded of me! She will be here soon, Necromancer! We all serve in her holy glory!"

"Duth Dumak Arazeg serves no one! Remember that, Ollpheist." yelled the unnatural voice.

"Yet, you are here, when I summoned," mocked the melodic voice who must have been Ollpheist. "Do not forget it was she who raised you from your eternal sepulcher and allowed me to save you when you failed against the mortals. You were once a god Arazeg. Perhaps you should start acting like one? How could a band of horsemen defeat you and your invincible hell horse?"

"Damn you!" yelled Duth Dumak Arazeg furiously, "That collection of glue and rotting Slavine food is no hell horse, I did not lose. That damn horse failed me. These mortals are unlike the ones she has met on other shards, there is divine— "

Ollpheist spat on the ground, "How pathetic you have become."

Dumak bit his lip trying not to scream, "Mark my words, Ollpheist. Shangri will rue the day she thinks these mortals normal. She must allow me the full might of her demon army. "

"That will not be happening," remarked Ollpheist, almost amused, "if not for the need of your technomancy to unlock the final seal, Shangri would have done away with such filth."

Dumak could not believe how he was being spoken to, "I WILL GAIN COMMAND AND EARN MY REVE— "

"No, you will not. The Dark Mistress has already ordered a proper raid against the troublesome humans."

"WHAT, WITHOUT ME?" roared Dumak, "If she kills PenRuger, I will tear her down from her Celestial perch and destroy— "

Ollpheist laughed at Dumak, "As the sun cannot burn out, neither can our lord and master. You would burn a thousand deaths before you could get near her. She rose you from your imprisoned crypt and— "

Something slammed into the woman's crate and shattered. The woman screamed and jumped, slamming her head against the ceiling. She struggled to right herself and peaked through the tiny cracks, the smell of bitter alcohol filling her cell.

Ollpheist rolled his eyes disappointedly, "That was my favorite mug."

If Ollpheist sounded annoyed, then Dumak was positively fuming, "I would have escaped those cursed bonds without her help! My cult of blood worshipers would have freed me. No power in all of creation can hold Dumak forever!" As he yelled, his voice became even more unnatural. "I am the most powerful creature in this demon army!"

From her limited view through the crate, the woman could see the two creatures arguing nearby. One looked like a man, but deformed and ugly, he was Duth Dumak. Ollpheist was one of Shangri's Rurapenteii, a highly evolved demon abomination that helped keep order inside the demon ranks. This one though seemed larger and far more decayed. His skin oozed something out of every pore. The woman was surprised at how stunningly green and red the Rurapenteiis' eyes were.

"Second most powerful" stated Ollpheist, his dark melodic voice sounded bored. "Otherwise, my master would not have seen fit to bind your life force to mine."

"You are *nothing*! A glorified tether, a fail-safe!" screamed Dumak. "She fears my abilities. I grow in power each day and when I am back to full strength, she knows I will kill her!"

"Silence!" yelled Ollpheist, now furious. He spoke quickly and with passion. There was truth in his voice. "That's the second time you have threatened my darkness in front of me, NO MORE! You would do well to watch your words, filthy necromancer! Our lives are linked. If you ever raise a finger to our master, I will kill myself. I will gladly die knowing you will be dragged to the depths of Bellows alongside me."

Dumak screamed "You dare threaten me, Duth Dumak Arazeg? You know not what you do, what pain these words will bring down on you."

"SILENCE! You will speak no more!" Ollpheist flicked his wrist in Duth Dumak's direction. Dumak clawed at his throat, surprise and fear in his eyes.

"As you gain power, so do I! Shangri created me as the perfect counter to you and a GOD is never mistaken!"

Dumak tried to respond, but couldn't, Ollphiest flicked his wrist once more.

"That woman is no god! I have things to do, Ollphiest, *important things*. Why has she summoned me here?"

"The Morustranconatra. "

Dumak tried to hold in his surprise at hearing those words. How could they have known about her?

"You can try to hide your surprise, but we already know you knew about her existence. I am sure she will deal with you and your lack of sharing information. Luckily, Lorux was sent to retrieve your horse, he saw her with his own eyes."

Dumak tried to deny knowledge of the Morustranconatra, "I have no idea what you are telling me, Ollpheist."

"She was located last night with the horsemen during our raid to reclaim the war wagon that *you* lost to the mortals!"

"The Morustranconatra is a myth." Duth Dumak laughed at Ollphiest, with no regard to the remarks of his failure "It does not exist. No vessel can contain the Prime."

Ollphiest was unmoved by Dumak's outburst. "Shangri has seen the vessel with her own eyes, peered into its soul, seen the flame. Our master is certain this time."

Dumak began to walk away from Ollphiest, "She was certain when she tried to create a fake Morustranconatra herself!" Dumak pointed towards the woman's crate, "Yet there she rots as a reminder to your master's failure."

The woman saw Dumak approaching her crate, and she fell into the fetal position. Tears ran down her cheeks, she feared what the deformed man might do. Dumak slid the small slat open, and peered in.

"Honestly, why doesn't she rid us of this mistake? Why keep it around?"

Dumak waved his hand over the crate and it began to levitate.

"I could kill it now, it's too weak to even save itself." mocked Dumak shaking the box around with magic, causing it to spin and turn, "Or I could rip her soul out from her body and change it into a shriek, at least then it would be mildly useful." The woman felt herself begin to retch. She fought to keep her sick in her mouth.

Ollphiest snapped his fingers, and the crate floated back down to the ground, "She is not to be touched! We may still find a use for her. We have been ordered to study the vessel and prepare it."

Dumak folded his hands and laughed, "Face it Ollphiest, this myth will never pan—" Dumak did not finish his statement. Ollphiest's eyes had suddenly glowed yellow.

"Has she finally arrived?" asked Dumak flippantly.

Ollphiest's eyes continued to glow yellow and he did not move for several seconds. "Trouble has arisen in one of our sanctuaries in the Aedunic lands. It seems the horsemen are causing trouble on multiple fronts."

"*PenRuger!*" yelled Dumak, "I will destroy him and his allies!"

Ollphiest nodded, "They bear the same markings as the ones heading east. We have been ordered to engage the horsemen before they discover the sanctuary's secrets!"

"As she orders" Dumak gave a sadistic smile, and grabbed the jewel on his necklace, "You do know, one day I will kill you, Ollphiest!"

"I look forward to the day you try," mocked Ollphiest.

A bright flash lit up the area and there was a loud pop, followed by silence. The two had vanished inside the burst of light, leaving the woman in the crate alone, crying, and bleeding, left with only her thoughts of white horses and sandy beaches.

***

The confidence that the battle of Callan's field brought the expedition had been burned away much like the village of Mystique. As hard as it was to believe the members of the expedition were adjusting and accepting the fact there were hooded shrieks with razor sharp claws, corrupted and possessed people, an ancient hell horse seeking redemption, and a lunatic, deformed necromancer out to kill Thaddeus' bloodline, now a new terror was added to the shroud of mystery that surrounded the enemy. A terror that was almost invisible and very dangerous. As the sun rose the next morning, many were shocked at how much damage the shrieks and shadows had managed to cause in such a short period of time.

Wrench worked through a daze of pain and exhaustion, trying to fix what the creatures had broken. Many of the steam powered wagons had been flipped and pieces of the engines and boilers were torn apart. The consensus of the professor, Thaddeus, and Italicus, was that the shrieks were searching for something or someone. Closing the engine hatch to the latest wagon he had been working on, Wrench went to find the professor. He shook off the sense of déjà vu watching the parade of the bandaged and injured. *Thank the Maker for the Equinauts.* Wrench didn't want to think about where they'd be without protection.

Wrench approached the professor, who seemed to be having an argument with Thaddeus. Both men hushed once they saw Wrench, still shocked to see the large man in such a frail state.

"Sorry to interrupt, professor, but I wanted to let you know several wagons are finished and ready to go. There's a few though that are just too far gone, too much damage to their engines." Wrench yawned and scratched at his neck. "I can junk them and use their parts to fix what we need to repair the rest."

"Make it so. We can convert those we need to to horse-drawn," replied the professor. "Thank you, Wrench. Your determination is admirable in your current state. But please try to get some rest!"

Wrench nodded and shuffled away.

"Time is of the essence! Isn't that what you have been repeating since this expedition started?" Exclaimed Thaddeus? "Edryss' life and the lives of your godchildren are at stake! The longer we wait, the smaller the chance that they get out of this alive."

"Our first priority is the injured and getting ourselves back to working order," stated the professor. "I can't have you and your men gallivanting into Veilwood, leaving us vulnerable. Those creatures were after the war wagon and those rock/eggs that we recovered. What is to stop them from trying again?"

"That is cold, even for you. We *know* where their camp is! We can be there and back in no time!"

"No! And don't presume to use your officer voice on me! The Intel you have is from a talking head! How do we know he can be trusted?"

Thaddeus was trapped. The head could not be trusted. As Thaddeus tried to construct an argument, Italicus approached with a piece of parchment in hand.

"I'm sorry to interrupt."

"No bother, Italicus," said the professor, turning to leave. "We're done here."

Thaddeus sighed deeply. "What is it, brother?"

"The Butcher's Bill," answered Italicus solemnly, "A cook and one of the professor's drivers didn't make it far past sunrise. Everyone else is expected to survive."

Thaddeus took the parchment and read it, "And here I thought we all made it out of that fight alive, small blessing it was only two."

"It is, but I know you, Thaddeus. The only acceptable number is zero."

"All life matters and a single loss is a failure on us all." agreed Thaddeus, standing. "I will not let that bill go any higher today. We cannot wait a moment longer. Prepare the men. We are going to get our people. We'll be back before the professor knows we're gone."

Italicus smiled, "The men were ready an hour ago."

Thaddeus smiled, "Gather them, we leave in fifteen minutes!"

Leora was gathering the small number of items she had left from Thaddeus' tent. A bunk had opened in a tent after last night's battle. Leora feared it was rude for her to ask so soon after one of the cook's death to take her bunk, but she could not stay another night in Thaddeus' tent. If she had another pair of clothes she would not be wearing the outfit he had given her. Placing her journal into a leather bag, she moved to leave the tent but was blocked as Thaddeus rushed in. At first, Thaddeus ignored Leora and rushed to his chest and began pulling out items.

"I am sorry, I just need to gather some of my gear and I will be out of your way." said Thaddeus, trying to sound nonchalant, but in reality, it pained him to know she was mad at him.

"Do not worry about me anymore!" responded Leora coldly, but curious to why Thaddeus was in such a rush. She quickly noticed everything he was grabbing was some sort of weapon, several daggers, a chakram, and a tesla whip.

"What? Why?" Thaddeus looked back and saw the bag she was carrying.

Thaddeus' eyes saddened, "Please, when I offered you my tent there were no strings attached. It's yours for as long as you want or need. "

Leora tried to stand tall, "Well, I don't want nor, do I need. I found a bunk. "

"Oh, well I, "Thaddeus wanted to tell Leora everything, but he couldn't find the words. "I hope that I um, "the silence that passed between them was awkward and Thaddeus hated himself for not being able to say what he wanted, "hope it works out. If it doesn't, you are always welcome here."

"Thanks, but I'll be fin— "Leora lost the words she was going to say as well, she was now very concerned with what Thaddeus was doing. Out of the bottom of his chest he proceeded to pull out pieces of armor that was very unusual. They looked almost mechanical with wires coming out of the ends. "What is happening, are we about to be attacked?"

"We are going to save our people, Italicus is gathering men as we speak." spoke Thaddeus as he put on the mechanical greaves and connected them to wires that ran up to his Tesla Pack.

"You're what? "Leora nearly gasped at the thought of Thaddeus going into the forest and facing the demons. Part of her wanted to cry out and say don't go, that it was stupid, but the other part of her was still angry at the man.

"The professor is against it," he remarked, "so we have to hurry and leave before Belladon realizes it. I will not let Edryss, Glut or Andi die!"

"Garret!" said Leora sharply.

"Garret, who's that," asked Thaddeus?

Leora looked at Thaddeus like he was stupid, "Andi's brother! His name is Garret."

"No, it's not, its Glut." corrected Thaddeus, "Garret would be a better name though."

Leora shook her head frustrated, "No, he told me himself that it was Garret."

"Then he fooled and lied to you?"

Thaddeus cowered slightly at the evil eyes Leora glaring at him with, "If anyone should know how to fool people it's you!"

Leora felt proud of herself that she was able to say that to Thaddeus, feeling like she had said her peace, she turned to leave.

"Leora wait, please."

Against her better judgement, Leora stopped.

"Leora, I am sorry I panicked. In these past few weeks I, uh, I felt like we were getting close. I think it scared me, I haven't been this close to someone in nine years."

Leora tried to look angry or at least stoic, but she couldn't fully hide her feelings, "Nine years?"

Thaddeus' face blushed and looked away, "There are things about my past, things that happened, awful, painful, things. I don't like talking about the pain, it is too great. "Thaddeus tried to look at Leora, but tears were rolling down his cheek, he turned away again. "I wanted to tell you, and I still want to tell you, but every time I opened my mouth the pain would came back." Thaddeus tried to sound cheerful, but he failed," I was scared, it's one of the few pains my medallion can't heal." He reached out for Leora's hand, "The idea of being close or intimate with someone brought up a past that I tried to forget. I needed to make sure what I was feeling was real and not remnants of my past coming back."

Leora's eyes had softened greatly, "I don't understand. What happened in your past that was so bad?"

Thaddeus took a large breath and hugged Leora. She at first resisted but gave in and wrapped her arms around him as well. "I will tell you everything when I get back, but first I have to save them."

Leora had almost forgotten what Thaddeus had been doing, all her anger left her. Suddenly she was scared and didn't want Thaddeus to go. "Don't go, or at least let me come with you!"

"No Leora, you need to stay here. "

"But I can help!"

"No, I need you here to help keep the expedition safe. " Thaddeus prayed that she would understand and that he wouldn't have to say what he really felt, that he would be devastated if she got hurt, or worse. "Veilwood is not without its own perils and dangers. Keep the professor safe and watch him, he is very worried about his godchildren."

Leora nodded, she squeezed Thaddeus tightly, placed her lips against his ear and whispered, her voice was soft but passionate, "Please come back to me. You may have a past, but I don't. I only see the future and I want that future to be with you."

Thaddeus pulled back, he starred warmly into Leora's perfect blue eyes. He ran his hand through her thick, red hair and parted it away from her face. She cooed and leaned into his large, warm palm. He moved into her, their lips were almost touching, a second and an eternity between them. She could feel electricity build inside of her, certain a spark would form if they didn't touch soon. She gazed up with her eyes into his, her heart melted as she could see he felt the same for her. "A future of dancing is… "

Leora's heart exploded, she didn't care or need to hear what he had to say. All she wanted in that moment was Thaddeus' lips. She could not wait and did not wait. She pressed her soft lips against his and kissed him with such passion and ferocity it took Thaddeus by surprise. It was being like kissed for the first time and the last time, so many emotions ran through their hearts and minds. Leora never wanted to stop kissing him, but she was forced to stop to breathe. She let go of his lips, biting his bottom lips as she pulled away. Thaddeus' face had become like a puppy longing to be loved, she sighed and rested her head against his chest, breathing hard.

"Promise you will come back to me. "

Thaddeus kissed the top of Leora's head, his mind mingled with images, the battle that was to come, Leora, and of Alana. He took a large breath, "I promise!"

Thaddeus left leora in his tent and met up with a handful of men. They were going to head into the forest on foot since riding a horse was nearly impossible through such thick brush. The professor had taken notice of the odd activity some of the Equinauts were up to, he was amazed at the audacity of these men. Ready to risk everything to save lives and rescue one of their own. *Would my men risk that much to save me?* he wondered. The faces of Andi and Glut appeared in his mind, and how scared they must be in the heart of the demon controlled territory. The professor grabbed his top hat and scurried over to them as they left camp. Thaddeus saw the professor and prepared for another battle of wills.

"Please don't try to stop me, professor."

"These are the men that you are taking? Perhaps you should take a few more with you?"

"More men?" asked Thaddeus, surprised, "I don't understand, don't you want as many men here as possible to guard the column."

The professor lowered his head, "I want you to bring my godchildren back safely."

Italicus' eyes widened, *"Your godchildren*!? I didn't know that. Hell, why didn't you let us go sooner?"

The professor's face was red with shame, "The whole shard is at stake, I couldn't let my personal connections interfere with the wellbeing of the cause!" The professor looked up at Thaddeus, "Please, I was wrong, their lives are as important as everyone else's, even more so to me. Please, just bring them back safely. They are the only family I have."

***

Andi struggled against the lid of the crate that she, her brother, and Edryss had been imprisoned in. Unable to stand upright, Andi and Edryss felt awkward trying to stand and push. They feared their time was being whittled away, while Edryss was confident that Gladthorn and Thaddeus would come to rescue them. It was impossible to know when that would happen. They knew the longer it took their rescuers to find them, the greater the chance the demons would come back.

Their fears were realized in the early morning when hundreds of goats awoke them with their annoyingly loud brays. They watched through slivers and cracks in the crate as a shriek herded in the goats that they must have stolen from a local, independent farmer. Mere seconds after the goats had made their way into the demonic walls, shrieks, shadows and other demon creatures converged onto their location. The braying instantly turned into blood curdling cries for help. The demons ripped and tore into the goats, eating them alive. Fearing that the demons would soon converge on them, the three knew there was no time to wait to be rescued, they had to escape on their own. Pushing as hard as they could, the wood began to slightly crack.

"That's it, keep pushing." urged Edryss on.

"Stop!" yelled Glut, acting as a look out, "That large creature is walking back."

Edryss and Andi stopped pushing and got on their knees to peer through cracks. Glut was correct, the decayed and deformed human/demon was approaching. The three moved against the wall behind them as if it would protect them. The crate lid sprung open, Edryss leaped up ready to attack, but the demon was ready for an attempt to escape and swung his left arm, striking Edryss across the face with such force that she fell to the ground. Glut just barely caught her head in time.

"YOU!" ordered the demon, grabbing Andi by the front of her shirt and jacket, easily lifting her out of the crate and quickly shutting it.

Andi fought to free herself but was unable to break the creature's grasp, "Let me go! LET ME GO!"

The creature did not listen and dragged Andi away. He brought her near the ruined temple, the blood stone was within sight. He grabbed her by the hair and lifted her onto a table. Andi hollered in pain. The creature turned and left her on the table. Andi was confused, she wasn't strapped or tied, she was simply on the table. She watched the demon that brought her walk away. She noticed to her left was a gate wide open, *a chance to escape*! Andi leaped off the table and headed for the opening. Her eyes caught something that stopped her dead in her tracks, it was her father's travelling bag. There was no choice for Andi, she had to have that bag. She ran straight for it, not caring if there were other demons around. Her heart leapt out of chest as if she had actually discovered her father, she reached for the bag and began to open it. A rush of memories and emotions overtook her. Inside she found clothing that once belonged to her parents, items like her father's pipe and comb, and to her astonishment, another journal. Andi began to go through the pages, it was a log of everything he had done since leaving the Citadel.

Andi began to read the last few pages through tears of joy and anxiety.

Today, the four hundred and twenty third day of our journey, has ended in failure. My fears are coming true. I have come to the dreadful realization that Nikolas has been correct the entire time and it breaks my heart. This entire endeavor has been a fool's errand and I have spent my time unwisely away from my darling girl. I cry knowing my sweet, innocent Andi may never be cured of her terrible and frightening ailment. I was so sure, so cocky and confident that I could save her. I fear I have sold my soul to save my daughter in vain, these people from beyond the shard that we encountered were so promising, but I fear I may have let the fox into the hen house, that they aren't what they claim to be. How many lives will be lost because of my selfish need to save my daughter?

Andi almost dropped the journal. She was crying and did not fully understand what she was reading. *What did you do, Dad? What aliment is he talking about? What lives are going to be lost?*

"It's difficult isn't it, to see a loved one through another lens. That they are not the infallible people we dreamed them to be." Andi gazed behind her and gasped, it was another human demon hybrid. This one's body had decayed greatly, but its face was more intact. "That they are like you, only human."

Andi took several steps back.

"I am Adaran," spoke the demon trying to smile, "I worked with your father, and I hope to work with you as well."

Andi held her father's journal tightly, "Liar! My father would never, how did you get my father's stuff!? TELL ME!" demanded Andi.

"I promise you, daughter of Giatros Kimball, I will never lie to you. The dark one, lady of the celestial light, found your parents in the forest alone, being stalked by an elemental that they failed to trap. She used her power to save them. When your parents saw how great her power truly was, they fell to their knees in adoration, thanking their deliverer for saving them." said the demon almost happily, "What a fortuitous occasion it was, our master sensed their blood and saw divinity. You have been foretold, a chosen vessel. "

"Divinity? What are you talking about?" Andi yelled annoyed, "I do not believe you!"

"You must because it is true. Your father spoke of you, spoke of your ailment and was quick to ask for help thinking they could use my mistress' power to save you. She gladly offered an exchange, your father, so determined to save you offered to do anything. "

"Nooo!" yelled Andi, "My father would never work for demons."

"Of course not, our master is not some hideous beast, she is the everlasting beauty of the celestial plane. She told your parents they were here to save the shard. Your parents worked with our human cultists and myself, greatly covered up of course. We worked with your parents for months. "

"I don't believe it!"

The demon laughed, "My dear, why should I lie when I have proof." He pulled a pendant out of his flesh. Andi began to cry, it was part of her father's pendant, an anvil broken in half.

Andi's world was falling apart, and she dashed to the side trying to get away. The demon twisted his wrist, causing Andi to grab at her neck. Her pendant was pulling her back, the chain was choking her. Unclasping her necklace, the pendant flew into the demon's hands. Andi fell to her knees breathing heavily. The shadow of the demon overtook her. She tried to get up and run, but her legs betrayed her, she fell to the ground. The world around began to fade, and she began to fall asleep. For first time in her life, Andi remembered every time this had happened. She remembered as a kid how scared her father was, she remembered the dark evil laughter that awaited her in her dreams.

When Andi awoke, she was unable to move. She was lying pressed down against a hard, uneven, cold surface. Her head was still groggy, her mind begged to go back to sleep, but she could hear unusual noises and forced her eyes open. The area she was in was right up against the tall, temple ruins. Large glass cylinders stood next to her. Each cylinder filled with green fluid with creatures at different stages of development swimming. Next to the glasses were hideous creatures chained to the stones. They had large bodies with small, oval heads, spider-like flesh legs, and a large, muscular tail that pointed up. The tails were constantly sparking energy out of the ends. The strange creatures were devouring pieces of dead goat. Andi realized there were people in white and red robes on their knees around her chanting and prostrating themselves while others were wheeling in a large machine towards her. Adaran appeared over her head looking down.

"As I suspected, you awoke the moment I placed your pendant on your chest." He spoke delighted, "The Genesis ore must block the connection. Tell me," Adaran bent down closer to Andi, she could smell his fowl decaying odor, it made her gag. "Do you remember the voice? I know it speaks to you when you're in your slumber, calling to you, beckoning you to allow it in."

"What the Bellows are you talking about?" Lied Andi, she remembered now, she could still hear its laugh.

"You lie as well as your mother. "Adaran walked over to a nearby table and grabbed something, "She never fully trusted me."

"At least one of my parents had some sanity!" said Andi trying to mock the demon.

Adaran easily turned the tables on the young girl, "So, you do believe they were here, that they worked for us. With your father's technomancy skills, we discovered a whole new field of possibilities, something the Ethereal could not have foreseen and countered with their many spells and locks. Your father sped up everything we had planned and gave us new ways to free the Prime."

"Technomancy!? WHAT ARE YOU TALKING ABOUT? The Prime!?"

The demon smiled, "Yes, the true and appropriate master of the universe, a god among gods! The Prime was the glorious leader of the Fallen, the only one strong enough to lead us against the wretched Ethereal." Adaran's voice when he said the word Ethereal was fused with hatred and disdain, "While the Ethereal watched the Maker's creation suffer and die, the Fallen wish to end all suffering, to end— "

Andi mockingly laughed, "How, by killing us all?"

"YES!"

Andi gasped at how matter of fact Adaran was in his comment.

"Life was the Maker's only mistake, such beauty and complexity in his design. Nature perfectly balanced. Laws to the universe like gravity and matter, order in all things. When he created life and that balance, that order was destroyed, and while the infection of life grew like a cancer, the Maker vanished and left us to see all he created wither away and be destroyed by the mortals."

Andi tried to counter his argument, "Why create all this if not for the living? Didn't the first act of creation lead the Maker towards creating the life that you supposedly hate? Are you not, or at least were alive at some point? If life is such an abomination, a plague or cancer, why don't you end your own suffering? Actually, PLEASE, do us all a favor and slice your own throat. If life is meaningless, do us all a favor and kill yourselves first!"

Adaran laughed, "Please child, mind games will not work on me. Shangri created me, forged me out of the essence of life. No, I will not die. When the Prime burns this universe to the ground, I will ascend to the Celestial and be one with Fallen."

Andi stared wide eyed, "You actually believe that? What an idiot you are, they are the bad guys. Bad guys never keep their word. Honestly, read a book! You're only fooling yourself. At least if I burn I'll die knowing you will burn right alongside me!"

"Oh, no, Andi Kimball, you will not burn. Your life will be eternal. You are the one. The one we have sought for so long. You will be the instrument that burns all of creation!"

***

Little is known about Veilwood forest. Scholars consider it ancient, before the Barren Age, it was believed the forest was once a paradise where a great city once stood. The more common belief however, is that the forest is cursed, inhabited by large Naga snakes, Chuul Snappers, and Dryad wood creatures. There are even stories of a territorial elemental creature that lurks through the forest, killing anything that crosses its path. Regardless of the stories, few people would travel through the forest due to its immensely dense, rugged terrain, and the fact that it is a border between the Slavine and Citadel territories.

With these dangers in mind, Thaddeus led his men cautiously off the path and towards the heart of the forest.

"I wish I was on Moose right now!" complained Italicus, annoyed at the constant chopping away of brush. "He would plow right through this crap!"

"And spook at the first bird or squirrel to make a noise!" mocked Thaddeus, cutting his own path.

"Maybe, but that would have been better than slogging through this for the past three hours!" said Italicus annoyed. "How do we know this isn't their whole plan?"

"Their plan?"

"Yeah, that demon bitch, Dumbcrak, and every other demon we've encountered!"

Gladthorn laughed, "So their evil plan was to capture three people, tire us in this forest and do what? Kill us here??"

"Exactly!" said Italicus, unabashedly. "You don't trust that demon head, do you?"

"I'll trust in anything if it means we will find Edryss safe!" stated Gladthorn forcefully.

"That's just stupid. Blind belief will get you killed." advised Italicus, ripping his pant leg on a thick thorn bush.

Thaddeus laughed and pointed at Italicus' face, "Says the man who blindly believes that gold feather will protect him!"

"That's different!" Italicus declared

"How so?" asked Thaddeus.

"Mine is true!"

Thaddeus laughed while Gladthorn chuckled, slightly his mind focused on saving Edryss.

"Mark my words, both of you!" advised Italicus, "If this isn't a trap, then there is something in this forest more vile, more evil than any demon threat."

Thaddeus laughed, "Italicus, do you really think this forest is haunted?"

"You don't?" Italicus halted and glared, "Demons and myths of gods you believe, but a good old-fashioned haunting is too much for you?"

"Italicus' claims of haunting do come with many sources of collaboration." called a voice from behind the three men.

"Balin!" exclaimed Italicus, "Our resident historian! You have got to be going crazy with all these academics we are protecting!"

Balin smiled, a very rare occurrence while the men were on a mission. Balin was short with black hair and a goofy smile. Though he was a decent shot with the Tesla, Balin lacked any other real skill to really call himself an Equinaut. What made Balin special was heart. He would give a stranger his jacket in the height of winter and freeze rather than see someone cold. That was all Thaddeus needed to see before he asked the poor, homeless kid to join his mercenary family.

"Sir, I find most of them to be severally lacking in any knowledge of life before the Citadel was formed," stated Balin, "But that's modern education for you. I think it's just one factor of many that proves the Citadel's culture is dying. Recently—"

"Balin! Heel, boy! Heel!" joked Italicus, "Stay on topic, please! You were saying that I had validation for my concern about the forest?"

Balin pulled back his black, long, wavy hair and smiled, "Yes, sir, over fifty years ago, during the last war with the Slavine, back when we had a King. King Magnus sent an entire battalion of soldiers into Veilwood forest and for an entire year, they vanished."

"See guys? An entire battalion vanished in this forest," mocked Italicus.

"What happened to them?" asked Thaddeus.

"Actually sir, you will probably recognize this name," stated Balin. "King Magnus sent Colonel Wesley Oberon and Royal Mage Alinus into the forest to investigate the disappearance."

"Aye, Colonel Oberon is still to this day one of my biggest heroes!" declared Thaddeus, and he pointed his sword at Italicus. "And don't you dare make a remark!"

Italicus bit his bottom lip and winked.

"What did they find?" asked Gladthorn, intrigued.

"Most of the battalion alive, but scared, all of them very confused. Each soldier reported tales of supernatural creatures." stated Balin.

"See guys, *haunted*!"

Just as the severed head had warned, the forest grew thicker the further Thaddeus and his men marched. Their steady hacking was slowed only when several Naga snakes thought they could stalk the men.

"Thaddeus are we sure on this?" asked Italicus, severing the foot-long head of a particularly large Naga snake. "I'm beginning to feel like this a fool's errand, there isn't anything out here. "

Thaddeus grunted, "We should be getting close."

Another hour went by and still there were no signs of the dense forest thinning. The men stopped, and Thaddeus considered retreat. He didn't feel comfortable leaving the camp short-manned for so long. Gladthorn offered to scout ahead, looking for an easier path.

"One man can move quicker than the lot of us," Gladthorn reasoned. "I'll be back within the hour."

While the men waited, Balin entertained them with facts he had collected about the Slavine and the forest.

"Because of their particular appetite, the Slavine have thousands of untouched acres of fertile land, most of it not being used, wasted…. Just fathom how much food the Citadel could grow if we had access to those lands. There wouldn't be a food shortage." recited Balin.

"Is there really a food shortage?" asked Thaddeus. "You saw all that farmland sitting empty in the Diamin theme, how many people could those fields feed?"

Balin thought about it for a moment. "That's true, but the Steward ordered the Diamin theme vacant forty years ago and it's a travesty that we can't use it. But what I find troubling as well is that just beyond the eastern edge of Veilwood, where the Scather river breaks off into the Scathy, there's rumored to be large tracks of farmland, miles away from any Slavine town. Land the Slavine find to be useless. if it wasn't for the Slavine fort in the forest, people could sneak through and farm that land. To be honest, I don't understand why the Slavine wouldn't let us use that land in exchange for something else like—"

Thaddeus' brow furrowed, and he raised his right hand to quiet Balin, "What Slavine fort in the forest?"

Balin looked at Thaddeus, confused, "The same fort that the battalion encountered fifty years ago. In fact, it was because of that fort and the Slavine soldiers working together that everyone survived the supernatural threats."

"You didn't say anything about a fort," Italicus said darkly. "Where in the forest is it?"

"I'm sorry, I don't know," answered Balin. "The only reference to its location was its proximity to the north path. I assumed you guys already knew about the fort."

Thaddeus and Italicus looked at each other with wide eyes.

"We left Faramal in command. If he encounters that Slavine fort, he wouldn't attack it, would he?" asked Italicus.

"Not with 15 men," reasoned Thaddeus. "But if the Slavine harass them-, who knows?"

"I told you we should have left Gladthorn in command."

Thaddeus looked at Italicus severely, "Zapp will keep an eye on Faramal, but Gladthorn is our best tracker, if the lead doesn't pan out, he is our best chance at finding something. Plus," Thaddeus, wiped the sweat from his forehead, "plus I doubt he would have stayed at the camp while…" Thaddeus raised his eyebrows and shrugged.

"Really, those two?" asked Italicus with a surprised look, "I didn't know that!"

"You didn't know that? Everyone knows it! They try to live by the regulations, and I applaud them for that, but, well, why do you think they left camp unattended in Mystique?"

"Honestly, I did not think that was it. "Italicus faked several tears and sniffed, "My boy Gladthorn, he has grown up so fast! One day in a tavern he is being slapped by a woman, to now he is secretly dating one. I could be proud as a parent."

"Ha," remarked Thaddeus, "well, he obviously didn't learn it from you."

Instead of arguing Italicus shrugged and nodded, "Yeah well, women and I haven't had the best track record recently. That is why I have sworn off women, they're nothing but problems and creation is at stake, right?" Italicus paused and stood in a noble stance, "No, I must do what is right for everyone, not just myself. I pledge to not pursue a woman until this crusade is complete. Women everywhere will be devastated, crying tears of great pain, but in the long run they will thank me for sacrificing."

Thaddeus groaned, "Keep pledging all you want. "

"Mock me, good sir, but it is true. I am done with women." Italicus continued to whack away at the brush creating a path, "Plus, there is no woman out there for me. I can't be contained by just one. If there is a special woman out there just for me, my work is too dangerous. No, in the end I am bad luck for woman, my mother even said so."

"That's because you do it all wrong! Every woman you meet you try to charm and flirt with. "

Italicus beamed, "I am pretty charming, not many can say no to this face!"

Thaddeus rolled his eyes, "You do it because you know they aren't the one for you. You are waiting for the right one to fall right out of the trees for you, waiting for the universe to give you some big signal saying she is the one. Well guess what, it doesn't happen like that. You actually have to get know them to find the one."

"I thought Meg could have been the one, she really got me." Italicus said in a moment of honesty, but the sensation of being vulnerable made Italicus uncomfortable. His defenses came back up, "Hey now, how did this topic get turned on to me, I thought we were talking about Glad and leaving him in command. I just don't trust Faramal to do the right thing if the Slavine show up."

"I thought everything was about you?" joked Thaddeus.

"Har Har." mocked Italicus.

Thaddeus nodded his concern but there wasn't anything he could do about it. "Maker willing, the Slavine are busy doing things other than patrolling a small forest road."

As if on cue, Gladthorn broke into their small clearing through the brush and spoke in a hushed and hurried tone, "We are being followed!"

"Are you sure?" asked Italicus, already throwing out hand signals to the rest of the group to employ stealth tactics. "How did they even know we were on our way?"

"I don't think it's demon." stated Gladthorn, out of breath, "I think it's Slavine!"

Thaddeus looked at Italicus and raised an eyebrow as if to ask whether there could be a Slavine connection to all of this after all? In the end, it didn't matter. Saving Edryss, Glut, and Andi was the most important thing. Slavine, demon, they would all die if they must.

***

Andi's stomach was on fire and the rest of her body recoiled at the pain she was feeling. Adaran's robed followers had brought some sort of device and strapped Andi's stomach to it. The machine sounded like it was steam-powered but it glowed like it was not natural. Large arms and pipes ran from her stomach and into the machine itself. Adaran was watching a gauge and controlling a lever when his eyes rolled to the back of his head.

"Yes, my lady, " answered Adaran, "I am sure she is the one we are looking for, yes."

Andi listened and looked for another demon nearby, but Adaran seemed to be talking to himself.

"Obviously Giatros lied, his child was alive the whole time. I don't know how she could have stayed hidden. Our Citadel operatives must have not have been as thorough as we thought all those years ago. I promise you they and their families will be dealt with. No, her mother was the last of Ambrosius' bloodline and she only had one child."

Arcadia's ghost, they don't know Glut is my brother, thought Andi, knowing now that she had to protect the secret of her brother from Adaran.

"Who are you talking to, creep?" yelled Andi, "AND WHAT ARE YOU DOING TO ME!?"

Adaran ignored Andi and continued to talk to himself.

"Yes," Answered Adaran to the air, "this place is adequate to get what must be done, done. It is an honor you allow me to conduct my experiments in such a hollowed place. It's not as well-equipped as my lab, but I could not take Dumak's insufferable complaining. And I do not trust him near the MORUSTRANCONATRA. No, no need to repeat yourself, great one. I understand that we need him to unlock the final—yes, yes, yes. The machine is working as designed." Adaran's voice trembled, "Forgive me, your greatness, I did not mean to sound so abrasive. Yes, Dumak's knowledge of technomancy has increased greatly since we lost Giatros."

Andi gasped, *what did he mean by lost?* "WHAT HAPPENED TO MY FATHER, stank breath?"

"She is not ready, she still can only hear in her sleep. Years of Genesis ore proximity has dampened the connection her divine genes have. We are siphoning that energy as we speak. Within a few hours she will always be able to hear all that she needs."

Andi did not want to admit it, but she was already feeling a change inside of her. She was, of course, remembering the times she fell asleep as a child. She was also remembering she wasn't alone, that her entire life, she was never actually alone. That a presence had always been there in the back of her mind, she had been unable to hear it, but she had always felt it. It was familiar to her, warm and powerful but also angry and evil. The wall in her mind was collapsing, she could hear its hypnotic song calling out to her. It desired her, above all things.

The feeling of being desired and loved was something Andi had always yearned for. The closest she had of that was her brother, they were inseparable, they were family. Though she lost her parents, she was never going to lose her brother. She thought for a moment that maybe Thaddeus could desire her, but how could anyone want her when a beautiful woman like Leora was around. Andi did not understand why she was feeling the way she was, this was not her. Leora's face blinded her mind and she felt annoyed with her. So pretty, smart, tall, beautiful. Her feelings though quickly became anger, almost hatred towards the woman. Images of her dying popped into Andi's mind and for a tiny moment she felt desire, and it was good.

Shocked by how good she felt, Andi's mind twisted as she fought the images. She did not hate Leora nor did she want her to die. She found Leora annoying, and perhaps she was jealous of her, but she did not want Leora dead. In fact, Leora had never even been rude to her even when she heard Andi's out of line comments. Andi knew these images in her head were not hers, they were being placed there and it scared her. The images inside Andi's head changed dramatically and she saw Thaddeus embracing her, staring into her eyes and kissing only as a lover can. Andi did not fight these images at first, they were pleasing to her and it made her body feel amazing. But the images increased in their lewdness. They were no longer just kissing, Thaddeus was tearing her clothes off and ravishing her in ways she had never been touched before. Despite the overwhelming pleasure her body felt with these images in her head, she fought back. She desired Thaddeus, but not like that. She wanted more than the physical from him.

Andi tried, but she could not fight the images. The emotions and power running through her body increased, rising in intensity until she couldn't take it anymore. It was frightening and the most pleasure she had ever felt. Her body shivered and shook, and she cried out for it to stop.

Andi was at the point of collapsing, she was at the peak of the rush, any higher or stronger and she would probably be rendered unconscious. Suddenly, without warning or signal, it stopped. The images ceased and so did the feelings inside her body. Andi felt empty, alone, lost, but most of all, violated. If she had been able to, she would have brought her legs up to her chest and cried into her knees. *What is happening to me? Why is it happening?*

Adaran laughed and smiled, "I see you are moving along faster than I had anticipated, you are seeing the perks of this connection. It can give you amazing power and pleasure beyond mortal comprehension, but it can also bring you pain and suffering. Embrace the connection, allow it to become part of you."

Andi was crying, but she managed to force out, "Never!" through her lips, "I will never give in to it."

Adaran was not impressed, "Brave words, but without this," He grabbed and held Andi's pendant, "there is nothing you can do to hinder the connection."

As soon as her pendant left her body, she felt the darkness over take her, struggling to keep her eyes open. She tried to focus on the pain the machine was causing her stomach, but she could not fight it. Moments later she fell into the abyss.

***

For over an hour, I have stalked my prey. The deeper they struggle through the forest, the more determined I feel to follow. My enemies are shrewd, but I am far more astute. That they are up to something, something horrible and evil, I am certain. I am unconcerned with their motives and plans. Now I have their scent, their deaths are inevitable.

I will not be detected. I have rules that protect me. Always know where your prey is located, stay down wind, don't make a sound, even a heavy breath can give away your position. Dexterity, strength, cunning, all are needed if you are to survive the onslaught this world provides. Instinct is key to the hunt, without it you are dead. My instincts have been honed to perfection, years of practice, years of training. I have been forged by the hammer and re-forged by the anvil. Heated in fire and set in water, I emerged stronger. Reborn into a hunter, a soldier, a killer.

Prey. it's always about prey, for as long as I can remember. Each hunt unique, men never stood a chance. Peering down through leaves and shadow, I see him. He is slow, he is clumsy, he is dead, and he doesn't know it. It is beautiful and dismal, the fragility of life. Because I live in deference to the sanctity of death, I can gift finis to others.

***

At Italicus' suggestion, the Equinauts broke into smaller groups. If they were being hunted, whether by Slavine or demon, it would be easier to evade them in smaller groups, and easier to fight in close quarters if they weren't tripping over one another. The landscape became far more rugged than they had anticipated, but the tree line was now thinning, and patches of sunlight came down through the trees.

Italicus smiled as he crept through the thick brush, his senses on high alert. He had always preferred hunting on his own rather than as a team. For most of his life he had been on his own. Before becoming an honorable defender of the innocent, before becoming an Equinaut, he would probably have been called a scoundrel. He met Thaddeus in a tavern shortly after Alana's passing. Thaddeus was in rough shape, but it was a pivotal moment in both their lives. Thaddeus had pissed off some of the locals, the ones that couldn't hold their temper after a mug or two, and they never really stood a chance against Thaddeus. Except that Thaddeus was totally drunk, barely able to stand. If not for the timely arrival of a certain scoundrel, whose life had just fallen apart as well, Thaddeus probably would have been stabbed in the back by the pointy end of a broken bottle. Why save the life of a man who you don't even know? That's tough. Perhaps the Maker played a part, or perhaps two men at the same place in life found each other when it was needed by both. Thaddeus offered him a spot with the Equinauts soon after his tavern rescue, and the rest, of course, is history.

The sun had fully broken free and was illuminating most of the ground now. Italicus, feeling sneaky, slowly worked his way along the remaining shadow. If he hadn't stopped suddenly to scan the crepuscular rays, he wouldn't have noticed the slight wind pass behind his back. Something had jumped from a branch above his head. His response was swift. He pulled out a readied dagger, spun and knelt, thrusting the blade straight out, hoping to stab the would-be-trapper's legs. Italicus was taken aback. He was staring at the very long, very slender thigh of a pale, smooth skinned woman. As he followed her form up, he realized that this woman was stunning, her long hair blonde and her large eyes pale gray. *Perfection*, he thought.

"Why, hello." Italicus said, smoothly, "What's a lady like you, with such amazing skin, doing in a creature-infested forest like this?"

The sound of rope tightening forced Italicus to tense, but he found his eyes unable to look away from the woman's face. He tried to convince himself that he wasn't mildly excited that she could defend herself, that she would be just as beautiful had she not had an arrow drawn and pulled, ready to be fired into his head.

The woman's face remained stony, her eyes were cold and still, determination was painted across her face. Italicus had seen that look before on a certain man in the Equinauts, the kind of look that comes from years of training and experience, the look you bear when you know that you are the best at what you do.

"Drop it." she ordered. Italicus opened his hands, and the dagger fell near his foot, within reach. "Good. Why are you here? Are you working with the creatures?"

"Listen honey, I know the angle you're seeing me at isn't my best, but do you really think a handsome devil like me would be working for hideous beings like those?"

"Handsome devil?" replied the woman.

Italicus shook his head, annoyed at himself, "Uh, poor word choice."

The woman's eyes narrowed, "You do know the creatures."

"I know *of* them, yes!" Italicus could tell that the woman did not completely believe him, she was deciding whether to let go of the arrow and end the conversation. "Allow me to introduce myself, I am Italicus, second in command for the Equinauts, perhaps you have heard of us?" asked Italicus with as much charm as he could muster.

Her demeanor changed instantly, and when she smirked, Italicus thought for a moment he was safe. "I have heard of you, there's a pretty big bounty on your head," Italicus could hear the bend of the wood as she pulled her bow even tighter, "and the reward doesn't specify dead or alive!"

Italicus blinked and smiled broadly, "Well, I hate to make that pretty little face of yours frown, but you're not taking me in, sweetheart."

"Strong words for a man who has an arrow pointed at him from arm's length away. *Sweetheart.*"

"My dear, if you truly have heard of me, you know that arrow will never make its mark."

Without waiting for her to respond, Italicus swung his left hand forward, knocking the woman's bow away while grabbing his blade from the ground with his right. He swung, and sliced at the taught bowstring, leaving it hanging loose and useless. He then spun on one knee and hooked with his other leg, knocking the woman off balance. He leapt at her, pinning her arms and legs down against the ground.

"Normally I get a woman's name before I get on top, but for the ones trying to kill me, I make exceptions." mocked Italicus, looking triumphant.

"You idiot," said the woman through clenched teeth, and then she spat at Italicus. "Don't insult me with your bravado., just kill me!"

"Obviously, you haven't heard of me or the Equinauts, we will defend ourselves, but we're not killers! Now you are going to tell me, why are the Slavine near a demon camp? Are you in cohorts with those creatures?"

"What makes you think I am Slavine?" asked the woman, offended.

Italicus looked pointedly at her left arm, "Don't lie to me! That is a Slavine wristband made specifically for their human slaves!"

"I am no one's slave!" yelled the woman, her voice dripping in hate. The woman went limp and looked at something behind Italicus.

A sudden pain on the back of Italicus head sent him into a dizzy spiral.

"Tie him to the tree, I have questions for him!"

Italicus was dazed, he could feel some movement around him and rope being pulled around his waist and shoulders, but the stars in his head kept him too busy to care or fight back. Italicus tried to open his eyes, but the sun was too bright. He closed his eyes. The stars in his head were slowing, but he still felt woozy.

The heat from the direct sunlight was uncomfortable on Italicus' face. The burning sensation stopped and Italicus was shaded by a hulking mass. He didn't have to open his eyes, he knew from the smell what he would see. About 8 inches from his face was a giant head, a head that was connected to a giant body that was bent over, so that the giant head could be level with Italicus' face. The Slavine brute stooped and starred with his strong, reptilian, yellow eyes. His face was long and wide, his jaw was thinner than what you might expect from such a large creature. The scales on the creature's apish face pushed Italicus to feel that the man in front of him was more reptile than it was person. Slavine skulls were heavily plated on their foreheads for hunting and had three distinct horns that curved out at the base of the neck in, which then curved skyward at their tips. If a foe got too close to a Slavine's back, he could thrust his head down, and impale the man behind him with these horns. Slavine were known for their large built bodies, their strength was that of two or three men, and once their minds were made up, they will move heaven and earth to see their will done.

"He is awake!" called the Slavine, in a deep low voice.

"Thank you, Kojhot" said the woman, putting her hand on his shoulder. Kojhot seemed to be both appalled and soothed by her touch. Italicus was impressed, he had never seen a human command a Slavine brute before, save for the Lord Chamberlain.

"You have them trained well, you'll have to teach me your secret!" taunted Italicus.

The Slavine lifted his hand to Italicus' throat.

"Kojhot! No! Not yet!" insisted the woman. She approached Italicus and bent down to whisper into his ear, "I can make this really easy and enjoyable for you, or I can make it rough." Her nose grazed Italicus' ear. "It's your choice." she said seductively, rising back up and smoothing out her leather armor, "Though I hope you choose the later."

Italicus licked his lips slowly, "Lucky enough for you, I do like it rough."

The woman nodded to Kojhot. Koj smiled and punched Italicus in the face, the back of his head slamming against the tree. He shook his head to rid himself of the returning stars. The woman sighed, "You can answer my questions candidly, or you can die from severe head trauma."

"I'll tell you what. You ask me a question, I'll answer, but then, you have to answer a question of mine." offered Italicus.

"Fine, I'll go first."

Kojhot looked at her incredulously, "You can't really mean that!"

"I do. You will remember your place!" She pulled Kojhot's face to hers, and said more quietly, "I will get honest answers quickly, and then you will kill him. Our answers won't leave this tree."

She looked down at Italicus and demanded, "Why are you here, Equinaut? Did the Citadel send you?"

Italicus' smile became conniving, "That's two questions. We were not sent from the Citadel. We're simply looking to retrieve our friends, they were taken by the demons." Italicus tried to gauge the woman's reaction, but it was difficult. Her face betrayed little emotion. "My turn why are you here?"

The woman eyed Kojhot calculatingly, "We heard rumor a Slavine's human had been captured by the demons. We were sent to investigate, but it was untrue. She was not a Slavine's human."

"A Slavine's human? Oh, a slave, gotcha. When someone is owned by someone else, they're called slaves, just so you know. So, wait, because she wasn't a slave, you left her there? That's cold, even for the Slavine!"

The woman faced Italicus blankly, "aA least the Slavine sent us to look, can't say that for the Citadel!"

Italicus was confused by that last remark, but he definitely heard the disdain in her voice.

"How many demons are in Veilwood forest?"

Italicus looked at her confused, and tried shrug and raise his shoulders, "I don't have the slightest clue, lady! I just told you we have nothing to do with the demons."

Italicus' captor nodded to her brute subordinate who didn't hesitate to punch Italicus directly in the nose. "You will tell me what I want to know."

Italicus grunted from the pain and shook his head several times, "I am trying to tell you toots, I- Have-No-Clue!"

"I know you know more than what you are telling me!" yelled the blonde woman furiously.

She pressed the tip of an arrow head against Italicus' neck.

Italicus pressed his head back against the tree he was tied to, the arrow was beginning to pierce his skin. "No, I get another question. you asked me two in the beginning, remember?" yelled Italicus like he would to a subordinate.

The woman sighed and brought the arrow down away from his neck, "Very well. Speak quickly."

Italicus smiled, "What is your name?"

Kojhot sighed impatiently, and offered Ishsta his bow, "I have tolerated this behavior long enough. Kill him now. if you don't, I will. It's rude to play with your food."

The woman placed the arrow in her hand onto Kojhot's bow. Italicus stared into her eyes, unwilling to break his gaze. if she was going to kill him, he could at least force her to watch his life drain.

"My name is Ishsta, Ishsta Leohanstar."

Her voice changed, it was soft and gentle. Her eyes softened. A final kindness, Italicus thought. He could hear the bow's string being pulled taut. *At least she's going for a clean kill, though a sword across the neck would probably be quicker, less painful. If she doesn't hit the right spot, this could get really touchy and prolonged.* Italicus willed his mind to quiet. During the slight hesitation on Ishsta's part, a humming sound wisped by his right ear, then another, followed by a third. Italicus saw the surprise and then pain in Ishsta's eyes as she fell backwards.

"It's about damn time you got here!" remarked Italicus, extremely annoyed. "The plan was to walk into the trap, then trap the trappers, not walk into the trap and then let Italicus get pummeled by the giant Slavine!" The ropes around him loosened and fell to the ground. Gladthorn emerged from behind the tree, his Tesla rifle trained on Ishsta and her companions, "What the hell, guys?"

"Gladthorn was there the whole time, close enough to activate his shield if the archer had let go of her arrow." assured Thaddeus, stepping into the clearing with his rifle drawn, "Weapons. Give them to him."

"Still, why did you wait so long?" asked Italicus, gathering the bows and swords of Ishsta and the Slavine.

"I wanted to see what you would ask her." Thaddeus paused, and scoffed, "'What's your name?' Such a romantic. Plus, how often does the Maker allow a woman to fall from the trees for you."

Italicus held in a smile, he had not thought about Ishsta leaping out of the trees like that. He pulled out a handkerchief and pressed it against his nose, "Yeah, well, shut up. You'd better hope this doesn't leave a scar!"

Thaddeus laughed, "Men have scars. While you were flirting with your girlfriend, Sulla spotted the camp and made visual on our people, they're alive."

"That's good news. What will we do with them?" asked Italicus.

"I am not sure. Gladthorn, any idea who she is?"

"That's Ishsta Leohanstar, one of the best rangers the Slavine have!" The respect was apparent in Gladthorn's voice.

"Ah, damn. Well, we can't take her with us. Tie them up." ordered Thaddeus. "By the time they free themselves, we'll be long gone."

Ishsta glared up at Thaddeus, "You, you are letting us go?"

Thaddeus nodded "Yes, put your hands together behind your back. If you try anything, we will shoot you. Otherwise, we mean you no harm."

"You are unlike the description given to us." Ishsta remained suspicious.

"Do not make me regret this. We will rescue our people, and then leave this forest. I expect we won't see you again." Thaddeus tightened the knot around her hands.

"You're taking our weapons?" grunted Kojhot.

"After what your government and the Citadel have done to us, I can't much trust anyone on either of their service!" Thaddeus sighed, wrapping rope around the wrist of the unnamed Slavine.

Italicus knelt down in front of Ishsta, whose jaw tightened "What do you want?" He pulled a small brown bottle from his pocket and with it wet a clean handkerchief.

"How many of those do you have?" Ishsta asked.

"Enough," Italicus jested. He attempted to press it up against her wound, but she pulled away. "It's ok. it's just a numbing agent with some aloe for the burn."

Ishsta stiffened but allowed Italicus to apply the salve. Instantaneously the pain lessened. While Italicus inspected her wound, Ishsta stared at the lines on his face. Deep furrows around his mouth and eyes, he laughs often. Lines etched across his forehead, he knows pain too. When Italicus glanced up, he saw her staring, and quickly her face returned to icy disinterest

"I just want you to know, no hard feelings. I know you didn't want to kill me."

Ishsta simply starred over Italicus' shoulder.

"Italicus, we've work to do," called Thaddeus, who had already pushed into the forest.

"You can fall out of a tree for me anytime you want!" Italicus tucked the handkerchief into her sleeve and leaned into Ishsta's hair, "Keep it, something to remember me by." Italicus set her useless bow on the ground, turned, and marched dutifully into the forest.

***

The small meadow where the demon camp was located was probably at one time an amazing and beautiful place. It was no wonder that the Progenitors would have built such a temple in this spot. What beauty there may have been was gone, the entire area was dead and decaying. The tall, dense grass which ringed around the clearing had turned brown and straw-like. Death hung about the camp like a cloud, fauna was absent, and the flora showed signs of decay. A putrid smell filled the air, like that of a rotting animal carcass. Shrieking howls echoed through the surrounding forest.

The most intimidating aspect of the camp was not the large ruins of the forgotten temple, but was the wall around the camp. It was putrid and wretched, a combination of bones and flesh. How they managed to build such a monstrosity was beyond comprehension.

Gladthorn returned, his expression was grim, his face and jacket were covered in mud and sludge. He threw the severed head of a demon onto the ground and smashed it with his boot, "He saw me and ran, didn't get far."

"How bad is it?" asked Thaddeus.

Gladthorn kicked the remnants of the head further into the woods, several Equinauts had to dodge it. Gladthorn was in an angry rage, "It's heavily fortified, Italicus would get a date with one of the demons before we could crack open those gates."

"Whoa, hey now. "Italicus defended himself and pointed at the walls of the camp, "I think I could do a little bit better than that."

"Were you able to see inside at all?" asked Thaddeus

Gladthorn nodded, "I saw at least eight shrieks, half a dozen or so shadows, three big, intimidating demon/human hybrids and several other creatures we have never encountered."

"Did you see our people?" asked Thaddeus.

"Yes, Andi is strapped to a large rock at the foot of the temple. I didn't see Glut or Edryss. "

"Were there any other prisoners?" asked Italicus.

Gladthorn nodded, "There was a small crate south of the center. One of the larger demons was terrorizing whoever was in it. I could hear a woman crying out from it, but it wasn't Edryss."

Thaddeus looked at Italicus, surprised.

"Ishsta mentioned the demons had another prisoner." clarified Italicus, "We can't leave her here to rot."

Thaddeus agreed, "Our people come first, but of course, we will try to free whomever is in that crate. Did you see any sign of this demonic woman of darkness?"

Gladthorn shook his head and spoke with anger, "No."

"Don't worry," assured Thaddeus, "Edryss is alive and we will find her."

Gladthorn's composure almost broke down but he managed to hold a stoic stare and nodded.

"Well guys, if we are getting in, they have to open the doors. We are going to need a pretty good plan." insisted Italicus.

Thaddeus smiled, "Well I have one, but were going to need some bait." Thaddeus smiled at Italicus, "How fast can you run?"

Italicus held up his hands, "Oh no, I am not being bait again, it's not my turn."

Italicus and Thaddeus both looked at Gladthorn, "Don't look at me, I am not fast and there is nothing getting in the way of me being the first to Edryss."

"An impasse, I see" joked Italicus, "Alright gents, odds on the poke, go!"

Thaddeus took a large breath as he snuck up to the flesh walls of the demon camp. *What are the odds that I would lose both games of odds on the poke*, grumbled Thaddeus in his head? *That is the last time I go against Italicus!* He looked back towards the woods, Italicus and Gladthorn watching him with their rifles at the ready. Italicus waved and gave a thumb up while Gladthorn was wearing his serious, unmoving face.

Thaddeus approached the camp's western gate, armed heavily. He was surprised at how close he got to the wall before being noticed. The cracking of a fallen tree branch beneath his feet alerted a shriek, who screamed, warning the camp of the nearby intruder.

Thaddeus shot several blasts from his rifle then bent slightly over, and patted himself on his own arse, yelling "COME AND GET SOME, UGLIES! PRIME BEEF RIGHT HERE!"

The shriek took the bait, the demon gate swung open and the shriek charged Thaddeus. Standing completely still, Thaddeus waited for the shriek to nearly reach him before activating his sword. He waited just for the right moment when the shriek raised its own sword to slash at him. Striking down, Thaddeus severed the shrieks arm, making the shriek wail in pain. Thaddeus kicked out with his right leg and knocked the creature to the ground. He began yelling insults at the fallen shriek and kicked it several times. The creature continued to cry out for help. A half dozen or more shrieks and several shadows emerged from the camp gate and charged towards their fallen comrade.

Thaddeus did not wait or hesitate this time, he ran as fast as he could from the coming demon horde.

Despite his head start, Thaddeus could see the shadows and shrieks beginning to darken the ground before of him, they were getting closer. Thaddeus unburdened himself of his tesla pack, lowered his head, and tried to put in a little bit more speed. He had to make it to the two giant rocks ahead of him.

As soon as he was close enough, Thaddeus dove between the boulders, and letting out a string of curses as he tumbled forward. The shrieks slowed and approached him on the ground. The lead shriek drew its sword and to Thaddeus' surprise handed it to the one-armed shriek, allowing it to claim its prize. A hum started up behind them, the shrieks wheeled about to see a line of Equinauts standing with their shields activated. Before they could react, more Equinauts appeared from the tops of the boulders in formation, charging them from either side, Plaz swords glowing and swinging.

Italicus helped Thaddeus up.

"Hell, of a run!" said Thaddeus, out of breath.

"Yeah, how's it feel, being the bait?"

"Keeping track, are we?" bantered Thaddeus, clasping his knees and looking up.

"All I have to say is Portus Novanum," chuckled Italicus.

"Am I ever going to live that down? I didn't know the girl had a twin!" remarked Thaddeus, rolling his eyes.

Shrouded in rotting, black cloaks, Thaddeus, Italicus, and Gladthorn entered the camp undetected and made quick and quiet work of several shadow creatures who found themselves too close to the flesh wall. So far, the severed head had given them accurate information. Stabbing through a shadow with a plaz sword will force it into its physical state. From there, you can kill them with a quick, second swing before they phase back out.

The three broke off, Thaddeus headed for Andi. Italicus insisted to go after the woman in the crate, while Gladthorn was determined to find Edryss and Glut. Sneaking around the camp was not easy, several shrieks hovered by Gladthorn, making an unnatural sound like they were acknowledging their fellow shriek. When Gladthorn did not make the noise, they stopped until Glad did his best impression of the noise himself. The gargled squeak must have been enough because the shrieks went about their business.

The hood on the shroud was terribly cumbersome and the smell was rank, Gladthorn could barely see out of it. He had made two full laps around the perimeter of the camp and still had no clue where Edryss and Glut were. Thaddeus and Italicus were already in place, they were waiting on him to give the signal. Gladthorn was getting angrier and more scared by the second, he desperately needed to find Edryss. Emotionally to the point of an actual panic attack, Gladthon pulled back the troublesome hood.

His face was riddle in pain and covered in worrisome tears.

"GLADTHORN!?" called out a voice, seemingly out of nowhere, but right next to him.

Gladthorn leapt into the air making a loud high-pitched squeal similar to the one he had given to the shrieks earlier on. The next sound he heard was nectar to his ears, Edryss laughing. "Some brave soldier you are, scaring that easily."

Gladthorn spun and saw two perfect eyes peeking through a crack in a crate and ran to it. "Girl, you did not see that ok." He began to fidget with the lock, "That never happened!"

"Oh, it happened, my good sir!" Spoke Edryss in delight to see Gladthorn again, "And I am telling that story to everyone at our wedding."

"Ha, ha, funny, telling them at our— "Gladthorn dropped the lock and bent down so his eyes were level with hers, "Did you just say our wedding? Are you saying yes?"

"Of course, I am!"

Gladthorn's smile was larger and brighter than ever before in his entire life. "We can have it in the village where you grew up, so you father can be there. I'll hire four white horses and the best carriage we can find. There will be doves flying, a full band, and I am sure Thaddeus will want to do an Equinaut gun salut— "

"Umm, can we plan this wedding of yours once we are free?" interrupted Glut, "I still have to find my sister."

Gladthorn's cheeks turned red, he hadn't noticed Glut's eyes peering through next to Edryss. He nodded, "Don't worry, Thaddeus is already with her. They are waiting for my signal."

Gladthorn melted the lock with the blade of his Plaz sword and handed Edryss the hilt of the extra sword he brought. "Stay with Glut, once you see my, signal run for it. Right out of the camp. There are several large boulders piled together, got there. Don't wait up, ok? We will be right behind you."

Edyrss grabbed Gladthorn and kissed him. "I'll see you when this is done."

Gladthorn slyly made his way towards one of the human looking demons. He was nearly upon the demon. His sword was ready to pierce its spine. Gladthorn was completely noiseless in his approach, but the creature possessed either a sixth sense or perhaps just had good luck. As Gladthorn raised his plaz it spun on him and snarled, unsheathing an obsidian looking blade. The creature yelled in two distinct tones and faced Gladthorn, it struck and parried with swiftness and ease.

Chaos in the camp ignited the moment the creature cried out.

Thaddeus had been waiting next to Andi for several minutes now, she was lying on the rock unconscious. Thaddeus was worried for her, the machine she was connected to looked painful. He was also appalled by the unnatural creatures in the glass jars and the apparatuses around him. What unholy activities happened here?

Once Gladthorn had engaged the enemy, Thaddeus dropped the costume and sliced Andi's bonds. She was still unconscious and did not react at all to her bonds being free. Thaddeus swung his sword and destroyed the machine's arms and began to tear it off her stomach. He pulled a large needle that kept coming out, he was shocked at how long it was. Andi still wasn't moving, he looked around frantically for her pendant, but he could not find it. He reached into his jacket and placed his medallion around her neck. Andi's eyes immediately began to blink.

"What's happening?" asked Andi.

Thaddeus helped her sit up, "It's a rescue, where is your pendant?"

Andi looked around, her head still slightly fuzzy, until she remembered, "Adaran has it around his neck."

"Who?"

"A human like demon, decayed flesh and stuff." answered Andi trying to find words.

"Well, use my medallion for now, we will find him and kill him." insisted Thaddeus trying to rush her off the rock.

Andi followed Thaddeus until she remembered and turned back.

"What are you doing?" asked Thaddeus in surprise.

"I have to find it, it was on this table." answered Andi, throwing things off of the table where Adaran had placed her father's journal.

Two shadows saw Thaddeus and charged him. Activating his tesla pack, the new armor he had put on came to life, his gloves, arms, and greaves shining a glowing blue aura. As the shadows charged him, he punched out with his left arm and kicked out with his right leg at the shadows. The moment the armor came into contact with the shadows, they phased back into physical form. Thaddeus leapt in the air and swung with his sword, slicing both shadows in half. "Andi, we need to go, now!"

"No, I have to find it. "Andi yelled, she threw everything off the table in frustration, but it wasn't there. She spun around and began canvasing the area.

Thaddeus could see Gladthorn was in trouble with the larger demon, "Andi, now! We must go!"

Andi was about to yell when she saw her dad's travel bag on the ground, his journal, and half his pendant on a nearby crate. She ran to them, "I got it!"

Thaddeus grabbed Andi by the arm. He didn't care if she dropped whatever she was looking for, they had to go. He rushed her to the gate and told her to run to wait by the large boulders. Thaddeus rushed to his master scout. The humanoid demon was relentless in its attacks against Gladthorn. Thaddeus tried to relieve him, but they quickly realized the demon/human hybrid could comfortably fight two opponents at once. The demon's skin was oozing pus where Gladthorn's sword had struck him, his nose was thin and severed, and his eyes were solid red, the color of blood. What little hair it had was matted, thin, and unkempt. Thaddeus threw his shield up at the demon, smashing the creature in its face. Gladthorn tried to plunge his sword while it was preoccupied, but the substantial demon spun, knocking both men to the ground.

"Italicus!" yelled Thaddeus, regaining his balance and shielding the still down Gladthorn. Italicus pulled out a small horn and blew, signaling the rest of the men to enter the camp.

Gladthorn was beyond frustrated, "How are we going to kill this thing?"

Thaddeus swung his sword, it missed, "Alley oop!" he yelled as he dodged a swing from the creature.

Gladthorn almost lost his breath, "Are you serious?" he asked, bending to miss a side swipe from the demon's sword. The demon turned its wrist quickly and used the pommel of its blade to smack Gladthorn in the face. The force sent him flying backwards.

"Yes! Now!" yelled Thaddeus, managing to slam his shield in the creature's face once again. Gladthorn shook his head and said a small prayer. He rushed to put space between himself and the fight, then turned and ran back towards it. Thaddeus crouched down as low as he could and waited. The moment Gladthorn's foot made contact with his commander's back, he sprung up to his full height. Gladthorn flew into the air with a massive amount of speed and force. Crouching in the air, Gladthorn's whole body spun like a circular saw. Leaving a faint afterglow of his orange sword. The creature was completely unprepared for the man's insane acrobatics. The demon fell to the ground, its skull in pieces.

As the Equinaut reinforcements rushed into the camp, the demons slowly fell to ground, dead. Not a shriek remained, and the shadow creatures were nearly all dead as well. Only one other human/demon hybrid was found in the camp and like its brother, it was becoming a hassle to kill. The creature was getting angry and nearly killed an Equinaut who had gotten too close. Keeping their distance, the Equinauts fired their tesla at the creature. The energy discharges were clearly having a small effect. The creature screamed in anger and pain as it absorbed more blasts, its flesh was burning and pus spewing from its wounds. The creature was nearly dead, but before it took its last breath, it spoke in a two-toned voice., a melodic chant that it repeated over and over again.

The aura of the demon camp suddenly changed, a deep chill ran down every Equinaut's spine as nature itself became angry. The men could feel the static electricity build up on their clothes, the wind started to blow, and the sky became blanketed with shades of gray. Thaddeus looked around for the source of the phenomena. He could not tell where it was coming from, all he could see was his men clasping their ears as a high pitch hum filled the air. This harsh sound was clearly descending from the sky. The intensity increased, it grew louder and more powerful with each passing second. The men felt the ground vibrate from the reverberation of an ear shattering shock wave and they fell to their knees, hands holding their ears, some crying from the intense pain. They all looked up to the sky for the source of the sound. They were met with the unimaginable. They were met by the intense, unremitting blaze of a fireball.

A single clap of thunder sent even the bravest of Equinauts flat against the dirt in fright. As the men recovered from the jolt, they realized the phenomenon had fallen to the ground inside the camp. For a moment, it seemed like a second sun had arrived. Out of the fiery glow, a figure began to come together. The figure was tall and willowy. It mesmerized everyone as it left the fireball behind, walking with all the grace and assuredness of a phoenix. As she moved closer to the plane of their existence, no one was able to move. She enchanted every man and woman watching. They realized this being was the personification of womanhood. Her beauty was unique and hypnotic. She was the essence of femininity but with all of the power and strength of a deity.

Thaddeus watched in amazement, she was the most hauntingly beautiful woman he had ever seen. As this figure turned towards him, he saw that she was enveloped in celestial auras of gold. Her head was bestrewn with amber feathers intertwined by even more burgundy feathers, whose long cerulean tips blessed the air around her face. Each feather seemed to be dappled with the finest gold dust. These feathers were long and swept back towards a headpiece that sat upon her delicate head. This regal headpiece made of intertwining fine and phalerae metals, extended down in chains which hung against her temples and rested about her long, graceful neck.

As her face cleared, she was beyond captivating, it reminded Thaddeus of satin spar gypsum. Her cheeks favored rose petals in color and texture. Her forehead was adorned with finely spun gossamer lace enhanced by gold filigree. More feathers arose from each shoulder and fell down her long, supple back. Her slender body was covered in a sheath of champagne silk with a decadent design of gold and burgundy throughout. The fabric twisted in a toga about her long frame and fell loosely around her ankles. Though the outfit she wore was celestial, glowing with an aura of delicateness and elegance, a warrior such as Thaddeus could see it was tailored for war. Her smooth feet were wrapped in dainty sandals that entwined gold chains around her firm calves. Thaddeus wondered whether her feet even touched the ground. Her height was so that she looked like she was still in the heavens. She was a goddess amongst them.

"Thaddeus PenRuger, you may approach." allowed the woman, her voice as mellifluous as it was and commanding.

"I am PenRuger!" called Thaddeus, looking up towards this woman who seemed to float in the heavens. He held his sword and shield handsomely.

"Lay down your sword, child, I offer parley, a cease to hostilities during our negotiation."

Negotiations thought Thaddeus surprised to hear her say those words. Thaddeus nodded to his men to stand down, "You have my attention. With whom will I convene?"

The woman looked down her long nose at Thaddeus mockingly, and for a moment he did feel like a child.

"I am, Shangri!"

"You led this demonic assault on our shard?"

"I presently command the horde." Answered Shangri, "With the MORUSTRANCONATRA found, soon our true leader will come forth and take command of his battalion!"

"I am sorry your grace, but I cannot allow that. That Morust- can notta- person you are talking about, well that young woman is under my protection and from what I have heard about your leader, he doesn't really like the living or even creation for that matter. This shard, it's our home. It belongs to us and many others. If you give up this foolish crusade to destroy creation, we may be willing to share parts of our shard with your kind. You must realize and understand that we will not yield its care and bounty to abominations. Though we are weak, we are many. Though we are small, we are smart. We can avoid much suffering by collecting the shard's leaders and caretakers to discuss our future. We are open to discourse, but don't mistake our preference of words to mean we will not act when threatened."

"You speak like a celestial. Your words are elegant and spoken with meaning and determination that is usually not heard from by mortals. But know this, "spoke Shangri, "nothing will stop me from freeing my master or ceasing our assault against creation. We will end all suffering and find the answer we seek."

Thaddeus sighed, "We are not without steel, we will defend our homes and our lives, to the death if we must. But we will not lie down and simply die to fulfill your purposes."

"Your steel, homes, and lives are no concern of mine. I am only here to prepare the deliverance for my master!" Shangri smiled, and the softness of her face drew a harsh juxtaposition with her words. "Through your deaths and the deaths of your kind, we will set in motion a plan which was set thousands of years ago!"

"If that's truly your purpose, why are we alive?" asked Thaddeus, matter of fact. "If you are as powerful and calculating as I fear you are, then there must be a reason you didn't obliterate us the moment you landed here and taken your MORUSTRA- whatever!"

Shangri stared at the man. He was arrogant, but in this, at least, he was correct. Thaddeus refused to break eye contact. He felt small, trying to represent his race and creation, though he knew enough not to let it show. "You want something."

"For one so young, you are perceptive. Because of this, I expect you do realize the futility of your attitude and words. Your kind has no chance standing up to my forces. We have yet to reveal ourselves to this shard. Creatures that would suck the courage from the bravest of knights are waiting on my cue." Shangri's delicate features now seemed sharp.

"You are lying!" accused Thaddeus, "You may have legions of demons at your command, but they can't travel through the mountains, can they? I think you and only a small handful were able to cross the threshold. Otherwise, we would be overrun, and you could take whatever you wanted."

Shangri tipped her hat to Thaddeus by the look of anger on her face, but her face changed instantly once commotion at the west gate pulled her attention. She smiled at the sight of several shrieks gliding into camp. Thaddeus' jaw dropped. "Your efforts are useless and any threat you make is hollow. The lot of you couldn't put down throng of shrieks!"

"State your terms." demanded Thaddeus, "What do you want?"

"It is simple, PenRuger." stated Shangri, who descended to the ground in front of Thaddeus. She was easily seven feet tall towering over him. "Give me the girl, Andi Kimbal. The man you call professor has in his possession several scrolls written by a race that you refer to as Progenitors. I want those scrolls. I want the war wagon you recovered from the Mystique village, with all of its contents, and I want Lorux! Bring these things to me and I will be merciful and allow you all to live. Not for long, but long enough for you to make peace with the Maker and say goodbye to your wives."

Thaddeus considered for a moment, "How do I know you will honor your word?"

"You don't." stated Shangri.

"When my people speak of this war, it will be remembered that first, I asked for peace. But through your own word and actions you are the one who brought us to war." Thaddeus bowed his head, low. From that position, he took up his swords and shield, and shouted, "NOW!"

The shrieks threw off their cloaks, revealing Equinauts with charged tesla rifles aimed at Shangri. A volley of tesla fire was let loose against her. The steady pulses of light did little to harm her, but like bees, they swarmed. Shangri threw her arms up and deflected as many shots as she could.

"ENOUGH!" shrilled Shangri, furious at these mortal's arrogance. Slamming her fist into the ground, a shockwave exploded and threw everyone backwards. In the time it took for everyone to get back to their feet. Shangri had erected a sphere of energy around her.

Thaddeus feared the sphere was similar to the destructive one Dumak had nearly killed him with. "KEEP FIRING, ORDERLY RETREAT!" ordered Thaddeus.

The tesla bolts were easily absorbed by the shield. Shangri began to laugh, seeing herself in an unbeatable position. She patiently watched the mortals slowly make their way towards the opened gate, waiting just for the first one to reach the opening. The ground around the gate abruptly exploded as energy shots fired from out of the sphere. Several Equinauts were sent flying through the air landing hard nearby.

Thaddeus called for a halt and ordered his men to spread out, not to clump together. He had hoped the sphere was a two-way function. Energy can't get in nor get out, but he was wrong. More explosions occurred. Thaddeus watched as Shangri toyed with his men. None of the shots were hitting their targets, she was corralling them together. A large explosion happened near Thaddeus' feet forcing him to cover his face with his arm, but he did not move. He stood his ground. Shangri threw another barrage at Thaddeus, but he still didn't move. He was not going to play whatever game she had in mind.

"HOLD YOUR GROUND MEN!" yelled Thaddeus at the top of his lungs, "SET TESLA PACKS TO BEAM SETTING AND FIRE!"

Thaddeus fired his weapon, moments later every other Equinaut fired as well. Streams of blue and white energy fired at the sphere. The barrier began to vibrate and shake, it was having trouble absorbing so much energy at once, "KEEP FIRING! DON'T CROSS THE BEAMS!"

Shangri growled, howled, and made other noises that were unnatural and completely frightening. She tried to attack the mortals again, but the shield she had formed was to unstable to work properly.

"We are not doing enough damage!" yelled Italicus to Thaddeus.

Thaddeus knew Italicus was right, but he also knew how dangerous it was to run the packs at that level of output, "INCREASE THE ENERGY FLOW! MONITER YOUR GUAGES, DON'T LET YOUR PACKS PEAK!"

The barrage of blue and white beams turned to orange and then to red, and a choir of whistles and alarms began to sing from everyone's backs, some warning that energy cells were low while others warned of impending explosions if they kept firing at this rate and overheating the boiler chambers.

The increase of energy was working, the shield was beginning to crack.

"JUST A LITTLE LONGER!" yelled Thaddeus urging his men on.

"Hey Thad, um, what are we going to do when this shield breaks?" asked Italicus concerned.

Thaddeus' arms, like everyone else's, were vibrating trying to wrangle their riffles in from the extremely intense force flowing out of their barrels. "Be ready to run."

Thaddeus looked for the nearest Equinaut to the Sphere, "MR. AKASH, PHAETON INITIATIVE! NOW GO, GO, GO!"

Akash quickly nodded, understanding the command. He stopped firing and dropped to his knees, taking off his tesla pack. Adjusting several levers and ripping off the restrictor plate, he threw his pack against the sphere and ran like hell.

"KEEP FIRING BUT COVER YOUR EYES, BOYS!" ordered Thaddeus

Italicus tried to keep a straight face, but the idea Thaddeus had chosen was incredibly risky, "That is your plan? That's a really bad plan!"

Thaddeus ignored his friend's comment and continued to fire his beam.

A very loud mechanical sounding alarm wailed over all of the firing, it was a Tesla pack's last warning of an impending build up in the boiler of the pack. The alarm grew louder and more intense, for a brief moment it stopped, and then the pack exploded in a massively large fireball. The energy from the blast rippled through the sphere, causing the entire thing to implode on itself.

Thaddeus peeked early, the light was nearly blinding to him. His mad idea had worked, the professor would have been proud. The force of the sphere imploding focused all of the energy into the center where Shangri was. He didn't wait to see how much damage it did to her, all he knew was she was momentarily lying on the ground.

Thaddeus quickly ordered, "RUN! RUN NOW, TO THE TREE LINE!"

Italicus was already several steps into his dash before Thaddeus had finished his order. Everyone ran as fast as they could for the open gate. They turned to their left and headed straight for the large set of boulders where they had killed the shrieks. Andi, Glut, and Edryss were yelling and urging the Equinauts on.

"Run! Run! To the forest's edge!" yelled Thaddeus frantically, knowing he had just poked a lion in the face.

Andi and Glut made a beeline for the trees, while Edryss waited for Gladthorn to reach the boulders.

A loud and horrific sound emanated from the demon camp like a hurricane had been awakened. Thaddeus feared what was behind them and hoped they could lose Shangri in the dense forest.

Thaddeus ran as fast as he could, following his crew towards the forest's edge. He could see Andi and Glut ahead of him, Edryss and Gladthorn to his right, and Italicus with a black-haired woman who resembled a skeleton over his shoulder. They were almost to the tree line when Thaddeus was beginning to think they were going to be ok. Edryss abruptly lifted off her feet like an invisible force had wrapped itself around her and was pulling her back. Only Gladthorn's grip on her hand kept her from flying off towards the camp. He grabbed her forearm and fell limply to the ground, trying to anchor her with his weight. Thaddeus ran and leapt into the air, wrapping his arms around her torso. Still, she rose. Italicus rushed back from the brush, yelling wildly, motioning behind them.

Akash had just reached the forest's edge when he turned and saw Thaddeus, Italicus, and Gladthorn trying to hold Edryss down. Without hesitating, Akask turned back away from the forest and towards them. "Everyone grab a hold of each other!"

Every Equinaut around Akash followed him. Edryss' body began to rise despite the three's best efforts to hold her down. Akash dashed forward and wrapped his arms around Thaddeus. Another Equinaut grabbed Akash's waist followed by another and another. Nearly ten men, forming a human chain tried to anchor Edryss down.

Slowly Edryss descended, but the invisible force was not ready to go down without a fight. She suddenly shot forward, backwards, left, right, up, and down. it was complete chaos, and everyone struggled to hold on. When that did not break the Equinaut's grip, Edryss began to spin widely to the left. She spun faster and faster until most of the human chain broke and went soaring through the air.

Only four were able to hold on to Edryss, a ball of energy raced towards them. It collided with Edryss in a bright burst of light, and Thaddeus, Italicus, and Akash crashed to the ground. The light enveloped Edryss and part of Gladthorn who refused to let go. It pulled them back towards the demon's camp.

"Let go!" yelled Edryss, tears in her eyes, "Get away from this thing!"

"No! I just got you back! We are getting married remember?" Gladthorn cried out at the top of his lungs, as he tried desperately to dig his feet into the ground. "Give me your other hand!"

"You have to let go or she'll kill us both," pleaded Edryss. "I will not be the cause of your death. Now Gladthorn Deon Jones, LET ME GO!"

Gladthorn's world was crumbling around him, large, painful tears flowing down his cheeks, "You know I won't!" looking straight into her eyes pleading with her not to give up. Edryss could see the conviction in his, but it wasn't enough. She loved him more than she loved herself, she had to keep him safe.

"I'm sorry!" she yelled crying, "I am so sorry! I LOVE YOU!"

Gladthorn knew what she was about to do, and he braced himself for pain. She repeated I love you over and over as she used her free hand and stabbed Gladthorn's wrist with a small dagger from her belt. He clenched down until his hands failed him, and he felt her small hand slip through his massive fingers. Gladthorn fell to the ground, and without his weight, his love flew away from him.

Thaddeus, Italicus, and Akash, rose to see Shangri walking out of the camp, her eyes glowing like molten metal, her white teeth reflecting off the sun. Her dress, armor, and feathers were dirtied from the mud of the camp and flowed without gravity. Edryss flew fast and straight into the open arms of Shangri. Thaddeus had his rifle pulled out, pointed at the banshee.

"Fools!" screamed Shangri, and the trees and ground began to shake, the wind whipped furiously. Her voice was haunting, "I am as a god to you! I offer you life, I offer you your friends' release, and you think you can outsmart me? I was there when the Maker created your universe, I was there when he left it, and I will be there when it is destroyed!"

Gladthorn bolted towards Shangri, pulled his rifle, and fired, hitting Shangri square between her eyes.

"Impressive marksmanship," replied Shangri, flicking her wrist and sending Gladthorn flying backwards into the air.

Edryss cried out, trying to escape. She kicked, clawed, punched, and bit, but Shangri held her easily with one arm

"THIS I SAY TO ALL OF YOU WHO THINK YOU CAN OPPOSE ME. SEE THE RESULT OF YOUR ACTIONS!" Shangri placed her free hand onto Edryss' heart. Shangri's body began to illuminate light and it spiraled around her arm for several seconds. Had the show of light not been from a horrific creature, it could have been beautiful to behold. The energy around Shangri's arm built up, getting brighter and brighter and then suddenly shot straight into Edryss' chest.

Edryss screamed, she could feel the heat and power radiate out of her captor's hands and straight into her body. Edryss felt swelling and melting inside of her, and she used every last bit of strength fighting to stay conscious. The pain flowed through her in waves, from her heart to the tips of every extremity. The pain was unbearable. She could feel the flesh around her chest begin to burn, and then her entire insides began to boil. In those moments, she wished for death. Turning her head, she glimpsed the horrific eyes of Gladthorn staring helplessly at her, praying for a miracle. As loud as Edryss screams had been, it was equally as loud as when they stopped. To everyone's horror, her body went limp, unconscious. Her body convulsed, and her eyes rolled in their sockets. Gladthorn, guided by anger and rage, rushed Shangri, unsure how to stop her, but as Edryss' body burned black. Gladthorn collapsed to the ground in front of her. Shangri threw the smoking corpse at his knees.

Gladthorn moaned and whispered slightly, "Maker, why?" and fell lifeless next to the husk, losing all will to fight. Out of Edryss' body an orb of light exited from her chest. Shangri smiled wickedly and held out her hand, the orb of light danced about her forearm until she placed it into her mouth and swallowed it.

Shangri now smiled sweetly at the two bodies, "Pray to the Maker all you want. He is gone, left, never to return! The only constant in this universe is death!" She then looked at Thaddeus who rushed forward to collect them.

The pain was obvious on his face. The anguish made Shangri giggle maliciously. Thaddeus felt the weight of a broken promise, the promise he made to Edryss' father the day she joined the Equinauts. Thaddeus forced himself forward, broken.

"Do you see, PenRuger? You are like flies to me! You and all your men will face the same fate. I make my offer again. Bring me what I desire, and I will allow you time to say goodbye to your loved ones."

Thaddeus had known grief before, but never had he faced such anger as his anger towards this creature, this abomination that laughs at the thought of exterminating them like pests. His anger towards the threat she posed to his men, anger at the death of Edryss and the pain of Gladthorn, and anger at himself.

She was right. She would kill them all and he would be forced to watch, useless against her power. Thaddeus let out cries of fury as he ran. He knew he stood no chance, but neither did Gideon facing the mammoth, but somehow against all hope he vanquished Dumak, defeating the evil. This was his moment and he prayed and called out to the Maker. "Please, let this be the time I know you are there!" He felt his veins begin to bulge, his blood pumping hard and fast. Inside his chest, he felt warmth like never before. His veins coursed with an energy that could only be described as divine in origin.

In the woods, Andi felt strange. She suddenly realized it was the way she felt when Thaddeus' medallion was healing him. She grabbed the medallion and cried out in pain. She dropped the medallion as it began to glow as bright as Shangri's fireball.

Thaddeus felt strength like never before. He was almost to Gladthorn's position, he felt resolve. His plan suddenly changed, he wasn't going to grab Gladthorn and run, he decided instead to charge and attack Shangri.

He raised his sword. His shield began to hum, and his eyes became like steel. His cries of anguish transformed into a powerful war cry.

Shangri smiled sadistically, she was impressed with the man's bravery and she welcomed the fight, instantly readying herself. Her arms began to glow, and balls of energy formed floating above her palms. She threw them at the man and laughed. Thaddeus passed through them without missing a step. Shangri was puzzled by this and threw more balls of energy, but each and every strike was futile. Thaddeus continued towards her, unaffected.

He was nearly upon her, Shangri could see and feel the change inside of the man. She was struck by the sudden feeling of familiarity and suddenly recognized the aura emanating from her foe. Shangri was at once afraid. Not since the beginning of creation had she felt this type of power.

"What is this!?" Shangri demanded, as Thaddeus collided with her.

Thaddeus attacked. All his rage, all his hate, all his anger, all his hurt boiled within him and he charged like never before. Shangri produced a pure, white sword of energy from her hand, and parried as he pummeled his sword against her, fear frozen across her face. Thaddeus did not relent, striking at her with the force of a god. He added a new attack, throwing her off balance with constant smashes with the boss of his shield, never tiring. In fact, each strike was gaining in strength. As Shangri spat energy at him, he deflected and swung, anticipating her every move. Never in all the battles and wars she had fought in the millenniums of her existence had she met a being with such strength and ferocity. Thaddeus' blood chilling war cry continued, more horrible up close. Gladthorn, slowly gaining consciousness, watched his leader from the ground, fighting the fight he was unable to, and praying to the Maker that Thaddeus would slay this demon.

"How can this be?" screamed Shangri, bewildered, "No mortal should possess such power!"

Lifting her hands towards the sky, Shangri called down energy from the heavens. The clouds and sky began to swirl. The heavens released their celestial energy. It came, flowing over her, forming a massive fireball in one hand. Thaddeus kicked out at her as hard as he could in the chest, sending her flying to the ground, the fireball energy still held in her hand. Thaddeus approached her, uncontrollable rage in his eyes. Shangri panicked, fearing what this mortal was about to do. Throwing out her hand Shangri tried desperately to hit Thaddeus with the celestial energy, a beam of energy so bright and powerful any other man's flesh would have been vaporized being near it. Thaddeus collected the beam with his Gladius, unharmed. He continued to approach.

Thaddeus was upon her, Shangri tried once more to hit him with her celestial energy, but he struck swiftly with his sword, severing Shangri's hand!

Shangri let out a cry that went on for miles. Gladthorn was deafened, but Thaddeus stood, unaffected.

"IMPOSSIBLE!" she screamed, as Thaddeus stepped upon her, pinning her to the ground.

"This is for Edryss!" He raised his sword into the air and lunged it down at Shangri's head.

"NOOOOOO, it will not end this way!" hollered Shangri, and before the sword could reach its target, a sudden explosion of light sent Thaddeus backwards and onto the ground. Thaddeus looked up into the sky, and the rage, heat, and pain seemed to subside. He knew Shangri was gone and for now, everyone was safe.

When Gladthorn got to him, Thaddeus was out cold.

Echo from the Past

The battle for the planet had begun, and the fight for who would be its god was just beginning. Dumak was too slow to dodge the first blast of energy. He sailed through the wall of the temple courtyard and fell dozens of stories down to the ground. The blast was not powerful enough to kill him, we would have to weaken his defenses before a spell could penetrate his skin. His protection spell was similar to the ones the Ethereal and Fallen used on themselves during the Great War. He returned to the courtyard in the blink of an eye, transporting in behind us. We turned to see his eyes fill with anger. Dumak volleyed his own shot of energy. We easily dodged it, sending him into a further rage.

As we fought, the crystal began to shake violently, sending out a dense ripple of energy that threw my vessel and me to the ground. My vessel and I were greatly weakened, but we shared the brunt of the shockwave. The ripple had momentarily zapped Dumak of his energy, causing his spell shield to power down, and we had our chance. I communicated my idea to my vessel and in less than a second, she agreed. Dumak arose, angered, and tried to stay on the offensive. He lunged at us once more and let out a fury of constant energy towards us. As Dumak let out his final attack, I separated from my vessel. Dumak witnessed my true form for the first time. He blinked in terror, unprepared for a second target. I rushed towards him, my hands burning hot with pure ascended energy. I touched the side of his face and he howled in pain, sheer, unadulterated pain. I cried out in jubilation, there is nothing sweeter than the sound of your enemy screaming in misery. I should have kept my hands on his head, I should have killed him when his spell shield was down, but I looked back to see if my vessel was relishing in his pain the same as I was. She wasn't. Without hesitation, without thinking, nor realizing what I was doing, I rushed to my vessel and left Dumak alone. I had not killed him, and I did not care.

I flew to my vessel, she was lying motionless with a serious wound to her stomach. It smelt of burnt flesh. I tried to heal it but could not. I began to panic. I merged with her once more. I knew I could heal her body from within. The pain had pushed her to unconsciousness. I was sure she would regain consciousness, she had to regain consciousness, she had to!

Dumak stood, his face burnt and deformed. He fired at us once more. I returned the volley, hitting him in the chest, but his spell shield was back up. I knew my vessel's body could take little in this state. I needed to get away and heal her. I needed to get to the seele stone. Instead of firing at Dumak, I aimed for the stone roof above his head, covering him in a ton of rock. I knew that wouldn't hold him for long, but maybe long enough to get the stone.

I rushed desperately towards the holy alter, next to my Sanctum Sanctorum. My vessel was weakening. Her body was failing, despite my efforts to heal her. I could not lose her, losing her would be like losing part of myself. We were to rule this planet together. Entering my sanctuary, I rushed to the holy alter. The seele stone it was not there, it was gone… It had to be here, none but a few even knew about the stone! I was filled with the shock of betrayal at the realization that Dumak was right! His warnings, we had been broken, defeated from within. A traitor lived among us. Shock gave way to rage, I would level the whole city if I had to, to find this renegade! I would never stop looking until I had my revenge.

As I turned to leave, Aaron walked into my sanctuary. His face was red, he looked far better than he had hours ago, he was still bruised and hurt, but he was obviously healing fast. Too fast, in fact. At my presence Aaron was startled, but his lips formed a smile. I remembered the first time I looked upon him so many years ago, when he saved my army from a rout and turned it into a victory. He had served me well, I considered him my most faithful servant. His devotion to me was beyond any other. Yet, there in his hand was the missing seele stone. He had stolen it! How could he be the one who betrayed me, who risked the life of my vessel?

Aaron took a step forward and lifted his hand with the seele stone towards me. He was about to speak, a spell taught to him by Dumak no doubt. I was not going to let him fire first and have the pleasure of seeing me hurt. I threw out my arm and let out lighting from my fingertips towards my most faithful. Aaron stood there, he was unable to dodge. In fact, he didn't even try. I hit him square in the chest and sent him flying against a pillar. The fool was still alive. I lifted him into the air and began to choke him. He tried to say something, but I silenced him. I wouldn't be assaulted by his traitorous words. I flung him across the room, his body slammed against the holy alter, smashing it into pieces.

Filled with anger, filled with hate and betrayal, I was ready to kill the man. I was prepared to inflict so much pain that death would be a mercy. I raised my hands to finish him off, pure energy flowing through my entire body. I let lose my power towards Aaron when my vessel suddenly regained consciousness. Realizing what was occurring, she ripped herself from our mergence and fell upon Aaron, using her body as a shield and taking the blast of my energy in the back.

I stood there in my true form, stunned, floored, and unable to comprehend what had just happened. I could not understand why she would shield the traitor. My mind raced to put the pieces together. What a fool I was, how ignorant I am of corporeal beings. At the time my heart broke and I felt empty and alone. My mind could only conclude one thing, she was my real betrayer. Oh Maker, how could I be so blind? Aaron wasn't the only traitor. My vessel had betrayed me as well. How could I have missed it, I should have seen it. I had known I could trust no one, and yet, how could I have been so foolish? I witnessed creation, I witnessed the universe expand and grow, I waged war on a plane of existence no man or woman could comprehend. Over a million ascended beings were at my command, smiting entire worlds at my very whim! I understand all kind of warfare except for maybe the cruelest, love. I loved my vessel as much as I loved myself, yet she betrays me, ME!

My chest filled with fire. Thoughts of Dumak and the battle outside left me. I was filled with a single desire: revenge. If my vessel thought she could get away with betraying me, she would learn I would make all pay. I hissed as I looked down at her. She was still laying face first on Aaron. She was still alive. I could hear her heart beat. It was shallow and weak, but it was still there. I would make sure the remaining beats would be ones of pain. My vessel was gaining consciousness. Good, she would be awake to feel the torment I had in store. She turned and looked at me, her face distorted in sadness and what looked to be pity. Her eyes suddenly bulged, her face froze in anger. She reached for the seele stone in Aaron's hand. I poured all my hate, all my anger into one single ball of energy. It left my hands with such velocity I could not keep my balance. Using the stone, my vessel let out her own attack and missed. I thought I had trained her better. Her attack was so far off it passed over my right shoulder. I laughed at the fool hardy attempt she made. My energy ball was nearly upon her. I slowed my perception of time, so I could enjoy watching every last moment of pain and agony on my betrayer's face. Oh, how I wish I could have made it an eternity.

My joy became shock and fright when I heard the most hideous guttural sound from behind my back. I turned to see my vessel's energy ball hitting a sneaking Dumak square in the chest.

Realization hit me in waves, how my hate and anger blinded me. How could I have doubted her, she who had been with me for so long? I looked back towards my vessel. The energy ball was just hitting her, her face engraved with the look of betrayal and confusion. She did not understand why I had attacked her. Her body lay still, her chest open and smoldering. Dumak was on the ground as well, and everything began to clear in my head. What have I done? What have I done!? I screamed a thousand screams shaking the foundations of my city.

I looked at Dumak. I was filled with anger and sorrow once more, but now it was aimed at the right creature. I wanted to kill him. He was unconscious, I could have done it, as I should have once before, but death was too easy for him. He had to suffer! I dragged his body with what little hair he had left on his charred, burnt head into the court yard. I placed him in the crystal prison, and before I sealed it, I placed inside with him an eternal fire to forever let him burn! I cast the crystal far from sight. It shot into the distance with such power I knew it would be buried deep within the crust of the planet, never to be seen again.

I went back to my sanctuary, where Aaron had regained consciousness. He sat, crying over my vessel, holding her hand to his heart. He looked up at me, his face a mix of anger and fear. I stared back at him, daring him to challenge me, but he bowed his head and stared at my vessel. She was barely alive. I had no clue what to say, no clue what to do. Her wounds were far too great for even the seele stone to heal. For the first time since the dawn of time, I began to cry. Large tears ran down my face and hit my vessel's cheek. She opened her eyes.

"My angel," she whispered softly, like when she was a girl.

"Forgive me!" I pleaded.

She had only moments left. She nodded weakly, she forgave me. The last words I heard from her were, "My angel, what is your name?"

It was hard for me to speak, but I knew she was about to die, "Aura'Eris Ponosia."

My vessel smiled at me for the last time. I could not believe what I had done. In spite of the knowledge that it would never be heard, I prayed to my father, I prayed to the Maker.

"Why did you let this happen? Why did you have to create all this? Create hunger, anger, humor, life, death, love, why did you have to leave us! The war, everything, that has happened to me is because you left me!" I cried for hours, the weight of millennia seeping through my eyes. The howls of my cries went for miles in every direction.

Aaron approached me and knelt down before me. Even after all I did to him and all that I had done to my vessel. His faith in me was unwavering. He led me to the courtyard, away from my vessel's body. I looked out onto the city. It was burning, but the battle was won. I was sole god on this planet. The city's inhabitants bowed before me and praised me, but without my vessel, my companion, it felt empty.

Even after all this, the Universe had something else in store, another twist in the tale. The crystal began to erupt. The cracks split wider, and energy and power began to burst through. I could sense its power, but it was even more than I could comprehend! Power on that level is uncontrollable. It doesn't follow the rules of nature. Suddenly, the release of energy reversed. The crystal began to attract, and not just energy, but everything! Everything began to move towards the crystal, the temple began to collapse on itself. I used all of my strength to keep myself in place. I had been too focused on myself. I did not react quickly enough. Aaron cried out for help, and I reached for him, but it was too late. He was forced into the crystal. Everything was being destroyed. Everything was being consumed. My city was tearing itself apart in a violent twister of annihilation. My people cried out for help, their screams shattering my sanity. In a matter of minutes everything was gone: my vessel, Aaron, all my people, most of the city, gone... all sucked in to the crystal. When it was over, I stood motionless in the rubble for several minutes, beside the lifeless crystal. I touched the crystal with my finger. It shattered.

On the ground lay a creature I had never seen before. Was it a man? Was it an Ethereal? Was it a Fallen? I had no clue. I reached out and touched it. My head filled with images that were not my own. I saw my master, the leader of the Fallen. He was not dead, but alive, imprisoned somewhere. Protected by locks, puzzles, keys, and spells, but he was alive, and that meant the crusade was not yet over. The war was not yet over. I had a new purpose, a new meaning in life.

The creature awoke. I could sense its power, but I could not understand it. With round soft eyes, the creature looked up at me the way a lost puppy might look to a stranger with food.

"Where am I?" it asked. "Who am I?"

I stared down at the creature and smiled, "You are on the planet Aurelia, and you are mine. Now come along, we have a lot of work to do!" I held out my hand. The creature took it and we began walking out of the debris that used to be my temple and city.

The creature looked up shyly, "Who are you?" It paused for a second and smiled like a child would to his mother, "What is your name?"

I stopped walking and tightened my grip upon the creature's hand. It cowered for a second, fearing it had made me angry. Twice in one day I am asked the same question. I thought to myself long and hard about everything that had just happened. I bent down on one knee and looked into the creature's eyes, "My name… My name is Aur…" I cleared my throat. My mind was filled with only one image: my vessel, my family. "My name is Shangri."

AFTERWARDS

The professor scanned the forest's edge for the hundredth time that night. He found himself in a very precarious situation. He laughed at himself, his talent for leading a large group of people into dangerous areas had become quite apparent, and now that large group of people were sitting still in a dangerous area without their needed protection. Faramal was inexperienced. Thaddeus was needed, and the wait for the rescue team's return had become daunting. It was nearly sunrise when the rescuers hobbled into the camp. The Equinauts were exhausted. They limped in without answering the professor's hurried cries for his godchildren. When he spotted Italicus and Gladthorn carrying an unconscious Thaddeus into the campsite, he feared the worst.

"Professor!" Andi appeared at the edge of camp, her brother astride her, equally bedraggled.

"Thank the Maker!" exclaimed the professor, pulling the two of them into a close embrace. His unceremonious reception surprised all three of them.

"I was dreadfully worried!" he huffed into Glut's shoulder.

The professor looked over Andi and Glut. They seemed unharmed apart from the trauma apparent in their expression. "Tell me everything. Did they hurt you?"

"Thaddeus." Mumbled Glut, "He and the Equinauts saved us."

Andi eyes swelled, "Edryss, she um, didn't make it."

After a brief conversation with his godchildren, the professor found Italicus in the medical wagon. He was leaning over Thaddeus, unbuttoning his jacket. He reached inside and was surprised he didn't find the small, silver box inside of it. He descended into the chair beside his friend and sunk forward until his head was nearly between his legs. He rubbed at the back of his head slowly.

"Great Scott!" sighed the professor, seeing the full extent of Thaddeus' dishevelment. There was not a bruise on him, but his clothes showed the marks of a brutal battle.

Leora busted through the door to the medical wagon and rushed to Thaddeus. She gasped and began to cry, "What happened?" she asked weeping.

The professor hugged her and looked at Italicus, "Yes, what happened? Andi and Glut seemed confused, poor dears."

"We got our asses kicked by a god," stated Italicus between deep breaths.

"A god?"

"Best way I can describe it," answered Italicus. "That rhyming bastard was right. A dark lady controls the demons. She is calling herself Shangri, came barreling down out of the sky inside a fireball. The power this she-creature radiated was just unfathomable. It was something evil, professor. Pure evil."

Gladthorn spoke up from his place in the corner, "This 'thing' spoke to Thaddeus, it didn't last long before negotiations broke down. We hit that she-devil with everything we had." Gladthorn slid down the wall. "Best we could do was annoy her, so we ran for our lives. We ran as fast and as hard as we could. But then she, she uh." Gladthorn couldn't finish his words. He collapsed into himself crying over the loss of Edryss.

"As we ran from the camp, she ripped Edryss right off the ground and pulled her back. She grabbed her from a hundred yards away," interrupted Italicus, avoiding Gladthorn's gaze.

"And?" asked the professor, frowning.

"Then ah, she killed Edryss," answered Italicus. The words were hard for him to swallow, "right in front of all of us."

Gladthorn covered his face with his hands and spoke through his fingers, "She didn't just kill Edryss, she obliterated her from the inside out. She was cooked alive!"

Italicus picked up the story, "Thaddeus grew enraged, cursing at Shangri. I don't know why or what, or even how this next thing happened, but his medallion, according to Andi, it glowed brightly, but he wasn't dying or being healed. He somehow tapped into its energy I think and then he attacked her. Never in all my life have I seen Thaddeus fight like that, and I've fought against armies beside him. It was like two alpha Hastaran apes battling it out for a pride of females. Thaddeus was a strike away from killing her, but Shangri vanished in a violent explosion. When we got to Thaddeus, he was like this. I don't know how he still alive."

"Will he wake up?" asked Leora staring at Thaddeus pleadingly.

No one answered her, because no one knew the answer.

"By the Maker, this is a lot to take in," said the professor with an uneasy expression, "But I am afraid—"

"I think we're all afraid, professor," interrupted Italicus. "Silver lining is at least you guys weren't captured by the Slavine. Balin was going on and on about this secret Slavine fort that has been here in the forest for over fifty years."

The professor gave Italicus a grim smile, "There may be something I need to tell you."

Before Italicus could question him, a loud pounding at the door of the medical wagon begun, shaking the entire structure.

"BELLADON! GET OUT HERE IMMEDIATELY!" Roared a very low, gruff voice. "Armed men have been seen entering the camp, Colonel Leohanstar demands they lay down their arms as you have already done."

Italicus and Gladthorn's heads picked up, their faces twisted in agony and surprise.

Italicus saw the Belladon's eyes drop, "professor?"

"Ah, yes. That would be Graum, second in command of that secret Slavine fort. Not so secret anymore. I'll tell you the whole story when I get back. Needless to say, we are all now prisoners of the Slavine Kingdom."

The Equinauts will return in:
Ethereal Legacy
Part Two: The Slavine Kingdom

Acharyapolina

A special Thanks to Acharyapolina for all of his amazing 3d artwork. A Talent beyond measure, if you need any 3d artwork created please consider Archayapolina. Please take a moment and visit his

https://www.fiverr.com/acharyapolina

To see more of his Ethereal Artwork please check out EtherealLegacy.net

About the Author

William F. James was born and raised on a small farm in West Central Florida. He graduated with a B.A. in Business Administration from St. Pete. College. William is a voracious reader of Roman History, Ancient History and Cultures. William started his writing career in between partnering and working with his father full time as a farrier shoeing mostly hunter-jumper show horses. Having been raised on a farm he has a love of the land and animals. Along with his wife Lisa, William lives with his horses, dairy cows, chickens and many other animals that have wandered onto the farm. For more information on William and his projects contact him at EtherealLegacy.net